MW00936691

E.G. FOLEY

THE GRYPHON CHRONICLES, BOOK SIX:

THE BLACK FORTRESS

Books by E.G. Foley

The Complete Gryphon Chronicles Series:
The Lost Heir (The Gryphon Chronicles, Book One)
Jake & The Giant (The Gryphon Chronicles, Book Two)
The Dark Portal (The Gryphon Chronicles, Book Three)
Jake & The Gingerbread Wars (A Gryphon Chronicles Christmas)
Rise of Allies (The Gryphon Chronicles, Book Four)
Secrets of the Deep (The Gryphon Chronicles, Book Five)
The Black Fortress (The Gryphon Chronicles, Book Six)

50 States of Fear Series:
The Haunted Plantation (50 States of Fear: Alabama)
Bringing Home Bigfoot (50 States of Fear: Arkansas)
Leader of the Pack (50 States of Fear: Colorado)
The Dork and the Deathray (50 States of Fear: Alaska)

Credits & Copyright

The Gryphon Chronicles, Book Six: The Black Fortress

Cover Illustration by Josh D. Addessi – www.joshaddessi.blogspot.com
Cover Design by Kim Killion – www.thekilliongroupinc.com

TABLE OF CONTENTS

PART I

PROLOGUE
The Devil's Own

Deep beneath the burning crater in the desert of Karakum, the demon Shemrazul sat in chains...

And waited.

Endlessly.

Rivers of lava sludging past his feet. Giant manacles of pure adamantine clamped around his ankles.

Forever.

But he had plans. And he dreamed. Hell was full of dreams. It was part of the torment.

Memories of his former estate persisted, seasoning his agony. Millennia ago, he had been pure spirit, one of the boundless Light Beings. He still remembered soaring over galaxies, flying past planets and suns in boundless exultation—free!—before this cruel, cruel injustice.

Now the only thing harder and more ancient than his chains was the demon's hatred. Not even the screams of the doomed souls filling the forsaken lands around him cheered him anymore.

Soon. One day, he would be free again, he vowed, and that day was fast approaching. For, through the blackest of magic, Shemrazul had sired a son almost forty years ago.

He was determined that this creature should be of use to him.

Nathan, the Earl of Wyvern, had been born and bred for a purpose: to lead the warlocks of the Dark Druid brotherhood that had been founded centuries ago by Shemrazul's loyal servant, Garnock, a medieval alchemist with an insatiable greed for supernatural powers.

Ah, good old Garnock the Sorcerer. Power-hungry fool. The Welsh wizard had been all too happy to work with—and 'ere long—*for*

Shemrazul.

True, he made it worth the wizards' while, but in return for his favors, he demanded their worship and total obedience.

Unfortunately, that was the source of his present dissatisfaction.

Zolond, the current Dark Master, was old now. Worse, he'd grown lazy and complacent.

But, far more seriously, Master Zolond was wavering in his loyalty of late, and that could never be allowed.

Oh, yes, Shemrazul was aware. Like the angel he had once been, as a demon, he could still read men's hearts. Peer into their thoughts.

That was how he knew.

Master Zolond had been dallying with dangerous ideas ever since his battle three months ago against the Elder witch, Ramona Bradford.

This would not be tolerated. The old man must be made an example of. And so, it was time for a change of leadership among the Dark Druids.

New blood. *His* blood—Shemrazul's son. His only comfort in this foul underworld, with its burning pits and sulfurous fumes.

Wyvern alone would not fail him.

Then the ancient chains clanked at Shemrazul's feet and he unfolded his ruined, leathery wings, his long dragon tail uncoiling behind him as he rose to summon his Nephilim offspring.

They were rare on earth these days, the half-bloods. But when they *were* successfully created and survived their violent births, they were magnificent to behold: stronger, smarter, bigger, better than mere humans.

Proud and ruthless. Made in the image of their fallen-angel fathers, endowed with supernatural gifts.

Once, long ago, in a lost age before history began, the Nephilim had nearly overrun the Earth, ruling over humans with an iron fist, thanks to their innate superiority.

But then the Enemy had wiped them out from the skies, all the proud Nephilim. The Tyrant above had scoured all the demons' half-blood children off the face of the earth with that unimaginable Flood, drowning their wondrous cities, their proud towers and palaces...

Such a howl had gone up from Hell that day that Shemrazul still shuddered to recall it.

Ah well. Maybe they'd never retake Heaven, but Shemrazul had a plan in place for how to claim the Earth.

All he needed was a little human cooperation—alas.

He hated it that he could do nothing without the help of those puny blood bags, those meat sacks, those dung beetles, those grubbing, scurrying, busy little ants: the humans. Oh, how he despised them, every one a mirror of his Enemy's face.

At least *his* son was a little better than their kind.

Nathan, Shemrazul said into the black void of Hell's sky. *Come. I would speak with you.*

* * *

Yes, Father. At that moment, Nathan, the Earl of Wyvern, was standing in the control room of the Black Fortress, talking to the engineer on duty.

But he paused mid-sentence, staring blankly at nothing for a second when he heard the demon's voice inside his head.

He'd heard it there since he was a boy.

"Sir?" the engineer asked, puzzled. "You were saying?"

Wyvern blinked away his distraction, filled with the urgent need to obey.

He'd been showing the whole bridge crew how the small black cube—one of the pre-Flood artifacts of Atlantis he'd brought back from the Mediterranean—could be inserted into the control panel, adding considerably more electromagnetic power to the infernal mechanism that allowed the Dark Druids' castle to jump from place to place undetected.

"This will extend our range and shorten the time it takes to rematerialize at our destination," Wyvern concluded. "We'll be better able to pinpoint our landing coordinates, as well."

"Fascinating, sir... But how does it work?" the navigator asked, while the lieutenant marveled, looking on.

"I have no idea. But it does. That is all I care about," Wyvern said, his voice as cold and low as ever. Then he nodded their dismissal. "As you were."

All the tidy, gray-uniformed men stepped back and saluted, then returned to their duties as Wyvern left the bridge without delay, eager to find out what Shemrazul wanted.

He hoped the demon was not displeased with him. The Horned One was not the sort of father from whom any son would've wished to receive discipline.

As far as Wyvern knew, he had done nothing wrong of late—not since the Nightstalker debacle, anyway, when his unsanctioned plan to kill Jake Everton by sending phantom assassins after the boy had failed.

Shemrazul hadn't seemed concerned about that, but Dark Master Zolond had scolded Wyvern afterward for attempting it.

The old man had called him rash and unthinking. Wyvern still smarted from the insults. "I will *tell* you when it is time to eliminate the boy!" the chief warlock of their brotherhood had snapped at him.

Wyvern growled at the memory. The thought of being called to the carpet like some common henchman made him grit both of his double rows of teeth.

Eh, the old crank was always coming down on him about something. It was tedious and insulting. As if the "great" Dark Master could ever run this place without him.

But Wyvern hid his scoff and checked his resentment as he entered the corridor where the doors to the sorcerer-king's private quarters were located within the mazelike passageways of the Black Fortress.

As usual, Zolond's own praetorian guard of tall, scaly reptilians stood sentry outside his door.

Seven feet tall and olive-green, with muscular humanoid bodies and crocodile heads, they wore shiny armored breastplates over their light, Egyptian-style tunics and carried tall spears in defense of the ancient sorcerer-king.

They stood at attention as Wyvern, the second-in-command, approached; the Black Fortress functioned much like the flagship of a navy, with Wyvern as the captain, running things from day to day, and Zolond as the admiral-in-residence.

"At ease," Wyvern said to the pair, then lowered his voice. "How long has he been in there?"

"Four hours, sir," one of the reptilians gurgled.

There were only six of the creatures in Zolond's service, but dashed if he could tell them apart.

"Hmm." Wyvern nodded, then leaned closer—as a Nephilim, he was the only humanish man aboard the castle-ship who could look the big lizards in the eyes. "Any idea what he's doing in there this time?"

Both elite royal bodyguards shook their toothy heads.

Well, it had been worth a shot asking. But Wyvern dared not keep the Horned One waiting, so he marched on with another terse, "As you were."

The two bored reptilians watched him walk away.

As he hurried on through the labyrinth of polished black granite that made up the castle's first floor, Wyvern's footfalls echoed down the sleek corridor while he continued puzzling over what the blazes Zolond was up to in his private chambers these days.

The old man had been acting so suspicious of late, locking himself away in his apartments for hours on end. Perhaps he was brewing up some new potions or spells, or even designing new creatures, as he was wont to do.

Wyvern didn't know. He was just glad the old snake was too distracted by whatever he had up his sleeve that he forgot to nag him as much as usual.

Of course, Wyvern suspected that Zolond only nagged because he was jealous. They all were.

They should be.

The other twelve members of the Dark Druid Council had to plead and make blood sacrifices to bribe the demons into heeding their requests. But not Wyvern. All he had to do was ask Daddy.

A smug smile curved his lips as he jogged down a set of black granite steps, his boot heels ringing on the cold stone as he mused on the very special bond he shared with his immortal sire.

Shemrazul of the Ninth Pit gave his half-blood son secret information that Zolond and the others only *wished* they knew about.

Knowledge was power, after all, especially among the array of super-villains who'd earned their seats on the Dark Druid Council.

Wyvern was the newest member, number thirteen, and that made him the lowest-ranking among the leadership (which bothered him, of course), but he had mighty ambitions.

He knew how to make himself useful, as well. His inside knowledge from Shemrazul was what had guided Wyvern to retrieve the treasure trove of Atlantean artifacts from that deep-sea trench in the Mediterranean called the Calypso Deep.

The cube he'd been showing the engineer was just one of several astonishing finds—rescued bits of wondrous Nephilim science.

He had found them just where his demon father had promised they would be. Retrieving them had been no easy feat. Wyvern had then stored them in a cave in Greece and, with all due haste, brought a few of the most useful pieces back to England to show off to his colleagues.

With the help of this ancient Nephilim technology, Wyvern had boosted the capabilities of the Dark Druids' fortress-ship, just as he'd shown the engineer.

Unfortunately, they would never know what the rest of the ancient artifacts might've been able to do, for that intolerable boy, Jake Everton, and his friends had uncovered the cave and destroyed the rest of the evil treasure trove.

Wyvern clenched his six-fingered fists at the thought of that brat.

What a plague he was! Little beast.

Wyvern had never liked children before, but ever since he'd first become aware of that vexing thirteen-year-old, he had no use for the creatures at all, except perhaps as shish-kebabs.

Ugh, the thought of Jake and his pesky band of friends set both rows of Wyvern's teeth on edge as he marched on.

Why won't Zolond just let me kill the brat and be done with it? That would solve the problem in a trice. How hard can it be? He's a kid.

But no, no, no. Master Zolond wanted Jake alive on account of Duradel's prophecy.

So, they'd laid a trap for the boy three months ago instead. A trap that should've worked by now.

But for some inscrutable reason, the canny ex-pickpocket still refused to take the bait.

How is the bait doing, anyway? Wyvern wondered. Pausing, he stepped around the corner and glanced down another black, torch-lit hallway.

At the far end of the corridor lay a dungeon cell, where Jake's magnificent, scarlet-feathered Gryphon prowled back and forth behind iron bars. The boy's beloved pet and protector, just like the gryphon rampant engraved on the Everton family crest.

Red, as he was known, had just enough room to take three steps in his cage before turning around to pace back the other way.

When the Gryphon saw Wyvern, he banged his golden beak angrily against the bars and screeched, hissing and slashing with his deadly lion claws, his tufted tail thrashing.

In response, Wyvern's own pet, Thanatos, sprang out of the shadows where he'd been lurking, keeping watch over Red. The manticore roared at the Gryphon, his tawny lion body ready to fight, his scorpion tail thrashing.

Red answered with a war cry and lunged at the bars.

Oh, those two wanted each other's blood, Wyvern thought with a chuckle.

"Down, Thanatos! Leave him be!"

The growling manticore slunk back to his corner on command.

"And you, settle down!" Wyvern ordered Red. "Don't worry, your precious boy will come to save you soon enough. And when he does, the two of you can share that cell."

A piercing sound—half eagle's screech, half lion's roar—followed Wyvern as he turned away, smirking at the creature's fury. Then he hurried on, heading for the throne room.

Yet, as Wyvern walked away, the sight of the caged Gryphon left him uneasy.

Truly, what was taking so long for their trap to work? Why wouldn't the brat take the bait?

It worried him. The others said to be patient, but Wyvern could not understand why an impulsive young would-be hero like Jake Everton had not come storming in by now to try to save his beloved Gryphon.

That was what the Dark Druids had expected him to do—indeed, what they had counted on him doing.

But so far, nothing.

The boy was crafty. That much, Wyvern supposed he could respect... Suddenly, an electrifying thought occurred to him. Maybe Shemrazul had summoned him today because he'd changed his mind about Jake.

Maybe Wyvern was about to receive fresh orders to finish the brat off for once and for all.

The possibility excited him as he jogged down the final flight of stairs.

Oh, I hope so, he thought, for maybe he was overly cautious, but Wyvern did not like Duradel's prophecy about the boy at all.

It made no sense, as it offered both a promise and a threat. More to the point, it pricked at Wyvern's jealousy. All he knew was that the easiest way to head off the danger that the oracle presented was to kill the boy *now*.

Before he grew any more powerful.

Yes, that must be it. Father wants me to kill him. Finally!

The tantalizing thought of ridding the world of Jake Everton for once and for all brought a chilly smile to Wyvern's face as he reached the bottom of the stairs.

A smile the two Noxu warriors on duty outside the throne room seemed to find disturbing. The pair of hulking half-trolls stood at attention as Wyvern approached, but eyed him uneasily.

He nodded at them to step aside. "He wants to see me."

They grunted, uncrossed their ax-headed spears, and stepped apart.

Wyvern grimaced at the brutes' unpleasant smell. *Bloody Noxu.* They stank like a pair of wild boars.

Only Master Zolond got the elegant royal reptilians for his bodyguards; here, and throughout the rest of the Black Fortress, the dull-witted, thick-bodied Noxu mercenaries sufficed well enough. They were a warlike tribe, competitive and stupid, with grayish skin and small tusks jutting upward from their lower jaws.

Wyvern took a deep breath and lifted his chin, bracing to see his father as the two Noxu guards hauled the massive doors of the throne room open to admit him.

Blackness yawned ahead: the castle's very inner sanctum.

Wyvern caught a faint whiff of sulfur wafting out of the ceremonial chamber, and a shiver of awe ran down his spine. It was heady stuff, standing this close to so much power.

Then he stepped past the guards into the darkness, eager to find out what malevolent new mission his demon father had for him now.

CHAPTER 1
Palace Intrigues

~ Merlin Hall ~
Wiltshire, England

Spymaster was not a role in which a thirteen-year-old lad generally found himself. But gazing down upon the colorful whirling chaos of the ballroom far below his shadowed balcony, Jake Everton, the young Earl of Griffon, knew for a fact that somebody down there tonight had to have some information on his Gryphon's whereabouts.

He just needed to find it—any sort of lead. And he would. With the help of his secret team of spies.

Standing alone in the gloom of a high, curved balcony overlooking the vast ballroom below, formally dressed for the gala in progress, Jake braced himself against the polished railing before him, his hands planted wide.

The gryphon rampant on his signet ring gleamed by the glow of the chandeliers. They hung several feet beneath his high perch, up near the gilded frieze encircling the noisy ballroom.

All the while, from beneath his blond forelock, he scanned the gathering with hawklike intensity. He had eyes and ears everywhere down there tonight, and they all would report back to him with any sort of clue they could find.

For now, the dull roar of several hundred conversations floated up to him, threaded with strains of the lively Renaissance music in progress. He could feel the brisk pounding of the drums, hear the winding melodies of woodwinds and lutes that filled the tapestried chambers of the great medieval palace.

Delicious smells from the kingly feast on offer wafted up to his nostrils, as well. Too bad he'd lost his appetite ever since they'd told him three months ago that the Dark Druids had captured Red.

But Jake would find him. Aye, tonight's stealthy operation offered the best chance of doing just that, for the ballroom down there was crawling with VIPs from all over the world.

Representatives from the far reaches of the British Empire had been arriving at the palace in recent days for the opening of the magical parliament.

Likewise, September marked the start of another six-week round of training for all the various kinds of magical students.

As a result, everyone who was anyone in Magick-kind was down there right now.

Except for those who'd gone missing, of course.

In any case, tonight's annual Harvest Home feast was merely the Elders' way of welcoming everybody back to Merlin Hall for autumn sessions before official business began tomorrow morning.

Personally, Jake found the party completely inappropriate at such a time.

War was brewing. His Gryphon was missing. His parents' bodies had not been in their caskets.

And they're here bobbing for apples. Adults. Jake shook his head.

So be it. He would turn this foolishness to his advantage.

With a roomful of visiting dignitaries, *someone* down there had to have a lead on where the Black Fortress had last been seen.

Wondering if any of his mates had heard anything yet, he homed in on them, one by one, around the ballroom.

There, a glint of golden hair revealed Cousin Isabelle, discreetly using her empath skills to learn what she could in a palace swirling with secrets.

On the opposite side of the vast room, Henry DuVal, the boys' tutor, leaned against a marble column, drawing on his wolfish instincts to sniff out any information from the visiting shapeshifter clans.

And over there, dressed all in black with a glittered orange spider pin adorning her spiky jet hair, the young witch, Nixie Valentine, sauntered past the sweets table, looking even more furtive than usual. Listening, no doubt, to conversations all around her, nonchalant as a little black cat.

Jake did not see his cousin, Archie, however. *Probably outside talking to the giants.* Jake doubted their thickheaded friend, King Snorri, knew much of anything, but perhaps Queen Kaia, his wife, would have something intelligent to say.

He'd know by the end of the night. But forget the towering Norse giants—for the smallest of his spies checked in a moment later.

Gladwin Lightwing of the royal garden fairies swept back and forth in broad S-curves over the heads of the crowd, trying to look casual as she made her way toward Jake's end of the ballroom.

As she approached, she shut off her sparkle trail and suddenly zoomed away from the throng, racing up past the chandeliers to hover before Jake's dark, galleried overlook.

"Nothing so far," she reported in her high, tinkling voice.

Jake hid his disappointment.

With Gladwin's position close to the court of Queen Victoria herself, he'd had high hopes that, of all his secret agents, the tiny royal courier might've heard something useful.

Gladwin landed lightly on the banister and gazed up at him. "Are you coming down to join the party soon? Everyone's asking for you. Especially Dani."

Ah, Dani.

Jake felt a twinge of guilt mixed with great fondness at the mention of his trusty carrot-head.

Ever since Sicily, when she'd rowed out to sea and saved his life, the two of them had reached a sort of understanding that they were more than friends.

All Jake knew was that, these days, the dauntless redhead was the only person who didn't run from him on sight, on account of his having been in a horrible mood for three months straight.

He had reason.

Dani understood. He wasn't *trying* to be mean to anyone. It was simply that he was in the middle of enduring the most agonizing months of his life, and that was saying something.

He would never admit it aloud, but his heart was broken over Red, and all the pieces were dagger-sharp.

In short, he hadn't been very nice to be around lately. But her loyalty never faltered. She was a sturdy little Rock of Gibraltar planted by his side, going through it *with* him.

To him, she was just the best and most necessary person in the world.

"Tell her I'll be down in a few minutes," he said. "I'm waiting for Maddox."

Gladwin raised her eyebrows. "Since when is a Guardian ever late?"

Jake merely snorted. It was true, the stern soldiers of the Order tended to be both disciplined and prompt.

But that just went to show how out of sorts both boys had been ever since they'd heard the news that had come out of that desert battle in June.

While Jake was distraught to hear that Red had been captured, Maddox's birth mother, Guardian Ravyn Vambrace, had not returned from the fray, either.

Nobody knew whether the proud warrior woman had been captured or killed.

The worst part for Maddox was that he had not said goodbye to her on the best of terms. No surprise in that. Maddox liked to give Ravyn (and nearly everyone else) a hard time.

Now, however, the seventeen-year-old suffered continuously over what might have become of the woman who had given birth to him.

As for Jake, the worst part of it all was knowing that he was ultimately responsible for this happening to Red.

The Gryphon was as fierce in battle as he was gentle with children. Red had made it clear that he wanted to go and join the fight. But it was Jake who had given his noble pet permission to participate.

Why, oh, why did I ever let him go? He tormented himself with this question day and night.

Even now, the thought of his own role in his beloved pet's possible destruction brought a lump to his throat, but, at once, he stiffened his spine.

He could not afford to be weak or muddled with tangled emotions. He needed a clear head tonight; the pain would only cloud his mind.

Lord knew it had already begun messing with his telekinesis. His gift had gone wonky in recent weeks, due to his continuous state of churning anger and grief.

Why, just the other day at his studies, he had reached for a glass of water and sent the cup flying before he could ever touch it. Accidentally splashed water all over poor Henry.

Blimey, this whole situation was turning him into a proper menace. He had to get Red back before he went barmy. Then he thrust off his roiling thoughts.

"Maddox will be here any minute," Jake told the waiting fairy. "Then we'll both be down."

Gladwin nodded and lifted off from the railing. "Very well. I'll keep digging."

"Be careful," Jake warned. "You, of all people, can't afford to get caught."

Spying on the Queen of England and her court was highly illegal, after all.

"I don't want you taking any unnecessary risks," he added.

"Yes, well, it's worth it for Red—and for you, dear boy." The fairy fluttered up and gave him a tiny kiss on the cheek. "Don't worry, Jake, we'll find him."

He managed a smile. "Thanks."

"Not at all! I owe you, remember?" she teased. "If it weren't for you, I'd still be stuck in a box in your Uncle Waldrick's basement. And if it weren't for Red and his wonderful healing feathers, I wouldn't have these."

She pirouetted in midair, fluttering her bright new wings.

Jake gave her a nostalgic smile, and Gladwin zoomed off again to continue the search.

Amused at how well the fairy had taken to her role as secret agent, Jake watched her sparkle trail as Gladwin flew figure eights over the crowd.

Now that she'd mentioned Uncle Waldrick, though, Jake started thinking about that miscreant again.

He hadn't seen Uncle Waldrick since he'd been hauled off to prison, but lately, Jake had been wondering whether, in all fairness, Uncle Waldrick still deserved the life sentence he'd received.

The man had supposedly committed murder, but Jake had seen for himself that neither of Uncle Waldrick's victims—Jake's parents—had been in their caskets in the family mausoleum.

He'd checked. It hadn't been pleasant opening the tomb, but he'd forced himself to look after Fionnula Coralbroom had made such shocking claims.

The incarcerated sea-witch had given Jake reason to hope that his parents might still be alive. *Where* they might be now—and where they'd been all these years—were questions for another day.

Questions Jake would begin seeking answers to as soon as he got

Red back.

Until then, he could think of little else.

Fortunately, another one of his palace spies arrived to give his report before Jake could sink back into his brooding: Constanzio, the jolly Italian ghost who'd been dubbed "the King of the Tenors" by the newspapers until his demise a couple of years ago.

He was Jake's favorite ghost, of all the dead folk he'd ever met.

Materializing in midair a few feet in front of Jake's balcony, the portly spirit looked smart in a spectral tuxedo for the occasion, just like he would've donned for his worldwide opera performances in real life not long ago.

With his love of food and wine, the famous singer seemed to be having trouble letting go of mortal life.

He was clearly enjoying the party tonight, a ghostly glass of champagne in one hand, a little plate of hors d'oeuvres in the other. *"Bounasera, ragazzo!"*

"Bounasera, signore," Jake answered wearily. He had no patience for small talk this evening. "Anything?"

Constanzio floated closer. "Actually, yes."

Jake straightened up. "Good man! I knew I could count on you, Constanzio. What have you got?"

"Well, I was over there, by the champagne fountain"—he lowered his magnificent voice—"when I heard the Djin ambassador telling one of the wood elf courtiers that the Black Fortress was sighted a month ago—"

"Where?" Jake interrupted, holding his breath.

"In the Mesopotamian Marshes," he said gravely.

"Huh?" Jake scrunched up his nose.

"It only stayed for an hour or so before it jumped again," Constanzio said. "What they were doing there, the Djin fellow didn't know, but it hasn't been back since."

Jake stared at, or rather *through*, his semi-transparent friend as he digested this strange information.

"What the devil are the Mesopotamian Marshes?" he said. "I never heard of that before."

Constanzio shrugged. "Marshes in Mesopotamia, I should think."

"Hmm! Well, at least that's something," Jake said, mystified. "I just wish there was some way we could track that blasted castle. This is so frustrating! Why does a building need to move around, anyway?"

"I know, I know." Constanzio shook his head. "The Order has tried for ages to come up with some way of tracing its various jumps. But it's too well shielded. Black magic, no doubt. The cloaking spells must be as strong as the dome over this place."

Jake nodded with a sigh. That was the reason the Order had not been able to rescue Red yet. They simply couldn't *find* the blasted building where he was being held captive—otherwise, the Elders would have sent a rescue team.

Jake had never seen the Black Fortress, nor this Wyvern fellow who supposedly ran the thing, but he already knew that he hated them both.

Wyvern was the chap who had personally taken Red hostage, had tortured Jake's mentor, Guardian Derek Stone, and had captured their Lightrider friend, Tex, the crazy cowboy from the Wild West. The same rotten blackguard who had trapped Aleeyah the djinni in her smoke form with a dark spell (though Archie was working on that).

It was Wyvern who had captured the angel, Dr. Celestus, and treated him with unspeakable cruelty.

And, last but not least, Lord Wyvern had tried to kill Jake by sending Nightstalkers after him.

Jake shuddered at the memory of how he'd been hunted that night by three phantom assassins.

There was no question in his mind that he'd have been dead, dead, dead if it weren't for Prince Janos.

Derek could say whatever he liked about the roguish vampire, but the rebel of the Order had swooped in and saved Jake's life that night, right when all hope seemed lost.

In any case, Jake had heard that the Dark Druids shielded their moveable castle by some inscrutable blend of magic and science that allowed the whole building to materialize wherever they wished, and then vanish again without a trace.

Cowards. He shook his head in disgust. What a cheap strategy. Rather than staying to hold a fair fight, they'd make their sneak attacks then jump away again—strike like snakes, then quickly slither off into the weeds.

Jake didn't realize he was scowling until he saw Constanzio scanning his face with a look of concern.

"Never fear, my young friend," the tenor said gently. "Sooner or later, we'll find a lead. I'll keep working the room. Perhaps I can charm some information out of one of the clairvoyants."

"Worth a try. Just mind that you're discreet."

"Always, m'boy. *Ciao.*" Constanzio lifted his glass in a toast, then dissolved.

"Grazie, signore," Jake murmured, but the ghost was already gone.

Finally, Maddox St. Trinian came prowling down the side hallway that led to Jake's balcony.

The tall, black-haired lad greeted him with a curt nod. "Let's get this over with."

Jake turned from the railing, arching a brow when he noticed his friend's clothes.

Guardians were usually dutiful in all matters, but Maddox had decided to state his protest of the Elders' holding a party at a time like this by boycotting formal attire. Instead, he wore the brown leather jacket that marked him as a Guardian apprentice, along with a plain tan shirt, sturdy canvas trousers, and his rugged work boots.

"Well, don't you look smart," Jake drawled.

Maddox flicked an equally dismissive glance over Jake's tuxedo. "At least I'm not a penguin."

Jake smirked at him and left the balcony. "Let's go."

Maddox nodded. It was time to get down there and do a bit of spying for themselves.

CHAPTER 2
Fathers & Sons

With the musky odor of the Noxu guards lingering in his nostrils, Wyvern found his eyes adjusting quickly to the darkness of the throne room.

The half-trolls pushed the doors shut behind him, and he began striding down the slick black granite slab that served as a walkway into the ceremonial chamber.

Twin rows of small blue flames illuminated the walkway on both sides; their eerie glow played over the carved cloven hooves of the huge ebony devil statues that served as columns in the throne room, each holding up portions of the very high ceiling on its shoulders.

The carved devils' ugly faces leered down at Wyvern as he stepped off the walkway into the throne room itself. Here, thirteen tall black chairs were arrayed in a triangle shape, with Zolond's elevated throne at the apex of the pyramid.

For now, of course, all the thrones were empty. The Dark Druid Council was not in session.

Wyvern slipped in between two of the thrones and walked into the triangle.

In the center of the floor lay a mysterious round hole—a bottomless pit, about ten feet in diameter, that dropped away into the underworld.

From right there in the middle of the chamber, Shemrazul would sometimes rise to give the Dark Druids his counsel—or, more often, their orders.

Unfortunately, this was about as far into the mortal world as the Horned One could come on account of his chains.

But perhaps that was a good thing. For even among the warlocks, it was deemed prudent to contain the demon somewhat.

Mighty as he was, not even Shemrazul could cross the ring of arcane symbols, powerful sigils, and spells engraved in gold on the floor encircling the fiery pit.

Wyvern stopped when he reached the outer band of gold-carved symbols, and there, he went down on one knee, bowed his head, and pressed his fist over his heart. "I am here in answer to your summons, oh, Horned One. What is your will?"

He heard the sound of fire whooshing up from the pit. Quickly jumping to his feet, Wyvern backed away to avoid getting singed.

A column of flame blazed up from the depths as Shemrazul rose from the pit. Wyvern lifted his head and found his father towering up out of the flames.

Looming over him, Shemrazul's face was not easy to look upon. Grotesque, long, and cruel beneath the span of his horns, it was the stuff of nightmares. Especially those yellow eyes, with their pupils slit like a serpent's.

The eyes glowed with pride as the demon gazed at him. "Nathan."

"Father." Wyvern bowed with a reverence that he showed no mortal on Earth. "You wished to see me?"

"Yes..."

Wyvern looked up attentively at the huge, ghastly face in the flames.

"I have read the stars, my son." Shemrazul flexed his tattered, leathery wings. "Your time is almost at hand."

"Sire?" Wyvern lifted his head, startled but eager.

"My son, I've summoned you because, this very night, my servant Zolond will make a...remarkable announcement."

"Oh? What sort of announcement?"

"You'll see. The point is, when he does, you will take it as your signal that the power I have so long promised will soon be yours. I hope you are ready."

"I am, sire." Wyvern stepped closer, amazed. He had not been expecting this at all!

"Good." The cruel face in the flames shimmered and twisted. The horns buckled and the cheekbones warped in the shifting orange blaze. "When Zolond makes his move, that shall be your sign to begin—*quietly*—setting up your palace coup. For, soon, you will supplant him."

Wyvern could scarcely believe his good fortune. He'd always expected to overthrow Zolond one day, but so soon?

No matter. He was Nephilim: he was ready. He stood up tall, his heart thundering with the lust for power. "What must I do?"

"I will guide you, never fear. But, of course, in the final moment, it must come down to you. Only a warlock powerful enough to seize the Black Crown can bear to wear it, my son.

"Likewise, just as Zolond once wrenched the Master's ring off the dead hand of his predecessor, you will have to do the same to him. But you must be as subtle as a snake." A rattlesnake sound from inside the pit emphasized Shemrazul's point. "If the old man discovers you are plotting to overthrow him, he will crush you."

Wyvern was not afraid of anything, but the thought of having to kill the mighty warlock who had ruled the Dark Druids for the past three hundred years did give him pause.

"How shall I begin?"

"First, you must gather your allies, consolidate your base of support. And trust no one. Not yet. The other members of the Council still fear Zolond. Some may hesitate to cross him. You cannot risk allowing them to betray your plan."

"Right," he murmured, his thoughts sweeping over the list of formidable super-villains on the Dark Druid Council. "Do I have your blessing to destroy those who refuse to join with me?"

Shemrazul smiled. "I would never punish anyone for murder. Of course you may kill them if need be. But I will tell you this: Duradel is already with you."

"Is he?" Wyvern murmured, surprised—although he shouldn't be. Blind from birth, the dark elf, Duradel, prophet and priest of the Dark Druids, saw all. "Well, that is good news."

The tips of his horns nearly scraped the high ceiling as Shemrazul nodded. "Unlike Zolond, the priest's full loyalty is to me. Duradel already knows I have chosen you as the next leader of the Council. But you will need more allies than just the Drow prophet. Securing their loyalty will be your first task."

Wyvern pondered the awesome chance he was being offered, if he was strong enough to seize it.

Then he looked up with a troubled frown. "Father, if Zolond has offended you somehow, then let me punish him to defend your honor."

Shemrazul let out a sinister laugh. "Ah, dear boy, you're such a comfort to me. Overthrow him, and that will be punishment enough—until he joins me down here. Then I will see to him myself. For all eternity."

Wyvern shuddered at the thought. "I beg you, Father, tell me what he's done to lose your favor so that I never make the same mistake."

The demon's cynical snort nearly singed Wyvern's eyebrows off. He jumped back but did not complain.

"Suffice to say that Zolond's loyalty to his Horned Lord has been wavering of late. Merely do as you're told and that will never happen to you. Now, forget about Zolond. He's the past. You are the present, my boy! But we must also see to the future."

"What do you mean?"

"A king must attend to the succession of his throne, Nathan. When you take the Black Crown, you will also need an heir, a son to train up in the ways of our line. One to follow in your footsteps."

Wyvern's heart fell. "But Father..."

"Don't fret, son." Shemrazul smiled almost gently.

It was terrifying.

"Yes, yes, I know. Because of...what you are, you can never have children of your own," the demon said.

Wyvern lowered his head, both pained and shamed by the fact. But it was true. As a half-blood, he could never reproduce. It was apparently just a fluke of Mr. Darwin's evolution. Same with mules.

As the offspring of two different creatures—horses and donkeys—mules were something else entirely, born sterile. So it was for all the half-demon Nephilim. He kept his head down. He might despise children, but even more than that, his great pride hated this flaw in his design.

"Shall I steal a child, sire? Or...I suppose there is Zolond's great-great nephew, that horrid young what's-his-name—"

The ghoul scoffed. "Don't be silly!"

Wyvern looked up in surprise. He did not have one silly drop of blood in his body.

"Come, Nathan, I am surprised at you," Shemrazul taunted. "Is the answer not plain?"

Wyvern gave him a blank look.

Shemrazul lifted his fiery eyebrows and gave him the answer: "Your heir is the boy from Duradel's prophecy, of course. Jake Everton shall serve as your son, and his title shall be the Black Prince."

Wyvern's mouth fell open, flashing both rows of teeth while Shemrazul's shocking words echoed around the black stone chamber, surrounding him.

Like a curse.

"But sire!"

"What?" the devil asked.

"Surely you can't mean—the Griffon heir?!"

"Certainly!" Shemrazul let out a volley of ominous laughter. "Who else could I mean?"

"Anyone b-but *him*!" Wyvern found himself sputtering. "Jake Everton? Th-the boy i-is impossible! He's un-unruly, impatient, destructive. Utterly disobedient! Impulsive and stubborn, ill-mannered and rude. Sneaky as blazes. Not to mention—a thief!"

"Precisely. He already takes after you!" Shemrazul was laughing with that bellowing chuckle of his that sometimes caused earthquakes.

"But Father!"

"Don't be an idiot, Nathan. Every 'flaw' you've just listed explains exactly why the young ruffian is perfect for our needs. He belongs on our side."

Wyvern stammered and huffed, but he did not dare protest outright.

"Oh, don't be obstinate, Nathan. Let me open your eyes about this..." With a swirl of a clawed finger, Shemrazul sculpted the smoke, causing thick gray billows to begin revolving over his palm like a globe.

He blew on the smoke with a puff of his sulfurous breath, and the gray clouds parted, revealing a vision to Wyvern.

"Look," Shemrazul ordered.

Wyvern ignored the smoke making his eyes sting and stared...

There, in the billows, he saw Shemrazul's vision for his future and went very still. By the Furies, it was so far beyond even his own grandiose dreams that he could only stand there in awe.

In the vision the demon had spun for him, he saw a dark royal family: king, queen, and prince.

Wyvern stood tall in the vision, dressed in flowing midnight robes, the jagged Black Crown on his head, armies bowing down at his feet. By his side stood a beautiful queen with long, wavy hair, blue-black as the sea. Her white skin glistened like an iceberg, and her red lips crooked in a treacherous smile.

But at Wyvern's right hand stood...*his son.* The Black Prince, as was the traditional title for the heir apparent.

Wyvern stared at the boy with his heart in his throat.

He had never dared hope for a son of his own, knowing the limits the Enemy had placed on his kind. But this brash, handsome lad was nothing short of magnificent.

Lightning flew from his fingertips. Phantoms fled from his glance. He could call swarms of flesh-tearing gryphons down upon an enemy.

Dressed all in black, the proud lad wore a simple iron circlet adorning his bright golden hair. His chin was high with lordly pride, his shoulders were squared, and his blue eyes burned like he'd gladly stomp down the world if it crossed him.

Or if his parents told him to.

"Do you not see?" Shemrazul whispered. "He is a boy with no father. You will soon be a king with no son. Tame the wild lad to our ways, and he will be yours to command."

Wyvern's heart cried out when Shemrazul whooshed the vision away with a wave of his hand. He had never hoped for a family. Never realized a creature like him could want one.

He could hardly find his tongue for a moment. "But Duradel's prophecy, sire. This boy is dangerous."

"Indeed," Shemrazul murmured, his tone ominous. "That is precisely why you must get control of him soon. After the feats he's already accomplished, imagine what he'll do at age twenty or thirty. You must bring Jake over to our side...lest the *other* half of the oracle comes to fruition."

Wyvern looked away and was silent for a long moment, shaken by what he had seen. "I understand."

"Best take good care of that Gryphon, son. It's the key to my grandson's heart."

Grandson... Son. Wyvern tasted the strange words in his mind. Could he really become the impossible boy's adoptive father? Would he one day dote on cheeky Jake Everton like Shemrazul doted on him?

"A-and the woman in the vision?"

"She is waiting for you, though you'll have to rescue your damsel. She is locked in a tower that not even she can break out of. Trust me, she's earned our regard. Besides, she has a history with Jake."

"Yes...I see. M-my son will need a mother."

"Precisely," Shemrazul said. "And she's very beautiful. Well—sometimes."

Wyvern could barely wrap his mind around this. Then he looked up at the demon and gave him a smile full of wonder. "You are truly great, sire."

"Aren't I, though?" Shemrazul whipped his dragon tail with pleasure at the praise, and the vertical slits of his snakelike eyes glowed. "I always look out for my own. Now, go. And prepare to lay hold of your destiny—son."

With that, he sank back down into the fire pit. The flames followed him, and their bright orange light vanished as the demon returned to the darkness.

Why, I'm going to be a father. Still marveling at the news, Wyvern wondered if he ought to break out the cigars.

CHAPTER 3
A Right Plum Lass

"Mesopotamian Marshes?" Maddox echoed as the boys marched down the stairs, heading for the ballroom.

"Aye, that's what the ghost said." Jake shrugged. "Any idea why the Dark Druids would want to go there?"

"Not the foggiest," Maddox said with a mystified frown.

"Well," Jake said, "maybe tomorrow I'll try the Merlin Hall library. That place is huge. Old, too. They must have something. I'll see what I can find."

The older boy looked askance at him. "You, at the library? You must be desperate."

Jake snorted, and the two strode on.

The frolicking Renaissance music grew louder as they proceeded down three flights of stairs and arrived in the soaring white marble lobby of Merlin Hall, beneath its domed ceiling.

From there, they headed to the wide entrance of the ballroom, where the Harvest Home was in full swing.

Jake had to admit that the whimsical autumn theme made the elegant ballroom look decidedly quaint. Sheaves of wheat flanked the doorways, while the cinnamon smell of mulled cider spiced the air. Cornucopias strewed small gourds across the dining tables. Scarecrows and corn dollies had been affixed to the ballroom pillars and stared at the guests with painted-on smiles.

Overhead, rustic garlands of woodland boughs covered in bright autumn leaves crisscrossed the dance floor, and everywhere dangled little, hollowed-out turnip lanterns.

Their warm glow twinkled over the hundreds of magical folk milling about.

Jake looked around, businesslike, assessing the situation. "Right. You start with the merfolk."

He nodded toward their friend, Princess Sapphira, and the contingent from the royal court of Poseidonia. The gorgeous mermaid and her entourage had come ashore for the occasion, thanks to the Landwalker spell that turned their tails into legs temporarily.

Maddox followed Jake's glance and nodded. For a second, both boys stared at the glamorous *Bellissima*, as they had nicknamed her before they had any idea who she was.

Tonight, the mermaid was transformed into a proper human-looking princess, from her glittering gown to her tiara, elbow gloves and all.

"She looks good," Maddox said wistfully. He had always got along well with the strong-willed royal and her trusty bodyguard, Captain Tyndaris.

"Looks like she's been practicing her walking, too," Jake replied, giving his friend a wry look. The first time they'd met Sapphira, she had been the clumsiest walker they had ever seen, lurching along like a hunchback, knocking over furniture. Little had they known the reason why. The haughty mermaid had been a fish out of water, indeed.

"I'm sure she'll help," Jake said. "Especially if you're the one asking."

"We'll see." Maddox shrugged, but he was a good-looking lad and he knew it. Older girls were always fawning over him.

Jake found it annoying. "Once you've talked to the merfolk, see if Finnderool will introduce you to any of his relatives from the wood elf court."

Maddox frowned. "Why don't *you* talk to him? You know him better than I do."

"Because Finnderool's a Lightrider, and we're not supposed to be doing this," Jake said oh-so-reasonably. "I don't intended to be passed over for the Lightrider program on account of our snooping. *You* need to handle this one."

Maddox eyed him skeptically. "Fine. But he's going to know you're the one behind it."

"Then try to be slick!" Jake said.

Maddox gave him a sardonic look, and Jake realized the futility of that request. Tough? Sure. Brave? Yes. Stubborn? Very much so. But slick?

Not Maddox. Not at all.

The brusque young Guardian seemed to enjoy being brutally honest.

"Just do your best," Jake said. "Better yet, take Sapphira with you and let Her Highness do the talking. The wood elves are snobs, but she's a princess. At least they'll be polite to *her*."

Maddox looked relieved at this suggestion. "Very well." Then he glanced around at the crowd. "Who are you going to talk to?"

Jake braced himself and looked around. "Everyone else."

He was dreading it, frankly.

To a boy of thirteen, the task of mingling with strangers at some fancy party and trying to chat up adults had to be some special form of torture.

Oh well. It was worth it if it could help Red.

Then Maddox, who was a few inches taller than Jake, nodded toward the center of the ballroom. "Here comes your wife."

Jake blushed at once. "Shut up."

"Who did you assign her to spy on?"

"Nobody." Jake sent him a grim look. "I'm keeping Dani out of this."

Maddox glanced at him in surprise, and Jake's blush deepened.

But he would not change his mind. What they were doing was risky, and he didn't want her involved.

Dani O'Dell had already risked her neck enough times for him. Besides, Jake wasn't taking any chances on the adults sending her away.

She was a commoner, after all; Dani had no magical powers, no family connections, only Jake and his cousins. Technically, the cute, cheery redhead was only here as lady's companion to Isabelle.

The Elders neither knew nor cared that, for all her humble origins, the Irish lass was the only thing keeping Jake sane through all this.

She was his best girl, and the only aspect of his life that was going right these days.

Then the crowd parted and there she was: the carrot-head in all her glory.

Her freckled face lit up when she saw him.

Jake felt an easing in the tension that had gripped him all evening as Dani joined them, nearly skipping over to the boys in her enthusiasm for the night's festivities.

"You came!"

Jake could not resist a rueful smile in answer. "Aye, I'm here."

"Even Maddox? I'm amazed." She gave the older boy a pert look. "I thought you for sure weren't coming."

"Hullo, Daniela," the gloomy Guardian replied, for not even Maddox could resist her lively Irish warmth. He nudged Jake. "This one talked me into it."

"Well, good! It's fun here," she said with a twinkling smile.

Jake tried not to stare, but he was stunned at how pretty she looked this evening.

Soon to turn twelve, Dani wore her shoulder-length auburn hair smoothed back from her face with a black velvet headband.

Her green silk frock matched her emerald eyes. A small ruffle of white lace trimmed the collar, the sleeves, and the skirts that hung to her shins. Below them, her white tights disappeared into fancy black ankle-boots.

Blimey, other than the mischievous sparkle in her eyes, there was hardly a trace left of the tough little rookery lass who'd stuck by his side through thick and thin on the streets of London, her clothes threadbare, her face smudged with dirt, her wee dog Teddy in a satchel on her back.

No, it seemed that Dani had finally got her ultimate wish: Isabelle's governess, Miss Helena, had clearly succeeded at turning her "respec'able."

She bobbed on her toes with excitement, skirts swinging. With a glance over her shoulder at the party, she beamed at them.

"Everything's so pretty! I was on the decorating committee, you know. And just *wait* until you see the food. They have a whole roasted pheasant with his tail feathers on, and his head! Can you believe it? I don't think I could eat it with the poor bird looking at me like that, to be honest, but it's impressive, anyway. And, Jake—they have roly-poly pudding!"

"Really?" he asked with a startled blink. He hadn't had his favorite food in a hundred years.

"Maybe that'll whet your appetite," she added, giving him a sympathetic smile. "Anyway—everyone's been asking for you."

"Oh." Jake's enthusiasm ebbed as he remembered his quest again.

He wasn't here just to pal around with Dani and Archie and the rest of the gang. He had serious business to attend to.

He glanced at Maddox, who also knew that time was of the essence.

"I'd better go," the older boy mumbled.

"Go where?" Dani asked brightly.

"Gonna say hello to Sapphira." Maddox nodded toward the merfolk.

"Oh." Dani's smile thinned a bit at that.

She had never really taken to the mermaid princess after the older girl had tried to work her feminine wiles on Jake. Dani liked straightforward people, and the watery folk were known to be a bit shifty.

"Well... Give Her Highness my best," she said oh-so-politely.

Miss Helena's training at work.

Jake regarded her in amusement as Maddox walked away. Then they were left standing together at the edge of the party.

"Well, come on!" Dani swished over to his side and playfully grabbed hold of his arm. "Let's go have some fun and cheer you up. You need it."

"Um... I can't quite yet."

"Why ever not?"

"I gotta talk to some people."

"Who?"

"What are you, an owl? Different people. Adults." He made a face.

"Oh." She furrowed her brow. "That's odd. Want me to come with you?"

"Nah, it's Order stuff. I'll get it over with, then I'll come find you."

Now she was suspicious.

"Who are you going to talk to? And why can't I come?" She tilted her head. "Is it a girl?"

"No! You widgeon, it's not a girl." Jake laughed at her.

The mention of Sapphira must have brought back that little jealous streak Dani had shown regarding the mermaid princess. But she was as persistent as her Norwich terrier.

Propping a hand on her hip, Dani narrowed her eyes, searching his face. "What are you up to now, blockhead?"

He heaved a sigh. It was no use lying to Dani. She knew him too well.

"I'm just going to do some askin' around to see if any of these mumpers know where we can find the Black Fortress these days."

"Jake!" Her green eyes flared wide for a moment, but she kept her voice down. "Are you mad? You'll get in trouble. You know you're not supposed to interfere—"

"But I have to."

"You promised to let the adults handle it this time!"

"Oh, and a fine job they're doing, aren't they?" Frustration bubbled up inside him. "I mean, just look at how hard they're trying to save my Gryphon!"

He flung an angry gesture toward the party—and accidentally sent a stray bolt of his telekinesis zinging through the air.

It knocked a tray of appetizers right out of an elven waiter's hands as he circulated among the guests.

Stuffed mushroom caps and little squares of cheese went flying up beneath the chandeliers. People cried out and ducked from the rain of hors d'oeuvres.

"Oh blast it," Jake muttered, humiliated by his blunder. He yanked his hand behind his back, bunching up his fist to contain the uncontrolled power. "Er, sorry!" he called, cringing.

Dani's lips twitched with stifled laughter when he looked at her.

"It's not funny," he snapped.

"You need to calm down."

"Don't tell me to calm down!" he huffed.

"Aw, Jake, don't be cross about the party." She laid a comforting hand on his forearm. "You know the Order has been working nonstop on the situation for the past three months. Derek and Sir Peter and your aunt and Finnderool and nearly everybody else. They're allowed to take a break for one night.

"Besides," she said, "the Harvest Home is a grand old tradition. If the Elders were to cancel it out of worry and fear, it would be like letting the Dark Druids win. Don't you think?"

Jake scowled, but he had to admit that she had a point.

"Now stop being a stick and let's go try some of that roly-poly pudding."

Jake shook his head. "You're a right plum lass, Dani O'Dell, but I've got to do this."

"I'm going to eat it all!"

"No, you're not," he said wryly.

With a sigh, she let him go. "Have it your way, then. Let me know if you need any help. Or if you find anything. And *don't* get in trouble."

He nodded. "See you soon."

Then they parted ways.

Jake looked around, then began moving through the crowd, wondering where to start.

Magical folk of all kinds clustered here and there throughout the ballroom, dressed in their richly colored autumn finery. They seemed engrossed in their own conversations: laughing, sipping drinks, eating hors d'oeuvres.

God, this was going to be awkward.

Then Jake spotted a few stately centaurs chatting with some leafy-headed Green Men. Centaurs were usually rather pompous and high-strung, in his experience, but the Greenfolk were always down to earth, notorious for being kind to children and other living things.

Yes, he thought in relief. That group seemed approachable enough, at least to get warmed up.

Insinuating himself into their conversation was still going to be fairly excruciating. He had no idea what to say. Would rather be fighting gargoyles, actually.

Ah well. Anything for Red.

He'd figure something out.

Here goes nothing. Jake took a deep breath and headed toward them.

CHAPTER 4

A Momentous Announcement

After his meeting with Shemrazul, Wyvern returned to the control room still slightly dazed by the news that he was about to become not *just* the sorcerer-king, but a family man. A warlock of his abilities was difficult to impress, let alone surprise, but that had done the trick.

Lo and behold, just when he started feeling normal again, settling down after this exciting twist in his fate, he received his *second* summons of the night.

This time from Zolond.

One of the royal reptilians appeared in the doorway of the bridge. The impressive creature stood at attention, its crocodilian head held high.

"Lord Wyvern," it rasped, "His Majesty wishes to speak to you."

Wyvern's pulse leaped as he turned to the creature in surprise. *Already?*

Shemrazul had told him that Zolond would make an announcement, and that would be Wyvern's cue to begin preparing to overthrow the old man.

Quickly hiding his eagerness, Wyvern gave the reptilian a cool nod. "Of course. Take me to him."

The reptilian bowed, then left the bridge and led Wyvern down the same hallway he had traversed an hour ago. But, this time, the scaly royal bodyguard showed him over to the closed double doors of Zolond's private chambers.

The creature opened the door, and Wyvern drifted in, on his guard.

He could not deny that he was just a little frightened, going up against the Dark Master, even though the old man had no idea of his intent.

There was no way Zolond could've seen what he and the demon had been scheming—not with Shemrazul's powers to keep matters hidden.

Still, Wyvern was glad he had his wand tucked in its sheath by his side.

Ugh, look at this place. No style at all, he thought as he glanced around at Zolond's decor.

All of the guest chambers and living quarters inside the Black Fortress were covered in magical mirrors, from which the occupant could materialize any sort of setting he or she preferred.

Master Zolond had chosen a most ordinary-looking parlor, such as might have appeared in any comfortable middle-class home across Queen Victoria's England. Persian rug. Lace doilies. Corner curio covered in knickknacks. Cherry-wood end tables, and a cozy wingchair across from a fireplace.

The place reeked of old man.

Wyvern hid his disdain as the reptilian trudged through the parlor and leaned its toothy head politely into the open door of the adjoining chamber. "Lord Wyvern is here, Your Darkness."

"Thank you, Druk," came a frail, scratchy voice from within.

A moment later, the unlikely leader of the Dark Druids ambled out of his bedchamber.

During rituals and incantations, when he was up to his eyeballs in his alchemy work, the Dark Master bedecked himself in black hooded robes like those of a medieval monk. His bony white hands, so gnarled and frail, would clutch his wand and his dagger, and when the dark spirits merged with him, his eyes would glow almost red from the shadows of his hood.

But in ordinary life or when he had business of some sort in the human world, the great sorcerer once known as Sir Geoffrey DeLacey appeared as the most harmless of tidy, well-mannered, little old Englishmen.

Mostly bald and clean-shaven, with grayish eyes, the elderly fellow was short and trim and always dressed in impeccably tailored clothes.

From his black bowler hat and starchy white cravat to his plain black frock coat, gray trousers, and simple leather shoes, he might have been an aged banker, or perhaps an ex-butler who had started his own enterprise in the City and grown prosperous.

He would have appeared right at home feeding the pigeons on a bench somewhere in Hyde Park, with his black bowler hat resting atop his briefcase beside him.

Other than the unusual ring on his finger, a ring of untold power—the Master's ring—there was nothing unusual about him at all.

People passing would've smiled at the sweet-looking old man, and Sir Geoffrey would no doubt have smiled back.

No one by simply looking at him could tell he was quite possibly one of the most evil men upon the Earth, and the most powerful warlock in generations.

Zolond adjusted his sleeves with a little tug, and then smoothed the scarlet silk handkerchief tucked into his jacket pocket.

Wyvern bowed. "You wished to see me, Your Darkness?"

"Yes." Zolond craned his neck back to meet Wyvern's gaze. "I am leaving for a while, commander."

"Leaving?" Wyvern blurted out, shocked by the pinpoint accuracy of the devil's prediction, not the announcement itself, as Zolond must've assumed.

The old man sighed. "I am taking a holiday, Wyvern. It's been ages since I've taken time off. A century, at least."

Wyvern blinked. "Oh. Right. I see. Well then. Very good, sir." A trio of reptilians filed past him, carrying the Dark Master's luggage out of the bedchamber. "Are you quite well, sir?"

"A bit tired these days. I am old, you know. So very old."

The tidy warlock slid his hands into his pockets and studied the floor thoughtfully. "That desert battle in June took it out of me, I'm afraid. Believe I'll go to my mountain retreat for a few weeks and, you know, rest up before it's time for the great rites of autumn and winter. I daresay Samhain will be here before you know it. Then winter solstice."

"Of course, sir." Wyvern hid his glee.

Zolond sent him a penetrating look. "I trust I can rely on you to look after the Fortress while I'm away?"

"Always, Your Darkness. It would be an honor."

"Good." Zolond gazed into the empty fireplace in a faraway mood. He seemed strangely distracted, but he came back from his musings abruptly.

"I will bid you adieu, then, ol' boy. Do keep in touch if anything comes up, won't you?" He was already walking toward the door.

Wyvern took a wide, quick step across the parlor and got the door for Zolond. "Of course, Your Majesty. I'm at your service, as always."

"There's a good chap." As Zolond walked past him, exiting the chamber, he only came halfway up Wyvern's chest.

Such a little man, like a goblin. It was hard to imagine that such a frail person could wreak so much havoc as Zolond had done in his day...

But his day was passing.

Wyvern hid any sign of what Shemrazul had promised him, politely escorting the chief warlock to the bridge, where the old man personally gave the officer of the watch his coordinates.

"Set a course for the Balefire Mountains."

The whole bridge crew glanced at the Dark Master in surprise, but quickly lowered their gazes.

"Aye-aye, sir," the navigator responded.

Zolond held on to the back of the nearest chair to steady himself as the navigator logged in the coordinates.

One of the reptilians approached the frail old man. "Would you like a chair, sire?"

"No need. I invented this thing, did I not?" Zolond smiled.

"Your Majesty is indeed a genius," the lieutenant said earnestly.

Zolond arched a brow.

The officer cleared his throat, then got back to business, flipping switches, adjusting controls. "Preparing to jump." He picked up the communication transmitter and spoke into it, addressing the whole Black Fortress: "All stations, brace for transport, in ten, nine, eight..."

Down in the barracks, the Noxu took heed, holding on to the hand loops. It could be a bumpy ride sometimes. Likewise, in Zolond's potion room, racks securing the vials lowered into place, and in all the mirrored chambers, lights began to flash a polite warning that the Black Fortress was about to leap—never mind that all the guestrooms were empty at the moment.

When all systems were ready, the lieutenant nodded to the chief officer of the watch, who then turned the key.

With that, the infernal machine that powered their jumps roared to life. The entire Fortress began to vibrate and hum. Energy crackled from its four spiky towers.

Familiar as it was, Wyvern still found the whole process thrilling. He accepted a pair of dark glasses that the engineer offered to him.

The bridge had a view down into the large, open courtyard in the center of the castle, allowing the crew to monitor their progress. Presently, they watched the revolving metal shaft of the dynamo rise from its squat brick housing in the center of the courtyard.

The thick metal column spiraled up to its full height, a little taller than the battlements. It locked into the upright position, spinning ever faster.

The whole crew took care to protect their eyes from the dazzling ball of pure energy that formed atop the whirling mechanical pedestal.

Blinding white and brilliant blue, the energy ball swelled and expanded as it danced atop the spinning dynamo.

Lightning bolts now began to leap between the castle's four corner towers.

Great, vicious bolts of it zapped and sizzled back and forth in thick, jagged blue lines. Its intensity grew until, moments later, the four courses of lightning flew toward the middle.

Wyvern had always thought the pedestal looked like some lost little lighthouse, but instead of giving off light, it attracted it, channeled it somehow—and used it to fly.

There were a few mighty pulsations. The lieutenant continued counting down the seconds: "...three, two, one."

Then they leaped, winking out of the Karakum desert, to rematerialize on some desolate plateau in the Balefire Mountains.

"We're here," Zolond quipped.

So they were.

The officers exchanged smiles, and Wyvern shook his head to clear it. It could be a little disorienting.

Mere moments later, they lowered the drawbridge and the tiny head wizard strolled out of the castle with his bowler hat on, a black briefcase in one hand; in the other, he idly swung his walking stick.

Only, Wyvern knew that it was not a walking stick at all, but the scepter of the sorcerer-king in disguise.

The six reptilians marched out in formation around Zolond, all of them armed, most carrying luggage.

Wyvern was happy to see the lot of them go.

Zolond glanced at his fob watch, then waved idly over his shoulder. "Candle-call me if you need anythin', Nathan."

"I will, sir. Enjoy your holiday!"

"I'll be back in time for the full moon at All Hallows' Eve. Cheerio."

"You rest up now!" Wyvern called, lifting his hand in farewell, while the last two members of Zolond's party marched down the drawbridge.

Bringing up the rear, the two largest reptilians trudged out carrying Zolond's sedan chair on its long poles.

They set the old-fashioned vehicle down, and the old man stepped inside. He took his seat, made himself comfortable. Then the two lizard men lifted the sedan chair up by its poles, balancing them on their green, scaly shoulders.

As idly as though he were taking a hansom cab through the streets of London, the elderly chap gazed out the window while the reptilians began carrying him up to his private retreat atop the mysterious Mount Woe, highest peak in the Balefires.

The place was well known to the Dark Druids as a natural vortex where many flowing currents of powerful earth energies converged. One could do great magic there, or draw on deep healing energies. It was an excellent place to go when one was wounded, weary, or planning something big.

No wonder Zolond had established his private hermitage in a cave somewhere on that mountain ages ago, as a mere sorcerer's apprentice.

After all, the crest of Mount Woe was also the sacred spot where the Black Brotherhood crowned their sorcerer-kings. Wyvern could hardly wait till it was his turn, but, for now, he lingered on the open drawbridge, watching the unlikely royal procession head up the slope.

A holiday, eh? Shemrazul was right. The old fox was up to something. No doubt this supposed vacation was tied to the disloyalty Shemrazul had hinted at.

But Wyvern shrugged off the question. One thing at a time. Zolond's exit was clearly the signal the demon had told him to watch for. Now was his chance to start working on his coup.

He strode back inside. "Raise the drawbridge," he ordered, then returned to the bridge.

"Commander, is Master Zolond all right?" the engineer asked timidly.

Wyvern shrugged. "He says he's tired."

He made sure to speak this news loud enough for the whole bridge to hear.

All the men and the nearby Noxu guards on duty looked shocked not just that Zolond was tired, but that he would admit it, for all committed evildoers knew better than to admit to such weakness.

Frankly, Wyvern was shocked by it, too. Perhaps it was a lie, a trap, a deception. Wyvern didn't think so, but, either way, the old man was definitely up to something.

What it might be, he had no idea, and, at the moment, really didn't care.

Perhaps, after three hundred years of his unnatural, long life, the old codger was merely losing his marbles.

All the more reason to remove him from power.

The officer of the watch turned to Wyvern. "Your orders, commander? Where shall I put her down next?"

Wyvern thought it over. Another mountain range came to mind...

Yes, yes, Shemrazul had instructed him to start his to-do list by securing some allies right away.

But Wyvern chafed at the assignment. The prospect of finally having a family of his own proved too hard to resist.

Too bad! he decided. The other bit could wait.

Well, the demon shouldn't have shown him that glorious vision of himself as the sorcerer-king with his cruelly beautiful queen by his side, and his magnificent son at his right hand.

That was what he desired most. Freeing the sea-witch would be easy; his way of doing things was to do the hard part first and get it over with.

The hard part was obviously the boy.

Having had some time to let the news of his destiny sink in, Wyvern had fully embraced the command to take that little hellion for his son.

Oh, the boy was a handful—as he should be, considering—and they'd had their conflicts in the past, even though they had not yet met face to face.

But even Wyvern could admit that, as vexing as the bold lad was, by his own deeds, Jake had already proven himself worthy to become the Black Prince.

Winning him over would be tricky, though.

Especially after Wyvern had tried to have him killed. Not that it had done him any good. He grinned at the thought.

Now he felt almost proud of the lad, looking back on it. Why, the young rogue had, first, destroyed the rock golems he had conjured. Turned them to dust with a wave of his telekinetic hands.

Next, Wyvern had sent three Nightstalkers to snuff the boy out while he was on holiday in Italy, enjoying a Grand Tour with his cousins.

The children had been escorted on their travels by Jake's formidable great-aunt, the Elder witch, Ramona, Lady Bradford.

Wyvern had warned his three phantom assassins not to try going after the lad when the old witch was there. *"Don't worry, he's a wayward young rascal. He'll sneak away at some point. That's what boys* do. *That's when you finish him."*

The Nightstalkers surely would have obeyed these simple orders, yet, somehow, all three had ended up dead—or whatever form of dead could befall phantom wraiths.

Wyvern beamed with pride in Jake now, in hindsight.

Still, no boy of thirteen, not even Wyvern's future son, could defeat even *one* Nightstalker on his own without a darkling blade, and only one kind of folk in the magical world carried those.

Vampires.

Wyvern snorted and shook his head. Oh, yes, he knew exactly who'd helped Jake survive the attack.

That maddening Prince Janos.

Once upon a time, Janos had been a knightly Guardian of the Order. But that was years ago. Before the rebel's fall from grace.

Be that as it may, Jake and Janos seemed to share some sort of bond.

Not that Wyvern was jealous.

But perhaps that smart-aleck vampire could give him some insight into his future son. Explain what made the boy tick. After all, if Jake had not yet responded to the capture of his Gryphon, what on earth was it going to take to lure him?

Janos knew Jake fairly well. He might just have some advice.

Not that the vampire could be trusted. The ex-Guardian was a known spy and a double agent.

But Wyvern had ways of forcing compliance, so he decided to risk it. That smarmy bloodsucker owed him a very large favor, anyway. Wyvern's mind was made up. Never mind what Shemrazul said about his to-do list. Gathering allies could wait.

It was just too exciting to think that he, a Nephilim, would finally acquire a son of his own. So he gave in to temptation.

"Set a course for the Carpathians," he ordered the bridge crew. "Land as close as you can to the stronghold of Prince Janos Gregorian.

It's rough ground there, but no matter. Get us in range, and I'll take my chariot the rest of the way."

"Aye-aye, sir." The navigator checked the maps, and then began dialing in the coordinates.

When the lightning started flying once more from the towers, Wyvern put the dark glasses on, a cold smile curving his lips.

CHAPTER 5
The Sorcerer-King

What are you up to, Wyvern? Where will you go next, I wonder? Zolond stared out the window of his gently rocking sedan chair as the solemn reptilians carried him up the steep, winding grade. His bowler hat resting on his lap, the old warlock watched night deepen over the ominous peaks of the Balefire Mountains.

They spanned out in all directions in this desolate place. Its emptiness comforted him. Nothing but forests and stars. A few night birds warbled in the brush, and their lonely trills let his questions about the Nephilim fade away.

Did he trust his second-in-command?

Of course not. But he was tired of it all, glad to be gone. For the truth was, the Dark Master had more important matters on his mind of late. Ever since that battle three months ago, the past beckoned to him...

At last, the reptilians reached the top of the treacherous path that wound up to Zolond's hidden refuge near the crest of the legendary Mount Woe.

The air was thin on the sacred mountaintop. Even the reptilians were winded as they set the sedan chair down on the stretch of flat, dusty ground outside of what appeared to be nothing more than an ordinary cave.

It was overgrown with weeds so thick that they almost obscured the rough-hewn steps Zolond used to take from his hermitage up to the stone altar on the mountaintop. But a smile tugged at his lips.

Ah, this place brought back memories. He had not been here in an age. But he had spent his youth here, discovering his power, learning how to use it.

With a nod to his trusty guards, Zolond stepped out of the sedan chair and stretched his weary old bones. Then he placed his bowler hat on his head, gripped his walking stick, and walked into the mouth of the cave.

A few little creatures flapped out, frightened—birds, bats. They were welcome to stay; he didn't care. The outer portion of the cave was only the vestibule of his former dwelling place.

As he moved deeper into the darkness, the womb of earth and stone surrounded him and seemed to shield him. Already he could feel the mountain's enormous power.

Cobwebs tickled his face as he ventured deeper into the cave's mouth. He smelled soil and vegetation, heard water dripping down the rocks. Advancing confidently to the cave's back wall, he tapped the living rock with his scepter.

With a rumble and a puff of dust from disuse, the stone portal slid back, revealing the hidden great hall of his mountain refuge.

He stared into his long-abandoned hideaway.

The place where he had ceased to be Geoffrey de Lacey, oh so long ago, and had become the warlock the magical world would eventually know and fear as the favored servant of Shemrazul.

He flicked away a thought of the demon who had given him so much—and who would soon want payment, no doubt.

Taking a deep breath, Zolond strolled into his old bachelor residence. Of course, he'd never married. He'd never had the stomach for it. Funny, that.

After all the terrible things he'd done, that was the one betrayal he could not bring himself to commit.

There was only one woman who ever could have ruled by his side, but she had refused. *She* hated what he had become more than anyone else on the Earth did.

Even Zolond himself.

Brushing off these unsettling thoughts, he took a wry look around at the cavernous chamber, stone-floored and broad beneath its soaring limestone vault. He remembered the cool, welcoming gloom of this place, and yet how the light angled in through the cracks where it could.

"Welcome back, Geoff," he whispered to himself.

It had everything he had needed for his studies. All of the ingredients in his large wooden cabinet of magical supplies would've long since lost their power, but it made him smile. *I ought to replenish them.*

Of course, his magic had moved far beyond mere potions and spells by now. Indeed, his favorite challenge in recent decades was creating living creatures from his own twisted imagination. Crossing things that ought not to be crossed. Men and lizards, like his servants. Men and insects...

Abominations, admittedly, but it made him happy to mock the Creator with his monstrosities.

His restless gaze moved on to his old scuffed worktable. *Ah, my old seeing bowl...* Various grimoires. *I ought to give them away to some deserving young warlock or witch,* he thought, for he'd long since memorized their spells.

Yet it comforted him, seeing his old books.

In truth, Zolond barely knew what was wrong with him these days. He had not been the same ever since *she* had joined that battle three months ago in astral form.

He had trounced her, of course. He had always been just a little stronger than her. Filled with hatred when he'd sensed her there, he had nearly strangled her on the astral plane in their clash, and yet...

Being with her again after their paths had split so long ago—one light, one dark—somehow still invigorated him. That brief tussle with her felt like it had shaved a hundred years off his age.

Most unsettling.

And if that one encounter wasn't bad enough, he was ashamed to admit that he had contacted her again, about a month after the battle.

Why? To mock her? Or to see if she was all right? If he had hurt her very much? He had no idea. All he knew was that he could not resist.

Who else could ever understand him but that blasted witch?

Three hundred years was a very long time to be so alone.

Zolond ambled across the stone floor and went to the arched opening in the cave that served as a balcony. He stood there for a long moment contemplating the valley so far below. Then he lifted his gaze to the indigo sky.

When the September moon appeared briefly through the clouds like an old friend, even *that* reminded him of her. How they used to sneak away from their training masters to meet in the moonlight...

What were they then—she, seventeen? He, nineteen, twenty?

He closed his eyes and cast about inwardly for the chunk of ice where his heart had once been, but he couldn't quite find it. The heart had begun to thaw.

Blast you, Ramona.

How he wished he had not encountered her again in that battle over the burning crater of Karakum this past June. They were too old for such antics, both of them. He sighed.

Where had the time gone? Why, it had stopped on that day so long ago when they'd parted ways. He winced at the memory of her twenty-something self staring at him in horror. *"Geoffrey! What have you done?"*

If she had been outraged when he'd sacrificed his first goat to gain favors from the darker powers of this world, it was after he had sliced the first man open in exchange for still more strength that he and his beloved witch had parted ways.

His true love had banished him from her presence forever. He could still see her shaking her head with tears in her eyes. *"Oh, Geoffrey, you've chosen magic over me."*

That was not his intention, but it was too late, and to this day, her words haunted him like a whole graveyard of ghosts.

Zolond bristled with disgust at himself for even caring.

Stepping away from the stone balcony, he handed his walking stick to his most loyal servant, Druk, the captain of the elite reptilian squad.

Zolond then turned to let Druk take his coat for him, as well.

Druk slipped the black jacket off Zolond's frail shoulders, smoothed it over his arm, bowed, and withdrew.

Zolond sighed, feeling more comfortable, then he slowly walked over to the small round table across from the foot of the moldering canopy bed.

On the table sat a black crystal ball.

He lowered himself wearily into the chair at the table and just stared at it for a moment.

This was what he and Ramona had been using to communicate in secret now and then ever since the battle.

For it was not just the one time that Zolond had contacted his old flame to see if she was injured.

No. Because, after that, the Elder witch of the Order had reached out to him, as well. Of course, it was only to ask him for a favor. He shook his head. Outrageous, that woman.

She said that the Order was aware the Dark Druids were planning a war, and she was right.

Ramona had contacted him in secret to ask if he was willing to open a back channel of negotiations with her. Her side wanted peace—as usual. She wanted to open talks between them to explore whether there was any suitable way their two sides might avoid all-out war before that calamity drew any closer.

Zolond had wanted to refuse her, but found that he could not. He wasn't taking it seriously, in truth, but at least her silly peace negotiations gave him an excuse to talk to her again.

"If nothing else, have mercy on our future generations, Zolond," she'd implored him in their first conversation on the matter some eight weeks ago.

Mercy? he thought with a scoff as dry as desert bones. *Foolish old woman, you know I gave that up long ago.*

But deep in the heart of his black crystal ball, a faint flame still flickered, it would seem.

Blast the woman—just like always, he couldn't resist her. Ah, back when they were young in Shakespeare's day, that sharp, feisty little witch had known just how to twist him 'round her little finger.

Now that they were old, so very old, she still knew how to reach him when he'd had long since concluded there was nothing left in him to reach.

And so, knowing her power over him, the Elder witch of the Order had been conversing with him in secret, suing for peace, and asking for favors that only he, the sorcerer-king, had the power to grant.

Of course, he was only leading her along, he told himself, unsure how much he dared concede. After all, Ramona knew as well as he did that if either of their organizations found out about these secret talks, their own sides would turn on them viciously as a couple of traitors.

How much Shemrazul knew at this point, Zolond did not care to contemplate.

On the outside, the Dark Master was still complying with the Horned One's orders, but, deep down, Zolond was in no great hurry for this long-promised war to begin. Shemrazul wanted it, not him.

Fortunately, he could afford to be patient for a while longer. After all, the hidden army he was gestating in the desert sands needed time yet to hatch. But Ramona didn't know that.

So he let her plead her case and told himself he was only toying with her, enjoying letting his former sweetheart try to persuade him.

It was true; he liked her attention. It made him feel...strange.

But Ramona had a point about keeping the balance between the Order and the Brotherhood. The truce that the two of them had managed to keep between their opposing sides for so long had become unstable of late, partly because of Wyvern's outsize ambitions, and partly because of that blasted nephew of hers.

Jake.

The boy was trouble, a walking earthquake, made for shaking things up. Unpredictable, smart, and just a little cocky.

Jake had not technically *killed* Garnock, but he had blocked the warlock ghost's attempt to bring himself back to life. By doing so, Ramona's nephew had gained the wrath of the whole Brotherhood.

At least, until Duradel had received his shocking prophecy about the boy.

Now the Dark Druids hardly knew what to think. But they had captured his Gryphon as a means of drawing the little hellion to them, and, one way or the other, getting him under control.

Gazing across the room and beyond the balcony at the night sky full of stars, Zolond pondered the prophecy for a moment. What did it mean? Might the dark and light come together in one young man?

Ah, but he was too weary for solving such snarls tonight. That was not why he'd come, anyway.

She was.

Zolond dismissed his reptilians. When they had gone, he laid his gnarled hands on the dark crystal ball, closed his eyes, then called to her in the silence from across the vast emptiness between them.

Ramonaaaa...!

Ramona? Come and speak with me.

By the gods, he was eager to contend with her again, though her effort to pull him back toward the light was quite futile.

More likely, he would pull her into darkness, finally gain his proper queen.

Or perhaps they'd reach a stalemate and turn the whole world a bleak shade of gray between them. At least then neither of them need be so alone.

"Where are you, you cantankerous old woman?"

"I'm busy, old mule. Leave me alone," came her startling reply

through the ethers.

Zolond could not resist a faint smile. *"Ever the spitfire, my dear."*

"It's not a good time. I'm with company, Geoffrey. I will speak to you later."

"Nonsense. I will not be kept waiting. I am the Dark Master!"

"Yes, yes, I know—"

"And don't call me Geoffrey!"

She paused. *"Would you rather I didn't call you back at all?"*

Zolond scowled at the black crystal ball. *"Fine, then. I'll wait. Though I really don't see what could be more important than this—"* he started. Then he remembered the date. *"Oh, right. It's the Order's annual harvest feast tonight, isn't it?"* His lips twisted cynically. *"How quaint."*

"I must see to my duties," the Elder witch said, terse as ever. *"I will contact you later."*

"Humph," Zolond said, but she was already gone.

Fool, he scolded himself, leaning back in his chair. What else could he do?

The most powerful warlock on earth could do naught but drum his fingers impatiently and muse that, perhaps, in time, the fate of all men, young and old alike, came down to this: waiting for women.

Ah well, he supposed, some of them were worth the wait.

Even if it took three hundred years.

CHAPTER 6
The Empath

In the ballroom, Jake's search for information had yielded nothing yet. Neither the centaurs nor the Greenfolk he'd started with an hour ago had had anything useful to say. But they'd been friendly enough, and that had made going on to the next group easier.

It was a remarkable thing. Simply by forcing himself to *act* outgoing, he actually started *feeling* more sociable. It got easier as he went on.

The adults he introduced himself to seemed pleased to make his acquaintance. It turned out they all had heard about him and were intrigued to meet "the lost Griffon heir," much to his surprise.

All in all, mingling with strangers was not as bad as Jake expected. He merely tried to emulate his cousins' glamorous parents, Uncle Richard and Aunt Claire, diplomats for the Order.

They were an elegant couple (though rarely at home), always smooth and refined, in control. Jake did his best to finesse the people he met just like they might have done on some ambassadorial mission to a faraway land.

Of course, from across the ballroom, Great-Great Aunt Ramona seemed to sense that he was up to something.

Tall and slim, with knife-hilt cheekbones and pewter hair gathered into a severe bun, the formidable Dowager Baroness Bradford wore a high-necked gown of plum-colored velvet, a brooch at her throat.

When she noticed Jake working the room, her eagle-eyed stare homed in on him.

If it had been Archie, always gregarious, she would not have thought twice. But for Jake, such behavior was wholly unlike him.

The shrewd Lady Bradford sent him a penetrating stare, arching a silvery brow, as if to say, *You don't fool me, Jacob.*

Not knowing what else to do, Jake had played it cool, lifting his glass of punch to her in a polite toast from across the ballroom.

She had pursed her lips in wry amusement at that in spite of herself. But, fortunately, as an Elder, she had hostess duties tonight, so she could not come and hound him. The next visiting dignitary had approached her to pay his respects, distracting her, and Jake had moved on in relief.

Presently, he was chatting up a red-bearded dwarf lord who'd come down from the north.

Good people, the dwarves. Hardworking, resourceful. Unpretentious—unlike many here. There was just something very trustworthy about the short, stocky folk, in Jake's opinion.

Admittedly, it was odd talking to an adult who was no taller than he was, but Laird Hamish Broadbuckle of the Deep Delves could not have been kinder. The chief of a bounteous clan up in Scotland, the proud forge lord wore a kilt and tam-o'-shanter. Full Highland regalia.

It turned out he was related to Emrys, the head dwarf who ran Jake's goldmine in Wales.

They laughed to discover this unexpected connection.

"You're Lord Griffon?" Broadbuckle boomed, thumping Jake on the back. "Good to meet you, laddie! Emrys wrote to me and me wife a while back and told us he finally got the chance to give you the golden key to the great vault in person."

"Ah, Master Emrys is an excellent fellow," Jake said warmly.

The dwarf lord hesitated. "May I say how truly sorry I am to hear about this distressing situation with Crafanc-y-Gwrool."

"Thank you, my lord." Jake was touched that the laird even knew Red's formal name. It meant *Claw the Courageous* in Welsh.

"If there is anything my people can do to help him or you, you have only to ask."

"All I really want is information," Jake said, keeping his voice down. "If you hear anything about the Black Fortress, any sort of lead would be most welcome."

Within the depths of his bushy red beard, Broadbuckle pursed his lips, then glanced around furtively and nodded. "I'm sure your auntie Ramona wouldn't want me mentioning it to ye, but I heard they were sighted in eastern France six weeks ago. Touched down in some valley in the Alps."

"Really?" Jake asked, startled that he'd actually found something. Or maybe it was nothing, some six weeks after the fact. But at least it was a crumb.

The Scots dwarf nodded. "But ye didn't hear it from me."

"I understand, sir. Thank you."

Broadbuckle cleared his throat and changed the subject. "So, when did you get in?" He nodded at the ballroom, indicating the palace in general.

"Oh—um, we've actually been here since the first of August."

Broadbuckle slurped his ale, but his bushy red eyebrows shot up at Jake's answer. "Aha. And what was that for? Some extra training, or...?"

"No, nothing like that, sir. It, um, it seems the Dark Druids are after me." Jake gave him a wry smile. "Guardian Derek Stone—he's my head of security. He decided it'd be easier to protect me and my cousins here at Merlin Hall, rather than at home. We had to have bodyguards watching us constantly there, in case the Dark Druids tried anything. We were starting to feel like we were under house arrest. It was maddening."

"Ho, I can imagine!" Broadbuckle's head bobbed emphatically. "Young folk need their freedom."

Jake gave him a look of heartfelt agreement. "So, Derek brought us here. The dome of protection spells covering the palace and the grounds at least lets us move about freely. It's a lot better than having Guardians following us around every second of the day."

Broadbuckle nodded with approval. "Safest place for you, no doubt. Especially with old Aelfric on duty out there on the chalk hill, standing guard. What is he, three hundred feet tall?" The dwarf grinned. "Seems a bit excessive to me."

Jake laughed at the dwarf's self-deprecating comment. "It certainly does. I'm glad he's out there, though."

"So am I." Broadbuckle lifted his tankard. "To Aelfric the Long Man!"

Jake smiled back. "To Aelfric." He clinked his goblet of punch against the dwarf lord's cup and drank.

Broadbuckle clapped him on the shoulder before moving off into the crowd. "You watch your back amid all this unpleasantness, laddie. And remember, if there is anything the folk of Deep Delves can do to help you get your Gryphon back safe, you've only to ask."

"My thanks, sir," Jake said, and bowed to the stalwart chieftain.

Broadbuckle nodded, covered a burp, and drifted off to continue speaking with other guests.

What a capital fellow, Jake thought, pleased. Then he pondered what he'd learned about the Black Fortress. *Eastern France, eh? I wonder what they were doing there.*

Henry and Helena came from that part of the world, Jake understood. He'd never been there, but he'd heard it was a heavily forested region in the foothills of the Alps. As he turned, wondering whom to speak to next, Maddox suddenly reappeared, his dark eyes full of urgency.

"Isabelle's in trouble," the older boy said before Jake could even ask if Maddox had learned anything.

He swallowed his questions, alarmed. "What kind of trouble?"

Maddox snorted. "The usual kind."

"Oh," Jake said in relief. "Where is she?"

Maddox nodded toward a distant corner of the ballroom. "Over there."

Jake followed his nod, but could barely see his pretty blond cousin, for Izzy was surrounded on all sides by smiling young men.

Not boys.

"Blimey." He frowned. "Aren't they a bit old for her?"

"Who cares? They're lords," Maddox growled, scrutinizing the situation with a cynical eye. "Figured you'd better do something, 'cause I'm already tempted to punch them."

"Right. We'd better go rescue her." Jake tugged at his waistcoat, then headed in the empath's direction.

Maddox stalked alongside him.

When the crowd shifted, Jake lost sight of Isabelle briefly. "What's going on with you two these days, anyhow?"

"Not a thing," Maddox said.

Jake sent him a skeptical glance.

His friend shrugged. "No point. She's highborn; I'm not. Besides, you know the rules."

Guardians were not permitted to become entangled in what the Elders called "romantic distractions."

"Your cousin's fate is already mapped out for her," Maddox added, as though he couldn't hold his tongue. "First, her debut in London society come the spring. And soon thereafter, marriage to one of these rich toffs."

Jake supposed he was right. "Sorry, mate."

"Doesn't matter." Maddox stared straight ahead as they walked. "Just a childish infatuation. It's done now, anyway."

"Oh really? Does Isabelle know that?" Jake asked, but his friend didn't answer, focused now on the knot of eager swains surrounding the wide-eyed soon-to-be debutante.

Pinned against a white marble column, Isabelle looked like a doe cornered by a pack of hunting hounds.

Jake realized in a glance what must've happened.

These flashy older chaps must have mistaken her friendliness for flirting, when all the lovely young miss had meant to do was ask a few questions in an effort to dig up information on Red.

Jake, in other words, was the one who had got her into this.

Well, he'd get her out of it, too.

He clenched his jaw as he strode toward his cousin, determined to rescue her.

The gentlemen seemed delighted with her, though all they could see of Isabelle's face at the moment was a pair of big blue eyes peeking over the edge of her fan.

Her crown of golden tresses was pulled back with ribbons and combs and hung past her shoulders in long, shiny spirals. Dressed in a short-sleeved ball gown of cream-colored silk trimmed with gold lace, she looked almost entirely grown up.

The bachelor lords surely viewed her as future wife material. And why should they not, Jake supposed? The aristocratic Bradford family had an excellent reputation in both the magical world and the human one, and she would have a generous dowry. Besides, marriages where the husbands were some ten years older than the wives were the norm, not the exception. Such was the case with Uncle Richard and Aunt Claire.

But Izzy was clearly fed up with their attentions. The sight of Jake and Maddox approaching brought her out from behind her fan.

She sent Jake a look of desperation that said: *Help!*

He quirked a smile to assure her he'd get her out of there.

What idiots, he thought when he came into earshot.

Men in their mid-twenties, he guessed, they were doting on her like she was some adorable child. Not the fierce young Keeper of Unicorns who had whacked Garnock the Sorcerer in the head with her ivory staff.

The fearless girl who had helped Jake face up to no lesser demon than the horrible Shemrazul himself.

"My dear Miss Bradford, you mustn't be afraid," a chap in a fluffy cravat assured her with a wink. "If war comes, we will win it in a trice."

"That's right. We'll trounce 'em, don't you fret," said a muscular fellow with perfectly sculpted sideburns.

"Personally, I can hardly wait to fight," a dapper gent declared, looking pleased with himself.

Maddox rolled his eyes.

"Enough grim talk of war. You're frightening her," Cravat Man scolded the others, his tone unbearably condescending. "Let us speak of something pleasant now. Tell us, Miss Bradford, what sort of debutante ball are your parents planning for you, hmm? I had better get an invitation."

"Me, as well!" said Sideburns. "Will that be April or May?"

"I'll be positively crushed if you don't promise me a dance." The third chap gave her what he probably thought was a charming smile.

"Um, gentlemen..." Isabelle shrank back against the pillar. "I fear we are w-well in advance of any such decisions."

They laughed and exchanged knowing glances that seemed to say, *Isn't she precious?*

"I'm gonna puke," Maddox said under his breath.

"Just stay back." Jake didn't want his Guardian friend taking a swing at any of these titled gents, or they could make Maddox's life miserable.

Frankly, Jake wasn't sure himself how to proceed.

It wasn't as though he wanted to start a fight with five grown men in the middle of the ballroom.

At once, a helpful thought surfaced: what would Cousin Archie do?

After all, Isabelle's brother had been helping her escape overzealous admirers since she was twelve. Her problem was she could never be rude to anyone. She didn't want to hurt anyone's feelings.

So she ended up getting trapped like this on occasion.

Jake decided to take Archie's usual approach: politely play dumb.

With that, he elbowed his way in between two of the strapping swains and planted himself by his cousin's side.

The gents seemed startled by his arrival, but in no way threatened by him, a mere thirteen-year-old.

They should be careful, thought Jake. He could act like Archie when the occasion called. But he wasn't Archie.

Archie was the nice one.

Though Jake kept his smile fixed in place, he was tempted to use his telekinesis to knock them down like bowling pins. And he just might, if they gave him cause. Of course, it would probably ruin Izzy's marriage prospects with any of these dunces, but he doubted she would mind.

"Excuse me, dear coz," Jake said sweetly, "the family's going to sit down to dinner now. They've sent me to fetch you. Shall we?"

He offered her his arm like the proper-est of gentlemen.

Archie would be proud.

Izzy clasped his arm as though it were a life ring tossed out to a drowning person at sea. She gave Jake a discreet look of gratitude, then smiled uneasily at her admirers.

"Good evening, gentlemen. My family needs me."

"Of course, my dear."

"A pleasure, Miss Bradford."

"Until the spring."

They all bowed to her, nearly bumping heads.

Izzy didn't answer or bother curtsying back, but shuddered as Jake led her clear of the pack.

Maddox closed ranks behind her, just in case any of those ponces tried to follow.

"Well, aren't you popular," Jake murmured in amusement as the three of them took refuge in the crowd.

"Ugh," said Izzy, pressing her fingertips to her temples. "That was unpleasant. Not all emotions are fun to read, I tell you."

Jake gave her a startled look, and Maddox growled like a guard dog.

"My head's ringing," she added. "I think I overdid it here tonight."

Jake frowned. He knew that Isabelle's empathic powers quickly became overwhelmed in large crowds. There were too many thoughts, unspoken conflicts, and swirling emotions for one person's mind to take in. "I shouldn't have asked you to do this."

"No, it's all right," she said. But when she wobbled a bit on her feet, he steadied her by her elbow.

"You should sit down."

She shook herself. "No, I—I'm fine."

Jake furrowed his brow. "Are you sure?" She looked a little green around the gills to him.

But Izzy nodded, resolute, and took a deep breath. "Feeling better already."

"Then would you mind telling me what the blazes all that was about?" Maddox burst out, as if he could not contain himself any longer. "Where is your governess? Where is your mother?"

"I beg your pardon?" Izzy glanced over her shoulder at him with an offended huff.

Maddox glowered at her. "You should not be talking to them unchaperoned. It isn't proper!"

"*What?* Don't criticize me! It's not *my* fault they wouldn't go away. I'm doing my part to help Red, just like the rest of you."

"Well, be more observant next time," Maddox said curtly. "You're going to get a reputation as a flirt."

Izzy's jaw dropped as she let out a gasp.

"Maddox, really," Jake chided.

The older boy pivoted away, muttering, "I'm going back to talk to Sapphira."

The empath narrowed her eyes. "I have a spotless reputation, as it happens!" she fairly shouted after him, but Maddox huffed off through the crowd.

"Of course you do," Jake hastily assured her. "The best."

Blimey, Isabelle was the most virtuous person he knew.

"Just ignore him. You know that's just Maddox being Maddox. He gives everyone a hard time."

"Not like he does me!" She shook her head, her blue eyes blazing with ire. "He really goes out of his way to drive me insane, doesn't he?"

"Nah, it just comes naturally. He doesn't even have to try."

She looked at Jake for a second, startled, then a rueful half-smile tilted her lips. She shook her head and sighed, letting the matter go. "Thanks for coming over to get me, coz. I couldn't seem to extricate myself. I didn't want to be rude, but those gentlemen *wouldn't stop talking.*"

"It's all right to be rude sometimes, Iz. Just ask Maddox."

"Or you," she shot back.

"Never!" he said with a grin. "C'mon. Let's go find the others. I believe Dani was trying to save us a table so we could all sit together."

Izzy nodded and waved her fan, still looking like she needed some air, but she walked along beside him through the crowd.

"So. He's spending time with Sapphira again, is he?" She went up onto her toes, nonchalantly searching the ballroom in the direction Maddox had gone. "Is *Bellissima* throwing herself at him again? Oh, never mind, I don't even care."

"You don't?"

"No! Well, maybe. I don't know. He's impossible. One minute he treats me like I barely exist, and the next, he's bossing me around."

Jake sent her a confused glance.

Izzy heaved a sigh. "Never mind. It's just—he's been a total stranger ever since Ravyn went missing. I know he's upset, but he doesn't have to shut me out. Then he overreacts like you just witnessed. It's so immature!"

Jake shrugged sympathetically. He had personally given up hope of making any sense of their relationship. The weird part was that Maddox St. Trinian was the only person Isabelle couldn't read. Her empath powers allowed her to sense the emotions of everyone around her. But not Maddox.

One of the clairvoyant advisers had told her it meant that their fates were inextricably tied somehow.

But that could mean anything—good or bad.

Shrugging off her romantic woes, he got back to the task at hand. "So, did your new admirers have anything useful to say about Red?"

She snorted. "No. They were too busy bragging about how brave they were going to be if there's a war."

"Guess they wanted to impress you."

"Then they should start by treating me like an actual human being with an actual working brain. Strike up a *real* conversation instead heaping me with stupid flattery. But no. They don't even care what's on the inside. All they see is my face. If one more idiot tells me how blue my eyes are, I'm honestly going to clobber him."

Jake glanced dryly at her. Isabelle was scowling. He could barely contain his amusement, for such an outburst from the demure young empath was rare.

"All right, then."

"Sorry," she mumbled, "I don't mean to complain. I just hope that when the time comes, my parents betroth me to a man who actually *cares* who I am as a person. Not just some silly china doll to set up on the mantel at his estate."

"Don't worry, coz, all that's still a long way off," Jake said. "You're not even making your debut until the spring. And what with the Dark Druids and all this talk of war, the world might've ended by then. You might get out of it altogether if there's an apocalypse."

She laughed. "Here's hoping."

Jake flashed a teasing glance at her, then spotted Dani waving eagerly to them from the round table she had secured for their group.

He had seen her sitting there earlier, alone, arms crossed, looking bored and disgusted with how this night was turning out. After all her high hopes about the Harvest Home party, she was having no fun at all.

He felt terrible for abandoning her, but it had only been an hour or so, and he was determined to keep her out of this as much as possible.

Beckoning them over, Dani must've noticed Isabelle's pallor, for her protective gaze homed in on the older girl. As official lady's companion to the viscount's daughter, Dani made it her business to look after Isabelle.

Abandoning the table at once, Dani rushed over to Izzy's side. "What happened? Are you all right? Do you need to leave?"

"Do I look that bad?" Izzy exclaimed.

"You're an interesting shade of green," Jake admitted.

"Come and sit down," Dani ordered, hurrying Isabelle over to the table before some other group could claim it.

Jake followed as Dani pulled a chair out for Izzy, going all mother hen. "Do you need some ginger ale? Almond biscuits?"

"That sounds wonderful, Dani. You are so thoughtful."

"Pish," the Irish lass said as the debutante sat down gracefully. Dani scampered off to fetch her refreshments.

"Honestly, what would we do without her?" Isabelle murmured.

Jake stared after the redhead. "I don't ever want to think about that."

Moments later, Nixie sauntered out of the crowd nibbling a lemon biscuit. She plopped into a chair at their table.

"Anything?" Jake asked.

The little witch shook her head, making the glittered orange spider brooch in her hair sparkle. "Nope. Not about your Gryphon, anyway. But I did collect a load of juicy gossip I could probably sell to the

Clairvoyant for a small fortune." Nixie finished her lemony treat in one irreverent bite.

Isabelle lifted her eyebrows.

"Where's the boy genius?" Jake asked her, since those two had become inseparable of late. "Still out talking to the giants?"

"Let's hope my brother didn't get stepped on," Izzy interjected.

"No, he's back. The giants were clueless." Nixie glanced around. "He's getting himself another cup of coffee."

"Ah." Jake nodded. "I take it he had another late night in his lab?"

Nixie shrugged. "You know Archie. He's determined. He takes an idea into his head and doesn't let it go until it either works or he finds some other way." She paused. "Say. Do either of you think he's been acting kind of weird lately?"

Jake and Isabelle looked at her intently.

"Weird how?" Izzy asked, but Jake quickly stifled the conversation when he saw Archie coming.

"Speak of the devil! Ahem."

Just then, Archie drifted over to them in his tweed coat and bowtie, one hand in his pocket, the other holding one of those little Italian coffees he'd fallen in love with during their Grand Tour.

He was chatting with the amiable Sir Peter Quince, the youngest of the Elders, who served as chancellor of Merlin Hall and dean of all student programs.

This place couldn't run without the easygoing wizard and his adoring wife, Jillian. Her official title, of course, was Lady Peter Quince, but with the couple's laidback manner, the chancellor's wife insisted that everybody simply call her Jillian.

Sir Peter wore his official black wizard robe draped over his clothes, along with his usual orange tie. Behind his tortoiseshell spectacles, his friendly eyes were thoughtful.

"Well, I have faith in you, Dr. Bradford," he was saying to Archie, who, in fact, did hold two university degrees despite being only twelve. "Keep me posted on your progress, won't you? If there's anything else you need for your lab, equipment and such, let us know. We will spare no expense to see our poor Aleeyah restored to her usual self."

Archie nodded. "Thank you, sir. I won't rest until the djinni is free."

As the pair joined them, the boy genius smiled a weary greeting at everyone, and Sir Peter paused at their table.

"And a fine good evening to you all," the chancellor said cheerfully.

The kids answered in kind.

They were all very fond of him and his non-magical wife. Jillian had been following a few feet behind her husband, delayed by all the people who wanted to chat with her.

A trim blond woman with a reputation for being supremely organized, Jillian Quince reminded Jake a bit of a librarian, though he wasn't sure why. It could've been her hair in a tidy bun, the spectacles dangling from a chain around her neck, or the modest cut and understated hue of her clothes.

Gray seemed to be her favorite color, but dull as it was, she looked pretty, nonetheless. She had fine eyes and a warm smile.

"Bit more exciting around here tonight than it's been the past few weeks, eh?" Sir Peter said.

They agreed it was.

"It's a lovely party," Dani chimed in as she came bustling back with Izzy's refreshments.

"Inn't, though? Compliments to this fair lady." Sir Peter hooked his thumb toward his wife, who now joined them. "Jilly-bean did all the work of planning it, organizing everything—"

"Well, Miss O'Dell was kind enough to help me put up the decorations," Jillian said as she reached her husband's side. As she slipped her arm around Sir Peter's waist, Archie glanced at Dani in surprise.

"Did you? I didn't know that."

"You've been *kind* of in your own world lately, Arch," Nixie said.

"Well, it looks really nice," Jake told the couple and Dani.

"Glad you approve, Lord Griffon! Enjoy the party, all. Cheerio." Sir Peter gave them a wink and then strolled on, tugging Jillian with him by the hand.

As an Elder, he had to assist with hosting duties, just like Aunt Ramona.

When he had gone, Jake poked Archie in the shoulder. "Did you talk to the giants?"

The boy genius nodded, but his dark eyes filled with regret behind his spectacles. "Sorry, coz. That yielded precisely zed."

Jake sighed. "I guess I'm not surprised. Worth a try, anyway."

"I'm just glad I didn't get squashed out there," Archie replied. "Bloody menace, those big feet." He sipped his coffee and gave Nixie's shoulder an affectionate squeeze as he stood behind her chair.

What an odd couple they were, Jake thought. Though they were opposites in every conceivable way, somehow they got along swimmingly together.

Perhaps it had something to do with the fact that they were both brilliant in their own ways, a pair of huge brains. As advanced as Archie was in science, Nixie was his equal in her magical studies.

Indeed, she was such an outstanding student that the Elder witch herself had volunteered as Nixie's official mentor in magic.

"So, are we ready to eat?" Archie asked after taking another gulp of coffee. "We can go and get in line for the buffet now, if you like."

"Shouldn't we wait for Mother and Father?" Isabelle asked.

"Oh, I saw them. They said to go ahead and eat whenever we want," Archie replied. "You know them. They'll be socializing all night."

Isabelle nodded to her brother, then glanced at her companion. "Thanks for the snack, Dani. This is really helping."

As the empath finished her ginger ale, Jake was glad to see the color had returned to her cheeks.

Dani nodded, then elbowed Jake. "Let's go nabble some of that roly-poly pudding before it's gone."

Jake smiled at her, gesturing politely. "After you, carrot-cake."

Dani grinned at the latest form of her nickname.

Nix and Izzy rose from their seats while the boys took off their jackets and draped them over two chairs to signal that the table was taken.

Izzy set her fan down in front of her place for the same purpose, but Nixie removed the glittery orange spider clip from her hair and gave it a tap with her wand.

The hair clip became animated, ready to scamper onto anyone who tried to sit down at their table.

"That would keep me away," Dani said in surprise.

With a clever smile, Nixie slipped her wand back into its holster on her waist.

Then they all headed toward the long buffet tables, where people were queuing up to heap their plates with the bounty of the harvest feast.

Since he really had very little appetite, Jake gestured to the others to go in front of him. He took his place at the end of the line, and then suddenly felt someone tap him on the shoulder.

He turned around to find his mentor and head of security,

Guardian Derek Stone, looming over him.

The dark-haired warrior looked even more intense than usual as he bent his head toward Jake. "I need to talk to you for a minute."

Jake's heart jolted at the serious look on Derek's rugged face.

Instantly, he realized that one of two things must've happened. Either Derek had found out that Jake and his team of "spies" had been making inquiries tonight about the location of the Black Fortress.

Which meant he was about to get a wigging.

Or the fearless Guardian himself had heard something about Red—something he could share.

Jake desperately hoped it was the latter. Because being scolded by the likes of the mighty Derek Stone was no fun at all.

The big warrior didn't look angry, though, so maybe it *was* the latter option. Jake prayed that was the case.

He nodded, his stomach knotting with anticipation to hear the news, whatever it might be. "Lead the way."

Derek straightened up and turned around. At once, he started plowing off through the crowd. Jake hurried after him with barely a glance behind. His friends were busy collecting their plates, chatting together, and peering ahead to see what food selections awaited.

They didn't even notice as Jake slipped away, hurrying after Derek.

Ahead, the wide-shouldered master Guardian strode out of the ballroom.

Jake followed anxiously, his heart pounding with suspense to hear what Derek had to say.

CHAPTER 7
Once a Guardian

Hundreds of miles to the east, night had only just arrived. Sunset faded, and a moody autumn twilight crept over the Carpathians, waking the owls, the bats, and other creatures of the night.

Including Prince Janos.

He had arisen from his coffin and was just finishing up getting dressed for the night, tying his cravat before the mirror—simply out of habit, of course. There was no reflection there anymore.

Pity, that.

He knew he had not aged a day since that fateful night in his early twenties when he'd made his decision to join the undead. Still, it irked him that he no longer got to see that handsome face, dark green eyes, and long, glossy black hair that had made him such a favorite with the ladies.

Hmm. On second thought, maybe it was better that he couldn't look himself in the eye anymore. He was not sure he could have done it even if he got the chance.

But so be it. He was what he was now, and there was no going back. No changing it, no undoing bad decisions. Some mistakes one simply had to live with.

Forever.

He heaved a soul-weary sigh. Immortality was such a bore.

At that very moment, a bloodcurdling scream rose from somewhere outside the front of his castle.

Not that this was terribly unusual.

Still, when the scream was followed by a flurry of diabolical giggling, Janos turned from the empty mirror with a scowl. "Oh, what now?" he muttered under his breath. Then whooshed over to the window to see what was happening.

There, by the silvery light of moonrise, he beheld an infuriating sight down in the stone courtyard below.

Not again!

It seemed his dear little hatchlings had lured yet another wagonload of unsuspecting travelers to their doom.

His children, some twenty or thirty of them—he could hardly keep track—the tallest of which, now stood about as high as his waist.

What the little darlings would do by the time they were up to his shoulder, Janos did not care to contemplate.

Cute as cherubs, vicious as wolves, they were chasing the peasants gleefully around the stone enclosure. They had been ill for so long, but now, thanks to that healing potion he had demanded from the Order in exchange for key information about the Dark Druids, his hatchlings had recovered.

And how.

The bigger boys were presently taunting their prey, trying to grab the poor souls hiding under the wagon, while the toddler-sized ones were climbing up to try and gnaw on the terrified horses' necks with their nubby little fangs.

Janos scowled. They were just children, though, and didn't know any better.

What really infuriated him was the sight of their beautiful mothers (three of the six) clapping their hands and cooing their encouragement to the little monsters.

"That's it, darling, bite the horsey! Good girl!"

"Terrify your prey, my dove, it improves the flavor!"

Janos rolled his eyes.

Once upon a time, he had thought it would be amusing to have a different wife for every day of the week, but he had lost interest in the game once he realized he was badly outnumbered when it came to domestic arguments.

He feared he was losing altogether when it came to how to raise the hatchlings, even though the children liked him best.

Thank God he had quit, bride-wise, while he was ahead.

The other half of his harem must not have arisen from their coffins yet, but that was just as well. Dealing with three of his ladies at once was challenging enough.

Look at them, he thought, shaking his head. They did not know the meaning of pity.

"Hurry, darlings!" Morgravaine called to her brood. "Don't let that fellow get away. Over there—he's trying to run!"

The peasant man fled with a scream as two ten-year-old boys sprinted after him with freakish speed, laughing.

"That does it," Janos muttered to himself.

A long time ago, he had been a Guardian of the Order, after all, serving under Derek Stone himself before his fall from grace, when his wicked, lovely ladies had led him astray.

Old habits died hard, it would seem. Defend the weak, protect the innocent. All that rot.

Well, he might be a vampire prince these days, but he would not sit around and let his children eat the neighbors.

Seriously perturbed, Janos left his chamber at once and marched out of the castle, his black banyan robe billowing out behind him, his boot heels ringing out over the cold, clammy flagstones.

The sounds of terror and childish hilarity grew louder as he stomped down the ancient staircase and through the dim, drafty great hall of his gloomy Gothic castle.

In the next moment, he flung open the double doors onto the courtyard and bellowed at his brood: "WHAT IS GOING ON HERE?"

The moment he burst out wrathfully from the castle into the courtyard, the children flocked away in a rush of wings and nails-on-chalkboard shrieks.

"Get back here!" he thundered.

To his relief, the vampire younglings came skulking back, ducking their heads. They all knew he was an indulgent parent. But there came a point!

Janos set his fists on his waist and looked around sternly at them. "Children, you know this is not allowed."

They started pointing at each other.

"He started it!"

"She made me!"

"No, I didn't—"

"Enough!" he barked.

"But Mummy said we could!"

"Husband!" His gorgeous blond wife, Deceptrix, glided over to him with a look of indignation. "What are you doing? Your children have to eat!"

"Not like this. Ladies, we discussed this." Janos gave his three beautiful brides a furious glare, then looked again at the terrified travelers. "My good people, I'm terribly sorry about this, er, misunderstanding. Let's get you sorted and send you on your way, shall we?"

"Janos! This must be one of your jokes." Hexella, his red-haired, milky-skinned wife, glided into his path, daring to defy him as Janos took a step toward the wagon. "The children caught these fools all by themselves! You ought to be proud, not punish them. They have to learn to hunt!"

"Not humans, Hex," Janos said patiently. "You know the rules. I am letting these people go. Now step aside—"

"Not so fast!" said Morgravaine, his fiercest wife, the cruel, raven-haired beauty. Always the ringleader, that one. She looked him over in disgust and shook her head. "You call yourself a vampire."

"Mind your tongue, woman," he warned, bristling.

She hissed. "Don't be a fool! We *have* to kill them now. They've seen us! If we let them go, they'll blab it everywhere, and we'll have a pitchfork mob here by morning, staking us all through the heart in our sleep. Is that what you want?"

Doesn't sound so bad.

He waved off her protest. "My darlings, do you really think I would ever let that happen to you? Don't worry, I'll oubliette them before I send them on their way, same as always. Children." He turned to the worried horde of juvenile vampires. "Go to your rooms. You will have no breakfast until you've thought good and hard about what you've done here. You've been very naughty."

Some of the littler ones started crying over their punishment, much to his dismay.

"But Papa—!"

"We do not eat people in this household! Do you understand? There is food aplenty in the forest without us ever resorting to this."

"Ignore him, sisters. We'll feed the children ourselves!" Morgravaine suddenly shouted, whooshing toward the peasants.

The other two vampiresses instantly followed suit; they hunted best in packs.

"Don't you dare!" Janos bellowed, sweeping in front of the three sinister beauties, and planting himself between the huntresses and the blubbering peasants.

He did not like to yell at his ladies, but sometimes they really left him no choice. He jerked his head to the side and violently shrugged his shoulders, donning his full vampire form to ward them off.

He roared a warning at them, baring his fangs. "No one touches these people!" he snarled.

"Get out of our way!" Morgravaine barked, taking her hideous vampire form back at him.

"You owe us!" cried Deceptrix.

"We made you what you are!" Hexella reminded him.

"And am I to thank you for that?" Janos thundered. Then he roared in their faces, bristling, fangs bared, lifting his clawed hands out at his sides, just a wee reminder of who was in charge here.

One of the peasant woman fainted.

But, fierce as they were, especially when they worked together in bloodthirsty elegance, the vampire brides knew they were no match for Janos. That was why they had chosen him, after all. A lesser man they'd have quickly torn apart.

That didn't mean they always liked him, though.

Still hissing, the angry vampire brides lowered their heads and backed down resentfully, retracting their fangs.

Janos delayed doing so, eyeing them with mistrust. He would risk no sneak attack from his females on these poor people, especially Morgy, that she-devil.

"Well!" Hexella finally huffed, returning to her gorgeous, red-haired human form. "I never!"

Deceptrix turned herself back into her usual blond goddess self and feigned a sniffy little sob. "You don't love us anymore!"

Morgravaine chose her weapons with greater care. "We should've chosen Derek Stone."

Janos hid his wince at his old team leader's name. "You tried. He rejected you, remember?"

Ah, Derek, the model of manly virtue.

Morgravaine harrumphed.

Then came the pouting.

Muttering about how mean Janos was, giving him countless dirty looks, the huntresses whooshed away, turning themselves into bats and flying off to their respective towers to sulk.

Perfect, Janos thought with a low snort. Now they'd all be in a bad mood for a week. *Typical.*

Calming himself back into his fully human form, he felt his razor-sharp fangs recede and his claws retract, and only then did he turn around and take a polite step toward the travelers.

They screamed and jumped back from him.

Their hysteria annoyed him. Had he not just saved their blasted lives?

Eager to be rid of them, Janos held up his hand and began to speak soothingly to them, drawing on the mesmerizing power of his vampire charm until he'd calmed them down a bit. "There, there, everything is going to be fine, my good folk. Just look into my eyes, and in a moment, you'll feel better..."

Once he had their full attention, he recited the oubliette spell over the baffled travelers, effectively erasing the past half-hour from their minds.

At last, he helped them turn their carriage around, still mortified by his little ones' horrid behavior.

"Wh-what are we doing here?" the peasants asked, blinking under the confusion effect of the spell.

"Why, you stopped to ask for directions, don't you remember?" Janos said sweetly. "And to answer your question, the north road is that way." He pointed politely to the road outside the castle. "You'll want to follow that for another mile up the mountain, then bear right at the twisted old oak. You can't miss it. But, er, I would pass quickly through these forests if I were you. There are wolves in these parts. Don't worry, they won't harm you as long as you keep moving."

The wolves around here answered to him.

"Right! Well, then, off you go. Good night and safe travels." He bade them adieu with a friendly wave.

When they had finally lumbered off, Janos blew out a weary exhalation.

This night was not off to what anyone could call a promising start, but as he would shortly discover, it was about get a great deal worse.

He should've known that something was wrong when his ancient butler, Creakwood, came shuffling out, looking like he'd just dragged himself up from his grave.

"Beg pardon, Your Highness. You have a visitor."

Janos looked at him in surprise. "A visitor? Here?" He had not heard anyone arrive. He glanced around, confused. "Where?"

Creakwood gestured up discreetly at the ramparts atop the castle walls.

Janos followed the direction that the butler's bony finger pointed, then he saw it—a wonder to behold.

He must've missed the sound of its arrival amid all the screeching and screaming. But up near the roof of his keep, he could just make out the silhouette of a dragon chariot against the night sky.

And he went very still, for he knew exactly who it belonged to. Not many people drove one of those flashy things, even in the magical world.

Wyvern.

So. He's finally come.

Janos felt his stomach tighten in a knot. But he looked at his butler with an unflappable smile. "I will receive His Lordship in the drawing room."

"Yes, master."

As Creakwood hobbled off, Janos squared his shoulders to go and greet the Nephilim warlock. The most dangerous foe he'd ever faced.

In truth, he had been expecting this visit for a long time now. Three months, to be exact.

For years, Janos had managed to avoid having to choose outright between the Order and the Dark Druids. He'd carved out a comfortable niche for himself in the shadows between good and evil, using both sides as he pleased to achieve his own interests.

But when he'd heard that the Black Brotherhood had captured Derek (and were no doubt torturing him), Janos had emerged from the gray zone to help the Order rescue the hard-nosed warrior who had once been like an elder brother to him.

He had fought on the Order's side that night in the desert, but even then, he'd known there would be a price to pay.

Well, it seemed the time had come to give the devil his due.

So be it. Janos lifted his chin, insolent as ever, and unimpressed by this Nephilim.

He wasn't sure how to kill such a creature, but he trusted he could figure it out.

As he began marching back across the courtyard, he checked the darkling blade at his hip.

Careful, he warned himself as he strode toward the castle entrance. *Use your wits before you attack.*

But look on the bright side. If Wyvern kills you tonight, that is not entirely a bad thing. To be sure, there were worse fates than death.

He should know. He was living one.

* * *

After landing his dragon chariot on the ramparts atop the castle's curtain wall, Wyvern had spent several fascinating minutes watching the vampire prince with his wives and children.

The jump had gone smoothly, of course. The Black Fortress waited a few miles away on a remote plateau the navigator had pinpointed amid this craggy terrain.

Once they'd rematerialized at their destination, Wyvern had taken his personal vehicle the rest of the distance. He knew the dragon chariot was a bit ostentatious, but it was nimble and fast; the Ruffed Orange Darter in the harness was a breed known for responsiveness and precision in flying.

Wyvern couldn't help it—he loved driving the thing. The speed, the elevation, the wind in his hair, the powerful rhythm of his dragon's wings.

When he pictured Jake riding on his Gryphon through the sky, it pleased Wyvern to imagine that he might have something in common with his future son. The Darter was trained for saddle as well as harness, so perhaps the two of them could go out flying sometime.

In any case, leaving the Black Fortress, Wyvern soon spotted Janos's spiky Gothic castle below. During his approach, he saw that the curtain wall surrounding the keep was as wide as a road.

He had easily touched down there. The Darter galloped a few paces atop the wall, gradually slowing.

"Whoa!" Wyvern tugged the reins until the orange-brownish beast had halted, and then set the brake.

Jumping out of the sleek vehicle, Wyvern instantly heard the commotion coming from the courtyard below.

Curiosity drew him.

With the sharp, pointy spires of the vampire castle reaching up into the dark sky around him, and his winged dragon flexing its long neck, shaking itself with a jangle of the harness, then settling itself down to wait, Wyvern walked over to the battlements to see what was going on.

What he witnessed had intrigued him—for personal reasons. For several long moments, he stared down at the strange little scene of vampire family life playing out below.

Wyvern had never much thought about it before, but it struck him now with newfound interest that Janos had a family. His wives were beautiful, his children too many to count, lively and strong, if a little bloodthirsty.

Wyvern smiled down upon them with a stirring of some fond, alien feeling inside as he watched the rowdy vampire hatchlings terrorize the hapless peasants.

How proud of his brood the vampire prince must be.

Truly, what Wyvern witnessed during those few short minutes had encouraged him in the wondrous new assignment he had received from Shemrazul. For if a creature of darkness like Janos could have a home and a family, then why not him?

Yes, Wyvern thought, this might really work.

Then the vampire's ancient butler had come limping out to escort him inside, and Wyvern left the scene of dark-world domestic bliss behind.

As he followed the butler into the castle, however, there was one thing he did not understand.

Why on earth would Janos value a bunch of peasants' miserable lives over the care and feeding of his hatchlings?

The old Guardian instincts must still be strong in the undead prince.

Wyvern made a wary mental note of that, then followed the butler down the tower's spiral stairs.

CHAPTER 8

The Best of Men

Following Derek out of the ballroom, Jake's heart thumped as he wondered whether he was in trouble or what.

Passing the corn sheaves and scarecrows posted by the ballroom doors, they left the constant roar of conversation behind, stepping out into the white marble lobby.

Here, it was quiet. Hardly anyone around. The only sound was Derek's heavy footfalls echoing ahead under the high, domed ceiling.

Jake's lighter steps reverberated more quietly as he followed the master Guardian across the milk-white floor of polished marble.

Directly across from the ballroom, the huge double doors of Merlin Hall's main entrance led out into the pleasant night.

But Derek did not go outside. Instead, he veered to the left, walking around to the side of the massive marble staircase to put some distance between them and the crowd.

Jake joined him there, waiting on tenterhooks to hear what he had to say.

The best-case scenario was that the Order had found the Black Fortress and were already organizing a team to go and rescue Red. The worst case, of course, was that Jake was about to be scolded for sticking his nose into the matter.

True, he had been ordered to let the adults handle it this time. But, so far, they weren't doing a very good job, now, were they?

In the shadow of the staircase, Derek turned to face him, his callused hands resting on his hips.

Dry-mouthed, Jake passed a worried glance over the Guardian's rough-hewn face, trying to guess what he was going to say.

But the big man was difficult to read.

The soldiers of the Order were trained to keep their emotions in check, and that usually meant hiding them.

The strong, silent type, Derek had returned from his ordeal at the hands of the Dark Druids even quieter than before. Jake had heard that Wyvern had tortured him. *That chap had better hope that he never crosses paths with me.*

Derek's dark, soulful eyes had seemed haunted ever since. He even looked different, for his captors had shaved off his previously long, dark mane of hair as part of his humiliation.

His hair had grown back since then, of course. He wore it short and neat now instead of long and wild; Miss Helena liked it better this way.

Jake was so glad that the big warrior had Isabelle's governess to care for him, after all he'd been through.

The genteel courtship between the two had been moving along slowly for the past year. And yes, Guardians weren't supposed to form romantic attachments, but, in this case, the Elders were prepared to turn a blind eye.

He was Derek Stone, after all.

As the big man turned to him, Jake braced himself for the news, whatever it was. He held his breath. "Well?"

"I have to show you something," Derek murmured. "But you can't tell the others yet. Especially the Bradfords."

Gulp. That didn't sound very good.

"A-all right," Jake said, his heart drumming. *Oh please don't tell me Red's dead.*

While Jake's mind conjured a hundred nightmare scenarios, Derek glanced around furtively, then reached into the breast pocket of his neat brown frock coat and pulled out a small velvet box. "Have a look at this."

"What is it?" Jake's first thought was that perhaps the box contained a message, a ransom note, or maybe some small Atlantean device like the ones he'd destroyed in Greece.

But when Derek flipped the box open, there, on a little velvet pillow, sat a diamond ring.

What the—?

Jake stared at it in confusion, then lifted his baffled gaze to his mentor's rugged face.

Derek gave an anxious gulp. "I'm gonna ask Miss Helena to marry me."

"What?" Jake's eyes widened with astonishment. It was all he could do not to burst out laughing with relief.

"What do you think?" Derek said, quickly snapping the box shut again and slipping it back into his pocket before anyone else could see.

Jake barely knew what to say.

He *wanted* to be happy for Derek. He *was* happy for him. And he was thrilled that he wasn't in trouble.

But his hopes of hearing good news about Red crashed and burned. Jake hid his flinch.

"That's...that's excellent, Derek," he managed. "I-I'm...really happy for you."

"Do you think she'll say yes?"

As Jake's initial reaction of breath-stealing disappointment faded, he realized how much Derek needed this, and heaven knew the man deserved it.

He'd done so much for others, especially Jake. Why, if it weren't for this big lug, Jake might still be out thieving for a living on the streets of London.

A genuine smile crept across his face. "Of course she will, you bloomin' mumper. Miss Helena adores you. I always told you so."

"That's true. You always did." Derek smiled.

"But does this mean you're going to have to resign from your post as a Guardian?"

"I got special permission from the Elders. I told them if they're going to make me choose between my post and the woman I love, I'm choosing her. Recent experiences have, um, put things in perspective. Life is short—" His words broke off awkwardly, and he dropped his gaze.

"I'm sure they didn't want to lose you," Jake said. But then he furrowed his brow. "Wait, are you still going to be my head of security?"

"Of course."

"You're not going to leave?"

"No, lad." Derek laid a hand on Jake's shoulder. "You've had enough adults disappear on you. I'm not going anywhere. Especially not now."

Jake was more relieved to hear this than he would've expected. It seemed that Derek Stone was the rock he had come to depend on.

They all did.

"But eventually," Derek added, "when the time is right, perhaps, after we've weathered this storm and maybe once your parents are back, if they're alive, Helena and I will be able to have a home of our own... But close to yours and the Bradfords', of course. Which reminds me. Don't tell your cousins yet, or you know they'll ruin the surprise."

Jake chuckled. "Especially Archie."

The boy genius couldn't keep a secret to save his life, let alone tell a lie.

As for Izzy, well, hiding such major news from the empath was going to be a challenge, but somehow, he'd just have to try.

Jake clapped his mentor on the arm. "I'm really happy for you, Derek," he said warmly. "You deserve this."

"Ah, she's too good for me. But thanks." Derek beamed, his chocolate-brown eyes full of gratitude. "I'm glad you don't mind."

"Why would I mind?"

"Things have been difficult for you, and I know change can be hard for a kid. I just...don't want to make it any worse on you. But I... Well, after what happened, I just want to be happy while I can."

"Of course you do. And you deserve it." Jake gave the big warrior a quick embrace, startling Derek, who chuckled and hugged him back in surprise.

Jake thumped him on the back, then quickly retreated. "You're good people, Derek Stone."

Derek looked so happy that, for a moment, Jake felt a little choked up. A rush of memories swept through his mind of all the things that Derek and he had been through together. Like that time they'd both been sent to Newgate Prison...

Shoving away his nostalgia, Jake cleared his throat and got back to the business at hand. He had to admit, he was excited for his mentor. "So when are you going to ask her?"

Derek snorted. "Soon as I work up my bloody nerve."

Jake laughed. The man wasn't afraid of anything. Except for little, no-nonsense Queen Victoria.

"Of course, I have to ask her brother's blessing first," Derek added.

"Why? Miss Helena's a grown woman."

Derek shrugged. "It's traditional to ask the man of the family first. Besides, he's her twin. I don't want to overstep my bounds and have to deal with Henry's wolf side."

Jake grinned. "That I can understand. Don't worry, I'm sure he'll approve."

"What about your cousins? Do you think they're going to mind me stealing their governess away from them?"

"Ah, they've had her long enough." Jake waved a hand. "Archie's still got Henry, and when Isabelle moves to London, Aunt Claire can find some other lady to be her chaperone."

"I hope you're right. I hope they're not against it."

Jake smiled knowingly. "Ah, c'mon, mate. It's hardly going to come as a *huge* surprise."

Derek crooked a lopsided grin. "Probably not. Now I just have to find the right moment. And not lose my nerve. If she says no, I'll—"

"Don't be daft! She's not going to say no." Jake gave Derek a jovial slap on his massive biceps, and the master Guardian arched a brow. "Courage, man!"

Derek laughed quietly and rumpled Jake's hair.

"Don't do that!" Jake ducked back with a playful scowl and took pains to fix his hair again as Derek started walking back toward the ballroom.

Jake followed, still fixing his hair and shaking his head over the strangeness of adults.

When they reached the doorway to the ballroom, Derek paused and stared wistfully at his sweetheart amid the crowd.

Miss Helena was chatting with some of her shapeshifter relatives visiting from France.

A little sigh escaped the mighty warrior. "Isn't she beautiful?"

"I've always said so," Jake agreed.

They both admired the elegant, black-haired Frenchwoman from across the room.

As always, Miss Helena was dressed in the first stare of fashion. Her gown of burgundy-colored satin had ruffled three-quarter sleeves and a bustle in the back. With her slim figure and delicate face, the shapeshifter governess was as striking as she was brave.

She had ivory skin, greenish-gold eyes, and silky midnight hair to match her appearance when she shifted into her black leopard form.

A governess with such abilities—not to mention sharp teeth and killer claws—had always made an excellent protector for the Bradford children growing up. Especially when paired with her twin brother, Henry. Archie's mild-mannered tutor could turn into one very fearsome wolf.

Jake had seen the ferocity the DuVal twins could unleash in their animal forms. But that was exactly why Helena's match with Derek made sense. Only a lady who could also hold her own in battle would have made a suitable bride for the likes of Derek Stone.

Jake looked askance at his mentor. "Humph, and you used to claim you didn't fancy her. But I knew. I told you. I knew it all along. Told you so!"

Derek smiled, then clapped him on the back. "Go get some food, lad. You're too skinny these days."

Jake had forgotten all about food, but now the suggestion sounded appealing. "Good luck popping the question," he whispered.

Derek gave him a conspiratorial wink and a nod, and Jake walked off smiling.

Finally, some cheerful news for once.

CHAPTER 9
Vampire Recruited

As soon as Janos stepped over the threshold into his castle, he could feel the dark, sinister presence of Wyvern in his house.

It was a cold, slimy sensation, like walking through a chill patch of air in a forest, unsettling.

He did not like it so close to his children, above all. They might be nightmares, but they were *his* nightmares.

Janos lifted his head to glance up the gloomy stone stairs. He wanted the Nephilim gone, and this meeting over with quickly...one way or the other.

When Creakwood eventually came hobbling back down to the entrance hall, Janos murmured to him to let the ladies know he might need reinforcements. Then he told his butler to bring breakfast up to the drawing room.

With that, Janos sprang up the staircase, stalked down the corridor, silent as a ghost, and paused outside the closed double doors to the designated chamber.

There, he lowered his head, stilled his mind, and scanned the situation behind those doors using both his inborn Guardian instincts and his more ethereal vampire senses.

Half-demon, eh?

Janos had seen many things in his day, but the nearness of the Nephilim warlock made the hairs on his nape stand on end. *Let's get this over with.*

He touched the hilt of his darkling blade one last time, reassured himself that he was ready, then conjured up his most smarmy flavor of vampire charm.

In the next moment, he threw the door open and went breezing into the candlelit drawing room with a wide smile, lifting his arms out at his sides.

"Lord Wyvern! Welcome to Castle Gregorian." Janos sauntered toward him. "To what do I owe this unprecedented honor?"

He found the earl lurking in the shadows as he waited: a thick, rectangular-framed man some six and a half feet tall. Wyvern leaned with his elbow planted on Hexella's harpsichord, which was as large as a grand piano, but older and more ornate.

"Janos," he greeted him, his tone wary. Then Wyvern stood up straight, and they both stared for a long moment, sizing each other up.

His smile pasted in place, Janos attempted to use his telepathic powers to scan the earl's mind, though it was risky, for he himself had much to hide.

But, alas, he could not read him.

Apparently, the Nephilim lord's demonic bloodlines gave him a certain protection, even from other creatures of darkness.

Wyvern arched a brow, as though he'd noticed the failed intrusion. "Careful, Your Highness."

"Pardon?" Janos asked with an innocent smile.

Wyvern smirked. "Cheeky as ever, I see."

"Why, I'm simply curious as to why you're here, my lord." Janos gestured to an armchair. "Care to sit?"

Wyvern shook his head. "I won't be staying long."

"Aw. Pity."

"But when I do go, you'll be coming with me."

Janos lifted his eyebrows. "Is that right?"

"Mm-hmm."

"And why would I want to do that?" Janos asked, his smile locked in place, murderous intent just beneath it.

It was Creakwood's arrival that cut through the tension between them in that moment.

The sepulchral butler wheeled in a squeaky serving cart with breakfast for two: normal food for the guest, and a nice pitcher of stag's blood for the host.

"Refreshments, my lord?" Janos offered pleasantly. "I took the liberty of telling my servant to conjure food for you, should you wish it. For my part, you must pardon me, I haven't had my breakfast yet. Most important meal of the day, I hear." Janos gave a knowing wink as Creakwood rolled the cart to a noisy halt in the middle of the room.

"How thoughtful," Wyvern said, amused to play along, it would seem.

They both sauntered over to the cart, where Creakwood removed the domed silver lid from a handsome plate of pancakes and sausage. It smelled heavenly.

Wyvern eyed it with interest, but then glanced at the pitcher full of Janos's usual morning beverage. "And what's that?"

"Stag's blood fresh from the forest, my lord, with a squeeze of orange juice and a stalk of celery," Creakwood said. "His Highness enjoys it each morning."

"Very nutritious," Janos said.

"May I try it?" Wyvern asked.

Janos looked askance at him, startled. "Of course. How delightful. Creakwood."

"Y-yes, master." The butler poured goblets of the stag's blood for them both. Creakwood's hand shook a little in the Nephilim's presence.

"Cheers," Janos said, lifting his glass.

Wyvern picked up the other goblet and clinked it to Janos's. But would he really drink it?

That question was answered in the next heartbeat when he lifted the glass to his lips.

Janos wasn't sure *what* to think as he watched the Nephilim warlock gulp down his glass of fresh blood with the gusto of a vampire.

Wyvern didn't have fangs, but Janos had heard rumors that the Nephilim lord had been born with double rows of teeth, like a shark.

He flicked a glance at the man's oversized hand wrapped around the glass, and just like the rumors claimed, Janos counted six fingers on the Nephilim's hand, thumb included.

Janos hid his shudder and swirled the stag's blood in his glass, offering up a silent thanks to the animal for its life before taking a sip.

"Delicious," Wyvern said, licking his lips. "I could develop a taste for that."

"So glad you like it."

They eyed each other, assessing.

Then Janos dismissed Creakwood with a nod.

The slow, rhythmic squeaking of the cart was ear-piercing in the tense silence while the two men waited for the butler to leave.

When Creakwood had gone, pulling the door shut behind him, Janos looked at Wyvern and cast off the mask of cordiality. "So, why don't you tell me why you are here?"

The earl crunched into his celery stalk and chewed, keeping Janos in suspense a moment more.

As a chap with fangs, you'd think it wouldn't bother Janos watching Wyvern eat, but he could not stop staring as the Nephilim lord devoured the stalk of celery, gnashing it between his double rows of teeth.

It was a little unnerving.

"Tell me, Janos," Wyvern finally said in a casual tone. "Do you ever wonder why you are still alive?"

He forced an idle smile. "Technically, I'm not."

"Don't be clever. I am in no mood." Wyvern set his empty goblet down on the harpsichord.

Janos followed suit, realizing he might well need his hands free.

Staring at each other, the two of them began circling slowly over the Persian carpet like swordsmen, but neither attacked.

Not yet.

"I am well aware that you've been playing both sides against the middle for years out of pure self-interest, Your Highness. Feeding the Dark Druids information when it suits you. Helping the Order when you can."

"So? I'm a vampire. We're free agents. Not all the world is black and white. Some of us are quite happy in the gray zone."

"But something's changed with you of late. Hasn't it?"

"Whatever do you mean?" Janos countered, bristling, ready to defend if the earl attacked.

They paced in slow, cagey rings.

"I think it's very clear you've finally chosen sides."

"Oh?"

Wyvern nodded. "For the last time we met, it was in battle. And you were fighting for the Order. Do you think I didn't recognize you despite the mask you wore over your face?"

"Aha..." Janos did not bother denying his involvement in the raid. "You mean the battle where your manticore killed my best friend?"

Submerged anger made his fists curl.

Urso had been Janos's last and only friend. The rugged German bear shapeshifter had even been the godfather to his hatchlings.

Both of them had always enjoyed a good battle. It had been a fun night up until Urso was impaled by the manticore's scorpion tail.

Vengeance rose up inside him at the memory, but Janos managed to leash it.

Wyvern narrowed his eyes. "Things happen in battle, vampire. Urso knew the risks. Besides, what about you? You helped two of my most important prisoners escape."

He had: Derek Stone and the angel, Celestus.

Janos snorted. "Well, we might've freed Stone and the angel that night, but you took other prisoners to replace them. You have the American Lightrider. And the Gryphon." He paused. "Are they still alive?"

"That is none of your concern." Wyvern left their ominous circling to saunter toward the harpsichord. "Do you know why I took the Gryphon, Janos?"

He shook his head, his senses on high alert.

"I have no specific interest in the creature myself," Wyvern said. "For me, the beast is but the means to an end. The bait to lure the prize I really want. Strangely, the trap hasn't worked yet, and I find I grow tired of waiting."

"And what exactly is this prize you're really after, dare I ask?"

Wyvern played a sinister, low chord on the harpsichord with his unnatural, six-fingered reach. "Jacob Everton. The Griffon heir."

Janos went very still.

"That is why I'm here, you see." A mysterious gleam crept into Wyvern's eyes as he glanced at Janos. Then he began playing a slow, eerie song to punctuate his words. "Everyone knows the boy is difficult, unruly... Moody, headstrong, undisciplined."

"He's thirteen—what else do you expect?" Janos retorted, wondering if he should block his ears. For all he knew, that song could contain dark magic of some sort.

"True," Wyvern said. "But the lad has turned out to be even more unpredictable than I anticipated. We've had his beloved beast for months now, and he's still made no effort to rescue the creature, though I'm sure it must be killing him. I am beginning to lose patience."

Janos folded his arms across his chest. "What could that possibly have to do with me?" Subtly, he eyed his daily glass of stag's blood waiting for him on the harpsichord.

He realized he'd need his strength if, or more likely *when*, this meeting turned ugly. He did not want to go any closer to the source of that unsettling music, but he must gulp the blood down soon or he'd start growing weak, having only had a small sip.

"You know Jake," Wyvern said. "He trusts you."

Janos laughed in denial. "Nobody trusts a vampire, Wyvern."

"True," Wyvern said as Janos crossed casually to the harpsichord and reached for his drink. "Except you gave the boy a darkling blade and helped him kill those Nightstalkers I sent after him, Janos. Did you think I wouldn't find out?"

Janos downed the whole glass of stag's blood in three swallows. It was reassuring, feeling his strength return, secured anew in every fiber and sinew as the gift of life coursed into his body.

He set the glass down and gave no outward sign that he was now ready for whatever the freak thought to bring.

"Oh, come, Wyvern," he said, carefully maintaining his façade of amusement. "It was most unsporting of you. Three deadly phantom assassins against one thirteen-year-old boy? All I did was even the odds a bit. Make the game a bit more interesting."

The earl snorted. "But you also disposed of my archaeologist in Greece for the sake of those children. Dr. Giannopolous—does the name ring any bells? Don't bother denying it, vampire. The two puncture wounds on his neck made it clear how the poor scholar died."

"Can I help it if I needed a midnight snack?"

Wyvern scowled. "Don't play games. You did it for Jake and his friends."

Janos smirked at him and uncrossed his arms. *Careful.* "What can I say, Wyvern? I have a father's heart. You wouldn't understand."

Wyvern gave him a dark look.

"As for your Dr. Giannopolous, that sniveling coward sent the kids straight into a nasty magical trap that could've got them killed. Far as I'm concerned, your drunken archaeologist got what he deserved."

"Hmm." Wyvern abandoned his disturbing tune and straightened to his full height. "It is a strange power we share, is it not? Deciding who lives and who dies."

"It is," Janos agreed. "But why are you asking me about this? Are you planning on sending more assassins after the kid? Because if so..." He took a step toward the towering Nephilim. "Why don't you try picking on someone closer to your own size for a change?"

Wyvern narrowed his eyes. Janos held perfectly still, staring him down, never mind that the earl was a half a foot taller than him.

"You don't want to challenge me, vampire. Cut the act," Wyvern said coldly. "I know full well you've been working against me for months. I should've killed you already for your treachery. But I had a feeling you might still be useful. I am here because I have decided to give you one last chance to redeem yourself. Join me or die."

Janos laughed in his face. "So dramatic!"

Wyvern knitted his eyebrows with a warning glare. "That is the choice before you. Don't squander it, or you may soon find yourself tied up outside to greet the sunrise—"

"Now, now, there is no need for ugly threats," Janos said, intrigued.

It sounded like the Nephilim genuinely needed his help. Well, that could be interesting.

"Very well, I'm listening. What exactly do you want from me, Wyvern?"

"Information. That is all."

"Oh really?"

"You will come with me to the Black Fortress and assist until I have secured the boy in my possession. Deliver Jake into my hands. *Then* I'll consider us even."

There was no way in the nine circles of Hell that Janos would ever do that. But he played it close to the vest. He was no fool.

"Tall order," he said, taking another subtle scan of the earl's mind to try and figure out why Wyvern wanted Jake.

It was no use. Wyvern's mind was locked down as tight as the Black Fortress.

Janos kept to his idle demeanor. "Jake might be just a kid, but this kid happens to be a doubler. Telekinesis from his sire, the ghost-sight from his dam."

"I'm well aware."

"Not bad with a blade, either," Janos said. "You might've captured his animal defender, but he's still got the whole Order protecting him—not to mention the Elder witch, his aunt, Ramona Bradford. Why do you want him, anyway? What makes him so important?"

"That is none of your concern."

"I'm not going to help you kill him, obviously."

"No one's going to hurt him."

"I see." The way Wyvern said it, Janos oddly believed him. He narrowed his eyes. "Is this for one of Zolond's ungodly experiments?"

"No, nothing like that."

"Well?"

"You are in no position to be asking questions, Janos. You will help me, or you will pay with the greatest torment that I can inflict."

"Indeed?" he asked with a laugh.

Wyvern nodded slowly. "For, you see, I already know your weakness, vampire."

"What, sunlight?" Janos taunted. "I'm so impressed you figured that out."

"No, dear prince. The other one," Wyvern said softly.

"If you say garlic, I shall lose all respect for you. Honestly—"

"I *mean* Isabelle Bradford."

Janos's mocking smile faded away.

CHAPTER 10
The Trouble with Shapeshifters

"Where did you go?" Dani exclaimed when Jake returned to the harvest feast.

Passing by their table on his way to the buffet, he saw the others had already loaded up their plates and sat down.

"Derek needed me for something," Jake answered with a casual smile.

Best to keep it vague.

Unfortunately, Dani knew him too well. She furrowed her brow, immediately suspicious.

Hmm. Maybe keeping Derek's secret from the others wasn't going to be as easy as he thought. Not for the world would he ruin the big man's surprise.

When Isabelle looked up from her plate and fixed him a penetrating gaze, Jake quickly moved on. Blimey, the empath would guess right away that he was hiding something.

He hooked a thumb toward the buffet. "Gonna go get some food."

"Good!" Dani said pertly. "You need it."

"Say, coz, bring me another of these lovely dinner rolls, would you?" Archie called after him, holding up a fluffy golden bun.

Jake nodded, amused. "Anything for you, coz."

Archie grinned back and took another bite of ham.

Heading over to join the long line for the buffet, Jake crossed paths with no less important personages than some of the Elders.

First, there was Aunt Ramona's friend, Dame Oriel, the Elder representing the clairvoyants.

A handsome older lady, Dame Oriel was a free spirit. She wore a loose, flowing gown with a peacock-feather pattern in rich greens and blues, but her most recognizable feature was her short-cropped, oddly colored hair.

During their visit to Merlin Hall last April, for example, Oriel's hair had been pinkish lavender to celebrate the spring. It was probably gray, left to its own devices. But she was far too creative for that. Now that autumn had come, she had dyed it a deep berry tone to harmonize with thc changing leaves.

Somehow, she seemed to carry it off.

Though she was speaking to other adults, Oriel smiled at Jake when he passed. He sketched a bow in answer, but did not interrupt.

Dame Oriel knew Jake, not just because he was Aunt Ramona's great-great nephew, but because she had conducted his mediumship Assessment the last time they were here, publicly testing his ability to see and speak with ghosts.

Thankfully, he had passed.

His stomach starting to rumble with all the delicious smells in the air, Jake got in the shorter of the two lines inching up both sides of the buffet. Two columns of diners flanked the spread on either side, helping themselves to the dishes on offer.

The line moved slowly, so Jake entertained himself by watching Dame Oriel introduce various guests to Master Balinor, the head Elder of the Order.

An ancient wizard with grand robes and cottony white hair, Balinor was one of the few sorcerers who still wore the traditional pointy hat.

Secretly, Jake thought he was a funny old thing.

He'd heard that Balinor sometimes fell asleep during meetings of the Elders.

Not that anyone seemed to mind.

Sir Peter was always there to smooth things over and pick up the slack. For while Balinor was ostensibly the chief of the Order, he was really just a figurehead, at his great age.

Sir Peter and his wife, Jillian, took care of the day-to-day running of Merlin Hall, while each of the other Elders oversaw matters in their respective fields of expertise: healers, psychics, Guardians, and so on. This left Balinor free to do whatever it was the old man did every day.

Jake had no idea what that might be. All he knew was that the dotty old wizard had accidentally let the secret slip weeks ago about how Jake had killed Garnock. Aunt Ramona had wanted the story kept under wraps.

But, thanks to one of Master Balinor's absentminded moments, now half the bloody Order knew.

As the line inched forward, Jake watched the elderly wizard interacting with guests from all of the magical realms.

Personally, this was the closest he had ever stood to the leader of the Order, and he wasn't sure he was too impressed.

The aged sorcerer had a faraway quality and seemed a little deaf, greeting one visitor after another as Dame Oriel introduced them. People had to yell for him to hear, especially in the clamor of the huge ballroom.

"Oh, yes, yes, very good," he'd say to each one, probably not hearing a word. "Welcome to Merlin Hall. And enjoy the feast..."

The owl on Balinor's shoulder, now, that was a far more imposing figure, in Jake's view.

He did not know what sort of owl it was, but it was a kingly creature, big and strong-looking, with white and brown plumage. Its leathery orange talons gripped the wizard's frail shoulder like a perch.

Master Balinor almost always had that owl on his shoulder, like a pirate might carry around his pet parrot. Jake figured it must be his familiar. Most witches and wizards seemed to have one.

The magnificent bird of prey seemed very intelligent, studying each guest who shook Balinor's bony hand. Jake loved how it could swivel its head all the way around backward.

But the owl's fierce golden eyes reminded him of Red's eagle half, and another pang of missing his Gryphon clutched Jake's heart.

He still felt it was wrong to be having a party at such a time as this. But, with a sigh, he continued moving with the double line.

At last, he reached the starting point of the buffet, where he collected a plate and a roll of silverware. His stomach began grumbling insistently. But when he looked up to assess his first food choices, his mood immediately soured.

Directly across the buffet table from him, the Elder in charge of the shapeshifters was assembling his plate.

Lord Badgerton.

Jake dropped his gaze and hoped to avoid the unpleasant fellow's notice. He knew full well that Lord Badgerton disliked him, though he wasn't sure why.

Well, as rude as the shapeshifter lord often was to him and his friends—to say nothing of Badgerton's obnoxious niece and nephews, the skunkies—the feeling was mutual.

The man seemed to have a real problem with Jake's past as a pickpocket. He also resented what he called Aunt Ramona's "favoritism" toward Jake.

Boris, Lord Badgerton, was a stocky, self-important little man with a dark mustache and beady eyes. Bushy brown sideburns with a white streak flanked his ruddy cheeks, and a potbelly mounded out from his middle.

Everybody knew how he marched around the palace in a state of self-righteous belligerence, taking offense where none was intended, and accusing people of not paying him the honor due his rank as an Elder.

Badgerton constantly complained that nobody gave shapeshifters the respect they deserved. But if the chap wanted people to admire him, he could've started by at least washing the dirt out from underneath his fingernails once in a while. They were filthy.

It was really quite disgusting.

Dani had been the first to notice. She had nudged Jake one day when they'd seen Lord Badgerton in the great library of Merlin Hall, where he had been scolding one of the elf librarians for daring to remind him that his book was overdue.

"Do you know who I am? I am an Elder, for your information! If I need a few more days to read this blasted book, who are you to tell me otherwise?"

Badgerton had tapped the overdue book with a filthy claw of a finger, and Dani had gagged, her gaze homing in on it.

"I want to speak to your superior!"

When the head brownie librarian had come out to see what was the matter, Jake and Dani had gone back to their study table, laughing and cringing at how gross Badgerton's fingernails were.

The aggressive little man had glanced over and glared at them, as if he sensed they were mocking him. But, really, an Elder ought to *know* enough to wash his blasted hands now and then.

Presently, Jake sneaked a glance across the buffet and saw that the shapeshifter's claws were still as dirty as ever. It nearly made him lose what little appetite he'd mustered.

Instead, he resolved not to look over at those dirty paws again, but he made sure to serve himself from the platters Lord Badgerton had not yet touched.

There were certainly plenty of choices.

A parade of tempting platters stretched down the endless buffet: roasted pheasant, turkey with stuffing, smoked venison and ham, pigeon potpies and Yorkshire puddings, roasted root vegetables, mashed potatoes with gravy, and a huge silver urn of squash soup.

Baskets brimmed with muffins, flaky rolls like the one Archie had asked for, and fresh-baked breads of all kinds. Nearby, the sweets table glistened with a dizzying array of sugarcoated treats: apple tarts, pear pies, almond torts and caramel custards; there were cheesecakes with berries, and towering striped trifles.

But Jake spotted his main quarry of the night up ahead: the roly-poly pudding.

His mouth watered, and he was glad to see that there was plenty left. He wondered if Aunt Ramona or even Dani had had something to do with his favorite dish being offered tonight.

Badgerton was helping himself to a scoop of mashed potatoes when he glanced across the buffet at Jake.

Jake happened to make eye contact, so he nodded respectfully.

Lord Badgerton seemed satisfied with that.

Relieved, Jake minded his own business, and the line moved along. Alas, when Badgerton set the spoon for the mashed potatoes down, Jake accidentally glanced at his nails. *Ugh.*

Just when he'd recovered from that bit of unpleasantness, things got worse when Badgerton's niece and two nephews arrived.

Naturally, the skunkies cut the line. Jostling and elbowing their way up to the buffet table, Prue, Charlie, and Welton crowded around their uncle, bringing their empty plates with them.

They must've snatched them on the end, reaching in between other people and doing whatever they pleased, as usual. Now they clustered around Lord Badgerton, whining at him so they wouldn't have to wait in line like everybody else.

"Please, please, let us stay here with you, Uncle Boris!"

"We're starving!"

"Children, other people are waiting," Badgerton said halfheartedly.

"But you're an Elder and we're your favorite relatives!"

"We're really hungry!"

"Oh dear, such pranksters..." Badgerton sent the centaur couple behind him in the line an insipid smile of insincere apology.

The centaurs looked indignant, but Badgerton clearly had no intention of sending his darling skunkies away. "Oh, very well, you may go in front of me."

And so the brats weaseled into line ahead of everyone else on that side of the buffet. The centaur lady swished her tail with disapproval, but nobody complained.

Jake heaved a sigh at their typical obnoxiousness but vowed to ignore them, focused on the roly-poly pudding. As soon as he got a couple of slices of that good stuff on his plate, he was out of here. Then he could finally enjoy spending some time with his friends.

Especially Dani. He'd kept the poor girl waiting around enough tonight. He was lucky she was so patient.

"Oh look," he heard Prue say. "It's Jake Everton. Hello, Jake!"

He knew they had seen him on the other side of the buffet, though he was a little ahead of their party.

Jake looked over slowly, suspicious of her friendly tone.

All three skunkies were staring at him with their beady, dark eyes.

Charlie Badgerton was the largest of the triplets, a husky, moon-faced boy with a bad haircut. Jake noted that Charlie had had a growth spurt since the last time he'd seen them in May, and appeared to have gained an attitude to go with it.

Welton was the runt of the litter, a wiry, bespectacled boy with a big nose, slightly bucked teeth, and a nervous giggle. He usually acted as the follower of the other two. Basically just a coward.

But Prue, a sturdy, black-haired girl, was the smartest—or rather, the most devious—of the three. She was usually the ringleader of their mischief.

"We're so sorry to hear about your Gryphon, Jake," she simpered.

Now he was even more suspicious. They were never nice to him.

"Thanks," Jake said slowly.

"Sure." Then Prue cast him a fluttery smile from across the buffet and tucked her hair behind her ear, and Jake's heart sank.

He was certainly old enough by now to tell when a girl was acting weird around him—and what it usually meant.

Oh great. He gritted his teeth, gave her a polite look, but very pointedly turned away, minding his own business. *Not. Interested.*

Prue was silent, but Jake could hear her brothers jeering at him under their breath. He ignored it. There was no point answering those idiots, especially here, surrounded by adults, let alone Elders. Because he knew full well who would get the blame for any sort of disturbance: Jake Everton, of course.

Happened every time, like clockwork, whether he deserved it or not.

Plus, the skunkies had a special talent for weaseling out of trouble, and Jake didn't need any more of *that* than he already had.

The line moved on, and Jake decided to try the ham. It looked juicy. As he reached for it, he heard the skunkies start taunting him on the subject of Dani O'Dell.

"Hey, Jake, where's Spot?" Charlie goaded him.

The trio called Dani that on account of her freckles. So mature.

"Yeah, where's your sweetheart?" Welton chimed in.

"She's not his sweetheart," Prue snapped at her brothers. "She can't be. She's just a *commoner*, and he's an earl." She rolled her eyes, then gave Jake another helpful smile.

"Aw, poor Spot!" Charlie said, then guffawed at his own cleverness.

Jake set down the serving fork for the ham. "Her name is Daniela Catherine O'Dell. *Miss* O'Dell to you. And, yeah, maybe she is my sweetheart. What of it?"

Prue narrowed her eyes, but Welton gave a haughty sniff.

"O'Dell? Ew, Irish. Why are they always O'Something? O'Malley, O'Murphy—"

"O'Leprechaun!" Charlie boomed.

"Beggin' yer pardon!" cried an actual leprechaun farther down the line.

The triplets stifled a burst of laughter and sent the green-clad fellow simpering looks of contrition.

"Sooorry," they chimed together in a snide little singsong.

"No offense," Welton added, elbowing Charlie.

"Humph." The dwarf-sized leprechaun scowled at them, but the much taller centaur lady turned her head and glared at the children, stamping her hoof as though warning them to show better behavior.

Lord Badgerton was oblivious to the skunkies' antics, as usual. He had turned away to talk to some dignitary who was not in the line, but just passing by.

Feeling the disapproval of the other adults around them, the skunkies simmered down for about thirty whole seconds.

Then Charlie muttered to his siblings, "I'll bet his Gryphon ran off just to get away from *him*."

Jake sent the largest boy a daggered glance.

"Oh, he didn't like that!" Welton snickered, elbowing his brother. "Gryphons are stupid anyway. I mean, whoever thought of such a dumb animal? An eagle's head on a lion's body? It doesn't even make any sense."

The centaur lady looked truly offended now—for obvious reasons. Her husband looked over, too.

"You shut your mouth about Red," Jake warned as he gripped his tray to keep his wonky telekinesis under wraps.

"Oho! Is that a threat?" Charlie said with a belligerent laugh.

"Sounded like one," Welton chimed in.

"What are you gonna do about it, *Griffon*?" Charlie whispered from across a tub of squash casserole and roasted carrots.

"Ooooh, maybe he'll kill us like he killed Garnock the Sorcerer!" Welton said with a sneer. "The great boy hero! We're *all* so impressed."

"Right," Charlie agreed. "Except now, if there's a war, everybody knows it'll be all Jake's fault. He's the one who started it. Broke that truce with the Dark Druids—"

"Shut up, you two!" Prue snapped. "Leave him alone."

Jake pressed his lips together to silence himself. He did not need some girl defending him. But oh, there was so much he wanted to say. His heart pounded with anger, and guilt squeezed his innards, because, of course, there was truth to the accusation.

What was I supposed to do? he wanted to yell back. *Let that evil ghost bring himself back to life?*

Trust me, you wouldn't have wanted to deal with the founder of the Dark Druids returning in the flesh to wreak havoc among the living. I stopped that from happening.

And if the Dark Druids don't like it, too bad!

But this was not the time or place for a confrontation with these idiots. He was embarrassed, though, because a few people in line around them had heard their accusations.

And probably agreed.

At least he'd finally reached the stupid roly-poly pudding. He didn't even care about it anymore, but since it was now right in front of him, he reached sullenly for the serving tongs.

It was then that a cherry tomato hit him in the cheek.

Startled, he jerked his head toward the skunkies, then angrily pointed a finger at them. "Don't mess with me—"

Unfortunately, his wonky telekinesis misfired just as Lord Badgerton turned back toward the line, having finished his chat with the dignitary.

To Jake's horror, the tiny bolt of lightning-like energy that accidentally flew out of his fingertip knocked Lord Badgerton's plate onto his chest and splattered food all over his chubby face.

Even the skunkies gasped with shock.

Jake stared at the shapeshifting Elder, frozen.

Lord Badgerton just stood there for a heartbeat, blinking, unsure what had just happened.

The entire line had gone silent, along with a good portion of the nearby ballroom. Folk of every species stopped and stared, open-mouthed, at the portly badger man wearing his supper.

"I'm so sorry!" Jake gasped out.

Henry DuVal appeared out of nowhere by Badgerton's side, rushing over to hand him a dinner napkin.

Glowering, Lord Badgerton reached up and wiped mashed potatoes out of his eyes. But through the food all over his face, his fury was evident.

"Ramona!" he bellowed in a rising crescendo, snatching the offered napkin out of Henry's hand.

"Boris!" the Elder witch said in astonishment.

Jake hadn't realized that Aunt Ramona was standing a few feet behind him, chitchatting with visitors. When he glanced over his shoulder at her, he had never seen her looking so shocked.

"I've had it with this little monster of yours!" Badgerton declared, passing the napkin over his chubby face in a quick swipe. "Look what he just did!" Bits of mushroom stuffing clung to his bushy sideburns. "This boy is totally out of control!"

"I-it was an accident, sir!" Jake stammered, bewildered at how such a mishap could've happened. "My apologies!"

"Boris." Aunt Ramona glided over to the buffet. People cleared out of her path. "Jacob didn't mean it. His gift is a little off these days because he's been so upset." She took out her wand. "Here, let me—"

"Hang your magic!" Badgerton roared at the Elder witch.

Aunt Ramona stiffened, and Jake frowned.

"There's no need to take it out on her, my lord," Jake said. "It was my fault. I already said I was sorry."

"You should be!" Badgerton boomed at him. "You're a walking

menace, Jacob Everton! It would've been better if you'd never have been found!"

"Boris, that is quite enough," Aunt Ramona said, lifting her chin.

The skunkies looked on, wide-eyed, at what they had started. Not just trouble with Jake, but a row between two Elders.

"Well, it's true." Badgerton flicked a morsel of bacon off his eyebrow. "That boy may have started a war! We'll be lucky if your precious nephew doesn't get us all killed—including his blasted Gryphon."

Shocked at his cruelty, Jake drew breath to tell Badgerton to leave Red out of this, but Aunt Ramona's bony hand clamped down on his shoulder.

"Jacob, go to your room," she said calmly. *You've done enough damage for one night,* her sidelong glance seemed to say, and Jake deflated.

He knew that she didn't mean it as a punishment, but to protect him, same as always. Protect him from himself, this time. Lord, he could not imagine how much of a burden he must be to everyone.

To her. To Derek. To all of them. Cleaning up the messes that he made. No wonder they hadn't picked him for the Lightrider program yet.

Still determined to be chosen one day so he could follow in his parents' footsteps, Jake reached deep down inside and swallowed his pride to try to smooth things over as best he could.

In such situations, his best course was always to imitate Archie. His amiable cousin might be an absent-minded genius, but no one could argue that the Honorable Dr. Archimedes Bradford was anything short of a perfect English gentleman.

Jake set down his plate, giving up on the roly-poly pudding.

"Ahem. Sir," he said in a loud voice so that everyone could hear, "my deepest apologies." Then he bowed his head, just like Henry had taught him, showing the utmost respect.

"Humph," said Badgerton, still wiping himself off.

At least one shapeshifter present looked impressed. Beside the offended Elder, Henry sent Jake a sympathetic glance.

At least the boys' tutor could see for himself that Jake had done his best to make amends, for all the good it did him.

Badgerton hadn't liked him to begin with. Now Jake was fairly sure he'd made an enemy for life.

Never mind that it really was an accident—and the man's own precious skunkies had started it. Jake did not lower himself to point out either fact.

Instead, he pivoted and abandoned the buffet, striding out of the ballroom with as much dignity as he could maintain.

At least Lord Badgerton wasn't the only one humiliated now.

But, somehow, Jake kept his spine straight, his chin high as he stalked across the ballroom, heading for the lobby.

His friends were on their feet at their table, looking dazed and bewildered. They stared at him, slack-jawed, as he passed.

Dani started to come after him, but Jake shook his head, refusing to taint her with guilt by association.

Besides, furious and mortified, he just wanted to be alone. The entire ballroom was staring at him. His skin prickled with the sensation of a thousand eyes studying him.

He couldn't wait to escape.

CHAPTER 11
The Underminer

Back at the buffet, Boris, Lord Badgerton, handed off his plate and food-smeared napkin to a passing waiter. The devil take this meal—this whole party!

For his part, he had lost his blasted appetite.

"Enjoy your supper, children. I'm going to get cleaned up," he muttered, giving the skunkies a look to inform them that Uncle Boris knew full well they were the ones who'd started it.

One wasn't chosen to represent one's entire species on the council of Elders by being a fool, after all.

But, as irked as he was by his clash with the Griffon lad and his holier-than-thou aunt, Badgerton was glad for an excuse to leave the harvest feast. He told himself he found these official celebrations deadly dull. He was sick of all these people, putting on their haughty airs.

Most unnerving of all, however, Balinor's hideous bird of prey would not stop staring at him. The thing sent chills down his spine.

Boris Badgerton had a horror of owls.

Those sharp, curved beaks. Those all-seeing eyes that could penetrate the darkness as easily as the light.

And gads, those claws! Deadly to rodents and weasels and other small, scurrying things.

Even now, he could swear that the feathered assassin sitting on the old wizard's shoulder was studying him. As if it could see through him. Read his innermost thoughts.

Penetrate his secrets...

Fixed in the unblinking stare of those ominous golden eyes, Badgerton shuddered and looked away with a gulp, then he shooed

Henry DuVal aside.

The gentlemanly chap meant well, to be sure, trying to cover for his miscreant pupil, but Badgerton was not fond of shifters who could turn into wolves or leopards or anything else that could eat his kind in nature.

Birds of prey especially gave him the chills—owls most of all, for they were the only natural predator of skunks.

Owls would scoop skunks right up off the forest floor and eat them alive.

Especially young ones.

"Behave yourselves," he warned his niece and nephews before huffing off to go and clean himself up.

He ignored the stares as he left the ballroom, still festering over what had happened.

He knew the skunkies were frequently naughty, but he couldn't help but indulge them. They were the dearest people in all the world to him. Such clever children! They were his pride and joy.

Aged eleven, they were sprightly and smart (even if their teachers didn't think so). In short, he was a doting uncle and found his sister's three young cubs adorable.

Which was why he could not let anything happen to them.

Suffice to say that after Lord Wyvern's recent demonstration, Badgerton's dread of owls had increased tenfold.

At least the children didn't remember anything about their brush with doom, for Wyvern had put the skunkies into a deep, magical sleep.

But Badgerton remembered. Oh yes, every terrifying detail. Egads. He gulped at the memory.

Wyvern's monstrous owl had stood nearly six feet tall—an ordinary woodland owl upon whom the Nephilim warlock had cast a Grow spell.

At that moment, the horned owl on Balinor's shoulder swiveled its head all the way around and looked at him just before he stepped out of the ballroom.

Badgerton nearly shrieked.

But the owl's pitiless stare brought his task back, front and center, in his mind. Wyvern had given him a job to do, and Badgerton knew the price if he failed to complete it.

His darling skunkies would become a midnight snack for the Nephilim's feathered monstrosity. He gulped.

Better get to work.

Badgerton had no desire to return to the party, anyway. In fact, now was the perfect time to resume his labors, while everyone was distracted at the feast.

With that, he scampered out of the ballroom. Heart pounding, he pattered across the marble lobby, and then hurried up the grand stairs.

Speeding to his suite in the Elders' exclusive wing of the guest block, Badgerton glanced around furtively, glad to see the hallways up here were empty.

Everyone was down at the celebration.

A few minutes later, he ducked into his bachelor apartments within the palace. Once he was safely alone, there was no point in changing into fresh clothes. The task he had ahead of him was a messy one.

Instead, he jerked his head at the same time that he gave a quick shrug of his shoulders, instantly turning himself into his badger form.

His soiled evening attire fell away as his stature shrank, leaving his furry body no bigger than a beagle's.

It was much easier to be stealthy when one was only knee-high.

At once, Badgerton waddled out of the pile of clothes and across his room, exiting through a small, curtained flap in the door.

The next thing he knew, he was hurrying out of Merlin Hall at top speed, his claws clicking on the polished floors. He hugged the wall as he scampered along the shadowed corridors, and then loped down a little-used staircase. It led to a back door out of the palace, and then he was free!

He sped across the cool, whispering grass of a large meadow. He was small, but on four legs, he could move very quickly.

Within a few minutes, he fled into the zoo on the palace grounds, where the Order's collection of magical animals were kept under the care of the kindly Green Man, Dr. Plantagenet, their veterinarian.

Badgerton was only passing through.

Hurrying along the winding paths of the menagerie at night, he passed numerous habitats and cages. He heard the Climbing Fish croaking from their posts on the dead trees in their mud-swamp pen. The Dreaming Sheep had already started to bounce up into the night sky, while the flying sheepdog chased after his flock, trying to herd them back down to the ground.

Around the next bend, Badgerton saw a pretty twinkling light in one pen, but he knew that it signified treachery. It was the glowing appendage that dangled from atop the head of that awful scorpion creature known as the Fairy Stinger.

Fortunately, the royal garden fairies knew not to be drawn in by the temptation of that shiny little light—fairies liked twinkly things—unless they wished to get eaten. Fairy flesh was that dreadful creature's favorite dish.

Meanwhile, the lazy three-headed Tritoise slept under its humped shell, oblivious, as usual. He stayed well clear of the yeti's cage and the newer corral for the hideous water horse, Nuckalavee. Only one person could control that wild creature, and that was the large, boorish troll-boy, Ogden Trumbull.

Og sometimes helped the Green Man take care of the animals, but, thankfully, Badgerton didn't see him either. The ugly, oversized lad was probably socializing out back with the giants.

Hurrying on, Badgerton slipped under the fence on the far end of the zoo, waddling out into the wild meadows on the other side.

The tall grasses rustled as he scurried through the pasture, panting with exertion. He was admittedly not in the best shape, but he was determined.

The rolling landscape dipped before him, and finally, he came to the opening of the tunnel he'd been digging for Lord Wyvern. For—let them mock—if there was one thing badgers were experts at, it was digging.

They were the engineers of the animal world. Their vast, elaborate burrows could stretch for miles, and badgers always kept them tidy.

Underground, for his kind, was home.

Indeed, as he scurried through the discreet opening of his tunnel, the cool soil of the autumn earth welcomed Badgerton into its cozy embrace. He rested his short, stocky legs for a moment and caught his breath, relieved to have slipped away from the palace undetected.

Then it was time to get to work.

As he trudged down to the end of the tunnel, the opening lengthened until it was tall enough inside for a man to stand upright.

And wide enough to let an army through.

He did not *want* to betray the Order. But what choice did he have? Wyvern's owl would eat his niece and nephews if he did not cooperate.

But the Nephilim lord had made promises as well as threats.

On that fateful night this past summer, when Wyvern had

appeared uninvited at Snugburrow, his country estate, the warlock had lured him out to the woods with a few mysterious notes of magical music that Badgerton had felt compelled to follow.

When he had arrived at the spot where Wyvern waited, the warlock had shown him his skunkies sleeping peacefully on the forest floor with that freakish, six-foot owl looming over them.

Badgerton had been horrified, but betraying the Order would mean his destruction, so he balked at Wyvern's proposal. In response, the Nephilim had sweetened the deal, offering a carrot as well as a stick, as they say.

The warlock had then made Badgerton an offer he couldn't resist.

The legendary Proteus power gave an ordinary shapeshifter like him the ability to turn himself into *anything*, not just his one, boring, token animal.

To be sure, he'd heard wisecracks all his life about how silly his power was—the ability merely to turn himself into a badger.

"What good is that?" people had jeered at him since he was a cub.

Just like they jeered at his darling skunkies now for what they were, the poor things.

He fumed at the thought of that rotten Jake Everton back in the ballroom tonight. Insolent, arrogant doubler. The lad possessed two of the most enviable powers anyone could want, yet he dared to mock innocent shapeshifter children simply because all *they* could do was turn themselves into skunks.

Well, Jake and his ilk wouldn't be laughing long.

For Wyvern's bribe had worked.

Boris Badgerton was a logical man, after all. Once Wyvern gave him the Proteus power, no one would ever mock him or his clan again.

If that decision made him a traitor to the Order, too bad. The weasels were also his kinfolk, so maybe treachery ran in his blood.

All Badgerton knew was that he was *done* being secretly ashamed of who and what he was.

Nobody around here gave him the respect that he deserved. All these self-righteous do-gooders thought they were better than him.

But once he finished his tunnel and joined the Dark Druids, then the likes of Ramona Bradford and her insufferable nephew would know he was not to be trifled with.

With that, Badgerton flicked out his sharp, dirty claws and began digging for all he was worth.

* * *

Upon leaving the ballroom, Jake did not obey Aunt Ramona and go up to his room.

Instead, he kept walking straight across the white marble lobby, marching right through the stately front doors of Merlin Hall and out into the night.

Full darkness had fallen and the moon rode high in the indigo sky.

As he walked down the wide, shallow stairs outside the palace, he found them lined with grinning jack-o'-lanterns, scarecrows, hay bales, and a scattering of autumn leaves. Torchlight flickered over the dramatic entrance to Merlin Hall from burning coals in the pair of tall braziers that flanked the foot of the stairs.

No doubt it all was the handiwork of Jillian Quince and her decorating crew. Including one disappointed little redhead.

Jake scowled, angry at himself for ruining the party for Dani—not to mention the disgrace of losing control of his wonky telekinesis.

When he stepped down onto the graveled drive in front of the palace, his nerves chafed raw from that debacle, he ignored the tiered fountain lilting in the stillness, and disregarded the opening to the giant boxwood maze.

He could hear the rowdy giants singing somewhere out behind the palace, but he ignored them, too, walking off by himself across the vast, dark lawns that surrounded Merlin Hall.

He welcomed the cloak of the darkness, the solitude. He was glad to leave the party behind. This whole night had been a waste. He'd learned nothing of Red's whereabouts; he'd let Dani down yet again; he'd spent zero time with his friends; he'd made an enemy of an Elder, and a fool of himself.

Perfect. Just perfect. He could feel his bad mood returning like a dark cloud settling once more over his shoulders.

It was the waiting that was killing him, he supposed.

Why was it taking so long? Trust the adults, they said. But no one even seemed to have a plan!

The truth was, Jake was beginning to lose hope.

With the lights of the palace gleaming in the distance behind him, he walked up onto the stone bridge that arched over the babbling stream where the naiads frolicked—freshwater mermaids, the guardians of all inland waterways.

Drifting over to one side of the bridge, Jake leaned his elbows on the rough stone wall and gazed down into the current.

Moonlight played on the surface of the swirling water. He did not know if the little river had a name, but it wrapped around the grounds of Merlin Hall and watered the fields.

A small distance upstream from the bridge, there was a half-submerged stone gazebo covered in moss where the water nymphs liked to sit. There were none there now, but underwater, the naiads were having their own autumn celebration to parallel the one going on inside.

If he listened hard enough, Jake could hear the soft, ethereal strains of their songs.

Those haunting lullabies were woven into his earliest memories, for it was to the water nymphs that his mother, Elizabeth Everton, the Countess of Griffon, had entrusted Jake as a wee baby in a basket on the terrible day Uncle Waldrick and Fionnula had attacked.

While Father fought to fend off the sneak attack, Mother had put Jake in the picnic basket and run to the edge of the stream that wrapped around Griffon Castle. There, she had begged the mysterious river maidens to take him away and keep him safe.

And they had.

Tricksy as the waterfolk were known to be, the naiads had taken pity on the newly orphaned infant, floating him down the brook until it joined the mighty Thames.

It wasn't really their fault they had lost him after that.

And now here he was, listening to the same songs that had calmed him when he was a terrified baby in a basket.

The water nymphs' wistful melodies comforted him now, just as they had then. But they also made his heart ache all the more, reminding him afresh of all the loss he'd already endured.

Maybe that was what made this situation with Red so difficult to bear.

Jake had survived by being tough both inside and out. But he'd let himself love Red and trust the loyal beast completely. The Gryphon had seemed so powerful that Jake hadn't thought that Red could ever be taken away from him.

The way his parents had.

I can't go through this again. Tears flicked into his eyes as he stared down into the swirling black water.

He saw his face in the reflection, silver-speckled with tiny pinprick stars.

While the watery strains of the naiads shimmered on the air, his chest welled up with sadness verging on despair. He'd never felt more alone. It was as if a piece of his soul had been torn away, and he needed it back in order to function.

On the verge of giving up hope, he lifted a teary-eyed gaze to the black, sparkling sky.

Please, God. Isn't there someone—anyone—out there you could send to go and save Red?

CHAPTER 12
Achilles' Heel

Janos stared at Wyvern in shock, feeling like he had just been punched in the gut. "What did you say?" he demanded.

His voice came out as little more than a whisper.

"You heard me," the Nephilim answered, his eyes gleaming in the candlelit drawing room. "Your weakness is no secret from Shemrazul. It's *her*. Your little friend, the Keeper of the Unicorns."

"That's absurd!" Janos stepped back sharply and turned away to hide his eyes from Wyvern, but his undead heart had started pounding. "I barely know the chit."

"It's no use lying, Janos. I already know the truth. My father told me, you see. Shemrazul has read your heart."

"Sorry, ol' boy. You've been deceived," Janos said in a taut voice. "Demons lie. They're rather famous for it, actually."

"So are vampires," Wyvern whispered. "This girl touches your heart in ways you thought you'd never feel again—"

"Don't be disgusting, man!" He turned back to Wyvern. "She's little more than a child. Or have you not seen my wives, one more luscious than the next? I may be many things, but I am no corrupter of innocents."

"I can see why she captivates you," the warlock mused aloud. "She is a lovely creature."

"Is she?" Janos drawled, then gave a one-shouldered shrug. "I hadn't noticed."

Wyvern laughed. "Don't look so panicked, Your Highness. I know you don't mean anything improper by it—which, in itself, is worrisome." He flicked a wary glance over him. "Perhaps I could understand a bit better if you merely wanted to drink the girl's blood and be done with it. But this is something...different. Something very strange. Isn't it?"

Janos shook his head, lying for all he was worth. "I have no idea what you're talking about."

"You *care* for this girl. Not romantically, perhaps. Not yet. But you look at sweet, little Isabelle Bradford and see the embodiment of everything you threw away. Don't you?" Wyvern taunted, impaling him with words crueler than any blade. "The light. The morning. The spring. She gives you *hope*." He fairly sneered at the word. "A faint stirring that perhaps there might still be some hint of goodness left in this world. Maybe even left...in yourself."

"I fear you've gone mad, my lord," Janos said crisply, folding his arms across his chest. "Shall I send for the doctor?"

"Oh, deny it all you please, my poor, ruined Guardian. But I understand you better than you think. You see, I already know that, deep down, some small part of you still harbors those pathetic ideals from your days with the Order. I witnessed it outside this very night with my own two eyes, when you let those peasants go.

"I admit, I was surprised when my father told me of your fondness for that simpering little empath," he continued. "But I suppose it makes sense. You've always had a weakness for the ladies, and Miss Bradford is a beautiful girl."

She is a beautiful soul, Janos thought, glaring at Wyvern. Anyone with eyes could see that Izzy had a pretty face. So what?

So did countless other females—he could charm them all, and it meant absolutely nothing.

But this one artless girl's gift at sensing others' feelings, combined with his own telepathic powers, had given Janos a glimpse of who Isabelle Bradford was on the *inside*.

And that was when he had been slain. Aye, as easily as one of her stupid unicorns—fierce creatures, easily slaughtered once they'd been entranced by the virtue of a pure-hearted girl.

It was her inner beauty that had dazzled, inspired him. Janos had not known, or perhaps had long since forgotten, that such simple goodness could exist.

But it still did, somehow, in her. One bright, pure flame in the ever-growing darkness of the world.

That was obviously why they had chosen her as a unicorn Keeper.

Even more remarkably, Isabelle had used her empath talent once to peer inside Janos, and he shuddered to think what she might've seen in him. To his surprise, though, that mere slip of a girl had not run away screaming.

Which told him that for all her quiet grace, the outwardly demure aristocratic maiden was as steely-spined as she was fair. She had searched the depths of the monster he'd become and hadn't flinched.

He later heard she'd even clobbered Garnock once, and that had made him smile.

Ah, Isabelle Bradford would probably be the death of him, he thought.

"You're more transparent than you realize," Wyvern said with silken cruelty. "Every chivalrous knight needs a lady to place up on some shining pedestal, after all. Even those who have thrown away their honor."

Janos looked at him in pain.

"I've no desire to hurt Jake Everton," the Nephilim continued. "But if you refuse to cooperate, I will throw your sweet little unicorn girl down to Shemrazul."

Something inside of Janos snapped.

Without warning, he grabbed Wyvern by the lapels and drove him backward with explosive force, slamming the warlock against the harpsichord.

It jangled out an ominous note.

"Touch her and I'll kill you," he snarled in the earl's face, baring his fangs. "So help me, I will tear you limb from limb. I don't care what sort of army you bring. I give you this one warning—"

Wyvern began laughing in his face, flashing his double rows of teeth. "Ah, I knew it. The truth comes out, even from a consummate liar! Well, it appears I've found the immortal one's Achilles' heel, haven't I? Who would've dreamt it? Six beautiful huntresses for wives, but it's the witless little empath who's stolen your poor, undead heart."

The drawing room seemed to darken as Janos's eyes turned black. He jammed his forearm across Wyvern's throat, bending him back across the top of the harpsichord.

Wyvern wrapped a six-fingered hand around Janos's forearm, trying to pry it free, to no avail. As the earl began struggling for air, not even the viselike hold that Janos kept on him was enough to shut Wyvern up.

"Come, do you not know how easy it would be for me to lure the chit away from her protectors and seize her?" Wyvern forced out. "All I'd have to do is torture some helpless little animal within range of her gift, and she'd come running to help the stupid thing."

Janos was horrified by the threat, for he knew in an instant it would work.

Of course it would.

Isabelle's empathic powers made her unable to ignore the suffering of any creature—even him.

But how could Wyvern even utter such things about her? Who could ever think of hurting Isabelle?

Human beings as kind and true and tenderhearted as Izzy Bradford only came along once in a hundred years in a world as dark as this, Janos thought. If there was one thing he knew, such creatures had to be protected at all costs. Like the very unicorns with whose care she had been entrusted.

Janos saw then that he had no choice. *"Once a Guardian,"* as they used to say back in the barracks.

And with that, his choice was made—as much as he hated being put in this position.

Sorry, Jake, he mentally told his favorite ex-pickpocket. *You're a tough kid. You're going to have to fend for yourself this time. I can't let them hurt her.*

"Fine." Forcing his anger at least somewhat aside, Janos roughly released the earl and backed away. "I'll tell you what you want to know about the boy. But no one touches the empath."

"Excellent." Wyvern rubbed his throat, straightened his cravat, and stepped away from the instrument. "I knew you'd see reason. Very well, come along, then. There's no point in delay. My chariot is on the roof. And Janos," he added with a baleful stare. "Never try that again."

It wasn't lost on Janos that Wyvern had made no real attempt to fight back. He wasn't sure what might have happened if the Nephilim had.

"Now, let's go," Wyvern ordered in a low tone.

His chest heaving with bottled-up wrath, Janos glared after the hulking Nephilim as Wyvern marched out of the drawing room.

He wasn't proud of the deal he had just made with that devil.

But, a moment later, when he followed the earl, Janos took care to hide the cunning half-smile that played at his lips.

For, really, Wyvern ought to know better than to trust a vampire.

* * *

Unfortunately, it was Wyvern who got the last laugh a little later that night.

Janos grabbed his coat, told his wives he was needed at the Black Fortress, and ordered them not to let the little ones eat anyone in his absence. The ladies had questions, but he had no answers, merely told them he'd be back when he could.

Then he went up to the castle roof where Wyvern waited for him. As Janos walked out onto the curtain wall, the breeze ruffled his hair, and a million stars blazed across the dark dome of the sky.

Ahead, he saw the earl's impressive vehicle waiting.

Wyvern was already standing in his chariot, the reins in his hands. The sinuous dragon hitched to the light vehicle was one of the small, fast variety—not much larger than a draft horse.

Derek would know what breed it was. He'd always been a fan of dragons.

This one didn't look friendly.

Wings draped at its sides, it pawed the ground restlessly, bobbing and swiveling its long neck. It hissed at Janos as he approached.

"Does that thing breathe fire?"

"No, but he bites. Best to stay out of range."

"Thanks for the warning," Janos muttered.

"Come, the night's wasting."

The dragon's golden eyes gleamed and it hissed at Janos again, flicking its forked tongue out as he walked warily past it to get in the chariot.

"Perhaps I should just fly myself," he said. "I could change into my bat form and—"

"No, the Darter would definitely eat you then. Besides, the defenses around the Black Fortress are considerable. Just come and stand in the chariot. There's plenty of room." Wyvern nodded to the empty space behind him.

Janos still didn't like it. But he went along with it, just like he'd gone along with too many foolish ideas in the past—both his own and others'.

"I'd hold on if I were you," Wyvern said. Then he stretched out his arm and snapped the whip over the Darter's scaly back.

Its leathery wings snapped out to its sides, and it began galloping forward.

Janos gripped the brass railing around the edge of the sleek mahogany chariot. The two-wheeled vehicle began rolling faster and faster down the road-like passage on top of the wall.

The brownish-orange dragon galloped on, pumping its twenty-foot wingspan; it extended its neck like a racehorse and the chariot barreled straight toward the old, broken battlements at the end of the wall. They had been destroyed in a siege centuries ago and no one had ever bothered fixing them.

The broken end of the wall rushed toward them.

Accustomed as he was to flying, Janos gripped the railing with momentary anxiety as the dragon raced toward the ledge.

He planted his legs in a wide stance as the beast leaped into the air, hurtling right off the side of the wall.

The chariot bumped over the remains of the battlements, then plummeted ten feet down when the wheels rolled off the edge; Janos felt his stomach drop. But Wyvern snapped the whip over the beast again, and the cart leveled out.

Janos let out a whoop. He could not deny it was exhilarating.

As the chariot lifted toward the moon, he saw various wives poking their pretty heads out of their tower windows. He blew the ladies a big kiss as they watched him fly away.

Wyvern just looked at him.

"What can I say, they adore me," Janos drawled.

"Didn't look that way in the courtyard," the earl said under his breath.

Janos ignored the remark and admired his lands from the air. The view was magnificent.

The forests and cataracts, high pastures and rockfalls of the mountainous countryside unfurled below in all of their raw, lonely beauty. He could see his wolves moving through the moon-silvered pines.

Then they passed over the pale ribbon of the North Road as it wound up the mountain, and Janos smiled when he spotted the wagonload of peasants he had directed that way.

At least I was able to save them, he thought.

But, alas, he was wrong.

For, at that moment, Wyvern pulled up his left sleeve, revealing a strange metal cuff on his forearm.

It was covered with subtle engravings like hieroglyphs of some sort, with what looked like advanced mechanical controls.

What the blazes is that thing? Janos furrowed his brow as Wyvern punched a couple of buttons on the cuff, then flicked a little metal lever sideways—at which point the bracelet lit up, came to life, activating somehow.

The engravings began to glow—and he suddenly realized.

"That's an Atlantean artifact!" he said. The words tumbled out, as much a question as a statement.

Wyvern didn't answer, peering down at the North Road. "Oh, look. It's your new friends." Staring down at the peasants, the earl lifted his forearm.

"What are you doing?" Janos asked in alarm.

With an evil little smile, Wyvern pressed a button on the cuff.

Instantly, a thin beam of brilliant orange light shot out of the bracelet and angled down through the darkness, racing toward the peasants.

When it reached them, the wagon ignited. Janos jolted with horror.

Screams erupted, but already the sound was receding behind them as the dragon flew onward.

Janos stared out the back of the chariot with his mouth hanging open, too shocked to react for a second.

All the while, the dragon raced. The wagon and its occupants grew farther away, a burning torch of people, charred wood, and screaming horses.

A column of smoke rose from the road where they were dying. *Oh God.*

Janos turned in a daze. "What have you done?" he cried when he found his voice a second later.

"I killed them, of course." Wyvern neatly deactivated the Atlantean device, then rolled his sleeve back down like nothing had happened.

Janos stared at him, at a loss. "Why?"

"Because it amuses me. Because I can." Wyvern shrugged. "And that, my friend, was *your* one warning. Cross me and I will rip your heart out."

The warlock gave him a pointed look, then gazed forward again and urged the dragon onward through the night.

Still reeling, Janos held on tight to the handrail as they flew.

In the distance ahead, the jagged spires of the Black Fortress waited. He could see the huge building now, parked on a plateau in the middle of the mountains.

Janos swallowed hard and summoned up his considerable courage as they headed for the belly of the beast. He was going to need it.

But he couldn't help wondering, *What in the world have I got myself into now?*

CHAPTER 13
The Pact

Maddox St. Trinian had been thinking.

A short while ago, Jake had gone storming out of the ballroom, but Maddox remained sitting at the round table where he'd opted to dine with his adoptive parents, who had come to visit for the occasion of the Harvest Home.

His father, the towering, mustachioed blacksmith and forge-mage Liam St. Trinian, was engaged in a lively conversation with a tipsy dwarf lord who headed a Scottish clan, the same chap Jake had mentioned talking to earlier—Laird Hamish Broadbuckle.

The two had hit it off, the giant blacksmith and the wee dwarf laird, swigging ale and swapping stories about mining and metals and what ratios each liked for making the strongest alloys.

Normally, Maddox would've taken an interest, for he was fond of metalsmithing himself. But at the moment, he was distracted by an idea that had begun churning in his head.

Tuning out the constant roar of conversation in the ballroom, he continued mulling his idea, weighing the risks and possible rewards. But then his adoptive mother, Ida St. Trinian, seated beside him, nudged him with a fleshy arm.

She nodded at his empty plate. "Did you get enough to eat, son?"

Maddox smiled warmly at her. She was always looking after him. "I couldn't force down another bite."

"What about dessert?" She gave him a knowing look, while Pa boomed a hearty laugh over some comment from the dwarf lord about the recent quality of iron ore coming out of Wales.

Maddox patted his flat stomach. "Can't, Ma. Guardians' rules."

"Pshaw, a little cake never hurt anyone," she teased, smiling. But she didn't push the matter, well aware that desserts were usually off-limits to those whose job required staying in top physical condition.

Deprivation when it came to sweets was just a part of being a Guardian. Along with the pulled hamstring and sore shoulder muscles from yesterday's training.

It didn't matter. He'd be fine.

"Just a little scoop of pudding?" she said.

"Don't tempt me, Ma!" he scolded her gently.

She chuckled and gave him a loving caress between his shoulder blades.

Maddox loved her dearly, both of them. Strong and steady, humble folk, they were down to earth and homey.

He was glad they were here. They were a great comfort to him, with his birth mother missing and possibly dead. Sometimes Maddox could only wonder where Derek Stone had found such a loving couple to raise him after Ravyn decided that keeping her Guardian career was more important than keeping him.

Oh well. It had all worked out, he supposed.

But Ravyn's choice had led Maddox to conclude that becoming a Guardian must be the most important kind of life anyone could have, and if that was the case, he wanted it too.

Besides, it was in his blood. When early signs of the usual Guardian talents had started appearing in him around the age of eleven, he'd been accepted readily into the program.

His adoptive parents had been supportive, as usual, but Maddox had heard much later that Ravyn had objected. The whole point of giving him up, she claimed, was so he could have some semblance of a normal life, not surrounded by violence and danger.

Too bad. In his view, she had lost the right to make decisions about what he should or shouldn't do. If anything, he devoted himself to Guardianhood all the more precisely *because* she didn't like it. He knew she meant it for his own good, but it still hurt sometimes.

At least he didn't have to worry about the St. Trinians lying to him about where he really came from. They didn't have a dishonest bone in either of their big, husky bodies. Nor were they jealous of the bond Maddox couldn't help feeling toward the woman who'd given birth to him. If it pained them, they were too generous of heart to say so.

Across the table, Pa's conversation with the tipsy dwarf lord moved on to the preferred shape of hammers and anvils.

Maddox would've ordinarily found this topic particularly interesting. But, of course, he had not been himself of late. With Ravyn missing, he was continuously distracted. What if she was dead and he had been rude to her? He wasn't sure he could live with that. All he really wanted was a second chance.

The uncertainty of all this was driving him mad. Sitting at the table, he stared into space, turning his butter knife slowly end over end beside his plate. Lately, it was all he could do to focus on his targets during weapons practice.

Thankfully, Master Ebrahim Sly, head of the Guardian training program, had not harassed him too badly for his rotten aim of late.

The head trainer understood his distress. After all, Ebrahim was a personal friend of Ravyn's.

Indeed, before she'd gone missing, their friendship had caused the herculean black man to go extra hard on Maddox, lest he be accused of favoritism. But even Master Ebrahim had gone a bit easier on him lately.

Still, Maddox was sure that if he could just help the Order find a way to bring Ravyn back safely, maybe *then* he would finally retrieve a little peace of mind. Until then, Maddox felt perennially uncomfortable in his own skin—and it wasn't because of the bruises, cuts, healed broken bones, and other injuries he'd sustained over the years in his training. It was all because of her.

Constantly on edge, he alternated between brooding and a restlessness that made him barely able to sit still. Lately, it seemed like there was always a part of him that wanted to punch something.

In the barracks, the Guardians liked to joke that, sometimes, violence *was* the answer.

Maddox scanned the ballroom with a moody gaze while Ma enjoyed a generous slice of pecan pie beside him. But, forced to attend this stupid feast, he was in an especially bad mood tonight.

He didn't want to be here in the first place, then the wood elves that he'd agreed to talk to had made him feel lower than a worm.

Sure, they were an elegant and graceful folk. But they had their noses stuck up so high in the air that it was a wonder they didn't drown in the rain.

Finderool, the elvish Lightrider that Jake idolized, wasn't as bad as the rest of them, but still. They had barely glanced at Maddox and wouldn't have answered his questions at all if it weren't for Sapphira.

Maddox wondered cynically if the haughty wood elves would've paid him more respect if they knew his birth father was actually a prince.

Probably not. But it was true.

Prince Maximilian von Kahlberg was the sovereign ruler of a small, idyllic principality hidden away high among the Alps. Ravyn had been part of the Guardian team sent to help protect the handsome royal idiot nearly eighteen years ago, when His Highness had run afoul of the Dark Druids.

So much for avoiding romantic entanglements.

They fell in love, the prince and his no-nonsense female bodyguard—at least for a while—and Maddox had been the result. But the prince couldn't marry her, and Ravyn could hardly tote a baby along while battling magical creatures.

True, she had nearly gotten kicked out of the Order for this affair, but the Elders had allowed her to keep her post once she made the decision to give him up for adoption.

Maddox watched Pa laughing with the dwarf lord and knew that, somehow or another, he had surely ended up where he belonged. The St. Trinians had wanted a child of their own. They showered him with more love than he probably deserved. He knew he was lucky. But sometimes he still felt sorry for himself. Of course, he'd never admit it, for self-pity was considered the absolute worst vice a Guardian could have.

Self-pity was deadly. It kept your focus on yourself when a Guardian's whole purpose in life was protecting others.

Anyway, Maddox doubted the wood elf courtiers would've been impressed to learn he was the illegitimate son of a loose-living prince.

But his annoyance at them was nothing compared to the rage he'd felt earlier, seeing Isabelle surrounded by drooling bachelor lords.

Not that it was very surprising. Boys and young men stared at her everywhere she went. He usually did his best to ignore it. But she looked particularly gorgeous tonight in her rich, creamy white ballgown that glistened with gold trim that matched her hair.

Maddox leaned discreetly to the right to catch a glimpse of her sitting with the others at his friends' table. Daintily holding her fork, Isabelle was nibbling on a cooked baby carrot; he knew she didn't eat meat.

Which he thought was madness. But it was because of her

telepathic bond with animals.

He supposed that *would* make it feel a little cannibalistic, but for him, life wouldn't be worth living without a good steak now and then, or Ma's barbecue...

"You're not missing much," she whispered, poking at what little was left of her pie. "Not as good as mine."

Maddox grinned. "That didn't stop you from eating it."

She gasped indignantly, then pinched him, laughing. "Well, it's just sitting there."

Maddox put his arm around her shoulders. "Of course yours is better, Ma. You're the best cook in the world."

"Aw, you." Her hazel eyes danced.

For a moment, Maddox debated telling her about Isabelle. It would be nice to have her sympathy, but he decided against it. Why bother? The aristocratic debutante would never be his, and that was that.

It didn't matter if they had liked each other at some point. It would never work.

Guardians weren't allowed to get involved in romantic entanglements. More importantly, she was too highborn for him. Her father would never allow it.

The elegant Lord Bradford was only slightly less arrogant than the wood elves, especially since Queen Victoria had recently elevated him from baron to viscount for his service as a diplomat to both the Order and the Crown.

Ah, yes, the diplomats, Maddox mused. They were the real elites of the Order. As a future Guardian, *he* was just a glorified bodyguard.

No, he concluded with a sigh. No doubt Lord Bradford's lovely daughter had a duke or an earl or maybe even some Continental prince in her future.

So be it.

Getting upset about it was stupid. Maddox put impossible wishes out of his mind with the discipline of a true Guardian.

Then his gaze moved firmly past Isabelle to survey the rest of the gang.

The others looked a little lost without Jake there, especially Dani. Maddox figured it wasn't long before the little redhead could no longer contain herself and had to go running after her Jakey-boy to see if he was all right.

Maddox's thoughts were moving along the same lines, but he had more of a plan of action in mind to suggest to the doubler, rather than fussing over him. Clearly, he had to get to Jake before Dani did, or he'd never get a chance to talk to him in private.

Dani O'Dell was probably Maddox's favorite out of the bunch. He admired her loyalty and courage, and thought of her as something like a little sister.

But she did tend to stick to Jake's side like a nettle, and what Maddox had to say was for Jake's ears only. If they followed the plan forming in his mind, they'd both get in a lot of trouble. He couldn't risk the little girl telling on them.

Maddox began thinking about how to extricate himself from the table when he heard his father say, "My son here is a fine crafter of blades, as it happens."

Laird Broadbuckle looked over at Maddox in surprise. "Your son? Why, I didn't realize!"

Maddox forced a smile. He heard that a lot. Yes, yes, he looked nothing like his supposed parents in the eyes of others.

So what? He had stopped explaining a long time ago.

Pa sent him a private wink, all too familiar with the same, tedious routine. "Taught him everything he knows. I'll have to send you one of the boy's recent ax heads. I think you'd be impressed."

"Why, that's very kind!" Laird Broadbuckle said, slurring his words a bit on account of the ale he'd been guzzling throughout the meal. His tam-o'-shanter hat had gone crooked. "But only if you can spare it."

"I'd be honored for you to have it, sir," Maddox assured him. "I hope you find it worthy." He nodded respectfully to the wee Highlander, but couldn't help wondering how long that crumb had been stuck in the dwarf's bushy red beard. "You know, um, you have something..." He started to point at Broadbuckle's face, but Ma poked him in the thigh under the table to shut him up. "Er, never mind."

Maddox smiled at him instead, and Ma relaxed.

Ah well. His bluntness was both a virtue and a flaw, he supposed. It was hard to know when to tell the truth and when to be polite.

Ma seemed to think that a mere forge-mage family ought to consider themselves lucky that the laird of a Scottish clan was talking to them at all. It was not their place, apparently, to go telling one of their betters about the wad of food he had stuck in his beard.

Broadbuckle was confused. "Wh-what? What's this?" The dwarf

glanced around uncertainly, but Pa changed the subject.

"Tell us about the Deep Delves, my lord. I've heard they are majestic. Just how deep do they run?"

Speaking of his homeland was clearly the dwarf lord's favorite subject. While he launched into a flowery description of the famous dwarven mines and underground palace, Ma sent Maddox a discreet nod of approval, then pushed her dessert plate toward him.

He gave her a mock frown. She shrugged.

With that, Maddox leaned over and gave her a kiss on the cheek. "Can I be excused? I'd like to go and talk to my friends."

"Oh, of course, dear. You've humored us long enough."

He smiled, took the napkin off his lap, and set it aside. Ma beamed at him as he rose. Pa had no objection to him leaving, and the dwarf lord smiled broadly, inspecting him.

"Fine lad you've got there, St. Trinian. You must be very proud."

"We are," Pa answered.

Then the dwarf lord beckoned to a waiter to bring them more ale. Maddox wasn't sure that was such a great idea, but who was he to judge?

After giving his father a slight bow and his mother an affectionate squeeze on the shoulder, Maddox sauntered off to find Jake.

As he crossed the ballroom, heading for the lobby, he could not help but notice in his peripheral vision a few more disapproving glances on account of his clothes. But he was not sorry for ditching the proscribed formalwear.

Tuxedos were stupid, but more to the point, now everyone would know that it was *he* who disapproved of *them* for having this party in the first place.

Traditions were all very well, but it seemed outrageously wrong, with Ravyn missing, and Red, and Tex, and who knew how many others.

Maddox had lost count of the number of Lightriders who'd disappeared. Too many. Were they dead? Kidnapped? Nobody really knew. It was a scary situation. But he could only focus on one crisis at a time.

When he stepped out into the gleaming white lobby, he noted small clusters of guests here and there chatting together, but nobody paid him any mind.

Then Maddox glanced around, wondering where Jake would've

gone.

He'd heard Lady Bradford order him to go to his room, but he seriously doubted the rowdy young troublemaker would've complied.

Maddox turned to the fancy marble staircase, then decided not to waste his time checking upstairs. The chances of Jake doing as he was told were slim.

Instead, he walked to the center of the lobby, pausing directly under the apex of the ceiling dome.

Glancing to the right and left, he peered down each of the wide corridors that branched off the huge foyer; they led into the two main wings of Merlin Hall.

The huge block of guest chambers was upstairs—rather like a grand hotel for all these visitors who flooded in on regular occasions to attend various magical events.

But the first floor contained the more public regions of the palace. The enchanted art gallery, the lecture halls and conference rooms, and many posh, quiet parlors. All of these were usually open to everyone, except on special occasions.

Other areas, like the magnificent Gothic chamber where the Fey Parliament held their official assemblies, could only be visited with a docent or a member of the palace staff. Sir Peter had taken them on a tour of it once, on one of those long, dull days during August when they'd sat around here with nothing to do.

Biting his lip as he debated, Maddox quickly decided that Jake would probably not have taken either of these routes.

Instead, he walked straight ahead to the threshold of Merlin Hall's stately main entrance.

The huge double doors had been propped open to allow the fresh night air to circulate into the ballroom. Otherwise, it would've grown too hot and stuffy with so many people in there.

Far too many people for his liking.

Lingering in the open doorway, Maddox scanned the darkness for that stubborn-headed doubler. His eyesight was very sharp; his hearing as well. It was part of being a Guardian, along with extra-fast reflexes. But he didn't see the boy out there.

On the plus side, he did not sense that Jake was in any danger. You never knew with that one. Then Maddox's Guardian instincts drew him toward the right.

He strode down the front stairs, past the pumpkins and hay bales and the tall, burning braziers.

The chilly night air was refreshing after the warm ballroom. He'd eaten a lot—though not as much as Ma, he thought in amusement—and it had made him slightly sluggish.

Overhead, clouds scudded across the moon. He nodded to a group of old men who had gathered outside to smoke. Wizards and their pipes, Maddox thought, shaking his head.

Old Balinor had come out to join them; the chief wizard's owl watched him pass, swiveling its head, its golden eyes gleaming in the darkness.

Maddox continued striding out across the sprawling lawns. *Where are you, you little pain in the neck?*

There. Finally, he spotted Jake leaning on the arched stone bridge over the little river.

Maddox marched toward him. Since he could see in the dark almost as well as Balinor's owl, he could clearly make out the younger boy's look of abject misery as he stared down at the water.

"You're not planning on throwing yourself in there and drowning, are you?" Maddox called with rude familiarity as he approached.

The mild taunt worked to pull Jake out of his woe. Anger was better than despair any day.

Jake lifted his head and turned toward him with a scowl. "That's not even funny, you know. Or have you forgotten that Archie nearly drowned in this stream?"

"Relax. I was only joking." Maddox slowed his pace as he walked up onto the bridge.

Jake's forelock hung over his brow, making him look as defiant as a colt that wanted nothing to do with being trained. His cravat dangled around his neck where he'd torn in loose, as though he couldn't stand to wear it anymore. "Whaddya want?"

Maddox frowned at him. "Easy! I thought I'm supposed to be the grumpy one."

* * *

Jake harrumphed.

"Well?" he demanded, glaring at the older boy. He really didn't appreciate the intrusion—or the taunt. Sometimes a chap just needed to be left the bloody blazes alone.

"I have an idea," Maddox said.

Something in his cool tone of voice brought Jake up short. A steely note beneath his usual nonchalance.

Jake turned warily, eyeing him. "I'm listening."

Maddox looked askance at him, as though choosing his words with care. In that brief silence, the stream lilted, flowing by underneath the bridge. A few small bats screeched, flapping back and forth among the trees.

"That little dwarf lord. Broadbuckle," Maddox said. "He told you the Black Fortress was seen six weeks ago somewhere in the Alps. Right?"

"Right." Jake nodded.

Earlier this evening, the boys had exchanged what little information they had found.

The Guardian apprentice leaned his elbow on the stone wall of the bridge with a casual air that made Jake suspicious.

"Well," Maddox said slowly, "Kahlberg's in the Alps."

Jake gave him a blank look.

"My father's kingdom? My birth father."

"Oh! Right... Blimey, it *is* in the Alps, isn't it?"

Maddox nodded. "I don't know if the royal idiot's even heard that Ravyn is missing yet."

Jake narrowed his eyes, looking intrigued. "What exactly are you thinking?"

"I'm going to write to him. Ask him to send out spies and use whatever channels he has at his disposal to pinpoint the location of this valley where they landed. The Alps are a big place, after all. But Prince Maximilian von Kahlberg's got connections throughout the whole region."

Ignoring the sarcasm in Maddox's voice, Jake straightened up with newfound excitement. His thoughts whirled like the stray leaves that skittered past his feet, rasping across the bridge's cobblestones. "You think he might actually do it?"

"He better." Maddox shrugged. "He loved her once. I know he's married now to his proper princess, but he owes my mother that much. Ravyn saved his life, after all. Besides, Prince Maximilian hates the Dark Druids almost as much as we do."

"Maddox, you're brilliant!" Then Jake tilted his head. "You're sure you don't mind doing this?"

The older boy smirked. "It doesn't matter. I'm sure he'll be surprised to hear from me. We don't have much contact, but I'm still his firstborn son, illegitimate or not, so..."

"Right," Jake murmured.

"Besides, I never ask him for anything." Maddox pushed away from the bridge, squaring his shoulders and standing up to his full height.

At seventeen, he was half a foot taller than Jake. His athletic silhouette blocked out the warm, glowing lights of the palace several hundred yards behind him.

"I'll write the letters tomorrow," Maddox said. "I could send it as a telegraph, but I'm afraid that wouldn't be secure, and this is sensitive information."

Jake nodded—and sniffled. His nose was cold. "While you do that, I'll get to the library and see what I can dig up on these Mesopotamian Marshes. Who knows? We might be able to get another lead."

"That'll get us started." Maddox's dark eyes glowed with newfound spirit now that he had some direction. "In the meantime, you and I need to start preparing—*without* letting anyone else guess our intentions."

"Our intentions? What do you mean?" Jake flipped his forelock out of his eyes. "Preparing for what?"

Maddox glanced around furtively, then peered over the side of the bridge, checking to make sure no naiads were eavesdropping on their conversation from below.

Satisfied, he lowered his voice. "If and when my father's spies bring back information, we need to be ready to act. I say we go there ourselves."

"Oh!" Jake raised his eyebrows, but instantly felt uneasy.

"I figure if the Kahlberg spies can at least tell us which valley the Fortress landed in, you and I can go there and have a look for ourselves."

"How? We'll need a Lightrider—"

Maddox smacked Jake lightly in the head. "We just need a train, you idiot."

"Hey!" Jake scowled, fixing his hair again.

"Well, a boat first, to get across the Channel, then a train," Maddox amended. "Then a couple of horses once we get across France."

"Why is everybody always messing up my hair?" Jake grumbled.

Maddox grinned. "Because you hate it."

Jake growled. The elder brother he never wanted. "You think there's any real hope of finding clues so long after the Black Fortress has been gone?"

"Maybe it'll come back," Maddox said. "Besides, anything's better than sitting around here doing nothing."

"Well, I can't argue with that." Jake thrust his hands down into his pockets and lowered his head, considering. "You know they don't want us taking any action on our own."

"Who cares! It's been months. How long are we supposed to wait? No. You ask me, we've been patient long enough."

"But Derek said—"

"All I know is that neither Red nor Ravyn would leave *us* to rot in some dungeon cell somewhere if *we* were the ones who'd been captured."

Jake winced. "You really think that's where they are? In a dungeon cell?"

Maddox deflated a bit. In the moonlight, Jake saw a ghost of regret for his bluntness skim his friend's square, uncompromising face.

"Your Gryphon probably is," Maddox admitted. Then he looked away, gazing off at the naiads' stone gazebo. "Ravyn might not even be alive anymore. One way or the other, I've got to know her fate. She's still my mother. Even if she did give me away."

Jake winced. Maddox was a pain, but his heart went out to the moody older boy.

After all, he was quite familiar himself with the torment of not knowing what had happened to his parents. He hated watching a friend go through it, too.

"Very well." Jake drew a deep breath and let it out, nodding. "I'm in."

"Good. We'll plan on it, then. But don't tell Dani! Or Archie. In fact, don't tell anyone. We'll only get in trouble."

Jake frowned. "What if Isabelle senses it?"

"She can only sense your emotions, not read your thoughts. And mine won't be a problem, since she can't read me at all," he added dryly. "So, do we have a deal?" Maddox offered his hand.

Jake hesitated, then nodded. He had tried his best to be obedient for three whole months. But tonight had not yielded anywhere near the results he'd been hoping for. What Maddox proposed was simply the logical next step.

It was risky, of course, the two of them going off by themselves to hunt for the Black Fortress. Especially since it seemed like the Dark Druids were after him.

But Jake cast aside his misgivings and shook Maddox's hand, giving his word in a mumble to keep their plan a secret.

Sealing their pact, the boys exchanged a hard look, both well aware of what this could cost them. There would likely be serious consequences once it was discovered that they had disobeyed orders and sneaked off on their own.

Maddox could get kicked out of the Guardian program, and Jake might never get selected for Lightrider training.

He might also get murdered by Dani O'Dell for leaving without her, but that was neither here nor there. There was no way he'd drag her into this.

Their instructions had been clear: *Let the adults handle it.*

Only, the adults were failing them once again. Not that Jake was surprised.

Adults had been failing him ever since he was a wee baby. Uncle Waldrick and Fionnula Coralbroom had sort of killed his parents. His parents, for all their Lightrider skills, had failed to fend off the attack. (Jake was sure *he* wouldn't have failed.) The naiads had lost him in the river. The orphanage had been a dismal place, his apprentice masters even worse.

No, Jake had learned through hard experience that if you wanted something done right, you always had to do it yourself in the end.

He was glad Maddox had thought of this plan, though, because Lord knew *he* was all out of ideas. But it seemed that until they heard back from Prince Maximilian's spies, they were stuck with more waiting.

Ugh. At least now they had a clear, sensible next step to follow. Maddox was right. Anything was better than sitting around, idle, waiting for somebody else to fix this.

Blimey, if Jake had to endure another month of that torture, he was sure he would go barking mad.

CHAPTER 14
Forbidden Waltz

Sometimes the battle of good versus evil involved great armies, mighty clashes across continents and seas.

But more often than not, it raged quietly within the hearts and minds of human beings.

That was where the battle must be won.

It was a war the Dowager Baroness Ramona Bradford had been fighting for three hundred years, and tonight once more, after the party, no matter how old and weary she felt, it was time to join the struggle again.

Leaving the harvest feast later that night, the Elder witch whisked up the marble stairs to her private quarters to keep her promise to Zolond.

She refused to indulge him overmuch, but she knew better than to try his patience or bait him with needless waiting. He was unpredictable, and she could not afford for him to abandon their talks.

When she reached the door to her apartments within the Elders' section of the guest block, Ramona closed the door quietly behind her. She lit the candles with a word, then let out a long exhalation, relishing the solitude of her room after all the hubbub of the party.

Drifting into the sitting room that adjoined her bedchamber, Ramona slipped off the Elders' loose ceremonial robe of black silk that she had worn draped over her gown. Then she kicked off her shoes and unpinned the brooch at her throat, loosening her prim lace collar.

A light knock at her door a moment later proved to be Oriel, showing up once more for moral support.

Ramona let her in. Her purple-haired friend flashed a freewheeling smile and held up a bottle of what proved to be cherry cordial, then wafted into the chamber.

"I stole this from the party," Oriel quipped. "I thought you might need a draught before you start."

Ramona snorted. "Good idea."

Her flowy peacock dress billowing out behind her, Oriel strode over to the slim table by the wall, where Ramona kept a pitcher of water and small plates, mugs, glasses, and such.

"It was a good party, don't you think?" Oriel remarked as she poured them each a small absinthe glass of the sticky-sweet cordial.

"Mm." Ramona nodded absently, but her thoughts were far away.

Oriel was only trying to make chitchat to put her at ease, but they both knew the seriousness of her endeavor here. The clairvoyant Elder was the only one Ramona had told about her forbidden communications with the Dark Master.

Her friend brought her the drink. They clinked cups with a murmur of "cheers," and each took a thoughtful sip.

Ramona made a face. "Oh, that's strong."

Oriel shrugged. "So what do you need me to do?"

Ramona smiled ruefully. "Send for a healer if I pass out."

Oriel winced. "Please be careful."

"Careful never got anybody anywhere in this life, my dear." Then the Elder witch sat down at the small round table where her white crystal ball waited.

She took another sip of cordial, mentally girding herself for battle once more against her greatest foe.

The man who had once been the love of her life.

Oriel retreated to her usual chair in the corner, where she watched and waited in somber silence.

Ramona took a deep breath and let it out, closing her eyes, stilling her mind. She knew what she was doing was extremely dangerous. But she wouldn't be taking the risk or wasting her time if she didn't think it could work.

Three months ago, she had attended the battle against the Dark Druids in the desert of Karakum, but not in person. In person, she had been at a pleasant seaside villa in Taormina, Sicily, chaperoning the children (as much as anyone could manage such headstrong little heathens) on their Grand Tour.

But upon receiving word of the Order's battle plans, the Elder witch had gone into her room, shut the door, taken out her crystal ball, and then journeyed to the desert of Karakum through the astral plane.

Invisibly observing the battle from the air, lending what aid she could at such a great distance away, the last thing she had expected was for Dark Master Zolond to sense her there and come whooshing out to attack her.

It was during their duel on the astral plane, as fierce and terrifying as it had been, that Ramona had realized there might still be a small part of Geoffrey DeLacey left inside the wicked Zolond.

He could have killed her, but he hadn't done it, and that told Ramona all she needed to know.

She still had some influence over him.

And *that*, in turn, encouraged her to think that perhaps not all hope was lost. Perhaps, in spite of how evil and how incredibly powerful the warlock had become over the three long centuries that had bound them here together with unnatural long life, there might still be a glimmer inside of him somewhere of the young man she used to love.

Maybe, just maybe, he'd be willing to listen to reason.

He might still destroy her, of course, but that was a risk Ramona was willing to take in the interests of trying to head off a great and terrible war.

Everyone could feel it building in the air, not just the Guardians anymore.

Though Zolond had defeated her that night, the fact that he had spared her life had convinced her that she still got to him. She knew he had loved her before evil had taken hold of his mind.

Her plan to try and reclaim him was bold, but she would not shrink from using what slight power she might still possess over him, in the interest of heading off this war taking shape between the Order and the Black Brotherhood.

Zolond could stop it from happening, if only she could stop *him*.

And so, when he had contacted her telepathically through his crystal ball about a month after their spirit-bound brawl in the desert, wanting to see in spite of himself if he'd hurt her too badly, Ramona had taken full advantage of the situation.

She'd been working on him in secret ever since. Her one goal was to try and pull him back, if only just a little, toward the light. Toward peace.

The danger, however, was that her darling Geoffrey had the same idea, and was working just as subtly to pull Ramona toward the darkness.

This endless battle of wills on the astral plane was exhausting them both. They were really too old for this nonsense. They both should've been dead centuries ago. *She* would've been, certainly, if not for that blasted spell the two of them had put on their love when they were both so young and naïve.

Before Geoffrey had chosen magic over her.

Ramona sighed, rested her fingertips on her crystal ball, and began staring into its white quartz heart. In spite of everything, foolishly, she could not deny that she was eager to be with him again.

Who else could ever understand what it was like, this strange life of theirs, cloaked in magic, watching eras come and go over such long, wearisome stretches of time?

She didn't like to admit it, but sometimes it was painful being apart. They were both so alone. In times gone by, they used to finish each other's sentences.

It was so easy to fall back into a wary friendship when Geoffrey chose to be pleasant.

Then she closed her eyes, centered her mind, and promptly left her chamber and her body, whooshing out onto the astral plane.

Ah, it was so freeing. No achy joints stiffened with arthritis, no weary eyes with dimming sight, no creaky old bones.

Here, she was spirit. Weightless. A roaming, sentient soul—like a ghost, but still alive, seated in her room with Oriel looking after her.

Reaching her destination took little more than a thought.

At once, a curious levitating walkway rose ahead of her amid the dark, soothing dreamscape of blue and purple mists. Pale and smooth, the path curved before her like the swell of a white marble wave.

Ribbons of lavender fog swirled around Ramona's whitish-gray, transparent form as she began gliding up the path toward their usual meeting place.

It was a fanciful location they'd concocted, witch and wizard, for their secret meetings—a nowhere, a no-when—with a shimmer of ethereal music sounding silvery notes now and then, vibrating the random chunks of crystal that hung, spinning slowly, in midair.

Stardust floated, glittering against the indigo clouds.

Her figure left ghostly wisps of white trailing out behind her as she sped without effort toward the spindly gazebo that domed up ahead.

Zolond was already waiting for her there, white and ghostly gray like herself. She could hear the tick-tock of his impatience as she approached with a slight flutter in her chest.

What a fool she was, she thought. Stealing away to be with him again, like a wayward girl.

"Well, if it isn't my favorite witch," the Dark Master greeted her.

In the next blink, Ramona had zoomed the rest of the way to her destination, rematerializing under the nebulous arch of the drifting gazebo. The charcoal-shaded structure bled its watercolors upward into the cobalt blue.

"Hullo, Geoffrey," she said. "I trust you are well."

"Hmm. Pleasant party this evening?"

"'Twas enjoyable," Ramona conceded.

Zolond snorted. "Frivolity."

"Why doesn't your side ever have any parties?"

"We do, sometimes. But things can get...rather bloody. Best to keep it to a minimum."

She gave him a sardonic smile. They floated in a wary circle, several feet apart. But neither broke their gaze.

"Did you go to your old hideaway, then? You mentioned you might," Ramona said.

Zolond nodded. "I'm there now. You?"

"Oh, just in my room at Merlin Hall. And how are the reptilians?"

He crooked a bushy white eyebrow. "You didn't really want to make small talk, did you, my lady?"

She smiled in spite of herself. "Not really. I've been doing that all night."

"Then let us skip the pleasantries, my dear." He stared at her. "I think we should discuss these matters in person. Why don't you come to the Balefire Mountains? We'll have lunch."

She laughed. "And what would Shemrazul say of that, I wonder?"

Zolond sighed. "I'd rather not imagine."

"Well?" Ramona said, circling with him while the silvery chimes made the crystals hum. "Have you considered my request?"

"I told you I would."

"And? Will you release our prisoners?" She held her breath.

"Er, no."

"Geoffrey!"

"However," he interrupted before she could protest further.

"Yes?" Ramona asked with a frown as they rotated around the

gazebo like the hands of a clock counting off the hours.

"I propose instead a hostage exchange. A swap of our princelings. Remember that old tradition? It was fading out of use even when we were young, but I think it might be a very suitable arrangement in this case."

"Aha," she said skeptically. In the olden days, enemy kingdoms would exchange young princes, with each boy being sent off to live with the opposite royal court until he was grown.

Each prince was guaranteed safekeeping in the opposite kingdom—so long as the other side did not attack.

"Then we can both be sure neither your side nor mine starts any trouble."

"Zolond," she chided, "your thinking is always creative. I give you that. But you must know I would never hand over one of our children to the Dark Druids."

"Don't dismiss it out of hand, stubborn old woman. I am prepared to give you my great-great grandson, Victor, and, in exchange, you may hand over your nephew, Jacob Everton. That is a fair arrangement. You said you wanted peace—"

"Let's leave the children out of this, Geoffrey."

"But they are all that matters, aren't they, Ramona? The future. The long game."

She shook her head, unwilling to budge. "Even if I trusted *you* with Jake, which I don't, I have no doubt that others of your brethren would kill the boy the first chance they got to avenge Garnock. *Who,* might I point out, really had no business bringing himself back to life in the first place."

Zolond shook his head, his white hair cottony in the dreamworld of their rendezvous. "You see, that is the difference between us, dear. To my way of thinking, if a warlock *can* do a thing, then why should he not?"

"Well, he couldn't, could he? So the question is moot," she shot back.

"He nearly did," Zolond said. "Would've succeeded, too, if not for your nephew."

"You are not taking Jake!" she exclaimed. "Not now. Not ever."

"Very well, then, give me your little scientist. What's-his-name, Archie? He could be a great help with my experiments—"

"Never!" Ramona whooshed across the gazebo to glare in his face.

"Don't you lay a hand on Archie! I will turn your reptilians to dust if you even—"

"Now, now!" Zolond laughed and lifted his hands, clearly startled by her ferocity. "Don't get yourself into a tizzy, ol' girl. It was only an idea! Why won't you work with me on this? At least I'm *trying* to find a solution."

She turned away, shaken by the mere mention of Archie getting dragged into all of this.

Threatening rough-and-tumble Jake was one thing. In many ways, the scrappy former pickpocket could take care of himself.

But Archie was a simple, trusting soul. He might have a genius intellect, but he possessed none of his roguish cousin's street smarts.

"This was a mistake," Ramona said tersely over her shoulder. "I should've known there'd be no reasoning with you." She swept around to face him. "Do you really want a war? It's been a long time. Perhaps you have forgotten how dreadful they are."

Zolond did not answer. His furrowed brow told her he'd grown annoyed with her for attacking him about Archie; his pale eyes were chilly.

"Goodbye, Ramona. Your company grows tedious tonight."

"Geoffrey!" she insisted, but he left the conversation, fading away into the purple fog.

"Blast it," Ramona said under her breath, also returning to her own time and place, in her body, in her room.

She drew her hands back from the crystal ball as its inner glow faded.

When the light had gone out from it entirely, a great wave of fatigue washed over her. Lord, she was more tired by their exchange than she had realized.

Drained.

"Well? How did it go?" Oriel asked, bringing her a glass of water.

Ramona sighed. "He has not agreed to any specifics yet. But I can't help but feel we're making progress."

Oriel searched Ramona's face worriedly. "You don't have to keep doing this, you know."

Ramona gave her a weary smile of gratitude. "But, my friend, I am the only one who can."

CHAPTER 15
The Prophet

Hours later, in the middle of the night, Archie Bradford awoke with a start and shot bolt upright in bed. He sat there for a moment, blinking in the darkness, a cold sweat dampening his face.

It took him a few breaths to get his bearings. His heart was pounding, but the room he shared with his cousin was quiet.

In the bed on the opposite wall, Jake slumbered peacefully, his pale gold hair illumined in the shaft of moonlight shining through the window.

Archie could hear his cousin breathing, but no other sound came from the rest of the Bradford suite. Jake's nearness was reassuring after that horrid dream had come back yet again.

Archie swallowed hard and touched his chest through his pajamas.

His heart was still thumping like it might yet burst out of his chest and make a run for it down the hallway. He strove to calm himself.

Unbeknownst to the others, it wasn't his little Italian coffees keeping him awake at night, nor his wrestling with the ongoing puzzle of how to free Aleeyah from her smoke form.

It was this...recurring nightmare.

Slowly, he lay back down on his pillow, but his eyes remained open wide. Nearsighted as he was, he could not quite see the ceiling clearly.

It didn't matter. His inward sight was all too keen, and lately, he'd been having another of his uncanny dreams.

A vision, he feared.

Archie was fairly sure the Kinderveil had lifted at last. After all, he was twelve now. Despite his best hope of being born with no magical powers—as if having a genius intellect hadn't already made him enough of an odd duck—recent evidence suggested there was a high statistical probability that he had, in fact, inherited a mild form of his father's psychic gift.

He had not yet officially announced the emergence of this latent talent, though he'd griped to both Jake and Nixie about his concerns occasionally.

He just kept hoping the thing might go away all on its own.

Like a rash.

He especially avoided his empath sister's probing gaze. Izzy sensed something was bothering him, of course, but Archie did not wish to alarm her or anyone else by revealing this horrid premonition. They were all upset enough over Red and everything that was happening. So, he let his sister think it was just the distressing situation overall gnawing at him.

Nixie also had noticed he was not quite his usual cheery self, but she was the sort of person who respected it when someone said, *"I don't want to talk about it,"* because she was the same way.

Archie's dearest wish was simply for everything to go back to how it was before—like it was at that gorgeous beachside villa in Taormina—well, with one amendment. That they got their beloved Red back, and soon.

Unfortunately, the nightmare that had begun plaguing him a few weeks ago made Archie fear that things might never be the same again.

He hoped with all his might that he was wrong. That this was no vision, just an ordinary dream. An unpleasant one, of course, but merely the result of something he ate.

A figment of his imagination. A spasm of his overactive brain.

It was comforting to think so.

He assured himself once again this was probably the case, then closed his eyes and did his best to fall back asleep.

Finally, his pulse eased back to normal.

Although the dream did not return, it left him with a foreboding sense of doom. A dark inner whisper of premonition warning him that, before all of this was over...

One of them was going to die.

PART II

CHAPTER 16
Chosen

Morning hatched like a great golden egg over Merlin Hall: a bright, cheerful Monday with a clear blue sky and the smell of autumn in the air.

Excitement was palpable throughout the palace as everyone from Elders to students dressed and eagerly hurried off to join the various activities they were scheduled to participate in during the week of magical business ahead.

Everyone except Dani O'Dell.

As the hired help, she saw the others off, wished them luck, and waved them out the door, holding her wee dog, Teddy, in one arm so he didn't escape.

When everyone had gone, she shut the door behind them, put the dog down, and looked at him, refusing to mope.

Wagging his stump tail, the little brown Norwich terrier gave her a double yip that seemed to ask, *"All right, what do we do now?"*

"Chores," she replied.

Then she got to work tidying up the Bradford family's suite.

Sunlight filled the high-ceilinged parlor that connected all the bedchambers.

Teddy followed her from room to room as she made the beds, smoothing coverlets, plumping pillows, and straightening up as she went, folding castoff clothes into neat piles or tossing them into the laundry basket.

Did she mind her chores? Not in the least. Dani took her post as Isabelle's companion very seriously, and rather than chafing at her tasks, she considered herself lucky just to be here.

A magical palace? With fairies? The chance to be with the one and only Jake on all of his adventures? Plus, Isabelle and Archie, Nixie and Maddox?

Dani loved them all. Even the half-terrifying Elder witch.

Besides, she'd have a *lot* more chores to do than this light work if she were back at home in the squalid tenement house where her wild tribe of older brothers lived with Da—none of whom ever thought to pick up after themselves, let alone say thank you for all her labors.

She shuddered to think how close she had come to being stranded permanently in the harsh, dreary world of the London rookery.

Once Jake had been reunited with his aristocratic relatives, she had feared she would never see her pickpocket friend again. But it turned out, to her joy, that she was as essential to Jake as he was to her.

They had survived by relying on each other in London's harshest quarters, and he had refused to leave her behind. Her golden-haired hero had come back for her, insisting to his formidable aunt Ramona that Dani be allowed to tag along.

It was only at the young Lord Griffon's insistence that his great-great aunt had taken pity on her, appointing Dani as lady's companion to Isabelle.

The Elder witch had decided that Dani's rookery toughness could be a boon to the sometimes too-delicate Miss Isabelle.

Well, Dani believed she had helped Izzy grow stronger. And she knew for a fact that Isabelle (and Miss Helena) were helping *her* to smooth out her own rough edges in return.

In any case, becoming a lady's companion was a higher rank in life than she had ever aspired to. A paid companion to an aristocratic girl was no common chambermaid, but ranked among the genteel folk of the world, equal in respectability to a governess or tutor.

As far as Dani was concerned, her getting this position at all was the luck of the Irish, plain and simple.

Moving on to Isabelle's chamber, she carefully cleaned a spot off one of the older girl's white kid gloves, as she'd been asked to do. She also got Izzy's dinner gown ready for this evening, hanging it on the front of the wardrobe and dusting the rich blue satin with a lint brush.

Returning to the sitting room, Dani tidied up the informal dining table, then arranged the pillows on the couch.

She returned Archie's extra pair of spectacles to his room or he'd never find them again, then she spotted a pair of shoes Jake had left under the coffee table. She went and tucked them under his bed.

When she came back out to the parlor, she looked around to make sure she hadn't missed anything.

It was then that a splash of white beneath the table caught her eye. She tilted her head. *What's that?*

Going over to the table, Dani bent down and crawled halfway under it, reaching to retrieve what proved to be a white feather.

Climbing to her feet again, she stared at it, puzzled. It was soft and fluffy, about five inches long. But where had it come from?

Not the Gryphon, clearly. He was in the clutches of the Dark Druids. Besides, Red's feathers were a rich scarlet hue, except for the few mysterious gold ones that had grown in after he'd molted.

No, this lovely, soft wisp of pearl-white reminded Dani of the feathers on the wings of the angel who had saved her life more than a year ago in London—Celestus, who disguised himself as a nice blond physician that tended to arrive with his doctor bag right when he was needed. Only in private did he reveal his magnificent angel wings.

But the feather couldn't belong to poor Dr. Celestus, either, Dani thought. Because, much to her horror, the Dark Druids had cut his wings off when they'd captured him and held him captive with demons for guards not long ago.

The Order had rescued him, but not before he'd been maimed.

Normally, it wasn't possible to contain one of the Light Beings, from what she understood. But, apparently, one of those Nephilim artifacts that were part of the Atlantean treasure trove had the ability to turn spirit beings into flesh.

By using the winged disk artifact from Atlantis, Lord Wyvern and his minions had projected a field of the same frequency the Light Beings sometimes used to manifest themselves in fleshly mortal form. (So Archie and the smartest wizards in the Order theorized.)

Once the evil warlock had trapped the angel in corporeal form, it had been easy for Wyvern to take Celestus prisoner, holding him, as it were, in an invisible cage made of silent sound waves.

It made little sense to Dani. All she knew was that once Lord Wyvern had captured poor Celestus, he had treated him unspeakably.

No doubt the devil the Dark Druids served had ordered Wyvern to do it, for Shemrazul had a special grudge against that particular Light Being. They seemed to have known each other for a very long time.

Eons.

On that day in Wales when Shemrazul had nearly escaped the underworld after Jake had killed Garnock, it was Celestus who came down to stop him—in warrior form this time, not as the gentle doctor. The Light Being had slammed down to earth with three of his fellows, all wearing armor like Roman centurions. Then Celestus had led the quartet of archangels to deal with the would-be escapee.

The four mighty angels with their shining spears and brightwield swords had shoved the giant red devil back down into the pit.

Thinking about it made Dani shudder. Well, Shemrazul must've enjoyed taking revenge on his nemesis for those few weeks before the Order managed to rescue Celestus in that same desert battle where Red had been taken prisoner.

Dani had heard it was Janos who had actually saved the angel.

The quick-thinking vampire had turned the winged disk artifact on the lesser demons who'd been guarding Celestus, thereby forcing *them* into flesh-and-blood form. Then he'd hacked them to bits with his darkling blade.

For all his charm, Dani could well believe that Janos could be very, very mean when he chose.

Alas, despite his heroics, the rescue team had not managed to get to the angel before the Dark Druids had maimed him.

She couldn't believe they had chopped off his wings.

No one had seen Celestus since the night he had been freed three months ago. Dani hoped he'd be all right. She had heard he had vanished in a beam of light right there off the desert sands, returning to the heavenly realms to heal.

She didn't know whether an angel's wings could ever grow back. She doubted even a Gryphon feather could help one of the Light Beings, the way it had regenerated Gladwin's fairy wings when Jake's evil Uncle Waldrick had snipped them off with a pair of scissors.

Hmm...

Twirling the white feather between her fingers, Dani looked around, still puzzled.

Since it couldn't belong to either Red or Dr. Celestus, she could only conclude that it must've fallen off one of those fancy hats that Isabelle's mother liked to wear.

Sometimes the younger Lady Bradford even wore a dashing feather in her hair. It was very fashionable.

Aye, that must be it. Satisfied that she had solved the mystery,

Dani ventured into the master chamber and respectfully left the pretty feather on Her Ladyship's dressing table, next to her silver-handled hairbrush and little pots of face powder and rouge.

With that, all her chores were done at last. She made sure Teddy had a fresh bowl of water, then finally turned her attention to her own studies.

She could not deny that her education had been neglected as a poor rookery lass. But Archie, one of the smartest people on Earth, had been kind enough to design a whole curriculum of independent study for her that would last her through Christmas. He had even lent her his old textbooks, outlining suggested lessons in history, mathematics, geography, English composition, and art.

Each day, she was allotted three hours during which to pursue her own education. Sometimes the others checked her papers for her. But Dani did not mind learning on her own.

As she collected her bookbag from her little cubbyhole of a bedroom in the corner of the suite, she paused to gaze out the window at all the activity on the sprawling green lawn below.

Kids from magical families were hurrying back and forth to attend the orientation for whichever supernatural studies class they belonged. Around their waists, each wore a color-coded sash designating which talent they possessed.

The healers-in-training sported green sashes, for example, the young Guardians brown. The clairvoyants wore blue, the telekinetics red—Jake had one of each of those, but "doublers" like him were rare.

The wizards and witches like Nixie proudly showed off their orange sashes; the shapeshifters, purple.

Dani wrinkled her nose, thinking of the skunkies and Jake's regrettable mishap last night. She had nearly burst out laughing when pompous Lord Badgerton had ended up wearing his supper...

Then she spotted a lone girl with elvish ears hurrying by, and *she* was wearing the rarest sash of all: a snowy-white one, shot through with silver thread.

Ooh, that was the one Jake really wanted. The coveted silver sash was worn only by the lucky few kids chosen for the Lightrider program.

That wasn't something you were born with, but something for which only a few kids were chosen.

Lightriders were special. The elite agents of the Order, only they had the ability to open portals anywhere along the ley lines that crisscrossed the Earth, allowing them nigh-instantaneous travel to any other point upon the globe.

Jake and Maddox had twice had the chance to travel down the ley lines with a Lightrider, but Dani had only done it once—when Finnderool had been sent to bring them back to England from Sicily. They had got there by boat and coach and train, but they came home through the Grid, as it was called.

It had been one of the most remarkable experiences of Dani's whole life. She still marveled to think of how all her molecules had tingled as she'd watched her entire body dissolve into fizzy particles, as though she were made out of ginger ale bubbles.

Teddy bounced insistently beside Dani at that moment, breaking into her reverie. The little dog jumped nearly as high as her waist in his determination to try to see the view out the window.

With a laugh, Dani caught him in midair on his next jump and held him up to look, though the lawn was clearing out now.

"Come on, silly. We'd better hit the books." She carried him back to the sitting room, put him on the couch, then plopped her bookbag on the table.

Taking out her textbooks, she couldn't help but sigh over all of those colorful sashes. In truth, it was hard not to feel a little inferior in this place when she was poor and lowborn and couldn't do anything more impressive than whistle loudly through her fingers.

But she bucked herself up with a short pep talk. *Oh, come, you might not have any magical powers, but you've always had a good head on your shoulders. Even Lady Bradford says so. You're loyal to your friends, and you never run away from a fight.*

All of that was true, and it was just going to have to be enough.

Cracking open her history tome, Dani resumed reading the story of Hannibal. When she'd last left off, the ancient general had been trying to cross the Alps with an army of elephants to go and fight the Romans.

He had a famous quote that had been his reply when people told him that his quest was impossible: *"I will either find a way or make one."*

It sounded like something Jake would say. Dani quirked a smile at that thought and read on.

She had barely reached the bottom of the page when, suddenly, she heard a faint knock at the door to the Bradford suite.

She looked over and would've written it off as her imagination, except her dog heard it, too. Teddy's ears pricked up and his fuzzy head swiveled toward the sound.

There it was again, ever so faintly: a tiny *tap, tap, tap.*

At once, Teddy leaped off the couch where he had curled up and raced toward the door, barking.

"Teddy, be quiet! Coming!" Dani called. She scooped her dog up with one hand to quiet him and opened the door with the other.

To her surprise, who should be fluttering there but her favorite fairy courier. "Gladwin! Oh my goodness, how nice to see you. Come in!"

She opened the door wider, and the wee fairy flew right in, leaving a trail of sparkles behind her.

Dani closed the door with a smile as Gladwin landed on the end table next to the curve-backed velvet couch.

Teddy jumped up on it again and scampered toward the fairy. Placing his front paws on the arm of the couch, he sniffed Gladwin, stump tail wagging.

Dani went over to the fairy with a smile. "What are you doing here?"

"Actually," Gladwin said, "I am here on official business."

"You are?" Dani's eyebrows lifted.

Gladwin nodded and reached over her shoulder for the cylindrical leather case strapped across her back, like an archer's quiver of arrows.

She popped the lid off the case, then pulled out a small parchment scroll and presented it to Dani. "Message for Miss Daniela Catherine O'Dell."

"For me?" Dani stared at her in disbelief.

Gladwin nodded, but Dani read a trace of worry on the fairy's tiny oval face.

"Who's it from?" she asked with a prickle of suspicion.

"The Elders," Gladwin said.

"What? Why?" Dani felt the blood drain instantly from her face. "This can't be good! What do the Elders want with me? Am I in trouble? Have I done something wrong? What is this about?"

"I don't know! You have to read it." Gladwin held the tiny scroll out, but Dani was afraid to take it.

The Elders never paid the slightest attention to her. She wasn't even aware they knew she existed.

She ran a quick mental review of all her recent behavior and couldn't think of any infractions she might've committed.

But then, suddenly, she remembered Lord Badgerton and the mashed potatoes. And her stomach flip-flopped.

Jake was the one always getting into trouble, and he was already on thin ice with the Elders.

What if they had decided to punish *him* for last night's mishap by sending *her* away?

Then it dawned on her that the messy incident at the buffet wasn't the only mischief Jake had got up to last night.

He'd been asking questions all night long about the Dark Druids, nosing into business that he shouldn't. Especially after being warned to let the adults handle it for once!

Dani had a sinking feeling in her stomach that she was right. They couldn't do much against the famed Griffon heir, the golden boy of the Order, but they could teach him a lesson by sending her away.

Oh God. Her heart started pounding. Dani's greatest fear was being sent back to the dismal rookery. What if—?

"Just see what it says," Gladwin said, but even she sounded nervous.

"You haven't read it, then?"

"No! I don't read the messages. I just deliver them." Gladwin flew up off the table and kept holding the scroll out to Dani. "Here. You have to take it."

Dani gulped, backing away. "M-maybe you could pretend you couldn't find me?"

"I'd get fired! I-I'm sure everything will be fine, Dani," Gladwin said, but she didn't sound convinced. "I think you'd better just look at it, a-and see what it says."

Dani stared at her, her heart thumping, but she knew perfectly well that there was no escaping the Elders. Gathering her courage, she bravely stepped forward and took the tiny scroll from the fairy's outstretched hand.

The message was no bigger than a matchstick, but she was still scared to read it, afraid that once she cracked that little wax seal, things would never be the same.

Oh, quit being a coward, she ordered herself. *It's just a tiny message. You've faced up to shark men and yetis, gargoyles and ghosts, and even Jake's nasty Uncle Waldrick and his sea-witch sidekick, Fionnula. Whatever it is, Dani O'Dell, you can face this, too.*

Fine, she thought. *If they want me to leave, then I'll go.* With that, she took a deep breath and unrolled the tiny scroll, then held it up and forced herself to read:

> *Miss O'Dell,*
>
> *Kindly come at once to the Yew Court. A gnome will be waiting to conduct you through the maze.*
>
> *Regards,*
> *Ramona, Lady Bradford*

"Mother Mary." Dani clutched her chest. This was even worse than she had imagined!

"What is it?" the fairy tinkled.

Dani looked at Gladwin, wide-eyed. "I've been summoned to the Yew Court. I-I'm ordered to come r-right away."

Gladwin drew in her breath then buzzed closer, landing on Dani's shoulder. "Don't be afraid, Dani. I'll go with you as far as the maze."

Dani swallowed hard. "Thank you, Gladwin. I...I wish I knew what this was about."

Being summoned to the Yew Court was never good news.

The empty space in the middle of the great green maze was where all the magical youth were forced to undergo their Assessments, testing their gifts. It was a place of legal consequence, as well, and had served as the courtroom where Jake's wicked Uncle Waldrick had been sentenced to life in an Order dungeon somewhere far away in dragon country.

The Yew Court was also where Janos had been sentenced to execution after turning vampire, but then had received clemency from the Elders when they couldn't quite figure out how to kill him—or, more likely, just didn't have the heart.

Well, if they spared Janos, maybe there was hope for her, too, but Dani wasn't holding her breath. The truth was, she wasn't really needed here anyway. She had no true place here. She was nothing but Jake's sidekick, and now she was being sloughed off like a snake's old skin.

But, by goodness, if they were going to give her the boot, she would face her fate with dignity. She paused for a quick glance in the mirror that hung next to the door of the suite, making sure her hair was combed and that she didn't have anything in her teeth.

Then she bent down and, with a hand that trembled slightly, gave her dog a pat. "Wait here, Teddy. Don't worry, boy. If they send us away, at least we'll still have each other."

Teddy let out a small whine and sat down, sensing the seriousness of the situation.

Dani turned to Gladwin in a daze. "Do I look all right?"

"Beautiful," the fairy assured her.

Dani gave her a skeptical look. She knew she might be able to pass for cute on a good day, but beautiful she was not. That was Isabelle's territory.

"Let's just get this over with," she muttered, opening the door.

Gladwin clutched a length of her hair like a ship's rope to hold herself secure as Dani began marching down the corridor, heading for the lobby.

She knew the way by heart, but the walk through the white marble hallways of the guest block passed in a blur as she struggled to think of some other explanation for why the Elders might've summoned her.

She couldn't think of anything.

In moments, she reached the wide main staircase. The lobby below bustled with wizards in robes, and parents of all species congregating here and there, chitchatting about their children's accomplishments, now that they'd seen them off to their sessions.

Dani's mother was dead and her father was probably waking up in a pub somewhere in the East End. There was never somebody there to be proud of *her*.

But she paid the happy parents no mind, crossing the lobby underneath the dome. Then she went out through the massive front doors of the palace and down the wide, shallow steps out in front.

The hay bales and jack-o'-lanterns she'd helped Jillian Quince set up were soggy with dew, but Dani walked right past them. Though the temperature outside was comfortable, fear had given her a chill.

Wisps of morning fog still floated over the emerald lawn.

When she stepped down onto the courtyard at the bottom of the steps, the gravel crunched beneath her feet.

Overhead, the cobalt sky arced like a bright crystal dome. All around the tree line, a gold tint gilded most of the still-green leaves, but a few trees had already broken out in burnished oranges and reds, like the colors of her hair.

The distant sound of a splash revealed the water nymphs taking a morning swim in the little river; she could hear their haunting laughter echo across the sprawling lawn as she crossed the courtyard with jerky strides.

Gladwin lifted off Dani's shoulder and fluttered alongside her as she marched with a deepening dread toward the entrance of the towering boxwood maze.

Already she could see one of the little gnome servants of Merlin Hall waiting to escort her through the labyrinth.

They didn't speak, the little servant gnomes of Merlin Hall. Instead, they used gestures to communicate.

Some people thought the knee-high fellows were cute, with their pointy red hats, curly shoes, and big white beards.

Dani thought they were creepy.

They were so similar-looking that it was hard to tell them apart. They had no expressions on their faces other than a vague irritation with everyone around them.

Unfortunately, the gnomes were the only ones who knew the way through the ever-changing maze to the Yew Court in the center, home to the Old Father Tree.

The massive boxwood labyrinth was booby-trapped to defend itself from intruders. Moreover, the pattern of the maze rearranged itself each night by some inscrutable magic, ensuring that anyone trying to find their way to the Yew Court unauthorized would become hopelessly lost.

As Dani approached, the gnome beckoned impatiently to her. He also stepped back, as though he feared she might step on him.

Apparently, people kicked the gnomes by accident all the time, or tripped over them. The centaur lords and ladies had to be especially careful not to trample them under their hooves.

Outside the neatly clipped hedges of the labyrinth's thirty-foot walls, Dani turned to Gladwin. Her hands felt cold and clammy as she bunched them into fists. "Are you sure you can't just tell the Elders you weren't able to find me?"

"I'm sorry, Dani. You know I can't lie to my superiors. Try to be brave. You always are," Gladwin offered in distress.

"Just promise me one thing," Dani said. "If they banish me and oubliette me so I don't remember any of this, or you, or any of my friends, please just promise you'll look after Jake. He's a mess without Red, and if they send me packing, he's going to feel even worse."

Gladwin nodded sadly. "Don't worry, my dear. I'll look after him. But chin up. Let's not jump to the worst possible conclusions straightaway."

Dani hoped the fairy was right. She managed a nod in answer, then turned to the gnome. "I'm ready," she told him.

His red-capped head bobbed, then the gnome pivoted and began waddling ahead of her into the maze.

With one last glance over her shoulder at the fairy, who hovered in midair, anxiously watching after her, Dani looked past Gladwin at the magical palace with the morning sun shining behind it, fanning out in great golden rays.

Oh please, don't send me back to the rookery, she thought. *My spirit will die there.*

But when the gnome hissed at her to hurry up, she had no choice but to follow. Fists balled by her sides, Dani stepped through the tall green opening into the labyrinth. Forcing one foot after another, she began trailing her grumpy little escort.

To go and learn her fate.

CHAPTER 17
The Unlikely Scholar

Jake, meanwhile, was already deep in a different sort of maze. He was prowling through the unfamiliar alleys of what was, to him, a dangerous and foreign land: the great medieval library of Merlin Hall.

Constanzio floated along beside him, keeping him company.

"Good Lord," Jake muttered, glancing around at the towering shelves on all sides. "What do they need so many books for, anyway?"

"You should try reading one once in a while," the ghost said pleasantly.

Jake snorted. "Oh, believe me, Henry's given me a list of readings I'm supposed to be doing every day."

"Hmm, and why do I get the feeling you haven't been keeping up with it, *ragazzo*?" Constanzio asked, half hidden in a tall bookcase full of travel guides.

"I dunno," Jake said with a shrug, scanning the shelves. "It's hard to concentrate with all that's been happening."

"Might help to take your mind off things— Hold on!" the ghost suddenly said. "Shouldn't you be at the session for telekinetics?"

Jake gave him a sardonic look before venturing down another dim, narrow aisle full of musty books. "I decided not to go."

He had dashed off from their suite this morning with every intention of attending the orientation session for the telekinesis kids. He had his red sash and everything.

But even as he walked toward the classroom where it was being held, his bookbag over his shoulder, Jake had seen a few girls giggling and waiting by the door for him to arrive.

Ugh. He had seen them smiling at him last night at the party, too. But he didn't have time for girl nonsense right now.

And the reaction from the boys had been even more problematical.

Word must've got around that his gift had gone wonky, and everyone was all aflutter about the Badgerton incident.

The other boys didn't seem to know whether to congratulate or mock him; the self-important Lord Badgerton wasn't the most popular fellow.

Still.

"Those sessions aren't really optional, Jake," Constanzio said with a frown.

Jake huffed. "*Signore*, I already blew up a rock giant and turned him into gravel. Those sessions are for beginners. Blimey, I could teach the class."

"Not so much these days," his spectral companion murmured wryly.

"Oh, come on!" Jake glanced at a row of cookbooks, then scowled at Constanzio. "That was only because I was upset. The skunkies threw a tomato at me! Everything will go back to normal, I'm certain, just as soon as I get my Gryphon back. Until then, I have more important things to do."

"If you say so, my bold young friend."

"Lord, this place," Jake said under his breath, lost. "Where do they keep the— Ooh!"

Jake spotted the head librarian hurrying past the intersection between the shelves ahead and dashed after him.

"Excuse me!"

House brownies were always obliging, even when they worked in libraries instead of people's homes. Jake knew because two wonderful house brownies worked for him at his cozy Welsh estate.

His housekeeper there, Snowdrop Fingle, did the cooking and cleaning, while her husband, Nimbus Fingle, tended the grounds and the stable. The house brownies took pride in keeping things in shipshape.

But house brownies were always so intent on their work that it was hard keeping up with the little whirlwinds as they rushed about their chores, completing them to perfection.

Jake raced to catch up to the brownie librarian, a four-foot-tall fellow with hairy feet, a tidy vest, and a pair of spectacles perched on the end of his blunt nose.

The library was nearly empty this morning, so the head librarian had been trundling back and forth re-shelving books that the patrons had left lying about.

"Pardon me, a moment of your time, please!" Jake hurried after the creature. Constanzio sped along beside him.

Portly yet weightless, the ghost flew *through* the rows of tall bookshelves when Jake proved too tricky to keep up with, darting down lanes and whisking around corners.

Trying to find his way in this dimly lit labyrinth of knowledge reminded Jake of his old days sneaking around the back alleys of the East End, trying to stay a step ahead of Constable Flanagan.

"Oh! Hello there. May I help you?" the brownie librarian said.

Jake nodded, skidding to a halt near the little fellow. "Yes, please. I need to find an atlas on Mesopotamia."

The brownie blinked. "Ancient or modern?"

"Modern, I think."

"Historical, topographical, ecological, or demographic?"

"Uh, not sure."

"Pfft," said the brownie with a wave of his hairy-knuckled hand. "Follow me, my young scholar."

Scholar? No one had ever accused Jake of being one of those before. Especially his long-suffering tutor.

Jake gave Constanzio a humorous look, then had to hurry to keep up as the brownie librarian pattered ahead, his callused bare feet slapping along over the cool stone floor.

It was the only sound in the hush beneath the high, vaulted ceiling. More like an ancient cathedral with bookshelves than a plain, simple library, Jake thought. They passed shelves with grimoires and spellbooks, recipes for potions and field guides to the study of various species. There were histories of elvish kingdoms, fat tomes chronicling ancient wars...

Jake noted these topics with interest, but bypassed them all, hurrying after the librarian. They wove through more twisting, turning aisles until they reached the reference section, where the little chap halted midway down a row.

He pushed a wheeled ladder several feet sideways, then climbed up on it and squinted through his little round spectacles, examining the contents of a shelf near the top.

"Hmm...yes...this one, I think..." His slightly clawed finger trailed over the spines of several huge books.

Tilting his head back, Jake watched in wonder as the librarian, making small sounds of thought to himself, slid a very thick book off the shelf.

Jake's eyes widened as he saw the book was nearly half the size of the little librarian.

"Oh, this one's rather heavy—" The brownie pulled too hard on the tome and went toppling backward off the ladder with a shriek, the massive book clutched in his arms.

Instinctively, Jake threw up his hands and fired out a net of energy, catching the librarian with his telekinesis.

To his relief, it worked just fine this time. The brownie's shriek of alarm faded as he found himself safe; Jake set him down gently on the library floor.

"Oh—why, thank you, young man. Thought I was a goner."

"Not at all." Jake quickly took the heavy book out of the little fellow's arms. "Are you all right?"

"Yes, y-yes, I'm fine. Oh...!" The librarian suddenly studied him with a closer eye. "You're Lord Griffon, aren't you?"

"Guilty," Jake admitted.

"I see."

"Probably not a good idea for him to start wondering why the notorious Lord Griffon is looking up the Mesopotamian Marshes," Constanzio warned, not bothering to lower his voice, since the brownie could not hear him anyway.

The opera ghost was right. The last thing Jake was supposed to be doing was research on one of the locations where the Black Fortress had most recently been seen.

But not even Constanzio knew about the plot Jake had hatched with Maddox, who was in his room right now writing that letter to his birth father, the Prince of Kahlberg.

The brownie librarian adjusted his spectacles, which had gone askew after his near-fall. "I say, my lord, aren't you supposed to be at the session for telekinetics?"

"They threw me out," Jake lied with a sheepish smile. That, at least, the brownie could believe. "Thought I'd come here and work on the assignments that my tutor gave me until the session lets out."

"Hmm. Very well. Does that look like the sort of book you need?" the librarian asked, nodding at the giant tome in Jake's arms.

"Yes, thank you. I think I'll peruse the shelves a bit here and see if anything else in this section looks helpful."

"Oooh, *peruse.* A fine word," the librarian said with a smile of approval. "I've always been fond of a good Latinate verb. Very well, Lord Griffon! If you need anything more, just let me know."

"Thank you!" Jake called after him. The brownie was already pattering off to continue his tasks. Jake sent Constanzio a relieved glance. "That was close."

The cheerful ghost raised his thick black eyebrows. "Good to see your gift still works well enough when it needs to."

Jake nodded, then he climbed the library ladder himself and chose another two atlases to *peruse*: one on ancient Mesopotamia and one on the modern-day Ottoman Empire. Nodding to Constanzio to follow, he then found his way to one of the study tables. He could not avoid the loud bang that echoed in the quiet when he set the atlases down on the scuffed wooden table.

He clomped his backpack onto the chair, but remained standing as he flipped the first book open. It was full of maps, but with a glance at the table of contents, he narrowed in on the region known as Mesopotamia.

Sure enough, at the southernmost reaches of the Ottoman Empire, just above a body of water labeled the *Persian Gulf,* the map showed a mass of squiggly sideways lines representing a vast stretch of swampland.

Studying it in the dim light of the library, he moved aside so the sunshine filtering in through the stained-glass window high on the nearby wall could shine down on the page.

Fortunately, there was a column of basic information down the left side of the page.

"Blast," he mumbled as he skimmed it.

"What's wrong?" Constanzio asked.

"It says the Mesopotamian Marshes cover nearly eight thousand square miles. There's no way to pinpoint where the Black Fortress might have landed within such a huge space."

Constanzio drifted down to perch on the edge of the table, peering at the page. "What else does it say? Maybe we can find some clue to tell us why they went there in the first place."

"All right..." Jake shared the information as he skimmed. "The Marshes are fed by the Tigris and Euphrates. Those are rivers, right?"

"Right. Some say that's about where the Garden of Eden once

existed."

"Oh really?"

The ghost nodded.

Jake made a face of surprise, then read aloud from the book: "'The shallows that cover this vast region vary in salinity as well as depth, ranging from an average of four to six feet, up to depths of twenty-two feet measured in some places.'" He glanced curiously at his spectral companion. "So I guess the Black Fortress has no trouble landing in a few feet of water, then."

The ghost shrugged. "If it can land at the bottom of a burning crater, I don't think it would have much trouble with a swamp."

"Good point," Jake said, then turned the page. Instead of a map, this held other interesting tidbits. He trailed his finger over the page. "Seems hardly anybody lives there. Small population of fisherfolk known as the Marsh Arabs. Well, this is interesting—it says they build their houses out of reeds that grow on the marshes."

"Interesting, but probably irrelevant. What else?"

Jake skimmed the next page. "There's animals there—water buffalo, lions, and foxes—so I guess there must be some dry land to walk around on, too. 'The marshlands are home to many species of fish, snakes, and birds, including the sacred ibis.' Sacred ibis?" Jake echoed. "That could be something. Couldn't it?"

At that moment, the librarian came trotting toward them—finished re-shelving, it seemed.

"The sacred ibis is frequently featured in ancient Egyptian art," the brownie informed them, overhearing. "The bird is associated with Thoth, god of wisdom from the Egyptian pantheon. Would you like information on ancient Egypt, Lord Griffon, or perhaps on waterfowl species in general?"

Jake sighed. "Might as well. Thank you," he added.

"Delighted to help." The brownie was already whizzing off again to find more reference books.

When Jake glanced at Constanzio, he noticed his jovial friend frowning. "I hate to say it, *ragazzo*, but this feels like a dead end to me. Not wrong, per se, just not...very significant."

"I don't disagree," Jake admitted, pulling the next atlas toward him. "But a false lead is better than none at all."

Constanzio nodded with a heartfelt look, then Jake checked the second book's table of contents. It all felt a little pointless, but he refused to be discouraged.

Red was counting on him. He continued reading.

Onward.

But he did pause to wonder what Dani was doing today...

CHAPTER 18
In the Maze

The grass beneath Dani's tightly laced half boots was still slippery with dew, the morning air as cold and clammy as her hands bunched up at her sides.

Her heart was thumping, but she kept putting one foot after the other, her skirts swinging back and forth about her shins as she hurried to keep up with the gnome.

She didn't *want* to follow him, but it was either that or risk getting lost forever in the shifting aisles and pathways of the maze—or worse yet, skewered, maimed, or otherwise blown up by one of the labyrinth's countless booby traps.

Still, she wished she'd never received Gladwin's message. To her mind, this summons to the Yew Court could only spell doom.

All the while, the dark green hedges walled her in on either side, blocking out the cheery morning sunshine. The temperature had dropped in the shadows, and she shivered in the chill, skipping a step now and then to keep up with the gnome.

They were fast for such small creatures.

As he led her through the turning, twisting alleys of the maze, Dani kept her gaze fixed on him, struggling to rehearse something she might say to the Elders in her own defense.

But how could anyone mount an argument if you didn't even know what you'd done wrong?

Besides, the way the gnome's pointy red hat rocked back and forth with his short-legged gait was making her a bit dizzy. Already queasy with nerves, she redirected her attention to the birds instead, listening to their rowdy morning clamor.

She could only hear them now, but yesterday, she had seen them:

a huge flock of dark little birds had covered the treetops, massing for their migration southward in a whirring cloud of wings.

She didn't know what kind of birds they were. Swallows? Starlings, maybe? But listening to their boisterous cacophony, she wondered nervously what they were talking about.

Isabelle would know. She could talk to the animals and understand their replies. But Dani, devoid of magical powers, could only guess.

I'll bet they're discussing flying south for the winter.

At the moment, Dani wished she could fly away too.

She just hoped she didn't start crying in front of the Elders, blubbering like a baby and begging to stay. No, she must keep hold of her composure, for such humiliation would only add insult to injury.

It was hard to tell how many minutes had passed, let alone how far they'd actually gone in the maze, but when they turned the next corner, she spotted the Yew Court ahead.

In the center of the maze lay a long green rectangular space, not unlike a sports field. The last time they'd come to Merlin Hall, she had seen Jake tested there in the Assessments. Nixie and Maddox, too.

Now it was her turn.

With a silent gulp, Dani marched slowly toward the opening in the maze.

She hadn't realized she had drifted to a halt until a tug on her skirts startled her out of her dread-filled daze. She looked down and saw the gnome pointing impatiently to the far end of the field.

"I know," she mumbled. Well, there was no point in stalling.

She took a deep breath, mustered up all the courage she could scrounge, then smoothed her skirts, lifted her chin, and strode out calmly onto the sprawling Field of Assessment.

Never mind that her knees were shaking.

Ahead, through the last whorls of morning mist, she could see the Elders' chairs arrayed in a single row on either side of the Old Father Tree.

Not all of the chairs were occupied, thankfully, so at least they hadn't called the entire council of Elders to deal with her.

Her mind churned as she walked at a dirge-like pace down the field. This was her last chance to think of an angle to take in pleading her case.

Please. I know I don't really belong here, but you can't send me away. Even though I don't have any magical powers, the others need me, don't you see?

I'm the glue. I mean, look at Archie. He might be a genius, but you need someone with common sense around here. Trust me on that.

And Nixie? She might be a spell-casting prodigy, but when she first came along, she didn't trust anyone. Now she's finally started to see that we really are *her friends. She's finally started letting down her guard.*

As for Isabelle, well, you must already know how special she is. But being an empath is difficult. She can't help taking in everyone else's emotions around her; it overwhelms her sometimes. That's why she needs me. I have to be here to protect her. That's my job, and I do it well.

And Maddox, well, I'm the only one he'll listen to when he gets all dark and broody.

And then, ladies and gentlemen, there's Jake.

A lump rose in her throat at the thought of him. She shuddered at how her darling blockhead might react if they sent her away. He was already on the edge, struggling with what he had to endure.

Don't do this to him. Please. He lost his parents, his Gryphon was taken, and now you're going to send me away too, just when he needs me most?

For his sake, not mine, I beg you, don't do this to Jake. Not even the Dark Druids would be that cruel.

But, of course, she didn't dare say any of this aloud. She wasn't *that* bold.

In truth, she would've been too scared to utter a word as she came to stand self-consciously before the row of seated Elders in the shade of the Old Father Tree.

She tried not to stare too much at the massive yew tree, ancient as he was, thousands of years old, with his huge trunk and soaring branches covered in soft, silver-green needles.

But, really, it was astonishing to stand there before a living tree with a face.

The Father Yew had bushy eyebrows of moss and kindly brown eyes as he gazed thoughtfully at Dani. His nose was a nubby knot of wood, and his lips were barky.

As for the others, now that she was here, she saw it wasn't all bad.

Jake's aunt Ramona was there. The Elder witch sat all the way to the left. Her patrician face nearly quirked a smile when she saw how frightened Dani was.

Next to her sat the ancient Master Balinor, his mysterious owl perched on the lowest of the Old Yew's branches.

Beside Balinor, Sir Peter Quince lounged in his chair, legs crossed. He was garbed as usual in his long black academic robes. Dani was most relieved to see the cheerful wizard there.

She was almost positive that if she was in trouble, Miz Jillian would've used whatever influence she had on her husband to put in a good word for her. The non-magical had to stick together around here.

Beside Sir Peter, Dame Oriel sat in a meditative pose, her plum-colored hair burnished in the glow of the morning.

Lord Badgerton fidgeted in the chair next to the clairvoyant, looking disgusted with everything, as usual, but at least he had cleaned the mashed potatoes out of his mustache.

To Dani's surprise, the last person present on the dais was not an Elder at all, but a Lightrider.

Waiting in the shadows beneath the tree leaned none other than Finnderool, the slim and graceful wood elf who had brought them back from Sicily.

His long, pale hair seemed to glow in the shade as he offered Dani a princely nod, his hand pressed to his heart in the standard greeting of his people. A slight smile played about his lips, but he always looked secretive and slightly superior. After all, he was quite highborn, kin to elvish royalty. Still, the Lightrider had a no-nonsense manner that Dani and the other kids agreed was decidedly intimidating. He was not unkind; he was simply all business.

As she waited to hear what they had to say, Dani was mystified that so many important personages had assembled here this morning for the sake of one magically talentless girl.

I must be in even bigger trouble than I thought.

Her heart skipped a beat, but Dani offered her audience a respectful curtsy. "Y-Your Excellencies wanted to see me?"

"Sit down, Miss O'Dell. We'd like to talk to you." Sir Peter rose from his chair and, with an idle flick of his wand, instantly conjured a wooden chair for her to sit on, out in front of them all.

"Thank you, sir." It was always a little disconcerting when the gifted did that sort of thing, but Dani sat down, folded her hands on her lap in a demure pose, and tucked her feet under the chair, doing her best to look well behaved.

"Now then," Sir Peter said, as though he could practically hear her thumping heartbeat. He was used to conducting the Assessments, after all. He had a talent for putting nervous kids at ease with his breezy manner. But today, even Sir Peter seemed somewhat solemn. "You must be wondering why we've called you here."

"Yes, sir," Dani forced out, but at that moment, a flicker of motion caught the corner of her eye.

One *more* person appeared, stepping out of a small arched opening in the side of the maze. Her eyes widened in disbelief when she saw him.

Da? She had not seen her father in over a year!

To be sure, Patrick O'Dell, Sr. was the last person in the world she'd expected to see, but this was no conjured illusion.

It was him, all right, her papa, in his same shabby coat and scuffed work boots. Ruddy-nosed and potbellied, the lowly Irish laborer was holding his old wool hat in his hands and looking even more out of place than she was here in the magical world.

"Mornin', lass," he greeted her in a low tone, then he sat down on the chair that had been provided for him a few feet apart from the Elders.

Dani couldn't even blink. Her heart was suddenly in her throat. *Oh no. They've sent for him to take me away.*

"Good, then. We're all here," Sir Peter continued in an easy tone.

Then he started rambling on with a sort of introduction about what they were all doing there, but Dani failed to hear a word.

Because she knew now for certain they were sending her home.

If Da had come all this way from London, then obviously, the Elders must have sent for him to come and fetch her. Take her back to the city with him. Back to the rookery, with its drab lanes and crumbling buildings, its sewage-stinking curbs and brawls in the streets. Its violence and poverty...

No fairies. No magic. No Jake.

She sat there in shock, her stomach twisting, her mouth dry. She felt her lower lip start to tremble as she realized her worst fears had come to fruition.

All because Jake had accidentally flung a glob of food at Lord Badgerton?!

It must have been the last straw, after all his wayward behavior.

But why were they taking it out on her?

The adults were all talking; she could see their lips moving, but she registered not a word of it.

The seconds were ticking by and Dani knew it was only a matter of time before they handed down her sentence. She couldn't even think. She wanted to jump up and flee, but the maze would murder her if she ran, so she sat frozen, her heart in her throat.

They'd at least better let me say goodbye.

"It's really very exciting," Sir Peter was saying, while Father Yew smiled at her in leafy benevolence.

Dame Oriel, however, tilted her head slightly and studied her, as though she, at least, had realized Dani wasn't paying attention.

"Peter," the clairvoyant Elder interrupted him.

"Yes, Oriel? Is there something you wish to say?"

"I...don't think the girl is catching all this," Dame Oriel said with an arch smile.

The younger wizard grinned. "Or perhaps she is in shock."

"Um," Dani said, trying to look like she'd been paying attention the whole time and wondering what she'd missed. "Sorry. What?"

The Elder witch arched a silvery brow at her.

Balinor had missed at least as much as she had, for he had dozed off, his arms folded across his chest.

"Tell her again what you said," Oriel suggested, nodding at Sir Peter.

"Of course. I was just saying it's not every day that Gaia makes her choice so clear, but she took to you right away, it seems."

"She said you're down to earth, Miss O'Dell," the Father Yew himself rumbled to Dani. "'Tis the highest compliment Mother Gaia can give."

"Indeed," Sir Peter agreed, beaming. "When Master Finnderool came and told us her wishes, I must say, we were all quite pleased." The Elders glanced around at each other and nodded—except for Lord Badgerton.

"You have great potential, Dani," Lady Bradford said. "I've always thought so."

"We are all so happy for you, my dear," Oriel chimed in.

"Me too, lass," Da said, hat in hand.

Wait, what? Dani stared at them blankly.

"Well, speak for yourselves," Lord Badgerton huffed. "I want it noted in the minutes that I am against this appointment. We barely know this urchin. Her selection smacks of nepotism, frankly."

"Nonsense, Boris!" Sir Peter said. "There was no favoritism at play here. Think of all she's done—without a whiff of magic at her disposal!"

"I agree," Oriel said firmly.

Dani's head turned back and forth, tracking each speaker, as though she were watching a game of tennis.

"It's all come from the girl's own, well, gumption!" Sir Peter declared. "Most of the children here were born into this life, but this plucky young lady has *earned* it by her own brave deeds." The wizard sent her a knowing wink and sat back down.

Finnderool was nodding as well, as he sauntered out of the shadows. "Ultimately, my lord, it doesn't matter whether you approve of her or not," he said to Badgerton. "*We* don't pick the program's applicants; Gaia does. As you are well aware."

Badgerton harrumphed. "She's a nobody," he muttered.

Da threw down his hat and shot to his feet. "I beg yer pardon! What did ye say about me daughter?"

Badgerton gave Mr. O'Dell a pugnacious look, which her rookery Da returned.

"That will do," Lady Bradford interjected sternly, and the two simmered down.

Dani still wasn't sure what in the blazes was happening.

"Master Elf, kindly continue your explanation," the Elder witch said to Finnderool.

The wood elf bowed to her. "Gladly, my lady." Finnderool sauntered across the row of chairs, heading toward Dani. "Miss O'Dell: I trust you remember when I came to fetch you all from the villa in Taormina and escorted everybody through the Grid."

Dani gave an anxious nod. "Yes, sir."

"And what did you think of your first trip through a portal?"

In spite of her confusion, the memory brought a faint smile of wonder to her lips. "Why, 'twas the most amazing thing I've ever done."

She still tingled at the memory of her molecules gently dissolving into light particles and then whooshing over the earth along the invisible ley lines from one portal to the next.

"Did you feel at all queasy afterward?" he asked.

"No, sir." She remembered that the others had, though.

Even Jake and Maddox had gone a little green when they stepped out of the shimmering portal onto the lawn at Merlin Hall. Archie had puked. Isabelle had staggered with dizziness, and even tough Nixie had needed to lie down and chew a piece of the medicinal ginger candy that Finnderool had passed around to settle the stomachs of anyone who needed it.

Dani had wondered what was the matter with them. To her, it had just sort of tickled.

Of course, those who tried to travel through the Grid without an authorized Lightrider to escort them would be instantly vaporized. It was part of Gaia's defenses, she'd heard.

Whatever the reason, Dani had had no ill effects from the trip. In fact, she had found it exhilarating. Her molecules had reassembled quickly and easily as they neared the terminus, then she had skipped right out of the shining tunnel, landing on her feet while her friends lay around retching on the grass.

"Gaia liked your energy a great deal," Finnderool said. "That's why you had such an easy time of it."

Dani stared at him, not quite comprehending. "My...energy?"

"Your life force, dear," Dame Oriel explained. "It's the sum of who and what you are. Your heart, mind, spirit. Your experiences. Strengths and weaknesses—and talents waiting to emerge."

"That is why we have summoned you here, Miss O'Dell—and your father, too." Finnderool gestured at Da. "The program can be dangerous at times, so no aspiring Lightrider can begin the training without parental permission."

Dani's eyes flew open wide. *Wait, what?*

"The Elders have discussed the particulars with Mr. O'Dell," Finnderool continued, "and I am happy to say he has given his blessing."

Da gave her an encouraging nod. "It's yer choice, lass, but I say go'n'make yer mother proud."

Balinor awoke with a jolt, having been elbowed by Sir Peter.

The old wizard cleared his throat and rose to his feet, then took something out of the deep pocket of his voluminous wizard robes. "Ahem! Miss Daniela Catherine O'Dell, you are hereby cordially invited into the Lightrider training program."

Dani's jaw dropped. It was possible her heart stopped briefly.

Then the old wizard held out the object he had slipped out of his pocket, and Dani stared at it in shock. Draped across his palms lay a white cloth sash, its silver threads glistening in the sun.

The Lightrider sash.

"Do you accept?" Balinor asked.

"Hoo!" said his owl.

"My thoughts exactly!" Dani burst out. "Who, me?"

The Elders chuckled, but she was in earnest.

"Is this real?" she cried, heart pounding. "Are you serious?"

"This is no jest, young lady," Dame Oriel said with amusement.

Sir Peter tried to stifle his laughter behind his fist; even Finderool smiled. Lady Bradford gazed at her, waiting for the news to sink in.

Dani just sat there like a lump, her mouth hanging open. "You want *me*...for the Lightrider program?"

"Correct," said the Old Father Yew.

"There must be some sort of mistake," Dani spluttered.

"That's what I said," Badgerton mumbled, and Balinor frowned at him.

"Gaia chose you," Finnderool reminded her. "She said you seem very well grounded."

"She talks?" Dani asked haplessly.

The stern wood elf cracked a smile. "Only to the Green Men, Miss O'Dell. But Lightriders can sometimes sense her reactions—like Guardians can sense danger. Now, do not waste the Elders' time, child. Either accept the sash or decline." Finnderool swept a graceful hand toward Balinor, who was still holding out the prized silver belt.

Dani gulped. "Oh...oh, yes. Thank you. I most certainly do accept." Still in shock, she rose from her seat and gave the Elders her best curtsy. "I-it would be my honor."

"Come forward, child," Balinor said, a slight smile quirking his lips beneath his bushy white beard.

Heart thumping, Dani walked toward him slowly until she reached the chief of the Order.

"Wear it with pride," Balinor said as he presented the sash to her.

Once she had taken it, Sir Peter burst out with fervent applause. "Well done, Miss O'Dell!"

Oriel joined in, and even Lady Bradford and Master Balinor clapped politely.

Finnderool merely bowed to Dani, his hand on his heart.

But Da jumped out of his chair and applauded the loudest, laughing. "That's me wee girl!" He even whistled through his fingers, just like he'd taught her to do.

Finnderool looked over at the rowdy Irishman in shock.

But Sir Peter rose from his chair, gesturing to Dani to return to her seat. She walked back to the chair he had conjured for her, fingering the Lightrider belt with a sense of unreality.

Was all this a dream?

Her amazement doubled as she realized what this meant.

Not only did she have her own rightful place here now in the magical world—no longer a tagalong—but when they chose Jake for this program, as well, which the Elders undoubtedly would when the time was right, they could go through all of it side by side. They'd become Lightriders *together*!

She sat down in her chair again, but now she was so happy and excited that she could hardly sit still. This was the best day of her life!

Twisting the soft cloth belt around her hands, she began swinging her feet with her eagerness to run and tell her friends the incredible news.

When Balinor returned to his seat, Sir Peter strolled past his colleagues with an easy, swinging gait, hands in pockets. "Well! Now that we've got all that sorted, I call this meeting adjourned.

"As for you, Miss O'Dell, you'll start your training this week. You will join Finnderool's group of Lightrider students tomorrow morning at nine o'clock sharp, and I know you will take good advantage of this excellent opportunity."

"Yes, sir."

The bespectacled wizard smiled warmly at her. "Congratulations, Dani. You've earned it."

The Elders echoed his sentiments and started getting up to return to the palace. Dani watched them with stars in her eyes. She couldn't believe this was happening to her, that she was finally a real part of the magical world all on her own, not just holding on to Jake's coattails.

And an important part, too!

"Lightriders don't have to have magical powers, you know," Dame Oriel said fondly, as though reading Dani's thoughts. "You've met our own dear Tex, haven't you? Well—Agent Munroe. Unfortunately, he is missing just now, but when we get him back, I'm sure that mad cowboy will enjoy regaling you and your friends with the tale of how it was when he was chosen."

Dani gave her a tremulous smile. "Thank you, ma'am."

Dame Oriel smiled back, then turned away to get on with her day.

"Come along, Mr. O'Dell," the Elder witch said to Da. "Would you care for some breakfast in the dining hall? I have a feeling your daughter wishes to share the news with her friends straightaway."

A grin broke across Dani's face. "Oh, am I allowed to tell them now, milady?"

The Elder witch snorted. "Of course you are, dear. I know the lot of you have no secrets among you. You may have lunch with your father before we return him to London."

"Thank you, milady." Dani gave the baroness a heartfelt look of gratitude, then ran to hug her father. "I'll see you at lunchtime, Da!"

"Aye, I'll look forward to that, poppet."

As soon as Da released her from his hearty embrace, Dani ran like a maniac across the Field of Assessment, clutching the folded silver belt in her hand.

She could not wait to tell the others. She leaped off her feet, punching the air over her head with a laugh of wild victory. Then she raced on, heading for the opening in the maze through which she had arrived.

The same gnome was waiting for her there—or maybe it was a different one. Who could tell? She wanted to scoop the grumpy little fellow up in her arms and dance him around like a doll.

But she refrained from that particular show of enthusiasm, otherwise, he might take offense and lead her into some spiked booby trap to teach her a lesson.

Her knee-high guide beckoned to her to follow and trudged back into the maze, but this time, he couldn't go fast enough for Dani. In her excitement, she hurried him along as quick as his stubby legs could carry him.

Bursting to tell her friends this astounding news, the return trip seemed to take forever as they went traipsing back and forth through the endless twists and turns of the labyrinth.

Considering this was the biggest thing that had ever happened to her, Dani decided to gather the whole gang into one place so she could make her announcement to everyone at the same time.

At last, she spotted the end of the maze ahead. A straight green lane headed out to the lawn, where she'd last left Gladwin.

The fairy courier must've had to go back to work, for she had disappeared.

Unable to hold herself back anymore, Dani set her sights on the opening ahead and raced past the gnome, yelling, *"Thank you!"* over her shoulder.

Clearing the maze, she sprinted off to go and collect everyone, especially glad of the chance to give poor Jake some good news for once.

He was going to be so surprised. But she knew he would be as happy about this as she was. Because it meant that as the future unfolded, they would undertake this adventure the same way the two of them had survived everything else.

Together.

Dani barreled across the grass and the graveled courtyard, pounded up the steps, flung through the front doors of the palace, rushed across the lobby and down the steps to the basement, where she found Archie and Nixie hard at work in the lab.

"Meet me on the bridge in ten minutes!" she yelled through the door, startling both prodigies out of their no-doubt complicated thoughts before racing on.

She yelled the same message up to Maddox a few minutes later out on the Guardians' training field, where he was climbing a dizzying obstacle course with objects being magically hurled at him from all directions.

The young soldier batted a rock away with the club in his hand, then frowned in Dani's direction. She never asked anything of him; he would know it was important. Rather than yell, he sent her a salute to let her know he'd be coming soon.

Dani dashed off again and found Isabelle feeding a baby unicorn a bottle of milk in a quiet pen at the edge of the menagerie. Dani kept her distance from her empath friend, not wanting Isabelle to guess her surprise before she could tell it herself.

The older girl certainly sensed her crazed excitement, but, happily, Izzy agreed to come and meet the others on the little stone bridge across the stream.

Finally, Dani raced off to find Jake. Saving the best for last, she supposed. Oh, they were going to have so much fun going through the Lightrider training together!

She had no doubt the Elders would probably be calling him next to the Yew Court. Strangely, though, she did not find her roguish friend where he was supposed to be—at the orientation for the telekinetics.

She peered in through the classroom window, but the handsome blond rascal was absent.

Oh, you dunderhead, did you get thrown out already? she wondered, but laughed. No matter. Wherever he was, she would find him. And when she told him her news, why, she could hardly wait to see the look on his face!

CHAPTER 19
The Doubler

Constanzio had left, but Jake still slumped at the library table, poring over the atlases on the Mesopotamian Marshes.

He had spent the past hour racking his brain and breaking pencil points as he hurriedly took notes, but it all amounted to very little, and by the time a yawn seized him, he wasn't sure that any of it even mattered.

Just as he started thinking about winding up his research excursion for the day, the sound of running footfalls barreling into the library arrested his attention. He perked up a bit, glancing toward the sound.

The wild staccato of racing footsteps clattered across the stone floor and echoed beneath the vaulted ceiling. Tucked away in the reference section, Jake stared toward the unseen intruder in amusement.

Whoever it was making all that noise, the brownie librarian would be shushing them in an instant. Then he heard a familiar voice calling his name in a loud whisper: "Jake! Jake, are you here? Hullo?"

"Carrot?" He furrowed his brow. "Psst!" he called when he saw Dani go dashing past the end of his aisle. "Over here!"

A heartbeat later, she came scrambling back, nearly sliding past the opening this time, but skidding to a halt. Regaining her balance, she rushed down the aisle toward him, wearing the most mischievous grin he'd ever seen.

"Jake! You have to come quick!"

He jolted to his feet. "Is there news about Red?"

"What? Oh—well, no. There's news! But it's not about Red. Sorry."

"Ah." He flashed a knowing smile. "About Derek and Helena,

then?"

Dani frowned. "No. What about them?"

Jake's eyes widened as he realized he was on the verge of giving away the Guardian's secret. "Uh, nothing—never mind. What were you saying, now?"

"I have to tell you something. All of you. I have news of my own, and it's *huge*. If you want to hear it, come to the naiads' bridge!"

"When?"

"Now," she said gleefully. Then she bolted off again like her head was on fire, leaving him confounded.

"Well, isn't she mysterious today," Jake murmured to himself. But curiosity got the better of him.

Quickly closing the atlases and leaving them for the brownie librarian to shelve, he slung his knapsack over his shoulder and strode after the redhead, tickled indeed to find out what "huge news" had her all a-tizzy.

A few minutes later, he walked up onto the little stone bridge where he and Maddox had made their secret pact just last night. To Jake's surprise, everyone else was already there.

Archie had doffed his lab coat and dragged Nixie out into the sunshine to hear Dani's big secret. Maddox had shown up still sweaty from training, while Isabelle leaned against the quaint stone wall of the bridge, still wearing the ruffled apron that she wore to protect her dress whenever she worked with animals.

Dani held court at the top of the bridge's gentle arch.

The Irish lass stood with her feet planted wide, her fists braced on her waist. Her green eyes sparkled, her cheeks pink with excitement.

Her smile beamed as everyone gathered around. "All right, you lot," she said. "Is everybody listening?"

Jake arched a brow. *She's even starting to sound like me.*

They all assured her they were.

"Very well," she said, clearly relishing her secret. "Ladies and gentlemen, the most astonishing thing in the whole world happened this morning. Gladwin brought me a message, and I—yes, me, just little old me—I was summoned to the Yew Court."

"The Yew Court?" Isabelle murmured.

Dani nodded emphatically. "I have never been so terrified in my life. Not even when that rock monster almost squashed me—you remember."

Jake certainly did. The thought of how close she'd come to dying still made him shudder.

"But it wasn't bad news," Dani continued. "On the contrary! My friends"—she held up a remnant of cloth in a color Jake instantly recognized—"you are looking at the newest recruit to the official Merlin Hall Lightrider program!"

Not a sound followed as they all stared at her without comprehension.

Dani laughed merrily. "That was my reaction, too! But it's true. Gaia picked me! Can you believe it? I start tomorrow. I'm supposed to join Finnderool's group!" She let out a whoop and jumped up and down, her fists in the air.

Archie was the first to splutter congratulations. "W-well, that's most, most extraordinary! M-my dear Dani, do you mean to say— How now, are you having us on?"

"No, it's the truth, I swear!" She held up her right hand.

"W-well, that's stupendous!" the boy genius cried, then he hugged her and clapped her on the back. "Isn't it marvelous, you all?"

Even Nixie looked impressed. She started applauding slowly for Dani, shaking her head in amazement.

Beaming with joy, Izzy rushed over and gave Dani a hug and sisterly kiss on the head. "I am so proud of you, Dani! You're going to be absolutely brilliant, I have no doubt."

"Congratulations, little red." Maddox thrust out his hand, and Dani shook it with a proud grin. "Maybe someday they'll send us out on missions together," he said. "Wouldn't be the first time I've had to guard you, eh?"

Dani laughed and pumped his hand eagerly. "I know I'd have nothing to fear with you watching my back, Guardian St. Trinian. Oh, wouldn't that be something? I really can't believe it. Gaia liked me! She chose me herself. Master Finderool said he suspected it the moment he saw I didn't get sick after my first trip through the Grid like the rest of you did."

"We have to celebrate. Tonight," Nixie declared.

"Quite so!" Archie exclaimed. "Dani, this is truly incredible and so well deserved. Isn't it, coz?" He glanced at Jake, who'd been silent, dazed by the news.

His cousin's pointed look jarred him out of his stupor.

"It certainly is," Jake forced out. But he felt a little queasy. His limbs seemed made out of lead.

Dani took a sprightly step toward him. "Oh, Jake, it's the happiest day of my life! Don't you see what this means?"

He shook his head, knots in his stomach.

She grasped him by his arms. "It *means* we'll get to be Lightriders together! Isn't that amazing?"

"Well—yes, but...I haven't been invited yet," he said with an uncomfortable laugh.

She waved this off. "Don't worry, I'm sure Gladwin will be bringing your summons any day now. Maybe even tomorrow! After all, why in the world would they ever pick me and not you? You're the Griffon heir, for goodness sake. Both your parents were Lightriders. I wouldn't even *be* here if it weren't for you."

Her reassuring words sank in and made him feel better. His tension eased a bit, and he finally smiled. "You're right. They're probably still letting kids know this week whichever programs they've been assigned to."

"Exactly," Dani said, nodding, her face radiant. "You know Sir Peter. He's not exactly prompt."

"Was he there too?" Jake asked.

"Yes. And your friend, Lord Badgerton. He was against my selection, of course. He made that very clear."

Jake smirked at that.

"Even Balinor was there," Dani added. "He's the one who gave me this." She then handed Jake her Lightrider sash and let him hold it.

He marveled at the soft, glistening material. It was the closest he'd ever got to one of these.

The craving to earn one of his own filled him, but he handed Dani's belt back to her with a roguish smile, for at that moment, he spotted Aunt Ramona coming out of the palace.

"There's my aunt," he said with a sudden spark of mischief. "I think I'll go see if she'll at least give me a hint as to whether or not I should be expecting a note from a certain fairy courier."

"Oh, yes, do!" Dani urged him.

"This is so exciting," Isabelle said as Jake took off running. "What shall we do to celebrate?"

He didn't hear the suggestions they proposed. Leaving the others on the bridge, he jogged off to intercept Aunt Ramona before she went back inside.

"Aunt Ramona, wait!"

Hearing his call, the Elder witch turned toward him, her head held high, her tight bun of silver hair shining in the late morning sun. As Jake pounded toward her, his knapsack bouncing against his back, she stopped and glanced down the shallow stairs at him.

He grinned as he approached; she gave him a cordial nod as he came bounding up the steps.

"I just heard the news about Dani!" he said, slightly out of breath.

"Yes, terribly exciting, isn't it?"

"It is! I'm really happy for her. Best news I've heard in months." He squinted against the sunlight glinting off the windows of the palace. "But, um, I was wondering if..."

"Yes, Jacob?" She eyed him with a guarded stare.

"Well," he said awkwardly, "are there any other kids you know of who might...also be invited into the program this week?"

"You know I'm not at liberty to share that information, nephew."

"Not even a little hint?" he asked with his most charming grin.

"Hmm." Her high cheekbones sharpened as she gave him a dubious smile. "I'm afraid I have no news for you at this time."

"But maybe I'll hear something soon?"

The baroness had started to turn away, but she paused and seemed to run a brisk mental calculation; then she turned back to him with a look of regret. "I am sorry, Jake. There are no more invitations being issued for the Lightrider program this session."

Jake stared at her. "Wait, what? You mean...?"

She gave a slight shrug and tilted her head sympathetically. "I'm sorry, dear boy. Dani is the last one for now."

She started to walk back inside, but Jake finally reacted out of shock.

"Hold on—is this because of Badgerton?" Jake ran in front of her. "Is he blocking my selection?"

"No, nothing like that."

His jaw dropped. Somehow, this answer only made it worse. "So, that's it, then? You just picked Dani and not me?"

"Jake!" she chided, startled. "Don't be unsportsmanlike."

"Unsportsmanlike?" he fairly shouted. "Being a Lightrider is *my* dream, not hers!"

"Well, that hardly matters. Look to your own actions!" Aunt Ramona snapped. "If you have not been found worthy, you have no one to blame but yourself. 'Tis within your own control to do better, Jacob. I am sorry, but unless we hear otherwise from Gaia herself, I'm afraid the answer is no."

He stared at her, at a loss.

"Well, don't panic, boy," she added, softening just a bit, and sounding annoyed at herself for it. "You're only thirteen. You still have plenty of time to qualify for the program. You'll simply have to work harder. Good day." With that, Aunt Ramona marched back inside.

For a long moment, Jake just stood there, incredulous.

I don't believe this. What else could go wrong? His Gryphon was missing. His parents were not in their coffins. He might've started a war, and now Dani had been chosen for the Lightrider program instead of him. How unfair could life be?

Sorry to say, but Dani O'Dell was the last person he wanted to see right now. Her smiling face filled him with rabid frustration as she came running over to him, the others just a few steps behind.

"Well?" Dani asked eagerly. "What did she say?"

Jake paused, checking his temper. "I wasn't chosen this round. Congratulations, carrot. I'm really happy for you," he said, his voice a monotone. "I'm sure you'll do great. You'll have to tell me all about it. On second thought—maybe not. If you'll excuse me," he said to everyone, "I have to go."

Dani looked wounded by his surly tone, right in her moment of glory. But Jake couldn't deal with her or the others right now.

He was too upset.

"Jake!" Isabelle shouted as he took off, walking quickly to escape them.

They had all just better leave him alone right now. He did not want to blow up at Dani or anyone else—he knew they didn't deserve it—but he already felt like his head was going to explode.

"Ignore him, Dani," he heard Maddox say as he huffed away. "What an egotist."

"He's mental," Nixie muttered.

"Jake, don't be a cad!" Archie called after him, sounding annoyed. "Jove's beard, he's always got to make it all about him."

Jake heard what they were saying—and he hated himself for ruining Dani's moment of triumph—but he couldn't seem to snap out of it.

After everything that had happened, this was just the last straw.

One more major disappointment on top of everything else that had gone so disastrously wrong in his life for the past three months.

But Archie sounded truly angry at him on Dani's behalf. "Badly done, Jake!" his cousin shouted.

I don't care! Jake thought, stomping off by himself to the zoo. With the way he was feeling, he figured he belonged among the wild beasts.

Even before he strode under the arched entrance of the menagerie, he could smell the animals' pens and hear the noises they were making—the bleating of the dreaming sheep, the occasional yawp of the yeti.

Passing under the wooden arch, he saw the Green Man zookeeper and veterinarian, Dr. Plantagenet, dressed in overalls and pushing a cart full of buckets around the paths, feeding all the animals. His helper, Og, was asking him a question, so neither the Green Man nor the irritating troll-boy noticed Jake slip by a few rows away.

For his part, Jake was impressed by the showy golds and reds of the autumn leaves atop Dr. P's head. He wondered if the tree man would just have bare branches for hair over the winter. Probably so.

Hurrying on his way, Jake strode down the winding paths of the zoo, past the mud-swamp habitat of the climbing fish.

Some of the fat, squishy fish had wriggled up the old, dead trees in their dismal enclosure. Jake could hear them croaking as they enjoyed the morning sun.

When he passed the corral for the dreaming sheep, the winged sheepdog that tended the flock wagged his tail at him, but Jake kept going.

Both the unpleasant Fairy Stinger and the three-headed tortoise were lurking somewhere out of sight in their pens. The yeti grasped the bars of its cage and glared at Jake, beating its chest and grunting.

Jake was tempted to grunt back, but he left the yeti alone, rounding the bend and heading up the hill.

Inevitably, he found himself drawn once more to Red's old molting nest atop a rock formation near the back of the zoo.

The poor Gryphon had built the big nest for himself months ago in preparation for the miserable process of shedding his old feathers and growing in new ones. Coming here comforted Jake; it made him feel closer to his missing pet.

As he found a handhold and started climbing, he thought back to Red's time in the molting nest with wistful affection.

A molting Gryphon was quite a sight, to be sure, half bald and mangy-looking. The normally magnificent beast had hidden himself away here in shame, embarrassed and chilly until his splendid new feathers had filled in.

Jake had taken good care of him with Dr. Plantagenet's help, although no one was quite sure why a few of Red's scarlet feathers had grown back in tones of gorgeous, sparkling gold.

His red feathers had healing properties, but what the gold ones did was anyone's guess.

Jake just hoped that Dark Master Zolond was not making experiments to solve that mystery, but he probably was.

His stomach clenched, but he warded off the awful thought by concentrating on climbing. Placing one foot carefully after another, he mounted the rough stone ledges and scaled jutting boulders until he had gained the top of the rocky pinnacle.

It wasn't terribly tall. Maybe a little over twenty feet high.

Dusting off his hands, he walked across the flat top of the natural tower, but the place was forlorn without Red.

The big nest looked abandoned. But Jake could still picture his lion-sized pet there, his paws tucked under, his wings folded around his body.

He missed Red so much—and now this. Nothing in all his recollection had ever come between him and Dani before.

He sat down heavily on the brim of the five-foot nest, his heart heavy, his whole existence one big, tangled knot of misery.

Unfortunately, he had only a few minutes of privacy to sulk and brood and hate the world before his cousin arrived.

Of course.

Isabelle.

The perennial Voice of Reason. Arriving right on cue to try to smooth things over. He rolled his eyes when she called up to him.

"Jake? Are you all right up there?"

"I don't need a lecture!" he called, not budging from his spot.

"You do need to apologize, though. You hurt Dani's feelings."

At that, Jake scowled down over the rock ledge.

Isabelle was standing at the bottom, shielding her eyes from the sun as she gazed up at him. "You made her cry."

"What? Dani doesn't cry!"

Isabelle just looked at him. Her silence spoke volumes, and Jake felt his heart sink like a stone.

Ugh. What a toad I am.

"Just leave me alone, Iz," he said with all the grace of that yeti. "I'm not good company right now."

"You don't say," she answered lightly, and then, to Jake's consternation, Isabelle started to climb.

This I've got to see. He peered over the ledge to find the proper young lady hitching up the hem of her skirts and beginning to scale the rock tower.

"What are you doing? You're in a long dress! You'll trip and break your head. Oh, never mind, I'll come down—"

"No, no," she said. "I'm almost there..."

"Isabelle!"

True to her word, the empath climbed the stony tower; Jake frowned as he watched, ready to catch her with his telekinesis if she slipped.

A couple of minutes later, he gave her a hand up over the final chunk of boulder, and she arrived safely beside him, her cheeks pink with exertion.

She glanced at Red's nest, and understanding flickered in her blue eyes.

"Well," she said, going over to sit on the brim of it like he had, "at least now you don't have to be miserable alone."

"Why are you so nice to me?" he asked.

"Oh, coz, you know I have a great fondness for all the wild beasts." She sent him a teasing smile and wiped the dust off her hands on her apron.

Jake looked at her for a long moment. "Did she really cry?"

"What do you think? You ruined the happiest moment of her life."

Jake heaved a sigh and hung his head. "They're all mad at me, aren't they?"

"I'm not. I'm not sure about Teddy." Isabelle leaned forward, resting her elbows on her knees. "Come, Jake. You know Dani deserves this. She saved your life—and mine—without any magical powers. In hindsight, I'm not surprised in the least that they picked her. It makes perfect sense."

"I know, I know. She deserves it," Jake said, heaving a disgusted sigh. "But I still don't like it."

"Are you jealous?"

He scoffed. "I'd be lying if I tried to say I wasn't, but it's not just that! Don't you remember when I interviewed the sea-witch? Fionnula pretty much admitted that the Dark Druids have some secret project underway that has them rounding up Lightriders. That's why they took Tex. *And* why they may have kidnapped my parents twelve years ago. Now the Order's going to make Dani a Lightrider, too? How am I supposed to protect her if she's out there on a mission somewhere without me? The Dark Druids took my parents from me, Iz. They've taken my Gryphon. But I swear, if they ever lay a finger on Dani—"

"Jacob, relax," Isabelle said. "She was invited into the program less than an hour ago! It takes years to become a full-fledged Lightrider. That's a long way off! Can't you just be happy for her today? Let her have her moment? Truly, Jake, it's the least the poor girl deserves."

Jake gazed at her, crestfallen. "God, I hate it when you're right." Then he looked away, staring out at the miles-long view. "I really made a muck of things this time, didn't I?"

Isabelle shrugged with a sympathetic smile.

He raked his fingers through his hair. "I really don't mean to be such a bear to everyone. It's just—I feel like I swallowed a box of nails these days."

"I know."

"I'm not sure how much more of this I can take. If only we had word."

Isabelle reached out and squeezed his forearm. "Don't give up, Jake. You've got to have faith. Something good is bound to happen soon. I can feel it."

CHAPTER 20
The Double Agent

At that very moment, Janos was wondering how the devil he had got himself into this. True, he had been locked up in a small, windowless meeting room for ages awaiting Wyvern's return. But considering that he was still alive after a whole twelve hours in the Black Fortress, he had to count that as a plus.

Not that it was his first time here.

In his role as a vampire prince, assumed to be a basically evil being, he'd been asked to attend various functions at the warlocks' headquarters before. A couple of unpleasant rituals and such. Annual informational meetings. Lord, those were tedious. Evil was very hierarchical, with lots of bureaucracy...

In any case, Janos was used to the slick black corridors and the strange sounds in this place. He was even accustomed to the bizarre process of jumping from location to location. Thankfully, his inborn stalwart nature as a Guardian gave him the ability to take all the weirdness in his stride.

Happily, he had managed to maintain an outward show of his usual cheeky nonchalance throughout his visit so far.

Upon their arrival last night, Wyvern had flown the dragon chariot into a wide opening that appeared in a lower story of the black castle during their approach.

The earl had brought the Ruffed Orange Darter to a halt in a large, empty hall with a loud *"Whoa, boy! Whoa!"*

Then they jumped out, and the Nephilim had left his horse and carriage, as it were, in the care of three Noxu.

Funny creatures, the Noxu. For some reason, they had always reminded Janos of rhinoceroses.

He wasn't sure why.

In any case, next, they had gone up to the bridge, where Wyvern ordered the crew to prepare for the next jump—and where Janos heard the navigator call out the coordinates.

He had memorized them instantly.

It seemed Wyvern and his minions didn't care if Janos *did* find out where they were going. Why should they be concerned? As far as they knew, he was evil, one of them, and, moreover, had no means of getting the word out to his former colleagues in the Order, anyway.

With a smile on his face and the coordinates seared into his brain, Janos had casually put the dark glasses on like everybody else and braced for the jump, steadying himself when they crashed down at their new location.

A rocky stretch of coastline in Scotland, of all places.

No one told him what they were doing there. But, a while later, Wyvern had given the crew a few more commands, then nodded at Janos to follow him.

Janos had done so at once, pretending to cooperate. Let Wyvern believe he was sufficiently intimidated by what the demon spawn had done to those poor peasants.

In truth, by turning those innocent people into a human flambé, Wyvern had only sealed Janos's resolve to thwart the blackguard in any way possible.

For the time being, however, Janos let himself be led around obediently through the eerie black corridors. Wyvern had shown him into a sparse meeting room with a table and chairs and left him there to wait, but, along the way, Janos had noticed something strange.

Namely, the absence of Zolond's reptilians.

Since the old warlock never went anywhere without his scaly bodyguards, was it possible the Dark Master was not at home?

If so, that was an extraordinary development. Indeed, it might also explain the faint whiff of rebellion in the air that Janos had never sensed here before.

Hmm. Something was definitely afoot inside this windowless maze of polished black granite.

His certainty about this grew when Wyvern eventually returned to the meeting room and began grilling him about Jake.

Leaning across from Janos with both hands braced on the table, the Nephilim fired off question after question about the boy.

Janos was mystified but pretended to cooperate.

"I want to know what motivates him," the earl said, drumming a six-fingered hand slowly on the table.

"Food," Janos said lightly. "The kid eats constantly. He ought to be the size of a barn, but where it all goes, I couldn't tell you."

"What else?"

"Fun! He's a boy." Janos shrugged. "I dunno. Pranks. Mischief. Shiny objects that do interesting things."

"Like darkling blades, hmm?"

Janos ignored that. "Minor acts of destruction. Rude sounds at inappropriate times— Weren't you ever a boy, my lord?"

"No," Wyvern replied with a dead stare.

"What, did you hatch from an egg? My own hatchlings started as larvae. It was really quite disgusting—"

"Stop fooling around, you witless vampire! You are evading the substance of my queries."

"Well, tell me in plain English what do you want to know!" Janos exclaimed. "It would help if I had some inkling of the point of all this." Janos paused. "Don't you trust me?"

Wyvern growled, a flicker of flames in his eyes.

Janos's lips quirked. *I think I'm getting to him.*

"Very well. I want to know..." Wyvern hesitated.

"Yes?"

"How to get on Jake's good side," the Nephilim grumbled.

Janos's eyebrows rose slowly. "Well."

Not exactly the answer he'd anticipated. *Extraordinary.*

Baffling, too. But he went with it, choosing his words with care. "In that case...you might try returning his Gryphon?"

"No! I can't take that chance." Wyvern scowled at Janos, pushing away from the table to pace back and forth across the dismal room. "Right now, the Gryphon is the only means I've got to draw him to me. But I can't wait forever! And since this bait is clearly not working, I'm going to have to use something stronger. I mean to snatch one of his friends. So, tell me—with none of your nonsense—which one of the other children should I take prisoner?"

Janos stared at him, his undead heart dying just a little more to have to answer such a question.

He lowered his head, reeling, and pretended to debate it with himself. But he felt ill.

"Hmm," he said, stalling.

Wyvern glared at him, waiting for an answer, but Janos had no idea which of Jake's friends to throw to the wolves.

Not Isabelle, obviously. She was the point of all this. Keeping her safe.

Archie was too valuable to the world with that magnificent brain of his.

Dani O'Dell? He stifled a shudder at the thought.

No. Impossible. Blazes, Jake would kill him if Janos brought the little redhead to the Dark Druids' attention.

Only one option remained.

His stomach twisted at the prospect of the answer he must give, but he didn't dare try anything clever with the kids' lives at stakes.

Forgive me, Stick.

"There is," he said, then cleared his throat, "an older boy Jake holds in the highest regard. A Guardian apprentice. About seventeen. Derek Stone introduced them. Jake looks up to him like an elder brother."

"Oh really?" Wyvern's eyes narrowed; he sounded intrigued.

Janos nodded and told himself that Guardians were supposed to give their lives for the cause if it came to that.

Which it wouldn't.

Somehow or another, he would not let them harm Maddox.

Still, betraying young Stick made Janos hate himself just a little more than usual.

"Yes, Jake and he are quite close," he said, his voice taut. "Their hope is that one day, they'll be assigned to the same Order team. Jake as Lightrider, Maddox as Guardian."

"Maddox who, exactly?" Wyvern murmured.

Janos took a deep breath. "Maddox St. Trinian."

Don't worry, Stick. I won't let them anywhere near you.

Of course, the kid hated him anyway. Such a good little Guardian, he could neither understand nor forgive Janos for abandoning the Order. But forget young Stick—if Ravyn ever heard about this, she would thrash Janos clear across the Continent for bringing her son to the Dark Druids' attention.

Unfortunately, Janos wasn't sure if his old friend and fellow soldier, Guardian Vambrace, was even still alive.

But at least Wyvern appeared to believe him.

Absorbing this tidbit of information, the towering Nephilim nodded slowly. “Very well. Maddox St. Trinian. Now, was that so hard?”

Janos forced a smile.

Then the earl asked several more questions about Jake in general. His powers, his education, his daily routines.

Really? thought Janos. They were bizarre questions, and he didn’t know the answer to half of them, so he just made up any old answers that popped into his head.

He figured if he kept Wyvern talking, the questions themselves might eventually give away a more solid clue about why the warlocks were so interested in Jake.

Though Janos found the earl’s avid interest in the boy creepier than a whole circus full of clowns, (he had never trusted clowns, even as a child), he told Wyvern whatever he wanted to hear.

Fortunately, vampires were excellent liars.

And yet, with every smooth response that left his lips, Janos was keenly aware that the price he’d have to pay for his deceptions must be climbing higher and higher if and when he eventually got caught.

But, of course, if they tortured and killed him, at least that would finally bring an end to all his bad decisions in life. He’d be glad to have it over with.

When Wyvern finally finished interrogating Janos, he seemed anxious to get on with the next item on his to-do list.

Janos tried to access what that might be, but the Nephilim’s mind was impenetrable. Wyvern summoned a pair of Noxu guards to show Janos to a guestroom, and he was dismissed.

With his heightened vampire senses, he could smell the Noxu coming even before the creatures arrived. Lord, they had a foul, musky odor that could singe the hairs in your nostrils. He could hear the ominous thumping of their footsteps and the leather squeaking of their primitive armor when they were still quite a distance from the meeting room.

Janos stepped out into the hallway as they arrived. Then the pair of hulking, tusked guards marched him through the onyx maze. They brought him to a guestroom and shoved him rudely inside.

“Watch it!” he said, catching his balance at once.

Slamming the door with a grunt of laughter, they locked it behind him, removing any doubt as to what sort of “guest” Janos actually was.

He scowled at the door, then glanced around uneasily at his stark black-and-silver room. A blue-flamed lantern on the bedside table revealed the most basic accommodations.

But he shuddered with unexpected horror at the room's most distinctive feature.

Mirrors on every wall.

Alas, the magic in them to create one's own preferred environment only worked if one had a reflection in the first place.

Janos didn't. As his gaze traveled around the gray emptiness of his chamber, it was as though he wasn't there at all.

That got to him, oddly, out of all the dangers awaiting him here.

His own un-being.

Like he didn't really matter to any other living creature in this world and might as well not even exist.

He lowered his head, more trapped by his choices in life than he was by this room. But he shook off the never-ending pain of his existence and vowed to make himself useful.

He might be a failed Guardian, but he could still reach out with his vampire telepathy and let the Order know where the Black Fortress was right now.

At least, he could bloody well try.

It wouldn't be easy. It might not even be possible. The coast of Scotland was a long way from Wiltshire, after all, and both castles, good and evil, were wrapped in many layers of protective spells.

In truth, it would probably be a miracle if he could squeeze one thought out through the cracks.

But surely one of the Order's clairvoyants would hear him. He decided to start with Dame Oriel. She seemed like a reasonable person, and quite a gifted sensitive.

Janos sat down on the bed, closed his eyes, cleared his mind as best he could, and tried to contact the woman.

He gave up with a wince several minutes later when he felt a headache start to throb in his right temple.

Maybe someone else, then. Balinor, he decided. Yes. All the old wizard's sleepiness was merely a sign of his deep immersion in the other realms, the world of spirits and dreams.

But Janos's attempt to make contact with Balinor likewise proved fruitless. He could sense the owl and believed the owl sensed him, as well. But the creature was hardly equipped to take down a long series of numbers.

Derek? Janos tried his old team leader next, well aware the master Guardian would hardly be happy to have his mind invaded, especially by the likes of him.

Well, it didn't work anyway, and now he was tiring. The headache pierced sharper through his skull. Still sitting on the bed, he leaned against the wall, his brain weary with the effort to make the connection with someone, anyone out there.

It was depressing that no one could sense him. He might as well not even exist. A terrible loneliness gnawed at his innards, but he pushed it away as usual.

Blazes, should he try Jake?

Better not, he decided. The Dark Druids already had an unhealthy interest in the rambunctious ex-pickpocket.

That left only one person as his last hope. Janos dragged his eyes open and frowned, his head throbbing.

He *really* did not want to drag her into this. Besides, he told himself, it probably wouldn't work.

No, it will, his mind said. *We've made contact before. Besides, she's an empath. This is what she* does.

Not with you! the remains of his conscience retorted. *Leave her alone. Stay out of the girl's head.*

It was dangerous in more ways than one. After all, his proposed visit into her mind would offer *her* a glimpse into his head, as well.

Hadn't she already seen enough of the nightmare he was? Janos did not want that girl getting any more dangerously close to him than she already was, in his heart.

But he knew he had no choice.

Somewhere deep inside, he was still a Guardian, however inadequate; the Gryphon was being held prisoner here somewhere, and once the Order had the location, they could send a rescue team to break him out.

Then Janos could fight alongside them. Maybe even kill that filthy Nephilim. Considering Zolond was gone, now was the perfect time to strike.

With that, he shoved aside his foolish, halfhearted scruples and turned his attention to a far more appealing recipient for his message than old Balinor.

Closing his eyes again, Janos leaned his head back against the wall, ignored the stabbing headache, and concentrated on a vision of loveliness that always brought a smile to his face.

He focused in more tightly, feeling his way through the ethers until he sensed her in the distance, her brightness like a flame in the gloom of his existence.

A happy little candle glowing in the window.

So peaceful. So pure.

He homed in on her light, flew toward her in his mind like a suicidal moth. *Isabelle?* he whispered into her awareness. *Isabelle, can you hear me?*

CHAPTER 21

An Uncanny Connection

"Thanks for coming after me, coz," Jake said as he jumped down off the rocks, then picked up his knapsack and slung it over his shoulder.

Izzy smiled at him, still dusting off her hands from the climb down. "Of course."

She was glad she had managed to help him calm down and stop being angry about things he couldn't control.

She felt bad for her cousin, though.

Jake was a fighter by nature, a headstrong young man of action. Being forced to sit and cool his heels while the adults supposedly handled the matter was clearly wearing away what little patience he possessed.

As they walked back down the winding path through the zoo, leaving behind the stony pinnacle where Red's molting nest perched, Izzy gave her wayward cousin a quick sideways glance, discreetly scanning him with her empath abilities.

He seemed all right now, thank goodness. He'd been furious before—and nobody was safe around an angry doubler. Now she could sense him feeling sheepish for his outburst. He knew he'd acted badly, poor thing.

She could also feel him dreading the thought of having to grovel to everyone, especially Dani. He'd never been very good at apologizing.

"Don't worry, she'll forgive you," she said with a knowing smile.

Jake sent her a startled glance, his blue eyes uncertain beneath his straw-blond forelock. But he smiled ruefully. "Sometimes I wonder why you all put up with me."

"Ah, we're your family, Jake." She grinned and threw an arm

around his shoulders. "We love you!" She embarrassed him with a big-sisterly kiss on the cheek that made him say *blech* and pull away.

Izzy laughed. Archie usually had the same reaction.

Then Izzy waved, spotting Dr. Plantagenet in the distance. Sometimes she came here to help with the animals, so the two of them were well acquainted.

The Green Man had finished feeding the animals and was now sweeping the front stoop of the quaint little cottage tucked away in the zoo that served as both his home and veterinarian office.

Izzy didn't see Ogden, but then realized it was the hour when the troll-boy usually took Nuckalavee out for his morning gallop. Nightmare that he was, the water horse needed his daily exercise just like any other equine.

When Izzy waved, Dr. P waved back, but she and Jake didn't stop to chat.

She nudged her cousin. "When you get Red back—and I do mean *when*, not *if*—be sure and have Dr. P give him a thorough exam to make sure he's all right."

Jake nodded. "Good idea. I'll do that. The Dark Druids better *hope* they haven't hurt him."

"Don't worry. You remember what Aunt Ramona said? He's too valuable."

Jake gave her a glum look. "I hope so."

They exited the zoo beneath the arched wooden entranceway and set out across the lawn, heading toward the palace.

Izzy savored the warm September sun on her face.

The misty morning had blossomed into a gorgeous fall afternoon. The emerald greensward stretched out on all sides of them, and the woods that surrounded the lawns gleamed in a riot of jewel tones like one of Queen Victoria's best necklaces. Topaz, ruby, amethyst...

All of a sudden, she stopped in her tracks with a strange tickle in the back of her brain.

She stared straight ahead, her eyebrows knitted, like she'd just remembered something important.

Then she heard it. The voice was very faint.

Isabelle! Can you hear me?

Confused, she looked at her cousin. "Of course I can hear you. I'm right here. What?"

"Huh?" Jake looked at her, scrunching up his nose.

Izzy stared at him. "You didn't say anything?"

He arched a brow. "Er, no."

"Oh..." She frowned. "That's odd."

He eyed her skeptically.

"Never mind," she said, but she had the strangest feeling of a nameless urgency inside. As if someone were desperately calling out to her for help.

She could've sworn she'd heard someone call her name. But where was it coming from? She glanced uncertainly toward the palace, but didn't see Mother, Aunt Ramona, or even Miss Helena trying to get her attention.

Deciding she must've imagined it, she shrugged off the odd sensation. Jake gave her a strange look, and they walked on without further incident.

Then it came again, more clearly now, but still faint.

I'm terribly sorry to barge in on you like this, Miss Bradford, but I seem to have found myself in a bit of a pickle.

This time, Isabelle stopped and pivoted to Jake. "What are you talking about? What pickle?" she demanded.

Jake squinted at her, then started laughing. "What's this about a pickle?"

"You just said you were in one."

"No, I didn't."

She studied him. "You didn't?"

Jake shook his head with a quizzical smile. "Are you feeling all right, coz?"

Isabelle, please! I need your help.

All of a sudden, a stabbing sensation shot through her head. She doubled over with a small cry of pain and raised both hands to her temples.

Jake grabbed her elbow, steadying her. "Izzy, what's wrong?"

She couldn't answer. Tears filled her eyes from the blinding ache in her skull. It felt as though someone had plunged a sewing needle right through her head.

Jake was talking to her. "Izzy, what's happening? Talk to me!"

But there was *another* voice talking to her, faint and sardonic, so familiar...

It couldn't be. He'd gone back to his horrid vampire wives. He was hundreds of miles away.

Forgive the intrusion, dearest. I don't mean to frighten you. But I really must insist that you listen very carefully to me right now.

Ohhh, she knew that voice. She couldn't believe it, but went very still as recognition filled her.

"Janos?" she whispered, and her heart began to pound.

"Janos?" Jake echoed, glancing around and looking even more bewildered than she was. "Where? What about him?"

"Hush." Izzy held up a finger to silence her cousin, her chest heaving as the pain began to recede.

She had to concentrate.

Can you hear me now? the vampire asked gently over the distance, obviously using his telepathic powers to place his thoughts inside her mind.

He had done that only once before, to rebuke her when she'd tried to read him with her empath skills.

"Barely," she answered, steadying herself. "Where are you? What's wrong?"

I don't have much time. I'm inside the Black Fortress—

"What?!" she nearly shouted.

Jake was staring at her like she'd gone mad, talking when there was nobody there. Of course, he did it all the time, with his ghosts.

They're watching me, Janos said. *Again, I apologize for the intrusion, but this was the only way I could get your attention. I...hope it didn't hurt.*

"It's fine, I'm all right." She waved it off. "How can I help?"

I have a critical message you must take to the Elders at once. Will you do that for me?

"Of course. Ready," she answered, telling Janos in her thoughts, while her lips also formed the words so Jake could follow along.

Her cousin stared and listened in confusion.

Isabelle nodded to the distant vampire, concentrating on the voice within. "Go on. What's the message?"

Tell your aunt Ramona to ready a strike team. Wyvern's up to something and Zolond's not here. Tell her to send a team of Guardians after nightfall, and I'll let them in. Now take out a pencil and paper, because I'm going to give you the coordinates for where the Black Fortress is currently located.

Izzy turned to her cousin, wide-eyed. "Jake—pencil, paper!" She gestured at his bookbag. "Jake is here with me," she told their vampire friend.

Oh? Tell him I said hello, Janos said dryly while her cousin scrambled to pull paper and pencil out of his bag.

Isabelle didn't bother with greetings, reporting just the facts: "Janos is in the Black Fortress. He's going to give us the coordinates."

Jake gasped. "Tell him they have Red!"

"They have the Gryphon," Izzy repeated.

I know, Janos said. *Tell Jake not to worry. I'm going to find Red and get him out of here. Tonight.*

"How?" Isabelle asked while Jake fished frantically in his knapsack for a pencil.

No idea yet. But don't worry, I'll figure something out.

At last, Jake pulled out a pencil. "Tell him Ravyn might be there somewhere, too, if she's alive! And don't forget about Tex!"

Izzy repeated his reminders.

Sheesh, anything else? Janos retorted.

"Just give me the coordinates." Isabelle nodded at Jake to write them down as she delivered them aloud from the vampire.

Ready?

"Go," Isabelle said.

Latitude: fifty-six degrees, twenty-eight minutes, fifty-eight seconds north. Longitude: two degrees, forty-three minutes, thirteen seconds west.

Janos repeated the coordinates, and Isabelle echoed them aloud so Jake could double-check his work.

"Got it," her cousin said. One glance at him showed his eyes brimming with newfound excitement and the first real hope they'd had in months. "But where exactly is this?"

Isabelle repeated the question.

Scotland, somewhere east of Dundee, I believe. We've landed at some deserted, rocky beach overlooking the North Sea.

"Why did the Dark Druids go there?"

I don't know. I'll try to find out.

"But Janos, what are *you* doing there?" she persisted.

Long story, no time. Run and give the Elders my message. Make sure they get the team here tonight. Oh—and if I'm not already waiting for them outside the Fortress with the Gryphon, tell the Guardians to scale the north tower. I'll let them in there.

"How will you do that?" Izzy asked, amazed. It was so strange to encounter Janos like this—all business, very little joking around. And even less of his absurd, meaningless flirting.

She realized abruptly that he was in Guardian mode.

What do you mean, how? he retorted. *Lord, you ask too many questions. Just go.*

"Janos!" she insisted.

Yes, my darling? he said, as though striving for patience.

Nevertheless, his breezy endearment made her toes curl.

"Be careful," Izzy said.

He gave a wry snort of humor at that. *Au revoir, cherie.*

"Anything else you want me to tell the Elders?"

No. He was quiet for a beat. She could feel his dismay. *I just hope they believe me.*

"I'll make sure they do," she promised.

She felt his pleasure at her faith in him.

I knew I could count on you, Iz.

She smiled dreamily. "Anytime."

Right, then! Standing by until the team arrives. Think I'll go and do a bit of spying. If I learn anything else important, I'll contact you again.

"I'll be listening."

Same here. Now, hurry. We need to get this done tonight.

"On my way," she replied. But in truth, when she came back out from under the hypnotic connection he had somehow established with her over those hundreds of miles, she still felt woozy and dazed.

Jake was watching her anxiously, holding the notebook. He tapped the numbers with the pencil. "This is where the Black Fortress sits right now? He's sure?"

She nodded. "He's there."

"Why?"

"He didn't have time to explain. Never mind, Jake. We need to take those coordinates at once to Aunt Ramona. You're faster than me. Go on, run. I'll catch up in a moment. I'm still a little...lightheaded."

"Are you sure—"

"Go. I'll be fine." She waved him on.

Jake nodded, tossed the pencil into his bag, then shouldered it. As he raced off toward the palace, Isabelle could feel her cousin's spirits surge.

See, coz? she thought. *I told you, have a little faith.*

For her part, Izzy was still in a state of wonder over what had just happened. She glanced around, turning to gaze at the northern horizon.

Dundee, Scotland, was hundreds of miles away. She marveled at the focus her vampire friend must possess to have been able to contact her telepathically over such a great distance.

It felt very odd, indeed, knowing he had the skill to drop into her mind whenever he fancied. However, she was grateful for his ability, because now the Order might finally get the chance they had needed for months to rescue the captives.

The one thing that mystified her was why Janos had reached out to *her* instead of to someone like, oh, Dame Oriel. There were far more skilled clairvoyants here at Merlin Hall than her modest talent as an empath.

But then again, she supposed, almost all of them mistrusted Janos. And Isabelle was sure that Janos trusted none of them.

It was sad, the way he'd been vilified. He didn't deserve it. Somewhere hundreds of miles to the north, the vampire prince was risking his neck for them all yet again, while everyone here called him nothing but a scoundrel.

Thank you, she told him, wherever he was.

Ah, anything for you, Izzy love.

Surprised he was still listening, she grinned at his sardonic response. Leave it to Janos to enter the belly of the beast cracking jokes.

"You're not afraid of anything, are you?" she whispered.

Only you, Miss Bradford. Only you.

Izzy shook her head, blushing. "Absurd vampire."

A little unnerved by their connection, she hurried after her cousin, eager to see what the Elders would say about this, and quite prepared to argue on Janos's behalf. They simply had to believe him and send the team, as he'd asked.

Surely Derek would listen, if nobody else would. Isabelle shook off the disoriented feeling and strode on, trailing Jake across the field.

Even now, in the distance, she could see her cousin bounding up the front steps to the palace, taking them two at a time. Jake raced inside, but it would take her another few minutes to catch up.

Her exchange with Janos had left her still feeling a trifle giddy. But if she was honest...

It usually did.

* * *

Ramona had returned to her chamber to freshen up before going down to luncheon in the dining hall. In truth, she was eager to steal a few minutes of solitude in her room. So much socializing wore her out.

As did dealing with her headstrong nephew.

Ah, Jake. She pursed her lips as she changed her earrings in front of the mirror. She could understand the boy's disappointment, but what was she to do? Let him claim honors he hadn't earned? Now, *that* would be the nepotism Badgerton had accused her of.

Besides, to put Jake in a program he clearly wasn't ready for would only set him up for failure.

No. Until her rascally nephew proved that he could follow orders instead of doing whatever reckless thing popped into his head—or until Gaia told them otherwise—he was not yet Lightrider material.

Now, Dani...

A smile played across Ramona's lips before the mirror as she recalled the little redhead's joy at her selection.

When Finnderool had brought Gaia's choice of the girl to the Elders a week ago (there had been processes and paperwork to set it all up), Ramona had fully agreed that Dani O'Dell deserved it.

She had shown many fine qualities in the time she had been with them. She was humble, hardworking, grateful, unselfish, unfaltering in her loyalty to the others, with a clear understanding of right and wrong. And she was always able to find her courage somehow, even in the darkest of moments.

Not to mention her talent for helping Ramona manage Jake.

The wary ex-pickpocket trusted Dani, and, for Jake, trust did not come easy, Ramona knew. As her thoughts drifted over the children one by one, Ramona also took great pride in Nixie's excellent progress at her magical studies, in which she was mentoring her.

Yet the spiky-haired image of her star pupil led Ramona back to Jake. If even a born rebel like Nixie Valentine could apply herself with discipline and hard work to learning her craft, then why should Jake get a free pass?

Just then, Ramona heard a distant clamor down the hallway beyond her chamber door. A flurry of running footsteps coming closer.

Ramona arched a brow, for she had a feeling she knew who it was.

Her nephew, of course, the young human whirlwind.

In the next moment, he was pounding on her door.

"Aunt Ramona! Aunt Ramona!"

"Come in, Jake!" she called.

The door burst open at once, and the boy practically tumbled in, his cheeks flushed, his blue eyes bright with excitement.

"We have news!" He held up a notebook with some scrawls on it and ran to her. "Janos contacted Izzy telepathically and gave us the coordinates for where the Black Fortress is right now! He's there! He said for you to send a rescue party. He's going to free Red!"

Jake kept talking a mile a minute while Ramona took the notebook from him and stared at the coordinates.

"He says it's somewhere in Scotland."

"He contacted Isabelle? Telepathically? From all the way in Scotland?"

"Yes, ma'am."

Oh, this was disturbing news, indeed. Ramona was taken aback. "And where is Isabelle now?"

"On the way. She's a bit behind me. She got lightheaded afterward and needed to rest or something. Janos said to get these coordinates to you right away so you could send out a team!"

"Yes, yes, of course. This is excellent news." Ramona nodded, setting aside her alarm on her great-great niece's behalf for the moment.

Jake seemed ready to burst with excitement. "Finally, this is our chance! Maybe I could go along on the mission—"

"Jacob Everton!"

He gave a slight pout. "It was just an idea."

"A daft one," she said archly. "Now, make me three extra copies of those coordinates. We'll need to distribute them to Sir Peter and others. But, Jake, tell no one else what has occurred. We must keep this to ourselves for now."

"Yes, ma'am." Jake tore a fresh piece of paper out of his notebook, ripped it into thirds, then copied down the coordinates onto each piece.

Ramona opened the door of her chamber and saw Isabelle hurrying up the hallway.

"Aunt Ramona!" the girl called.

"Come, dear." Ramona beckoned to her. "Jake's already here."

As Isabelle walked swiftly toward her doorway, Ramona could not deny she was a doting aunt when it came to her little Izzy. Nor could she help noticing with fond pride what a lovely young woman her niece was growing up into, with her cascading golden tresses, china-blue eyes, creamy skin, and delicate features.

She would cause a sensation in London at her debut this spring, Ramona thought. How the quiet girl would hate all the attention!

Any other young miss with her beauty surely would have been vain, but not Isabelle. She was too busy struggling against what she counted as her own flaws.

In the eyes of the world, the sensitivity that made her a powerful empath resembled weakness. But it was not. It was strength, of no ordinary kind. The strength of goodness, of softness. The unexpected might of love itself. And to be sure, Isabelle wielded that power in full force when confronted with real darkness.

This was why she'd been chosen as a Keeper of the Unicorns.

And yet in ordinary life, Ramona feared the girl's trusting nature, her innocent faith in the goodness of others—and her beauty—all made her vulnerable to...unsavory characters. She bristled with protectiveness of her favorite as Izzy closed the distance between them.

A moment later, Ramona had shooed the girl safely into her room, where Jake was just finishing up his copies of the coordinates.

Ramona laid a hand on Isabelle's shoulder. "Jake told me what happened. Are you feeling all right?"

"I'm better now, thank you, aunt."

"I could conjure up some ginger ale—"

"No, no, I'm fine, really. Never mind me." She smiled, and Ramona detected a particular breathlessness about her. "What about this new information? Will you send a team, Aunt Ramona, as Janos has asked?"

"Of course she will." Jake looked over and straightened up from the table. "Won't you?"

Ramona hesitated, studying her niece. "Did you sense any deception from Janos, my dear?"

Izzy seemed taken aback at the question. "Why, no, aunt. Of course not. I know he was telling the truth!"

"Did he say what he was doing there?"

"No, but he was nervous. He said they were watching him. We only communicated for a few minutes."

"I see." Ramona nodded, her mind churning. It did not *seem* like a trap.

"Aunt Ramona, Janos wouldn't lie about something like this," Izzy said.

"He saved my life," Jake reminded the Elder witch.

"Very well." Ramona nodded at Jake. "Take a copy of the coordinates to Guardian Stone straightaway. Tell him everything you've told me, and that I said he's authorized to begin forming a strike team."

Jake paled, taking a sudden step toward her. "But ma'am—you can't send Derek, surely. He just got free of the Dark Druids—they tortured him! There must be someone else you can send. Why not Master Ebrahim—"

"Are you going to question everything I do?" Ramona asked him sharply. "Whether Derek feels ready to go on the mission or not is entirely up to him. But I want him at least to plan the thing—and I want the team underway within the hour if possible. Now, go!"

Jake lowered his head. "Yes, ma'am."

"Wait." Isabelle halted her cousin. "*Whoever* is chosen for the team, be it Derek or someone else, they cannot undertake this mission until nightfall."

"Why?" Ramona turned to her.

"Because, otherwise, Janos won't be able to leave with them. He's a vampire, remember? He can only go outside when it's dark. If sunlight touches him, he'll die. If the team goes by daylight, Janos will be stuck in the Black Fortress. They can't leave him behind. Once the team arrives, the Dark Druids will know he's the one behind this. They will punish him worse than they did Derek."

"She's right, aunt," Jake said with a firm nod. "The team can't leave Janos behind. Not when he's risking himself for us like this."

"Quite right." Ramona nodded reluctantly. "Very well. You may go, Jake. Tell Derek all of this, and then do whatever he asks of you. He may have further errands for you to help in this matter."

"Yes, ma'am." Jake looked relieved, finally having specific actions he could take in the effort to get Red back safely.

"What can I do, Aunt Ramona?" Izzy turned to her as Jake dashed off to find Derek. "Who else needs to be notified? Sir Peter? Finderool? I could take the coordinates to any—"

"In a moment, dear." When the door had closed behind Jake, Ramona stared hard at her niece.

Izzy's soulful eyes filled with worry. "Is something wrong, aunt?"

Ramona laid a hand on her shoulder. "Darling, I want to ask you a question."

"Yes?"

"Has Janos ever contacted you like this before?"

"No. Well—" She began blushing. "He did, but it wasn't his fault. I tried to probe *his* emotions once, and he scolded me for it. T-telepathically."

"I see." Ramona pursed her lips. "He's very handsome, isn't he?"

Isabelle turned bright red.

"And charming...?"

"It does not signify, aunt. Prince Janos is married. And a vampire."

"Precisely," Ramona told her in a stern tone.

Yet Izzy's blue eyes flickered with a rare show of defiance. "But just because he is—one of the undead doesn't mean he's a bad person, does it? He is trying to help us. He's risking his life! I believe in him."

"Yes," Ramona said. "That's what worries me."

Izzy frowned. "People should give him a chance."

"We'll see."

Be careful, child, Ramona thought.

"Do you want me to take the coordinates to Sir Peter and Finnderool?" Izzy asked, shifting her weight with an air of impatience.

"Yes, go on. There. Jake made copies." Ramona gestured wearily at the slips of paper on the table. "But leave one for me. You may go."

Izzy collected the two extra slips, leaving the original for Ramona. Then she strode toward the door, pausing to give her doting old aunt a quick kiss on the cheek before bustling out to see to her task.

When her niece had gone, Ramona drifted over to the window and gazed down at the lawn for a long moment.

She could not deny she was a little shaken by the news of this uncanny connection between Janos and her darling Isabelle.

Maybe it was nothing, but it made her uneasy.

Or perhaps it was simply that she, herself, as a girl had shared a similar bond with a dangerous young man who had ultimately chosen the path of darkness.

Geoffrey.

Ramona cast a guilty glance toward her crystal ball, bound to him still. *Heaven forbid that my sweet girl should ever make the same mistake.*

CHAPTER 22

The Woman in the Walls

Janos felt better once he'd got the information out to the Order. Talking to Isabelle had also lifted his spirits with a pointed reminder of *why* he was doing this in the first place.

Now all he had to do was escape from his room, find out where the Dark Druids were keeping the Gryphon, come up with a way of rescuing the creature, learn whatever he could about the fates of poor Ravyn and Tex, and try to puzzle out what the Dark Druids were up to on this craggy Scottish beach.

Am I forgetting anything? he thought wryly.

Ah well. At least the first part was easy. With a smirk for the fools who had thought that some silly locked door could contain him, Janos dissolved into his black smoke form, then drifted out of the guestroom with ease, filtering underneath the crack in the door, silent as a vapor.

Since nearly everything was black here, it was easy to float down the hallway undetected. After all, vampires might be bloodsucking liars, but even the Elder witch would've admitted that they made excellent spies.

Gliding through the cold, echoing corridors of the Black Fortress in his smoke form, Janos did his best not to get lost in the onyx labyrinth, but at least in this windowless building, he didn't have to worry about sunlight hitting him. Really, it was coming up on noon; he wished he was back at home in his coffin having a good day's sleep.

He just hoped that Wyvern didn't have cause to summon him from his guest chamber while he was out snooping around.

Why *had* the Nephilim brought the castle here to the edge of the North Sea, anyway? Janos wondered. And where the deuce was Zolond? *Hmm.*

His questions faded away, however, when he turned a corner and saw a very bored-looking Gryphon lying in his cage, growling occasionally to himself. The tip of Red's tufted lion tail tapped slowly with impatient frustration, like a person might drum his fingers.

Poor boy. After twelve weeks of no flying, Red was probably wondering if his wings still worked.

Floating closer, Janos assessed the situation. *Well, this shouldn't be too difficult.* There weren't any guards on hand who'd need killing, though a fat iron padlock fastened the cage door. *Blast.*

On the bright side, Janos detected no telltale glow of magic on the lock. In his smoke form, he could usually see the aura of magic on an enchanted object or a person under the influence of a spell.

He was relieved that no such glow surrounded the padlock on Red's cage. If the lock did not have to be opened with a wand, that meant someone around here must have an ordinary key.

All right, then, who would Wyvern entrust the key to? Janos zoomed closer.

Red did not sense him. Janos decided it might be a good idea to let the beast know he was there and that rescue was imminent. That way, the Gryphon would be ready when the time came.

But just as Janos started filtering back into solid form, a flicker of motion in a dark corner to his right caught his eye.

He gasped, quickly reversing the process and whooshing back up toward the ceiling. For there, lurking in the corner, keeping guard over the Gryphon, it seemed, was Wyvern's own horrible pet.

The manticore that had killed Janos's best friend, Urso.

An invisible wisp of vapor near the ceiling, anger filled Janos at the sight of the monster that had impaled his last remaining friend.

He hungered for revenge, glaring at the beast.

But, though Janos feared no man, a full-sized lion with a venomous scorpion stinger for a tail did give him pause.

After all, Urso the big German bear shifter had been a magnificent fighter, but this monstrous beast had laid him low. For all Janos knew, if *he* battled the manticore and were struck in the heart by that blade-like hook on the end of the creature's tail, that might be enough to kill even a vampire.

Then his mission would fail. And the Guardian team were on their way.

There was also the small fact that Janos had no weapon at the moment.

Wyvern had forbidden him from bringing one. Ah, how he wished he had his darkling blade.

It was the one tool that could change with him from smoke form to solid and back again, the one weapon capable of skewering dark spirits. Yet for all their effectiveness, darkling blades were but a cheap imitation of the swords the Light Beings carried, known as brightwields.

A brightwield could kill just about anything, but they were very rare, and rumor had it only certain individuals could use them.

Janos would've been glad for even the most ordinary sword at that moment, staring down with hatred at the manticore.

It was lying idly on its belly, licking its front paw like an ordinary lion.

The thing was huge. Its tawny body was a little bigger than Red's, but the segmented scorpion tail gave the beast a long and deadly reach.

Janos hissed a mental curse. Unfortunately, even if he had a weapon to fight with, this was not the sort of beast he could battle quietly.

Nor was revenge on the menu, frankly. He seethed at the fact, but killing the manticore was not why he was here.

Remember your mission. Lesson one to baby Guardians like Stick. The same mantra had been drilled into Janos's head, too, in his day.

His primary task was freeing Red.

He forced himself back to it. Scanning the area once more, his gaze was drawn back to the manticore—and suddenly, Janos spotted the key!

To his utter dismay, it was hanging on a leather strap around the manticore's neck. His heart sank. *Eh, why me?*

Realizing the pickle he was in had just gotten rather more sour, Janos retreated for now. He could do nothing until he got his hands on some weapons.

With grim resolve, he left Red behind for the time being and began searching the surrounding hallways and rooms in his vapor form, peeking into open-doored rooms. Finding nothing of interest, he wafted down a set of black stairs and continued his perusal of the place on the next floor down.

The Black Fortress had about ten floors, and he supposed he should get a look at them all. He pressed on, finding a few rooms of note, but nothing hugely helpful.

For example, he came across the fabled star chamber, with a pentagram hewn into the floor. This was where those who had displeased the Dark Druid Council were summoned to be judged.

Floating on, he eventually happened upon an indoor swamp sort of room, with a pond and a tangle of low palm trees growing all around. It was unnaturally warm and humid there, heated by he knew not what, and dimly lit around the edges by strange, glowing rocks. Crickets sang inside the long, rectangular chamber and dragonflies buzzed above the water, which bubbled here and there on occasion.

Janos was baffled. Then he deduced that this habitat must've been specially set up for the enjoyment of Zolond's royal reptilians, but, of course, they weren't there at the moment. He still wondered where they'd all gone.

Continuing on his way, Janos found nothing either interesting or helpful, until, finally, in a dark corner of the same lower floor that housed Wyvern's chariot and the Orange Ruffed Darter, he came across what appeared to be a guardroom.

It certainly smelled of Noxu.

Still in vapor form, he went closer, carefully gliding in to take a look around.

There were worktables for cleaning weapons, lockers where the guards could keep their things. Wooden racks here and there for storing weapons, wall pegs for hanging bits of armor.

There were long benches, too, and on one of these, Janos spotted a lonely Noxu mercenary picking his toenails.

Charming.

He made short work of the creature, materializing behind it and snapping its neck with elegant precision before the brute even knew he was there.

Janos caught the heavy body as it fell, laying it down quietly. Then he helped himself to the creature's large, serrated dagger.

He frowned at the weapon. It was heavy and awkward, lacking all finesse. Not his style at all, but it would have to do.

He glanced around at the guardroom and realized one of those long Noxu halberds leaning in the rack might be very helpful with the manticore.

It would allow him to strike the monster while keeping him out of reach of that venomous tail. He helped himself to one of those, too.

Then he saw another toy—and his eyes flared with delight.

You, he mentally told the crossbow. *You're coming with me.*

Stalking across the guardroom, he slung it across his back, along with a nearby quiver of arrows. He helped himself to a knife belt and sheathed the blade he had borrowed.

Then he stood up straight, pleased with his plunder. *Time to go.* He had located the Gryphon. His next task was to figure out what had happened to his former teammate.

Good ol' Ravyn Vambrace.

Ah, back in the old days, she could drink half of the barracks under the table, and once—once only—she had beaten Derek himself in an arm-wrestling match. She had never let him live it down.

Good times.

Janos did not know if Maddox's birth mother was alive or dead after three months unaccounted for, but he was certain that if the Dark Druids had killed her, she would've taken at least a dozen of them or their minions with her.

Slipping out of the guardroom, Janos proceeded deeper into the Fortress, intent on searching the sections of the building he had not yet seen. Now that he was back in corporeal form—for he had to carry his weapons—he took care to keep his footfalls silent, using all his vampire stealth.

Again, it was quiet as he stole along the sides of the corridors, pressing his back to the wall now and then when he heard someone coming. He ducked into rooms until they passed and managed to stay out of sight.

He couldn't stop wondering about Ravyn as he sneaked along. Perhaps he would find her being held in a cell here somewhere, much as the Dark Druids had held Derek for a time, and poor Celestus, the angel. Much as they now held Red.

But, surely, if they were holding her prisoner, the Order would've heard about it by now.

No, the sad truth was that Ravyn was probably dead. The thought depressed him. The loss of such a proud and skillful fighter—not to mention an old friend—was a very great shame.

Even though Janos knew Ravyn had been as disgusted with him as every other loyal Guardian, he still cared about her like a sister.

But, as it turned out, mere moments later, it was *she* who found *him.*

And the greeting Janos received when he slipped around a corner somewhere in the bowels of the Black Fortress was a knife to his throat. A viselike grip slammed down on his shoulder.

He froze, expecting one of the palace guards.

"Hello, old friend!" came a harsh, barbaric whisper instead. "Imagine seeing you here, vampire. Selling us out to the enemy yet again—vampire?"

"Ravyn?!" Janos glanced over his shoulder in astonishment. "You're alive!"

"Don't look so surprised," she said through gritted teeth. "I, for one, took my training to heart. So, any last words before I cut your head off?"

He lifted his hands up cautiously in a token surrender. She sounded half wild. "Let's not do anything hasty—"

"What are you doing here? Come to grovel your way back into Wyvern's good graces again after you helped us in the battle? No doubt you're still trying to play both sides against the middle."

"Don't be absurd!" he whispered. "I'm your advance rescue team."

She was silent for a moment, weighing this.

"I'm working with the Order," he insisted.

"Ha. I've heard that before. Why you?"

"A situation presented itself. Wyvern needed me for something. I decided to take advantage—"

"Oh, but that's what you do, isn't it? Twist everything to your own advantage—"

"Would you shut up and listen to me?" he whispered. "There's a team coming tonight. I'm here to rescue the Gryphon, find you, and try to figure out what the devil happened to our Lightriders. Now, you can either help me or proceed with my decapitation. Either way, I don't have time for this."

Her fingers tightened on his shoulder. "Cheeky as ever, I see."

"That's why you love me," Janos drawled.

With a growl of annoyance, Ravyn spun him around and stared at him, sizing him up.

For his part, Janos was shocked at the sight of her.

Normally bronzed and black-haired, she had always been a muscular woman, but as a highly trained soldier, Ravyn Vambrace was far more dangerous than any mere athlete.

He had no idea how she had been surviving for the past three months, but she looked wild-eyed and fierce, the sleeves of her shirt cut off, her sculpted arms bare. Her brown canvas breeches were filthy and her knee-boots were scuffed.

Her skin was almost as pale as his from being in this lightless place. And there was no fat left on the woman.

It was clear her experience living secretly as a fugitive within the castle had further hardened her as a warrior. Her dark eyes, so like her son's, blazed with hungry intensity.

And serious distrust of Janos.

"How are you alive?" Janos asked softly.

"You mean how have I avoided getting captured?"

He nodded.

"I found Zolond's potion room. Helped myself," she said with a cold smile.

"What, all this time?" Worry filled him. Taking potions for too long could wreck a person's health. "What about the side effects—"

"What choice did I have?" she snapped. "At least I'm alive."

Janos stared at her. "Just what have you been taking, love? Do you feel all right?"

"Do I *look* like I feel all right? Idiot," she retorted, still menacing him with her knife. Then she grumbled, "I found a vial called Camouflage, and another called Invisibility. But that one gives me a headache."

This is bad.

No wonder she seemed a little crazy at the moment. He'd be too if he'd survived on potions and sheer grit for three months in his place.

"Well, don't worry," Janos told her with more calm assurance than he actually felt. "When the team comes tonight, we're going to get you out of here."

"Really?" Tough as she was, Ravyn stared desperately at him, clearly longing to believe.

Janos lifted his right hand. "I swear it on the life of my hatchlings. We'll get you back to Merlin Hall by this evening—to your son—and the healers can fix...whatever needs fixing."

Ravyn stared at him for a long moment. Her voice caught as she asked, "Is he all right? My boy."

"He's fine," Janos said smoothly, ignoring a twinge in his conscience over what he'd told Wyvern. "He's more like you every day, truth be told. Now, are you with me?"

Without warning, Ravyn lunged into his arms and hugged Janos tight. A faint, sudden sob escaped her. "If you're lying, I'll gut you like a trout, I swear." He could hear her fighting back tears. The poor thing was traumatized.

"I would never lie about something like this. I'm here to save you, ol' girl." He hugged her back for another moment. "Don't fret now."

She sniffled. "I could kiss you!"

"Please don't," Janos said with a smile. "You smell like a Noxu."

Ravyn stepped back, blinked away a single tear, then hauled off and punched him in the chest for that jest.

"Ow," Janos said, but he could not have been more pleased.

Just like old times.

Having teased her back to some semblance of her usual self, Janos rested his hands on his hips. "Now, how are we going to rescue that Gryphon?"

Ravyn's chiseled face grew somber. "I've been trying to do that for three months. Maybe now that there's two of us, we'll have better luck. Still, rescuing Red is the easy part."

Janos furrowed his brow. "What's the hard part?"

"Tex." Her jaw tightened and her eyes turned even grimmer.

"You've seen him?"

She nodded. "They're keeping the Lightriders in the basement. Come on, I'll show you." Knife in hand, she stole off silently down the corridor.

Janos glanced around, uneasy for Ravyn's wellbeing, but awed by her will to survive.

And people wondered why he loved women. *Remarkable creatures.*

He shook his head with admiration, but Ravyn was getting away, heading for another lightless stairwell ahead.

Summoning up all his vampire stealth, Janos gripped his knife and glided after his former teammate.

Just like old times, indeed.

CHAPTER 23
An Excruciating Wait

That night, scores of people congregated on the lawn of Merlin Hall, anxiously awaiting the return of the rescue team the Elders had sent.

The mood was tense, voices kept low as adults and kids alike clustered in small groups beneath the stars or sat on logs around the towering bonfire they had built; its blazing light glowed in defiance of the darkness.

The fire filled the air with a pleasing, rustic scent that blended well with the smell of autumn leaves. It sent a plume of orange sparks snapping skyward, where the waxing moon glowed gold on a silver-sequined field of navy blue.

As Jake walked across the lawn, hands in his coat pockets, he was glad to see so many people concerned about the outcome, but he still couldn't believe that Derek had gone on the mission.

The master Guardian had admitted when Jake had asked today that he hadn't even popped the question yet to Miss Helena.

Hadn't found the right moment, he said.

Now, if anything happened to Derek while he was out there, he might never get the chance. Jake shuddered at the thought, flipping up the collar of the light wool jacket he had put on to ward off the chill of the autumn night.

He avoided the crowds around the bonfire, rounding the lawn to take cover in a scant grove of slender birch trees. Maddox was already there, leaning against one of the ghost-white trunks, arms folded across his chest as he waited in silence for word.

Jake nodded a greeting; Maddox nodded back.

Both of them were more or less a wreck, he supposed, wanting with all their hearts to see their loved ones return safe, and so scared of something going wrong that they almost didn't dare breathe.

Jake sat down on a boulder, running one of Red's scarlet feathers back and forth between his fingers. Maddox pushed away from the tree and moved about restlessly. He picked up a large stick and swung it at the leaves in his path as though it were a golf club. Jake wished he'd hold still.

"What's taking so long?" the older boy finally demanded, turning to Jake. "They should've been here by now, don't you think?"

Since Maddox seemed to be in even worse shape than he was, Jake pulled himself out of his brooding as best he could and, curious, struck up a bit of conversation. He didn't answer the question, though.

"So if he rescues your mother, do you think you might finally start being nice to him?"

Maddox stopped swinging the stick. "The bloodsucker, y'mean?"

Jake nodded, but Maddox's face hardened in the moonlight.

"Why should I? He promised me he'd keep an eye on Ravyn when they left for that battle, but he came back without her. Now he claims he's going to rescue her." Maddox shrugged. "But he did betray the Order once before, so I guess I'll believe it when I see it."

"He did not *betray* the Order." Jake rose. "He just didn't want to be a Guardian anymore."

"Same thing."

"No, it's really not," Jake said emphatically. "He just got sick of protecting ungrateful VIPs who treat Guardians like cannon fodder. If Janos were a *real* traitor, he wouldn't have saved my life like he did."

Maddox let out a sardonic sigh.

"You should've seen him battling those Nightstalkers in Taormina," Jake insisted. "Even you would've been impressed. I could swear he was having fun taking them out one by one. Bloke's a serious fighter."

"Well, he should be. He was trained by Derek himself."

"Come on, man. Give him a break. He's trying to help us."

"And why do you think that is?" Maddox asked flatly.

Jake sat back down on the boulder. "Because he's not as bad as everybody thinks."

"Don't be naïve."

"What are you talking about?"

Maddox stared at him. "It's because of Isabelle. He loves her."

"What?" Jake waved this off with a chortle. "You're out of your head, St. Trinian."

"He does. I have eyes," Maddox said. "He can't help it. He doesn't mean to. He just *does*."

His friend's somber tone gave Jake pause for a second. Was it possible? Then he snorted. "Don't be a doorbell, man. He just flirts with her. He flirts with every female he sees."

"Not Dani, not Nixie."

"They're younger. Isabelle's nearly a grown-up lady. He doesn't mean it one iota! He's just joking around, and everybody knows that, especially Isabelle. Everyone, that is, except you." Jake grinned. "You ask me, he does it just to needle you—Stick. Personally, I think it's pretty funny."

"You would. You're just like him," Maddox said with a huff. "Couple of troublemakers."

Jake scoffed. "Compared to you, who isn't, Mr. Perfect? Mr. Everyone Should Do Exactly As I Say Because I'm Saint Better Than You Trinian?"

"A: I usually *do* know better than you," Maddox retorted. "And B: at least I'm striving for excellence. You just want everything handed to you—milord."

Jake jumped to his feet. "That's not true!"

"Seriously, how are you surprised they didn't put you in the Lightrider program?"

"Now, look here—" Jake took a step toward him, but Maddox wasn't through.

"You can't follow orders. You started as a thief. You scoff at rules or just figure out a clever way around them—"

"That's rubbish! I've been doing *exactly* what Derek and Aunt Ramona tell me for the past three months—"

"And it's nearly killing you, isn't it?"

"Why don't you get off my back, Maddox?" Jake pushed him, but thanks to his wonky telekinesis, he shoved the older boy harder than he'd meant to.

Maddox slammed back against the tree trunk with a *woof*! Then fury filled his face.

"You brat!" He lunged forward and swung the stick at Jake.

Jake ducked the blow then grabbed the other end of Maddox's makeshift bat, and they proceeded to have a tug of war over it.

"How now! Cease and desist, you two!" Archie exclaimed, marching into their midst with Nixie a step behind.

She had her wand out and looked prepared to use it to zap them apart if necessary.

"Stop this ridiculousness at once!" Hands planted on his hips, the boy genius frowned at each of them. "Steady on, lads. We're all on the edge here. Let's not take it out on each other. Both of you, just calm down."

"Or else," Nixie growled, her wand at the ready.

Jake let go of his end of the stick, then Maddox cast the thing to the ground and sullenly retreated to lean against the tree trunk again.

Nixie rolled her eyes and shook her head.

"What time is it, Arch?" Jake asked, sulking a bit at the insults. What a pain Maddox was. "They've been gone for ages."

Archie pulled his fob watch out of his vest pocket and held it up to squint at it by the light of the distant bonfire. "Coming up on midnight," he said, then put it away.

Jake paced across the grove, fallen leaves crunching under his feet. He flung back down onto the rock where he had sat before. "This is intolerable! Why couldn't I go with them?"

"Uh, because you're a kid," Nixie said.

"A kid who defeated Garnock the Sorcerer, not to mention Davy Jones, the Lord of the Locker. I think I know what I'm doing!"

"Relax," Nixie ordered. "You've managed to keep your head together this long, Jake. What's a few more hours?"

"She's right," Archie said. "You can do this, coz. So can you, Maddox. You'll have them back soon and everything will be all right. You'll see."

Nixie plopped down onto the big rock beside Jake and elbowed him. "In the meanwhile, have you apologized to Dani yet?"

Jake glanced uneasily at her. He had been so distracted all day by these new developments that he had not got around to that yet.

Archie gave him a chiding frown. "Go and talk to her, ol' boy. It's the least you can do after you were so beastly."

Maddox gave him a matter-of-fact look. "Jealousy is not an admirable quality."

"Look who's talking!" Jake said, but stood up stiffly. Nixie was right. He owed Dani an apology. He just hoped she accepted it.

Jake let out a sigh. "Any suggestions how to begin?"

"Just make sure to grovel," Nixie said with a bland smile.

Archie nodded ruefully. "Girls like it when you grovel."

"Well, I hope she doesn't plan on lording it over me until the end of time," Jake said.

Maddox frowned. "Dani's not like that."

"Courage, man." Archie slapped him on the shoulder as Jake trudged past.

"Good luck," Nixie called.

Jake sent her a dry look, then smoothed his waistcoat and wished that, for once, he could borrow just a dash of Janos's charm when it came to females.

Of course, the carrot-head was likely to clobber him if he tried mimicking any of those suave moves.

But he truly did feel awful for ruining her big moment, and for, well, being an all-'round jackanapes today. He knew he'd been hard to live with for the past twelve weeks, but maybe tonight, Red would come back safe, and things could finally go back to normal.

He drifted over to the bonfire, where he saw Dani sitting on a log beside Isabelle. The girls were talking, heads together, but when he walked over, their conversation ceased.

Jake stood there awkwardly while they both just looked at him, Isabelle distracted, Dani stiff and cold.

Why, he had never seen her so angry at him before, not like this.

Usually, her anger or exasperation at him involved yelling, but those flareups of her Irish temper passed quickly, like a summer storm.

The cold stare the future Lightrider gave him when he approached was something else altogether. It unsettled him, made him unsure.

"Um, could I talk to you?" he mumbled, already feeling embarrassed when the other people around the fire glanced curiously at him.

Dani just sat there.

"Please?" Jake prompted, the fire warming his back as if to make up for the chill coming from the pretty redhead in front of him. "It's really important."

"Fine." Avoiding eye contact now, Dani rose to her feet and smoothed her skirts. "I'll be back in a moment, Isabelle."

"Take your time." As Dani marched ahead, Izzy sent Jake an encouraging look.

He nodded a discreet thanks and followed the redhead.

When he came up alongside her, he noticed in surprise that nowadays, she was only as tall as his shoulder. Why, he must've undergone another growth spurt without even realizing it. It did seem like every other week, he was walking around with his ankles hanging out and had to buy new trousers.

"Whaddya want?" Dani asked, staring straight ahead as they walked away from the bonfire and the crowd.

"I feel really terrible about how I reacted to your news today."

She didn't even look at him. "You should."

"Please. I'm genuinely sorry. I didn't react well at the time, but I truly am happy for you. I think it's amazing that they're going to make you a Lightrider. You deserve it, you really do. Blimey, I'd be dead a couple of times over if you hadn't been there for me, like you always are."

She stopped walking and turned to study him. "You hate it, though, don't you? You hate that I got your dream. That means you're going to hate me." Her eyes welled up with tears.

"No it doesn't!" he insisted, laying a hand on her shoulder. He leaned closer, feeling protective, and so very sorry for his thoughtless words. "I could never hate you, Dani O'Dell."

"It looked like you did today when I told everyone the news."

"Dani, I could thrash myself for hurting your feelings. I'm just stupid sometimes. You're the grandest girl in all the world to me. Don't you know that?"

She stared at him, her lips trembling a little.

Jake gathered up his nerve to get the words out. He wasn't usually the sort to wear his heart on his sleeve, but she deserved it. "You're going to make a great Lightrider, Dani. Just as good as Finnderool one day, I bet, once you're all trained. They wouldn't have picked you if you didn't have it in you. I admit, I was jealous. But not enough to let it come between us. You mean more to me than any silver sash."

"Really?" she asked in a small voice while the bonfire cast their shadows on the grass nearby.

Jake nodded, holding her hurt but still-trusting gaze. "I couldn't do any of this if it weren't for you. Just promise me you'll be careful out there. It's a dangerous life, and knowing I won't be there to protect you is already driving me mad."

She managed a nod, and to his relief, he saw the coldness leave her big green eyes. But the wounded look was still there, and it wrung his heart.

"You won't have to worry about me, Jake, because you'll be right there with me," she said. "I know you will. They'll pick you, too, you'll see. They have to."

He shrugged and shook his head. "I won't hold my breath." After all, Dani hadn't heard Aunt Ramona rebuke him today.

Dani took his hand and gave it a squeeze. "Just try to stay out of trouble for a while and they won't have any choice but to recruit you. You're the most talented kid here. Besides"—she nudged him—"once I'm established in the program, I could put in a good word for you."

He smiled ruefully. Her fingers felt warm in his grasp, but his hands were cold. "Thanks," he said, "but you don't have to do that. I just need to know we're all right, you and I. Can you forgive me?"

She tilted her head with a reluctant half-smile. "I suppose you've been under a lot of strain lately."

"Yes, well, that's no excuse." He faltered, looking into her eyes. "The last thing I would ever want to do is hurt your feelings."

"Well." She dropped her gaze with a slight blush, holding tightly to his hand. "Fortunately, I'm tougher than I look."

"Aye," Jake murmured with heartfelt admiration, "that you are, carrot-cake."

She flicked a glance up at him through her lashes, and her dimples showed this time when she smiled. His heart clenched, and relief at her forgiveness eased some of the bow-string tension out of him.

"You're a right plum lass, Dani O'Dell." Jake stepped closer and kissed her on the cheek.

"Aren't I, though?" She gave a happy little sigh as he pulled away.

Still holding hands, they gazed at each other for a long moment. Jake was stunned at what a huge relief it was to know that they were friends again—or whatever it was they were.

All he knew was that they were essential to each other.

At that moment, a deep vibratory hum erupted out of the darkness, rousing shouts and exclamations from across the lawn and around the bonfire.

People sitting on the logs leaped to their feet. Shouts and eager exclamations began filling the air.

"They're coming!"

"Stand back, the portal's about to open!"

Jake drew in his breath. "They're back. Let's go!" Still clutching

Dani's hand, he tugged her toward the sound.

Hand in hand, the two of them started running full-tilt toward the waypoint—a metal spike like a huge drawing pin driven flat into the lawn and running some twenty feet deep. Waypoints studded the ley lines of the Grid and marked the only known spots where portals could be opened.

As Dani and Jake barreled toward it, everyone else seemed to have the same idea. The crowd converged at that particular spot, but Sir Peter wasn't having it. The bespectacled chancellor strode out into their midst, his black robes billowing as he waved everybody back from the waypoint.

"Stand back, people! Let's give the team some room when they arrive. Excuse me! You there!" he shouted, gesturing to some centaurs. "Don't get too close to the portal unless you wish to be incinerated. That's right, everyone, back a little farther, please! Safety first, ladies and gentlemen."

Turning, Sir Peter pointed at someone in the crowd. Jake saw that it was Jillian. "Tell the healers on standby that the team is coming in!"

The tidy blonde nodded to her husband, then dashed into the palace.

The hum was getting louder, emanating from the space around the waypoint.

Jake and Dani struggled to reach the front row, but the adults jostling ahead of them were larger and blocked their view.

Jake stood on his toes just in time to see Sir Peter gesturing impatiently at one section of the throng. "Clear a path for the gnomes, if you please!"

"Out of the way!" a few people yelled.

Then several sets of gnomes trundled out onto the lawn in formation, each group together carrying a stretcher on their shoulders.

Jake and Dani exchanged a dire glance. Stretchers were merely a reminder of how dangerous this mission was. Oh, Lord, what if Derek didn't come back?

Or Janos?

Or Red...

Jake turned to Dani, dry-mouthed with fear.

"Whatever happens"—she gave his hand a squeeze—"you've still got me."

Thank you, he thought, but Jake could only nod, his voice trapped in his throat. He gripped her hand, his own icy with dread as the two of them stared toward the waypoint, waiting to see if the mission had been a success.

CHAPTER 24
The Price of Freedom

Dani prayed that everyone was safe and that Janos had indeed managed to rescue Jake's beloved Gryphon. But if that was not to be—whatever outcome the next few minutes might hold—she prayed above all for the wisdom to know what to say to Jake, how to help him if the mission had gone wrong.

Meanwhile, the sound of the energy throbbing through the ley line enfolded them, a deep vibrational resonance that pulsated like a heartbeat.

The sound grew louder as the team approached, and then, suddenly, the portal flashed open: an upright circle of dazzling light about eight feet in diameter, mirrorlike, its watery surface rippling with faint rainbow colors like a soap bubble.

She peeked in between the larger bodies of the adults in the way, trying to get a better view. Though she had seen portals before, it was different now, knowing that someday she would be one of the privileged few who could open them at will, travel through them anytime.

Of course, it wouldn't be much fun having that navigational device that Lightriders used, the Flower of Life, surgically implanted in her forearm. But she pushed that thought out of her mind. Considering she hadn't even been to her first class yet, it was far too soon to start worrying about that.

Beside her, Jake growled with frustration. Standing on his toes, he craned his neck this way and that. "Blast it, I can't see a thing! Too many people in the way!"

"Go." Dani let go of his icy hand and nodded to him. Any former pickpocket worth his salt could easily shimmy his way up to gain a front-row view in any crowd. "Just don't get incinerated."

To her surprise, Jake clasped her hand again. "C'mon, carrot, you're coming too."

He pulled her with him, and together, they wove through the crowd, dodging here, ducking there, and twisting under arms like it was the world's roughest game of London Bridge Is Falling Down. But they ended up in the front row. Jake winked at her, and Dani smiled back.

Then they waited, squinting as they stared down the brilliant tunnel of light. A shape began materializing in the glare, molecules collecting...

The shape wasn't human.

Jake gasped as Claw the Courageous himself came bounding out of the portal, his splendid scarlet wings outstretched.

Red roared the second he was free, all four paws pouncing down onto green earth again.

Jake shouted his name; the Gryphon spied his master and went racing to him.

Dani cheered along with the crowd as Red bowled Jake over, playfully rolling around with him like an oversized dog.

Jake's laughter brought tears to Dani's eyes. She covered her mouth with her hand to hold back a sob of joy. Then Maddox fought his way to the front of the crowd as Ravyn Vambrace came running out of the shining circle.

"Mother!" he yelled, a title he usually reserved for his adoptive mum.

Ravyn turned toward the sound of his voice. "Maddox?"

The Guardian lad ran over and hugged her, but Sir Peter quickly motioned them aside because Derek and Janos were on their way, materializing even now in the tunnel.

Dani drew in her breath, because the two fighters were carrying Lightrider Tex in between them.

They did it! They got him!

That was the instant she knew the whole mission had been a resounding success.

More members of the rescue team followed them out of the portal, but Dani was so relieved to see Tex. All the kids were fond of the crazy cowboy. His arms draped over Derek and Janos's shoulders, Tex looked barely conscious, his feet dragging behind him.

Jake climbed to his feet, one hand still resting on Red's back. Dani went over to them, and Red nuzzled her like a giant housecat.

Dani threw her arms around the Gryphon's feathered neck and hugged him hard. "Oh, Red, we missed you so much!"

"Becaw," the beast answered with affection. He seemed fine as far as Dani could tell.

"Looks like Tex is hurt," Jake said grimly.

Dani looked over and saw Derek and Janos easing the long, lanky Lightrider down onto the grass.

Jake and Dani ventured closer, Red prowling in between them.

"Is he going to be all right?" Jake called.

"You need to stay back," Derek said gruffly, but Dani could not see where on his body Tex was injured.

Janos noticed them gawking and sent Jake and Dani a grim nod. The streak of blood on his cheek looked like war paint, but Dani doubted it was his own.

"Thank you," Jake said. His voice was barely audible, but Janos heard with his acute vampire senses and smiled, sending him a little salute.

Then Sir Peter waved them back. "Clear the way, children! Too close!"

Jake and Dani obeyed.

"Welcome back, Tex!" Jake called as they retreated a few steps.

The cowboy lifted his hand wearily, tipping his hat. "Yeehaw, kid," he answered in a weak voice.

Jake and Dani both smiled when they heard it. Whatever he had been through, at least Tex *sounded* like his old self.

Then the gnomes lifted the wounded Lightrider onto one of the stretchers and sped him off to the healers inside the palace.

Ravyn refused to lie down on a stretcher, for her part, but limped toward the castle with Maddox holding her up on one side. The sinewy female fighter nodded at the well-wishers along the way.

Judging by how skinny Ravyn looked, Dani thought that rather than a visit to the healers, the fierce Guardian lady ought to start with a large meal.

Then Finnderool stepped through the portal, followed by towering Ebrahim Sly, another master Guardian like Derek. Exiting the tunnel with a firm step, the giant black man nodded at the wood elf; it seemed he was the last one through.

Dani knew Master Ebrahim was in charge of training the

apprentice Guardians like Maddox, but he still went out on missions all the time.

Finnderool, meanwhile, stood by, cool and elegant as ever. The tall, slender wood elf remained beside the portal a moment longer, as though he'd been holding the door for the others.

Dani watched in wonder. To think that one day, that would be her role, too...

Then she glanced around, amazed. It seemed that everything really was all right now.

The whole crowd was deliriously happy. Lady Bradford was there, applauding the victorious team. Archie and Nixie were jumping up and down gleefully, then rushing over to hug Red. Miss Helena was kissing Derek.

Dani wrinkled her nose at that and looked away.

She glanced around to find Isabelle just as the older girl exchanged a private nod with Janos from a distance. For a second, they stared at each other like no one else was there.

Then Finnderool closed the portal, and its brightness vanished in the night.

"Wait!" Janos said quickly, turning to stride toward the wood elf.

Dani's eyes had not fully adjusted to the darkness yet after that dazzling light, but she recognized the vampire's voice.

It held a strange undertone of fear she had never heard from Janos before.

"What is it?" Finderool asked. With his pale blond hair, he was easy to pick out in the darkness.

"Wyvern will know that I was the one behind this. Please transport me to Castle Gregorian so I can secure my home before he retaliates."

Finnderool glanced at Sir Peter, and the wizard nodded.

"Do as he asks," the chancellor said. "In fact, let's go with him." Sir Peter clapped Janos on the back. "Don't worry, man, we'll help you make sure your family's safe. I'd be happy to cast a few good protection spells around your castle, if you like."

Hands on hips, Janos gave him a weary nod. "I'd appreciate that." He sounded relieved. Looked it, too.

Dani's eyes had adjusted, so now she could see. All her friends were nearby, clamoring over the Gryphon, but Dani was quiet, and so was Isabelle, who had drifted over to her side.

Both girls watched the scene unfolding nearby.

"Open the portal," Sir Peter instructed the wood elf, then turned to Derek. "Guardian Stone?"

Derek gave a firm nod. "I'm in."

"Janos?" Finnderool called, beckoning him over. "Come tell me the coordinates to the waypoint nearest your castle. I trust you have them memorized?"

Janos nodded and went over to give him the numbers. Finnderool punched them into the magical-scientific device discreetly embedded in his left forearm.

Dani watched with avid interest from her spot a safe distance away.

"Derek?" Miss Helena pushed her way into the men's midst. "You're leaving again?" she exclaimed.

"This won't take long," Derek assured her, then gave the shapeshifter lady a quick kiss on the forehead. "Janos put himself on the line for us—twice now. The least I can do is repay the favor."

"I'm coming with you!" Henry hurried after them.

"Not you too?" Miss Helena exclaimed.

"It's all right, sis. I've been there before, remember?" Henry said. "I know the ground, the wolf packs there. Perhaps I can help."

"We should move quickly if we are going to beat Wyvern to the castle," Derek said with a grim glance around at the others who were going.

"Be careful, please, all of you," Miss Helena said.

As the portal flared open, dazzling their eyes once again, Dani saw Janos send Isabelle a slight bow of farewell.

Izzy nodded back to him, then Finnderool began waving his team into the tunnel. "Look lively, people. Who wants to go first?"

Janos ran in doggedly, his black ponytail flying out behind him.

"Next?" Finderool asked.

"After me," Sir Peter quipped, then ambled into the shining tunnel, wand in hand.

Henry jogged after him and Derek marched in last.

"I trust you're taking notes, Miss O'Dell," Finnderool said, arching a brow when he saw her gawking. "Nine o'clock sharp tomorrow morning. Don't be late."

Dani smiled eagerly. "I'll be there. Good luck!"

"Only the unprepared rely on luck, Miss O'Dell—lesson one. Farewell," he added, then he stepped through and touched another button on his left wrist, and the portal winked closed.

* * *

As Janos went hurtling homeward through the Grid, every one of his molecules was filled with a sharpening sense of urgency. His Guardian instincts were going mad with the certainty that his family was under threat, and as the ley line carried the team toward the Carpathians, the feeling only grew stronger.

In seconds, he could see the circular opening ahead. They were nearing the waypoint. He braced himself for the landing as his molecules started re-forming, buzzing back into place, reconstituting his usual shape.

Seconds later, he ran out of the shining circle of light and stepped aside for the next arrival. Sir Peter, Henry DuVal, and Derek followed, with the haughty wood elf bringing up the rear.

Fortunately, it had been years since any of them had suffered the adverse reactions to Grid travel that newcomers dealt with. The only symptom now was a brief second or two of mild disorientation.

Janos experienced it now as he landed in the woods, feet planted in the turf. The waypoint was hidden in the forest, about four miles from his castle.

Even before his momentary disorientation cleared, Janos could smell the distant scent of smoke. It was probably just some peasant's hearth fire, but it made his stomach clench.

Too late, his heart told him, but he refused to heed it.

"Come on," he said to the others while they were still trying to clear their heads.

He started running down a deer path through the woods, heading south for the castle over rough, hilly terrain.

The others were right behind him, Finnderool still punching buttons on the implant in his arm.

With every step, Janos's sense of foreboding increased.

The few short miles they had to traverse seemed interminable. The team pressed on, sticking together, climbing rock-strewn slopes and scrabbling down dales, through thorny brush and over babbling streams.

The way was harder than Janos remembered.

Sir Peter was no warrior—not in the physical sense.

Understandably, the bookish wizard lagged behind a bit, and even Derek, softened up by his ordeal as a captive of the Dark Druids, could be heard huffing and puffing a little.

Janos almost teased him, but the jest he might've made stuck in his throat. He pushed himself onward.

Only Finderool easily kept pace with him, bounding lightly over large stones and mossy logs. But while it was elven grace propelling the pale-haired Lightrider forward, for Janos, his speed came from pure dread.

The sensation of impending disaster rose higher every minute.

Something was very wrong, starting with the smoke smell. Instead of fading behind them, the scent was only growing stronger, and it held an acrid, unfamiliar tinge.

The woods around them seemed especially dark. And empty, Janos realized. Where were all the night birds? Where were all the bats?

It was too bloody quiet.

Then, beyond the ridge ahead, they could see an orange glow against the black sky.

They all paused. His companions panted. Janos suddenly felt sick.

Henry moved up beside him, grasped his arm, and gave him a meaningful stare. "Stay here. I'll go scout ahead."

The shapeshifter took his wolf form and galloped ahead, racing up the dark rise that waited for them.

The others kept going. There was no way Janos could hang back. But not even a vampire could keep up with a wolf.

Moments later, wolf-Henry reached the top of the rise and started barking a vicious alarm.

Janos understood and ran faster.

"Janos, wait!" Derek shouted, trying to stop him from seeing what awaited.

Even before he arrived beside Henry, Janos had a feeling he knew what he would find.

And he was right.

"Noooo!"

The castle was burning. His hatchlings, his children...

His brides!

Too late.

The unnatural blue intensity of the flames reminded him at once of Wyvern's cruelty to the peasants.

He raced forward with a war cry, barreling up as close to the castle as he dared. But Wyvern had been thorough.

The towers were torches, the keep a billowing inferno. Its very stone glowed, melting.

Janos threw his head back and roared, his fangs tearing forth.

Sir Peter lifted his wand, chanting as he strove to catch his breath; he summoned a torrent of rainfall from the skies to begin dousing the castle, but Janos already knew there was no point.

Nothing could survive such a blaze.

Derek set a hand on his shoulder, half to comfort, half to hold him back from throwing himself into the flames. But the Guardian instincts in both men registered no signs of life from within.

Janos tore away from Derek's hold and took a few steps to the side, at a loss, blind with rage, his hands on his head.

"I failed them," he gasped out. "I told them I'd protect them and I failed."

He dropped to his knees in the rich soil of the woods. Lowering his hands to his sides, he curled them into fists and unleashed a howl of futile agony under the moon.

The wolves of the forest howled back from their hidden places throughout the mountains of his kingdom.

Now they and the shadows were all he had left.

* * *

In the distance behind his dragon chariot, Wyvern caught only a wild echo of the clamorous howls coming from the forest.

A cold smile curved his lips as he glanced over his shoulder at the burning castle. *Betray me? I warned you.*

That blasted vampire had added insult to injury by wounding Thanatos in addition to freeing two highly valuable prisoners.

Wyvern had found his pet manticore bleeding from a stab wound in his hip and locked up in the same cell where the Gryphon had been caged. The poor beast would have died if Wyvern had not returned in time with his wand to work a healing spell.

Treacherous vampire. Well, now they were even, he supposed. He whipped his Orange Darter onward across the black sky.

Beside him, all the while, his voluptuous new passenger held on tight to the handrail of the dragon chariot. She gazed down, cooing with amazement at the ground so far below, her long, dark, wavy hair billowing wildly all around her, her red lips curved in a smile.

She was enjoying herself immensely, his future wife, but Wyvern didn't really care if she was or not.

All that mattered was that she paid him back for the favor he had done her tonight, springing her from her watery prison deep in the North Sea.

Transformed back into the beauty she once had been—thanks to *his* magic—the famed enchantress let out a laugh and lifted one hand in the air, glorying in her freedom as the dragon chariot flew onward to their next destination of the night.

They were heading into dragon country.

For while Janos might've betrayed him, there was still someone else Wyvern could turn to and recruit for his cause. Someone with an even closer tie to his future son.

Indeed, one of Jake's own bloodline. For who could possibly know more about the boy than his own dear Uncle Waldrick?

CHAPTER 25

The Prisoner

Waldrick Everton, formerly known as the sixth Earl of Griffon, had served but a year and a half of the cruel life sentence the Elders of the Order had handed down to him for kidnapping his nephew, Jake, and the fairy, Gladwin, and for harboring a known fugitive from justice, his beautiful (sometimes) accomplice, the sea-witch, Fionnula Coralbroom.

But what he was really guilty of—what they knew, but couldn't prove—was that Waldrick had murdered his elder brother, Jacob, and that vexing Elizabeth woman, his wife. That was why they had locked him up and all but thrown away the key.

At first, he had raged continually in his dismal dungeon cell, trying to shake loose the bars.

As if no one had ever tried that before.

Or ramming the dank stone walls with his shoulder like he'd break them down.

Absurd, of course. All he'd done was nearly dislocate his own shoulder.

When his fury had spent itself in futility, he had fallen back on his wits, plotting endless escapes.

They all had come to nothing.

After a dozen such failures, he had fallen into a miserable depression at the unfairness of it all, which lasted approximately four months by his reckoning, though time had lost its meaning here in this place, where he had been forgotten by the world.

Finally—indeed, not too long ago—Waldrick had begun to make his peace with his fate. His life was ruined and that was that. No use crying about it forever.

Much to the surprise of his guards, he had become something of a model prisoner after this epiphany.

That very night, lying on his cot and gazing through the bars at a starry September sky over the forest, he was musing without hostility on the good times he used to have with his pet spider, Malwort, before even his trusty arachno-sapiens had abandoned him.

Yes, even Malwort had run away from him.

Alas, in hindsight, Waldrick wasn't quite sure he blamed him. *I never really appreciated the little fellow as he deserved...*

All the while, Waldrick twanged a slow, melancholy tune on the mouth harp he'd fashioned from a twig and a piece of twine.

Did he regret killing his brother and his sister-in-law?

Sometimes.

Not enough to convince the Order that he deserved extra privileges yet, but he was making his way by slow, plodding steps toward an almost human sense of responsibility for his own actions.

He did not like the way that it made him feel.

He still dreamed of the days when he used to be a rich, admired lord in London. Ah, that was the life. Swanning about Town with the beautiful diva, Fionnula, on his arm—toast of the royal opera house.

But she too had gone to prison for her role as Waldrick's accomplice, and for that little matter of trying to overthrow the entire government of King Oceanus of the North Sea. In her true form, of course, Fionnula Coralbroom was a powerful sea-witch, a siren, whose wickedest magic was in her song.

None of her adoring London audiences had ever suspected this fact. They could not explain why the opera house was always packed when she was scheduled to take the stage. But there was enchantment in her voice—a gift she could use for good or ill.

It was no mystery which direction she'd gone. But, Lord, she had been a stunner back in those days. At least in her human form. Waldrick had relished squiring her about Town. He had loved feeling the envy of all the other rich and titled gents in London when he'd arrive at some party or restaurant with the ravishing star of the stage by his side.

Of course, he would never be seen with her in her sea-hag form.

Not even he liked a lady with tentacles. But with a little help from the magic in those Gryphon feathers, the sea-witch could turn herself into *quite* the prime article...

All of a sudden, a reptilian roar from the dragon-infested forests surrounding the Order's prison broke into Waldrick's reverie.

He shot upright on his cot. The formidable lizards roaming those woods out there terrified him. The ultimate deterrent against prisoners breaking out and running away.

At least watching the dragons from the safety of his cell could be interesting. Especially when one of the big ones caught a deer or devoured a luckless peasant who happened to take a shortcut through the woods, not realizing where he was.

More dragon roars answered the first, echoing from all around the valley. It was downright unnerving!

What's got them so riled up?

Waldrick swung his dirty bare feet over the edge of his cot and walked in his tattered clothes over to the window of his cell. He grasped the iron bars carefully and peered out.

Sure enough, huge reptilian shapes shook the trees below. A burst of fire in the darkness lit up their location. Leathery wings fanned the sky as a few more dragons alighted, drawn to one particular gathering point.

What on earth has got into them?

He'd never seen them act like this before, dozens of them swarming into the valley just below the prison.

Waldrick barely dared blink as he stared down the hill from his cell. A plume of flame curled into the sky as a long-necked beast lifted its head high and breathed fire.

But then Waldrick tensed. His shoulders bunched up with fear as he saw a tall, man-shaped silhouette striding right through the midst of the beasts.

Oh, they've found themselves a midnight snack, he thought, riveted.

But as he watched in morbid fascination, the dragons did not devour the man.

A massive green one with horns snapped at him, but the man held up his hand and bellowed at them in a language that Waldrick did not possess.

He knew magical words when he heard them, however. He could feel the power in the man's incantation resonating through the valley.

Then Waldrick's eyes widened as the dragons bowed down to the man.

He'd never seen such a thing.

"What's this?" he breathed.

The mighty dragons almost seemed to genuflect, tamely letting the man pass between them.

A dragon lord. He stared until his eyes stung. Why, he'd thought they'd gone extinct.

Against the glow of the fire one of the dragons had started in the underbrush with its blast of breath, Waldrick stared at the black silhouette of the man striding now up the hill toward the dungeon.

Instinctively, he moved away from the window with the uncanny sense that the dragon lord had been looking straight up at his cell.

He had no idea what was going on.

But he could feel the approach of a great evil. Nervous and unsettled, Waldrick hurried back to his cot and sat down, lifting his feet off the cold stone floor and tucking his bare toes under the edge of his rough blanket.

He was wide awake now, though, listening for all he was worth, unsure of what would happen next. Who was that person and why was he heading this way?

A few minutes later, Waldrick heard the prison guards scream somewhere below. He drew in his breath, yanking the blanket up to his chest and cowering a little.

Their screams were quickly cut short.

Through the thick walls of the prison, Waldrick could have sworn he heard a distant trill of feminine laughter. There was something oddly familiar about it, but his heart was pounding too hard for his brain to make sense of it.

Only one thing was certain: Waldrick knew trouble when he sensed it. And trouble was headed his way.

In the darkness, his eyes bulging with fear, he slid his gaze toward the corridor from whence he heard heavy, implacable footfalls coming closer...closer.

Dread overwhelmed him—then the man from outside stepped into view.

He looked like a gentleman, well dressed in Bond Street tailoring. He was unfashionably tall, though—clearly not a giant, just a bit too large for a normal human man. He had brown hair, a powerful build...

And the coldest eyes Waldrick had ever seen.

The dragon lord smiled blandly at him through the bars. "Are you

Waldrick Everton?"

Waldrick was afraid to answer the question. "Who are you?" he forced out.

His visitor sketched a bow. "Nathan, Lord Wyvern, at your service. You may have heard of me."

Oh, but he had.

Rumor had it he was Nephilim. Well, that would explain his height. Waldrick flicked a glance toward the stranger's hands wrapped around the bars of his cell.

Egads. Six fingers.

So it's true.

"Ahem. Yes. I-I am Waldrick Everton," he admitted, lifting his chin.

"Good. Just the man I've come to see."

Waldrick rose cautiously from his cot and hoped the Dark Druid could not hear his knees knocking together.

"And why is that?" he inquired, trying to seem as composed as his former lordly self.

"I have a proposition for you," Wyvern said. "How'd you like me to get you out of that cell?"

His first thought was that he was perfectly comfortable in his cell, thank you very much. Not for the world would he want to be indebted to any Nephilim. Even he wasn't that stupid.

"Well, you're very kind to offer, but even if you did, I wouldn't get very far out there." He nodded toward the window. "You've noticed the dragons?"

"Leave them to me," Wyvern said with the smile of an alligator.

Waldrick raked his fingers through his hair, trying to straighten his appearance in the presence of a fellow gentleman. "I, er, take it you are a dragon lord of some kind?"

"You guess aright, my lord."

I'm not actually a lord anymore, he started to say. But it was so nice to be addressed once again by his old honorific.

"I'm sorry," Waldrick said abruptly, "have we met?" He was sure he would've remembered the imposing fellow if he had; his visit here seemed inexplicable.

"No," said Wyvern, "but I am familiar with your case. Most unjust."

"Oh really?" Waldrick could not resist taking a wary step closer. "Well, I am touched by your interest in my legal troubles, but you are...?"

"The future leader of the Dark Druids," Wyvern finally supplied in answer to his open-ended question.

"Ohhh. Oh, I see." Waldrick paused, weighing this dire information with the utmost caution. "Is Master Zolond unwell?"

The Nephilim's eyes flickered, the pupils going longwise briefly, like a reptile's. "Something like that."

"Ah. Pity. Well—he's very old." Waldrick smoothed his disgustingly filthy shirt merely out of habit, a vague memory of his once-fine wardrobe dancing through his mind. "And, um, what exactly do you want with me, Lord Wyvern?"

"I am in a position to help you, if you will help me."

"Oh? How?" Waldrick asked, on his guard. He knew a liar when he met one.

After all, it took one to know one.

"I am interested in your nephew, young Jake, Lord Griffon. I understand he is the reason you are sitting in this cell."

Waldrick gave a noncommittal snort. Time had helped him start to see that his being here was his own fault, but just hearing the name of that little troublemaker gave him a headache.

The boy was the bane of his existence.

"I take it he's been wreaking havoc again." Waldrick sighed. "Very well. What's he done now?"

"Never mind that. I need to get him under control. That's all I am at liberty to say for now, Everton. I need an angle for how to get to him. I thought you might be of use. You are his kin, after all."

Waldrick flicked a flea off his arm. "Oh, I could help you, I'm sure. It's just, if you get me out of here and I should get caught again, it would be the gallows next time. You see my predicament." He really would prefer to stay in jail than go anywhere with the infamous warlock.

"Hmm," Wyvern said thoughtfully, as though sensing his reluctance. "Then let me sweeten the deal. What if I promised you your old talent back? A man with pyrokinesis could be a very useful ally to me when I head up the Council."

Waldrick froze at the offer. He was actually a little afraid of his fire-throwing talent. It had been too much for him as a boy.

There had been...accidents.

It had been his big brother, Jacob, who had performed the horrid Extraction Spell on him, with Waldrick's agreement. After tearfully swearing that he didn't want to end up roasting innocent people all because he couldn't control his gift, Waldrick had gone along with it when his handsome and always-brave elder brother, Jacob, declared they must take the talent out of him.

His brother had then nicked one of Aunt Ramona's extra wands for the excruciating spell and read the chant aloud, removing the pyrokinesis from Waldrick, and distilling the firepower (as they called it) into a vial.

Jacob had then stored it in the family's secret vault hidden away somewhere in the bowels of Griffon Castle.

Waldrick had never been able to find the vault, let alone open it. By family tradition, only the firstborn, the heir, had the privilege of learning where it was and how to open it.

That had been Jacob, not him.

But that hadn't stopped Waldrick from trying to find it. Because after a few years of being ordinary, he had regretted submitting to the procedure. He wanted his firepower back.

And why should he not have it? It was his, blast it!

By then—in his early twenties—he was more mature and knew that he could handle it.

His brother didn't think so.

They had argued, and finally, Jacob had confessed that he'd destroyed the vial long ago.

Waldrick had been stunned as the news sank in that he would *never* get his power back.

When he asked his brother why he would do such a thing, Jacob had accused him of not maturing at all, of only turning more devious and shifty with every year that passed.

Adding insult to injury, the arrogant firstborn had insisted that it simply wasn't safe for Waldrick to have it. That he couldn't be trusted with so much power.

So spoke the heir.

Waldrick had been enraged. He knew then he would never forgive his brother for this betrayal.

Jacob had destroyed not just something that *belonged* to him, but a part of Waldrick himself.

He didn't care if the vainglorious young Lightrider had only been trying to help him, as he claimed; that was the moment Waldrick had begun to hate his brother.

A hatred he had been helpless to act upon until he met Fionnula. Without her magic, he never would've managed to kill Jacob and his wife.

"Well?" the Nephilim asked.

Waldrick eyed him uncertainly. "With all due respect, my lord, it is not possible to give me my firepower back. My brother destroyed it. He told me so himself."

"He lied," Wyvern said.

Waldrick stared at him, astonished by this outlandish claim.

Was Wyvern suggesting that Jacob had been bluffing? That Waldrick had murdered his brother over a lie?

Impossible. He shoved the ghastly thought aside with a shudder. The vial was gone, and his power with it.

Besides, how could this stranger possibly know where the secret family vault was, let alone claim that his vial was still in there, intact?

Oh. Well—he's obviously lying, Waldrick realized. *He's just telling me whatever he thinks I want to hear. I wonder why...*

"Well?" Wyvern prompted again.

Waldrick chose his words with care. He did not want to reveal that he knew it was a lie. Because if there was any hope of getting out of this prison...

"Ahem. To be honest, my lord," he said, "the thought of a deal with the Black Brotherhood does make a simple chap like me, oh, just a trifle nervous."

The dragon lord laughed. "Well, if *I* can't persuade you, there's someone else here who might have better luck." Wyvern beckoned to someone down the corridor. "Perhaps you'd feel a bit better about joining the team if you knew a familiar face was already part of this."

The sound that followed made Waldrick's ears perk up: high heels clicking on the stone floor.

Echoing louder and louder...

He furrowed his brow, cocking his head to listen. There was something so familiar about the self-assured rhythm of that sassy stride.

In the next moment, his former ladylove stepped into view, gorgeous as ever, and planted a hand on her hip. "Hullo, Waldrick."

"Fionnula!" he cried in disbelief. "Is it really you?"

She laughed and threw her hands in the air. "In the flesh, darling!"

"Wh-what? How?" Waldrick was gobsmacked.

"Oh, darling!" Fionnula sashayed up to the bars, wrapped her hands around them, and fluttered her lashes. "Isn't it wonderful? Nathan's saved us!" She glanced adoringly at Wyvern. "Now we can both be free. The world is our oyster once again. Just like old times!"

Waldrick moved closer, gazing at his old partner in crime, amazed. "Fionnula...! I-I don't understand. How did you get out?"

"Bad girls must be rewarded," she said with a coy wink. "I knew the Dark Druids wouldn't abandon me forever."

"Zolond ordered you freed?"

"Oh, Hades, no. It was all Nathan's doing. He rescued me!"

Wyvern folded his arms across his muscled chest with a smirk.

"He's so clever, darling! He sent rock golems to smash through the walls of my underwater prison! Conjured them right out of boulders on some Scottish beach. It was sooo impressive," she purred.

The Nephilim smiled and shrugged.

Fionnula tossed the dark waves of her blue-black hair over her shoulder. "You should've seen it. At His Lordship's command, the boulder giants marched right down into the North Sea and punched a hole right through the wall of my cell—and here I am! Once we got to shore, Nathan healed me with his wand. Just like the Gryphon feathers used to do. So? How do I look?"

The diva set her hands on her waist and preened, awaiting Waldrick's praise.

"More radiant than ever," he said sincerely.

"Aw, you were always so sweet." She puckered her lips and offered a kiss through the bars, but when Waldrick puckered back and leaned toward her, Fionnula twirled away. "Oooh, you're too stinky! So, will you help us bring Jake to heel or not?"

She took the Nephilim's bulging arm and waited hopefully for his reply.

What on earth are these two scheming? Waldrick thought.

The sea-witch cocked a sly glance at her towering savior. "He is considering it, Nathan."

"He'd be a fool not to," Wyvern replied.

Oh, "Nathan," is it? Waldrick thought. The pair seemed awfully cozy. "I don't know," he mumbled.

"La, join the party, Waldrick! What do you have to lose?" Fionnula cajoled him. The hairs on his nape bristled with distrust of the woman. But, admittedly, it was much nicer seeing her like this than in her...*other* form.

He shuddered privately at the memory of her tentacles.

She beamed her theatre smile at him. "Remember how much fun it was when we had your nephew under that Oboedire spell, and he had to do whatever we said?"

A reluctant smile tugged at Waldrick's lips. "That *was* rather amusing." He had especially enjoyed ordering Jake to act like a chicken...

But this was no time for revisiting old jokes. Serious business was in play.

Waldrick wasn't sure yet what was going on, but these two clearly needed him. *Well.* Waldrick Everton didn't help anyone for free. "I'd have certain requirements."

"Name them," said Wyvern.

"Hmm. For starters, I'd expect fine meals like I used to enjoy. Proper clothing. Luxurious accommodations worthy of my lineage."

"Done," the warlock replied.

Waldrick tensed. *Too easy.* That was never a good sign.

He knew then that this was a bad idea. The man was a Nephilim, for heaven's sake.

But the thought of a table laden with chef-cooked delicacies and a closet full of Bond Street-tailored clothes was enough to persuade him after a moment's hesitation.

He was sick of staring at these four walls, anyway. And it would be so much fun making Jake miserable again.

After all, if not for that impossible boy, he never would've ended up here.

In truth, with the dark way the Nephilim was staring at him, it seemed pretty clear to Waldrick that he didn't actually have a choice.

"Very well." Of course, he still didn't believe that the warlock could deliver on his absurd promise to get his firepower back. But the prospect of escaping this cage brought a smile to Waldrick's grime-caked face, nevertheless. "Count me in."

"Excellent." Wyvern thrust the sea-witch aside, since she was still hanging on him, and took out his wand. "You might want to stand back, Everton."

Waldrick fled to the far corner of his cell, then ducked away as the warlock's shout of exertion blasted his cell open with a shattering bolt of magic.

Fionnula squealed with delight, clapping her hands in excitement and hopping up and down in her red high-heeled shoes.

With sparks still popping along the glowing metal of the bent and twisted bars, broken stones still shedding clouds of dust, Jake's wicked Uncle Waldrick slipped his feet into his ragged old shoes, then stepped out of his cell at long last.

A free man.

* * *

Something terrible had happened.

Isabelle could feel it in her bones. Waiting for the team to return once again, she closed her eyes and tried sending out a mental query to Janos.

What's wrong?

No answer returned. The dark skies were empty. The moon crept behind a cloud as though ashamed, and from somewhere near the glade where the boys had been waiting, an owl hooted mournfully.

Though her sense of impending disaster continued to grow, Isabelle could not discern quite where it was coming from.

At least Jake was happy. Of that, she was sure. He and the others had returned to the palace in triumph, making a well-deserved fuss over the Gryphon.

They all were somewhere inside, celebrating Red's return, along with Dani's selection for the Lightrider program.

Izzy had promised to join them soon. But, for now, something told her to wait out here till the team came back.

This thing wasn't over yet.

Miss Helena was waiting outside as well, keeping warm by the bonfire. Izzy's poor governess had double the reason to be worried. Both her twin and her beau were out there, in harm's way. Hopefully, the men would secure Janos's home and return without incident.

Privately, Izzy rather regretted that her vampire friend would not be coming back to Merlin Hall with the team, but she supposed he had to stay home to protect his poor little hatchlings and those glamorous monsters he called his wives.

Well, at least maybe now that he'd brought Ravyn back safely, Maddox would be satisfied and start being a little more civil to Janos.

Not that Janos seemed to care. The rogue had a splendid talent for shrugging off the world's disapproval.

Reckless, she thought.

At last, the pulsating rhythm of a portal preparing to open came coursing down the ley line that passed right through the grounds of Merlin Hall. Its deep, reverberating hum filled the night, rising and falling like a chorus of crickets at the end of summer, but on a much lower frequency.

Isabelle glanced at Miss Helena, who rose from the log. Then they both began walking warily toward the waypoint.

Most of the spectators who had come out to wait for the safe return of Red, Ravyn, and Tex had dispersed by now to go celebrate the captives' freedom, but a few people remained out on the lawn.

They gathered around the waypoint a safe distance back. Izzy braced herself, her heart pounding. She noticed Jillian waiting among them for Sir Peter.

Miss Helena looked pale. Izzy gave her governess's hand a reassuring squeeze. The elegant shapeshifter smiled at her with gratitude.

Then, sure enough, the portal blinked open, pouring out light, and those who had gone with Janos came stumbling out into the darkness.

Isabelle staggered back a step, overwhelmed with the blast of uproarious emotion that came roaring out of the tunnel.

Her stomach felt like it dropped beneath her feet. Her very bones felt afire. And the pain in her heart was like a knife.

That quickly, her sense that something terrible had happened out there was confirmed. Yet she saw no injuries on them: Henry and Sir Peter came out unscathed.

Then Derek stepped through, but he was holding on to Janos, who seemed mortally wounded.

Izzy held up her hand to visor her eyes, trying to see through the blinding light from the portal, yet her senses reeled. She felt ill with whatever this was she was sensing.

Why had they brought Janos back? And how could he be wounded? Vampires healed instantly.

Then she smelled the smoke that they'd carried back on their clothes.

Confused and alarmed, she saw Finnderool hurry out of the portal and close it. The cloak of darkness returned. Miss Helena hurried forward.

Isabelle followed as best she could, dizzy and seasick with all the wild fury and grief seething in her brain and her senses.

It wasn't hers.

Janos.

Some ten feet away, she saw him pull away from Derek angrily.

"Leave me be!"

Henry and Finderool tried to help him as well, but he cast them off. Fear and confusion seized hold of Izzy.

Are you hurt? she demanded of him.

Janos went very still, his back to her. He did not turn around.

They're dead. They're all dead.

Izzy gasped and covered her mouth with her hand.

He burned them all alive.

"Janos!" She jolted forward into motion, reckless with shared pain. Running toward him purely on instinct, she halted as he suddenly whirled around with a snarl.

"Stay away from me!"

"Janos?" She froze, at a loss.

The vampire stared accusingly into her eyes, and Izzy's jaw dropped as she sensed his emotions.

You blame me *for this?* The shock of it stole her breath. *Why?*

"Leave me alone," he growled.

"I-I don't understand."

"Of course you don't. You're just a little girl," he said bitterly. "Goodbye, Miss Bradford." Then he pivoted and began stalking away, but he vanished mid-stride into his black smoke form.

Disappearing into the night.

CHAPTER 26
Djinni Out of the Bottle

The next morning, Jake awoke and all was right with the world. Truly, it was the first day in nearly three months that he'd woken up, as they say, on the right side of the bed. Red was back; he was safe. Indeed, the Gryphon had slept curled up contentedly at the foot of Jake's bed, same as always.

Jake felt as though an anvil had been lifted off his chest. He'd cleared the air with Dani. His Gryphon was back and none the worse for wear.

Now, finally, he could think. And there was much to think about. Like why his parents hadn't been in their coffins in the family mausoleum...

But for now, he just enjoyed feeling normal again.

First thing in the morning, he sprang out of bed and got himself dressed, glancing constantly at the Gryphon. Red lapped up some water from his bowl in the corner, then sat down, wrapped his tufted tail around his haunches, and looked at Jake, as if to say, *What are we doing today?*

Jake laughed at the funny look on the Gryphon's face and patted his head, scratched his neck, half hugging him repeatedly in between moving about his chamber, splashing his face, and putting on his clothes.

"We need to get you checked out by Dr. Plantagenet right away," he told his feathered friend.

Red snuffled, not looking forward at all to a medical exam. But Jake needed to know if the Dark Druids had left his pet with any unseen injuries or a lack of nutrition that he should know about.

As soon as they had both eaten breakfast, he took Red over to the

Green Man's veterinary offices in the heart of the menagerie, and left him in Dr. Plantagenet's capable hands.

They wouldn't be parted long.

"Don't worry, Jake, I'll take good care of him." The Green Man scratched Red affectionately under his beak. "We'll look him over, run a few tests, and make sure he's ready for action. He'll be good as new in no time."

Jake welcomed the veterinarian's optimistic prediction as he leaned against the wall, in no hurry to get to his errand. Red, meanwhile, sat on the sturdy exam table, scowling a little to have to undergo the tests, but the Gryphon was never one to complain.

Jake gave his pet another hug goodbye.

"I'll be back soon to fetch you, boy. Be good for Dr. Plantagenet. He knows what he's doing, and this is for your own good. I've got to go."

"Becaw?" Red asked.

"Oh, Archie wants my help today with some experiment," Jake said. "He's been trying every way he can think of to help poor Aleeyah—you remember the djinni?"

"C-caw." Red nodded.

"Well, you might not be aware of this, but during the same battle where you got captured, Lord Wyvern apparently hit Aleeyah with some sort of heavy-duty spell. You remember how she can turn into a little puff of smoke to transport herself instantly from one spot to another?"

Red nodded. It was a familiar djinni trick.

"Wyvern's spell or incantation or whatever it was hit her right when she was in mid-transport, and she got stuck that way—in her smoke form! None of the wizards have been able to solve her predicament, so Archie offered to give it a go."

Red bobbed his head in approval. If the boy genius couldn't do it, no one could. Meanwhile, Dr. Plantagenet went over to his work counter by the wall and took his stethoscope out of the cabinet. Then he got a wooden tongue depressor and a thermometer. As he moved about, preparing for the exam, one of the brown leaves on his twiggy head suddenly fell off and wafted to the floor.

"Oh! How embarrassing." He quickly stooped to pick it up and throw it out the window.

Jake managed not to laugh, and looked again at the Gryphon. "I'll be back to pick you up this afternoon. You can either take a nap in your nest if you want, or just come and find me at Archie's lab in the basement. But knock first. You know Arch. His experiments can get a little dicey."

Red nodded, and Jake gave him another doting pat on the head. "Take good care of him for me, doc."

The Green Man smiled. "Will do, my lad."

With that, Jake pried himself away from the veterinary office and went to see what Archie wanted him to do in his role of assistant.

Jake jogged back across the grass to Merlin Hall and strode lightly inside, crossing the white lobby underneath the dome. His mood was buoyant; he didn't even mind that Dani had started her Lightrider training without him this morning.

Of course, he didn't let himself think about it too much. *Bully for her,* was all he said to himself.

As for Isabelle, he hadn't seen her this morning. She had been pretty shaken up by the dreadful news about poor Janos's family.

Jake also felt awful for his fanged friend, but they were vampires, after all. They drank people's blood. His wives were known murderers, his children probably ghouls. Janos was the exception, a vampire who refused to feed off humans. So, not to be callous—and he'd never say it to Janos—but Jake was with Maddox on this one. In the long run, the world was probably better off, and deep down, even Janos likely knew it.

Still, the poor fellow was devastated. This evening, Jake planned to take the others over to try visiting him.

Janos had holed up in an empty mausoleum over on the Merlin Hall Burial Grounds. He wanted to be alone and the little Gothic marble building would seal out the sunlight, so at least he would be safe there. Since day was night to him, Jake figured Janos was probably sleeping right now, but he and his friends meant to go and knock on his door after nightfall.

They all felt so bad for him.

Jake wasn't sure if the vampire would want to see anyone so soon after the tragedy, but he at least wanted to thank Janos for rescuing Red and to say how sorry he was.

All the same, after having been in a dark place himself all these weeks, Jake felt so good at the moment that he did not want to get bogged down in thinking too much about Janos's suffering.

He pushed the painful thoughts away, needing to enjoy his own happiness for a few days.

Bounding down the steps that led into the basement of Merlin Hall, Jake leaped off the bottom few and landed at the bottom with a pounce. Then he strutted down the dark corridor, whistling, until he found Archie's laboratory.

Admittedly, he found the place slightly creepy.

Buried mostly below ground level, the high-ceilinged room was spacious but dim; the only windows ran along the top part of one wall. Globular lamps assisted with lighting the worktables and dark wooden shelves, but the lab still felt chilly and dank on account of the drab green paint on the walls and the gray flagstone floor underfoot.

Worst of all, though, was the turpentine and burned-hair smell of all the chemicals. Ventilation was poor. But the lab had a sink in the corner and all the equipment the boy genius could want, given the circumstances.

Burners and beakers, bell jars and bowls lined the surrounding shelves. There were rows of test tubes in all sizes and sharp little tools resembling tweezers and scalpels.

There were thermometers, magnets, and dozens of little glass vials containing elements and minerals, like a collection of odd-colored rock salt. These sat alongside the mortars and pestles used for crushing things into powders and finely tuned scales for weighing them. On the center table sat no less than three different microscopes and a small spinny thing called a centrifuge.

These, at least, were the items Jake could identify, but there were other whimsical contraptions and odd apparatuses that he could not name.

In any case, as he breezed into the lab finally in a good mood, he lifted his arms out to his sides, presenting himself. "Dr. Frankenstein: your Igor is here!" he said to the boy genius.

"Ah! Excellent." Archie looked up from a clipboard, where he had been scribbling notes.

Nixie was also there, scratching her head idly with her wand and squinting up at the top shelf, where Malwort, a friendly spider the size of a dinner plate, scurried back and forth, fetching ingredients for her.

Archie had given the witch a few shelves of her own, where she could keep her magical equipment. The two geniuses liked working together. They made a good team.

Malwort stopped and plucked a vial off the shelf with his two front legs. "Oh look, it's the Jake!" the arachno-sapiens said in his clinkety little voice.

"Hullo, Malwort," Jake replied.

He had long since noticed that the talking spider seemed much happier in life as Nixie's assistant than he had ever been as Uncle Waldrick's pet.

As Malwort hopped back down off the shelves to bring Nixie the vial, Jake noticed that both she and Archie were wearing white lab coats.

He wondered if he'd get to wear one too—and a pair of those goofy googles. Then he strolled toward his cousin, and Archie studied him curiously over the rim of his spectacles.

"Well, look at this. I do believe my cheeky cousin's back. Good to see you, mate." Archie offered a handshake. "It's been a long time!"

Jake laughed, shook his hand, then clapped his cousin on the shoulder. "Aye, I'm officially back to m'old self."

"We've been warned," Nixie drawled, sauntering over to them.

Jake reached over with a grin and rumpled her spiky black hair. She hissed at him, but not maliciously.

"Did you get Red over to the vet?" she asked, fixing her hair with a scowl.

"He's there now." Jake clapped his hands together and rubbed them back and forth, ready to work. "Right! So what do you two brains want me to do?"

Archie glanced past him. "Nix, you ready?"

"Ready," she answered.

"Good." Archie nodded. "Then, both of you, follow me." He bopped through a side door that Jake hadn't even noticed was there, while Nixie turned to her creepy little assistant.

"Stay, Malwort. This could get dangerous."

"Yes, boss," the spider answered. Nixie gestured to Jake to go ahead of her, so he followed his cousin into the adjoining lab.

It had the same green walls and gray floor as the main lab, plus a few chalkboards, but no furniture, leaving the space clear for the bizarre mechanical wonder that took up most of room.

"What on earth...?" Jake murmured, staring at it. *Well now.*

The boy genius had come up with some odd inventions in his day, but this one had to be the strangest of them all.

The large, grayish metal contraption looked like an upside-down salad bowl with flat, shallow sides. Around fifteen feet in diameter, the center—or the base of the overturned salad bowl—stood as tall as Jake's chest, while the sides sloped down to the level of his shins.

A metal pole about six feet tall stuck up through the center of the contraption, a sturdy leather strap or belt wrapped around it, and as Jake's gaze traveled along it, he saw the belt was attached to a seat of gears several feet away.

Oh, how Archie loved making things with gears.

The upper sprocket was set horizontally, so that the belt from the pole could also travel around it, but the lower sprocket that it melded with was set vertically, at a right angle to the first.

Likewise, the lower sprocket had a leather belt wrapped around it—longwise in this case, while the other ran sideways.

But the belt on the lower gear was connected to the front wheel of, lo and behold, a velocipede.

Ugh, Jake hated those things: teetering, tall bicycles. You could break your neck on one of those things if you fell over. (Plus, they reminded him of Loki.)

In any case, this particular high-wheeler, or penny-farthing, as they were commonly known, wasn't going anywhere. It had been safely secured on wooden blocks a couple of inches off the ground.

Jake turned to his cousin in amazement. "What's all this, then?"

Archie beamed with pride and tucked his pencil behind his ear. "It's a giant centrifuge, coz! And guess what? You're the power source." He clapped him on the back, then pointed at the bicycle. "Riding that."

"Oh..."

"Maddox has been helping me with the welding..." Archie began bustling around and showing Jake the two large objects that were secured on the upside-down salad bowl, carefully placed across from each other.

One was a giant test tube, big enough to fit a full-grown adult. It rested at an angle, with the stoppered top on the higher end, near the middle.

Opposite the test tube sat a long sandbag of about equal size, well strapped in, like the test tube was.

Archie pointed at it. "When Aleeyah comes back, she'll be about the size and weight of that sandbag. We've measured it carefully. It's there to keep the centrifuge balanced. We don't want the poor woman flying off and crashing headlong into the wall from centripetal force the moment she's back. This thing is really going to get spinning, y'see. That's the idea, anyway."

"Huh," Jake said, staring at the contraption in wonder.

"The belts drive the motion using the power of mechanical advantage." Archie tapped his clipboard with his pencil. "According to my calculations, the gravitational force we're going to create will *squeeze* her molecules back together, *forcing* Aleeyah from a gas into a solid state."

Jake frowned uneasily. "That sounds pretty drastic."

"It is. I am not messing around." With that, Archie lowered his goggles over his eyes.

Lord help us, thought Jake. But, fortunately, he noticed that his cousin had worn his lucky bow tie. That should help.

Nixie, meanwhile, shut the lab door, then walked around the centrifuge to the other large structure behind it: a tall wooden platform on stilts.

It had a safety railing and a ladder leading up, which Nixie now climbed, holding her wand crosswise in her mouth. Like a pirate climbing the ship's rigging with his knife.

"What's that?" Jake asked, nodding at the structure.

"Oh, that's the observation deck," Archie said. "I'll have a good view from there of how the experiment is progressing. Right, then! We're almost ready to proceed. Now, where is our patient?" Archie glanced around the lab. "Aleeyah? Hullo?"

"There she is." Now atop the observation deck, Nixie pointed toward the ceiling, where a modest cloud of grayish smoke drifted with an air of nervous boredom. "Say hullo to Aleeyah, Jake."

Jake waved uncertainly at the cloud. "Morning, Aleeyah. You probably heard the good news about Red and Ravyn and Tex."

Nixie nodded with confidence. "We told her she's next."

Archie gazed up at the cloud. "Are you ready to get in?"

The cloud drifted up and down a tiny bit, like a person nodding. When it wafted down toward the test tube, the inventor climbed up onto the giant centrifuge.

The sheet metal warbled and reverberated under his movements as Archie clambered up the slope, then planted his knee near the top and pulled out the big rubber stopper using both hands. It came out with a *pop*.

The djinni hesitated, understandably.

"Do hurry," Archie said. "It's all been sterilized; we should minimize exposure to the air."

The Aleeyah cloud floated down into the test tube.

While Archie waited to make sure that all of the djinni's smoky bits were in, Jake noticed that the test tube already had stuff in the bottom. It was filled about halfway with a sloshy gray liquid.

"What's that in the test tube?" he said.

"Oh! That's, um, life soup, you might say."

"What?"

Archie shoved the stopper back into the test tube. "Nix and I have already assembled all the basic ingredients needed to build a human body."

Jake stared at him in shock.

Finished securing the stopper, Archie gave the test tube a reassuring pat for Aleeyah's sake, then dismounted the centrifuge like it was a slide as he explained.

"Nearly nine gallons of water provide the proper ratio of oxygen and hydrogen. A special nitrogen compound I invented. A generous helping of carbon, as well—that gives it its charcoal color, y'see. Then come the minerals: calcium, potassium, sodium, magnesium, iron, and so forth. Everything for building strong, healthy bones."

"And don't forget the magical ingredients." Nixie rested her elbows on the railing of the observation deck. "The two powdered Gryphon feathers that you gave us, plus... Should we tell him, Arch?" She flashed her beau a grin.

Archie grinned back. "You tell him, Nix."

"Tell me what?" Jake prompted.

She stood up straight. "Though the Gryphon feathers are renowned for their healing properties, we already tried it alone and it didn't work. Then it dawned on me that what we *really* need is a spell-breaking substance for a base. The most powerful magic-reversal agent we could get. After all, it was a dark spell from a Nephilim warlock that trapped Aleeyah in her smoke form."

Jake nodded. "Lord Wyvern."

"Correct," Nixie said. "So we knew we'd need something strong to undo his working. Thing is, the master wizards and witches that have already tried untangling this problem got nowhere with all of the usual solutions. But there's one ingredient they forgot."

"She's brilliant, that one." Beaming, Archie nudged Jake and nodded at her. "Tell him what you came up with, Nix."

Nixie lifted her chin. "Fairy tears!"

"Ohh, right!" Jake exclaimed, remembering. "They broke that dreadful spell Fionnula Coralbroom put on me once. What was it...? The Oboedire spell."

"Oh, that's a bad one." Nixie's eyebrows rose. "You were under that once?"

"Aye, before we met. The sea-witch put it on me. It made me obey whatever she and Uncle Waldrick ordered me to do for a while. I would've been stuck as their slave forever if it weren't for little Gladwin. She was kneeling on my palm when she cried a few tears. They dripped onto my skin, and that broke Fionnula's spell completely."

"Good to know," Nixie said. "If a couple of fairy teardrops got you free from the Oboedire spell, then this should definitely do the trick for Aleeyah. Because we put a whole quart of them in there."

Jake looked at her in astonishment. "How on earth did you manage to collect a whole quart of fairy tears?"

Nixie grinned at his question, but Archie poked Jake in the arm, then pointed at the velocipede. "You should go and get on the bicycle."

He nodded and walked over to it as Nixie answered his question.

"Have you ever heard of Charles Dickens?"

"The writer? Of course. I'm not that much of an ignoramus." Jake made sure the penny-farthing was secure before he dared climb up on it; he tried to shake it, but it remained firmly upright in the stand where it perched, secured by the wooden blocks.

"Well," Nixie continued, "I've kept this kind of quiet, but, for the past several weeks, I've been inviting the whole tribe of royal garden fairies down to the terrace, where, each night, I serve them their favorite bedtime snack and read them another chapter of Mr. Dickens' book, *The Old Curiosity Shop*."

"A classic," Archie chimed in, making final checks of his machine.

"They loved it," Nixie said. "You know how sentimental fairies are, especially when it comes to little children."

"Right." Jake nodded. Satisfied the penny-farthing wouldn't topple over, he used the metal step to climb up onto the bicycle seat.

"Well," Nixie said, "when the part I'd been waiting for finally arrived, Isabelle and Dani assisted. I had a whole box of tear-collecting vials ready to go. And on that particular night, we finally reached the chapter with the Death of Little Nell."

"Aw!" Jake burst out laughing.

Nixie shrugged. "It worked—like a charm, if I say so myself. The poor little fairies cried their eyes out."

"So did I!" Archie mumbled.

So did everyone who'd ever read the blasted thing, Jake thought, chuckling.

Indeed, some of Mr. Dickens's fans barely forgave the author for having killed off poor, sweet, innocent Little Nell.

"You're cruel," Jake said with a grin.

"I know," Nixie said sweetly.

"Enough jibber-jabber, you two. It's time to get this experiment underway." His final checks complete, Archie stood beside the centrifuge, his hands planted on his hips.

"Now, Jake," he continued, "in a moment, you'll begin to pedal, but not yet. There's going to be incredible resistance when you first begin, so Nixie and I will help get the centrifuge moving by giving it a good push." He beckoned to his sweetheart to come down from the observation deck.

Nixie hurried back down the ladder, then went and stood beside the centrifuge, opposite Archie.

"When I say go, Nixie and I will push, and you start pedaling. See, for every one revolution you do on the velocipede, the centrifuge will spin eight times. That's the mechanical advantage at work. Got it?"

"Got it." Jake nodded and gripped the handlebars.

From the corner of his eye, he noticed Malwort peering worriedly through the small window in the door between the two labs. Inside the giant test tube, Aleeyah was probably feeling even more anxious than the spider.

"Count of three," said Archie. "One...two...three!"

At once, Jake stood upright on the bicycle, mashing down all his weight on the right pedal while Archie and Nixie thrust the centrifuge forward in a counterclockwise direction.

The thing barely budged. Jake's bicycle stirrup scarcely descended by an inch.

"Again!" Archie said. "One...two...three!"

Once more, they all heaved together, and this time, the centrifuge creaked forward half a foot. The two leather belts groaned. The gears clanked through a few meshed teeth, grinding into sluggish motion.

Again and again, the three of them strove together until the front wheel of the penny-farthing was slowly gliding forward, moving the belt wrapped around it, and transferring the motion through the vertical gear to the horizontal one. The pole in the center began to turn, and finally, through their combined willpower, the upside-down salad bowl began to rotate slowly.

Then a little faster. And faster still.

Five minutes later, Jake was pouring sweat, standing up on the high-wheeler pedals, but the whole machine was now cranking. The big test tube still looked securely fastened in as it whipped around and around, as though it were a mad carnival ride of some kind.

Jake wondered if djinnis could get dizzy in their smoke forms. He certainly would if he were in the test tube.

The centrifuge was now spinning like a crazy carousel. The gears were whirring; the leather bands swept around their courses with a vibratory hum.

It got easier a bit to pedal, but Jake did not let up.

Archie was monitoring a pressure gauge, meanwhile, keeping an eye on how much force was being created. The centrifuge was now turning too fast for the inventor to touch the contraption without risking injury to his hands, so he waved Nixie back up onto the observation deck and went over to check in with Jake.

"You're doing great, coz!" Archie said. He had to speak loudly to be heard over the whirling, creaking, and whirring of his contraption. "You feel all right?"

Panting, Jake nodded and kept riding the bicycle like he was in a race. "Is it working?"

"Looks good. But we won't know for sure until Nixie zaps it with the lightning. Good thing she's a weather witch, eh?"

"Lightning?" Jake exclaimed, pedaling for all he was worth.

"Of course. Spark of life, some theorize—literally."

"Well, she better not hit me!"

"I'm not an amateur, Jake!" Nixie called down.

Archie nodded. "Don't worry, you're quite safe."

Unless my legs fall off. Jake dabbed sweat off his brow with his forearm. "How much longer do I have to do this?"

"Another five minutes at the most. The machine's own momentum should have it feeling a lot easier by now."

Jake nodded. That was true. At least it didn't feel like he was pedaling up the side of a mountain anymore.

"Very well. I've got to take my place up on the observation deck, so you just keep going, and don't stop until I tell you. All right?"

Jake nodded. His shirt was now sticking to him with sweat, his feet burning in his shoes. But he figured he owed his cousin the favor after being such a grump for the past three months.

Archie ascended the ladder and took his place on the observation deck. Jake watched his cousin at work, as he had so many times before.

The boy genius made notations, checked a timer, watched the pressure gauge, called encouragement to Aleeyah, and then ordered Nixie to ready her wand. He held up his hand, cautioning her to wait; Nixie adjusted her goggles over her eyes, then lifted her wand.

"On my signal, Nix. We're coming up on seven minutes now. Present rate of speed: eighty-seven miles per hour. She's reached four g's. Which means we are now ready for the lightning. Remember, one fast strike, and keep it under ten thousand volts. Brace yourself, Aleeyah!"

Egads, thought Jake. Eighty-seven miles per hour? Who could conceive of such a speed? But the two geniuses were throwing everything they had at the problem, and if Archie's science alone wouldn't be enough, now Nixie lifted her wand and began her incantations.

Dark clouds gathered up near the ceiling and began to roil. Jake warded off a shudder at the unnerving display of power and minded his own business.

Moments later, a rumble of thunder filled the lab. Nixie kept chanting, ordering the elements to gather and conform to her will.

No wonder Archie does whatever she says.

The magic-made clouds over the centrifuge were swirling in tandem with the motion of the machine. The thunder growled again; the air tingled with building pressure.

"Excellent, my dear! Steady on!" Archie said, nodding eagerly at what he was seeing. "Fire at will, Miss Valentine!"

Nixie flicked her wand with great precision and shouted, *"Fulmen percusserit nunc!"*

A lightning bolt crackled out of the clouds swirling over the centrifuge. Jake ducked instinctively and squinted against the flash, but he never stopped pedaling. The lightning hit the center pole, traveled down the metal sheeting to the test tube, and vanished.

The centrifuge kept whirling round and round. Nixie's summoned clouds were already dispersing.

"Did it work?" Jake called. The test tube kept passing too fast for him to see, and trying to watch it from here was making him dizzy.

Neither Archie nor the witch answered.

Up on the observation deck, they both were watching with absorption, leaning forward and gripping the hand rail, while the breeze from the centrifuge's motion fluttered their lab coats.

"I see her! Look!" Archie suddenly cried, pointing. "She's beginning to materialize!"

"Should I slow down?" Jake yelled.

"No! Keep going, coz! It's working!"

This excellent news gave Jake a renewed burst of strength. When Nixie let out a whoop, he glanced over and caught a glimpse of a blurry Aleeyah in the test tube, her hands planted against the glass, a look of shock on her face.

But she was conscious and alive...and with every wild rotation, she was coming more into focus, less smoke, more djinni.

Archie banged his palms on the railing. "By Jove, we've got her! Jake, I want you to slow the pedaling down. Give it some resistance. I'll get the brake. We need to get her out of there before she pukes."

Aleeyah looked bewildered and slightly green as she flashed by. Jake did his best to slow the pedals down while Archie zipped down the ladder.

Then the young inventor went over to the far side of the centrifuge, where he pulled a large upright lever that slid the wooden block brake against the whirling base of the machine.

Between this resistance and Jake's determination to slow the whirring pedals of the velocipede, the boys managed to bring the centrifuge down to seventy, sixty, fifty miles an hour, which was still much too fast—faster than steam trains!

But soon, the djinni was rotating at slower speeds, forty, thirty, twenty miles an hour, and within another few minutes, the boys finally managed to bring the centrifuge to a halt.

Jake's chest heaved and his legs felt like wet noodles. He could barely move to climb down.

Fortunately, Archie and Nixie were already on the task of freeing Aleeyah from the test tube.

Archie pulled out the stopper and cast it aside. Aleeyah lifted her hands out of the test tube. Archie and Nixie each took an arm and pulled the slim djinni spy up out of the glass container.

While Jake climbed down gingerly from the penny-farthing, his legs rubbery and sore, the two geniuses helped the reconstituted djinni down to the ground.

Aleeyah slumped onto the floor between them with a groan, holding her no-doubt still-reeling head in her hands. But they had done it.

She was back with all her parts in their proper places—even her clothes—a wispy purple top and baggy harem pants. Yes, the djinni spy was all there, Jake saw, from the vicious knife strapped to her waist, down to the tinkling silver bells she wore around her ankle.

The geniuses were making a fuss over her, crowding her.

"I say, are you all right?"

"How do you feel?"

"Give her a moment, you two." Jake also flopped down onto the cool stone floor, stretched his quivery legs out in front of him, and strove to catch his breath.

"Ugh," Aleeyah finally said. "Thank you all so much. It's so good to be back."

"How can we help you? What can we do?" Archie said.

"You must be starving. Thirsty?" Nixie asked.

"Just a little woozy." Aleeyah was already starting to look better.

"I'm all right, too. Just in case anyone was wondering," Jake said wryly.

Archie and Nixie ignored him, but Aleeyah looked over and stared at Jake for a moment in distraction—as though she'd just remembered something dire.

He lifted his eyebrows. "What is it?"

She didn't answer.

"Help me up," she said to the others, her ominous stare still clamped on Jake. "I must speak to the Elders this instant."

CHAPTER 27

Fair Is Fair

Jake had no idea why Aleeyah was eyeing him with such suspicion, but he shrugged it off and joined Archie and Nixie in taking her to see the Elders. Maybe the djinni was just surprised that a blockhead like him could've helped the brilliant pair free her.

The two geniuses were now supporting her between them, each taking an elbow and helping her up the stairs from the basement level. Jake followed. For his part, it was all he could do to pull himself up by the banister. His leg muscles still felt wobbly from all that frantic pedaling, but he was determined to walk it off.

Moments later, they emerged from the dingy basement stairwell and arrived at the lobby, where they beheld a startling sight.

A row of the knee-high palace gnomes stood guard across the opening to the grand hallway, down which lay all of Merlin Hall's official parliamentary chambers.

Jake's lips twitched with laughter at the sight of them, however, for these gnomes weren't wearing their usual little blue coats and pointy red hats.

Instead, they were dressed like tiny Beefeaters, the traditionally uniformed Yeomen Warders who kept watch at the Tower of London. Each one wore little black buckle shoes with red stockings and knee breeches, a resplendent red tunic adorned with gold and black trim, a white ruff around his neck, and a squat black hat.

One wee fellow carried a ceremonial staff and marched back and forth among the others with great pomp. He seemed to be in charge, so Archie and Nixie brought Aleeyah over to him.

Jake followed, biting the inside of his mouth to keep from laughing at the gnome in his official uniform. *Dani has to see this.* Carrot always said the palace gnomes were creepy, but even she would have to admit they looked kind of adorable right now, like grumpy little dolls.

Of course, she was no doubt having a fascinating first day of Lightrider training, so this was nothing by comparison.

The thought still brought a slight wince, so Jake focused on the matter at hand.

Obviously, the gnomes' formal garb meant the magical parliament was now officially in session.

There must be a great deal for the adults to discuss, especially now that Ravyn was back to report on what she might've discovered during her time hiding inside the Black Fortress.

Which was a shocking feat in itself, Jake thought. He wondered how she could have possibly eluded a castle full of villains for three months. Perhaps some good information might come out of it. After all, what Red could tell the Elders was limited, and Tex probably wasn't well enough yet to share anything he might've learned.

Happily, thanks to Archie's experiment, Nixie's brilliance, and Jake's tired legs, the Order could now add Aleeyah to the list of those who might have useful knowledge about what the Dark Druids were really up to.

Archie explained to the gnome in charge that the djinni needed to go and see the Elders at once.

Unfortunately, the chief gnome held up his gilded staff with a pugnacious look, signaling that the governmental hallway was a no-go. Of course, he didn't talk. They never did.

"You don't understand," Nixie said. "It's an emergency! This is the djinni who was stuck in her smoke form for so long. Dr. Bradford just brought her back. At least let the Elders see that she is here!"

The gnome considered this, tilting his head back far to get a good look at Aleeyah. Then he moved his staff aside, beckoned to the djinni, and started trudging down the parliamentary hallway, as if to say, *Follow me.*

But since Aleeyah still needed support to walk, they had to escort her. Jake quickly ousted Nixie as the djinni's second helper, determined to get a peek at what was going on.

"Hey!" the little witch protested.

"What? I'm just bein' a gentleman."

"Pfft," she replied.

Aleeyah gave Jake another wary glance, but did not shove him away.

Nixie followed right on their heels, ignoring the couple of gnomes who hissed at her to stay back.

"You do know I am Lady Bradford's only pupil, right?" Nixie said crisply.

At the name of the Elder witch, the gnomes stood down and let her pass. Nixie hurried after Aleeyah and the boys. As the head gnome conducted them down the opulent hallway, gilt-framed portraits of the Order's founders stared somberly at them.

In short order, they came to the first of three pairs of heavy wooden doors spaced out along the right-hand wall. Thanks to a previous tour of the parliamentary wing that Sir Peter had taken them on one day weeks ago when they'd been bored, Jake already knew that behind those massive doors lay the oldest part of the palace: the ancient, Gothic parliamentary hall.

The gnome stopped at the first pair of doors and used all his strength to haul one open. As the crack in the door slowly widened, it revealed the back half of the hushed formal chamber under its steep, vaulted ceiling.

A small but ornate auditorium with red-carpeted aisles, the parliamentary hall sloped down toward a dais in the front, but, presently, only the back half of the chamber was visible through the crack in the door.

Jake saw tall, narrow windows of stained glass casting colored light over the tiered seats, like wooden pews with desks. About three hundred representatives from all the magical lands sat there, resplendently dressed in their parliamentary robes—like a king's robe, only less fancy.

From centaurs to dwarves, wizards to wood elves, healers to djinnis, Greenfolk, and even a few ghosts present in their official capacity, they all sat listening intently to the speeches in progress.

At the moment, a female voice reverberated through the hall; Jake couldn't see the speaker, but the mood in there seemed grim.

Meanwhile, the gnome finally succeeded in opening the massive door wide enough for Aleeyah to enter.

Panting with exertion, the little fellow planted himself against it to prop it ajar, then he nodded at her to go in.

The djinni turned to Archie and Nixie. "Thank you both again so much for everything. You truly are brilliant."

"Pshaw." Archie turned so red that his freckles nearly disappeared, and even Nixie the cynic blushed, lowering her head.

Jake smiled at the djinni, open to being thanked as well, but Aleeyah glided past him with nothing but another leery glance from the corner of her kohl-lined eyes.

What the devil? Jake thought. *I had no idea she disliked me so much. What did I ever do to her?*

He snorted, puzzled and indignant as Aleeyah prowled into the chamber and slid into the nearest pew. The more he thought about it, the more he was offended.

Talk about ungrateful.

Just before the gnome started closing the door, Jake spotted some empty pews in the back and took a step over the threshold.

"Excuse me," he whispered to the gnome, "can we go in and listen to the speeches?" He assumed that any kid showing interest in learning about current events would be welcome to attend.

Archie nodded eagerly. "Oh yes, please, we'd like to observe the session, if we may."

But the gnome hissed—vehemently—and drove Jake back the one step he'd taken over the threshold by whacking him in the shin with his staff.

"Ow!" Jake yelped, not expecting the blow.

Some nearby representatives shushed him along with Archie, but Nixie snickered as Jake reached down and clutched his shin. As if his legs hadn't already suffered enough abuse today!

Closer to the gnome's eyelevel as he quickly rubbed away the pain, Jake scowled at his attacker; the gnome scowled back.

"That was unnecessary. But fine." Jake was beginning to see how *that* one had become the boss of the others. He seemed especially grumpy.

Meanwhile, sensing trouble, more of the tiny Beefeaters came jogging over in formation to help their sergeant shoo away all unauthorized persons from the parliamentary chamber.

Just before the big wooden door swung shut, however, Jake spotted Maddox sitting in one of the pews.

"Hold on—no fair!" he whispered, planting his hand stubbornly on the door to stop it from closing. "How come Maddox gets to go in there and not us? He's not that much older than— Oof!"

The chief gnome jabbed Jake in the stomach this time, pushing him back.

Archie chortled.

"Little menace!" Jake said, amazed, but he reluctantly backed off.

Nixie stepped between the boys, peeking into the chamber. "I don't think they let Maddox in because of his age," she whispered. "That's his birth mother giving the speech."

Just before the door closed, they heard Ravyn's final words.

"And so, ladies and gentlemen, I'm sorry to say I can now confirm that our worst suspicions are true. The Dark Druids are indeed building an army."

All three kids gasped, and so did most of the audience, then the door closed.

At once, Jake's curiosity was ignited. He had to know what was going on!

Alas, the whole troop of gnomes now surrounded Archie, Nixie, and Jake, hissing at them and herding them back from the door, prodding them up the hallway and out into the lobby once more.

Blast it! Jake thought in frustration.

Considering his own role in starting all this, when he'd stopped Garnock the Sorcerer from bringing himself back to life, surely he had a right to know what Ravyn had learned.

But how could he get in there? It wasn't as though he could just kick the gnomes aside and do whatever he wanted. Aunt Ramona had made it clear that if he followed his rougher instincts, he'd never be selected for the Lightrider program.

However.

On his way back up the hallway, a few feet from the lobby, on the same wall as the parliamentary chamber, Jake noticed something he had glossed over before.

His gaze homed in on a small side hallway under a pointy stone arch; the opening to it was draped with a pair of red curtains.

Immediately, he remembered from Sir Peter's tour that beyond those curtains lay a set of narrow wooden stairs that lead up to the gallery, where the public was usually allowed to sit in and observe the proceedings.

The fact the curtains were lowered right now signaled that this particular session wasn't open to the public. Which wasn't a surprise, with all that was going on. But Jake still didn't see why Stick should be allowed to go and hear the information and not him.

Maddox's mother had returned, true, but both of Jake's parents were still missing, taken by the Druids, if Fionnula Coralbroom was to be believed.

They certainly hadn't been in their coffins.

I'm going up there, he decided. Hang the rules; he was part of this. But he'd need a little assistance to pull it off.

Nixie looked askance at him, also noting the red-curtained passage. Archie glanced over at both of them, his dark eyes full of resolve behind his spectacles.

Well then, at least we're in agreement. He could see in their faces that they were thinking the same thing he was.

Of course, Jake knew better than to expect either of the geniuses to join him. Archie was not *that* much of a rule breaker, and Nixie would never risk her role as Aunt Ramona's only pupil. For the sake of her magical studies, she had to keep her nose clean. Jake could certainly respect that.

As soon as they gained the lobby, the gnomes left them alone. The three of them drifted a few paces away and congregated nearby, exchanging conspiratorial glances.

"I need to know what's going on in there," Jake murmured. "I'm going to sneak up into the gallery."

"How?" Archie asked.

Jake glanced at the witch. "Nixie, how's that invisibility spell you've been working on?"

"Are you crazy?" she whispered. "No way! Not for this. Spying on the government? Sweet Hecate, I'd get in way too much trouble."

"Well, I need some sort of distraction."

Archie leaned his head closer. "Use your telekinesis, coz."

Jake considered this, glancing casually back down the hallway. His gift had been wonky lately, but with Red back, it ought to be back to normal now.

"All right. You two just stand there and pretend like we're talking."

"We are talking," Nixie mumbled.

"Let's drift a little closer to the hallway," Jake said in a low tone, glancing toward the corridor. "I'm going to distract the gnomes and make a run for it. I just need to get through those curtains, then they won't see me."

"Clever," Archie said with a slight blanch. Unlike Jake, he did not enjoy defying authority, but he could be led astray on occasion.

They pretended to be having a delightful conversation, walking slowly as they talked, but it was just gibberish; they went as close as possible to the edge of the hallway, acting like they'd barely even noticed they had moved.

Some of the gnomes watched them suspiciously, but others paid no attention.

In truth, Jake was surprised any of them bought it, because, personally, he had never seen two worse fakers. Archie was famous for being a terrible liar, and Nixie had the most unconvincing fake laugh Jake had ever heard.

They never would've made it as pickpockets, these two, he thought as they drifted to another halt, still chitchatting about nonsense and laughing.

For his part, Jake kept an angelic smile pasted on his face, especially since he was the one facing the gnomes.

Sizing up the situation, he counted a dozen little Beefeaters guarding the entrance to the hallway. Once he'd distracted them, he only had to dash about fifteen feet down the corridor and then slip through those red curtains on the right.

He recalled that the cramped wooden staircase up to the gallery had been old and creaky, though, so he'd have to be careful not to make too much noise climbing it.

"You will let us know what you find out?" Archie murmured.

"Of course," Jake said, smiling widely. Then he grew more animated, telling them a story that required a lot of hand gestures. "So there's this new American game called baseball. Have you ever played it?"

His listeners eagerly said that they had not while Jake summoned up his telekinesis, praying it wouldn't go wonky.

"Well, it's kind of like cricket, only not as boring. You have two teams, y'see, and an umpire, with bases all around." He waved his hands to and fro, pointing and demonstrating everything as he talked. "Each team chooses a pitcher, and he *throws* the ball—"

Suddenly, a large portrait of one of the founders clattered off the wall and banged down onto the floor.

The gnomes whirled around to see what had happened. Why, he'd nearly scared them out of their little red britches.

Jake bit the inside of his mouth again to keep from laughing as a few of the gnomes glanced at him suspiciously, but the rest were peering down the hallway, their backs turned.

"Then the batter has to *hit* the ball—"

A second painting mysteriously crashed to the ground as Jake pretended to swing a baseball bat.

"If he makes a good hit, he's got to try to run. Run around *aaaall* the bases." He circled his finger in a wide ring, and, with a slight zing of power, a third portrait farther down the hallway plunged off the wall.

The gnomes, unnerved now, began running down the corridor to investigate.

"Go!" Archie whispered, waving Jake on.

He went. Already in motion, he dashed into the hallway, quick as a thief.

Five silent, speedy paces hugging the wall, then he dodged to the right, whisking through the red curtains while the gnomes were still trying to figure out why the portraits had fallen—as if it might be a sign of some sort.

As the red curtains stilled behind him, Jake was already lunging up the steps two at a time, landing as lightly as possible, ignoring his aching thighs. To his relief, the ancient stairwell quickly crooked to the left.

The moment he rounded the corner, he felt that his chances of not getting caught improved. At least now he was out of sight.

He kept climbing the creaky stairs, trying to keep his footfalls quiet—and hoping that the geniuses had had the presence of mind to get out of the lobby.

It would only draw the gnomes' suspicion if they returned to their posts and found that one of the three kids who'd been standing there a moment ago had disappeared, while the other two remained. Much more convincing if all three appeared to have moved on.

I do hope I didn't damage those paintings. In hindsight, he supposed that knocking the founders' portraits off the wall might seem a tad disrespectful if he got caught. He winced. A bit late now to realize that.

At least it had worked. That was what mattered, he supposed. That, and not getting caught. Well, Isabelle was the virtuous one, not him, Jake thought with a huff. The gnomes shouldn't have tried to keep him out.

A moment later, he reached the shadowed gallery at the top of the stairs.

He ducked down at once, not wanting to be seen by anyone in the auditorium below. It was noisy down there right now compared to the hush that had fallen over the crowd during Ravyn's speech. He could hear many voices arguing.

Eager to get a clear view down into the chamber, he crouch-walked forward past the few rows of empty wooden benches provided for the public, advancing to the solid half wall that overlooked the formal chamber below.

Tingling with the knowledge that he could get in serious trouble for this, Jake poked his head up just an inch or two, carefully peeking over the edge of the railing.

Then he watched and listened for all he was worth, determined to find out what was going on.

CHAPTER 28
Revelations

Guardian Ravyn Vambrace looked like a different person this morning compared to the wild and grimy warrior woman who had burst through the portal last night.

That was the first thing Jake noticed.

Today she looked entirely respectable, even ladylike, in her long brown bustle gown, her jet-black hair pulled back in a tight bun. She must've just finished her speech, because she was walking away from the podium.

But whatever she had said, Jake wished he hadn't missed it, for it was important enough to have set all the delegates at odds.

Across the chamber, members of the magical parliament were squabbling and pointing at each other, arguing amongst themselves, and shouting questions at Ravyn.

For her part, the weary Guardian was looking peaked and overwhelmed. Jake was startled to notice that she seemed unwell.

And, to be sure, her speech had caused a ruckus. There were boos and ayes flying all around the chamber. Unfortunately, the vaulted ceiling of the high Gothic hall made the voices blend and echo. From up in the gallery, it was hard to follow any one discussion—even for an experienced sneak.

Jake perked up when he saw Aunt Ramona hurry up onto the dais, lifting her hands.

"Order in the chamber! Come to order! Ladies and gentlemen, please!" The Elder witch rapped her wand sternly on the lectern. "Guardian Vambrace is still recovering from her ordeal! She's told us all she knows. Leave her be. We owe her a deep debt of gratitude for her courage and endurance. Ravyn, thank you. That will do for now.

You may take your seat."

Ravyn bowed to Aunt Ramona, then continued down the aisle, apparently headed to join Maddox in the pew where he was sitting.

But then a startling thing happened. Ravyn's usually taciturn son rose to his feet and began clapping loudly for her.

"Well done, Guardian Vambrace!" Maddox shouted, much to Jake's amazement.

Others joined in, giving the fighter a well-deserved round of applause for her sheer survival grit.

Ravyn waved it off with a self-conscious smile, then hurriedly slid into the pew beside her son, embarrassed by the applause. Maddox put his arm around his birth mum's shoulders and gave her a proud kiss on the temple.

Jake could barely believe his eyes. It seemed his friend had finally learned his lesson about appreciating the woman.

Thankfully, the round of applause also helped dispel some of the tension in the room.

"Settle down, please!" Aunt Ramona said primly to the crowd. "It's time for our next speaker. Ladies and gentlemen, Agent Josephus Munroe will be the next to give a brief report.

"But first, if I may, I must interrupt the proceedings to share some wonderful news Sir Peter has just brought to my attention. I know we all could use it right now." She beamed at the crowd, glancing around. "It seems my clever nephew, Dr. Archie Bradford, has just succeeded in retrieving the djinni Aleeyah from her smoke form." Aunt Ramona gestured toward the new arrival seated in a distant pew. "Welcome back, Aleeyah!"

The audience turned around and looked at the djinni with exclamations of surprise. Aunt Ramona started a round of applause in Aleeyah's honor, and the crowd joined in.

Aleeyah waved to them, half rising from her seat, but still looking nearly as weak and exhausted as Ravyn had.

Meanwhile, Tex limped up onto the dais, injured and walking with a cane, but clearly refusing to be daunted.

The red-haired cowboy had curled the ends of his handlebar mustache and donned his best duster coat to appear before the magical parliament. Ten-gallon hat in hand, he hobbled over to the podium and leaned against it.

Aunt Ramona backed away to give him the limelight.

Tex took a long, slow look around at the crowd. "Howdy, y'all."

"Howdy, Tex," a few in the crowd called back, chuckling, though many frowned at his unstatesmanlike language.

Jake grinned.

"Ladies and gents," Tex began, "y'all know the enemy's long had a hankerin' to make their own twisted version of our Flower of Life device." The American Lightrider held up his left arm where he bore the implant, just like Finderool, then he lowered it to his side.

"Again and again, they've tried and failed to reproduce one o' these here doodads—and thank the good Lord above for that. But you know that bunch. Once they set their minds to something, they don't give.

"Well," he drawled, "since they couldn't figure out how to make their own Flower o' Life, they resorted to stealin' ours, that dirty pack o' thieves. That's why they took me captive. Turns out they've been abducting Lightriders for a long time now. O' course, we all know Lightriders have been disappearin' and dyin' under mysterious circumstances for a while now. Ten years, I reckon. And from what I just witnessed, maybe even longer."

At this revelation, Jake thought immediately of his parents. He hung on Tex's every word.

"In the place where I was kept, they had scores of Lightriders—I didn't get a good count how many. Dozens, I'd guess. Maybe a hundred. Each one was confined in a sort of glass coffin. This took place in some huge chamber in the basement of the Black Fortress. A scientific laboratory."

He took a deep breath and continued. "I was kept in a dream state of some kind, comatose, with my arm rigged up to some weird machine that pumped m'blood and made my heart beat and kept me alive. Fed me by tubes inserted in my arm. It wasn't pretty," he said with a grim half-smile.

"They were careful not to kill me, though. They must've figured out by trial and error that once a Lightrider dies, the Flower of Life in his arm dies, too. Then it's of no use to 'em.

"It's not us Lightriders ourselves that they want, y'see. It's the Flower of Life. Why? Well now, that's hard to say." Tex glanced at Aunt Ramona, then at the crowd again, but Jake was reeling, wondering if this had been done to his parents, too.

Moreover, what Tex was describing sounded exactly like the vision Archie had confided in Jake that he was having back in Sicily...

"The best we can reckon," Tex continued, "they plan to open as many portals as they can all at one time and launch simultaneous attacks in multiple locations, sendin' that army through the Grid that Miz Ravyn just mentioned to y'all."

Jake stared, holding his breath.

The hall had gone utterly silent.

"That's about all I know," Tex concluded, giving the parliament a modest nod.

At once, Aunt Ramona glided over to him, taking the injured Lightrider by the elbow. "I know you all have questions," she addressed the crowd, "but we must let Agent Munroe rest. He's been through a terrible ordeal. For now, he's shared the essential points for our discussion."

Shaken as they were by his revelations, the delegates began clapping for Tex.

That pleased him, the ham. The cowboy tipped his hat to the crowd as he put it back on, and even managed to regain some of his Wild West swagger as he limped off the stage. "Thank ya, folks. Mighty kind."

Sir Peter helped him down the few steps from the dais, and Aunt Ramona returned to the podium.

"Very well, ladies and gentlemen, we have been given serious matters to think about. However, I suggest we now take our break for lunch to let the information sink in. When we return for the evening session to continue our deliberations, we shall begin to formulate our response to these findings."

"Wait!" someone shouted near the back of the auditorium.

Everyone turned.

Jake looked over as well, still in a state of shock from all he'd heard. He saw Aleeyah rising from her seat. The weakened djinni spy pushed herself up to a standing position and leaned on the pew in front of her.

"I, too, have news!" she said in a loud voice. "And you might as well hear it now, because I don't know if Archie's work will hold, or if I might still revert to smoke form. It's too important to risk waiting."

Aunt Ramona squinted at her. "Do you wish to come up to the podium, Aleeyah?"

"If it's all right, my lady, I would rather stay here."

"As you wish. But do speak loudly." Aunt Ramona gestured at her to proceed.

Aleeyah nodded, cleared her throat, and looked around at the assembly. "When I was trapped in my smoke form, I decided to make the best of my situation by gathering intelligence for the Order inside the Black Fortress while our wizards and scientists worked on the problem.

"Some of you may know that, as a djinni, I can blink myself into any place I've visited before, simply by picturing it. It's rather like our mages' conjurations. So even though I did not know *where* in the wider world the Black Fortress sat, I could nevertheless insert myself *inside* the building since I had been there before." Then she added an explanation for those who didn't know: "I was part of the rescue team months ago that recovered Guardian Stone and Dr. Celestus. That's how all this started. Wyvern hit me with a spell while I was mid-blink, and I'd been trapped ever since.

"In any case," the djinni continued, "with all the dark enchantments on the castle, it isn't safe to stay for more than a few minutes at a time, even for me. Moreover, not until now could I share with a single soul what I had learned.

"But, thanks to young Master Archie and Miss Valentine, I can confirm that everything Guardian Vambrace and Agent Munroe just told you is true. However, there is more."

Aleeyah paused.

As Jake peeked over the railing, he saw her gaze linger on Aunt Ramona up on the dais. The lovely djinni shivered in her light, scanty clothes, looking spooked by whatever was on her mind.

"Tell us, dear," the Elder witch encouraged her.

Aleeyah visibly steadied herself. "Most of you have heard of the dark elf, Duradel. The blind prophet of our enemies. The Drow priest is a great seer, though his talents have long been dedicated to evil."

The delegates sitting around Aleeyah nodded. She nodded back, as though reluctant to finish her tale.

But she couldn't quit now, Jake thought. The whole parliament waited on tenterhooks to hear her news.

"It seems that Duradel has given the Black Brotherhood a new prophecy. I'm afraid I…I barely know how to say it. For it concerns one of our own."

A ripple of alarmed murmurs ran through the ornate space. Jake stared down over the railing, riveted.

"Who?" several people asked.

Aleeyah gazed apologetically at Aunt Ramona before she said the words.

"The Griffon heir. Jake Everton."

Aunt Ramona's face turned ashen, and up in the gallery, Jake's blood turned to ice in his veins. He listened, frozen.

Aleeyah glanced around nervously at all the important folk of so many types and varieties.

"According to Duradel's prophecy, this boy has a destiny. Either to become the cult's nemesis, destroying them completely, or...the greatest leader the Dark Druids have ever had."

Low-toned exclamations raced throughout the chamber, but Jake barely breathed.

Aleeyah hesitated. "That's why they're after him. It's not because he ruined Garnock's attempt to bring himself back to life. It was, at first—but not anymore.

"Some want to destroy him. Others want to recruit him," she said in a loud voice. "Because Duradel's prophecy means that Jake will either smash the Dark Druids one day—or he'll smash the Order."

The parliament hall erupted at the news.

Jake drew in his breath and ducked behind the railing.

While shouts and exclamations exploded throughout the chamber below, he slumped with his back against the half wall and stared unseeingly at the floor. His heart pounded like it might bruise his ribs.

Me?

The delegates were beside themselves down there.

"This is outrageous! That boy started all this! *He* broke the truce—and now we all have to pay the price?"

"They say he destroyed Davy Jones, as well! He's far too powerful for any mere lad! It's unnatural!"

"It comes from his having two Lightriders for parents! Their match should never have been allowed!"

"Don't forget, his uncle was corrupted—a murderer!" someone warned. "What if he follows in Waldrick Everton's footsteps?"

Jake was appalled at the mere thought that that could even be possible.

He felt dizzy with dread as he listened to the clamor of the whole magical parliament yelling and arguing about him.

"What else does Duradel say?" someone cried.

"That's all I know!" Aleeyah shouted back.

"If this is true, we've got to get the boy out of here. He's dangerous! He can't stay here. We have to think of the other children!"

"Aye! Oubliette Jake Everton—and quickly!"

"Never!" Aunt Ramona boomed from the podium, silencing them. "You would believe the lies of the enemy? The blathering of this corrupt Drow priest? My nephew is a good boy—and he has already done great deeds beyond the capability of many in this chamber! He would *never* turn against us!"

Jake listened, stricken, to the Elder witch defending him.

"But, with all due respect, Lady Bradford, he has already begun to show signs of wickedness," someone shot back in a dire tone.

Jake recognized the voice of Lord Badgerton.

"Let none forget the boy was a thief when Guardian Stone tracked him down."

"He was starving!" Aunt Ramona yelled louder than Jake had ever heard her before.

The rebuke from the Elder witch rang throughout the chamber. "Listen to yourselves! Jake is just a boy."

"Well, Zolond was a boy once, too!" someone retorted.

That comment took Jake completely off guard.

Zolond? They're comparing me to Dark Master Zolond?

Perhaps the anonymous remark had taken Aunt Ramona aback too, for in the next moment, the firm footfalls Jake heard sounded like the angry dowager baroness marching off the dais.

"Order in the chamber, if you please! Everybody, please, just calm down..." Sir Peter smoothly asserted control over the chaos that returned across the chamber. "Let's all take a breath, shall we? I think it best if we adjourn now for the midday meal. We'll resume our meeting as scheduled after lunch, once we've all had some time to think about this."

While the representatives begrudgingly agreed and began rising from the pews, Jake sat on the gallery floor in shock, his back against the half wall.

He stared straight ahead at nothing, his heart slamming in his chest. His brain throbbed with incredulous horror.

Me? The greatest leader the Dark Druids ever had?

How can this be?

From the assembly room below, he could hear the general

rumbling of the delegates murmuring among themselves in worried tones and gathering up their papers. Their voices and movements echoed under the high, vaulted ceiling of the chamber.

As they began shuffling toward the exits, he heard creaking as the gnomes opened up the three pairs of heavy wooden doors. But Jake didn't dare look down to confirm any of this.

No, he was hiding. For if he peeked over the railing now and someone spotting him here spying, it would only seem to confirm that he was a bad seed, destined for evil greatness.

Am I? he wondered, aghast at the possibility.

As a thousand memories barreled through his mind, he could not deny that he was hardly the best-behaved boy in all the world.

For heaven's sake, he was only thirteen and he'd already spent a night in prison!

He remembered Newgate all too well. Of course, him being him, he'd broken out of there rather than waiting around to serve justice...

Then a rain of coins clinked through his memory as he thought of all the things he'd stolen as a pickpocket. Blimey, what if he had unknowingly taken the last pennies some of his victims possessed?

He thought of the times he'd hoarded to himself whatever extra food he could scrounge, instead of sharing it with the other orphans. And the fine summer days when he'd shirked his duties for his various apprentice masters, sneaking off to have fun instead. No wonder they were always beating him...

His constant bending of the rules, just like Maddox had accused him.

Maddox, who always did the right thing, even if it meant giving up Isabelle. Sure, the older lad could be mean sometimes, but then, so could Jake.

Just yesterday, he realized with a sinking feeling, he had ruined Dani's moment of triumph with his own petty jealousy.

He winced as this Duradel fellow's prophecy reflected him back to himself with more cruel truth than any mirror.

Maybe he wasn't quite Zolond.

Not yet.

But he rarely thought of other people's feelings, like Izzy did. He did not even know how to be humble and always unselfish like Archie, who had every reason in the world to be arrogant, with that brilliant mind of his.

He didn't always tell the truth like Maddox did. Far from it. He lied more than Loki.

He lacked the proper gratitude he owed to Aunt Ramona, and Aunt Claire and Uncle Richard, as well, and to Derek and the twins.

And to poor, heartbroken Janos.

Jake hung his head in shame at his own callous reaction of earlier today.

Why, the gallant vampire had sacrificed his own family to save Red, but Jake's private thought on the matter had been *good riddance* to a bunch of deadly bloodsuckers.

All in all, the realization hit him like a blow from a giant's war hammer.

Good Lord, it's true—I am *a terrible person!*

Yet he let himself get away with everything because he had the excuse of being an orphan. As if that had cleared him of having to follow the rules that applied to everybody else.

He thought of all the times he'd lashed out at the people he cared about with his sharp tongue and occasional quick temper. All his stupid fights with Maddox; his suspicions of Nixie when they'd first met her; always teasing Archie; his beastly behavior toward Dani yesterday. He was generally nice to Isabelle, because who couldn't be nice to Isabelle?

But he bossed everyone around constantly—insisted that he knew what he was doing—just so they should go along with his commands. How many times had he nearly got them all killed?

Jake felt sick, seeing it now. Even at this very moment, he looked around at where he was: exactly where he shouldn't be, of course.

What am I doing?

Oh, and he remembered Dani warning him back in the days when his abilities had first started emerging that such unnatural powers must be of the devil, but he had laughed her off.

Well, he wasn't laughing now.

This is terrible. I can't let this happen.

Become the Dark Master when I grow up? Destroy the Order? Betray everyone and everything I love? Turn out even worse than Uncle Waldrick?

Never.

Indeed, Jake realized what would ultimately happen if he ever did turn evil.

Red himself would come hunting him. Then he'd have to fight his own Gryphon.

The thought horrified him.

But in the next moment, the darkest memory of all returned—of that séance with Madame Sylvia in Wales, where he had first come face to face with Garnock the Sorcerer in his phantom form.

Staring at the floor, Jake wrapped his arms around his bent knees, pondering that night as the Gothic chamber finished emptying out below.

The night of the séance, all of the attendees had sat around a table holding hands while Madame Sylvia called down the spirits. A few ghosts had shown up to give messages to their loved ones—Jake could see them.

But no one had been expecting a visit from the evil spirit of the dead alchemist, medieval founder of the Dark Druids.

Garnock had come whooshing in through the wall as a terrifying wraith and immediately started attacking, consuming, the other ghosts.

It was horrible to see, just as bad to hear.

With his own two eyes, Jake had seen how Garnock gained strength from feeding off the other ghosts and even off the living, first projecting dark thoughts and sorrowful moods into his victims, and then draining their life energy to increase his own.

As a phantom, the dead warlock had been invisible to everyone else at the table, even Madame Sylvia, for she could only *hear* the spirit world, not see into it, as Jake could.

He alone had watched the whole thing unfold in horror. Thankfully, the phantom never realized Jake could see him.

First, Garnock had attacked the other ghosts and either destroyed them or scared them all away. Then he had gone around the table, feeding off the living.

Still a novice at using his powers, Jake had sat there frozen with fear, not knowing what to do.

Then Garnock had got around to him.

Without warning, the dead sorcerer had thrust a terrible vision into Jake's mind in order to frighten him so he could feed off his fear. Just for a heartbeat, Jake had seen himself grown up, rich and hugely powerful, sitting at the head of the Black Brotherhood...

The terrifying new leader of the Dark Druids.

Thus, Jake had already glimpsed that possible future, long before Duradel had ever made his horrid prophecy.

The vision had broken up quickly, for when Garnock tried to feed on his soul, he got a mouthful of Lightrider energy, thanks to Jake's bloodlines.

After coughing and gagging, the evil phantom had left Jake alone.

But what if the vision he'd given him was true?

Jake shivered with foreboding.

The image had unsettled him at the time, but he had refused to put any stock in it. He'd told himself that it was just Garnock's way of torturing him to get the most anguish out of him on which to feed.

But after what Jake had just heard down there in the parliamentary hall, maybe that wasn't the case.

Maybe Garnock had simply been showing him a picture of Jake's own dark future.

As the heir to the Black Crown.

He closed his eyes and lowered his head, sickened. *No. I can't let this happen. I won't. I've got to change. Right now, this very moment. Completely.*

Whatever it took, he would not allow this version of the future to become reality. No matter what he had to do, he refused to let this prophecy come to pass.

From this moment forward, everything changes.

He would straighten out his act—for real this time. Walk the straight and narrow.

Like Derek. Not Janos.

As much as they all loved the roguish vampire, he had ruined his own life with bad decisions.

Jake vowed that, from now on, he would be patient and polite, like Archie.

He would follow every rule they gave him, like Maddox. Always tell the truth, no matter how painful.

He would put his head down and work hard, like Dani—cheerful, uncomplaining.

He would, like Nixie, no longer expect special treatment just because he'd had it hard in life.

And like Isabelle, henceforward, he would be kind, curbing his temper and his tongue.

Most of all, like the noble Gryphon, he would learn to be unselfish.

At least, he would try with all his might.

From now on, Jake vowed, lifting his gaze slowly from the floor, *I am going to be good.*

Even if it kills me.

CHAPTER 29
Goodbyes

Dani had spent the morning at a classroom orientation with Finnderool's group of future Lightriders, but it was over all too soon. Barely able to contain her excitement, she rushed over to the library at Merlin Hall, eager to devour every book on Lightriding she could get her hands on.

There, she enlisted the help of the brownie librarian. While explaining the sort of books she wanted, she couldn't help but spill the big news, whereupon the wee fellow congratulated "the future Lightrider" until she glowed, then eagerly ran around fetching her a whole pile of books to help get her started.

Soon, books towered on the study table before her. She read until her belly rumbled and her eyes burned, but she was still excited to read more later.

Since there were too many books for her to carry, she chose three of the most interesting beginner guides and handbooks and checked them out proudly.

While the brownie librarian stamped them for her, Dani wondered if Jake had ever read any of these volumes.

Probably not. He preferred to learn by doing.

Well, Dani didn't mind extra reading and practice. On the contrary, she intended to dedicate herself to the program with all of the seriousness it deserved. She was not about to take this opportunity lightly.

For once, she felt her heart soaring with the thought that she could truly *be* something, *do* something important with her life.

Still walking on air over her brilliant future as a Lightrider, she headed down the graveled path across the quadrangle, then suddenly stopped in her tracks, for at that moment, an unwelcome sight appeared ahead. *Oh great.*

The skunkies.

Her favorite people.

Dani's heart sank. The shapeshifter triplets hadn't noticed her yet. Normally, she would glance around to find another route that she could take back to the Bradford suite to avoid crossing paths with them.

But future Lightriders didn't run from anyone, she decided, let alone a trio of obnoxious skunk shapeshifters.

Hmm. She wondered how they'd react when they saw her coveted silver sash. Then she snorted. They'd probably just make fun of her, as usual. At least on the outside. On the inside, they'd be green with envy.

Knowing that, she couldn't help gloating just a little as she continued on her way, hugging her books to her chest. But any faint hope that the skunkies might mind their own business wilted when the trio saw her coming and blocked the walkway ahead.

Big, moon-faced Charlie planted himself right in the middle of the path, where Prue told him to stand. The devious shapeshifter girl positioned herself on the right, while skinny Welton pushcd his glasses up higher onto his big nose, drifting along the left side of the graveled walkway. The runt of the litter looked nervous that the playful breeze zooming about the quadrangle might blow him away like an autumn leaf.

Dani wished it would. Then she noticed that Prue had dyed a front lock of her glossy black hair cobalt blue.

Showoff. She didn't want to admit it, but it looked rather dashing. Too bad. Dani would've been in a world of trouble if she ever dyed her hair, but Prue and her brothers could do whatever they wanted.

"Well, well," Prue said, putting her hands on her hips with a sneer. "If it isn't the latest recruit for the Lightrider program. Congratulations, Spot."

Dani checked her temper and pretended to take it as a compliment, ignoring the taunting nickname they had given her on account of her freckles.

"Why, thank you so much," she said sweetly. "If you'll excuse me, I have to get back to Jake. We're having lunch." Dani smiled, well aware that every girl at Merlin Hall had a crush on her beau.

Including Prue.

The spoiled shapeshifter's beady eyes narrowed to angry slashes.

"Not so fast, Spot!" she said when Dani moved to step between the triplets, determined to continue on her way.

"Where you going?" Charlie asked with a laugh, blocking her path with his large girth.

Welton tittered nervously.

"So. Gaia happened to like you. Who cares! No accounting for taste. I suppose you think you're very clever now." Prue folded her arms across her chest, and her two brothers stepped closer.

Dani lifted her chin. She always thought of her eldest brother, Patrick, in such situations.

Patrick O'Dell, Jr. had worked as a bare-knuckle prizefighter for a couple of years before sailing off with Her Majesty's Royal Navy. Patrick had taught her the value of a well-timed right hook.

"You three had better not start any trouble with me," Dani advised them. "Not today."

"Why? What are you going to do about it?" Charlie retorted. "Send your precious Jakey-wakey after us again?"

"I can fight me own battles," she said, her heart pounding.

Prue scoffed, but Dani shifted her books into her left arm. Just in case she needed her right fist free.

At that moment, thankfully, Sir Peter came striding across the quadrangle, whistling a tune, his hands folded behind his back. He was probably on his way home to the Chancellor's House nearby to have lunch with Jillian.

But, noticing them there, the dean and chancellor of Merlin Hall stopped, pivoted, and looked at them suspiciously. "Everything all right here?"

"Everything's just fine, Sir Peter," Prue simpered. "How are you today?"

He ignored the question. "Miss O'Dell?"

"Fine," Dani mumbled.

The wizard frowned at the Badgerton triplets. "You three, aren't you supposed to be somewhere right now?"

It was enough of a hint to make the bullies leave her alone. The skunkies made vague excuses and retreated, heading back toward the palace, but Sir Peter stayed planted.

"Thank you," Dani said once they were out of earshot.

"For what?" he asked in a mild tone, then gave her a wink and strode on. "Oh! I almost forgot..." He turned absently, his black academic robes swirling around him. "You'd better hurry along, Miss O'Dell. Lady Bradford was looking for you a while ago. Some sort of family meeting."

Dani drew in her breath. "Was she? Goodness. Thank you, Sir Peter."

"Cheerio," he said, and strode on, making his way homeward toward the elegant Chancellor's House.

Dani clutched her books and ran the rest of the way back to the Bradford suite, wondering what was afoot. Only now did she realize how she'd lost all track of time in the library. She was alarmed that she may have forgotten one of her duties in her pursuit of Lightriderdom.

I hope I'm not in trouble... Oh no! A dreadful thought occurred to her. *Teddy!*

She'd become so absorbed in her studies that she'd forgotten the need to take her dog out so he could do his business.

I hope he hasn't had an accident in the suite!

She ran faster, her heart in her throat, for the only thing worse than getting in trouble herself was when her dog made a nuisance of himself in the eyes of the Bradford adults.

After all, if she had little right to be there, Teddy had even less. He was a good dog, but every animal was sometimes a little naughty. All Dani knew was that if they ever tried to make her get rid of Teddy, she would pack up her things and leave too.

She pounded up the fancy marble staircase and went racing through the elegant corridors of the guest block, until she arrived at the door to the Bradford suite.

She flung open the door and rushed in, slightly out of breath. "Lady Bradford, you wanted to see me?"

She stepped into the suite, but the only one there was her dog. Dani looked at the floor, but didn't see any sight of doggy mess. *Whew.*

Teddy danced and yipped and ran in circles around her as Dani checked the various rooms. But she soon verified that, other than her terrier, no one was at home. *Where is everybody?*

Maybe they'd all gone down to lunch.

She venture into Izzy's room to see if the older girl had left a note. But the moment Dani peeked into her friend's little jewel box of a bedchamber, she gasped so hard that she nearly had an apoplectic fit.

All of Isabelle's things were missing!

Alarmed, Dani rushed to the boys' room and found the same situation. All of Jake and Archie's belongings had vanished too. Yet when she checked her own little chamber, her confusion mounted, for nothing had been touched.

What is going on here?

At that moment, she heard a faint knock at the door. It was a small knock, and it made her wonder if Gladwin had come back with another message.

Dani ran to answer it with Teddy barking at her heels. She scooped him up to contain him and opened the door.

Instead of a fairy, one of the little pointy-hat gnomes stood there, looking grumpy, as usual. The knee-high gnome held up a note that looked oversized in his tiny hand.

"Oh... Thank you," Dani said, taking the message.

The gnome just stood there without saying, *You're welcome.* What did it want, a tip?

"I'm sorry, I don't have any money."

It hissed at her but remained.

Dani looked down at the note. Her name was written on the front of it in the Dowager Baroness Bradford's own hand. She quickly opened it and read.

> *Miss O'Dell,*
>
> *Please join us in Parlor 12 downstairs as soon as possible. Follow the gnome. He will show you the way.*
>
> *Lady B.*

Dani looked down at the gnome again. "Will you take me to them?"

The gnome beckoned to her with its little gloved hand. Then it started trudging down the hallway, and Dani had to hurry. She set Teddy down in the suite. "Sorry! I'll take you out soon, I promise."

Teddy whined as she pulled the door shut in his fuzzy face, then she scrambled down the corridor after the gnome, her shoes slapping the marble floor loudly in the quiet.

The gnome led her to the first floor, through the lobby, and into a side corridor, and then, finally, to one of the many formal sitting rooms the palace had to offer.

As Dani approached the closed door to Parlor 12, she faintly remembered another occasion when Lady Bradford had called them all into one of these rooms to share serious news. That time, the Elder witch had told them she'd be taking them on a Grand Tour so they could stay ahead of the Dark Druids, who were after Jake.

Dani wondered if it was something big like that again. The gnome pointed at the door, then walked away.

Cautiously, Dani opened it and peeked in. To her surprise, the parlor was crowded with all of the major players in their lives.

The Elder witch leaned against the elegant writing table at the front of the room. Henry and Helena waited by the wall on the right, and Derek stood, arms folded, to the left of Lady Bradford's desk.

All her friends were there, Dani saw as she slipped into the room.

Jake stood gazing out the window with a faraway expression. He was dressed in gentlemanly garb, looking handsome enough to make her blush. Red sat contentedly beside his young master.

Archie and Isabelle were also there...

Hold on, Dani thought all of a sudden. *Why are they wearing traveling clothes?*

Maddox and Nixie had also been summoned, but they were dressed as usual, and looked as confused about all this as Dani felt.

"Oh good, you're here," the Elder witch said. "Please, come in, Miss O'Dell."

"Sorry I'm late. I-I was at the library." Pulling the door shut behind her, Dani noticed the grim, serious mood that hung over the room. Her pulse lurched.

Had something bad happened?

"It's all right, child. You are right on time. Please, sit down." Lady Bradford beckoned her toward a chair.

As Dani crossed the parlor, the Gryphon left Jake's side, prowling over to her and giving her an affectionate nudge. Dani patted him on the head, then sat down beside Nixie.

Her friend shifted sideways on the settee, making room. Dani lowered herself onto her seat, but as she waited to hear what was going on, she exchanged a worried glance with Isabelle.

The empath gave her a soulful look. Dani knew Izzy was still distraught over the murder of Janos's family, but even Archie did not look cheerful at the moment.

"What's going on?" Dani ventured, uneasy at how grave they all looked.

Jake turned from the window and walked somberly to the front of the parlor. Mother Mary, she had never seen such a haunted look on his face before—and for a boy who saw ghosts, that was saying something.

He seemed pale, shaken up by something.

Tensing with worry, Dani instantly wanted to give him a hug, but clearly, Jake had something important to say to the rest of them.

She braced herself to hear what it was. But, honestly, if some new disaster had happened, she was going to be furious.

Wouldn't they ever get a break? She had *assumed* that once Jake got Red back, everything would finally be all right.

Now it seemed perhaps she had been wrong. The next few minutes would tell. Lacing her fingers anxiously in her lap, she braced herself to hear whatever it was he had to say.

After a pause, Jake looked around at everyone. "Thank you for coming. The reason I've called you all together, as the adults already know, is that I am leaving Merlin Hall."

"What?" Dani asked.

"I'm going back to Griffon Castle. Derek and Red will both be coming with me. Henry and Helena have agreed to come along too, as Archie and Isabelle will be going home to Bradford Park. Aunt Ramona will stay here, however. As will Maddox, Nixie—and you, Dani."

She stared at him in confusion, then exchanged a baffled glance with Nixie.

"Will you be gone long?" Dani asked.

"I'm not sure," Jake said. "But you three need to stay here for the sake of your studies. Archie and Isabelle will have Henry and Helena for instruction, same as always."

In a heartbeat, Dani went from baffled to upset. "Why are you leaving? Did something happen?"

Jake glanced at Derek and Lady Bradford; they nodded to him as though giving him permission to speak.

Since when had that cheeky ex-pickpocket ever waited for permission for anything?

He was starting to scare her. Feeling uneasier by the second, Dani sat stiffly, waiting to hear his explanation.

"This morning, after Archie and Nixie freed Aleeyah from her smoke form—"

"They did?" Dani blurted out. "Sorry."

But she gave the geniuses a congratulatory look. This was the first she'd heard of this.

"As soon as Aleeyah was back in human form, we took her over to the parliamentary chamber. She wanted to see the Elders right away.

"Well, the session was underway and it sounded pretty interesting, so I asked if the three of us—Nixie, Archie, and I—could listen to the speeches. The gnomes said we weren't allowed." Jake lowered his head. "But, um, me being me—as I've explained to Derek and Aunt Ramona—I snuck in anyway."

"Oh, did you get caught?" Dani asked with dawning understanding. They must be sending him away as his punishment.

But Jake shook his head. "No. I freely confessed to what I'd done. Because what I heard in that session...scared me. By now, word is already spreading about the news Aleeyah brought back concerning me. I called you in here because I'd rather the rest of you heard it from me."

Dani frowned at him, increasingly concerned. "What news?"

Jake lifted his gaze and stared at her from beneath his blond forelock, an absolutely tormented look in his blue eyes. "Aleeyah found out that the Dark Druids have a prophecy about me."

"What?" Dani whispered.

"That, one day, I might turn evil and become the greatest leader they ever had. Either that or their nemesis."

Her jaw dropped. *"You?* Evil?"

Jake nodded. "I need to get away from here for obvious reasons. If I'm a threat, I don't want to draw the danger here to everybody else. Besides, I'm, er, not really welcome at the moment."

Red nudged him with his head as if to say, *Well, I still love you.*

Jake scratched the Gryphon's feathers. "I don't want to cause any more trouble than I already have. If there's any chance I really could become the leader of the Dark Druids someday, then, clearly, I need to buckle down and get serious about all the things I'm actually *supposed* to be doing."

"Like what?" Dani just stared at him in shock from across the room.

"Work on my studies with Henry. Train with Derek." Jake glanced at the two men. "*And* I'm going to start getting Griffon Castle ready for my parents when they come home someday.

"I know there are no guarantees. But after what Tex told the magical parliament, I've got to believe it really could be possible. Tex said the enemy has a program where they're keeping the Lightriders they've abducted unconscious but alive inside the Black Fortress as part of some nefarious future plan.

"Well, maybe my parents were taken as part of that plan. If so, that means there's a real chance that they're alive and I'm going to get them back someday. That it wasn't just some cruel lie from Fionnula Coralbroom.

"All I know is that if I ever *do* get to meet my mother and father, I want them to find me the sort of son they can be proud of. Not a scapegrace." Jake glanced ruefully at his aunt Ramona. "The way I see it, I've been a cocky know-it-all long enough."

"You are not!" Dani said, but Maddox gave a low snort.

"I am," Jake said softly. "And worse. But that's all about to change. It's time for me to be an ordinary boy and let the Elders do their job. I'm to go home and do the things a lad my age is supposed to be doing. I'm going to stay out of trouble, and, for once, I swear I am going to do as I'm told."

Dani's jaw dropped.

Never in her eleven years, ten months of life had she ever expected to hear him say something so un-Jake-like. Did he have a fever? Had someone put a hex on him?

Maddox seemed as confused as Dani was, while Nixie gazed at Archie with a pained look, realizing they would be separated, too.

"Sorry, Nix," Archie said. "Jake's family. He needs us right now." The boy genius glanced at his sister, and Izzy nodded.

"I don't understand," Maddox said to Derek. "Not to question your judgment, sir, but wouldn't it be safer just keeping him here?"

Derek sent the Elder witch an inquiring glance; it was she who answered.

"On the face of it, Maddox, you are not wrong," Her Ladyship conceded, sounding worried. "However... Last night, after Ravyn came through the portal, she sought me out privately, and gave me an additional warning that she did not share with the full assembly today in her speech." Lady Bradford glanced around at them. "We don't want this news getting out. But since this concerns our own dear Jacob, you need to know the situation—and I am confident that you can all be trusted."

Everybody nodded.

Dani sat with her spine ramrod straight, muscles tensed, her hands clasped on her lap. This sounded bad.

"What Ravyn also managed to learn during her ordeal is that the Dark Druids...have sent a spy into our midst."

Dani gasped, as did Isabelle.

"It seems we have a mole somewhere here at Merlin Hall. This spy is probably reporting back to the Dark Druids about all of Jake's activities, since they are obviously interested in him. Thus, it is better if we send my nephew elsewhere until the traitor in our midst has been caught and dealt with."

Maddox made a low sound of astonishment at this revelation, but the Elder witch sighed.

"At least now we finally know why our enemies are so interested in you, Jacob. I have already started adding more protective spells to both Griffon Castle and Bradford Park, and I have several more planned, one of which resembles the Kinderveil.

"Our enemies can scry for Jake all they like; they won't be able to find him. In addition, he'll have Derek and the twins to protect him. And Red, now that our dear Gryphon's back. Nor do I need to mention my nephew's rather remarkable ability to take care of himself."

"Even so," Dani said, staring at Jake in distress, "I should go with you."

"Not this time, Dani," Lady Bradford said gently. "You have been chosen for the Lightrider program. This is where you belong now."

Dani looked across the desk at the dowager baroness and her heart sank.

She could not believe the irony of her predicament. Her greatest fear for ages had been that she would be sent away from Jake and her friends because of her lack of magical powers. But now it was *she* who had been recruited into the Lightrider program, while Jake was the one being sent home.

And there was not a thing she could do about it.

"I'm sorry, but how is Jake supposed to be good without me there?" she blurted out, gesturing at him as she looked at his aunt. "I'm the one who stopped him from stealin' half the time in London.

Jake, you know it's true. You need me to keep you on the straight and narrow."

He gave her a tender smile. "I don't deny it, carrot," he replied. "It's just that the stakes are too high now. I can't rely on you to be my conscience all the time. I need to be, you know, responsible for my own decisions. Your sense of right and wrong is already sound. That's why Gaia picked you. Mine still needs a bit o' work."

Her heart clenched. But she realized that this was happening whether she liked it or not.

As the adults exchanged a few words on the logistics of returning to the two adjoining family estates, Dani's mind whirled.

She and Jake stared at each other, at a loss. They had been practically inseparable for as long as she could remember, so how would she possibly get through her day without him nearby? Let alone without Archie and Isabelle and Red?

The very thought of it frightened her. She felt as though *she* were the one being punished.

True, she'd still have Nixie and Maddox—and Teddy—but Jake was more or less everything to her, with the Bradfords a close second and third.

Yet her own panicked reaction told her something important.

It made her realize that if Jake needed to work on shoring up his conscience, maybe *she* needed to work on something, too.

Like figuring out who she was, other than just the tagalong friend of the famous Lord Griffon and his aristocratic cousins.

"When are you leaving?" she asked, already feeling desolate.

Jake gazed woefully at her. "Today. Our things are already packed. We'll go as soon as the meeting's over."

Far too soon, she was standing by the carriage, holding Teddy on his leash, and saying heavy-hearted farewells to all those who were leaving.

Archie gave her a hug and a brotherly kiss on the cheek. "Look after Nixie for me, will you?"

"You know I will, Arch. I'll miss you."

"Same here." His brown eyes were soulful behind his spectacles. "Good luck with your Lightrider studies. I know you're going to be one of the best the Order's ever trained."

She smiled gratefully at him, then turned to Isabelle. The empath gave her a pained stare. At least Isabelle knew exactly how Dani was feeling behind her attempt to seem brave on the outside.

Dani stepped closer and hugged her. "Tell me you'll be all right, Iz. You know I'll worry when I'm not there to look after you."

"I'll be fine, but of course I'll miss you terribly," Isabelle said.

Dani stepped back and looked into the older girl's sky-blue eyes. Izzy still looked troubled. "Any word from Janos?"

She shook her head. "We were all going to go and speak to him tonight, remember? But now I have to leave." She looked away. "Perhaps it's for the best. He did tell me to stay away from him. I don't know what I did that was so wrong, but he's been through so much, I suppose I should at least try and respect his wishes."

Dani squeezed Izzy's forearm. "I'm sure you didn't do anything wrong. You did exactly what he asked you to do. You got the coordinates right, you gave the Elders the message..."

Izzy shrugged. "I know. I just... Maybe if I go away for a while, I'll come back and he won't hate me anymore."

"Janos doesn't hate you."

"It seemed like it." She glanced across the grounds, but the mausoleum where their vampire friend had hidden himself away was not in view. Then she looked at Dani. "If you see him, maybe try to cheer him up. You're always good at that. At least let him know we still care about him."

Dani nodded. "I will."

"And if the Elders decide to take any action concerning him, will you write to me and let me know? I keep thinking surely they'll reinstate him as a Guardian after all he's done for the Order, but...I'm not sure he'd even want that."

"If I hear anything, I'll let you know," Dani promised. "But try not to worry. I really can't see how he'd be angry at *you*. He was probably just devastated over his family and you were just the first available target."

Izzy heaved a sigh and lowered her head, her blond curls swinging forward over her shoulders. "I don't know. It seemed more personal than that. If you do get a chance to talk to him, maybe you could... Oh, never mind."

Dani smiled haplessly.

Izzy smiled back and gave Dani another quick hug, then went to say goodbye to Her Ladyship. Then Dani bade Henry and Miss Helena stoic farewells and thanked them for everything.

She hugged Derek, too. The big warrior would always have a special place in her heart for the way he had tracked Jake down as an orphan and brought him back to his relatives. It seemed like a lifetime ago, but Derek was the first person that either of them had ever met from this whole magical world.

Next, Dani gave Red a hug. The Gryphon touched noses with Teddy, then went and hopped up into the carriage.

Finally, it came time for Dani to say goodbye to Jake.

As they stood together apart from the others, she felt like her heart was slowly tearing in half.

She read his face anxiously and saw the fear in his eyes over this situation with the prophecy. She'd be terrified if she were in his place, but seeing Jake scared unsettled her. Because this boy wasn't afraid of anything.

Not gargoyles. Not rock monsters. Not shark-men. Not even Garnock the Sorcerer. But this prophecy that he might end up evil had clearly shaken him to the core.

Dani rested her hand on his arm. "Listen to me. I know you better than anyone, Jake, and there is no way you could ever turn evil."

He swallowed hard and stared into her eyes. "Well, the Dark Druids believe it. And let's be honest, I'm not exactly *good.*"

"Yes, you are. Good enough," she offered, trying to coax a smile out of him.

He shook his head solemnly. "I've got to be better, Dani. I don't know how I'll ever manage to walk the straight and narrow without you pointing the way. But I suppose it's time I learned."

"You'll do it," she assured him. "You always succeed when you put your mind to something." She paused. "Say, can I ask you for a favor?"

"Of course. Anything for you, carrot."

"Take Teddy with you. He's better off at Griffon Castle."

Jake's eyes widened. "Really?"

She sniffled and nodded, a lump in her throat. "From what I'm told, Finnderool is going to have us running ragged from sunup to sundown with our Lightrider training. I mean, I don't want to part with Teddy any more than I want to part with you or...or the others. I'll miss him terribly, but he'll be cooped up in the suite all by himself for most of every day. It's not fair to the wee thing. He knows Griffon Castle. He always liked it there. Lots of room to run. He'll be happy there with you. And Isabelle will be just next door. You know how much he loves her. Plus, when you two are busy, he can keep Red company. I don't want him to be here alone all the time."

Like me.

"Of course. If that's what you want. I'll be glad to do it." Jake nodded and let her put the little brown dog, her greatest treasure in all the world, into his arms.

Teddy panted happily, unaware of what was happening. Dani patted his head and tried her hardest not to cry.

She couldn't believe that these, her two favorite creatures on the earth, would be leaving her any minute now. She didn't even know for certain when she'd see them again.

"Don't worry, I'll take good care of him for you," Jake said softly.

"I know you will, Jake." She looked away as his face blurred from the tears coming into her eyes.

"Hey, carrot, remember the time Teddy tried to eat one of the servants that Fionnula had turned into a frog?"

She couldn't help but smile. "What I remember most is how you changed them back into people with that spell from your aunt, and they were all bare naked."

They both started laughing, Dani in spite of herself. In spite of the tears in her eyes.

"Remember that fat chap with the hairy back?" Jake teased.

Dani made a face. "Blech! So disgusting!"

After laughing over the mischievous memory from their first magical adventure together, she gazed at Jake for a long moment. Once again, he had cheered her up.

"You don't think you'll be gone too long, do you?"

His smile faded. "I really don't know. I don't want to put the Order at risk, or any of you."

Dani felt a hundred protests rise within her at the mere suggestion that he might not return, but this was not the time to make them.

The decision had already been made. It was beyond her control. The situation was too serious, and they all would simply have to do what had to be done.

He must have read her distraught emotions on her face. "Aw. Come 'ere, you." Jake shifted Teddy into one arm and hugged Dani with the other.

She hugged him back hard and gave him a kiss on the cheek.

He held very still, as though soaking up her affection, memorizing how it felt to be together. "You will write to me?" he murmured.

"Of course." She nodded. "I'll ask Gladwin to bring you my letters. But you'd better write back!"

"I will," he promised. He gazed into her eyes. "You know, you're a right plum—"

"No. Don't say it or I'll cry. Just go." Her lips trembling, she stepped back from him and Teddy. "We'll see each other soon. I'll keep you posted on things here. Stay out of trouble and be safe."

"I will." His expression turned resolute. "Enjoy your Lightrider training."

She shook her head. "No. I won't enjoy it without you."

"No, enjoy it," he chided. "You deserve it, Dani O'Dell. You can tell me all about it when you write."

She managed a smile, her composure hanging by a thread.

Jake smiled back, then snuggled her dog. "Come on, Teddy. What do you say we go to Griffon Castle?"

Jake climbed up into the carriage, and Dani handed him the satchel with Teddy's things: his bowls, his blanket, his extra collar, and his leather chew toy.

Once Jake had sat down with the dog on his lap, he waved one of Teddy's front paws at her out the carriage window.

Dani chuckled, but more tears rushed into her eyes. Once again, she managed to blink them back by sheer willpower. Then she blew the whole carriage full of her loved ones a kiss as the vehicle started rolling away.

Henry was driving, but Derek had stationed himself atop the carriage, a rifle resting across his lap. Inside the coach, Miss Helena and Isabelle sat across from Jake and Archie, with Red lounging on the floor between them, his wings tucked around him.

The Gryphon gave Dani a silly look out the window, then the Bradfords and Jake waved goodbye to the three of them who were left behind.

In the tumult of her emotions, Dani was barely aware of Nixie and Maddox standing nearby.

The only thing that stopped her from breaking down in tears altogether was the knowledge that she would be a Lightrider one day. After all, elite future agents of the Order probably shouldn't blubber like a baby.

Already feeling forlorn, Dani watched the coach trundle up the arched stone bridge, over the naiads' stream, then continue rolling on down the drive, farther and farther away.

After a moment, Nixie and Maddox both walked off without a word, each in their own world of confusion and grief at this unexpected parting.

Dani remained behind, watching and waving goodbye until the carriage disappeared in a cloud of dust.

Only after it had gone, as she stood there in the empty drive, still fighting back a sob, she heard footsteps shuffle up slowly beside her.

"Well," drawled a deep Texan voice, "reckon they're off."

Her eyes blurred with tears, Dani glanced up at the wounded Lightrider. Tex was leaning on his cane, studying her from under the brim of his ten-gallon hat.

"You all right, little lady? Don't mean to intrude, but I promised the kid that I'd look after ya."

"You mean Jake?"

"Yep," said the cowboy, chewing on his toothpick. "Who else? You're the moon and stars to that there boy."

The thought of Jake's attachment to her gave Dani a pang in her heart. "Well, thank you, but...I'll be fine."

"Shoot, I know ya will. Lil gal's tougher than a pine knot."

Dani's lips quirked. "Oh, I don't know about that, sir."

"Well, I do—and it's a darn good thing, too. You're gonna need it."

She looked up gratefully at the cowboy Lightrider, squinting against the sun. "Do you think they'll be all right, Agent Munroe?"

"No question. Anyone comes along and gives young Lord Griffon trouble, he's liable to serve it right back to 'em twice over."

"I guess so."

"C'mon now, don't ya fret. I hear you got plenty to think about your own self these days."

She couldn't help but smile. "That's true. Have you heard the news? They picked me for the Lightrider program, Tex. I'm going to be just like you!"

"Well, shoot!" He managed a weary guffaw and clapped her on the back. "Yee-haw, Miss O'Dell!"

With that, he set his ten-gallon hat on her head.

"Yee-haw!" Dani echoed as the giant hat slipped down over her eyes and made her laugh.

She pushed it back up and smiled appreciatively at the

kindhearted cowboy. "You'd better take this back. It's a little big on me."

Tex looked pleased with himself for cheering her up as Dani gave him back his cowboy hat. He perched it atop of his own head, where it belonged.

"Now, you come on back inside, lil lady. Don't just stand out here a-mopin'. Let's go get us some vittles."

"Some what?"

"Lunch."

"Oh."

"You want my advice, you better rest up afore that Finnderool feller gets ahold of you. I hear he's tough." Tex turned her around, and they started walking back to the palace together.

The wounded man was moving slowly, limping with his cane. Dani kept pace with him. She was already feeling scared about sending Teddy away. But, of course, Isabelle would help take care of him...

"Nervous, tumbleweed?" Tex asked with a shrewd, sideways glance.

She nodded ruefully. "I don't suppose you've got any good Lightrider stories today?"

He grinned and squinted toward the palace. "*Weeell* now...as it happens, I was just thinkin' about this one time when I had to take a bunch o' diplomats down to see the squid people."

"Squid people?" she exclaimed.

"Dang ugly," he said with great conviction. "Got tentacles for beards. Even the females. Ink shoots out their noses when they sneeze..."

He proceeded to regale her, and Dani listened to his outlandish account with skeptical amusement as they slowly walked along. Though she was fairly sure this was just another of his Texas tall tales, somehow, it was exactly what she needed to hear.

CHAPTER 30

To Catch a Spy

As soon as Ramona had seen the travelers off, she lifted the hem of her skirts and marched up the staircase from the lobby, then down the Elders' private corridor into her apartment, seething.

Her blood boiled with indignation. Eyes ablaze, she had barely managed to hide her fury from the others. But now her wrath over all she had learned today would find its true target.

She slammed the door to the sitting room behind her and locked it. Then she crossed to the table with her crystal ball and dropped into the chair. At once, she projected herself into the dreamscape that served as their meeting place.

"Zolond? Zolond! Come here and face me, you treacherous old snake!" she shouted as she strode in astral form up the white, curling path toward the drifting charcoal gazebo.

The chimes sang on the air, but she was in no mood for their soothing tones.

"Geoffrey! Blast it, where are you? I demand answers, now!" She arrived at the gazebo and paced back and forth impatiently. "Zolond!"

He appeared suddenly across from her in the floaty gazebo, looking startled and sleepy, his snow-white hair sticking out in all directions, rather like a baby chick's. He did not look at all in that moment like the most evil person in the world.

"What on earth are you squawking about now, you old shrew?" he said, annoyed. "I was taking a nap."

"So sorry to wake you," Ramona said sarcastically. "But I demand an explanation!"

He sighed. "About what?" Then he dragged a bony hand over his hair, trying to squash it down.

Ramona glared at him. "As if you don't know!"

He lifted his hands out to his sides, at a loss.

"Don't play innocent with me, you slithering cobra! You sent a mole into Merlin Hall!"

He looked surprised. "Oh. Is that all?"

"All?"

Zolond frowned at her. "Why are you surprised, you daft witch? Of course we have spies. So does your side. It's the way of the world. Always has been, always will be."

"Well, who is it?" she demanded, pivoting at the edge of the gazebo. "If you've turned one of our own against us—"

"I have no idea!" He scoffed as though amused. "I am the sorcerer-king, Ramona. Sometimes I daresay you forget that. Such trivial matters are far beneath my notice."

"Zolond!"

"Don't bother me with these trifles. I'm going back to my nap. Figure it out for yourself. You're a clever girl."

Ramona inhaled angrily. "Tell me who it is or we are done here."

"Didn't you hear what I just said? I have no idea who the dashed mole is. Wyvern oversees such matters. I may receive occasional reports, but I have no involvement with the day-to-day running of such operations." He frowned. "Why are you taking this so personally?"

She narrowed her eyes. "Because it *is* personal, Geoffrey. You lied to me once again."

"Pshaw!"

"And—we know about Duradel's prophecy."

"Oh really?" He seemed a tad surprised. Then he folded his hands behind his back. "And how did that come about? Surely the *virtuous* Order has not been using spies, too?"

She lifted her chin, ignoring the question. "You'll never get your hands on Jacob."

He considered this. "Don't be too sure. If the boy wishes to join us of his own free will, you won't be able to stop him."

"He will never do that. He is a good boy."

Zolond smiled darkly. "We'll see."

Exasperated, Ramona left the conversation in a whoosh. She could still hear him, though, as she sifted out of astral form back to the here and now.

"Running away?" the Dark Master taunted her.

"Go to Hades!" Ramona shot back.

Zolond laughed. "Oh, I will, someday. All my friends are there!"

Fuming at his recalcitrance, Ramona flicked her eyes open, returning her awareness to the sitting room. "Maddening beast," she said under her breath.

But she had to admit that at least she believed him when he said he didn't know about the spy.

Still irked, Ramona pushed away from the table with her crystal ball and left her chamber, heading downstairs for a private meeting that she had previously arranged with a small handful of people whom she could at least be sure the spy was *not.*

Namely, herself, Dame Oriel, and Sir Peter.

She probably should've included Balinor as the titular head of the Order, but she deemed it too great a risk. It was not that anyone questioned the old wizard's loyalty, but he *was* growing slightly senile. If they included him, he might let something slip again and unwittingly tip the spy off that they were onto him or her.

Ramona had also invited Ravyn Vambrace to be a part of their confidential meeting, since she was the one who had discovered the presence of a spy in their midst. With her heightened Guardian senses, the warrior woman was sure to be useful in their enterprise of unmasking the traitor.

Exiting the palace by a back door, Ramona walked outside and proceeded down a graveled walkway, passing through the quadrangle and heading for the Chancellor's House, Sir Peter's home.

A small but stately Jacobean manor house set apart from the palace, the Chancellor's House dated from the late 1500s. It was three stories tall and built of reddish brick, its hue mellowed with time.

The ornate stone-carved entrance was tucked back cozily between a symmetrical pair of gabled brick wings that jutted forward on either end, and glistened with banks of mullioned windows.

Sturdy brick chimneys towered above the steep roofs, and matching topiaries flanked the heavy front door like a pair of green lollipops.

Because the Chancellor's House was not connected to the palace, Ramona was confident that they could talk here with strictest secrecy.

Moments later, she joined the others in Sir Peter's snug drawing room. It had a fine white fireplace, a Persian carpet softening the hardwood floor, and a low ceiling with dark timber beams running across the white plaster.

As they all exchanged greetings, Oriel smiled at Ravyn. "You're looking quite a bit better."

She was. There was more color in her cheeks, and the dark circles under her eyes were fading. She smiled back at the clairvoyant.

"I'm feeling better, thanks."

"I'm not surprised," Sir Peter said. "Never mind the healers—that son of yours has been acting like quite the mother hen."

Ravyn laughed. "It's strange, isn't it? I think he's actually starting to like me. At least that's one good thing to come out of all this."

"That, and you learning this news about the spy," Ramona said.

At that moment, Jillian poked her head in the door. "Would anyone care for tea?"

They all declined, and she retreated with a smile. "Very well. If anyone changes their minds, just ring for me."

Ramona thanked her with a nod. She had always found Jillian a charming woman—and her husband certainly did, as well.

"Give us a few moments, dear," he said as she withdrew. "If anyone comes by, we're not to be disturbed. I'll miss you!" he called, only half teasing, by the sound of it.

Ramona shook her head.

"I'll miss you too, dear." Jillian pulled the door shut with a chuckle.

Oriel smiled fondly, but Ravyn arched a brow.

Then Sir Peter turned back to the three ladies, gesturing to them to make themselves comfortable on the slouchy velvet furniture.

They sat down, and, at last, their little meeting was called to order.

"Well! It's certainly been an interesting day, hasn't it?" Oriel murmured.

"It's not over yet," Ramona said. "We have to get to the bottom of this, and quickly."

"Agreed." Peter glanced around at all of them. "Thoughts?"

They were silent for a moment, then Ramona glanced at the Guardian. "Ravyn, I know we can rely on you to use your preternatural senses to listen and watch around the castle for any signs of suspicious activity."

"Of course, ma'am."

"You know," Oriel spoke up, tilting her head, "Ravyn's not the only one who can keep watch. As head clairvoyant, I could certainly speak to the castle ghosts to keep their eyes and ears open. Ghosts make excellent spies—or counterspies, in this case. I'm sure they'd all be happy to help. At least the more benevolent spirits, like Constanzio, the Gray Lady, and perhaps a few others."

"Excellent idea, Oriel," Ramona said.

Peter nodded. "A good start. So...any thoughts of who our spy might be?"

Oriel hesitated. "Well, I hate to bring it up, but Prince Janos *is* on the grounds of Merlin Hall at the moment. And we all know his loyalties have been divided for a long time."

"You think Janos might be the spy?" Ravyn turned to Oriel in surprise.

Even Ramona raised an eyebrow.

"I doubt it." Sir Peter frowned. "The poor fellow just sacrificed his entire family for the cause."

Oriel shrugged. "Still. We know he's long been a double agent."

Ramona nodded to her friend. "I can understand why you would doubt him. But ever since the children came into the picture—Jake, I mean, and Isabelle, and all of them, really—Janos seems to have been sliding in our direction. He's very fond of them. I can't imagine he'd do anything to hurt them."

"Well, he's on our side now, whether he likes it or not," Peter said. "The Dark Druids will never have him back after he freed Red, helped Ravyn, and brought back Tex. If you ask me, they're probably out for his blood as much as ours, if not more."

"Good point," Oriel admitted.

"I could talk to him," Ravyn offered.

Peter gestured for patience. "Give the poor man a few days to mourn. I wouldn't try him yet. It's too soon to push him."

Ravyn nodded.

"I had another thought, though," Peter said.

"Yes?" Ramona asked.

"Whoever the mole is, our primary objective should be ending his or her communication with our enemies, correct?"

They nodded.

"Well, why not use a silencing spell so this traitor can't talk to anyone?"

A smile spread across Ramona's face. "You are much too cunning for so amiable a man."

Peter grinned. "I'll work the spell. It takes a few days to prepare, but it's sure to be effective. I developed a new variation as the ultimate means of quieting students who won't stop talking in class."

Even stern Ravyn Vambrace chuckled at that.

Ramona appreciated his jest. They were all on edge, but the young wizard had such a talent for defusing tension.

"Very well, what else can we do?" Oriel mused aloud after a moment.

"Here's a thought," Ramona said. "We would need some pretext for doing this, but what if we put together a panel of our most skilled and trustworthy empaths to interview our possible suspects? I'm not sure what excuse we could give for conducting these interviews..."

"But if we would say it applied to everyone," Ravyn chimed in.

Oriel nodded. "And if we started with the Elders, leading by example, it would demonstrate that everyone is expected to cooperate."

"Oh, I hope it isn't one of the Elders," Ramona murmured.

Ravyn gave a terse nod. "It's a good idea. Only someone who's guilty or at least hiding something would refuse."

"*Not*...necessarily," Peter said. "We wish to create harmony among all of Magick-kind here at Merlin Hall, ladies. I fear this tactic seems a trifle heavy-handed. 'Twould bring an atmosphere of needless paranoia for everybody. Only one is guilty; the rest are innocent.

"Besides, I hate to lie to our own people—or subject the public to such intrusive measures. It could especially cause problems among members of the magical parliament. You know a lot of them have giant egos."

Ravyn snorted. It was definitely true.

"An interview by an empath is no small thing," he continued. "That is serious inner scrutiny. We don't wish to become the Inquisition here."

"Fair enough," Ramona said, then she sighed, out of ideas.

It was only then that Ramona realized she herself had a very big secret to hide. She quickly masked a look of shock as she wondered all of a sudden if a panel of empaths would be able to tell that she had been meeting secretly with the head of the Dark Druids.

Good Lord, what would they think of that? She herself might come under suspicion for being the mole!

Her heart was pounding as Peter spoke up again.

"Perhaps we could compromise, though," the wizard said. "If all else fails, the interviews *do* sound like an effective last resort."

"I agree," Ravyn said, a warlike gleam in her dark eyes. "We could claim that the reason for them was that something had been stolen, for example. Some important artifact of Merlin Hall. A historic jewel of some sort?"

Ramona and Peter both nodded, but Oriel looked at Ravyn with amusement.

"I thought Guardians didn't know how to lie," the clairvoyant Elder said.

Ravyn grinned. "Oh, we do—but only when using deception as a battle tactic."

Oriel chuckled. "I see."

"Very well." Sir Peter looked around at the ladies. "It seems we all have our starting points, at least. Ramona, why don't you begin putting together a list of our most qualified empaths—just in case—while I get to work on the silencing spell? Oriel can recruit the castle ghosts as our counterspies, and Ravyn can use her Guardian senses to keep watch, and then question Janos in a few days, as well.

"But do be gentle with him, won't you?" he added. "I can't even imagine what the poor fellow's been through."

"I'll go easy on him," Ravyn promised.

"Good. Well, then! In the meanwhile, let's just keep our fingers crossed that whoever the traitor is, he hasn't told the enemy anything too important yet."

They nodded, clear on their tasks.

"Once we find this person," Ravyn said, "what do we do with them?"

All of their expressions darkened, but nobody said a word, for they all knew.

By tradition, the Order burned traitors at the stake.

CHAPTER 31

Dark Visions, Deepening Gloom

Archie stared out the carriage window, bleary-eyed, while the others dozed, but, lost in his brooding, he barely saw the sunlit English countryside rolling by.

The only one besides him in the coach who seemed fully awake was little Teddy. Snuggled next to Isabelle, the wee brown dog sat across from him, panting, watchful, and alert.

The carriage smelled of dog breath and Gryphon feathers.

Red snored quietly, taking up the whole carriage floor, and thus leaving the four human passengers no choice but to prop their feet on him as though he were a giant feathered footstool. He didn't seem to care.

As for the people, Izzy's head bobbed against Miss Helena's shoulder in time with the rumbling of the carriage wheels; the governess leaned her cheek on Izzy's blond hair.

Everyone's eyes were closed except Archie's. Beside him, Jake had nodded off with a newspaper over his face to shield his eyes from the midday glare.

The men were topside, of course, Henry driving, Derek waiting with rifle in hand to shoot anything that came at them with a bad attitude.

Archie wondered if he should go up there, too, into the fresh air. He felt restless and caged inside this stuffy coach; he had too much to think about, and he was sick of thinking.

It was all too grim.

Truth be told, he feared he was still a bit in shock, though he'd taken pains not to burden anyone with his horrified reaction to his cousin's revelations.

Jake was already horrified *enough* about the prophecy, and Archie refused to make it any worse for his best mate.

But, privately, Archie was aghast.

Everything Jake had reported overhearing in his eavesdropping session had only confirmed Archie's *last* round of visions, which had started months ago, during their Grand Tour.

All of it had just proven true, accurate down to the smallest detail.

Particularly the part Jake had shared about Tex's account of unconscious Lightriders being kept alive in glass coffins with tubes in their arms.

Archie had already seen this—months ago—in his dreams.

Of course, the Order would rescue them, somehow, someway, sometime. That was not what concerned him.

What had shocked him to the core was this ghastly confirmation of his gift.

He did not want it to be true. But the thing was unavoidable now. There was no more denying it. The Kinderveil had definitely lifted and revealed him to be some type of clairvoyant.

He knew that he should tell his busy, distant parents, and soon. But, frankly, he wasn't ready to deal with the headache of their reactions when he himself barely knew what to think.

Father was going to be so happy. And Mother was sure to make some big, embarrassing fuss. Lord, she'd probably throw him a party. Ugh.

Because Archie wanted no part of this talent he'd inherited from them, he feared his parents would be insulted. He didn't want to hurt their feelings. But didn't have the heart to pretend to be happy about this.

Still, like it or not, there it was.

As if the world did not think him eccentric enough—as if his head were not already overstuffed with more facts than one brain should carry—now it seemed the weirdo "boy genius" could also access hidden knowledge in his dreams.

Archie sighed and slumped down in his seat at the thought. He tried to cheer himself up with the reminder that some scholars believed his idol, Leonardo da Vinci, had possessed certain uncanny gifts, as well. Even Sir Francis Bacon had been a known visionary...

For once in his life, however, Archie was loath to follow in their footsteps.

Indeed, ever since Jake had shared his information, he had been in a quiet and polite state of private terror. The reason was simple.

If his first round of visions had been true, then the probability increased exponentially that the next one would come true as well—the vision that frightened him so much that he hadn't even mentioned it to Jake.

He felt as though saying it out loud would only make it real.

But it *was* real, wasn't it?

Eyewitness accounts had just confirmed that the Lightriders were being held prisoner, exactly as he'd glimpsed months ago. He had been right.

As usual.

But that meant the question now was not *if* but *when* one of their tight-knit group was going to die.

And, more importantly, whom?

He squeezed his eyes shut at such a hideous question. Teddy gave a small whine and cocked his head curiously, as though sensing Archie's distress.

Beyond distress. These questions were torture.

How awful to know in advance that death was coming for one of them, and yet to be helpless to do anything about it—especially for an expert problem solver like Archie.

That was the main reason why he hadn't told the others yet. What was the point of forcing them to share his torment, when he had so little information?

Should they go around petrified twenty-four seven, like him?

Certainly not.

They had enough troubles of their own. Jake, shaken by the prophecy. Isabelle, wrecked over the death of Janos's family. Dani, just starting out her bright future with the Lightriders.

And Nixie.

Her Archie couldn't tell most of all, because he knew she would go too far in figuring out how to protect them. His witchy little sweetheart wasn't always the *best* when it came to good and evil.

Rather like Jake.

They were both pragmatics, unafraid of stepping over certain lines if they had to, but Archie knew down to the marrow of his bones this wasn't wise. Himself, he was always very careful of staying within certain ethical boundaries.

He had to. His beloved science could be too dangerous if one started ignoring right and wrong. He did not want to turn into Zolond, after all, making monsters in the lab.

Plus, he had seen those dreadful screens showing battles past, present, and future in Odin's war room when he and Jake had visited Valhalla.

As the Norse god of war before he had retired, Odin had a whole wing of his gleaming white palace dedicated to the art of war.

Archie would never forget the scenes he had witnessed on all those countless moving picture screens. His heart had nearly broken to realize that, at some point in the future, mankind would turn his beloved flying machines into weapons of war. He did not *ever* want to become one of those scientists who helped take a wonder of invention and turn it into an instrument of death.

Nixie, however, wasn't quite as persnickety about such boundaries. She and Jake were more the type who'd do whatever it took to get the job done.

Archie did not blame them for this, of course. Both had been alone for a long time and struggled to survive. Who was he to judge? As the son of a lord, *he* had never had to endure that sort of hardscrabble life.

But it was just a fact. He knew that if push came to shove, his dear Nix might well resort to using her magic in ways that Aunt Ramona would not approve of.

Archie was banking on the hope that it would not come to that.

If only his visions would hurry up and give him more specifics! But, at present, he had insufficient information to take any sort of measures against this vague threat of impending doom.

He knew no variables: no who, what, when, where, or how.

So what could he do? Be ready around the clock to combat anything and everything?

Thus his addiction to the little Italian coffees.

But when the nervous energy they gave him wore off, he was oh-so-tired. More exhausted every day. He could feel fatigue starting to break him down. His mind wasn't as sharp as it had been.

Maybe he should sleep.

Up until today's eye-popping confirmation that his visions weren't just a figment, Archie hadn't been sure which was more important: sleeping to try and get answers, or staying awake to watch out for catastrophe.

He let out another sigh, heavy-hearted with his secret.

If he could not prevent anything from happening, then he wasn't sure he even wanted to know which of them was fated to die. Unfortunately, he couldn't stop obsessing over the matter.

What if it's me? What if it's Jake? What if it's my sister? Or Dani? God, what if it's Nixie? Or Derek or Helena or good old Henry? What if it's Mum or Dad?

Each possibility brought a different flavor of pain. His mind spun through the awful choices like the click-click-clicking of some dastardly carnival roulette game.

He shut his eyes again, queasy with the rocking of the coach and the torment of his dreadful secret.

Perhaps there was a chance that he was wrong. That it was all just a marvelous coincidence or maybe just a one-time thing.

His mathematical mind knew better, of course; the odds of that were ridiculous. Nevertheless, he clung to this threadbare hope.

But never in his life had knowledge felt like such a curse. Never had his brain posed questions whose answers he was too scared to learn.

He did his best to ignore the knots in his stomach and flicked his bleary eyes open once again, determined not to doze off like everybody else had.

For, unlike them, Archie was afraid of what he might see in his dreams.

PART III

CHAPTER 32
The Making of a Gentleman

For three weeks, Jake applied himself diligently to becoming a better boy.

It was grueling. Harder, maybe, than living in the rookery. Because back then, at least he'd had the freedom to do whatever he pleased. All he'd had to worry about—besides food—was staying a step ahead of the adults who would've liked to control him.

But now, each day, he squashed his own stubbornness and willingly submitted himself to Derek and Henry and Helena's just authority.

Anything was better than turning evil.

So, he often thought, *this is discipline.*

He began by holding himself strictly to the schedule the warrior and the scholar had designed for him. That in itself was rough. Wake at six. Promptly make his bed. Splash his face and dress for the morning's exercise. Run three miles, alone, thinking, Derek timing him.

Then a bit of sparring against the master Guardian, learning more fighting techniques, a bit of footwork—even learning from the hardened soldier how to better use his trusty blade, Risker.

It was the least he could do, considering the Norse god Odin himself had given it to him as a gift.

This was followed by as many push-ups as he could do on the shady terrace, sit-ups, and other painful things all meant to make him stronger.

Dash upstairs, clean himself from head to toe, and make himself presentable for the day. The gentlemanly clothes that a young lord had to learn to wear were stiff and well cut. Crisp linen shirts and a starched cravat that felt like a dog collar, but he was getting used to it. Waistcoats with neat, tidy buttons, tailored trousers and matching daytime coat, fine leather dress shoes.

No food was given to him until he passed inspection, then he ate sitting ramrod straight at the table.

Miss Helena watched over his table manners like a hawk. He learned how to manage a soft-boiled egg in a dainty eggcup, how and when to use a fish fork, how to sip his morning tea without slurping.

Next: read the front page of the *London Times*. Reflect on what a daft world it was. Return to his chamber. Brush his teeth.

Then arrive promptly in the library on the ground floor of the castle as the grandfather clock bonged nine times.

At precisely nine a.m., plop down onto a hard wooden chair—no, hold on; a proper English gentleman never plopped.

The new Jake whisked his coattails out behind him and sat down correctly, then cracked open the books without complaint. Then it was Henry's turn to have at him with the lessons, filling up his brain.

Monsieur DuVal was a much stricter tutor than Constanzio the ghost, to be sure, and, as a result, Jake actually started learning. Took an interest. Asked questions, wrote down notes.

Every now and then, he glanced up from under his forelock and noticed Henry studying him as though shocked by his transformation in progress.

Back and forth, Jake marched through his castle from one duty to the next without so much as a grumble, but each time he passed through the great hall, he took a long, searing look at the portrait of his parents above the fireplace.

As autumn settled in, they remained his inspiration for enduring all this discomfort.

He just *knew* they were coming back. They had to. Now that he knew there was a very good chance that they were still alive, he refused to believe otherwise.

One day, they would all be a family again, and when that day came, he intended to be ready.

That was why he worked so hard for once in his life. He did not want them returning from twelve years of captivity in the Black Fortress to find their only son had grown up into a wild, unlettered heathen.

He wanted with all his heart to make them proud of him when

they finally saw each other again for the first time—the first time he could remember, anyway.

The last time he'd seen them, he had been that little bald baby sitting on his mother's lap in that family portrait above the mantel. But nowadays he could look in the mirror and see that he resembled his father Jacob in that painting more and more every day.

Onward.

Continuing the rounds of each day: Jake's study time with Henry went along relentlessly till noon. Then he hurried over to Bradford Park, where he joined Archie in his lab for science class.

There was none of their usual joking around here. Archie had Jake scoop amoebas out of the pond and study them under the microscope, sketching what he saw.

He had him carefully weighing out tiny amounts of powdered chemicals and burning various combinations of them in test tubes, explaining how they interacted when heat was added.

These concoctions usually stank to high heaven, but Jake managed not to burn down the lab. Professor Archie wanted him to dissect a frog, as well, but Isabelle ran in and forbade it with exclamations of shocked horror.

She grabbed the frog and bolted out of the lab with the creature, tossing it into the pond. The boys just looked at each other and decided to pass on that experiment.

Three times a week, she became his teacher as well—his equestrian instructor. A gentleman had to know how to ride a horse. So Jake would change into his riding breeches and boots, his tidy jacket and hunt cap, mount up on various horses from the Bradfords' stable, and take a riding lesson from the empath.

It was a great advantage, learning how to communicate with horses from someone who could actually talk to animals. True, Isabelle had been glum and out of sorts and, well, just not *herself* ever since they'd left Merlin Hall, but during their riding lessons, she turned all business.

"Easy, coz, you're pulling too hard on his mouth. Don't kick; just press his side with your leg. That'll help him understand which way you want to go."

Jake quickly learned to post at the trot, holding the riding crop in his pinky finger just so, though Isabelle was very strict about never actually using it. Only the smallest of taps was permissible.

"Anyone who'd whip a horse does not deserve to get anywhere near one," she'd declare.

After his riding lesson was over, his duties included cooling the horse down and caring for the animal afterward. Give him fresh water. Remove the tack. Brush him down. Check his hooves. Give him an apple or a carrot for his reward.

Isabelle watched Jake pumping water from the well for his horse one day. "A good horseman always puts his animal before himself. That's a lesson that goes back all the way to the medieval knights..."

Sometimes they went on trail rides through the stained-glass October woods, soaking in the beauty of the changing leaves with the breeze rustling through them, and the gathering chill in the air.

Other times, Derek joined them on his big black steed. Whenever they approached the outer boundary of the cousins' adjacent estates, Jake could feel some peculiar form of energy in the air.

"What is that? Do you hear that sort of hum?" he asked Isabelle one day when they rode to the edge of the property.

He could almost believe it was just his imagination, but the horse heard it too; he could tell by the way the gray's ears swiveled about nervously at the sound.

"That is the magical perimeter Aunt Ramona established around our two estates," Isabelle replied.

"Protective spells," Derek added, riding with them that day. "Animals can usually sense it."

"Oh."

On the days when Jake did not have a riding lesson, he had to contend with the most challenging part of his studies: the elocution lessons he received from Henry.

Despite having been born in the forests of eastern France in the foothills of the Alps, where his kindred pack still ruled, the wolf shapeshifter spoke better English than Jake did.

"You must learn how to speak like a gentleman, my lord. But only half of that involves refining your accent. The other half is what you actually *say*."

That was what made it so difficult.

Learning to bite his tongue. Curb his sarcasm.

As a pickpocket who had owed allegiance to no one, Jake had had the luxury of snapping out with any rude comment that popped into his head, but a future peer of the realm had a duty to set a good example.

Words could wound others worse than any sword, especially when uttered not by witches but those with real power in the world.

Truly strong men, however, Henry taught him, followed the principle of *noblesse oblige*, which meant deliberately choosing to be kind, patient, and merciful to those of lesser standing in society. They saved their harsh, mean warrior side only for their enemies. Their equals.

The best example of that that Jake knew was the Gryphon, of course. He was gentle with all the kids and little Teddy, but when he went on the attack against a foe, he was savage.

Come to think of it, so was Henry, Jake thought. The unassuming tutor who could turn himself at will into a ferocious wolf.

All of Henry's lessons about life—never mind history and English—also helped Jake start to understand Archie better.

He was finally beginning to perceive how his famously chivalrous cousin viewed the world.

He had thought Arch had simply been born that way—polite, extra nice to everyone—but as three weeks of this discipline began to reveal, molding and sculpting him, Jake saw that true English gentlemen were not born; they were made.

He pondered this continuously as the days rolled by. But he couldn't help wondering what Dani would think of this new Jake.

True to her word as always, she wrote him letters every few days.

Gladwin delivered them, and it was always good to see her, too, and to hear the news from Merlin Hall.

Jake practiced his handwriting by writing back to Dani once a week.

That must've shocked her, he thought with a smile as he penned a dutiful response about what he had been doing and how Teddy was faring without her.

They both missed the carrot-head terribly. Teddy had been sad. There was no denying it. Little whines had escaped his snout now and then as he lay unhappily on the couch. But somehow he seemed to understand that none of them had a choice about what was going on.

At least the wee terrier had Red to keep him company when Jake was too preoccupied to play with either of them in his determined effort to change his wild ways.

It was tiring, but he was prepared to do whatever it took not to become the "greatest leader the Dark Druids had ever had."

He shuddered at the thought.

The prophecy gave him nightmares sometimes. Blimey, it even drove him right into the village church nearby on Sunday mornings.

He wasn't taking any chances. Sermons could be boring, but it was better than letting himself grow up to destroy the world.

In any case, for a few hours each evening, Jake was finally at his leisure.

He could just imagine how shocked Dani must be when she read in his letters how he chose to use his free time, getting the castle ready for his parents' return. Maddox probably didn't even believe it.

Each evening, he marshaled up the staff of family servants—those loyal but unfortunate souls who had once been turned into frogs by Fionnula Coralbroom.

Then he and half a dozen servants would attack a new room in Griffon Castle. Sometimes two, if they could manage it.

They'd clean the room from top to bottom, slowly getting their home ready, wing by wing, for the return of the famed Lightriders, Lord and Lady Griffon.

Jake knew he was getting his hopes up higher and higher, and it scared him to do so, more than walking on a tightrope over a canyon.

Perhaps he was setting himself up for crushing heartbreak. But he dared to lay hold of a different kind of courage than he usually displayed. The courage to have faith that, yes, the parents he'd loved and missed all his life without even knowing them were still alive and would be coming home someday.

Maybe even soon.

CHAPTER 33
Lightrider-in-Training

For three weeks, Finnderool had kept his students so busy that Dani had hardly had time to miss Jake.

Or his cousins. Or Red.

Well, except at suppertime, when only Nixie and Maddox were there. Neither of them were great talkers.

They just sat there and chewed, sunk in their own thoughts, one missing Archie, the other possibly missing Isabelle—or not. It was always hard to tell what Maddox was thinking.

Most of all, truth be told, Dani missed her dog. Her heart ached terribly without Teddy there by her side every day, or curled up in the bed beside her feet at night, but at least she knew he was in good hands.

Ah well, she had her new Lightrider friends to keep her company. There were eight kids of various magical breeds and races in her group, along with the crop of brand-new Guardians they were training with.

They all stuck together, because, to Dani's surprise, kids from the other programs were often rude to the young Lightriders out of jealousy.

In any case, the first two weeks of classes had been all about the overview: Lightriding 101. Some of the history, what qualities made a good Lightrider, a look ahead at some of the skills they'd have to learn.

By the middle of the first week, they had received all their textbooks and what would soon prove to be their daily routine.

First thing in the morning, Finnderool had them out on the Guardians' beginner-level obstacle course. *Whew, it's not easy!* she wrote to Jake.

Girls and boys alike had to run over tires, climb rope ladders, haul themselves over high beams, jump down on the other side, and keep running. There was sprinting, relay races, and long, grueling hikes on occasion.

She heard that, in the summer, there would even be swimming lessons from the naiads. They'd also be learning basic self-defense skills, but Dani had to laugh at that. She was well ahead in that department, at least, after growing up with five big brothers in a rookery full of fighting Irish.

Archery was new, though, and Dani found it fun. Of course, Master Wood Elf put them all to shame with his skill with a bow and arrow.

Finnderool could literally hit targets while blindfolded. It was amazing, but this was the favored weapon of his people and he'd begun learning it, he told them, when he was three.

In any case, after the day's physical training regimen, the students had just enough time to scramble back to their rooms, wash up, gulp down a quick breakfast, and then don their uniforms, before grabbing their books and dashing off to class.

Dani always felt proud to put on her uniform. Given all of their physical activity, the girls' sturdy, dark-colored dresses were a little shorter than was usually acceptable, at about knee-length in front, though they hung a little longer in the back. She liked how the puffy skirts swung. They were two-toned, with a band of rust brown beneath the waist, the rest navy blue down to the hem.

The dress came with a fluffy dark blue petticoat for added modesty, but their legs were covered with rust-colored tights, anyway, and sturdy brown boots that laced up to their shins.

The upper half of the uniform dress had a dark blue bodice with short puff sleeves and a neat, buckled waist, with two brown belts that held hooks for hanging gadgets and storing supplies. Out on a mission, after all, a Lightrider must be ready for anything.

But the uniform was not *all* business.

The Elders had at least tried to give the girls' version of it a feminine touch. A wide column of small, cream-colored ruffles adorned the center of the dress, from the waist up to the throat.

The high neck of the dress was then encircled by a smart, rust-colored ribbon with a buckle in the front. Dani thought all the girls looked very smart.

The boys wore similar colors, but for them, it was dark blue breeches with a rust-brown stripe down the side, and short jackets to match.

Their shirts were white, but they wore rust-colored neckerchiefs and wool caps. Their belts and knee boots were of brown leather, as well.

All eight of them revered having been selected. Dani's hands still trembled when she stood before the mirror in her tiny room and finished off her outfit by tying the white sash with silver thread around her waist.

Sometimes it all seemed like a dream. But the insistent ticking of the clock reminded her that it was indeed real, and Master Finnderool did not like to be kept waiting.

Once again, she grabbed her books and went barreling off to the classroom wing of Merlin Hall for her lessons.

There was so much to learn—much more than just how to travel through the Grid. The students had to tackle a wide array of subjects, in fact, like the history of the Order, and a great deal of maths—especially geometry—as well as extensive geography lessons with maps, calculating distances and miles between vortexes in the Grid.

The wood elf also had them memorizing capitals of countries and provinces, and learning the weather and topography of various regions.

Twice a week they had etiquette lessons, too, since they would be escorting fancy diplomats to various places around the globe.

Dani was grateful for the many hours she had already spent learning the basics from Miss Helena. Finnderool explained that they had to know how to behave around VIPs of all sorts of Magick-folk without embarrassing the Order or, worse, blundering somehow and accidentally causing an incident between magical species.

The Djin, for example, could take offense at trifles, Finnderool warned, and nobody wanted to see a djinni angry. The pixies were notorious tricksters (as Dani well knew), the shapeshifters clannish, the giants a bit slow, but it was important not to let on that you noticed.

The Greenfolk like Dr. Plantagenet considered impatience the worst possible form of rudeness and took their own sweet time about everything, just like trees growing. They were adamant, too, about doing nothing out of season.

The wood elves, of course, had no flaws whatsoever, according to their teacher. But the kids eventually realized he was only jesting.

Believe it or not, Dani had written to Jake, *Finnderool actually does have a sense of humor in there somewhere.*

Before any mission, the wood elf had further explained, it would be their responsibility to research any particular local customs, laws, and protocols that had to be followed. They were the ones—not just the Guardians—who had to keep their VIPs out of trouble.

It all sounded so exciting—and that was only the first two weeks!

When week three started, a momentous event took place, one she didn't even tell Jake for fear of making him jealous.

Dani and all the other Lightrider students were each presented with a training gauntlet, jokingly referred to as the Bud of Life—in contrast to the true Flower of Life implant that adult Lightriders had surgically embedded in their wrists.

For the kids, it was just a brown leather cuff that ran from their left wrists halfway up their forearms.

The Bud of Life had a compass and a communication device built into it somehow, plus six dials for entering in coordinates, with two small switches for the four cardinal directions: north/south and east/west. A small brass button at the end of the line of dials and switches read ACTIVATE.

Three leather straps with brass buckles fastened it in place, and it came with two rules, which, if you broke them, could get you thrown out of the program.

One, they were not to take the Bud off at any time without permission, and two, even more importantly, they were not to get it wet or it would break.

They spent all week trying to get used to wearing them. But, as big a development as this was, it wasn't all that happened in week three.

So did the start of afternoon group work.

That was when Finnderool had brought in the new crop of Guardians to work with them. *Their* teacher was a master Guardian like Derek, called Ebrahim.

He was a jolly, muscle-bound black man of about fifty who was rumored to be quite fearless. No doubt it was true. Big as he was, Master Ebrahim didn't need to be afraid of much, Dani guessed.

The towering, mocha-skinned man led a line of eight wide-eyed Guardian recruits into their class the next day like a trail of baby ducks.

Then the two groups were told to partner up.

"Get used to working together." Finnderool explained that on every mission, a team of three or more was sent. The team always included the Lightrider, the Guardian, and the VIP, whom Finnderool termed the conductee.

"The Lightrider escorts the diplomat or dignitary through the Grid. You're in charge of transportation, among other things. The Guardian is on protective duty, but you Lightriders will also be required to learn basic self-defense and survival skills. It's important to have at least some overlap in capabilities within the team.

"As for your conductees," he said, "it won't always be the same person. In fact, quite the contrary. It just depends on the mission."

The class nodded, jotting down notes.

Master Ebrahim then addressed the group: "My Guardians, you will be responsible for keeping your Lightrider and conductee safe. You should always be scanning. Watchful. Any threat arises, you want to sense it with your heightened instincts before it shows its ugly face. Avoid it if you can. We don't want to scare our conductees. Let's be honest." He sent Finnderool a mischievous glance, his dark eyes twinkling. "They're usually pampered aristocrats who aren't very good in a crisis."

Finnderool conceded this with a shrug.

"That means it's up to you to be prepared for any sort of threat that might arise," the towering Guardian continued. "However, you must work within the parameters your Lightrider sets for the mission, because he or she is the one who'll have researched the place. Now then, starting next week, Master Finnderool and I will have a special...surprise for you."

All sixteen kids talked excitedly at lunch that day what the surprise of week four could possibly be, but nobody knew.

Dani could hardly wait.

CHAPTER 34

Many Happy Returns

Nixie Valentine was not a sentimental person, despite her last name. She did not believe in all that drippy hearts-and-flowers stuff. She enjoyed gloomy days, liked to dress in black, and was generally against the color pink.

A hardheaded cynic with a hard-shelled exterior, she would never be the sort to wear her heart on her sleeve, à la Isabelle.

But she was the sort of person who never forgot a kindness, and aside from Archie Bradford (she missed him dreadfully, the egghead), no one had been kinder to her than the famed Elder witch.

And so, when the appropriate day came, exactly three weeks after the gang split up, Nixie worked up her courage to bring her intimidating mentor a cupcake for her birthday. Atop it she placed an unlit magical candle that she had made herself.

As she slowly carried it on a plate down the hallway toward Lady Bradford's apartments, she mulled over her private concerns about the Elder witch lately.

Something was definitely going on.

Nixie would never dare to pry into Her Ladyship's business, but she was really starting to worry about her.

Lady Bradford had been acting rather strange ever since that battle four months ago. Spending too much time alone in her chambers. Keeping odd hours.

Why, Nixie could almost smell the secrets swirling in the air where her aged mentor was concerned.

Of course, as a mere apprentice, she was not at liberty to share her concerns about the powerful old woman with anyone, not even Arch.

As much as she adored him, the boy genius could not keep a secret any more than he could tell a lie, and Nixie knew instinctively that whatever Ramona Bradford was up to, she did not want anyone knowing about it. Dame Oriel was the only one she seemed inclined to take into her confidence.

Well, whatever was causing her mentor to act so furtive and distracted lately, Nixie only wanted to help. And even though she had heard the Elder witch say she had no desire to celebrate yet another birthday, Nixie owed Her Ladyship too much to ignore the occasion.

That was how she found herself outside Lady Bradford's door that day, cupcake in hand. She shifted the plate into one hand and knocked with the other.

"Who's there?" the Elder witch called.

"It's me, ma'am," Nixie said loudly through the door.

It opened promptly, and Nixie lifted the cupcake with a hapless smile, suddenly feeling stupid.

"Happy birthday!" she said nevertheless.

Her momentary awkwardness melted as Lady Bradford's bony face softened with a modest smile. "Oh, my dear. Tut, tut, you shouldn't have."

"No, ma'am, I had to," Nixie blurted out earnestly. "I'm sorry—I know you didn't want anyone to make a fuss. But it's just one cupcake, and after all you've done for me, I had to let you know how grateful I am, f-for everything." She held out her offering. "Many happy returns, ma'am."

Ramona accepted the plate with a fond look. "Well, *thank* you, Miss Valentine. You're very thoughtful."

Nixie nodded self-consciously, blushing. Having made her delivery, she started to turn away.

"Well, don't you want to share it with me?" the old woman asked.

Nixie spun around, giving in to a grin as Lady Bradford opened the door to her sitting room wider. "It's all for you, ma'am! But I'll keep you company while you eat it."

"Nonsense. It's too big for one old lady. Come in, sit down. I'll get some forks."

Nixie was awed by this rare invitation from an Elder.

Feeling entirely honored, she went in and closed the door behind her, taking a discreet glance around at her mentor's rooms, while Lady Bradford marched the cupcake over to the table and set it down near her magnificent white crystal ball.

Nixie ogled the marvelous orb of rare white quartz perched atop its ornate silver stand.

"Oh, dear me." Lady Bradford turned to her expectantly, propping a hand on her waist. "I can't seem to find any extra plates. Would you mind doing the honors, hmm?"

The Elder witch was obviously fibbing, but Nixie beamed at the chance to show off her skills.

"Gladly." She focused her mind for a second, imagining the table set as nice and pretty and refined as Ramona's favorite, Isabelle, would make it. Then she snapped her fingers. *"Parare mensamque!"*

With a twinkle of magic, two dainty place settings appeared: little painted dessert plates of fine china with matching teacups and all the necessary silver.

Lady Bradford glanced at her with pride. "Well done," she said, clearly amused. She gestured to the chairs. "Shall we sit?"

"First you have to blow out your candle so you can make a wish. I'll light it for you."

"Hmm. Very well." Lady Bradford humored her by taking her seat at the small round table. She pushed her crystal ball farther to the side to make room for their tea party.

Nixie remained standing and took out her wand.

She could feel her cheeks heating with a blush over the magic she'd put into the candle. She hoped Her Ladyship wouldn't find it stupid.

Again, she had simply tried to think of what Isabelle would do. Mainly, she just hoped the silly thing worked once she lit the wick.

With the guest of honor seated and ready to blow out the candle, Nixie lit the wick with a tap of her wand and a simple *in flamma* spell.

As a seemingly ordinary flame leaped to life atop the candle, Nixie realized that, customarily, next came the singing. But she couldn't bring herself to do that. Certainly not as a solo. Instead, she just smiled and said, "Happy birthday, Lady Bradford."

"Thank you very much, my dear." Looking intrigued, the Elder witch leaned forward and blew out the candle—almost.

Instead of vanishing, the little flame atop the wick began to spark.

Lady Bradford sat up straight, her pewter eyebrows arching. The sparks shot higher over the cupcake, began changing colors, and turned into a miniature fireworks display.

Nixie held her breath; it was working! Lady Bradford watched the display with a smile.

But Nixie knew full well that that would hardly begin to impress an Elder witch.

Next, the colorful bursts of sparkling fireworks turned into artificial butterflies that fluttered all around them, only to transform yet again, this time into colorful confetti that scattered down over the table.

Lady Bradford clasped her bony hands together in delight, then applauded. “How charming!”

When the Elder witch laughed, Nixie knew she’d done well. Better than expected—in fact, this was the first time she had ever seen Her Ladyship laugh.

“Oh my goodness, this is truly sweet of you, my dear. Don’t worry, I won’t tell anyone about the butterflies,” Lady Bradford teased.

Nixie grinned. “It *would* wreck my image.”

The Elder witch chuckled and gestured to the chair across the table from her. “Sit down and let’s eat this thing.”

“Yes, ma’am.” Beaming, Nixie took the seat, while the baroness cut the cupcake in half, revealing rich chocolate cake under creamy white icing, with colorful icing flowers all around the edges.

Lady Bradford served them each a half, then picked up her dessert fork and took the first bite. “Mm, devil’s food cake. My favorite! How did you know?”

“Isabelle told me. I didn’t make the cupcake, though,” Nixie confessed. “I only ordered it from the kitchens. B-but I believe the pastry chef was a house brownie.”

“Oh, then it’s sure to be good.”

Nixie smiled. “What would you like to drink, ma’am? Tea?”

“Mm, I think a glass of milk sounds just the thing.”

“Me too.” With a snap of her fingers, Nixie caused two cold glasses of milk to appear.

Lady Bradford picked hers up. “Cheers.”

Nixie clinked cups with her. “Cheers, ma’am.”

Lady Bradford took a sip. “You know, I meant to congratulate you on your role in freeing Aleeyah from her smoke form. I understand it would not have been possible without your lightning generation, and yet, so far, all the credit has gone to Archie.”

Nixie smiled. “He thought of it. It was easy.”

"Don't minimize your own talents, my dear. You are a born weather mage. I know grown witches who wouldn't have been able to do that. Conjure the lightning? Maybe. But control it? *That* is another matter, indeed."

Nixie was touched yet a little embarrassed by the compliment and wanted to change the subject. She paused, chewing thoughtfully. Then she washed down her bite of delicious cupcake with a sip of milk.

"So," Nixie remarked after a moment. "An October birthday. Libra."

"Oh, yes. The Scales. Keeping the balance," the great witch said ruefully.

There was an indefinable undertone in her voice that hinted at great weariness and maybe even sorrow.

Nixie hesitated. "Why do you hate your birthday, ma'am?"

Lady Bradford shrugged. "Too many of them, is all."

Nixie leaned closer. "*How* many?"

The Elder witch paused, narrowing her eyes. "You really want to know?"

Nixie nodded.

"Three hundred and thirty-three," Lady Bradford announced. "But if you tell a soul, I shall vehemently deny it."

Nixie hid her shock, but smiled at the witch's arch tone. "You must be excited. That is a very powerful number."

"Yes. I suppose it is." Then Lady Bradford smiled. "But it's a ridiculous number of birthdays."

"Why so many? How?" Nixie dared to ask.

The Elder witch sighed. Her gaze wandered over to her gorgeous crystal ball. She hesitated, as though weighing whether to reveal her story. "Once upon a time, long, long ago," she finally said, "there was a silly-headed young girl not much older than Isabelle. A budding witch, much like yourself. And, like you, she also had a beau. But as this foolish young witch eventually learned the hard way, her beau was not the sort of truly good man that Archimedes will undoubtedly grow up to be.

"At seventeen, alas, our naïve little witch didn't know that yet. She and her beau—a young warlock—adored each other, especially doing magic together.

"They wanted to combine their talents and use our craft to make the world a better place. But even more than they both loved magic, they were devoted to each other. They thought they would be together forever. So, by using magic, they decided to make it so."

Nixie listened in amazement, forgetting all about her cupcake. "How?"

Lady Bradford took a bite and chewed for a moment, then swallowed. "Have you ever heard of the Montague and Capulet spell?"

Nixie shook her head.

"Never do that spell," Lady Bradford said flatly. "But you wouldn't. You're too sensible. The spell is, of course, named after Romeo and Juliet." Lady Bradford took another bite. "Pair of young dunces."

"Those, at least, I've heard of," Nixie murmured.

"It is a reckless potion, only for two fools in love. It's based on the same wish that motivated Romeo and Juliet in the play. The same fear that haunts everyone who loves. The desire—the need—never to have to live without the person you love.

"For some couples, they would consider this a fate worse than death. The Montague and Capulet spell ensures that if one dies, the other dies. Likewise, so long as one lives, the other lives, too."

Nixie made a wordless sound of awe at such a drastic working.

"For a time, our young couple carried on peaceably. But as a few years passed, the girl's unfortunate beau became frustrated that all the magic in the world could not seem to fix the ills of mankind.

"He began bending a few rules. Ignoring safety protocols. Blending spells in unsanctioned ways in an effort to achieve good outcomes. But good can't be forced on others, you see. It has to be *chosen* through a person's own free will.

"Geoffrey forgot that—or lost patience with it. He began breaking rules outright to try to *force* his will on the natural world. To make others behave as *he* felt they should. He made himself the arbiter of right and wrong, and if people wouldn't choose wisely for themselves, he'd impose it on them through enchantments. Virtually enslaving them."

Ramona shook her head. "This set him on the road to becoming a dangerous tyrant with no respect for others. Such pride starts the rot that soon leads to corruption."

Nixie stared at her. "Did he even try to control...the girl?"

"He wouldn't dare," Lady Bradford replied with a smile. "He would've liked to. But the witch in question has always been extremely strong-minded. Rather like you. Sadly, there was nothing she could do to make him stop or pull him back onto the straight and narrow.

"Finding success at bending the world to his will, Geoffrey decided that the ends justified the means, in whatever situation. And that is *always* the first major step into someone turning truly evil."

Nixie gulped.

"And so, the feckless young warlock was eventually deceived into following the left-hand path. He still loved his sweetheart—so he claimed—but he loved the power he was gaining more. She begged him not to pursue the black arts, that it would mean the end of their match. But he didn't listen. He was obsessed—and quite brilliant, like Archie. There was so much he wanted to do and to learn, but there never seemed to be enough time to take it all in.

"So, one day, he worked a powerful long-life spell on himself, and the witch was dragged along into it with him, because of the way the Montague and Capulet spell had already bound them together for the duration of their life span on earth."

The Elder witch paused. "This *impressive* old age of mine is Geoffrey's doing, not mine. In truth, 'tis a curse."

"A curse?"

"Why, yes." She smiled. "I'll still be here, you see, when you and Archie and Isabelle and Jake and the others are all old and wrinkled like me. I'll see you laid to rest in your graves, and I'll be left to mourn. Just as I've mourned the past eight generations."

Nixie stared solemnly at her, shocked.

"If it were up to me, I'd have been content to leave this Earth after, oh, eighty or ninety years. But as long as Geoffrey still employs every spell at his disposal to cheat death, then I have no choice but to go on living too.

"Not that I blame him for seeking to extend his life," she added ruefully. "If I had the sort of afterlife awaiting me that *he's* got in store, I'd probably do everything I could to escape death, too.

"But, sooner or later, Zolond's got to pay the price for the choices he's made."

Nixie's eyes widened. This Geoffrey, her old beau, was Zolond? The Dark Master? Sorcerer-king of the warlocks who could command the demons and made the Black Fortress their home?

Her heart pounded.

The Elder witch gave Nixie a pointed look that told her in no uncertain terms this was not to be discussed outside her suite. She took a sip of milk and continued in a cool tone. "So, until my old beau joins his lord, Shemrazul, in the Ninth Pit of Hades, for my part, I'll just keep on having these ridiculous birthdays."

With that, Lady Bradford took her final bite of cupcake.

"Well," Nixie said calmly, doing her best to take such devastating revelations in stride, "I, for one, am glad you're still here, ma'am."

The baroness chortled, then quickly regained her dignity. "Thank you, my dear. People like you make my sentence on this earth much more tolerable. So, tell me, what is the moral of this story, hmm?"

"Whew," Nixie said. It had been an overwhelming lesson. Stunned, she sat there, still taking it in. "Use magic wisely?"

"And?"

"Never use bad means to achieve good ends?"

The Elder witch gave her a wink. "Atta girl."

CHAPTER 35
A Heart-to-Heart

That night at Griffon Castle, Jake ate supper with his cousins, Derek, and the twins at the long, formal table in the red dining hall. Red and Teddy were stationed in the corner, as usual, scarfing down their food from their bowls.

Jake had been quiet for most of the meal, turning an idea over in his mind while the adults chatted.

He stared through the dancing flames atop the tall silver candelabra, only stirring from his reverie when Archie asked him to pass the partridge hash.

Absently, he floated the serving bowl down the table to his cousin using his telekinesis before the footman posted by the wall could even react.

Isabelle gave Jake a curious glance as she sipped another creamy spoonful of the cheese-and-walnut soup, no doubt sensing his wistful mood.

When a break in the adults' conversation emerged, Jake suddenly spoke up.

"I should like to throw a welcome-home party for my parents once they've been rescued," he announced. "I was wondering if any of you might have ideas about what might be suitable."

Everyone at the table turned to him, looking astonished that he, of all people, should make a civilized suggestion.

Henry's eyes began to glow with pride to hear him talking so proper, to boot. He lifted his goblet in a toast. "Capital notion, my lad."

Miss Helena smiled. "I think that is a lovely idea, Jacob."

"So do I," Isabelle said, perking up a bit. She had been glum on the whole ever since they'd left Merlin Hall.

Archie warmed at once to the idea and instantly began throwing out clever inventions he could rig up to really dazzle them when they came home. "Fireworks? A cannon that shoots confetti?"

"We'll need music," Derek murmured with a smile.

"And dancing," Miss Helena chimed in, dimpling at her beau.

But Isabelle sighed at the mention of dancing and lowered her gaze, looking downcast again.

This distant attitude was so unlike her that Jake decided to try to talk to her about it after supper that evening. See if he could help. After all, she was always there for *him* whenever he needed someone to talk to.

He was no empath, of course, but the least he could do was try and return the favor.

And so, after the meal, Jake went over to his cousin, who was sitting by the fire in the great hall, working on her embroidery loop by candlelight.

It surprised him because, for all her many talents, Isabelle was terrible at any kind of sewing.

Even as he walked toward her, she pricked her finger on the needle and let out a small cry of pain.

Jake smiled as she popped her fingertip into her mouth.

"Hope it's not fatal," he said.

She harrumphed and squeezed her finger, then shook it. "No, but it hurt. That's the third time I've poked myself in the past quarter hour! I'm starting to feel like a human pincushion."

He leaned over to look at her colorful project. "What's that you're working on?"

She sighed. "A sampler for Aunt Ramona's birthday. It was supposed to be done three days ago, but I've been procrastinating."

"When's her birthday?" Jake asked in surprise as he sat down in the other leather armchair across from the fireplace.

"It's today, Jake."

"Blimey," he said with a frown. "I didn't get her anything."

"Don't worry, she despises her birthday." Izzy gave him a look. "She's had so many of them, she doesn't like to be reminded."

"How old is she?" Jake murmured.

"I'm not sure, exactly. Mama says she's over three hundred." Isabelle shrugged. "I just thought I'd pass the time here in the country making her a handmade gift. No magic involved—obviously." Wryly,

Isabelle held up the embroidery loop, showing him her work, and Jake had to admit that the flowers in the design resembled lopsided bricks.

"It's nice," he offered, but Izzy scoffed at his tact.

"It's dreadful. I'm hoping it's the thought that counts."

Jake laughed. "Don't worry, I'm sure she'll love it. She loves everything you do."

Isabelle cocked her head with a rueful smile and set her embroidery project aside. "Maybe it would be better if we just took a stroll into the village tomorrow and bought her something nice."

"Oh, I would love a break from this place," Jake said heartily. "Let's ask Derek and Henry if we've earned a day off yet. Maybe they'll let us go."

Isabelle nodded, then her thoughts apparently drifted once again, as they had so often ever since their party had left Merlin Hall.

Her faraway stare fixated on the cheerful blaze dancing in the fireplace.

"Hullo?" Jake called.

She blinked back to awareness and glanced at him. "Sorry, coz, was there something you wanted?"

"Just to talk to you," he said.

"About what?" she asked with unusual bluntness.

"Maddox."

Her golden eyebrows lifted. She sat up straighter. "Maddox? What about him?"

"It's obvious you miss him. So, instead of moping around here or stabbing yourself with sewing needles, why don't you just write him a letter to tell him how you feel?"

She looked at him in surprise. "Write to Maddox?"

Jake nodded.

But Izzy stared back at him, looking tongue-tied. Then he noticed the guilty flicker in her blue eyes, and his brows arched as understanding dawned.

"Oh. So, it's not Maddox you've been moping over."

She dropped her gaze and floundered, her cheeks turning pinker in the fire's warmth.

Jake leaned forward, searching her face. "Talk to me, Iz. I'm worried about you. You haven't been your usual happy self since we left Merlin Hall. I tell *you* everything."

Izzy gave him a soulful look, then glanced over her shoulder, scanning the rest of the spacious, high-ceilinged great hall to gauge the whereabouts of the others.

Miss Helena was sitting at the pianoforte perusing a catalog of fabrics and fripperies, and jotting down items she wished to order. Derek was at the round oaken table, reading the *Times* sports page in between steps of cleaning one of his rifles.

Archie was playing chess with Henry at the game table over by the wall where the knight's suit of armor stood. As for the pets, Teddy was running circles around Red in the center of the room.

No one paid Jake and Izzy any mind.

"Well?" He turned to her again. "What's bothering you?"

"Could we take a turn out on the terrace?" she asked timidly.

Jake nodded. "Of course. I could use some fresh air."

They rose, and Izzy slipped her shawl around her shoulders. Jake pulled his jacket on again. He'd removed it after supper and hung it on the back of a chair.

"We'll be out on the terrace for a few minutes," he told the others.

"I got overheated sitting by the fire," Izzy added.

"Don't stay outside too long." Miss Helena glanced up from her catalog. "It's chilly out."

They agreed, then walked out onto the terrace behind Griffon Castle.

Though it was barely eight o'clock, the blue-black night enveloped them in shadows the moment they stepped outside. As they crossed the terrace, dried leaves skittered and rasped across the flagstones at their feet.

Above them, an uneven cloud cover hid the half-moon and veiled the stars. The outline of the trees bristled against the sky. The large topiaries throughout the garden made strange, hulking shapes in the dark. But straight ahead, down the central garden aisle, Jake could see the wide River Thames rolling by endlessly.

A glimmer of moonlight silvered the current.

In any case, the cool night air cleared Jake's head quickly after the heavy meal and the cozy warmth around the fireplace.

The two cousins strolled over to the far edge of the terrace, where Izzy stood pensively at the top of the shallow stone stairs that led down into the garden.

Jake perched on the wide stone balustrade nearby. "So, what's afoot?" he asked, resting his elbow atop his bent knee.

Izzy gazed up at the half-moon for a moment, the night breeze riffling her long skirts.

Jake waited, determined to be patient, per his lessons.

Finally, Isabelle looked at him. “Janos yelled at me.”

“What?” Jake wrinkled his nose.

“Well, not *yelled*, exactly. It was more of a snarl. ‘Stay away from me,’ he said.”

Jake looked at her in shock. “When was this?”

“Right after he came back through the portal with the team. The night his family died.”

“Blimey.” Jake pondered this, then frowned. “Well, you can’t really blame a chap for what he might’ve said at such a horrible moment as that.”

“No, I know!” she said in obvious frustration. “It’s just, his anger was very specifically directed at *me*.” She shook her head, distress filling her face. “I can’t imagine what I did to offend him. It was almost like he blamed me in part for what happened to his family. I just don’t understand how that could be.”

“Neither do I.” Jake was mystified. “Why on earth would he blame you? That doesn’t make any sense.”

“I have no idea,” she whispered with a shrug.

“Has he tried to, you know, contact you? Mentally? Telepathically, I mean. To explain or apologize or…?”

“No. That’s why I think he really meant it. If the words just slipped out, then surely he would’ve said something by now. Like he was sorry. That he didn’t really mean it. And I’d forgive him, of course. As you said, who could blame a person for lashing out at such a time?”

“You were probably just the first available target,” Jake said.

“That’s what I thought, too, at first. It’s not as though I would hold a grudge against anyone under those circumstances. But that’s just it. I haven’t heard a word from him. Nothing.” She shook her head. “I cannot comprehend why Prince Janos would blame me for their deaths. I had nothing to do with it!” She pressed her hand to her heart. “I did my best to help him, didn’t I? You were there. We did exactly as he asked.”

“We did,” Jake agreed, nodding. “You got his message down perfectly.”

“And yet he lashed out at me, as though, somehow, it was all my fault.”

Jake frowned and watched the river for a moment.

Isabelle toyed with a tassel on her shawl, moving restlessly across the top of the garden stairs.

"Let me ask you this," Jake said after a moment. "Have you tried scanning him with your abilities?"

"Lord, no." Izzy shuddered with a dire look. "I don't dare. He might sense it and get offended all over again. He's angry enough at me as it is."

"But it might provide some answers."

"I can't invade his privacy, Jake. He made it very clear he wanted nothing more to do with me."

Jake squinted, confused. "I don't understand. He's always adored you. You know it's true."

She looked away with a low, unhappy laugh. "What, you mean all his silly flirting? He doesn't mean anything by it. That's just his sense of humor."

Finally, his cousin smiled, as though remembering all the times Janos had informed her she was going to marry him when she grew up. The times he had given her and nobody else the most courtly of bows, and the way he clutched at his heart as though mortally wounded every time she rolled her eyes at his clowning.

Remembering all those instances himself, and seeing the look on Isabelle's face right now, Jake suddenly remembered what Maddox had said about the matter.

"Oh dear," he mumbled, leaning back on his hands. The stone balustrade was pleasantly cool and rough under his palms.

Isabelle looked over at him. "What?"

"Well, this is awkward," Jake said, debating whether to tell her Maddox's daft theory.

What if the grouch was correct after all?

"What?" Isabelle prompted, her long skirts swinging as she turned to him. She folded her arms across her chest. "Did Janos say something about me?"

"No, no," Jake answered. "I never did get a chance to talk to him before we left Merlin Hall."

"Well, what then?" she demanded.

Jake hesitated, but it wasn't as though the Guardian lad had sworn him to secrecy. "Maddox has a theory."

"About Janos?" Izzy snorted. "Then it's probably not very nice.

Maddox hates him."

"Well, hate's a strong word. But yes. A theory about Janos."

"Do tell," Izzy said in a skeptical tone.

An owl hooted somewhere in the trees.

Jake sighed and sat up straight again. "I probably shouldn't be telling you this, but Maddox thinks Janos loves you."

"What?"

"Like—really loves you. Up-on-a-pedestal kind of love."

"Me?" She gaped at him. But her voice caught when she added, "Don't be silly."

Jake shrugged. "Maddox thinks that all of the vampire's joking around with you is just him hiding the truth in plain sight. Like spies always do."

Isabelle went perfectly motionless, staring at him with her mouth hanging open.

At that moment, the moon peeked out from behind the clouds and illumined her face. She looked stunned, her lips parted, her eyes wide.

Then she turned away without a word, gazing at the river. Jake could practically hear her heart pounding.

"Well? What do you think?" Jake asked. "You're an empath. I mean, you can sense when someone loves you, can't you, Izzy?"

"Yes," she said faintly. Then she went and leaned against the empty stone urn at the end of the balustrade across from Jake. She looked a little shaken.

He waited for her to explain. "You're awfully quiet, coz."

Isabelle lifted her gaze from the ground and stared at him, clearly at a loss.

When Jake read the mix of wonder and alarm in her eyes, understanding dawned.

Then it was *his* turn to be amazed.

"You already knew," he murmured.

She shook her head, glancing toward the river. "I-I didn't know that that's what I was sensing all this time, until you just said it now. I never would've dreamed... I mean, he's so impossible! Oh, but every time I'm with him, Jake, it's such a beautiful feeling. He feels like no one else to me. Safe and sure. Undemanding and kind. Completely nonjudgmental." The words tumbled from her lips as though she could no longer contain them. "Everybody judges me. I always have to be *so* careful in everything I do! I try so hard.

"But he just...accepts me. Exactly as I am. And he *knows* who I am, because he can look right into my heart."

Jake studied her, amazed. "You love him too?"

"I don't know!" She seemed shaken merely to ponder the words. "All I know is that he's so easy to be with. Not many people are that easy for me to be with. But I swear I never thought it was *that.*"

"Love?" he asked slowly.

Izzy nodded, still looking dazed. "I-I thought it was just...Janos being Janos. His charm. His wit." She hesitated. "I know we share some strange sort of bond. I felt it, too. But I made light of it, just like he always has. Because, obviously, it would be impossible for us... Totally impossible. He's too old for me, for starters."

"No older than those other chaps your mother shoved in front of you at the harvest feast."

"He's a vampire!"

Jake shrugged. "He saved my life. He rescued Red. He makes you laugh. He has a good heart."

"It doesn't matter." She shook her head, her face solemn. "Father would never allow it in a hundred thousand years."

"Aye, probably not," Jake admitted.

"Anyway, whatever Janos might've felt for me before, it's clear he despises me now. I only wish I knew what I did wrong." Tears suddenly welled up in her eyes.

"Aw, don't cry, coz." Jake rose, determined to help her solve this. "C'mon. Let's walk down to the river and skip some stones. I'm sure the two of us can figure this out if we try."

She nodded absently, blotting her few tears away on the end of her shawl. Jake led the way down the center aisle of the garden. Izzy trailed after him, morose.

The grass was soft underfoot, but the breeze grew stronger and the soothing sound of the current grew louder as they approached the grassy riverbank.

When they reached the edge of the water, Jake searched around in the moonlight for a flat stone, found one, and tossed it out across the water.

Three skips, then it plopped into the Thames.

"I think I know," Jake said.

Izzy looked askance at him. "That was fast."

He smiled. "Skipping stones always helps me think."

"Well?"

"You're not going to like it."

"Tell me anyway," she said wearily, pulling her elegant shawl more tightly around her. "Please, give me one good reason why any sane vampire should blame an innocent bystander for the murder of his wives and his hatchlings."

"All right." Jake took a deep breath. "We know Lord Wyvern killed the vampire brood to retaliate against Janos for his role in freeing Red and Tex. Wyvern didn't just do it to be hateful; he had a very specific reason."

"Let's hope so. Yes." She nodded. "He did it to punish Janos for tricking him."

"Well," Jake said, "the way I see it, the only logical way that Janos could possibly trace the blame back to you is if he somehow did all that for your sake."

Izzy's eyes widened. "What? My sake? Wh-what do you mean?"

Jake found another stone, a good, weighty one shaped like a broken star. "Not to scare you, Iz, but you did help me destroy Garnock. You were there. You were crucial to the whole thing. Well, the Dark Druids want revenge on *me* for that—at least, they did until this prophecy emerged." He shrugged. "Maybe they want revenge on you for your part in it. Don't you remember how that horrible demon Shemrazul expected Garnock to sacrifice you to him?"

She shuddered. "How could I forget?"

"Well, maybe they're after you, too. And maybe, just maybe, Janos caught wind of that threat. Maybe *that's* the real reason why he backstabbed the Dark Druids the way he did. Not simply to rescue Red and the others. I honestly doubt he'd go to such extremes for any of them.

"But to protect *you*? The girl he teases all the time about marrying him someday?" Jake nodded. "He'd do it. In a heartbeat. He'd have no choice. It's who he is."

"God," she whispered. "If that is true, he surely never expected to have to pay such a terrible price. I'd hate me too, if that's the case—"

"Janos isn't a fool, Izzy," Jake interrupted in a flat tone.

She looked at him with surprise.

He turned toward the river, tossing his head as the breeze blew his hair into his eyes. "He's not stupid. He had to know what could happen. Let's be honest—he's been walking a dangerous line for a long time. I'm sure Janos was well aware of what sort of man he was crossing in this Nephilim warlock. If you ask me, he weighed the cost in his mind: six bloodsucker brides and a brood of future killers versus one valiant Keeper of the Unicorns. Well, they're evil, you're good, and he's still a Guardian at heart, fangs and all. A simple equation."

"What are you saying?"

"I know it sounds cold, but think of it. Janos had to know exactly how deadly his little monsters would grow up to be. There were, what, twenty, thirty of them? Each one living hundreds of years? Feeding on innocent human lives every night? How many thousands of people would they have murdered over time?

"Can you imagine having to be responsible for so much death and destruction? I can't. But he's freed of that, now that they're gone. In a way, he's got a clean slate. So, if you ask me, deep down, he's glad they're dead—he's relieved. And he hates himself for it."

She looked stricken. "Poor Janos..."

Jake nodded, fingering the stone in his hand. "You just stepped into the middle of all that at the exact wrong moment. The very person who finally inspired him to choose good over evil, for once and for all."

With that, Jake skipped the stone and watched it fly, making two white splashes in the dark before it disappeared.

Then he turned to her, feeling all the more certain he was right. "Janos doesn't hate you, Izzy. It was just bad timing. He might've lashed out at you in the moment that night, but I'd bet you this entire castle that the one he's really angry at is himself."

CHAPTER 36
The Fratricide

The next day, Waldrick Everton smoothed his new silk waistcoat as he stood before the mirror. Reflected behind him was the luxurious bedchamber he'd been assigned when he first arrived at the Black Fortress three weeks ago.

The cunning magic in the walls of these guestrooms allowed the occupant to conjure any sort of setting that he liked. So Waldrick had imagined for himself a bedchamber worthy of the Palace of Versailles. Lots of gilding. Crystal chandeliers. A magnificent canopy bed.

In one corner sat a bombé chest full of gourmet refreshments he could munch on whenever he pleased. By the opposite wall stood a towering wardrobe full of handsome new clothes that fit him perfectly. And through that white door there lay a splendid bathroom with gold-plated spigots and fine tile mosaics. It had a huge tub for his bubble baths, and large mirrors for making sure he had rid himself of unsightly nose hairs.

In short, Waldrick Everton was back to his old dapper self, living in the style to which he had once been accustomed.

Luxury suited him well. He looked much better, having regained some weight and shaved off that hideous prison beard, saying goodbye to all of its resident fleas. Smelled better, too. But, somehow, he didn't *feel* as happy about all this as he ought.

Why was Fionnula acting so distant? he wondered as he frowned at his tidy, clean-shaved, well-dressed reflection. She'd been excited to see him that first night, but then it was like he barely existed.

Well, Waldrick wasn't blind. He could see how his former ladylove was all aflutter over her precious Nathan the Nephilim.

Humph. No matter. Waldrick would soon win back her affections.

He just needed something that would put him on a more equal footing with the six-fingered freak—namely, getting his pyrokinesis back.

And that was supposed to be happening today.

Waldrick warded off a hint of apprehension at the prospect and flicked a piece of lint off his sleeve. True, he could still hear the screams of those peasants he had accidentally torched as a lad. But surely he was old enough by now to control his gift.

He was a man, after all, not a boy. Once he had his firepower back, then Fionnula and Wyvern would start to treat him as an equal, not some charity case.

Turning toward the door of his chamber with a resolute stare, Waldrick squared his shoulders, pointed an admiring goodbye at his reflection, then dragged himself away from the mirror, determined to get this day underway.

To be honest, though, he didn't much like going out there. His princely chamber was his refuge, but it made a jarring contrast to the rest of this stark black place. He knew by now that once he stepped out that door, there was no telling what bizarre thing might happen next.

Aye, over the past three weeks, Waldrick had learned that life inside the warlocks' castle brimmed with all manner of high strangeness. Still, it was a vast improvement over prison. At least here he was free.

More or less.

Bracing himself, he grasped the doorknob, then abandoned the safety of his chamber. Wyvern had ordered him to appear on the bridge at noon, which was only three minutes away.

Waldrick proceeded down the gloomy black corridor, but when he came to an intersection, he hesitated, unsure which way to go. Every dashed hallway in this maze of a castle looked the same: plain black granite.

Candles in wall sconces here and there provided at least some illumination to help him find his way. But this place was entirely disorienting—on purpose, he would bet. Half the time that he left his bloody room, he wound up lost.

Unfortunately, this was one of those times.

Waldrick optimistically decided to go left. Instead of the bridge, however, what he found was just another black hallway, another eerie intersection.

Well, that wasn't a good sign. He felt impatience tightening in his chest, along with a growing sense of claustrophobia. He turned his head to the left and the right, peering down both identical directions.

Again, the feeble glow of the wall sconces writhed on the polished black granite. There were doors along the hallway, but all of them were closed, giving no clues about where he was.

Blast it, the bridge had to be here somewhere!

He decided to try the right-hand turn this time, since the left hadn't worked out very well. Then he proceeded down the next slick, polished hallway of smooth granite, black as the grave. *This place really needs an interior designer. Someone with a little style...*

This time, he hadn't gone far when a strange noise reached him from ahead. An insectile chirrup, like the sound a cricket makes when it gets into the house.

Waldrick paused, furrowed his brow in suspicion, then continued on cautiously. There were all manner of perilous creatures around here. Half-trolls. Orange ruffed dragons. You could never be too careful when it came to the Dark Druids.

Again, the chirp rasped down the cold stone corridor. But it was much too loud for an ordinary cricket. Waldrick's pulse quickened.

On his guard, he proceeded down the hallway, because he had to locate the bridge. He did not care to find out what the Nephilim would say if he arrived late.

What if Wyvern changed his mind about taking him to Griffon Castle today to retrieve his firepower from the family vault?

Personally, Waldrick had his doubts that Fionnula's precious Nathan would ever be able to open the dashed thing—if he could even *find* the vault's secret location somewhere inside the castle.

But who could say? The Nephilim seemed to have all sorts of tricks up his sleeve. They'd see soon enough whether the too-tall brute was all boasts or could actually do as he claimed.

Then Waldrick heard voices ahead. *Oh good. Maybe someone here can point me toward the bridge.* He hurried toward the intersection of the two hallways.

But nothing could have prepared him for the trio he encountered there.

Two scientists in white lab coats were casually escorting a tall, spindly creature down the other hallway.

Waldrick stopped in his tracks as he realized the chirping sound had been coming from that thing. He swallowed an oath, frozen where he stood.

What is it? His heart pounded as he stared.

Some unholy blend of insect and man, the olive-brown creature stood over six feet tall, with twitchy double wings. A big-eyed insect head, complete with antennae, perched atop its muscular, humanlike body. Except the body had *four* manlike arms...and backward-bending knees.

Waldrick could not believe his eyes.

The bug-man's torso was encased in a hard exoskeleton; thankfully, its lower half was covered with simple brown trousers. It had insect feet.

His heart thumped as he gawked at the thing. It walked along tamely in between the scientists, its double wings flickering now and then, antennae waving.

That was the moment Waldrick knew he was in over his head in this place. That there were things going on around here that he wanted no part of.

Evil things.

He had no idea how that ungodly creature had been made, but he knew Zolond's work when he saw it...

Suddenly, all three passersby noticed him standing there in shock. They stopped in the middle of the intersection.

"You there!" one of the scientists said. "Where are you supposed to be? Security!"

Waldrick's eyes widened as he realized the scientists had a pair of Noxu guards following them—probably on hand to help them keep Bug Boy under control. Because that creature looked dangerous.

The brawny half-trolls now entered the intersection, and, seeing him, the larger one grunted aggressively at Waldrick.

"What are you doing there?" it demanded.

"Oh, n-nothing," Waldrick stammered. He began to back away.

The locust fellow apparently did not like strangers, for it whipped around and chirruped angrily in Waldrick's direction.

Waldrick nearly shrieked, stumbling backward. But the scientists held on to the locust creature's lower pair of arms and spoke soothingly to the monstrous thing, calming it down.

"Let's go, boy," one said. "You've done very well today. Now let's go and get you your lunch. Come along."

"You! Get back to your room," the Noxu ordered Waldrick, snorting gruffly through its tusks.

"I-I'm trying to find the bridge," Waldrick said, taking another backward step as the bristling half-troll stomped toward him. "L-Lord Wyvern is expecting me!"

"Is that so?" the brute retorted, cracking its knuckles.

Just then, a welcome sound reached them—the click-click-clicking of high-heeled shoes hurrying down the corridor behind him.

"*Waldriiiiick!* Oh, for goodness' sake, my little cabbage head, there you are!"

He turned.

To his relief, Fionnula was bustling toward him, looking magnificent in a long royal-blue gown.

"Did you get lost again, you silly boy?"

Waldrick nodded, and the sea-witch's cunning eyes slid to the Noxu warrior.

"It's all right. He's with me," she told the half-troll. "Mr. Everton is wanted on the bridge, posthaste."

The Noxu snorted, but bowed to her. "Yes, milady."

Fionnula certainly seemed to have some clout around here, Waldrick thought. As the leather-clad guard trudged off after the scientists and the locust man, she seized Waldrick's arm.

"Honestly, you great nincompoop," she muttered. "You must be more careful and quit wandering off like this before you get yourself into real trouble. Now, come along."

"D-did you see it?" he asked, still dazed.

"See what, dear?" She turned him around and began marching him firmly down the same hallway he had just traveled, retracing his steps.

"Th-the giant cricket with the body of a-a man!"

She laughed and waved it off. "Oh, that's just one of Zolond's experiments. You know how the Dark Master is, always trying fanciful new concoctions. But never mind that. Nathan's waiting."

The simpering way she said the earl's name jarred Waldrick out of his daze.

Unaware of the sudden souring of his mood, Fionnula squeezed his arm. "Well? Today's the big day! How does it feel? You must be so excited to be getting your power back. I'd be."

"Yes," Waldrick said in distraction. "If Wyvern's really able to pull it off."

"You doubt him?" She cocked her head.

"You know me, dear. Seeing is believing. Obviously, I won't be able to help much. That curse that my blasted Aunt Ramona put on me prevents me from setting foot again on the grounds of Griffon Castle. Wyvern will have to find the vault on his own. I hope he can manage to do it without me."

"Oh, la, darling!" Fionnula trilled a laugh. "I'm sure Nathan and I won't need your assistance. But it's adorable of you to offer." She giggled as if the mere suggestion were absurd.

Waldrick frowned at her, miffed, but then he saw the bridge room ahead, and the towering silhouette of Lord Wyvern standing in the doorway, his fists propped on his hips.

"You're late, Everton," the Nephilim said in his cold, deadened voice. He did not wait for Waldrick to apologize and looked at Fionnula. "Did you check your seeing bowl?"

"I did, my lord. We're all clear. No one's home at Griffon Castle. Apparently, they're all still holed up at Merlin Hall."

"Good." The smartly dressed warlock nodded at the glamorous witch. "A simple mission, then. We'll get in and get out." Nathan stood aside so Waldrick and Fionnula could enter the bridge. "The navigator has already logged in the coordinates. If everyone is quite ready"—he gave Waldrick a long-suffering look—"we can *finally* get underway."

"I'm ready," Waldrick said with a defensive frown. "You really ought to put up signs around this place. Some directions would be nice. Maybe paint arrows on the floor."

Wyvern handed him a pair of dark glasses. "Put these on and go sit down. Strap yourself in. It might be a bumpy ride."

"Humph." Waldrick snatched the dark glasses out of his six-fingered hand, then found an empty seat on the bridge and buckled himself in, nodding politely to the bridge officers.

They and the Nephilim were experienced enough just to stand and brace themselves during these mystical jumps, but Waldrick wasn't about to trust his safety to arcane Dark Druid technology.

He did not intend to go flying through that big glass window when they landed, because he still wasn't sure how all this worked.

As the loud, vibrating hum of the Fortress mechanisms started revving up, he put on the dark glasses then gripped the arms of his chair.

He kept his face impassive, but deep down, Waldrick was not looking forward to seeing Griffon Castle again. His childhood home...

The place where he had murdered his big brother.

CHAPTER 37
Return to Gryphondale

A day off. Glory! As a reward for all of Jake's hard work and dedication over the past three weeks, Derek and the twins gave him and his cousins permission to enjoy a day of leisure.

They were not allowed to stray far, of course, but since things at the castle had been completely quiet since they'd arrived, the three of them were allowed to take a stroll to the nearby village of Gryphondale so they could buy a small, belated birthday gift of some sort for Great-Great Aunt Ramona.

It had been Isabelle's idea the night before, after her sewing project had proved a damp squib.

The village was a charming place, quite safe, and only about a twenty-minute walk away through pleasant countryside. With just a mile or so between them, the village was actually named after the castle, for the two had coexisted for centuries.

The fact that angelic Isabelle was the one who asked on their behalf no doubt also helped to persuade the adults to set them free for a while.

Jake needed it—and empath Izzy told them so.

Their chaperones agreed with a warning to be careful, and in moments, the three of them were off, scrambling eagerly out the door.

After all his grueling discipline of late, Jake relished the precious hours of freedom as he and his cousins moseyed into the village at about eleven o'clock that morning.

The tiny town had cobbled lanes lined with wrought-iron street lamps and picturesque shops. A few half-timbered buildings from medieval days still stood in good order, like the ancient pub and the coaching inn. Others, like the apothecary shop, were housed in simple cottages under cozy thatched roofs.

But most of the shops along the high street were tucked into tidy Georgian terraces with bow windows where their goods were on display. Jake and his cousins wandered in and out of them, searching for a gift for Aunt Ramona.

Better late than never, after all.

Of course, for themselves, their *own* personal reward would be a visit to the glorious Confectioner's Emporium. But they were saving that for last.

The famous candy shop was down at the end of the high street, in a whimsical building that took up nearly the whole corner.

Biding their time, they ambled down the street, drifting in and out of different shops, but Jake couldn't help but notice that, everywhere, older folk among the villagers stopped and stared at him.

"Well, bless my eyes! For a moment there, I thought you was your father, young master," one humble peasant with an oxcart said.

Jake took this as the greatest of compliments, and introduced himself to the townsfolk with as much aplomb as his entire team of trainers could have hoped for.

Indeed, after all his recent education, he was beginning to understand what it meant to be a lord as he moved among the people—his people.

For generations, the folk of Gryphondale had looked to the earls of Griffon Castle as their local landlords and protectors. It was a cordial interdependence that had grown up from medieval days.

True, some aristocrats chose to treat their people shabbily, acting greedy and aloof, subjecting them to crushing rents just to line their own pockets.

Probably unpleasant fellows like that dreadful Lord Badgerton.

But when an earl or duke or baron obeyed the rules of chivalry, he was kind to the common folk who lived on his lands and looked out for them. In this manner, the local people and the earls of Griffon (with a few obvious exceptions, like Uncle Waldrick) had got along peaceably in the same traditional ways that England and most of Europe had known for at least a thousand years.

Of course, the entire village already knew Archie, the future Viscount Bradford, their *other* local lord. Indeed, they had known him since he was a baby.

Isabelle jokingly liked to call her brother the Mayor of

Gryphondale, for Archie greeted all the villagers by name, asked after their children, and chatted with the shop owners how business was going.

Izzy, for her part, didn't say much. She didn't have to. The soft and civilizing presence of a true lady seemed enough to inspire the common folk everywhere she went. She could bring out the best in the roughest, rudest, lowliest of peasants with a kind smile.

After all, as Jake now understood, if a gentleman was raised to become a benevolent protector of the lower orders, a lady's role was to be a good influence on others, warding off the harshness and barbarity in human nature by example.

Jake admired his cousins all the more for their success in these arenas as they all strolled on down the cobbled street, enjoying the bright autumn day.

"You're awfully quiet, coz," the boy genius remarked while a scattering of fallen leaves eddied across their path in a little red-and-gold whirlwind.

"Oh, I'm just thinking," Jake replied, hands in pockets.

"About what?" Isabelle asked.

Jake shrugged. "How different our lives are now from the last time we came here."

"Ah," said Archie. "That is true."

"We'd only just met you," Isabelle reminded Jake.

He nodded. "Aye, Derek had just tracked me down. Uncle Waldrick was still trying to kill me. And then I came here and met you lot... Why, I felt like I was in a dream. I'd never had any relatives before that."

They smiled at him.

"As for my powers, I barely knew how to use them."

"And look at you now. The golden boy of the Order," Archie teased.

"I don't think so," Jake said with a grim look. "Not after that horrible prophecy."

Isabelle gave Jake a pat on the shoulder. "Don't worry, Jake. We won't let you turn evil."

"Weeeell," Archie drawled with a mischievous glint in his dark eyes as they approached the end of the street. "Our cousin should be safe *so long as* the Dark Druids don't try to tempt him with candy."

Jake scoffed, but Izzy nodded, playing along. "You're right, Arch. That would probably work."

Maybe she was right, Jake thought wryly. For they could now

smell the delicious odors wafting out of the Confectioner's Emporium. He gave his cousins a grin. "C'mon, you lot. I hear chocolate truffles calling my name."

"Allow me." Archie marched ahead of them and hauled open the frosted glass doors of the magnificent candy shop.

Calliope music tumbled out, and Jake's excitement climbed.

Archie held the door for them, waggling his eyebrows as he swept a courtly gesture, inviting them to enter first. "Ladies and gentlemen, we have arrived!"

* * *

"Is this the place?" Wyvern asked in a deadened tone, scanning out the carriage window.

Waldrick managed a nod, feeling slightly queasy to be back once more at the outer boundary of his childhood home.

Griffon Castle lay just beyond those trees. They could see its picturesque towers in the hazy pastel distance, for the private parklands surrounding the Evertons' ancestral pile consisted of several thousand acres, mostly pastures and woods.

As for the Black Fortress, Wyvern had landed it in a remote cornfield a quarter mile away. This done, he then conjured a smart black coach-and-four with a servitor for a driver to take them the rest of the way.

Fionnula had been so impressed. Presently, Wyvern eyed the woods on the other side of the babbling stream.

The country road where they had come to a halt followed the brook's winding course as it wrapped around a portion of the castle grounds, on its way to join the Thames.

He and Jacob used to fish in that stream...

Waldrick thrust the memory of his brother out of his mind as Fionnula let out a throaty chuckle, gazing toward the castle. "Ah, this brings back some memories, doesn't it, Waldrick?"

When he glanced across the carriage at her, he found the opera diva dimpling at him with a shadow of their old flirtation.

He nodded, encouraged. "It does. We had a lot of fun here, didn't we, my dear?"

She winked at him. "We certainly did."

Wyvern frowned at their exchange. But better a frown than a smile from that one, Waldrick thought dryly.

On those rare occasions when the Nephilim smiled, it was possible to glimpse his double rows of teeth, and that made Waldrick's skin crawl—never mind that he had scarcely just recovered from his shocking encounter with the Bug Man.

"Well, boys?" Fionnula asked brightly. "Who wants to lead the first dance? Oh, right," she said before either could answer. "Waldrick's cursed. He can't set foot on the grounds. Looks like it's your waltz, Nathan."

The Nephilim gave Fionnula a look that made her blush.

Waldrick scowled at that. She had never blushed at any look from *him.* Indeed, he could barely believe the sea-witch *he* knew was even capable of blushing.

Then the huge man jumped out of the carriage and got the door for her, handing the dark-haired beauty down from the coach.

She took his arm as soon as she had alighted, and Waldrick could do nothing but sit there and stew.

Well, she'd always been a social climber, he admitted. There was no getting around the fact that her precious Nathan was an earl, but Waldrick no longer was.

That was the only reason she seemed to have transferred her affections to the Nephilim. For now, Waldrick supposed that both he and Fionnula owed the brute for their freedom, so he kept his mouth shut.

But he fully intended to gloat when Wyvern failed to open the magical vault hidden somewhere in the castle, as he surely must.

It would be fun seeing him fail. Maybe then Fionnula would stop hanging on the warlock.

True, failure here meant that Waldrick would never get his power back. But he wasn't so sure he really wanted it back, anyway...

Brushing off his doubts, along with the recurring sensation that there were dark plans afoot that he was not privy to, he followed the pair out of the coach.

"I'll go with you as far as I'm able," he said as he joined them on the road.

"Never fear, Everton," Wyvern said with an arrogant glance. "Between Fionnula and myself, I trust we can protect you from the Elder witch's curse. We may not be able to wipe it out entirely, but we should be able to roll it back considerably. Darling, care to give it a go?"

"I'd be delighted," Fionnula said pertly. "But first, we've got to get across this brook. Allow me!"

She went mincing daintily ahead of the men, her ocean-blue skirts billowing in the light breeze. Prancing down to the grassy bank of the little river, she began singing a footbridge into being.

Even here on land, the presence of water helped the sea-witch draw power. The wind began to blow, as always, when it came to her magic. It ruffled the surface of the water and rattled the colorful leaves that still clung to the branches overhead.

Waldrick looked up nervously, but Nathan lifted his eyebrows, looking pleased as a little wooden footbridge started materializing over the stream. Fionnula beckoned to them.

Amazed at her display, Waldrick hurried after her. Fionnula crossed the bridge first, still singing, but he was right behind her, clambering over the wooden planks she had conjured from thin air.

At top speed, Waldrick scrambled onto the opposite riverbank. The cursed side of the stream, for him.

The minute he stepped onto the Griffon side of the water, he could feel a slight tingle in his feet. He wasn't exactly sure how close he could go to the castle without his entire body bursting into flames, per Aunt Ramona's curse.

That sounded awfully unpleasant, so these two mad companions of his had better be able to do what they claimed.

Meanwhile, Wyvern's mode of getting from one side of the brook to the other was faster and considerably more athletic. Eschewing Fionnula's little bridge—no doubt because he wanted to show off—the dragon lord backed up, took a few running steps, then leaped all the way over the stream—almost like he was flying!

Waldrick's jaw dropped as Wyvern, in a running stance, floated horizontally for some twenty feet.

Fionnula let out an eager "Oooh!" and clapped her hands.

In the blink of an eye, the dragon lord landed beside her with a nimble motion, then straightened up to his full, unnatural height again and tugged on his waistcoat.

"Now, then. Shall we?"

All aflutter, Fionnula took his arm. "That was most impressive, Nathan."

"Thank you, my lady. But before we go any farther, let's find out exactly what sort of spells we're dealing with here. I don't trust that Elder witch any farther than I could throw her."

"I couldn't agree more," Fionnula declared.

Meanwhile, the tingle in Waldrick's feet was growing sharper, but those two seemed to have forgotten he was there.

"You've got a good Reveal spell, I trust?" Wyvern asked her.

"Of course," Fionnula said. "Good enough to unmask Ramona's handiwork, I warrant."

"Clever girl." Wyvern lifted her hand and pressed a light kiss to her knuckles, right in front of Waldrick.

Who scowled.

"Then let's go," Wyvern said. And with that, the powerful pair walked off ahead of him, Fionnula singing her sinister heart out, Wyvern lifting his wand and waving it about as he chanted something at the air.

Waldrick stared after them, irked as a soggy cat.

But he could not deny that their combined power was impressive. Whatever sort of Reveal spell they were working, he did not know. He'd never really taken much interest in spell-craft.

But he looked up in wonder as a bright, transparent, almost crystalline dome began to appear, arcing over the woods and the castle turrets in the distance.

It glistened, bright and beautiful, shot through with a myriad of delicate colors like a soap bubble. Musical notes like a gentle stroke of harp strings wafted out of the dome in time with the shifting hues.

Waldrick bunched up his shoulders and ducked his head, instinctively afraid. He knew white magic when he saw it, and Aunt Ramona was not a witch to be trifled with. She had terrified him and even Jacob on occasion when they were boys.

Waldrick knew it was dangerous for him to be here, no matter what those two said. Having just escaped prison, he had no desire to burst into flames, so he hung back, cowering in spite of himself.

Wyvern must've noticed his absence, glancing over his shoulder while Fionnula kept singing.

Her voice grew louder and fiercer, infusing the woods. Her magic intensified, the wind blowing darker and faster—until the center of Ramona's protective dome overhead began turning gray.

"Keep up, Everton! What's the matter?" Wyvern called back to him over the harsh notes that their mutual ladylove was belting out.

"I'm cursed!" Waldrick shouted. "Remember?"

The Nephilim smirked. "Don't be a baby."

"Easy for you to say!"

"Here." Aiming his wand at the ground, Wyvern created a weirdly glowing path of misty blue light. "Just stay on the path, and you should be fine."

"Should be?" Waldrick muttered. *Not exactly encouraging.*

"How do you even know where our secret family vault is within the castle, anyway?" he challenged him after he'd caught up.

Wyvern sent him a bland smile. "That is for me to know and you to find out. Now, stop being a coward and come on!"

With that, the warlock turned away and continued escorting Fionnula deeper into the windblown woods.

It was odd, though, as Waldrick followed. Some instinctive part of him wished to protect his family home from these invaders. But what could he do?

If these two had the power between them to dismantle even one of Aunt Ramona's spells, then *he* certainly had no hope against them. He had no choice but to do as he was told. At least until he got his pyrokinesis back.

With a grimace, he forced himself forward along the glowing blue path and hurried after them. After all, in the strange world of the Dark Druids, anything might happen. Staying close to the mad pair seemed his safest bet.

Meanwhile, all around him, the woods where he and Jacob used to play had turned dark and chaotic. The wind slashed at the trees and the tight spiral of storm clouds Fionnula had summoned overhead ground away Aunt Ramona's bright crystal dome.

Waldrick cowered instinctively. Just moments ago, the sky had been a clear cobalt blue. Now he had to shield his eyes from blowing bits of debris—bark and mulch, twigs and leaves. The birds were in a clamor.

Leaves blew around the three of them in wild swirls and eddies. Branches cracked and crashed. The thorny underbrush whipped and clawed at him as he ran past.

Overhead, meanwhile, the white protective dome was sizzling, turning smoky gray in places, and starting to crack. Lightning bashed at it from the outside, courtesy of the sea-witch, but the bolts were not yet able to pound their way through.

The evil couple were doing all they could to break down the Elder witch's magic.

Waldrick glanced up continually, taking care to stay right in the center of the misty blue path.

In the next heartbeat, however, he froze as a terrifying sound filled the air, revealing the fact that the magical duo weren't *quite* as clever as they thought.

No, indeed. Aunt Ramona must have tricked them, that canny old fox.

For, at that moment, a furious Gryphon roar filled the woods, warning them—too late—that Fionnula's seeing bowl was wrong.

Someone was very much at home.

CHAPTER 38
Bad Pennies

Loud calliope music tooted through the Confectioner's Emporium while the intoxicating odor of a thousand sugary treats filled the air, making Jake and his cousins very silly.

They wandered through the aisles of the marvelous candy shop, giddy and rowdy, making each other laugh at trifles, pulling ridiculous faces and throwing things at one another, puppeteering the stuffed animal toys for sale—in all, enjoying acting immature, a welcome bit of nonsense after all the pressure they'd been under.

Archie immediately acquired one of his favorite candy pipes and lipped it, looking very professorial. Isabelle took a sample of saltwater taffy and held it up over her lip like a mustache, then scarfed it down greedily, abandoning ladylike manners. Jake sampled jellybeans in a rainbow of flavors, tossing them up and catching them in his mouth, and piling up candy bars in one arm to purchase.

They laughingly reminisced on the time Magnus, the town blacksmith, had tried to murder Jake at the candy shop, poor fellow. It seemed like such an easy attack to ward off now, but at the time, it had been terrifying.

They had come a long way in their ability to deal with enemies. And, really, it hadn't been Magnus's fault, anyway. The big blacksmith had been helpless, under the control of some diabolical spell by Fionnula Coralbroom.

"Oh, look, it's soooo cuuuute. I need this!" Isabelle cried, hugging a stuffed lamb toy she found on the shelf like a child half her age.

The boys scoffed, but the Confectioner's Emporium *did* tend to turn one into a little kid again. Jake watched the miniature train go chugging by with great interest, for example. He stood happily munching on one of the candy bars he had bought up at the counter, while the store's toy train circled by on its little track through a candy landscape.

Archie began fooling around at the big calliope fixed against the wall, improvising songs and making up idiotic words. He'd had just enough piano lessons to be dangerous as he took over the keyboard. But as horrid as his playing was, Jake and Isabelle soon joined him there, all three feeling the effects of the sugar and singing along, not caring if they looked ridiculous and sounded even worse.

But, standing beside the towering musical instrument, their laughter faded, and, all of a sudden, Jake blurted out, "I miss Dani."

Archie gave him a rueful smile. "I miss Nixie something awful," he confessed. "But I miss Dani, too."

Izzy nodded. "Me three."

As the calliope notes faded away (someone needed to put in another coin), Jake leaned against the train track with a sigh. "I wonder what she's learning in the Lightrider program. She hasn't really said much about it in her letters."

"Maybe she's not allowed," Archie said. "Each of the big areas of study has its secrets, you know. There's lots Nixie can't tell me about her magical studies."

Jake snorted. "More likely, she's holding back from saying too much about it, after I acted like such a glock-wit. She probably thinks telling me how great it is would only make me feel bad."

"Would it?" Izzy asked, nudging him.

Jake shook his head firmly. "No."

"Come on, boys," Isabelle said, stepping between them. She took an arm of each. "We've wasted enough time here. Go buy whatever else you're going to purchase. We really should be getting back."

Archie's eyes widened. "We didn't buy anything for Aunt Ramona yet!"

"I'm going to get her something here," Jake announced.

After another quick search of the candy shop, Jake ended up buying the Elder witch a ridiculous toy monkey automaton. It had red pantaloons, a little bellhop's hat, and a pair of cymbals that it clashed in the most annoying way.

"Because, clearly, that's what every three-hundred-year-old witch needs," Archie said, staring at the thing.

Jake grinned. "It'll remind her of me."

"In more ways than one," Archie replied.

Izzy chortled.

It was funny, but Jake smacked him in the back of the head anyway, just like Dani's older brothers used to do to *him*.

"Hey!" Archie said, still grinning.

"Ye had it coming, mate."

Isabelle shook her head at their antics, then Jake went up to pay. While the aproned clerk behind the counter gift-wrapped the monkey, Jake hurried up and down the aisles, picking out an assortment of sweets to send to Dani. He just wanted her to know that he was thinking of her, and that coming here without her really wasn't the same.

Impressed with the notion, Archie tracked down some candy spiders and skulls for Nixie, while Isabelle begrudgingly picked out a large sour lollipop for Maddox. That seemed fitting.

At last, they left the Confectioner's Emporium and headed back to Griffon Castle. Their giddiness of earlier had faded away as they strolled down the shady side of the street in thoughtful silence.

The short break today had been refreshing, but Jake knew that, tomorrow, it was back to the routine.

They hadn't gone far, however, when Isabelle stopped, staring with a vacant look straight ahead down the high street.

The boys stopped too.

They glanced curiously at her, then at each other.

Jake shrugged. Archie shrugged back.

Isabelle suddenly lifted her hands to her temples and closed her eyes with a wince. "Ugh..."

"Ho! What's the matter, sis?" Archie's humor vanished as he turned to her.

"Either I ate far too much sugar...or something's wrong at Griffon Castle. Very wrong."

Jake drew in his breath as he realized this was one of her empath moments. Archie and he looked at each other with alarm.

"Wrong *how*?" Jake asked.

"I don't know." She flicked her eyes open again and shook her head. "Something's happening. Danger. Too many people."

Jake looked around. There was hardly anyone in the street at the moment. "What people?"

Listening to her own inner signals, Isabelle suddenly looked around wildly. "We need to go. Now!"

She bolted without warning down the street, and the bewildered boys had no option but to follow. They caught up to her shortly, all three pounding along the cobbled lane in a clatter of footfalls.

"Can't you give us a better idea of what's going on?" Jake exclaimed as they barreled out of the village and down the country road.

"I don't know!" Izzy said, her topknot tumbling askew as she ran. "The spells Aunt Ramona cast must be blocking my ability to sense it. I only know it's bad!"

"Perfect," Archie muttered.

They ran faster, tearing past the farmers' fields, their bags from the candy shop banging about. Cows stopped chewing to stare at them as they raced by.

Ahead, Jake noticed that the afternoon sky had darkened—but only over Griffon Castle.

"Well, that can't be good," Archie said, seeing it as well.

All three of them let out startled exclamations, stumbled to a halt, and ducked instinctively when a lightning bolt flew out of the sky and stabbed at the north tower of Griffon Castle.

"Blimey!" Jake said, uncovering his head. "Er, I don't suppose there's any chance that's Nixie come to visit?"

Archie shook his head, panting with exertion. "Not even in a bad mood would she lightning-strike your castle."

Exchanging fearful glances, they pressed on until, finally, they saw the little stone bridge ahead, spanning the brook that wrapped around this side of Jake's property. It was then they heard wild barking and spotted Teddy racing toward them at top speed.

"Teddy!" Jake cried. Though his stomach hurt from sprinting with a belly full of candy, he managed to run a little faster. Dani had entrusted her dog to his care, after all.

But the speedy brown terrier buzzed right past Jake and ran to Isabelle. *"Arf, arf, arf, arf, ruff!"*

"Slow down, Teddy!" Red-faced and panting, Izzy crouched down, and the wee dog jumped up to rest his front paws on her knee. "Start from the beginning, now, and tell me what's the matter."

The Norwich terrier began making those odd little warbling noises, yips, and growls that he always used when talking to the girl who could communicate with animals.

It really did sound like he was talking, but only Isabelle (and others with this rare gift) could understand.

She gasped and stared at Teddy. “It can’t be. Are you sure?”

The terrier tossed his head with another yip, then twirled around twice.

Even Jake could tell that was a yes.

“Well, what’s he saying?” Archie cried.

Isabelle turned to the boys with a look of shock. “He says Fionnula Coralbroom and Uncle Waldrick have returned. They’re at Griffon Castle right now.”

“What?” Jake’s stomach plummeted. “But th-that’s impossible. They’re in jail!”

“Sweet Bacon, they must’ve escaped,” Archie whispered.

Jake spun around to stare in horror toward his home. Fionnula’s presence would at least explain the lightning.

“That’s not all,” Izzy said with a gulp.

Jake turned back to his cousins.

“Teddy says they’ve brought somebody else with them. A third man he’s never seen before.”

“Who?” Archie asked, his eyes round behind his glasses.

Isabelle shook her head, looking dazed as she picked the little dog up in her arms. “Teddy doesn’t know. But he says...he says the stranger smells of death.”

* * *

Waldrick watched the chaos going on around him, taking care to stay on the glowing blue path that Wyvern had set for him. Fionnula was laughing gaily, hurling bolts of magic at the castle servants who ran out to try to confront them.

One by one, she transformed them into frogs.

“Not again!” said the butler, before he too collapsed out of sight with a *ribbit*, buried somewhere inside his discarded uniform.

The sea-witch marched on, jabbing her high heels into the smooth green turf of the lawn as she strode ahead of her two admirers.

Oh, she was in rare form, and Waldrick suspected she was merely showing off for her precious Nathan.

The Nephilim watched her with amusement, but Waldrick saw no humor in this. Frankly, he was worried.

Because, already, this visit was not going to plan. No one was supposed to *be* here.

Lo and behold, now they had to deal with that intolerable do-gooder, Derek Stone, his dead brother's best friend, not to mention Isabelle's shapeshifting governess, Miss Helena DuVal.

They had not yet encountered the wolf twin, but Henry DuVal couldn't be far off, Waldrick thought.

Personally, he was in no humor to have his leg bitten off by either twin in animal form today. Both genteel teachers could be vicious in battle mode; he'd seen it. That was why the family had hired them.

As far as Waldrick was concerned, the sooner they collected his firepower from the vault and got out of here, the better. Though he took a certain pleasure at the dread on Derek's face when the Guardian came running out of the castle, sword in hand, and saw the Nephilim, Waldrick's enjoyment was short-lived.

For at that moment, the Gryphon entered the fray with a terrifying war cry.

Waldrick looked up and gasped to see the magnificent beast take a running leap off the castle roof, where he knew it had a nest.

It launched into the clear autumn sky and then began to swoop and dive, attacking them, menace from above.

Waldrick shrieked and ducked. He had to take cover! That thing had cause to hate all three of them, but with him, Waldrick knew, it was personal.

The warlock might've held the Gryphon hostage for a few months, but Waldrick had kept him caged for eleven long years.

More importantly, Waldrick had murdered Red's last master. The beast wanted his blood in revenge for Jacob and Elizabeth.

"I'll see to the Gryphon," Wyvern clipped out, glancing at Fionnula. "Contain Stone and the woman."

"Contain?" she asked, sounding disappointed while Waldrick cowered behind the pair and between them.

"You heard me!" Wyvern snapped while Red circled like a giant vulture overhead, plotting his attack. "The boy is probably here somewhere. We can't kill these two in front of Jake or he'll never join our cause. Now, do as I say!"

"Humph!" Fionnula said, for no male had ever dared talk to her like that, Waldrick knew very well. But she nodded in begrudging agreement, then turned all business, lifting her wand to focus on Derek and Miss Helena. "Contain? Hmm, let's see... What would be fun?"

Red dived all of a sudden, swooped right at the Nephilim, and raked him with the claws of his front paw as he went by.

Wyvern bellowed with rage and clutched his bloodied shoulder.

Red screeched as though mocking him and rocketed back up into the sky.

Cringing and whimpering, Waldrick did not intend to be next. He wondered if the Nephilim knew the scratch of a Gryphon would weaken dark magic considerably. But he didn't bother warning Wyvern of this.

No, too scared to speak, Waldrick turned around and ran for his life back down the glowing blue path into the woods.

Behind him, he could hear the warlock ground out a healing spell on himself. *Good luck with that,* he thought. Dark magic could only do so much against a Gryphon scratch.

Other frightening battle sounds rang out behind him as Derek warded off zinging bolts of magic from Fionnula's wand with his sword, deflecting them off the blade. "Get back inside, Helena!"

The French governess replied with an angry leopard roar.

At least, Waldrick hoped it was the leopard. Barreling toward the woods, he stole a terrified peek over his shoulder to make sure it wasn't Red homing in on him.

In that quick glance, he saw Wyvern turn, wand in hand, to face the stone gate pillars flanking the entrance to Griffon Castle's long drive.

The stately pillars were topped with stone statues of gryphons rampant, just like on the Everton family crest.

While Waldrick raced as fast as he could away from danger, the warlock lifted his wand and began chanting in the direction of the stone gryphons.

As soon as Waldrick gained the cover of the trees, heart pounding, he dared to turn around and peek out through the branches to see what was happening.

Out on the lawn, Fionnula cackled as Miss Helena, in her sleek black leopard form, menaced her with another roar, tail thrashing.

Down at the end of the drive, however, the gryphon statues had started to move and come to life.

Waldrick's eyes widened. The gray stone gryphons stretched and bellowed in raspy voices, shaking off dust. Small chunks of cement crumbled free from their feathers.

He drew in his breath as they lifted off their brick pillars and, with magic crackling all around them, flew toward Red.

Meanwhile, leopard-Helena galloped toward Fionnula, who stopped laughing. Derek let out a war cry and ran at Wyvern as if to tackle him.

Waldrick shook his head. *Now, that was not smart. Idiot Guardian.*

But he did not wait to see what happened next, for the Gryphon suddenly spotted him. Circling over the castle roof as it plotted its next charge, Red's keen eagle eyes homed in on Waldrick hiding in the woods.

Red let out a mighty caw and swooped toward the ground.

Waldrick shrieked.

The stone gryphons were of no help yet, still getting their bearings and figuring out how to fly, and now the real one was coming after *him.*

His face contorting with terror, Waldrick turned and fled deeper into the woods, staying on the blue path so as not to be incinerated, but he glanced continually over his shoulder.

The beast dropped down from the sky and galloped up the path after him.

"Curses!" Stumbling in his fright, Waldrick raced on, putting more distance between himself and the castle.

But he needed some sort of hiding place—now!

He could hear the Gryphon's lion paws rustling over the fallen leaves behind him farther down the trail. He did not even want to think about those claws.

Pulse pounding, Waldrick spied a small white structure of some sort ahead among the trees.

For a second, he thought it must be a groundskeepers' shed, tucked away in the woods. These thousands of acres didn't tend themselves, after all. But then Waldrick remembered what the little building actually was.

The family mausoleum.

Aghast, he nearly stopped in his tracks.

I can't go in there!

Jacob and Elizabeth were laid to rest in there!

Of course. Now he remembered...

He even recalled pretending to cry in front of the elegant marble tomb on several occasions, when funeral guests had come to pay their respects.

No—please—I can't face them, he thought in agony.

But when Red screamed with fury somewhere in the woods, hot on his trail, Waldrick bit back a shriek and saw he had no choice. It was either that or get eaten by the Gryphon.

He ran on.

Stumbling over a branch in his fright, he steadied himself and raced toward the mausoleum, his mind made up.

It would be horrible being confined with the corpses of his victims, but built of marble in the style of a tiny Greek temple, at least its heavy stone door and solid roof should keep the beast at bay.

There was only one problem. To reach the tomb, he would have to leave the glowing blue path Wyvern had made.

Oh well. If it was a choice between being torn apart by a vengeful Gryphon or incinerated by Aunt Ramona's curse, the latter sounded like the better way to go. Quicker, anyway.

Besides, maybe, out here, he was far enough away from the castle itself to survive the Elder witch's curse.

Terrified, but with no choice but to chance it, Waldrick held his breath and veered off the misty blue path, darting toward the little building.

At once, his feet started feeling warm.

He kept running. The tingling sensation traveled up his legs. He sprinted toward the mausoleum, hearing snarls through the snapping twigs and cracking underbrush behind him.

At top speed, Waldrick careened past the memorial flame forever burning outside the little Greek temple. He seized the outer metal grate covering the thick stone door of the tomb.

Waldrick yanked the wrought-iron grate open, then pushed with all his might against the polished stone slab of the door.

He could hear twigs breaking, angry puffs of breath as lion paws galloped closer. The Gryphon was closing in.

Gory visions of being devoured filled Waldrick's brain as he slammed his shoulder against the stone barrier a few more times until it budged, ignoring the pain and the burning in his feet, until it suddenly gave way.

The crypt door swung open. At once, he flung himself into the dark, chilly space, then threw his weight against the back of the door as the Gryphon charged, just a few feet away.

The stone door banged shut in the Gryphon's face, just in the nick of time.

Red screamed outside. Waldrick heard the beast pound against the door. Its claws rasped down the stone like the sharpest of nails on a chalkboard.

Thankfully, the door held.

Then, by the sound of it, the stone gryphons that Wyvern had animated must've caught up to Red, for the real Gryphon withdrew, apparently forgetting about Waldrick for the time being.

It had to deal with new enemies.

Chest heaving, his ashen face pouring sweat, Waldrick turned around and leaned against the cold marble door behind him, trying to catch his breath and slow his hammering heartbeat.

Well, at least he hadn't burst into flames.

Indeed, come to think of it, in here, his feet no longer burned, though they were still smoking. Perhaps Aunt Ramona's spell did not apply inside the holy ground of this tomb.

It was extremely dark inside the mausoleum. Chest heaving after his ungentlemanly sprint, Waldrick shielded his nose and mouth with his hand, not wishing to breathe in air tainted with the foulness of dead bodies.

The bodies of people you murdered. Your own brother. Your sister-in-law.

Waldrick closed his eyes when they started adjusting to the gloom. He did not want to see. Some feeble light came in from small, high windows filled with thick glass blocks high up on the walls. But he refused to look at the twin sarcophagi—at first.

But then, after all those months in prison, brooding on his wicked deeds and trying his best to be a man and take responsibility for what he had done, he finally decided to face up to his crimes for once and for all.

Gathering his paltry courage, Waldrick flicked his eyes open and forced himself to look.

It was then that he got the shock of his life. He stared blankly at what he saw, then rubbed his eyes and looked again.

The picture didn't change. Incredulity sent chills down his spine.

How can this be?

Jacob and Elizabeth, as the Earl and Countess of Griffon, had been buried side by side in stately marble sarcophagi, each resting on solid stone pillars. Their coffins nested inside these white marble casings, well protected for centuries to come.

But something was wrong. Drastically wrong. Waldrick stared in utter confusion.

Both sarcophagi sat open, their heavy stone lids cast aside.

"What's this?" he whispered. Because even from the spot where he leaned against the door, he could see that the lids of both inner coffins had been propped open too. And inside...

The coffins were empty.

He stared without comprehension. *But I murdered them. I went to prison for it.* The question suddenly exploded in his brain.

Well, if they are not here, then where the devil are they?

Are they even dead?

What is going on?

His mind reeling, Waldrick lurched away from the door and took a slow walk around the dusky interior of the mausoleum, staring at the two empty coffins where their bodies should have been.

He felt sick with confusion, utter bafflement...and the dawning realization that somebody had lied to him.

His eyes narrowed.

Fionnula.

Waldrick looked up from the coffins, listening in the direction of the battle sounds.

Rushing into his mind came the memory of all those sly glances he had seen pass between Wyvern and the sea-witch. As if the two of them were sharing some deliciously conniving plot.

It was then, deep down in the pit of his stomach, Waldrick realized that Fionnula—his ladylove, his supposed partner in crime—had clearly betrayed him somewhere along the way.

He did not know how or why or any of the details. But he could smell her treachery a mile away. It was the only explanation.

His eyes narrowed. *What are you playing at, you soggy hag?*

Nobody made a fool of Waldrick Everton. *What have you done with my brother and his wife?*

Oh, by Jove, I will get to the bottom of this. Hardening his will, Waldrick marched back to the mausoleum door and cocked his head, listening intently for the Gryphon.

Hearing nothing close by, he pulled the door open a crack, peeked out, and confirmed that Red was busy battling the stone gryphons in the sky well over by the castle.

Relieved, Waldrick sneaked out of the tomb with the utmost caution. Then he pranced and hopped his way back to the blue, misty path with all haste, his feet smarting until he reached it.

On his way, he *did* notice more sounds of mayhem emanating from the direction of the castle, but he did not intend to stick around and find out what was happening.

As soon as he reached the glowing blue trail, he headed for the carriage, determined as ever to save his own skin.

This time, his did not mind wading back through the creek, as the water cooled off his feet. But as he climbed back up the other grassy bank, and then hurried down the road to wait inside the carriage, he made a solemn pact with himself to hide what he'd learned from the witch and the warlock.

It was tempting to ask questions, but something told him that it was better for his health to play dumb.

No matter. He could be devious when the occasion called—just like Jacob had accused him so long ago.

One way or another, he would get to the bottom of this. And if Fionnula had double-crossed him, by Jove, the sea-witch would be sorry.

CHAPTER 39
The Battle of Griffon Castle

After what Teddy had just told Isabelle, Jake and his cousins looked at each other and all thought the same thing: *Run!*

At once, Jake turned and darted off the arched stone bridge. He started pounding toward the castle.

Archie wasn't far behind. Isabelle scooped the dog up into her arms to keep him safe and raced after the boys.

Leaving the bridge, Jake and his cousins ran the rest of the way to the grounds of Griffon Castle. The closer they went, the more disturbing the entire scene grew.

Dark clouds swirled overhead, and a strong breeze blew, but only in the vicinity of his estate. Jake was worried sick about Red, Derek, and Helena.

Henry had returned to Bradford Park, since Jake's private classes had been canceled for the day. But the servants were all on duty at the castle, and Fionnula had turned the poor people into frogs before.

His dread mounted when he heard Red screech somewhere in the sky, but he could not see his Gryphon on account of the trees as he veered off the road, dashing through the open wrought-iron gates at the end of the driveway.

"Hold on!" Archie said, skidding to a halt a few feet behind him.

Jake turned; Archie pointed, panting.

"Aren't there supposed to be stone gryphons on top of those pillars?"

"Blimey," Jake mumbled.

The decorative gryphons were gone. A bit of cement rubble littered the base of the pillars.

"Oh no," Isabelle murmured as she caught up. She hugged Teddy closer as she gawped at the empty brick pedestals flanking the drive.

Jake had a bad feeling about this. "C'mon, you lot. We'd better stick together."

His cousins moved closer and, together, they sneaked toward the castle, taking cover behind a massive evergreen shrub.

Huddled there, they could finally manage to see what was happening on the lawn.

Jake clenched his jaw, his heart pounding; his home was under attack by a wand-wielding enemy he had never hoped to see again.

Blast it, Fionnula had turned his servants back into frogs!

His cousins fumed on either side of him, seeing this as well. Teddy growled. Izzy wrapped her fingers around his snout to keep him from barking.

Jake glared to see that Fionnula had also trapped Derek and leopard-Helena under a giant glass bell jar—like knickknacks or dried flowers to be put on display.

The sea-witch cackled with glee as leopard-Helena loped around the perimeter of the huge bell jar, trying to find a way out.

He could see Derek yelling at Fionnula, but the bell jar silenced him. His face stamped with fury, the master Guardian kicked again and again at the thick glass walls of the container without even making a crack.

"Sweet Bacon," Archie murmured. "I use jars like that in the lab to contain gases. They're airtight! Before long, Derek and Helena won't be able to breathe. We've got to get them out of there before they run out of oxygen."

Jake did not take his eyes off the scene before him. "How?"

"Well...let's see." Archie pushed his spectacles up higher onto his nose. "I've got a kerosene blowtorch in my lab at home."

Jake looked at him, then shrugged. "Of course you do."

"I could at least cut some air holes in the glass so they can breathe until we can free them."

Jake nodded. "Good plan."

"Um, Jake? I think I found the gryphons from your driveway pillars." Isabelle pointed discreetly at the sky.

Jake drew in his breath as Red zoomed into sight above the castle, circling from the distance.

Right behind him, the two stone gryphons gave chase, squawking at Red and doing their best to knock him out of the sky.

The animated gryphons were harrying and hectoring the real one, leaving Red unable to do anything about Fionnula—or Waldrick, if he was truly here.

Jake didn't see him anywhere. Nor did he see the third man Teddy had reported.

"Do you think it was Fionnula who brought those statues to life?" Izzy asked, peeking over Jake's shoulder. "It doesn't really seem like her style of magic, what with water and all.

"No, but we know of someone *else* who's very adept at manipulating stone," Jake said grimly. "Remember those rock golems in Greece?"

At that moment, an overly tall and muscular man with brown hair strode into view, wand in hand.

The kids ducked instinctively behind the bush, but the stranger didn't see them. He was watching Fionnula as he crossed the lawn, heading for the house.

He said something to her, but his voice was too low for them to hear.

"Sweet Euclid," Archie murmured, "is that who I think it is? Here?"

Jake stared at the oversized man, a cold knot of dread in his gut. "Well, it isn't Uncle Waldrick."

Their uncle had no magical powers to speak of, but the towering stranger now blasted the front door of the castle off its hinges with a flick of his wand.

Then he went inside.

Jake seethed at the intrusion into his home. But what was mere trespassing when one was already a member of the Dark Druid Council?

"Wyvern," he growled. "What's he doing in my house?"

Isabelle gave him an ominous look. "Probably looking for you, coz."

Archie nodded, worry in his eyes. "Because of the prophecy. Bet he's come to recruit you."

"Well, it's not going to work." Jake turned to them as they remained crouched down behind the huge green shrubbery. "Here's the plan. You two get to Bradford Park. Iz, put Teddy somewhere safe, then find Henry. We need his help. After that, send an Inkbug message to Aunt Ramona. Better yet, send a telepathic message to Janos that we're in trouble—"

"It's daytime. He can't help us." She shook her head. "But don't worry. I'll bring help, believe me."

Jake nodded, unsure what she meant, but, trusting the girl to her own devices, he looked at Archie. "You bring your blowtorch and make sure Derek and Helena can breathe. I'll cover you."

"What are you going to do, Jake?" Izzy asked.

"Help Red, for starters. Then deal with Fionnula."

"Be careful," Izzy warned.

He nodded. "Go. Keep an eye out for Uncle Waldrick. He could be lurking here anywhere—and don't let Fionnula see you, either, until I've neutralized the situation."

"*You're* going to neutralize Zolond's second-in-command?" Archie asked.

"Have a little faith! I'm not afraid of him," Jake said.

"That's what worries us," Izzy mumbled, but when Jake scowled at them, the Bradford siblings crept away, leaving their bags of candy by the shrub and sneaking off through the woods toward their adjoining estate.

"Right," Jake whispered to himself. At least he didn't have to take on both witch and warlock at the same time. But he was not going to stand by and let them wreak havoc on his home and the people he loved.

Fists clenched, Jake rose. His heart pounded as he strode up the rest of the driveway toward the lawn.

He watched the aerial battle overhead as he approached, assessing how best to destroy the stone gryphons attacking Red.

But then, while he was still marching up the drive toward the courtyard in front of the castle, a chilling howl echoed out across the grass.

Fionnula turned toward the sound. It was coming from the direction of Bradford Park.

The howl was unnerving, even though Jake knew exactly what—or rather, who—it was.

Henry must've smelled trouble all on his own, or sensed his twin's distress, for Archie and Isabelle had obviously not reached their home yet.

Jake was torn between relief that adult help was on the way and dread over what a shapeshifter could possibly do to the likes of Fionnula, let alone Wyvern.

He trusted his tutor to use his head, but the thought of anything happening to their oh-so-civilized Henry was terrible.

With this new factor thrown in, Jake suddenly wasn't sure how to proceed. Red had flown out of range again, so he couldn't do much there yet.

Keeping low, Jake approached the lawn, crouching behind the underbrush as he ventured closer to Fionnula. Her back was turned as she watched the distance.

Henry's howl seemed to have riveted her. No doubt it had been his intention to draw the danger to himself.

"Chivalry, Jake," as his tutor had told him so many times.

They did not have to wait long for the shapeshifting tutor to join the fray. Wolves were fast, especially when their assigned cubs were in danger.

It seemed only seconds later that a massive gray wolf exploded out of the underbrush, barreling top-speed toward the sea-witch, barking and snarling. All of the mild-mannered tutor's inner viciousness had been unleashed.

Closing the distance between him and Fionnula in a streak of thick gray fur, wolf-Henry leaped into the air to tackle her, fangs bared.

With a shriek, Fionnula brought up her wand.

Jake bit back a shout of protest as the bolt of magic hit his tutor.

Wolf-Henry froze in midair, motionless and floating. He didn't seem injured, but neither could he move. He looked rather startled, floating there, mid-leap, some three feet off the ground.

Jake could almost hear him: *"Oh dear."*

Inside the bell jar, leopard-Helena roared and pounced against the glass, no doubt threatening Fionnula not to harm her suspended brother.

Derek, meanwhile, had turned and seen Jake approaching. The Guardian paled, then began mouthing and gesturing at Jake to go away, somehow avoiding Fionnula's attention.

"Get out of here! Hide! It's Wyvern!"

Derek pointed toward the house, trying to warn him that the infamous Nephilim lord was inside.

Jake shook his head, giving his mentor a shrug that said, *I already know!*

Then he noticed Red heading back his way and forgot about Derek for now.

Summoning up his telekinesis, he took aim, then announced his arrival on the scene by exploding one of the stone gryphons tailing Red right out of the sky.

He took care to shatter it when it was well away from the giant bell jar. He didn't want to break the bell jar and send chunks of sharp glass raining down on Derek and Helena.

The second stone gryphon let out an angry screech and headed toward Jake. He brought up his right hand and launched a blow, blasting it into a thousand pieces.

Red roared with pride, then came gliding down to land by his side.

Fionnula glared at him. "Well, look who it is. Such a naughty boy."

She aimed her wand at him, but Jake was faster, knocking it out of the witch's grasp with a wave of his hand. It hurtled end over end through the air, and the bolt of magic she had tried to shoot at Jake flew wide.

The wand bounced harmlessly onto the ground, merely scorching the grass where it landed.

"Guard her, Red," Jake ordered.

The Gryphon growled, all too happy to obey. He leaped in front of Fionnula, blocking her path when she tried to retrieve her wand.

She stopped in her tracks, eyes widening as Red snarled and reared up, his wings out, his tufted tail thrashing. She stood frozen, too terrified to move, but not much use without her wand.

Red placed himself between the sea-witch and her most vital tool.

Jake got to work trying to lift the bell jar off Derek and Helena with his telekinesis, but Fionnula must have anticipated him trying that, for the thing wouldn't budge.

He kept trying anyway.

"There, there, kitty-bird," Fionnula said to Red with a nervous laugh, lifting her hands in token surrender. "Perhaps I can sing you a little ditty."

"Don't even try it," Jake warned her. "Start singing, and I tell him to attack."

Red roared at her for good measure; Fionnula squealed with fright.

"Nathan!" she hollered, glancing anxiously toward the castle.

Jake followed her gaze.

Trusting Red to guard the sea-witch, he turned his attention to the tall, cold-eyed man who now appeared, looming in the doorway of the castle.

"Nathan, do something!"

The towering stranger ignored the sea-witch, his stare homing in on Jake.

"Well, well. Who have we here?" A wary smile crept across his face as the stranger stepped out of the castle. "My little Lord Griffon. We meet at last."

* * *

Wyvern gazed at the boy in amazement. He could not deny he was impressed.

You see? Shemrazul whispered in his mind. *I told you.*

You did, Wyvern answered mentally.

It was one thing to hear secondhand about Jake's various exploits, but seeing them firsthand—seeing *him*—struck Wyvern profoundly.

Moments ago, he had been inside the house working to locate the vault and ignoring the mild queasiness he felt from the scratch of that blasted Gryphon.

A wound from such creatures contained a sort of venom noxious to those on the dark side. Eh, he'd had worse.

Walking through the castle, surveying its fine rooms, and gazing coldly at the family portrait of those two Lightriders with their infant son, Wyvern had soon found the place where the vault was hidden. Then he'd heard a long, haunting howl. He had rushed over to the nearest window and looked out just in time to see Jake use his telekinesis to explode the stone gryphons.

Wyvern had stared with astonishment at the lad's ferocity and skill. He had seen many things in his day, but never such ability in one so young. And then, when the young scoundrel had defeated Fionnula with a mere flick of his hand, Wyvern had been flooded with an even greater eagerness to meet his future son.

He knew he had to handle this carefully, though.

Already on his way, he was marching toward the door when Fionnula shrieked his name. (Wyvern had long since decided that his future queen was a little annoying. But so be it.)

At last, face to face with his future heir, Wyvern grasped the wisdom of Shemrazul's plan. This magnificent young hellion would indeed make a worthy crown prince.

Jake stood a little over five feet tall with a shock of straw-blond hair and blazing blue eyes; he had a lean build and a highborn bearing.

Though he was a bit tousled and rosy-cheeked from the fray, his tailored clothes were obviously Bond Street, giving him a well-dressed appearance.

Good. Wyvern could not abide untidiness.

Most impressive to *him*, however, was how Jake held his ground as Wyvern approached.

Remarkable. He could tell the kid was frightened, but Jake refused to back down. On the contrary, the boy forced himself forward a step or two, and Wyvern was delighted with his courage.

Why, grown men frequently babbled and sometimes even peed themselves with fright when they found themselves fixed in his sights.

Not the plucky Lord Griffon.

When Wyvern noticed Jake's silent gulp, however, he almost wanted to laugh with his first real flicker of genuine fatherly feeling. Pride surged through him as the cheeky young rogue scowled at him, refusing to flinch.

Given the difference in their height, Jake lifted his chin to keep holding Wyvern's stare as he approached. The boy glared up at him—as though Wyvern could not have squashed him like a bug.

Such spirit!

You're right, Father. He is the one.

Test him, Shemrazul replied in Wyvern's mind. *See for yourself what he is made of. But don't push him too hard. You'll need to take him with you.*

Wyvern smiled, studying the lad. Jake would probably go kicking and screaming, but for his part, Wyvern was going to enjoy becoming a father at last.

And it all started now.

CHAPTER 40
The Temptation of Jake

Blimey, but that oversized mumper was looking at him funny, Jake thought, feeling nervous under the warlock's scrutiny.

Wyvern had stepped out of the house and begun strolling toward him, leaving the front door open.

Jake stood his ground, prepared for anything, but he shifted his weight uncertainly. Why hadn't the brute attacked him yet? The question worried him, but he showed no fear.

On the contrary, he drew strength from his hatred of this man for all he'd done to Derek. To Janos. To Tex. To poor, wingless Celestus.

And most of all, to Red.

Ah, but it looked like Red had got a bit of his own back, Jake thought, noticing the torn cloth and bloodstains where Wyvern's fine coat clung to his giant shoulders.

The Gryphon growled from nearby, still guarding Fionnula.

"Stay back, boy," Jake ordered Red, and Wyvern's unnerving half-smile curved higher for some unknown reason.

"Nathan!"

"Keep your peace, woman." Wyvern gestured at the sea-witch, never taking his eyes off Jake.

Jake arched a brow at the earl's dismissive tone with the famed sorceress. Even more startling, Fionnula obeyed. He glanced over and saw her fold her arms across her chest with a pout, but she didn't argue.

He looked up at Wyvern again, rather impressed that he'd apparently tamed the wild sea-witch. But no wonder the warlock was so good at manipulating stone. Wyvern's gray eyes were as cold and unfeeling as the average boulder.

And he was Nephilim, all right. Jake's glance flicked down to the Dark Druid's hand, where too many fingers curled around his wand.

"I've heard a lot about you, young man." Wyvern sauntered closer, his heavy footfalls crunching over the gravel as he crossed the courtyard outside of the castle with an air of caution.

As if Jake could do much of anything to him. The bloke was nearly seven feet tall, for starters. And while Jake might be able to blow up any rock golems the warlock might create, it was important in life to understand one's limits.

Right now, all he had was his bravado. It had usually been enough.

"What do you want?" he demanded with an arrogant toss of his head.

Wyvern's half-smile grew to a whole one at Jake's rude tone.

From the corner of his eye, meanwhile, Jake could see Derek pounding on the glass, could hear the dull thumping of his fist, but his mentor's furious warnings to Wyvern not to harm him were barely audible.

The warlock did not seem inclined to do so.

Which was worrisome in its own way.

Of greater concern, however, was when Jake noticed Derek tug at his cravat. Jake tensed, realizing he and Helena were already feeling the lack of oxygen in there. Blast it, hadn't the man already suffered enough at the hands of the Nephilim?

Prepared to do whatever it took to keep his loved ones safe, Jake forced himself forward, going to meet his enemy halfway, right in the center of the courtyard. Frankly, he wasn't feeling all that bold, just protective.

He and Wyvern stopped a few feet apart in the middle of the now-sunny courtyard.

The storm clouds had stopped swirling overhead since Fionnula had lost her wand. They had begun slowly dissolving, still shifting between dark and light, shadows and sun. At least the wind had died down.

Dry-mouthed, Jake hoped that Isabelle had found the Inkbug by now and sent some kind of warning to Aunt Ramona. Maybe there was something the Elder witch could do long-distance.

But he doubted it.

And yet, still, Wyvern didn't attack him. For another moment, neither Jake nor the Nephilim spoke, sizing each other up.

Jake was not thrilled to see he only came up to the man's chest.

At this close range, he could feel the aura of evil emanating from the warlock. They said he was Zolond's enforcer. That he ran the Black Fortress and even had a seat on the Dark Druid Council.

Aye, Jake thought, and they also said his father was a demon.

He'd heard that rumor at Merlin Hall during the summer, after Derek had brought him and the others there. At the time, Jake wasn't sure he believed such a mad claim, but standing in the Nephilim's presence, he knew now it was true.

A dark, remote, otherworldly atmosphere surrounded the well-dressed man as surely as if he wore an apocalypse-scented cologne.

He did not seem entirely human, and now Jake knew why.

Wyvern was half demon.

Jake had heard that the earl's real father was not the previous Earl of Wyvern, but Shemrazul, the same devil with whom Garnock the Sorcerer had originally made his pact centuries ago.

Jake believed he had met the mighty Shemrazul briefly when he had stood on the edge of Hades after killing Garnock's ghost.

Indeed, the huge red devil might've come bursting up out of Hell to terrorize the world if not for Celestus and three other warrior angels, who had shown up in Roman-style armor with wings unfurled and shining swords of light in hand to drive Shemrazul back down where he belonged.

That, Jake thought, had been the most extraordinary thing he had ever seen in all his dealings with the magical world so far.

Wyvern, meanwhile, was studying Jake intently. "Well," he said, "here we are."

Indeed. Jake would've rather been anywhere else. The longer he stood in Wyvern's presence, the worse he felt, as if he were being drugged with a slow drip of despair.

At a loss, he glanced over at Derek for reassurance, simply out of habit.

The Guardian was watching their encounter with a look of dread. He had stopped pounding on the glass. This was the first Jake could recall ever seeing real fear on his mentor's rugged face. It shook him.

How Jake wished his father was there in that moment. But how could you miss a stranger?

Feeling more and more alone, he glanced at his Gryphon. Red's mane of feathers around his neck were standing on end. His golden eyes glowed with wrath.

He was still obeying Jake's order to keep his distance, but Red would certainly give his life if necessary to protect him, if it came to that.

Jake shuddered at the thought, feeling powerless and very much out of his league. He was well aware of just how dangerous this intruder was, after all.

The man had burned Janos's family alive.

"It occurs to me we've never been properly introduced," Wyvern said. "I am Nathan, Lord—"

"I know who you are." Jake stared coldly at him. "You're the man who stole my Gryphon."

Red snarled.

Wyvern tilted his head. "You're the lad who destroyed my Atlantean treasure trove."

"You sent Nightstalkers to kill me," Jake reminded him.

"And you fended them off. With a darkling blade, eh? I wonder where you got one of those." Wyvern sent him a knowing wink. "How's your vampire friend these days?" He made a mocking sad face.

Jake was stunned. His utter lack of remorse for having murdered vampire women and children was the thing that finally made Jake take a step backward.

Behind the glass, Derek looked even more alarmed to see him do that, while poor wolf-Henry hung helpless in midair, still poised to leap.

Jake shook his head to try to clear it; the manifestation of real evil left him disoriented. He'd faced Garnock, yes, but this was the first time he could recall encountering a *living* person with no conscience whatsoever. Even Uncle Waldrick and Fionnula showed mild traces of humanity on occasion.

But Wyvern's depth of inborn malice made him feel dizzy, as though he were in the presence of some alien life form.

Crikey, if the son was this bad, Jake didn't even want to think about what it would be like having to face down the father.

Somehow, though, he shook off the effects of evil's nearness and managed to regroup, laying hold once more of his bold façade. "Enough chitchat. If it's me you're looking for, well, you found me. So what do you want?"

Wyvern laughed at his insolence. "By Shemrazul's horns, lad, you are something, aren't you? Tenacious cub, just look at you. All flash and fire." The earl folded his arms across his chest, looking pleased. "I daresay you'd make any father proud."

Jake went very still.

Was that a threat against his father—who might still be alive?

After all, Jake now believed that his parents were being held somewhere inside the Black Fortress, perhaps in that comatose state he had heard Tex describe during the magical parliament.

Though he did not care at all for the way the earl was assessing him like a colt for sale at auction, Jake focused on the warlock's comment. "What do you know about my father?"

"Hmm, that is the question, isn't it?" Wyvern gave him a mysterious smile, then looked over at the two piles of crushed gravel littering the lawn. "You made short work of my stone gryphons, I see. Well done."

Jake shrugged, baffled that the massive man should congratulate him on this act of destruction. "It was a lot easier than ending the rock golems, actually." He could not resist a cheeky nod at the earl's bloodied shoulder. "Looks like my real Gryphon nearly made short work of you, my lord."

Wyvern shook his head and chuckled, seemingly in spite of himself. "Oh, you are a spitfire."

Why is he being nice to me?

"Come, Jake," Wyvern murmured. "What are you doing at Griffon Castle?"

"Uh, I live here," Jake said.

"That's not what I mean. What are you doing with the Order? Look at these losers. They're supposed to be keeping you safe, but Fionnula and I rendered them helpless in under ten minutes. You can't trust these people, and frankly, you don't need them." He glanced scornfully at Derek and the shapeshifter twins. "Deep down, you know your destiny lies with us."

"The Dark Druids?" Jake scoffed. "Don't make me sick."

"Oh, I could, if you like. Name your disease of choice. Measles? Mumps? The chicken pox? Oh, I know—how 'bout leprosy?" The earl waved his wand, and Jake felt a sudden burning pain burst through his right hand.

"Ow!" Lifting his hand, he gasped in horror to find it instantly covered with disgusting boils. Right before his eyes, the skin began turning white, and his pinky finger looked like it was rotting off.

It was the hand of a leper.

Jake looked at him in a panic. "Put it back!"

Wyvern grinned, flashing double rows of teeth.

Jake recoiled to see such a thing; Wyvern quickly shut his mouth with a wounded look.

"Nathan," Fionnula chided. "Don't torture the boy. He needs to see that he can trust you."

Jake glanced at her in disbelief. Trust Wyvern? She was dreaming. But he couldn't be bothered with her foolishness right now.

The ashy whiteness had begun creeping down his right wrist. Pus oozed from the boils.

"Oh, don't worry, dear," Wyvern said, "I'm only having a bit of fun with the lad. Of course we wouldn't wish to damage those telekinetic hands. They're too valuable."

Wyvern waved his wand again, and Jake's hand returned to normal.

Staring at his limb, his heart pounding, Jake wiggled his fingers then checked around his wrist and forearm. The skin was clear. Then he looked at Wyvern, at a loss.

"Really, darling," Fionnula said, "that wasn't very nice."

Nice was probably not a word in the Nephilim warlock's vocabular.

Wyvern looked at her, then back at Jake. "Just teaching him a little lesson, dear. The boy's got to learn to respect us. If we are ever going to be a real family."

"Wait—*what*?" Jake had barely just recovered from his bout of leprosy, but this shock was even greater. Family? With Wyvern and Fionnula?

Good God!

"What did you mean by that?" he demanded, but Wyvern ignored him, for just then, speaking of family, Archie came running to the rescue, his trusty tool bag in one hand, blowtorch in the other. He wore thick leather safety gloves on his hands, while his welding goggles perched atop his head.

"And who is this little fellow?" Wyvern asked. "Is this that Maddox boy the vampire spoke of?"

"No," said the sea-witch. "It's Archie Bradford. Ramona's *other* nephew. He's rather famous in his own right."

"I've never heard of him."

"They say he is a brilliant scientist."

"Really?" Wyvern murmured. "How intriguing."

"You leave him alone!" Jake warned the pair fiercely.

Both Derek and Helena had also reacted to Archie's arrival. They ran to the far edge of the bell jar facing Bradford Park, where Derek started banging on the glass and trying angrily to wave Archie back.

Leopard-Helena let out a muffled roar, while wolf-Henry whimpered, straining against his immobilized state, no doubt burning to protect his star pupil.

"Archie, stay back!" Jake yelled, terrified of what Wyvern might do to him.

"Can't, coz! Derek and Helena are about to run out of oxygen." Skidding to a halt, Archie tossed all his sciencey accoutrements down on the grass beside the bell jar, tools clanking.

Jake whirled to face Fionnula. "Get rid of that thing!" he pleaded. "Let them out of there!"

"Humph!" She turned away with her nose in the air. "I'd need my wand for that."

"Keep them where they are," Wyvern ordered her.

Jake scowled while Archie began knocking on the bell jar here and there, listening to the sound it made, apparently looking for a thinner section of the glass.

Choosing a spot, Archie pulled down his goggles and frantically pumped the pressure handle on his blowtorch, then he twisted the valve open.

"What on earth is he doing?" Wyvern asked, watching with curiosity.

"Fixing things," Jake snapped. "It's what he does."

"Extraordinary," the earl murmured.

Jake glared at him. "You hurt one hair on his head, and you make a permanent enemy of me. You got that, you oversized oaf?"

Wyvern smirked. "Never fear, Jake. I'm well aware that boys your age need at least one good mate. I should've liked to have one when I was young, too. Fionnula, no killing Mr. Bradford."

"It's Dr. Bradford, actually!" Archie shouted, then fired up his blowtorch and stood back while it flamed.

Jake was awed at his intrepid single-mindedness. The boy genius just ignored the danger, same as in the lab.

Archie waved Derek and Helena back to a safe distance while the blowtorch burned off the charge in the flash pan, then began climbing to operating temperature.

When the flame streaming out of the nozzle burned blue, Archie picked up the blowtorch with care and started melting a hole in the glass.

"I'll tell you what," Wyvern said quietly, turning to Jake. His chiseled face softened a bit, but his eyes remained flinty. "You come with me and Lady Fionnula right now, and I'll let you bring your Gryphon and your little friend. No harm will come to them. You have my word. You'll be quite content with us. I promise, Jake. You'll have your heart's desire. You've seen what we can do." Wyvern nodded toward the sea-witch. "With our magic, Fionnula and I will grant your every wish like the mother and father you never had."

"I had them!" Jake said, enraged by his filthy offer. "*Your* side took them away from me! What have you done with my parents?" he shouted, his voice climbing with the echo of pain. "Are they still alive or have you murdered them?"

Wyvern didn't answer the question. "Let us look after you, Jake," he said instead. "Come. You've been through so much, poor boy. You don't need the rest of this sorry lot. You belong with us."

Jake shook his head, incredulous. Truly, he could not believe what they were suggesting. The notion was preposterous. He would've liked to see Archie's reaction to the ludicrous proposal, but his cousin could not hear their exchange over the hum of his blowtorch blasting the glass.

Wyvern nudged him with a knowing smile. "Wouldn't you like to be a prince?"

Jake shrugged. "Not in the slightest. But, just out of curiosity, how would I do that? How would going with you make me a prince?"

"You would serve as my heir when I am the sorcerer-king."

Jake scoffed. "I want no part of your stupid prophecy!"

"You know about that?"

"Of course!"

"How?"

"Pfft, I'm not telling you that. You're a Dark Druid. The lot of you are loony."

Wyvern quirked a brow. "If it's fate, Jake, there's nothing you can do."

"If it's fate, then I choose the Order. Not you."

"Hmm." Wyvern's eyes narrowed. "I was worried you'd say that."

"So, what now? You gonna kill me? Go ahead! It's probably best for the world."

"Oh, Jake, if I were going to kill you, you'd already be dead. But, lucky for you, that wouldn't serve my purpose at all. Not anymore."

"Uh-huh," Jake said with the utmost skepticism. "So, let me see if I have this right. You and the squid want to become my new parents."

"I beg your pardon!" said Fionnula, but Wyvern could not hide his amusement.

"That's right. More or less."

Jake snorted. "Not interested, thanks."

"I can get you an army of gryphons. You like gryphons, don't you?"

"Just the one," Jake replied.

"Riches?"

"I already own a gold mine, mate."

"Hmm." Wyvern narrowed his eyes, looking a little frustrated yet amused. "How about additional powers?"

"Doubler. Keeps me busy enough. Don't you get it?" Jake exclaimed. "All I really want is to get my parents back!"

Wyvern stiffened. "Well, that's not possible."

"Why? Are they dead? I know Uncle Waldrick didn't really murder them. He thought he did, but Fionnula tricked him by putting magic bullets in the gun. She told me so herself."

"Oh, did she?" He sent the sea-witch a reproachful glance.

"I had no choice!" she said. "The boy came to see me in prison. What else could I do? Information was all I had to bargain with!"

"We'll talk about this later," he replied.

Jake shook his head at the sea-witch. "Fionnula, you really need to think about your taste in men."

"That will do, sir! I've had about enough out of you." Losing patience, Wyvern rebuked Jake with a zap from his wand that sent him sprawling facedown on the driveway. "You need to learn some manners."

The unexpected face plant knocked the wind out of him, and when his chin hit the gravel, he bit his lip as his jaw snapped closed.

It hurt. Jake was now on eyelevel with Wyvern's polished black boots. Dazedly, he touched his lip, and his fingers came away bloody.

"You *do* realize there is no one on your side who's even a match for me, don't you? Who can stop me, really? Balinor? Please," Wyvern said. “The old man’s a joke. Your aunt, the Elder witch? She’s afraid of her own power. Or, what’s his name—Peter Quince? He’s an amateur compared to me.

“Face it, Jake. The Order’s going to lose. I’ll make sure of that. Trust me, you’re going to want to be on the winning side by the time it’s over. With us, you can learn the real meaning of magic.”

His heart pounding, Jake refused to stay down and started climbing back onto his feet.

Wyvern stopped him, planting a big boot on his back to smash him flat onto his stomach.

“Hey!”

“Do you know what it means to wear the Black Crown?” the warlock continued, warming to his speech. “Can you even imagine it? It means cheating death, for starters. Look at Garnock. He was well on his way to bringing himself back to life after centuries in the grave.”

“Till I stopped him,” Jake boasted, never mind his inglorious position.

“You got lucky,” Wyvern said, then added more weight to the foot he’d planted between Jake’s shoulder blades to try to still his struggling. “The only reason you were able to stop the great Garnock is because, deep down, you’re already one of us and you know it. Play your cards right, and you might even supersede our founder in time.”

“No thanks.” Pressing upward with all his strength, Jake nearly succeeded in making it onto his hands and knees before his would-be adoptive father squashed him flat again.

“Oof!” Jake bumped his chin again and winced, but was not giving up. He ground his knees into the gravel as he fought to rise.

“Don’t you realize the chance you’re being given here? The Dark Master has the power to guide world history in any manner he fancies. When I invite you, boy, to serve as my son, to stand by my side as the Black Prince, I am offering you the Earth, in due time. The Order might be able to make you a Lightrider, but me, Jake? I can make you a god.”

Burning with defiance, Jake peered up at Wyvern from underneath his forelock. “There’s only one God, gov, and he whupped your father’s hide a long time ago.” With a sudden war cry, Jake shot his hands up and hurled the most vicious wave of telekinetic energy he could summon at Wyvern.

It jarred the Nephilim, forcing him to take his foot off Jake’s back to catch his balance.

Jake jumped to his feet, pressing his attack without hesitation, blasting the earl with the full force of his telekinesis.

Wyvern planted one foot behind him, refusing to be bowled over. He held up his palm, shielding himself somehow, though not very well.

Red cawed encouragement. Jake clenched his teeth and intensified the onslaught, ignoring the blood trickling down his jaw from his split lip.

Blimey, this amount of force should have sent the earl flying into the next county by now. But the warlock barely budged.

With a low grunt of effort, Wyvern held his hand steady and blocked the double-barreled energy attack that Jake continued blasting at him.

"Children," the earl quipped through gritted teeth. There was fury and exasperation in his eyes, yet admiration.

Theirs was a battle of wills.

But, to Jake's fury, Wyvern started laughing.

"The boy has spirit, doesn't he, dear?" he called.

"Stubborn, like you," Fionnula answered uneasily.

Jake concentrated harder, pouring more energy out through both palms. He was giving the fight all he had, but it still had minimal effect.

Wyvern adjusted to his attack, now staving off Jake's furious assault with one hand, arching an eyebrow like he was bored.

"Honestly, Jake. You think I've never dealt with telekinetics before? Enough! Your determination is adorable, but I have things to do."

Jake disregarded the mild scold, but he knew he was in trouble when all the power he'd put into his attack began to sap his strength.

Suddenly, he didn't feel so good. He knew he'd overdone it, but he kept up the attack. The energy streaming out of his palms was waning fast. A headache started throbbing in his temples.

But only when he felt blood trickle out of his nose did he finally quit.

Chest heaving, Jake dropped both hands to his sides, exhausted.

"Well," Wyvern said sardonically. "Now that you've got that out of your system, are you ready to be reasonable?"

Jake looked at Derek, who watched helplessly from beneath the bell jar. The warrior gazed sorrowfully at Jake's bloody nose and scraped chin as if he already knew what would happen next.

The look on Derek's face was what made Jake realize it too. *Oh my*

God, they're going to kidnap me for their stupid prophecy. They really think they can force me to become a Dark Druid.

Wyvern gave him a fatherly smile. "Now come along quietly—son." He reached out and offered Jake his hand.

Jake looked down at it, with its huge grip and extra finger.

He despaired. He had just subjected the Nephilim to the strongest attack he could inflict, and it had had no effect. Now Wyvern was offering an olive branch? He'd expected a counterstrike.

This unexpected reaction threw him.

Was that what it was like, having parents? You could blast them with all your anger, and they'd still stand there, still caring about you, just waiting for you to calm down?

Well, he'd probably never know.

Fionnula was a liar, after all. His parents probably *were* dead by now, or had been kept in that comatose state too long to ever be revived.

Imperfect as it was, this might be the only chance he'd ever get to have a real family of his own. Wyvern and Fionnula were repulsive as parents, true. But it wouldn't be half bad being a prince, anyway.

Indeed, *that* offer had been enough to tempt Janos.

But as Jake gazed down at that overlarge hand with its too-many fingers, all he could think of was his real dad, who had the same telekinesis talent in his hands that he had passed on to *him*. The blond, smiling stranger and the beautiful, sable-haired woman in the portrait hanging over the fireplace.

His throat closed.

Tears blurred his eyes.

"Do as he says, Jake," Fionnula said quietly.

It was a warning for his own good if he'd ever heard one. A subtly spoken message that even the sea-witch feared the Nephilim.

Jake looked at Fionnula in desperation. She stared back at him matter-of-factly, and Jake realized that she was as trapped by "Nathan" as he was.

Derek shook his head, at a loss. Miss Helena roared, but she and Henry were both helpless. Aunt Ramona was nowhere to be found.

Archie stopped melting glass, turned off the blowtorch, and lifted his goggles to reveal eyes filled with concern. "Coz? Whatever he's telling you, I promise it's a lie! Don't listen to him! Jake?"

"Stay out of this," Jake replied in a weary monotone.

Wyvern paid Archie no attention, still holding out his hand. He searched Jake's eyes, well aware his strength was spent. "Come along, my lad. Take my hand, and together we'll change the world."

Jake shuddered. He knew what he had to do.

He realized he was going to be destroyed where he stood, but maybe that was safest for all of humanity.

Somehow he scrounged up his courage to make a final stand, and stared at the towering man with his last measure of defiance.

"Stay out of my house," Jake said slowly, emphatically. "Get off my land. You keep away from the people I care about, or I'll smash you. You hear me? I won't stop until the *other* side of your prophecy comes true. I'll see you and all the Dark Druids destroyed."

Wyvern looked at him in amazement. "Did you hear that, Fionnula? Threatening total annihilation, and he's only thirteen! Baal's beard, he already talks like one of us!" He let out a bark of laughter. "Shemrazul was right! This *is* my son."

"No, I'm not!" Jake roared.

"Close enough," said the earl. Then he waved his wand and lifted Jake off his feet, using his own sinister version of telekinesis.

"Hey!" Jake kicked his legs and swung his arms, but he couldn't get down. It was the same sort of prank he liked to play on Dani from time to time, letting her dangle in midair just to tease her. He could suddenly appreciate how annoying it was. "Put me down!"

Wyvern ignored him, nodding at Fionnula. "Let's go."

"But my wand!"

Red snarled, planting himself in the way.

"Leave it," Wyvern said. "You've got twelve more at home. It's time to go."

"What about the item we came for?" Fionnula said, backing away from the Gryphon.

"We'll try again some other time. The boy is a far more valuable prize."

"You'd better put me down right now!" Jake bellowed. But there was nothing he could do other than kick and squirm helplessly and float along like an infuriated helium balloon.

"Settle down before you hurt yourself." Wyvern left the courtyard and walked out onto the lawn, using his wand to steer Jake ahead of him, some four feet off the ground.

Red roared, seeing this, still guarding Fionnula's wand.

"Stay back, Red!" Jake said. He did not want his Gryphon getting captured again.

Then Archie yanked off his goggles and started stomping toward them. "I say! Let my cousin go this instant."

"Archie, don't be stupid!" Jake yelled. "Stay out of this, both of you! He's too powerful!"

"Smart lad," Wyvern murmured.

Archie faltered. Apparently, he could tell that Jake absolutely meant what he said.

He did not want them involved.

After what had happened to Janos's hatchlings, they knew Wyvern did not scruple over hurting kids.

Floating along, Jake stared back anxiously at his cousin, filled with a sense of doom. He had a feeling that when his evil new "parents" said they were taking him home, they meant to the Black Fortress.

The thought made him queasy. Because, after all those months of waiting for Red to be rescued, Jake knew all too well that once they got him inside the warlocks' moving headquarters, the Order would never be able to pinpoint his location.

He wasn't telepathic like Janos; he had no way to get the message out. *Then I'll escape. Aye. That's it. No problem...*

But if Lightrider Tex and even Ravyn Vambrace hadn't been able to do it...

Blimey. I'll figure something out.

His main concern at the moment was to avoid getting anyone he cared about maimed, mangled, or killed. As Wyvern steered him across the lawn with Fionnula following a few steps behind, it hit Jake like a punch in the gut that, once more, he was alone...or was he?

For, at that moment, a strange sound began drumming in the distance. It was coming from the direction of Bradford Park.

Fionnula turned to Wyvern. "What is that?"

He furrowed his brow. "How should I know?"

The deep, thunderous noise grew louder. The woods between his cousins' house and his own began to shake.

Jake stopped squirming as he caught an inkling of what it might be.

Isabelle had said she'd be bringing help...

All of a sudden, the herd of unicorns she tended burst out of the woods in a blaze of white and charged straight toward them, a glorious cavalcade of flashing horns, pearly hides, and pounding hooves bearing down on them.

With a whinny of righteous fury, the mighty stallion Belarex led the charge, with three dozen bright, shining mares barreling on behind him.

They swept across the meadow, leaped the post-and-rail fence, and galloped onto the lawn of Griffon Castle.

Fionnula screamed. Wyvern dropped Jake with a shocked curse, turning toward the stampede. Jake tumbled free onto the ground—but all of them were in immediate danger of being trampled.

Including wolf-Henry.

Jake roused what little strength he had left to lift his frozen canine tutor higher off the ground, quickly floating him over to the nearest tree, where he set him down, still frozen, on a fat, low branch.

While the frog servants leaped out of the way, croaking with alarm, Belarex lowered his head and aimed straight for Lord Wyvern, the sunlight glinting on his swordlike horn.

If the threat of being impaled by an angry unicorn stallion did not scare him, not even Wyvern could withstand the rippling wave of white light that rolled out several yards ahead of the unicorn herd.

The beautiful creatures embodied pure goodness, and when the sweeping wave of their power struck Wyvern, it made him bellow with pain and clutch the spot where Red had scratched him.

Belarex was bearing down on him, flying over the ground like a racehorse.

As the white stallion lowered his head to run Wyvern through, the warlock grasped Fionnula by the wrist, rasped out a spell, and circled his wand around himself and the sea-witch.

The pair vanished in a puff of black smoke.

CHAPTER 41
Call in the Cavalry

"Jake! Archie! Stand still!" Isabelle hollered, mounted side-saddle on her usual white riding horse at the back of the unicorn herd, her Keeper's staff in one hand. "I've told them not to hurt you! Don't move!"

Jake froze in place. Archie did the same.

Isabelle had warned the boys many times that unicorns didn't trust human males; the animals felt threatened by them after centuries of being hunted, and usually attacked them.

His heart in his throat, Jake hoped the creatures would listen to their Keeper as the herd galloped straight toward them, a bristling phalanx of bright, shiny spears.

Derek and Helena were safe behind the bell jar, but Red flapped up into the air, zooming out of the way.

Then the wave of light energy hit him, blowing Jake's hair back. The herd of stampeding unicorns followed.

The next thing he knew, he was in their midst.

They thundered past him on both sides, their pounding hoofbeats shaking the ground beneath his feet, the breeze from their passing riffling his hair. Jake stayed motionless somehow. He barely dared breathe to avoid provoking the creatures as they flowed past him.

He only flinched when one of the shining mares barreling by slapped him in the face with her lavender-tinged tail. It stung, but at least he had not been impaled.

In the next moment, the stampede had passed him by. Still holding his breath, Jake turned to watch the unicorns gallop away.

It was an awe-inspiring sight. The herd arced around the lawn and swept behind the castle, circling back toward Bradford Park and the safety of the woods that were their home.

Jake gradually exhaled.

Isabelle split away from the herd and cantered her horse over to the boys. "Are you all right?"

They nodded.

Archie threw an arm around Jake's shoulders. "We owe you one, sis."

"Happy to help. Um..." Izzy frowned up at the frozen wolf resting on the tree branch nearby, looking nervous. "What is Henry doing up there?"

"Oh—I thought he'd be safer out of the way," Jake said. "I'll get him down." He used his telekinesis to float wolf-Henry safely back down to earth.

But their poor tutor was still frozen.

Isabelle swung down off her horse. "How can I help?" She hurried over to kneel next to Henry while Red flapped down onto the lawn. Archie gave Jake a *whew* sort of look, then trudged back to the bell jar to finish making air holes for Derek and Helena.

Jake glanced around uneasily, making sure that Wyvern and Fionnula were really gone.

There was no sign of them. Nor had he seen any sign of Uncle Waldrick the whole time they were here. Maybe Teddy had been mistaken.

Red hurried over to Jake and pushed his head against his side, nudging him like an oversized housecat and nearly knocking him off his feet. "Becaw-caw?"

"I'm all right. You?"

Red snuffled and shook himself, which seemed to mean *fine*.

"That was close, boy. Too close," Jake whispered.

Red bobbed his head in solemn agreement. Then the Gryphon offered one of his healing feathers for his split lip, but Jake declined. Though it was painful, this slight injury would keep his mind sharply focused on exactly why he would never join Wyvern's side.

"I'm just glad he's gone, and that horrid sea-witch, too," Jake said. His gaze fell upon Fionnula's wand lying on the grass. Narrowing his eyes, he walked over and picked it up, then smashed it over his knee.

The instant it was broken, wolf-Henry finished his leap, finally able to move. As the big wolf landed nimbly on the ground, the frog servants instantly returned to their human form as well.

Shrieks of embarrassment filled the air as, once again, the staff found themselves either half-naked or with their clothing all askew, either tangled around them, trousers on their heads, or uniforms on backward.

Jake winced. "Sorry about that, everyone!" he called awkwardly.

"Sorry, my foot!" the first footman burst out. "I *quit*!"

"Me too!" the scullery maid piped up. "Bein' turned into a frog once is bad enough, Yer Lordship, but twice? Why, it ain't natural!"

"She's right!" The second chambermaid threw down her apron. "These ain't acceptable workin' conditions for nobody! I quits, too."

"Come on, everyone!" a stable groom yelled. "Let's get out of here!"

"You shall do nothing of the kind!" the ancient butler suddenly thundered, silencing them all.

Old Potts looked around grandly at the rebelling staff, never mind that his starchy black tailcoat was on backward.

The gray-haired butler had served under Jake's parents; indeed, he had been the lead frog in the pond for a very long time.

"Shame on you all!" Potts said. "We shall not abandon the young master in his hour of need! But to those of you who are such craven cowards as to abandon your post with one of the first families of the magical world over a few trifling minutes as an amphibian, then begone! You are not worthy to serve this noble house. But I assure you, you will not get a reference from *me*. Humph!"

The mutineers reconsidered, glancing around at each other.

Jake nodded to Potts in appreciation, but he really couldn't blame the others for wanting to escape this madhouse.

"Um, I should like to offer anyone who stays a ten percent raise," he told the staff as they continued righting their clothes.

"Becaw!" Red agreed, for the Gryphon was really the one in charge of the gold.

"Well..." The feisty scullery maid cocked her head. "That seems like a reasonable offer."

As the others nodded reluctantly, Jake thought of giving them all the rest of the day off, but many seemed badly shaken up, and he had learned from Aunt Ramona that, in times of crisis, sometimes it was best to stay busy.

So he cleared his throat and gave them a task to take their minds off their ordeal. "Ahem, once you're sorted—anyone who's staying, that is—would you please check the house to see if Lord Wyvern stole or damaged anything while he was inside?"

Potts lifted his chin and tugged at his waistcoat. "My lord, 'twould be an honor."

"Thank you," Jake said, then he nodded their dismissal. He gave Potts a particularly grateful look, and the old butler sent him a wink, then marched toward the open front door.

As the rest of the servants began drifting after their supervisor, Jake noticed that the giant bell jar was slowly dissolving into thin air. Its erasure must've started the moment he had cracked Fionnula's wand. That was what had freed Henry and the servants, after all.

It seemed Archie's skill with a blowtorch had been all for naught as Derek and Helena's glass prison drifted into nothing. A moment later, there was no trace left of the bell jar but a ring on the lawn where its weight had smashed down the grass.

Then Jake, his cousins, Red, and wolf-Henry ran to Derek and leopard-Helena, and they all hugged each other with relief, exchanging worried questions and making sure everyone was all right. Wolf-Henry ran over to his sister, tail wagging, and leopard-Helena gave him an affectionate meow.

Derek grasped Jake's shoulders and looked into his eyes with a soulful expression, then pulled him into a protective embrace. Guardians didn't say much, but the big fellow needed no words at the moment.

"Don't worry, I'm all right!" Jake insisted, his voice muffled by the warrior's chest.

Wolf-Henry offered an apologetic whine before trotting off toward Bradford Park, presumably to change back into his regular self—and get his clothes.

Leopard-Helena remained, her gown lying on the grass where she had apparently transformed. She seemed in no hurry to return to human shape. Indeed, the governess could be heard purring as she stayed close to Isabelle. She seemed very proud of her charge.

Jake certainly was. Derek released him from his bear hug, and Archie went to gather up his tools.

"Well done, sis. I shudder to think what would have become of us if you had not convinced the herd to come to our aid."

"Jake would've been abducted," Derek said grimly. "The whole Order could've been jeopardized. The entire balance between good and evil. Jake—I failed you."

"No!" Jake said, and his cousins echoed his protest. Even Helena agreed with a scolding hiss.

Derek seemed unconvinced. He rested one hand on his hip and lowered his head. "I should've done better."

"Don't do that to yourself," Isabelle chided him. "I'm just relieved the unicorns didn't hurt the boys. They're somewhat used to Archie, but Jake...?" She shrugged, but her words triggered a realization in his mind.

"Hey!" Jake said. "If I were really evil, Belarex would've trampled me to death. Wouldn't he?"

Isabelle nodded. "It's his nature to attack evil when he sees it." She smiled at him. "The fact that he went right past you should finally convince you that you're a good person."

Jake absorbed this. "Wyvern claimed I belonged on their side."

"No, Jake. No," she said.

"I told you not to believe him," Archie said.

Jake lowered his head, and Derek rested a brawny arm around his shoulders.

Now that Jake had faced down Wyvern for himself, he felt an even deeper bond with his mentor. What the Guardian had been through at the warlock's hands, he didn't want to imagine.

"We can't stay here any longer," Derek said. "Your aunt's spells on this place have obviously been breached."

"How did they know we were here?" Jake asked. "We didn't tell anyone where we were going. Dani and Maddox and Nixie wouldn't have told."

"The mole inside Merlin Hall must've found out and passed the news on to Wyvern," Derek said.

Isabelle shook her head. "I...am not convinced they knew we were here. I couldn't read much off them—it's not safe to try reading someone like that for more than a moment or two. But I kind of got the feeling they were as surprised to see us as we were them."

"Well, that's strange," Derek murmured.

"*I* want to know how the devil Uncle Waldrick and Fionnula escaped from prison—and, more importantly, why we weren't told!" Archie's face wore a rare look of anger. "If the Order can't keep Jake safe—"

"The Elders probably didn't want to frighten us, is all," Isabelle said.

"Frighten us?" Archie exclaimed, turning to his sister. "Seeing Derek and Miss Helena nearly asphyxiate before our eyes, now, that's frightening! Blast it, the Elders simply *cannot* continue keeping us in the dark like this just because we're children! They're going to get us killed! I can put up with many things, by Jove, but being deliberately kept ignorant is not one of them!"

Directing his words at Derek, Archie pointed at Jake. "If my cousin hadn't spied on the Fey Parliament, the three of us would still be oblivious to the Dark Druids' prophecy, and the threat against the Lightriders, a-a-and all of it! Nobody would've told us! Not even Mother and Father! I know you're all trying to protect us, but, blast it, don't the Elders understand that lack of knowledge is the most dangerous thing of all? Th-this is unacceptable!"

Shocked silence followed.

It had been an extraordinary rant from the mild-mannered lad.

Derek, Isabelle, and even Red looked amazed. Some of the servants had also paused to stare on their way back into the castle.

Jake arched a brow. "You really need to get some sleep, coz."

"Well, it's true!" Archie folded his arms across his chest and didn't budge.

"He does have a point, you know," Izzy murmured.

At that moment, the butler poked his head out the front door. "Lord Griffon! Guardian Stone!" Potts beckoned to them with an air of great agitation. "We found something! Come quick!"

They exchanged startled glances, then hurried toward the castle.

* * *

Waldrick, meanwhile, had been waiting in the carriage, drumming his fingers and examining his nails, when Wyvern and Fionnula reappeared on the road in a puff of black smoke.

He looked out the window. *Finally!*

Waldrick immediately saw that the backstabbing sea-witch was missing her wand. *Well, well.*

As for Wyvern, the warlock's glare seethed with silent rage. Then Waldrick noticed that the earl was not carrying the promised vial of his firepower.

Waldrick's lips curved in a sour smile as smugness bloomed in his heart, but he hid his reaction as the two stomped over to the coach.

Dear, oh dear. Failure, Nathan? Waldrick nearly drawled. But he wasn't stupid.

It was pretty clear at once that things hadn't gone well.

The carriage rocked as the pair climbed in angrily and plunked down on their seats, Fionnula beside him, Wyvern across from him in the coach's backward-facing seat.

Wyvern barked at the driver to go, but the coachman was only a spoon changed into a servitor. They hadn't wanted any actual human witnesses to their break-in.

So much for that.

It appeared the whole mission was a bungle. Everyone at the castle had seen them. All the people who weren't supposed to *be* there.

And now their fearless leader had come back empty-handed.

Waldrick basked in his rival's failure, even though it was to his own disadvantage.

"What are you looking at, Everton?" Wyvern growled as the coach rolled into motion, heading back to the Black Fortress.

"Oh...just wondering if you managed to get my firepower back," he said with a bland smile.

The Nephilim glared out the window, gnashing his double rows of teeth.

"Ah...I see," Waldrick murmured, loving this in spite of himself. Then he eyed the traitorous Fionnula.

She, of course, had no idea that he was onto her. After taking shelter in the mausoleum and finding the empty coffins, he had good reason to suspect she had lied to him. But he hid this knowledge.

Instead, he gave the sea-witch a discreet look that said, *Told you he couldn't do it.*

Fionnula made a face at him. "What happened to you back there?" she demanded. "Oh, let me guess: you ran away."

"The Gryphon attacked me!"

She rolled her eyes. "Useless."

"I beg your pardon, I'm not the one who botched this operation," he declared. "You're the one with the seeing bowl, my dear. As for you, my lord, I warned you you're not dealing with an ordinary boy."

Wyvern cracked the knuckles of a six-fingered fist. "Don't tempt me, Everton."

"Believe me, he knows that now," Fionnula said under her breath.

"Aha." Waldrick tried his best to stay quiet, but after a moment, he could not resist. "So...Jake bested you, didn't he?"

"No!" the earl snapped, but Waldrick didn't believe him.

"There's no shame in it, Wyvern. I'm just saying, remember how you mocked me about being beaten by a 'mere boy'?"

Wyvern's eyes flamed orange in reply, and his pupils shifted longwise, changing shape briefly, like those of a reptile, be it snake, lizard, or dragon.

It was a sufficient reminder of his devilish bloodlines, so Waldrick swallowed his snicker. But inwardly, he continued gloating.

He pushed his tongue into the side of his mouth to conceal his smile. *Well, Jacob, he's your son, all right. Chip off the old block.*

His brother used to have the power to exasperate everyone around him. Just. Like. That.

The memories of their childhood together made Waldrick wistful for a moment, especially after that visit to their boyhood home. Indeed, a newfound hope stirred within his half-rehabilitated heart that, maybe, just maybe, he wasn't a murderer after all.

It had been terrible living all these years with what he had done—or, at least, what he *thought* he had done.

As for his ex-talent, he wasn't even cross that Wyvern had failed to retrieve it. Truth be told, he was delighted that the haughty Nephilim had fallen on his face today—and that Fionnula had seen it.

Waldrick ought to be angry, he supposed. But, at the end of the day, he didn't really want his pyrokinesis back anyway.

Let the cursed vial remain hidden. No one should possess such power.

It was a dreadful gift.

* * *

Jake and the others hurried into the castle to find the butler waiting anxiously for them at the bottom of the grand wooden staircase.

Potts beckoned, and they hurried across the great hall. "We just noticed it, milord."

"Noticed what?" Jake replied.

"This way." Potts escorted him up the first flight of stairs to the quarter landing, where the staircase turned, but there, Potts held up a spindly arm, barring the way. "Watch your step, sir!"

Jake's eyes widened when he looked down at his feet and saw a black, gaping hole beneath him.

The wooden floor of the landing had opened up like a trapdoor.

"Careful, everyone!" Potts warned them as Derek arrived behind Jake.

His cousins followed, with leopard-Helena and Red bringing up the rear.

Jake crouched down and peered through the rectangular hole in the floor. Incredibly, he saw a spiral staircase twisting down, down, down into the dark recesses of the castle's undercroft. He hadn't even known there was a basement under this section of his home.

"Sweet Bacon," Archie whispered.

"Do you think the vault's down there?" Isabelle asked, peeking over his shoulder.

"I do," Jake said in fascination.

The hole looked extremely deep. He could not see the bottom of the spiral staircase. It was cloaked in the subterranean blackness down there.

"Potts, quickly, bring some torches," Jake said.

"Yes, milord." The butler hurried back down to the great hall.

Jake moved aside so the others could see better. "At least now we know what Wyvern came for—provided Izzy's right, and they weren't just hunting for me."

"But how could he possibly have known it was here?" Izzy murmured.

Derek looked at Jake. "Your father was the only one who knew how to find it. Do you realize what this means?"

Jake held Derek's stare in shock as the realization hit him. "He really is alive."

"The question is..." Archie leaned forward to peer into the hole. "How did Lord Wyvern extract the information from him?"

Nobody answered. They didn't need to. Only Red let out a low, mournful *caw*. Jake closed his eyes.

Derek laid a hand on his shoulder. "Steady, lad. He's a tough man, your sire."

"But twelve years?" Jake whispered, a tremble in his voice. He flicked his eyes open with just a hint of tears burning in them. "Who could withstand that? And my mother, too?" Anger gripped his heart.

"Jake." Izzy stroked his arm. "Remember what Tex said. They need the Lightriders alive."

"The glass coffins," Archie reminded him, his dark eyes somber.

Jake reached out to rest his hand on his Gryphon's head, steadying himself. "Yes... You're right."

This was no time to give up hope. Indeed, as of this moment, he had more reason to hope than ever before.

Derek was correct: Wyvern's knowledge of where to find the vault was the closest thing to real proof they'd had so far that his parents really were alive—at least his father. But the thought of all that the Dark Druids must've put them through for all these long years hardened Jake's resolve.

As he stared down into that deep, dark hole in the heart of his castle, he made a decision.

Isabelle searched his face. "Coz? Are you all right?"

He nodded, righteous anger catching fire within him and burning with a white-hot intensity.

"What is it?" she murmured.

"I'm not going to let them get away with this."

"The Dark Druids?" Archie asked.

"They've gone too far. But I'll tell you what," Jake said. "It ends now." He rested his foot on the edge of the opening that led down into the dark. "If I'm the key to all of this, as their prophecy claims, then I can't afford to hide here trying to stay out of it. I need to join the fight."

He looked at Derek. "I tried it your way. To follow all the rules and do as I was told. But I see now I don't have that luxury. You all stand as witness to the promise I make you today. I swear on the bones of my ancestors, I'm gonna take that prophecy and shove it down their throats." Jake glanced around at them. "I'm going to be their worst nightmare. From this moment forward, the gloves are off."

Red screeched and reared up in full agreement.

Then Potts returned.

Jake seized a torch from the butler, stepped through the opening, and headed down into darkness.

CHAPTER 42

The Training Simulation

Week four of Lightrider training had finally arrived, but Dani and her classmates were still in suspense over what the promised surprise was going to be.

Everyone could tell that their two teachers had something up their sleeves, but, so far, Master Finnderool and mighty Ebrahim had kept their mixed group of budding Lightriders and Guardian apprentices in the dark.

Dani and her new pals were all abuzz, trying to guess, but no one had any real idea. Considering they were at a magic palace, it could be literally anything.

They tried to charm the information out of Tex, as well, since he was rather indulgent with "the young 'uns." But the cowboy wasn't talking.

Maybe the teachers had changed their minds, they debated, because Monday came and went, and it was business as usual. Tuesday was the same.

Ah, but then...then came Wednesday.

It seemed to start out like any other day: athletics in the morning, rush home, get clean, change clothes, morning classes, then lunch.

Lunch was followed by afternoon classes, and it was then, on Wednesday, when the group of sixteen future Lightriders and Guardians returned together from the dining hall, eager to see if the surprise would finally be unveiled, that they were startled to find that a third adult had joined their two usual instructors.

Sir Peter Quince was lounging in their classroom, waiting for them, along with Finnderool and Ebrahim.

The students exchanged eager glances and took their seats with newfound excitement. It was hard to anticipate what might happen next, but if Sir Peter was involved, then it was bound to be fun. And perhaps a little terrifying.

Finnderool welcomed the kids back and took attendance, then both the Lightrider and the master Guardian both gave way to the wizard.

"Ladies and gentlemen." Sir Peter jumped up out of the chair and strolled over to the classroom door. "Follow me," he said with a mysterious smile.

Then he marched out.

Everybody knew Sir Peter was a little unpredictable, so they looked at their teachers in confusion, making sure they had permission to leave the room.

Ebrahim chuckled, and Finnderool gestured elegantly toward the door. "I'd hurry if I were you."

Dani shot up from of her seat and rushed to join the stampede out into the hallway. The teachers followed.

Well ahead of them down the corridor, Sir Peter was whistling cheerfully as he strode along, his black robes flowing. Everyone scrambled to catch up.

"Where are we going, sir?" Dani asked breathlessly.

"You'll see, Miss O'Dell," he answered in his breezy way. Then he pushed through a door to the outside and kept going.

Dani and her classmates followed him out to one of the flat green playing fields. It had woods on both sides.

Though it took her eyes a moment to adjust to the brilliant autumn sunshine, she noticed there was a large, brightly painted box of what she guessed was sporting equipment already waiting for them at the edge of the field.

Sir Peter ambled past the box and the thick, chalked boundary of the playing field, but Finnderool called, "That's far enough, children! Give our wizard some space."

The students stopped, but Sir Peter continued walking alone a few yards farther down the field.

There, he turned and looked expectantly at their two teachers.

Finnderool nodded to him, then looked at the kids. "Ladies and gentlemen, you have made excellent progress over the past three weeks. Now that week four has come, you've started to develop a good, basic grasp of all the sorts of things that Lightriders and Guardians need to know. You've realized by now that you must apply yourselves to your studies with discipline in order to gain knowledge. That it won't be all just adventure.

"Of course, mastery will take you a lifetime of learning. But you've applied yourselves diligently, we've noticed. Therefore, you've earned...a little reward."

Dani smiled; excitement rippled through the group.

"Today," he continued, "you have earned the opportunity to try your hand at your first field training. If it's adventure you want, it's adventure you'll get. At least for today. Then it's back to the books." He turned to the wizard. "Sir Peter, if you'll do the honors."

"With pleasure." Sir Peter sent the wide-eyed class a conspiratorial smile, then lifted his wand and began to chant.

Before Dani's eyes, currents of magic began shooting forward down the field and out to the sidelines, clear in color but distorted, like the shimmers off a hot roof in August. Here and there, it crackled like lightning carefully kept under masterful control.

It was just like when he changed the Field of Assessment in the maze to serve whatever purposes were needed to test the gifts of each magical child. He had conjured a dizzying obstacle course for Maddox, challenges involving the four elements for Nixie, and a miniature Stonehenge to test Jake's telekinesis.

Now, in a way, it was Dani's turn, but by the time Sir Peter was finished, she could see very little change in the playing field.

In fact, the only difference—at least for now—was the steady beam of white light that shone straight up at the sky from a spot on the ground at the far end of the field.

"What's that?" someone asked, pointing at it.

"That, children, is your designated waypoint," Finnderool said, nodding his thanks to the wizard. "The purpose of today's simulation is to give you your first taste of what it's really like, being out on a mission with a team."

Dani gasped, as did the others.

"Pair up," Finnderool ordered.

Excitement buzzed in the air as everyone found a partner. Dani ended up with Brian, a nice, dark-haired American boy with whom she often worked. He was easygoing and didn't give her grief, like certain blond ex-pickpockets of her acquaintance.

The brief thought of Jake gave her a pang. Amiable as Brian was, she would've given anything to be doing this today with him.

After nodding to Brian, she turned and raised her hand. "Master Elf?"

"Yes, Miss O'Dell?"

"What about the third member of our team? According to the handbook, there are always a minimum of three on a mission, aren't there?"

"Right you are, young lady." His lips twitched as he bent to reach down into the box of sporting equipment, the afternoon sunlight glinting on his platinum hair.

The wood elf fished around inside the big, colorful crate for a moment, shoving aside rugby balls, cricket bats, and hockey sticks. "It's here somewhere. I just saw it..."

Dani looked on, brow furrowed, as she heard the equipment clattering about inside the crate.

"Ah! Here she is." When Finnderool finally straightened up, he blew a lock of long, pale hair out of his eyes, then showed them what he'd retrieved: a round cannister like a coffee tin or a can of paint. "Allow me to present your conductee for the mission."

He pried off the lid, reached into the cannister, then held up a small pink pellet or gelatin capsule no bigger than an acorn.

Master Ebrahim flashed a knowing grin and folded his massive arms across his chest, glancing around at the kids.

"Watch this," Finnderool said. Holding up his hand so they could all see, he pinched the pellet in between his finger and thumb until it popped, then he tossed it onto the ground.

There, the capsule began blowing up like a thick-skinned balloon, swelling into a life-sized doll or mannequin that was shaped like a giant bowling pin...and decorated to look like a she-elf in a fine lavender gown.

The doll had a painted-on face with big, blank eyes, pointy ears, long blond braids, and a crown. Rocking back and forth on its rounded base, it seemed weighted to remain upright.

Finnderool set his hand on its head to stop its wobble. "This," he said, "is Princess Pansy. She will be your conductee for the mission."

The kids couldn't help chuckling. The training doll was the silliest thing Dani had ever seen.

"Don't worry," said the wood elf, "I keep a large supply of Pansy pellets on hand. As many as might be needed. For, as many of you will soon discover, they tend to get destroyed. That's the day's challenge. Keep Her Highness alive for the duration of today's mission.

"She's your official VIP—why, she's elvish royalty. For all I know, we could be related."

Sir Peter laughed at his jest.

"Lightriders, it's your job to get Princess Pansy to the waypoint." He jabbed a finger down the field at Sir Peter's column of light. "Guardians, take note. There will be challenges along the way that might try to stop you from reaching it."

"Just like on a real mission," Sir Peter said.

Finnderool nodded. "Once you arrive at the waypoint, the Lightriders will use the Bud of Life to open a portal. You will each be given a different set of coordinates that you must memorize while waiting for your turn. No writing down the numbers. You must do this from memory, just like in the real world.

"Once you've got the portal open, you will then escort Her Highness through safely to the other side. Remember, Lightriders, as team leader, *you* are ultimately responsible for the dear lady, so do try and keep her all in one piece.

"Guardians: as always, it falls to you to protect your Lightrider and the diplomat. No matter what sort of obstacles you might unexpectedly encounter."

He folded his hands behind his back and strolled past the row of pupils. "Now then, children, since your first time in the simulation is a very big occasion, those of you who complete the trial successfully will find yourself transported to the dining hall, where the gnomes have prepared an ice cream party for you."

A chorus of eager gasps filled the air.

"However," the wood elf continued, holding up a finger with a gleam of mischief in his pale eyes, "if you should fail, you will land in, shall we say, a less *pleasant* situation. Good luck." Then he glanced around at them. "Very well. Who wants to go first?"

Nobody spoke.

Dani thought of Jake. He would've already elbowed his way to the front of the line, no doubt. But she and Brian exchanged a look that agreed, *Not us.*

"What, nobody likes ice cream?" Finnderool taunted.

Ebrahim unleashed one of his loud, jolly laughs. It broke the tension.

Everyone was nervous. Nobody wanted to go first and serve as the lab rats. But, fortunately, both the Lightrider and Guardian programs attracted adventurous kids, so it wasn't long before Finnderool had three pairs of volunteers willing to go first, second, and third.

Dani and Brian agreed to go fourth.

It was better than going last. Having to wait until the end would be nerve-racking. But with three teams ahead of them, they could watch the simulation unfold and hopefully get a better sense of what to expect and how to do this.

"Very well, let's get started," said the wood elf.

Master Ebrahim began handing out quarterstaffs to his Guardians, as usual. Simple training weapons, the thick wooden rods were about four feet long.

Meanwhile, Finnderool passed around small slips of paper to his Lightriders, with instructions not to let anyone else steal a peek at their coordinates.

Dani unfolded hers and saw six two-digit numbers with two corresponding cardinal directions.

"These coordinates are for testing purposes only," the wood elf said. "You will memorize your numbers and hand the paper back to me when it's your turn. You can't take it with you. All right, everyone ready? Who's first?"

Two girls stepped forward.

The Lightrider-in-training was Chloe, a cat shapeshifter, the *other* redhead in their class, though she was more of a strawberry blonde. Chloe was clever and quick, with stripy, red-tabby-colored hair. Unfortunately, the poor girl had barely had two minutes to memorize her numbers.

The Guardian girl paired with Chloe was a tall, determined centaur named Stasia, short for Anastasia. Her hair was wheat-blond (in a ponytail, of course); her horse parts palomino. *She* was most famous as a star hockey player; when centaurs played that game, it was something closer to polo, and very competitive.

In any case, Dani had come to suspect that Stasia had a crush on Maddox, for she always managed to trot over to say hello when they were sitting together with Nixie at supper in the dining hall.

Watching the two girls go up to the teachers, awaiting any further instructions, Dani wondered if Stasia's horse-tall height and Chloe's catlike reflexes would prove an advantage in their quest.

That remained to be seen.

Since the teachers were still conferring quietly with Sir Peter, Chloe prowled back and forth, scanning her slip of paper with the coordinates continuously. Stasia stretched out her shoulders and swung her quarterstaff, warming up. The athletic centaur pawed the ground with impatience to get going.

Dani fidgeted with the Bud of Life on her wrist, watching them. She knew she should be memorizing, but was too distracted with anticipation to see what would happen next. She thought the two girls very brave for volunteering to go first.

"All right, ladies," Finnderool said. "First, take your Princess Pansy."

Stasia reached into the tin and took out a pellet. She nodded to Chloe, then pinched it and threw it on the ground. At once, the doll blew up. Dani wondered if the Pansies were made out of rubber or what. She shrugged off the question as Chloe picked it up.

"Is it heavy?" someone asked.

"No." She gave the rest of them a nervous smile.

"Good luck," several of them said.

"Right. You've got your equipment." Finnderool put out his hand, and Chloe placed her slip of paper reluctantly on his palm. He closed his fist around it. "Ready, girls?"

They gathered themselves and nodded.

"Go!" Finnderool said.

All the other kids watched eagerly.

The pair jogged down the field, on their guard, Chloe hefting Princess Pansy with an arm around the doll's waist. Stasia cantered ahead and then circled behind Chloe by just a few paces, scanning the field in all directions.

"Down!" the Guardian girl suddenly yelled.

Chloe dropped to a catlike crouch, pulling Princess Pansy with her.

Stasia galloped back to the Lightrider and shielded her and the doll from a flurry of bats that flew out of the woods to the right of the field and swooped by overhead.

Well. Dani folded her arms across her chest as she grimly realized Sir Peter had indeed rigged the playing field with magical obstacles to complicate their getting to the waypoint.

The wizard smiled innocently at the group.

As soon as the bats had passed, Chloe stood up again. Stasia and she picked up their pace, running the rest of the way down the field to the beam of light.

"Just some bats? That wasn't so bad," Brian murmured.

"We'll see," Dani said.

By the shining faux waypoint, Chloe set the doll on its feet. Princess Pansy bobbed around a little from side to side but didn't fall.

While Stasia kept watch, Chloe lifted her arm and began dialing in the coordinates on the Bud of Life.

They all saw her hesitate.

"Hurry up!" Stasia said.

"I'm trying!"

"You were supposed to memorize the numbers!"

"Well, I didn't have much time, did I? Just be quiet for a second and let me think!" Chloe moved about, pressing her fingers to her forehead.

Dani felt for her.

Stasia twirled her quarterstaff, waiting impatiently. The horse girl was kind of intimidating...

Dani felt an elbow nudge her. It belonged to Brian, standing beside her as they awaited their turn. The tousle-headed boy cast a pointed nod at the slip of paper she was supposed to be memorizing.

"Right," Dani mumbled. Better quit watching the show and make sure she had drummed *her* coordinates into her head by the time it was their turn. To flounder like Chloe was now would be so humiliating.

She turned away to focus, when, suddenly, an ominous sound came out of the woods to the left of the playing field.

Dani whirled around to see what was happening.

Stasia reeled to face it as well. The centaur girl gripped her quarterstaff as the underbrush started crackling.

The trees began to shake, and the whole group heard a garbled moan blare out of the woods.

"Open the portal!" Stasia cried.

Chloe gasped as a large, gray-skinned ogre suddenly bounded out of the woods and landed right on the midfield chalk line with an earthshaking boom.

It caught its balance and sniffed the air. Some seven feet tall, weighing hundreds of pounds, and dressed in rags, at least the ugly creature could not see the girls, for it was wearing a blindfold.

Sir Peter smiled generously.

Dani gulped. Ogres were stupid, but without Jake and his trusty telekinesis here to ward the creature off, she realized she was more scared of it than she'd normally be.

But it's not real, she reminded herself.

Well, it looked real. It sounded real, too. It even smelled real. The dirty-washrag stink of ogre traveled downwind to the group looking on.

The two girls on the field looked horrified for a moment. They stood frozen while the ogre sniffed the air, trying to detect them through its blindfold.

Dimwitted they might be, but ogres had a fine sense of smell. Snuffling eagerly, the brute turned toward the team, holding its massive arms up. It started walking around searching for them by smell—as if this were some highly perilous game of blind man's bluff.

Sir Peter waggled his eyebrows at the kids while Ebrahim grinned. Finnderool flipped his long hair over his shoulders with a toss of his head, smirking with amusement.

Dani frowned. The teachers were enjoying this far too much, and that was never a good sign. Brian gave her a worried look.

Meanwhile, the pair on the field were whispering anxiously to each other. Stasia planted herself in front of Princess Pansy and the Lightrider, her quarterstaff at the ready.

Luckily for Chloe, the sight of the blindfolded monster hunting them must've jolted her memory. She lifted her left forearm and finished dialing in the coordinates.

To everyone's relief, the tabby girl remembered correctly, for a kid-sized portal opened right above the waypoint.

It was not as big as the real one that Derek's team had gone through to rescue Red, but it had the same silver shimmer, like an upright, watery mirror.

Now, per Finnderool's instructions, the girls had thirty seconds max to grab Princess Pansy and run through the portal. But it was then that an unexpected feature of the doll kicked in.

"Hurry, they're coming," Princess Pansy said in a lifeless monotone.

The ogre heard it.

The creature whipped around at the sound. With a bellow, it leaped and then leaped again, slamming down just a few feet away from them.

Chloe shrieked and darted to the right with feline speed. Stasia stumbled to the left, nearly tripping over her own hooves in her fright.

The ogre swung its long, gorilla-like arms trying to tag them, and pandemonium broke out down at the far end of the field.

The teachers looked on, nonchalant.

The doll, abandoned now, swung back and forth. "Hurry, they're coming. Hurry, they're coming."

Dani watched wide-eyed, her heart thumping as the blindfolded ogre tried to catch her two panicked classmates.

The girls were dodging this way and that.

Even though it was just a training simulation and the ogre wasn't *technically* real, the doll's deadpan words added pressure to an already stressful situation.

"Hurry, they're coming."

Grazed by the ogre's swinging knuckles, Princess Pansy got knocked down and rolled several feet away.

Chloe crouched down, catlike, and bounded after their VIP. Bravely, Stasia took it upon herself to distract the big, clumsy monster. She galloped swiftly to the right, stopped several yards away, and let out a piercing whistle through her fingers. It drew the ogre's attention.

The brute sprang after her. Though she zigzagged enough to elude it, unfortunately, the ogre was now blocking the centaur's return path to the portal—and she had only seconds to get there.

"Hurry up!" Chloe yelled. She had recovered the doll and stood waiting for her partner at the edge of the shining portal.

Dani winced, for it was the ogre who harkened to her call. Perking up, the blindfolded brute chased after her voice.

Chloe screamed as it charged her, and in her panic, turned into her cat form and leaped through the portal with a *reer!*, leaving behind both her uniform and Princess Pansy.

"Chloe, get back here!" Stasia bellowed.

But her partner was gone.

"Hurry, they're coming," said Princess Pansy.

With a determined look, Stasia galloped around the ogre, her ponytail flying. She grabbed the doll with one hand as she passed it, but when the ogre leaped again right in front of her, she, too, lost her cool. Someone chortled as Stasia threw Princess Pansy at the monster, as if that was going to help.

It did distract the ogre momentarily. He grabbed the doll and started bashing it about back and forth gleefully on the ground.

Stasia galloped into the portal just as the ogre popped the inflatable doll between its massive hands.

The portal blinked closed, and, at once, the ogre faded away.

The field was left empty, but for the waypoint's beam of light and the tattered remnants of poor Princess Pansy, which, every few seconds, still continued to warn, "Hurry, they're coming."

A ripple of excitement ran through the class, as the kids had now gained a better understanding of how this would work.

"Where did they land?" Dani wondered aloud.

Brian shrugged. "Not at the ice cream party, I wager."

"No, indeed. Now then." Hands on hips, Finnderool looked around at the class while Master Ebrahim scowled at one of his best students' failure. "What were their mistakes?"

Max shot up his hand. A dwarf lad barely up to Dani's shoulder, he was another Lightrider-in-training. "Chloe forgot her coordinates. And their timing was off, sir."

"Correct. Again, children, you will have only thirty seconds until the portal closes."

"They froze up when they saw the ogre," Huang chimed in, his arms folded across his chest. "Wasted valuable time."

The supremely confident lad was one of the best in the Guardian class, having already mastered some unique martial arts training he had learned in the Orient, where he had been born.

He'd brought with him moves from the Far East that some of the adult Guardians did not even know. Huang had been happy to teach them, since this only gave him more of a chance to show off.

Ebrahim nodded in approval. "Huang is right. Guardians must stand their ground. However, Stasia did well with her distraction technique. The only other hint I will give you is to open your eyes, look around, and use what you find on hand."

"No one warned us there'd be ogres," someone mumbled.

Dani didn't see who had said it, but Finnderool merely smiled.

"My dear people, the rules of the game will rarely be spelled out for you in real-life situations. You're going to have to learn to think on your feet." The wood elf smiled slyly. "Hmm, I wonder if anyone will be eating that ice cream today."

"I will if they don't!" Ebrahim said, and Sir Peter laughed.

"But what was their greatest mistake?" Finnderool persisted, searching the kids' faces. "They broke one of the primary rules. Can anyone tell me what it is?"

Dani raised her hand tentatively.

"Yes, Miss O'Dell?"

"Um, don't use Princess Pansy as a weapon?"

Some laughed at the way she had phrased it, but that was what Stasia had done, lobbing Her Highness at the ogre.

"Exactly." Finnderool nodded. "They both abandoned their conductee when the ogre charged. You can't just hurl your VIP at oncoming threats. Understand me well, children. You Lightriders are very pleased with yourselves for being chosen, I know. And you Guardians are proud of your strength and speed, as you should be. But, on a real mission, neither of you are what really matters to the Order. The important one is this lady here."

He popped another Pansy pellet and dropped it to the ground, where it began inflating.

"The real missions you'll face can come with the highest of stakes. After all, maybe your VIP is a diplomat sent to negotiate a peace treaty between two warring factions, or to smooth ruffled feathers at some royal court that otherwise could have dangerous consequences. Our diplomats deal with high-level matters, often life or death. It is not our place to ask why the Elders send our ambassadors and agents to their various destinations. Our job is simply to support them in that however we can and, above all, get them there and back in one piece."

Dani blew out a breath and thought about Isabelle and Archie's parents. The glamorous Viscount and Viscountess Bradford were diplomats.

Until this moment, she had never much thought about why the sophisticated couple were always whisking away halfway around the world. *Hmm.* Maybe they had a good reason for largely ignoring their children, Dani mused.

Finnderool lifted his chin. "Now then, it is time for our second team of volunteers. However, I can now reveal another aspect of the game."

"Pay attention," Sir Peter advised in a low singsong.

"The simulation is going to look different for all of you. The first team got the easiest set of challenges." Finnderool smiled. "It just gets harder from here."

Dani's jaw dropped, and every kid gasped.

"It's not going to be the same?" Brian blurted out.

Finnderool shook his head. "The easy setting was team one's reward for volunteering to go first. Each team after them will find your challenges increasingly difficult."

The last kids groaned at the prospect of what they might face. With a crafty smile, Finnderool handed team two their Princess Pansy.

"Aw, don't look at me like that, children." Sir Peter sauntered forward again to change the playing field with his wand for the next team. "One day, you'll look back at all this and laugh at how easy it actually was."

Ebrahim nodded sagely. "It's always got to be hard before it gets easy."

"Quiet now, everyone," Finnderool said so the wizard could work.

Sir Peter invoked his magic again, and the playing field began to change.

Trees appeared, sprouting full-sized in seconds right out of the smooth green turf. The waypoint shifted to the far corner, and a meandering stream suddenly gushed out of the woods on the right-hand side of the field, cutting a path through the turf and wending its way across the green, to disappear into the woods on the left.

He pivoted. "Voila."

"Nicely done," Finnderool murmured.

The wizard bowed as he passed him. "Proceed, Master Elf." Sir Peter walked clear of the chalk line marking the playing field, his black robes flowing out behind him.

"You're up, team two. Good luck—but, mind you, Princess Pansy doesn't like to get her feet wet!" Finnderool called after them as they headed off.

Team two consisted of Max, the dwarf Lightrider kid, and Guardian-in-training Tyra, who was actually Ebrahim's niece. She had cocoa-brown skin and pretty green eyes, and she was one of the strongest girls Dani had ever met.

Tyra could do nearly as many push-ups as Maddox. Maybe that was why she walked with bit of a swagger—but then again, many Guardians did.

In any case, Dani and Brian exchanged a private glance of amusement at the funny pairing of the tall, imposing girl and the short, bespectacled boy.

Max stared at his slip of paper for another long moment, then handed it back to Finnderool with a grim look.

"Max shouldn't be nervous," Dani whispered to Brian. "He's one of the brightest kids in my class. He always knows the answers."

"Neither should Tyra. She could probably beat up that ogre, from what I've seen," he whispered back.

With that, team two set out. Little Max jogged to keep up with Tyra's long, sure strides as they headed for the waypoint glowing in the corner.

The bats whooshed by, just as before. Then they came to the stream.

Tyra bent down and let Max climb on her shoulders, carrying Princess Pansy in her free hand. As the dwarf boy balanced astride the Guardian girl's strong shoulders, he started dialing in coordinates already.

"Max, don't do it too soon!" Tyra warned, wading across the stream.

Dani was relieved to see that the water was only knee-high on the girl.

"Don't worry, I'm not going to activate the portal yet," Max said. "I'm just putting the numbers in while they're still fresh in my mind."

"Clever lad," Sir Peter murmured, looking on with the rest of them.

"Oh," Tyra said. "Good idea." Striding up onto the other side of the stream, she tossed Princess Pansy to the ground, then bent forward and let Max hop off her shoulders.

He whispered something to her, pointing toward the stream. Tyra nodded, then went back to the water's edge and picked up a good-sized rock.

"What's that for?" Dani whispered to her partner.

Brian shook his head. "Maybe she's gonna use it to bash the ogre. Master Ebrahim did say to use what we find."

"Right..." Dani looked on with renewed interest. It was clear that team two had some sort of plan as they began jogging toward the waypoint.

They hadn't gone far when the woods to the left rustled and the trees began to shake. Anticipating the reappearance of the blindfolded ogre, team two signaled to each other to keep silent and ran faster.

When the ogre burst out of the woods, Tyra seemed ready. Thankfully, the creature was still blindfolded. But, again, with her usual bad timing, Princess Pansy chose that moment to say: "Hurry, they're coming."

The ogre turned toward the sound.

Tyra took the stone from the stream bed and threw it far into the woods to the right of the field. It clattered into the underbrush and fell somewhere in the loud, crispy leaves.

The ogre bounded after the sound and disappeared into the woods.

Finnderool nodded and Sir Peter clapped for them. Ebrahim looked quite proud of his niece. Out on the field, team two did not pause to celebrate outwitting the ogre, but continued jogging toward the waypoint.

Things were looking good for the pair—until they passed through the glade Sir Peter had conjured.

It turned out the trees were unfriendly.

As the kids hurried through the grove, the trees came to life and started taunting them, throwing little crabapples at them and yelling crabby things.

There was nothing they could do but run.

"Open the portal, Max!"

"It's too soon! We only get thirty seconds before it closes!"

"I don't care! I've got a bad feeling."

Uh-oh, thought Dani. It was always bad news hearing that from a Guardian.

"Hurry, they're coming," Princess Pansy said over and over.

It was nerve-racking, that toneless refrain echoing down the field.

"Open it!" Tyra insisted as they ran, still getting pelted with miniature apples.

"Fine!" Max muttered, then he must've pressed the activate button, for right on cue, the portal winked to life ahead of them.

They had almost escaped the grove when, suddenly, two little gray squirrels jumped down from the tree onto the ground right in front of them.

Though they were small and fluffy and cute, they were surprisingly aggressive. The squirrels began stalking toward the pair, chattering angrily and baring their little buckteeth at them. They seemed determined to block their path to the waypoint.

Team two was nonplussed at this unexpected obstacle.

"Do they bite?" Max exclaimed.

"How should I know? Maybe?"

"They have really big teeth!" Max said. "You're the Guardian. Do something!"

"Fine, I'll distract them. You take Princess Pansy to her destination." Tyra handed off the doll to Max.

This was a bit of a problem, since he and the doll were about the same height, but he hurried away nonetheless, dragging the doll's feet on the ground.

The portal was waiting, after all, and they had less than twenty seconds now.

Tyra used her quarterstaff like a shepherd's hook to stop the squirrels from following him, brushing them back.

They could hear her trying to make friendly noises to the animals, as if the little attack squirrels were dogs. Bending down cautiously, she picked up some of the crabapples the trees had been throwing at them and tried to tempt the squirrels with them, as if they were treats.

The squirrels were not interested. They scampered after Max and managed to get between him and the portal.

Tyra ran to his aid. Each time the kids tried to sneak around them, the squirrels blocked their path, chattering away as if they knew they only had to hold them off for another few seconds.

They were strangely intimidating, especially to Max, since they stood as high as his knee.

Tyra started getting angry. "Get out of the way, you little vermin!"

She threw the crabapples at them, trying to drive them away, but that only seemed to make them angry.

"All right, here's the plan," she said to Max through gritted teeth. "I'm going to whack them and you run. Take the doll with you."

"You can't club them to death! They're just a couple of cute little squirrels."

"They're ruining our test! Do you want to fail? I don't!"

"Fine! Just don't *hurt* them."

Tyra huffed. "You do your part—I'll do mine." She held her quarterstaff out in front of her like it was a bat and slowly bent down. "Ready? *Go!*"

She whooshed her staff to the side, whacking the squirrels none too gently out of the way. They tumbled aside, rolling heads over tails, screeching with anger and perhaps a little pain.

At once, Max ran at top speed for the portal, dragging Princess Pansy with him. He raced into it and disappeared with his VIP.

"He did it!" Dani murmured. She turned to Brian.

He was staring down the field, watching Tyra.

The girl sprang to her feet and, with all the speed in her Guardian blood, raced after her partner. But the vengeful rodents recovered, and, this time, they attacked, leaping up onto Tyra's back.

She shrieked and squirmed to get them off, but the portal closed and the squirrels disappeared. The simulation ended, and Tyra was furious. She threw down her quarterstaff with a muffled curse.

"Temper!" Ebrahim boomed at his niece across the field.

Tyra picked up her weapon, still looking furious. "Sorry, sir," she muttered.

She returned to the rest of the group with her head down. She was clearly incensed at herself, so they all gave her plenty of space.

"Consider yourself lucky, young lady," Finnderool said. "At least you didn't land where your partner did."

"Didn't Max get ice cream?" someone asked in surprise.

"Absolutely not. He left a teammate behind."

Dani and Brian exchanged a worried look. This game just kept getting harder and harder.

"Have you memorized our coordinates yet?" he asked with a gulp.

"I'll keep working on it."

Dani turned away and concentrated on her slip of paper while Sir Peter rearranged the landscape a bit. Determined to memorize her coordinates—after all, this was the main part of her future job—she only half paid attention to team three.

The Lightrider was a slim, quiet wood elf girl called Peregrine with lavender eyes and hair the color of moonbeams. Her partner was Huang, and even now, he seemed very sure of himself. Rather like Jake, Dani couldn't help thinking.

As the pair took off down the field, Princess Pansy in tow, Dani noticed their challenges were considerable.

For them, the babbling brook grew wider and deeper and became a rushing river, and although a wooden footbridge was provided, it looked very rickety.

Fortunately, Peregrine had the usual grace of the elvish folk, so she tiptoed first across the bridge to test it out, leaving the mannequin with her partner.

"Hurry, they're coming," Princess Pansy said all the while. She started sooner this time. It was maddening.

Once Peregrine had landed neatly on the far side of the river,

Huang followed, carrying the doll. He, too, was skilled at moving stealthily, but when he reached the halfway point, the bridge started cracking apart.

Huang hurled Princess Pansy clear across to the other bank, where Peregrine caught her. Then the bridge cracked. The cocky young Guardian fell into the water with a yelp and was immediately washed several yards downstream.

But, like most Guardians, he was strong, so he managed to break free of the current and swim to the far bank. In short order, Huang climbed out of the river, drenched and embarrassed and very annoyed.

Sir Peter laughed quietly, watching. He seemed very pleased with himself for thinking up all these tricks. It all must be relatively safe, though, for Finnderool and Ebrahim did not look concerned in the least.

Do teachers actually enjoy tormenting students? Dani wondered. But instead of watching their test, she bent her head and focused on learning her coordinates.

She and Brian would be next, after all.

Meanwhile, team three was racing through the field. The bats flapped by overhead on cue, the grumpy trees threw crabapples and insults, and the squirrels attacked once again.

Huang had apparently been thinking about them. During his dunk in the river, he had scooped up some pebbles from the riverbank, possibly taking his inspiration from Tyra and Max's strategy.

He threw the pebbles at the squirrels, and when he hit them, to everyone's surprise, the critters disappeared in a puff of colorful magic smoke.

"Hurry, they're coming," Princess Pansy said for the umpteenth time as team three arrived at the waypoint.

"Isn't there any way to shut that thing up?" Huang exclaimed.

"Do not talk to our VIP that way," Peregrine scolded him. "She is more important than both of us, remember? Now, please, be quiet. I am thinking."

Setting Princess Pansy aside, the elvish girl started entering the coordinates into the Bud of Life. She was still working on it when the woods to the left began to rustle.

Huang turned, quarterstaff at the ready.

Dani's heart skipped a beat. She knew what was coming.

The ogre.

Sure enough, out of the woods leapt the ogre—only, this time, it wasn't wearing a blindfold.

Its gaze locked on to team three at once. It let out a barbaric roar and then began galloping toward them on its knuckles.

"Open that thing!" Huang hollered, twirling his quarterstaff like he actually knew how to use it.

Getting into position, the young Guardian planted himself in between the ogre and his delicate teammate.

Peregrine glanced over her shoulder with a look of dread—*"Hurry, they're coming!"*—but with another touch of her gauntlet, she brought the portal to life.

At that moment, the ogre landed mere feet away from them. Huang let out a war cry that raised Dani's eyebrows.

The Asian boy twirled the quarterstaff, and the ogre seemed momentarily mesmerized by its pinwheel motion.

"Go!" he yelled.

To her credit, Peregrine hesitated, as though loath to abandon her partner to face the ogre alone. "I can't leave you behind! It's against the rules!"

"I'll be right behind you. Get Pansy out of here!"

The doll tucked under her arm, the Lightrider girl didn't listen. Instead, she remained standing at the threshold of the portal, watching Huang dart and weave.

Dani got the feeling that Peregrine was counting the seconds.

"Come on!" she urged, but Huang was engrossed in the fight, showing off just a little for the teachers and the chancellor and the rest of the class.

"Over here, ugly!" he shouted.

The ogre swung its big, long arms, trying to catch the nimble boy, but he tumbled and rolled clear, then sprang to his feet and whacked the brute in the side of the knee.

The ogre bellowed and staggered to the side. Huang grinned and sprinted after his quarry, but Peregrine lost patience. She grabbed him by the jacket as he passed.

"Come on, the portal's going to close!"

She tossed Princess Pansy through the shining circle, then leaped in herself, pulling the protesting Guardian with her.

His feet had hardly vanished into the light before the portal winked closed.

Finnderool turned to them triumphantly. “And *that*, ladies and gentlemen, is how it’s done!”

The rest of the kids uncertainly applauded team three, even though the winners weren’t there to hear it.

They were off eating ice cream, thought Dani. For her part, sugary treats were the farthest thing from her mind. On the contrary, she was suddenly too queasy to think of food as Finnderool turned and glanced around at everyone.

“Now, where is team four?”

CHAPTER 43

Open Sesame

Lifting the torch higher, Jake ventured down the dark spiral stairs. Before him, the shaft stretched deeper and deeper into the subterranean regions beneath Griffon Castle.

The flame from his torch unveiled cobwebs and a few pale spiders lurking on the clammy stone walls, but its dim glow was not bright enough to reveal the bottom of the shaft, where he hoped to find the long-hidden family vault. The gloom below him was inky.

There was no railing on the staircase. It seemed a very long way down; he took care to mind his footing, hugging the wall as he descended.

Behind him, Potts distributed torches and lanterns to his cousins, who followed a moment later. Jake also heard Derek ask Helena to patrol outside in her leopard form, in case Wyvern and Fionnula returned.

"Roar if you need us," the Guardian said. "Red, why don't you go with her? Keep an eye on things from above."

The Gryphon snuffled in agreement and padded off with Helena to stand guard.

Jake waited for Archie and Isabelle to catch up, and when Derek followed, bringing up the rear, they pressed on in silence.

The temperature dropped the farther they went. No sunshine ever made it into this hole, Jake thought.

"Not looking forward to the return trip," Archie said after a bit.

"Me neither," Jake mumbled. Even his legs were starting to hurt, despite his daily jogs.

"How much farther do you think the bottom is?" Izzy asked.

"No idea," he answered.

"It's got to end sometime," Derek said.

Around and around, the spiral staircase twisted, circling ever deeper into the earth. The flickering flames of their torches and lanterns danced over the dank walls enclosing them, while the treacherous stairs stretched down endlessly. Jake started feeling slightly claustrophobic. He brushed a spiderweb off his face with a grimace.

"Ew!" Isabelle mumbled, two people back.

"Spider?" Jake asked.

Whack!

"Thanks, Derek," she said.

"That's what I'm here for, dear."

Jake smiled at the wry response. "Hey, I think I see the bottom!"

"Thank goodness," Archie mumbled. "M'legs are about to fall off."

"Oooh! I think we're almost there." Squinting into the gloom, Jake saw a simple stone chamber awaiting them below.

They hurried down the rest of the way, and what he saw removed any doubt they were in the right place. Jake's pulse pounded with excitement as he crossed the chilly stone chamber.

Lifting his torch, he stared at the long-lost Everton family vault. It was beautifully made but formidable.

The round metal door was massive, clad in glossy green jade and covered in a complex array of twisting brass gears and interlocking sprockets.

Deadbolts and padlocks, strange knobs and cylinders, metal pins and hinged shackles, latch-channels and bars—all seemed to feed into the silver set of eight numbered dials right at eyelevel.

When Jake saw that all the dials were set to zero, he knew exactly what this was: a puzzle lock. They'd been a problem back in the days when he was a thief, for they required a combination.

His heartbeat quickened as he went and set his torch in one of the metal torch holders flanking the vault. "No wonder nobody ever found this thing till now. My ancestors hid it well enough."

"I daresay." Panting, Archie leaned forward to brace his hands on his legs. He was not the most athletic boy.

Izzy groaned. "I can't feel my feet." She let Derek step past her, then plunked down onto the bottom step and set her lantern aside.

Jake glanced over his shoulder at them. "Maybe I can levitate you two back up to the top when we're done here."

His cousins peered up at the pitch-black height they'd have to float, then gave him dubious looks.

"Er, I don't think so, coz."

"But thanks, though," Isabelle said.

"My gift's not wonky anymore. Honest!"

"No. You strained yourself enough already today taking on Wyvern," Derek said. "Your cousins can walk up on their own two feet, like anyone else."

Jake shrugged, then Derek marched past him and stood looking up at the vault.

The metal door was a head taller than the big man and four times as broad. It took up nearly the whole wall of the little stone room.

"I wonder what all is in there," Archie murmured.

"We'll soon find out," Derek said. "I'm just glad Wyvern didn't manage to reach it. Jake must've interrupted him before he could make it this far." Derek scanned the array of knobs, latches, and locks. "I can't believe my best mate never told me about this. I hope he didn't think he couldn't trust me."

"Oh, I'm sure it's not that, Derek," Archie said cheerfully. "After all, I never showed Jake the safe where I keep my finished prototypes—Oops..."

The boy genius smiled sheepishly as Jake turned to him in surprise. Even by the dim torchlight, he could see his cousin redden.

"Sorry, coz. You *did* used to be a pickpocket. But don't worry, a bunch of daft inventions wouldn't interest you anyway, I'm sure."

Jake harrumphed. "Anyone care to guess at the combination?"

They all looked at Archie.

Mechanical things were his forte, after all.

"Righty-ho." Still looking embarrassed for keeping such a secret from his best mate, the boy genius pushed his spectacles up higher onto his nose and approached the vault door. "Let's have a look at you. Hmm, yes..."

Archie peered at the horizontal brass cylinder, where the correct sequence of numbers had to be rolled into view all in a line. Beside the final dial was a red button, presumably pressed last to register the sequence. "Oh, dear."

"What?" Jake asked.

"Eight digits." Archie looked at him uneasily. "That means there are"—he did a quick calculation in his head—"precisely one hundred million possible combinations."

"Um, gentlemen?" Isabelle said.

When they turned around, she pointed discreetly at the darkest corner of the chamber, tucked behind the stairs.

Jake's eyes widened. "Bones!"

An ancient human skeleton slumped in the corner, draped in cobwebs.

Derek inhaled slowly at the sight.

"Sweet Bacon," Archie whispered.

Izzy rose to her feet. "Who do you suppose that is?"

Jake stared at the skeleton. "A dead thief."

"So, the vault is booby-trapped, then," Derek said grimly.

"They usually are, in my *vast* experience as a hardened criminal." Jake shot his cousin a sardonic look.

Archie shrugged apologetically.

"We should abort this mission," Derek said at once, his voice terse.

"But we can't." Jake turned to the warrior. "The vault's been compromised. I'm not going to abandon my family's treasures just so Lord Wyvern can come back and steal them."

Derek sighed. "Very well. You might as well get going up those stairs. I'll handle this."

They all protested at once, wanting to stay and see what was hidden in the vault.

"Children, this is bound to get dangerous," Derek said, gesturing at them to pipe down. "As it is, you three are lucky to be alive after what just happened."

"Nonsense," Izzy said. "I can't face those stairs again so soon. Besides, we stand a better chance of figuring out the combination if we work together."

"She's right," Jake said with an earnest nod. "Archie's the one who understands how these kinds of complicated mechanisms work."

"We need Jake here, too!" Archie said. "His presence as the rightful Griffon heir may be a necessary component for unlocking this thing. He might have to validate it somehow. In fact, it's probably safest for Jake to be the one to enter in the numbers. This vault was obviously made with both science and magic. I daresay, if anyone else like you or I should try to get in, we'll probably end up like him." Archie pointed at the skeleton.

Jake lifted his eyebrows. This was turning into quite the

dangerous day.

"Very well," Derek grumbled. He went and rested his torch in the other torch holder.

Archie brought his lantern closer and set it on the floor. "Unfortunately, the safe probably won't give us many tries before it locks us out entirely."

"Or worse," Isabelle murmured, folding her arms across her chest.

"Which means we have to come up with an eight-digit number that would have been of significance to Uncle Jacob and Aunt Elizabeth." Archie looked around at them. "I suggest we have ourselves a good, hard think."

They did exactly that for the next ten minutes. Milling around the stone chamber, they racked their brains trying to guess the combination. The stakes were high. Skeleton man had obviously failed.

"Hmmm" echoed repeatedly in the tomblike space. Derek tapped the flat of his favorite dagger against his opposite palm. Archie muttered more than once that he wished he'd worn his lucky bow tie.

Isabelle twirled a lock of hair around her finger, tilting her head as if she were trying to sense the combination with her gift. Which, of course, was impossible. Her telepathic powers didn't work on even insects or fish, so how was an inanimate object going to tell her anything?

Jake stood stationary—arms folded, feet planted wide—staring intensely at the vault. *Come on, Dad, what's the combination?*

Eight digits...

"How about—" Isabelle started, then shook her head. "Never mind."

"Could it be your birthday?" Derek turned to Jake. "May first, and the year. That would fit, if you use the zeroes."

"I dunno." Jake stroked his jaw. "A date *does* fit, with the eight digits. But, speaking as a former thief, your only child's birthdate seems a little obvious. Something other people could easily find out. Archie?"

The boy genius shrugged. "I can't think of anything better. Might as well give it a go. Unless you've got any safecracking talents from the old days?"

Jake smiled wryly. "That's an entirely different course of study than pickpocketing. Very well, I'll try my birth date." He walked up to the huge vault door, but hesitated as he reached for the first dusty dial. "Be ready for anything, you lot, in case I'm wrong."

"Wait," Derek ordered him. "Isabelle, go back up twenty steps. If anything happens to us, run and fetch your governess."

Izzy nodded, picked up her lantern, and dutifully retreated to a safe distance up the spiral stairs. "I'm clear."

Derek nodded at Jake to continue. Archie and the Guardian glanced around, unsure of where the best spot to stand might be in case Jake failed.

Anything could happen if the combination was not May the first, 1864.

"Here goes nothing." Jake began rolling the dials in succession to show the appropriate number. *Zero, one, zero, five, one, eight...*

He glanced around. So far, so good.

Six...

With one number left to go, he checked over his shoulder, his pulse pounding. "Everyone all right?"

Derek and Archie mumbled affirmatives.

"You're doing great, Jake," Isabelle said from up on the staircase.

"Right, then. Here we go. The final digit."

Then he turned the dial to *four* and boldly pressed the red button.

Isabelle shrieked. Jake pivoted and saw her flailing her arms to try to catch her balance. All the stairs below the one where she stood had simply vanished!

With no railing to grab hold of, Izzy teetered on the edge of the broken staircase, which now ended abruptly some fifteen feet above the floor.

Derek bounded across the chamber to catch her. Archie shouted with alarm. Jake brought up his hands to use his telekinesis, but Izzy managed to save herself in the next heartbeat by throwing her weight backward.

"Oh my goodness!" she said with a gasp, landing safely on her sit-upon.

"Are you all right?" her brother cried.

Izzy clung to the stairs.

Jake was still braced to use his telekinesis if she slipped.

"I'm fine," Izzy said, obviously shaken. "I just...wasn't expecting that."

"Blimey." Jake dropped his hands to his sides, his pulse still drumming.

Derek scowled over what had just happened, then glanced around at the chamber. "I see. If your first guess is wrong, the stairs disappear. If we had come down here without someone who *happens* to have the telekinesis that runs in the Griffon family line, I'd say we'd be trapped."

"That's probably what happened to him," Archie said, nodding at the skeleton. "Maybe the stairs waited until he was dead to rematerialize."

Izzy winced.

"Don't worry," Jake said, trying to sound more confident than he actually felt. "I can float the two of you back up easily onto the stairs."

"And who's going to float you?" Derek retorted.

"I'll go get some rope," Izzy said.

"Not yet, please," Jake answered, glancing at the safe. All the dials had reset back to zero. "We need to come up with another combination to try. Now, everybody, think. Because I don't care to find out what happens if we're wrong a second time."

"Very well." Izzy remained, lending her wits to solving the puzzle.

More silence and *hmms* as they racked their brains in the torchlight.

"What if it's not a date at all?" Archie said after a moment. "What if the combination is a set of coordinates? They were Lightriders, after all. Coordinates would've played a big role in their lives."

Jake shook his head. "Not the right amount of numbers. And there's no way to dial in the directions—north or south, east or west."

"Oh, right," Archie said.

Jake was pleased (and a little shocked) he knew one thing at last that Archie didn't.

But blimey, this was getting painful.

"I do like a date for the combination, though," Derek said. "I can't think of any other sort of number it might be."

Archie nodded. "Agreed."

"But what date?" Jake asked, hands on hips. "What would be of significance to my parents, other than my birthday?"

They all looked at Derek this time. He brooded for a long moment. "Their wedding day. That's my best guess."

The Bradfords nodded, but Jake wasn't sure. Considering that his father was all but a stranger to him, how should *he* know what date would be meaningful to the man?

Then he thrust away a fleeting thought of Wyvern's preposterous invitation to become *his* son and heir...

"What about the date that Uncle Jacob became a Lightrider?" Archie suggested.

"Eh," Derek said with a shrug. "Elizabeth meant even more to him than his service to the Order."

"Very well, then, when did they get married?" Izzy asked.

"Good question." Derek lifted his fist to his forehead and squeezed his eyes shut. "Oh, when was that? Let me think... It was a June wedding. Elizabeth insisted on that. Very traditional. It was, um, a...a Saturday. Um... Blast it!"

Jake arched a brow. "Weren't you their best man?"

"It was a long time ago!" Derek said. "I was worried about making the toast in front of all those highborn people, not memorizing the date. No, wait—that's it! I think I put a mention of the date in the speech... Give me a moment. It'll come back to me."

Jake and Archie exchanged a bemused look as Derek struggled to drag the best-man toast out of his memory. Unfortunately, he had to start at the beginning, the same way he'd memorized it.

"To Jacob and Elizabeth..." He continued mumbling the speech from the beginning, repeating parts over and over again when he stumbled.

The kids waited, exchanging amused glances.

"It's all right if you can't remember—" Jake started.

"No! I've almost got it. I rehearsed it a thousand times so I wouldn't mess it up. God, I hate making speeches. Jacob was the ham, not me. I think it was near the end... Something like: 'So let us raise a glass on this—'" He snapped his fingers. "'On this most auspicious date.' That's it! Twenty-first of June!"

"Are you sure?" Jake asked eagerly.

"I'm certain of it." Derek looked exhausted from the effort. "Your Aunt Ramona picked it for them. She said the date was a good omen—three sevens in the number twenty-one, *and* the summer solstice, to boot. Yes, I'm positive that's it. I can't believe I nearly forgot."

"What year?" Jake asked, heading back to face the cylinder.

"Would've been the year before *you* arrived: 1863."

He nodded. "I'll try it. But first, I want you and Archie out of harm's way."

"We're not going to leave you down here alone, coz. What if the answer's wrong?"

"If it's wrong, then there's no point in you dying with me. But if I do, don't worry," Jake said in answer to his cousin's look of protest. "I'll haunt the blazes out of Wyvern before I'll let him raid my family vault."

"Jake!" Izzy said, frowning at his graveyard humor.

"Up you go," he said to Archie, then used his telekinesis to levitate the boy genius up onto the staircase with his sister.

Izzy made room for her brother.

Derek turned to him with a dark look. "I'm not leaving you."

"Bye," Jake said sweetly. He grinned at Derek's scowl as he floated the big warrior up onto the stairs as well.

It took rather more finesse to get Archie's lantern up to them, but he figured they would need it for the return trip if anything went wrong. Derek's torch, he was keeping. Just in case he ended up down here alone like that skeleton.

Once all three were back to what he at least *hoped* was a safe distance, Jake turned to face the vault once more.

Beautiful as it was, with all its gleaming jade and shiny brass, that skeleton in the corner was enough of a warning that the safe was also deadly.

What might happen if his parents' wedding day was not the right answer, he did not care to ponder. He did not want to end up like the pile of bones in the corner, poor bloke.

He stepped forward, wiped off his sweaty palms on his trousers, and summoned up whatever skill for this sort of business he might have gained during his pickpocket years.

Then he began dialing in the numbers. *Two, one, zero...*

"Where *was* my parents' wedding, anyway?" he asked over his shoulder, making conversation to distract himself from his climbing dread. "London? Westminster Abbey? Merlin Hall?"

"No, it was right here at the castle," Derek said. "The ceremony was in the chapel, and the reception was out on the lawn."

"Aww," Izzy said.

"Concentrate, Jake," Archie ordered.

"I *am* concentrating! Almost there."

Six. One. Eight...

A bead of sweat rolled down his face as he pondered the significance of the day. A wedding on the grounds of Griffon Castle sounded much more pleasant than what had happened out there earlier.

An idea suddenly popped into his head. "Hey, Derek, you and Miss Helena can get married here too, if you like."

"How now?" Archie said, turning to the warrior.

"What's this!" Isabelle exclaimed. "Derek? Is this true?"

"Blast it, Jake, you weren't supposed to tell them yet."

Jake snickered. "But if I'm about to die."

"You'll do nothing of the kind!" Archie said sternly.

"Don't even joke about it!" Izzy chimed in.

"Well, he probably hasn't even asked her yet, the big baby."

"Actually, I have," Derek said. "Just today, in fact."

"Really?" With only two numbers left, Jake turned to face the others. "Well? Don't keep us in suspense. What did she say?"

Derek lifted his eyebrows. "She meowed. So...I'm not really sure."

His cousins burst out laughing, but Jake's jaw dropped. *"You asked her while you were under the bell jar?"*

His cousins let out exclamations of mixed humor and disapproval at his utter lack of timing, but Derek shrugged.

"I thought we were going to die. There wasn't any time left to procrastinate. Hey, I never said I was some big romantic. I'm not Janos."

Izzy blushed, but only Jake noticed.

"So it's official, then?" Archie asked eagerly. "You're getting married?"

"I don't know! I think so. I have to wait till she's a person again to find out for sure." With a bashful grin, Derek rumpled Archie's hair. "And, of course, that's provided that I have you and your sister's blessing to steal your governess away from you."

"Of course!" they both said.

The Bradfords cheered and hugged him. Derek hugged them back, yet huffed, still trying to be stern.

"People, do you mind?" Jake said in amusement.

They left off with their little celebration, and he turned around again, eyeing up the formidable vault door.

"Righty-ho," he said, then he dialed in the *six*. The brief laugh had helped relieve some of the tension, but his muscles still strained.

"All right. I'm down to the last number." Jake dialed in the *three*.

As he reached to press the red button, Archie cried, "Wait!" and nearly made his hand jolt.

"What?" Jake said in exasperation. "Whatever's going to happen, I'd like to get it over with, Arch."

"Yes, but are we really sure we want to open that thing?"

They all looked at the boy genius curiously.

Archie shrugged. "I mean, for all we know, it could prove a real Pandora's box."

"We don't have that option, little brother. Lord Wyvern, remember?" Izzy said.

Archie sighed. "I suppose. Yes, yes, of course, you're right. Never mind. Carry on."

Jake shook his head. "Wish me luck," he mumbled. Heart pounding, he slowly pushed the button.

The moment it clicked in, a terrible grinding noise roared out of the edges of the room. The whole stone chamber seemed to shake. The dials, quickly this time, flipped back to zeroes. The torches flickered and all three people on the stairs began shouting at him.

"Jake!"

"Get out of there, coz!"

"The walls are moving, Jake! Hurry!"

"Guess that wasn't it," he said wryly over the din. But even his cheeky humor flagged when he glanced to the right and the left and saw the thick stone walls on both sides slowly rolling toward him.

"Jake, come! I'll pull you up." Derek whipped off his jacket and moved onto his stomach on the stairs. "Archie, Isabelle, help anchor my legs."

The Bradfords threw their weight against Derek's calves to secure him while the Guardian hooked his feet through one of the risers and reached down, dangling his sturdy canvas jacket over the edge for Jake to catch hold of and climb up like a makeshift rope.

But Jake looked from Derek's jacket to the vault dials.

Think. Yes, the walls were literally closing in, and all three people on the stairs were clamoring for him to hurry, but he wasn't ready to give up yet.

He knew he could get this. If the combination was neither his birth date nor his parents' wedding day, then what *other* date could have been special enough for the last Earl of Griffon to use?

It would have to be something he could easily remember, Jake thought. Historical dates? *History...* His mind whirled through all the lessons with Henry.

"Jake, c'mon!" Archie roared.

"I'm thinking!" Jake yelled.

"Stop fooling around and get over here!" Derek bellowed.

"Please, Jake!" Isabelle cried while the massive stone walls crushed the skeleton to powder.

Within a few moments, Jake knew he'd be next. But he refused to give in to terror.

Instead, he searched his brain for everything it meant to be the Earl of Griffon. The history, the heritage, the castle, the London house, the hunting cottage in Wales, the gold mine... *Hold on!*

The Gryphon!

Of course!

The answer was Red himself!

"Jake, *now!*" Derek roared, dangling over the edge while the wall rolled toward the broken-off bottom of the stairs.

His cousins were screaming, but Jake ignored them. The answer came to him readily, for he had memorized it during all those long, lonely months when his beloved Red was missing.

He rolled each digit into place with nimble pickpocket's fingers, though he had to squeeze himself sidewise to keep entering in the number as the walls started pressing in.

0-4-0-4-1-1-3-2

The fourth of April, 1132. The date his medieval ancestor, Sir Reginald, had first found the Gryphon egg—and changed the entire course of their family history.

The second Jake smashed the red button, the walls stopped.

His cousins stopped screaming. Derek stopped yelling, too.

There was a pause, then a mighty clanking of chains and a clattering of gears as the walls started retreating.

A moment later, they slammed back into their proper places at the edges of the room.

Jake exhaled, then the missing bottom of the staircase magically rematerialized, and he became aware of his own thumping heartbeat and his cousins cheering him.

"You did it, coz! Brilliant!"

"Jake, you're alive!"

He gave them a shaky wave, then something clicked behind him and he whirled around. He looked at the door and his eyes widened; the vault had awakened.

All of the deadbolts and padlocks, latches and gears across the face of the giant door were twisting and turning in the torchlight, gyrating, clanking, and sliding toward the unlocked position. It was mesmerizing.

Derek and his cousins hurried down the stairs, but Jake took a swift backward step as the door suddenly popped loose and let out a long hydraulic hiss.

A rim of glowing blue light appeared around its circular edge, coming from inside.

"Blimey." Steadying himself after his second brush with doom in one day, Jake reached uncertainly for the sturdy brass handle of the vault.

Massive as it was, the door swung easily on its hinges.

The bluish glow from inside spilled out into the stone chamber and illumined the faces of Derek and the Bradford siblings as they joined him at the threshold.

Then the four of them stared through the round opening at the vault's interior.

It wasn't large, for all the trouble it had cost them. Maybe twelve feet wide by twenty feet long. The light inside came from three floating orbs that must have been activated when the door was opened. Nixie knew how to conjure such things—illumination spheres, she called them.

They floated gently in the air, and by their light, Jake beheld a dazzling array of riches and precious family heirlooms. Velvet-lined shelves flanked the walls, right and left. Here, the smaller items were stored, all marked and cataloged in orderly fashion.

Larger objects ranged along the back wall. These included a few scrolled-up tapestries leaning in the corner, a complete set of shiny horse armor, and a life-sized alabaster statue of a beautiful lady with long, flowing hair. At her feet, three open treasure chests yawned. The first brimmed with gold coins, the second with silver, while the third gleamed with a glistening rainbow of loose gems.

Stepping cautiously into the vault, Jake stared all around him. His companions ventured in as well. They were welcome to come and see the family's most precious possessions.

Wyvern, on the other hand, was not welcome at all. There were plenty of things worth stealing in here, but not if you were a powerful sorcerer.

What did he want? Jake thought, scanning the safe.

The shelves burgeoned with priceless objects, works of art, vases, ornate candelabra of solid gold, cases of important papers, mysterious old books, and a fortune in jewelry—tiaras, necklaces, rings.

Every piece made him feel closer to his parents, even though he did not know their significance, the stories behind them.

Moving deeper into the vault, Jake scanned a wondrous display of gifts and souvenirs that his parents must have collected from various magical realms during their Lightriding careers. Then he came to a small niche in the left-hand wall, where he stopped and stared at a pair of kingly robes on display.

Draped over his and hers dress forms were long scarlet court robes made of rich velvet and trimmed with white fur. Between them gleamed a pair of his and hers coronets—the simple crowns an earl and countess were entitled to wear as marks of their rank on the most formal parliamentary occasions.

"Blimey, did my parents really wear these?"

"Your grandparents did," Derek said as he sauntered over. "Your father's parents would've worn these to the coronation of Queen Victoria when she was a young girl."

Jake gave a whistle. "Fancy enough?"

The warrior smiled. "All lords and ladies have to wear outfits like this to the coronation of a new monarch. It's required."

Archie nodded as he and Izzy came to see. "Our grandparents have them, too."

"And then, usually, just the men have to don theirs once a year, to attend the opening of Parliament. The one in London, I mean," Derek said, "not Merlin Hall."

"Do you have robes like this?" Jake asked him.

"Me? Nah, I'm just a commoner. But you'll wear one—my lord."

"I think I'd look pretty silly in that," Jake muttered, moving on.

Other pieces of family history had also been carefully preserved, like a tattered battle pennant from some long-ago war, and the ceremonial sword and helmet of another revered medieval ancestor that he had never heard of.

Dizzied by the display of all these treasures connected to his lineage, Jake knew that every item in here must have a story of its own, but that still didn't explain what Wyvern had come for.

He continued searching. "What am I going to do with all these things, now that Wyvern knows the location of the safe? I don't want him stealing them."

"Why, you can store them in my inventions' vault, of course."

He turned to his cousin. "Are you sure?"

Archie nodded. "Plenty of room! They'll be safe there. Even you didn't know my vault exists until today, and you're m'best mate."

"And here I thought you couldn't keep a secret." Jake sent him a rueful glance. "Proved me wrong, didn't you, coz?"

"*Weeeell,* when it's in the name of science." Archie grinned, then waved a hand. "Don't worry, we'll organize the servants to help carry everything over to Bradford Park and have it done in an hour."

Jake nodded. "Thanks, Arch."

"How beautiful," Isabelle murmured, admiring a magnificent bejeweled egg.

Derek held up a men's-sized gauzy white shirt that had a silvery sheen when it moved. "Giant Silkworm body armor."

Though the fabric looked fragile, it was well known in the magical world that Giant Silkworms produced a thread that was nearly impenetrable to bullets and blades, and also offered some protection against low-level spells. It was extremely valuable and rare.

"I wonder where your father got this."

"Take it," Jake said. "It's yours."

"No! I couldn't—"

"No, I insist. It looks like it'll fit you, and I already have another one of those in the Archive in Wales. Consider it my wedding present—to Miss Helena." Jake gave his mentor a pointed smile. "You may balk, but I think she'll be glad to accept anything that helps keep you out of trouble. Besides, my father would want you to have it."

"Your father might like to keep it for himself, considering we are now almost certain he's still alive," Derek replied with a smile.

Jake glanced at him, still awed by the thought. "No, you take it. You may need it when it comes time to rescue him and my mother." He felt a lump in his throat as the possibility drew ever nearer.

He shoved off the wave of emotion, clearing his throat, furrowing his brow, and focusing on the task at hand. "Now if we could just figure out what Wyvern was after."

"We'd better keep looking." As Izzy gave Jake one of her penetrating gazes, he realized his businesslike demeanor didn't fool the empath.

Ah well. Jake turned away. Crouching down, he proceeded to scan the lowest shelves—when suddenly, he spotted it.

A small, sparkling orange potion vial in an ornate footed stand.

Fine gold metalwork swirled down the neck of the little bottle from the stopper, made in the shape of a dragon.

Jake knew at once that this had to be the item his enemies had come for.

But still, he couldn't believe his eyes.

Father was supposed to have destroyed it long ago...

Uncle Waldrick's fabled firepower. Oh, Jake had heard the stories. He was shocked to find it intact.

He reached out and picked it up slowly.

"Ho! Careful with that," Derek warned, closing the distance between them with one swift stride.

As Jake straightened up, he barely paid attention. Lifting the vial higher, he stared in fascination at the isolated talent.

It was beautiful.

The few ounces of liquid inside the fanciful container were a reddish-orange hue, with gold sparkles floating around inside it like the sparks that popped out of a bonfire.

The gift of fire in a bottle.

"This is what they wanted," Jake murmured. He couldn't take his eyes off it.

Derek lifted it gently from his grasp. "I'll hold that."

"What is it?" Izzy asked while Jake frowned.

Derek gave his cousin a grim look. "I believe it is your uncle Waldrick's pyrokinesis."

"But how?" She knitted her eyebrows. "Uncle Jacob smashed it years ago. Didn't he?"

"Apparently not." The Guardian shook his head. "That trickster."

"So, you're saying Uncle Waldrick attacked Jake's parents for nothing?" Archie demanded.

Derek looked troubled. "It would seem so."

Jake digested this shocking information as best he could.

"Teddy told us Uncle Waldrick came with those two today," Isabelle murmured. "I didn't see him. Did any of you?"

Derek and the boys shook their heads.

Jake was seriously displeased. "Wyvern must've wanted my uncle to be a more useful ally. Like Fionnula."

"With this, he would've been," Derek said.

"Sweet Euclid," Archie muttered.

"What do they do with that? Drink it?" Jake asked.

"Aye," Derek said. "But this one's getting stored in the potion room at Merlin Hall. No chance of your uncle getting his hands on it there." He placed the vial in his vest pocket for safekeeping. "Now let's do as Archie said and transfer all these things over to *his* vault."

Derek glanced around at Jake and his cousins. "As I mentioned outside, you can't stay here any longer, now that Lady Bradford's spells have been breached. We leave as soon as possible. Today."

"Where will we go?" Izzy asked.

"Back to Merlin Hall," Derek said. "You'll be safe there, at least. Then the Elders can decide what to do with us."

They nodded, and Derek heaved a sigh, glancing around at the contents of the vault.

"We might as well get started moving this stuff." As the Guardian gathered an armful of Everton family treasures to carry up, Jake shook off the strange spell the glistening dragon bottle had cast over him.

As the tension eased, he was glad they were going back to Merlin Hall.

It had been too long since he had seen the carrot-head.

CHAPTER 44
The Test

"Team four? Where is my team four?" Finnderool looked around expectantly at the group of anxious students huddled behind the chalk sidelines of the playing field.

But when the wood elf's piercing gaze homed in on Dani, she blanched.

"Ahem. C-coming." Heart thumping, she stepped forward with her quiet Guardian partner, Brian.

If only Jake were here. Then this test would be fun, not scary. He would make short work of that ogre; he'd float her across the raging river in a trice; and he'd laugh his head off at those little, angry squirrels.

Oh well. She knew they'd take him into the program someday—they had to—but for now, she would have to make do with the quiet, steady-tempered boy from some mysterious place called Indiana.

As Brian and she moved toward the front, passing Sir Peter, the wizard gave Dani a look of regret. "Sorry in advance, ol' girl."

Her eyes widened. Would it be so bad that he actually felt the need to apologize? But she checked her climbing dread. Maybe he was joking.

And besides, Gaia had chosen her for a reason, Dani reminded herself. She could do this. "I-it's all right, sir. You're only doing your job."

Her answer seemed to startle him, then he chuckled. "You are such an amusing child," he said under his breath.

Finnderool snapped his fingers, growing annoyed with waiting. "Spit-spot! Lightrider, come and claim your conductee. People are waiting."

"Yes, sir, sorry, sir." Dani quickly reached into the tin cannister and helped herself to a Pansy pellet.

Up close, she saw it was a capsule with tiny pink balls inside. When she pinched it in between her fingers, it gave a startling little pop. She then dropped it on the ground the way Finnderool had done.

Meanwhile, Sir Peter was waving his wand over the playing field, and it transformed in ominous ways.

Many more trees began rising out of the turf, a whole forest of them. Then a fog descended, obscuring the cheery autumn sunshine.

Dani gulped. *I guess he wasn't joking.* The way ahead looked scary.

Finnderool scanned the field in approval, then turned to the group and made a horrible announcement: "Ladies and gentlemen, the first three teams got the easy setting for the test. For the next three, we now move to the medium setting. The last two teams will have the field set to difficult."

"What?" someone yelped in the back.

Three other kids groaned.

Apparently, these were the last two pairs of partners. One girl looked like she might cry.

Finnderool smirked. "Henceforward, children, this should enlighten you as to how much the Order appreciates eager volunteers. Our agents are people who are willing to step boldly into danger and face the unknown."

The kids glanced grimly around at each other.

"Note to self," someone muttered.

But Princess Pansy had finished inflating, so Dani checked her Bud of Life one last time, making sure the gauntlet was safely secured on her left wrist and forearm. She knew that when they reached the river—if it was still hidden somewhere inside the woods—she'd have to keep it dry no matter what. The Bud seemed secure on her arm, so she collected her fake VIP.

She picked the Pansy doll up and wrapped her arm around its waist. It was not heavy, just a few pounds, but Her Highness was almost as tall as Dani, so carrying it was a little awkward.

"Don't worry, Dani," Brian said bravely, though his grayish eyes looked frightened. "Whatever comes, I've got your back."

"Thanks, Brian. Yours too." She managed to smile at him, but he looked scared, and once again, she sorely wished it were the invincible Lord Griffon by her side.

"Your coordinates, Miss O'Dell." Finnderool held out his long, willowy hand for the slip of paper. She stole one last glance at it, then handed it over. "Thank you," he said. "Now step up to the starting line."

They did, putting their toes onto the chalked line edging around the playing field. Ahead of them, the conjured forest waited, with what dangers lurking inside, who could say? Brian and she were about to find out.

"Ready. Set... Go!" Finnderool said.

At once, they began jogging forward.

Dani gradually began to realize that the fluttery feeling in the pit of her stomach wasn't just fear. It was also excitement. After all, this was just a test, she reminded herself. She had faced *real* enemies many times with Jake and the gang.

Like Fionnula Coralbroom and nasty Uncle Waldrick.

Rock golems that tried to squish her.

Pirates who could turn into terrifying shark-men.

Ghosts, goblins, and gargoyles. Why, she had even helped face down Garnock the Sorcerer.

All of this might *look* scary, but the teachers wouldn't really hurt them. Reflecting on all this shored up her courage and got her past the fear as she jogged farther into the medium-level playing field.

While the first three teams had a few groves of crabapple-throwing trees, Dani and Brian got woods. Dark, spooky woods with swirls of fog snaking through them. Here, the afternoon sunshine had turned to twilight. The trees weren't too close together, but they were large and twisty, thick and gnarled, and Dani could swear some of them had old man faces like the Old Father Yew—only, these ones weren't friendly.

No wonder Sir Peter had apologized. She could swear the nasty-faced trees watched them pass.

Brian must've read her mind. "If the last ones threw crabapples," he murmured, "I dread to think what these might do."

"Let's try and get past them quickly."

He nodded, his quarterstaff at the ready. They hurried on to the riverbank, where they realized that the medium-level setting also got the rushing river instead of the babbling brook.

For them, even the rickety footbridge had now vanished. All they got to aid their crossing was a fat fallen log.

"I'll go first and check it out," Brian said. "Do you want me to take Princess Pansy?"

"Would you? My main worry is not getting water on the Bud of Life."

"Sure. You can borrow this if you want." He offered her his quarterstaff. "It might help your balance—like the circus lady on the tightrope."

"Oh, good idea!" She traded Pansy for the wooden rod.

Brian gave her a businesslike nod and headed out across the log with the silly-looking doll tucked under his arm. Dani watched nervously. He had no trouble getting across, she saw with relief. After all, the log was mossy but reasonably wide. It would probably be thinner for the next kids.

Upon reaching the other side of the river, Brian set Princess Pansy down and glanced around at the trees, making sure nothing was about to attack. Then he beckoned to show Dani it was safe to come across.

"I see a path!" he added, pointing toward the woods.

"Oh good." Dani nodded, then stepped onto the log. *Next time, I am volunteering to go* first.

Then she set out across the log, holding the quarterstaff like the tightrope lady, who, decades ago, used to entertain the carnival-goers at Jake's old hideaway in London, Elysian Springs Pleasure Gardens.

The thought of the abandoned pleasure grounds with its old swan boats and the fading pastel ice-cream-scoop turrets on the once-grand main pavilion made her smile. She had always loved going there, the one place where a scrappy girl from the rookery had always felt safe.

It was probably all because of him. Back in the old days, homeless pickpocket Jake had ruled the abandoned carnival grounds like a lonely king, camping in one of the ancient garden follies.

She had found the whole atmosphere enchanting. It had made their hard life bearable then, and thinking of it now gave her a much-needed dose of encouragement.

As she left the shore behind, venturing out across the river, its watery music filled her ears. The current flowed briskly beneath her feet. She kept her eyes on her footing, but whenever she did glance down at the water, she saw fish and rocks and foam.

She reassured herself that it was just like going on an ordinary hike. To her right splashed a little waterfall, where the current sang louder as it cascaded over some dark rocks.

It gave off a faint, pleasant spray. She could feel it as she walked past slowly. *This isn't so bad.* At least the log was dry. She really didn't even need the quarterstaff for balance. This was easy.

"Doing great, halfway there!" Brian called from the other shore.

She stepped carefully over a knotty whorl in the log and kept going, rather relaxed about it now.

Just when she was musing on how *real* Sir Peter's magical landscape looked, smelled, sounded, and how impressed Nixie would be if she were here, Dani glanced down at the water.

And saw a face glaring up at her.

She froze with a gasp, recognizing in a heartbeat that it was a naiad, a freshwater mermaid.

While their songs were enthralling and the creatures themselves were fascinating to observe from a safe distance, they had a scary reputation if you got too close.

Aye, they were known for grabbing people—pulling them underwater and occasionally drowning them.

She had never really trusted naiads, and seeing one sneering up at her from the river beneath her feet made her jerk back with a small cry. She nearly flailed herself off balance for a second while Brian looked on in panic.

"What's wrong?" he shouted.

She didn't answer, concentrating on keeping her balance. Usually Jake was there to catch her with his telekinesis, but this time, Dani was on her own.

While she wobbled with the quarterstaff, the green-skinned naiad rose up out of the water.

"Come on in, the water's fine!" it taunted her with a cackle.

Dani whimpered, teetering. If she fell into the river like Huang had, the Bud of Life on her arm would be ruined, and that might get her kicked out of the program.

Brian started back across the log to help her.

"Don't abandon Princess Pansy!" she yelled, regrouping.

After all, she had the quarterstaff to keep the naiad at bay, and if Brian turned his back on Princess Pansy, something would probably come out of the woods and steal her.

Just as Dani found her footing, planting both feet securely on the log, the naiad splashed her with another nasty laugh.

She yelped but managed to protect the Bud of Life from getting wet. To her relief, the naiad sank back down into the river and swam away.

The next team probably wouldn't be so lucky.

Dani's heart was still pounding as she scurried the rest of the way across the log and fled back onto solid ground on the other side.

"Blimey," she said, panting. She gave Brian back the quarterstaff.

"You all right?"

She nodded, accepting Princess Pansy in return. "That was close."

"Too close," he agreed, glancing uneasily at the water.

"C'mon," Dani said. "We've got to find the waypoint."

"You know your numbers?"

"Aye," she said firmly, then they marched into the woods, taking the path Brian had found. The river sounds faded behind them, but it wasn't long before another worrisome sound reached them from ahead.

Thud...! Thud...! Thud...!

"Mother Mary," Dani whispered, clutching Princess Pansy. "What was that?"

It continued.

Brian shrugged, scanning the woods ahead with a look of fierce determination.

"The ogre?" Dani whispered.

"I don't think so. Let's keep our eyes open. We haven't even seen the waypoint yet."

"Right."

They pressed on deeper into the forest, nervously watching for the source of the dull pounding noise to reveal itself from wherever it was hidden among the trees.

The thumps grew louder, their rhythm slow but steady.

Brian gripped his quarterstaff tighter—prepared, Dani hoped, to meet whatever sort of threat showed up to greet them. They walked softly over the bed of dried leaves and soft dirt, doing their best not to make any noise.

But as they approached the source of the thumping, Dani also heard splintering sounds along with the thuds. Brian must've already picked up on that with his excellent Guardian hearing. At last, they could take a reasonable guess at what the sound might be.

"It sounds like someone's chopping wood," Brian said very quietly. "Maybe trying to cut down one of these awful trees."

Dani drew in her breath. "A woodcutter? Like in the fairytales?"

"Maybe."

"Well, that's not good!" she said in a hushed voice.

"Why?"

"Because the woodcutter is always bad in the fairytales, Brian! Hansel and Gretel's father was a woodcutter, and he abandoned them to die in the woods!"

"Huh." Brian thought this over for a beat, but remained unflappable. "Well. It's just an old story. On the other hand, I guess it also means he does have an ax."

"That too."

They exchanged a dire look, then ventured onward, keeping as silent as possible. Hiding behind the trees as they sneaked along, they hadn't gone much farther when they saw him: a huge woodcutter, just like the cold-hearted father of the poor breadcrumb kids.

His back was toward them, but they could see the towering peasant man's broad shoulders. He was simply dressed but built like a bear. He swung his ax again and again, mindlessly crashing it into the nearest tree trunk. Splintered bits of wood flew with each powerful chop.

"Guess we get him instead of the ogre," Brian whispered. "He seems slow."

"Really focused on his task, too."

"That's good. He's distracted. With all the noise he's making, maybe we can just sneak past him and he won't even notice us."

With a mutual nod, they decided to try. They gave the giant, husky man a wide berth, rounding behind him at a healthy distance while he continued chopping away at one of the massive trees.

Of course, their effort to go around him took them off the path they had been following, and, as Dani recalled, in the old fairytales, leaving the path was usually a very bad idea.

Unfortunately, they had no choice if they were going to slip past this ax-wielding woodcutter.

Scrambling up a small, weed-covered hill, they were nearly clear of the woodcutter when, suddenly, Princess Pansy piped up: "Hurry, they're coming."

"Shut up!" she whispered instinctively at the doll.

It was too late. The woodcutter had heard it. Through the trees, they saw him leave off chopping wood. He turned around slowly, holding the ax in a murderous grip. But when they saw his face, both Brian and Dani gasped.

His eyes were sewn shut!

Dani recoiled. "Oh, that's disgusting!"

Brian grimaced. "It's like the ogre's blindfold, I guess," he mumbled. "Well, at least it'll make getting past him a lot easier."

"Hurry, they're coming," said Princess Pansy.

Brian scowled at the doll. "Is there any way to shut that thing off?"

Dani shook her head. "It's supposed to drive us crazy. That's the whole point."

The woodcutter lifted his chin and sniffed the air—a warning that, just like the ogre challenge, he, too, could track them by sense of smell.

"Come on, we've got to get out of here," Brian murmured. "I have a bad feeling."

Dani winced. "Oh, don't say that." Whenever a Guardian said, *I have a bad feeling,* mayhem usually followed soon thereafter.

This time proved no different.

Perhaps, as the fictional father of poor Hansel and Gretel, the woodcutter was used to dealing with children. And he clearly didn't like them.

He also must've adapted to living with his eyes sewn shut, for even though he couldn't see them, he chased after them with horrifying speed.

Dani bit back a shriek as she and Brian sprinted through the woods, the woodcutter in hot pursuit. She could hear his heavy footfalls crackling through the underbrush behind them.

He was large and fast and on a mission, apparently, to chop them into bits. But, thankfully, he was clumsy.

He ran into trees several times as he strove to home in on them. He kept swinging his ax, and half the time, it would crash into one tree trunk or another, sometimes getting stuck in the wood. Then he'd have to stop and wrangle it free.

But as soon as he pulled the blade out, he'd keep trying to find them.

"You don't think the teachers would let him actually kill us, do you? I mean, Sir Peter isn't evil!" Dani said, glancing over her shoulder as Brian and she raced on through the brush, far off the path now. "That ax is probably m-made of rubber or something, right? L-Like a stage prop!"

"Let's not stick around and find out."

Clumsy or not, the woodcutter knew this conjured forest far better than they did and managed to corner them in a small clearing a few minutes later.

"I'll distract him!" Brian cried. "You find the waypoint so we can get out of here!"

"I'll take that deal gladly. Be careful." As Dani tiptoed away, praying Princess Pansy kept her painted mouth shut, she felt very proud of her partner's valor.

Brian sneaked behind the woodcutter, then poked him in the back with his quarterstaff. "Hey, ugly! You missed me!"

The woodcutter turned around slowly with a guttural sound. Brian ducked and dodged as the ax swung. It was almost like the boy knew where the weapon was going to arc before it came at him.

Still, Dani slipped away through the trees with her heart in her throat. She had to remind herself that this was just a training simulation. Their teachers would have a lot of explaining to do if somebody got killed. No, she told herself, they would never let that happen. Wood elves didn't make mistakes, after all.

Then Dani focused on finding the waypoint. It had to be here somewhere. Still hearing the sounds of the woodcutter trying to decapitate her partner, she scanned the woods for the column of white light.

Creeping deeper into the forest, she opted to ignore the nagging thought that, in the old fairytales, the only thing worse than leaving the path was splitting off from one's companions.

"Hurry, they're coming," Pansy said.

"Yes, I know!" Finally, Dani moved around a great, thick oak tree and spotted the light ahead.

Still worried about separating from her partner, she memorized the spot and headed back in his direction, but in the next moment, she saw Brian sprinting toward her.

"Run!" He waved her on.

Dani bolted. "Follow me!"

"Did you find it?"

"It's up ahead!"

"Yes—I see it now!"

"Are you all right?"

"Just dandy," he said.

She smiled at his confident tone, tearing along through the trees. She glanced back and saw Brian racing after her, his cheeks pink with exertion.

Several yards beyond him, she could also see the woodcutter falling behind. In the next moment, he stopped, as if he'd given up or maybe reached the boundary of *his* section of the medium-level playing field.

Whatever the reason, he did not pursue them further, much to her relief. It seemed they had succeeded in getting past him.

Lord only knew what would come next. Maybe nothing, she hoped, if she got them out of here quickly. But this would entail opening her very first portal with the Bud of Life. She started getting nervous.

Following the light of the waypoint, Brian and she finally reached the edge of the woods.

Alas, no pleasant meadow awaited them. No sunlight broke through here, despite the absence of trees.

Instead, the same misty twilight that veiled the woods persisted.

Dani and Brian stopped to stare at what awaited them in the clearing: a small graveyard with about twenty old headstones.

Around it wrapped a broken wrought-iron fence with creepy, rusted gates under an archway, whose metal sign warned: *Hush, We Are Sleeping.*

Brian and she exchanged a wide-eyed look. He lifted his finger over his lips, but she hardly needed to be told to keep quiet at such a time. She had no intention of waking the dead.

Silently, they began to sneak past the cemetery. This situation obviously called for the utmost stealth, because if they triggered *this* challenge, she barely dared wonder what might come out of that graveyard.

Zombies? Unfriendly ghosts? The thought made her wish yet again that Jake were here. He wouldn't even be nervous. Knowing him, he'd be having a grand time.

Inspired by the thought of her hero, she shored up her courage as Brian and she crept past the graveyard.

They made it as far as the rusty gates when Princess Pansy said, "Hurry, they're coming."

Dani clapped a hand uselessly over the doll's painted mouth.

Immediately, the turf in front of every gravestone started shifting around. Something was moving underground in those graves.

She gasped when a bony hand and forearm shot up through the grass.

"Skeletons!" Brian cried. "Let's get out of here!"

“Hurry, they’re coming,” the doll intoned.

But Dani just stood there, staring for a moment in astonishment.

Skeletons were climbing out of the graves, dusting off the soil on their bones, and making sure they had their skulls on straight.

She gasped as they started walking toward Brian and her, their white limbs clattering, their jawbones clacking as if they were trying to talk or shout.

Dani knew the skeletons were only simulations, figments of Sir Peter’s warped sense of humor, but they were unnerving, nonetheless.

Brian tugged on her arm. “Let’s go!”

Thankfully, the skeletons were slow to get started. They seemed confused by the gate. This gave Dani and Brian and their bigmouthed conductee enough time to race toward the glowing beacon of the waypoint.

Unfortunately, the bony crew got better at walking with a little practice, and began picking up speed.

“Here, guard Princess Pansy.” Dani handed the doll to Brian as they reached the glowing waypoint marker. “I’ll dial in the coordinates.”

He set the doll on the ground behind him and got into position with his weapon, ready to take on the skeletons shuffling toward them. “I like these better than those creepy little squirrels, anyway. At least skeletons won’t give you rabies.”

“Good point.” Dani strove to focus and started punching in the coordinates she had memorized...

Or thought she had memorized.

The first two numbers were easy, fresh in her mind: *81* and *54*. But at the third, she hesitated.

Hold on, was that 19 or 91? She squeezed her eyes shut, forcing herself to see the numbers scrawled on the slip of paper in her mind.

Oh wait—what am I saying? She rolled her eyes. The minutes and seconds *had* to be a number under sixty. *Dummy!*

She turned the dial confidently to *19*, then flicked the latitude switch to *South*, her fingers trembling only slightly.

Halfway there.

She had made a little singsong of the numbers and sang it again and again in her mind. *What’s next, what’s next?*

With all her will, she ignored Brian, who was shifting the quarterstaff in his hands to hold it like a bat. He changed his stance, planting his feet sideways, bending his knees.

"Good thing for us I love baseball."

Dani refused even to look over. She didn't know anything about this newfangled American sport, nor did she care at the moment. Her stare stayed fixed on the number dials of the Bud of Life.

But when the skeletons approached, jaws clacking, she heard an odd, hollow *thunk* and looked over just in time to see Brian send one of the bony fellows' heads sailing off into the trees with a hearty swing of his bat.

The head went flying into the forest.

Unfortunately, the rest of the body only needed a brief pause before regrouping, as though this were a minor inconvenience. The headless skeleton then continued moving toward them, along with his bony band of friends.

Dani strove to block it all out, trusting her partner to keep them at bay.

Several more *thunks* followed, while she forced the next number into focus in her mind's eye: *41.*

"Hurry, they're coming."

"Shut up!" Dani snapped at the doll.

"How are we doing?" Brian yelled, whacking the legs out from underneath another skeleton.

"Working on it!"

He was starting to sound nervous. "Do you know the numbers or not, Dani?"

"I only have two more to go! Let me think!"

"I'm just saying, it's ten to one here and more are on the way!"

"Don't mention numbers, you'll confuse me!"

Brian shot her a scowl and then shoved his quarterstaff into a skeleton's ribcage to drive it back. "Go away!" he yelled at the thing.

"Hurry, they're coming."

Dani yanked the doll closer to keep it out of harm's way, then pressed her fingers to her forehead. *Come on, come on, get the stupid portal open, carrot.*

The next number blossomed in her mind. *That's right!* Maddox's age: *17.* She dialed it in and quickly flicked the longitude switch to *West*; of that part she was sure.

Just one more number to go.

Oh, what was it?

She inhaled slowly, trying to calm herself while another head went sailing. It didn't matter if Brian reduced the skeletons to a heap of bones, because they just sprang up alive again. No wonder he was getting frustrated.

"Can you please hurry up? Ow!"

One of the skeletons had picked up a companion's lost tibia and whacked Brian on the shoulder with it, its mandible working like it was laughing at him.

"Hurry, they're coming."

Dani racked her brain, but she simply wasn't sure about the final number. Thirty-something?

I think it's 34. Or was it 32? Her fingertip hovered over the last dial while her heart pounded.

Sweat formed on her brow as she agonized over the final number. *Think, think, think.* It was fifty-fifty as far as her memory was concerned, so, rather blindly, she opted for *34,* and then pressed the all-important button that said ACTIVATE.

Nothing happened.

The portal didn't open. *Blast it! It must've been 32.* Unfortunately, after a wrong number was entered, the Bud of Life needed one full minute to reset before you could try again.

They were the longest sixty seconds ever.

"Hurry, they're coming," Princess Pansy said again—and, this time, she was right.

More skeletons were closing in on Brian.

He was in the rhythm of it now, knocking back the skeletons as fast as they could come, using both ends of his quarterstaff like he was rowing a canoe. The odds against him were extremely unfair, however, so Dani sought to help her partner while she waited for the gauntlet to reset.

She picked up a skull that had rolled past and hurled it at another approaching skeleton. The skeleton collapsed in a clatter of bones. Dani found the strike oddly satisfying, like some macabre form of lawn bowls.

They went on like that for a little more, until she was confident that sixty seconds had gone by. Then, heart pounding, Dani tried again, turning the last dial anxiously to *32* and hesitating only for a second before pressing activate again.

It worked!

"I did it," she whispered as the radiance of the portal flashed, enveloping them in its brightness amid the gloom of the woods. "I can't believe it. *I* opened a portal. Me!"

It was the prettiest thing she had ever seen, shiny and round, beckoning them to safety, but for a split second, she could only stare at it with a dazed smile.

I *did that. Not Jake. Not Archie, not Nixie. Not Isabelle.*

No one but me.

"You did it!" Brian yelled, squinting over his shoulder at the light shining behind him.

Dani grinned and grabbed Princess Pansy. "Let's go get some ice cream, shall we?"

Unfortunately, the skeletons had other ideas.

Two of them reached out and wrapped their bony hands around Brian's arms, preventing him from running through the portal.

"Hey! Get off me!" He struggled against them, but more joined in the effort to keep him from going through the portal. He was starting to panic.

"Let him go!" Dani shouted.

The thirty seconds they had were ticking along, but her partner was having trouble extricating himself.

"I said, leave him alone!" Angry all of a sudden, Dani set down their inflatable conductee, picked up a lost femur, and started batting the skeletons away from her partner.

"Leave him be!" she hollered. *Tick-tock.* "We've got to go!"

Brian kicked away the skeleton on his right but was unable to pry off the grip of the one on his left. Instead, he whacked its arm with his quarterstaff.

Dani grimaced as the arm tore off the skeleton, but the bony hand stayed attached to Brian's biceps.

"Ew," she said with a wince, but at least her partner was free.

"Let's go!" No doubt Brian thought he was only following protocol when he pulled Dani into the portal.

"Wait!" Frantic, Dani reached back out through the portal where the horde of skeletons crowded around, jaws clacking. "We forgot Princess Pansy!"

Flailing, she grasped the stupid doll at the last second and pulled it halfway into the portal.

"Hurry, they're—"

The portal closed, and Princess Pansy got cut in half at the waist.

"Aw, cheese it!" Dani yelled.

The next thing she knew, she was flying through the silvery tunnel of light, still clutching the deflated upper half of Princess Pansy.

Brian was flying along ahead of her—or rather, below her. Their molecules had gone fuzzy and out of focus, so he looked blurry to her.

In fact, her own body looked blurry too, but since this was just a simulation, she supposed they had not dissolved entirely, the way they would if this were a real trip through a real portal to the outside world.

"Where are we going?" Brian shouted.

"No idea, but I doubt there's any ice cream there!"

She was right.

In the next moment, they discovered the destination Finnderool had prepared for the losers.

The training simulation dumped them out in midair several feet above the ground, so that they each sent up a muddy splash when they landed unceremoniously in the menagerie's mud-pen full of climbing fish.

Dani shrieked and got a mouthful of swampy water for her pains.

Brian punched the surface of the muddy water and let out a stream of words that kids were not supposed to say.

The climbing fish stopped croaking and eyeballed them here and there from the dead trees.

"Oh, I could strangle that wood elf! He thinks he's funny, doesn't he?" she shouted as she stood up, stewing. "Well, it's not funny! It's not funny at all!"

Brian's face was splashed with mud like war paint as he turned to her angrily. "What happened? I thought we made it!"

"Not *all* of us!" Dani held up the severed trunk of their royal VIP.

It was only then that she remembered the Bud of Life and yelped, lifting it higher to keep it out of the swamp water.

A quick glance at the gauntlet revealed that somehow—surely it was sheer Irish luck—she had managed not to get it wet in the fall.

Brian scowled.

"Gross!" Dani muttered. It would take a house brownie or a major magic spell to get her dashing uniform back to its spit-spot shape.

"Stupid skeletons," Brian muttered.

"What are you lookin' at?" Dani grumbled at the climbing fish, who were staring at her and her partner as they climbed out of the creatures' swampy habitat. "Sorry to bother you!"

They were harmless, of course. She actually wasn't sure if they were true fish or amphibians or something in between, but over eons, they had developed weirdly strong little fins that allowed them to squish their way up into the dead trees that graced their desolate habitat.

As Dani and Brian climbed over the post-and-rail fence around their pen, along came Dr. Plantagenet.

"Sorry about this, Dr. P," Dani said wearily.

"It's not our fault," Brian hastened to tell him.

"Hmm." The Green Man looked at the fishes' pen and then the muddy footprints that followed Dani and Brian onto the walking path, and sighed. "I really must have a word with Master Finnderool before one of my climbing fish suffers an injury. He really has a wicked sense of humor."

"The Green Man's worried about the climbing fish?" Brian huffed privately to her as he and Dani walked away. "We're the ones who got dumped out of the sky."

"At least we didn't land in the yeti's cage," she replied.

Brian grumbled under his breath.

After dropping the dead Princess Pansy in the dustbin near the zoo entrance, the two of them shuffled back to Merlin Hall in a state of muddy humiliation.

By St. Patrick's nose, if she ran into the skunkies right now and that Prue Badgerton said one wrong word to her, Dani swore she could not be held responsible for her actions.

Fortunately, she was spared an encounter with her archenemies. As Brian and she walked up to Merlin Hall, cold and covered in mud, the gnomes were waiting outside with hoses.

"Well," Brian said in a philosophical tone while the gnomes blasted them with water, clothes and all, "we were doing pretty well right up until the end there."

Dani gave him a glum nod. "You did *very* well with all those skeletons. And the woodcutter."

"You remembered the coordinates in the end."

Considering they had seen two other teams fail before them, they didn't take it too hard, all in all. It had been a hard test. Well, medium-hard. Still.

At least I didn't get the Bud of Life wet.

It made them both feel slightly better to remember that each team after them would have it even harder than they did.

They wondered aloud together what the future teams' challenges might entail. A more aggressive attack from the naiad? More skeletons? Maybe the woodcutter would only have one eye sewn shut instead of both?

"I guess we'll find out tomorrow," Dani concluded. "That was exhausting."

Brian nodded, then the gnomes handed them each a towel. They dried off a little, then parted ways, each trudging back to their rooms in their still soaking wet, somewhat less muddy uniforms.

Dani was glad the long school day was over. She could not wait to take a bath and get the icky, slimy mud of the climbing fish cage off her. The gnomes' hosing them down had barely begun to wash away the filth.

Still feeling yucky and worn out, she pulled open the door to the Bradford suite, then stepped (or rather squished) onto the little carpet just inside the entrance.

Normally, it was quite lonely coming in here these days, but for once, she was glad the whole gang was not there to see her in this embarrassing state, awash in failure and the stink of climbing fish.

Head down, she pulled the door shut behind her, when she heard a familiar voice. "Why, here's a right plum lass. Finally."

Dani lifted her head with a gasp. "Jake!"

The handsome blond rogue was sitting in an armchair with one ankle resting across his opposite knee, his fingers steepled.

He took one look at her in her bedraggled state and lifted his eyebrows. "Getting into trouble without me? What is this world coming to?"

"Jake—what are you doing here?" she exclaimed.

"Tell you all about it, but first, special delivery," he said, then Teddy leaped off the chair, where he had snuggled in beside his temporary owner.

Dani cheered and Teddy yipped with glee, scampering across the room to her. She knelt, not wanting to get water and dirt everywhere.

But she couldn't resist bending down to hug and pet her dog. Teddy bounced with a few insistent leaps until she conceded and caught him in her arms.

"Good boy!" The wee brown terrier licked her cheek. Teddy never cared how much of a mess she was. "Oh, I missed you, too! Did you behave for Uncle Jakey?"

"He did." Jake rose from his chair. "In fact, that dog of yours once again proved himself a furry little hero."

"Really? How?"

"In due time, Miss O'Dell. But first"—he gestured at her muddy self—"should I be concerned?"

Dani laughed. "No. Just another day of Lightrider training. How are you? You look good," she blurted out, then was embarrassed.

Well, it was true. He seemed different somehow, she noticed at once. She couldn't quite put her finger on what it was, but something about him had changed.

Perhaps he stood a little straighter; he came across a little calmer. Sauntering toward her, the ex-pickpocket seemed lordlier and more self-assured than ever. Strangely mature, compared to his usual rascally self.

"Thank you." Jake nodded, looking a little embarrassed at her compliment. "I'm doing well. Yourself?"

"Oh...I'm good." She gave Teddy a doting squeeze and begged her brain to think of a change of subject. What was this strange awkwardness between her and Jake? But he looked so handsome. She swallowed hard. "Thanks for watching him for me."

"Of course."

The conversation floundered again. A stilted silence descended. After all their warm, joking letters back and forth, actually being in the presence of this new Jake felt a little strange. It gave her butterflies in her stomach.

In truth, Dani wanted to hug him, to say welcome back, but she was such a mess. She didn't want to get his gentlemanly clothes all muddy.

Feeling very odd, she kept staring at him, trying to figure out why he seemed different. But Jake started blushing, as though he had noticed her ogling him, and then Dani blushed, in turn, because she was.

She couldn't help it. Her old friend looked cuter than ever. "So, um"—she tucked a mud-crusted lock of hair behind her ear—"are you just visiting Merlin Hall or are you back for good?"

"For good, as far as I know."

She managed to stifle a whoop of joy at that news. *Stop acting like an idiot!* she scolded herself. *It's just Jake. You've known him all your life.*

"Why did they bring you back?" she forced out, trying to sound intelligent despite her racing heart.

"Oh, it's a long story. Griffon Castle didn't, um, it didn't work out."

Jake was looking at *her* strangely, too, but that was probably because she looked like a swamp monster.

Blast. If only he had come when she was in her pristine uniform. He would've been so impressed by her then.

"I'll tell you all about it," he said. "But, um..." He gestured at her. "Did you fall in a puddle or what?"

She laughed halfheartedly, mortified. "The climbing fish pen, actually."

Jake's eyes widened.

She waved it off. "That's just Finnderool's evil sense of humor."

Jake flashed a grin, and Dani's heart fluttered. What on earth was wrong with her?

Maybe it was true that absence made the heart grow fonder, for they were gawking at each other and blushing like a couple of idiots. For her, it was just weird, but for cool-nerved Jake, it was unheard of.

"Um, you have a..." He took a gentlemanly step toward her, whipping a neatly pressed handkerchief square out of his breast pocket. Hesitating, he lifted his hand toward her face, then gently wiped a glob of mud off her cheek that the gnomes' hoses must have missed.

Dani stared at him, amazed.

"There you are," Jake whispered, suddenly turning embarrassed. Clearing his throat, he stepped out of her way and gestured her on toward her room. "Well—I'll let you go and clean yourself up, then."

"Thanks," Dani said slowly. *Huh.* Something weird was definitely going on here. Then she put Teddy down and bent to unlace her boots. She dared not get the carpet muddy.

"What's that on your arm?" Jake suddenly asked, pointing at the gauntlet. He seemed recovered from his bout of tender affection for her.

Too bad. She had rather liked it.

"Oh—it's called the Bud of Life," she told him as she untied her laces. "It's the junior version of the Flower of Life they embed in the Lightriders' arms."

"Really?"

She nodded, desperate that he not feel jealous. "It's such a pain. I have to wear it all the time. Trust me, you'll hate it when you get one." She continued unlacing her boots. "If I had got it wet when I fell in the climbing fishes' pen, I'd be in *so* much trouble."

"Blimey." Jake came toward her for a closer look.

Dani held up her arm, letting him inspect the gauntlet.

"This is fantastic." He studied it in fascination, then lifted his gaze and looked into her eyes. "Why didn't you tell me about this in your letters?"

She hesitated. "I must've...forgotten?"

"Dani, it's all right. I'm not jealous anymore." Jake paused, searching her eyes. "I really am sorry for how I reacted when you first told us that you had been selected. Sometimes I wonder why you put up with me."

Because I...

"I'm happy for you," he added while Dani stared at him in mixed shock and delight at his kind words.

"Listen." He took her hand in his—her left hand, the one on which she wore the gauntlet. "You don't have to avoid telling me about your Lightrider training just to spare my feelings. I promise. I'm a big boy. I can stand the disappointment. If they pick me someday, so be it. If not, I'll live."

"Well, *I* won't!" she retorted. "Every hour I'm there, all I can think about is how you should be there too. It's not fair that we can't do it together!"

"It's all right." He gave her a reassuring smile. "Believe me, I have other things to think about these days."

"Like what?"

"Oh, like Lord Wyvern attacking us earlier today at Griffon Castle."

"What?" Dani gasped with horror while Jake flashed an uncomfortable smile.

"It's fine. We're all fine," he said. "We managed to chase him off. But you'll be happy to know it was actually your dog who saved the day."

"Teddy?"

He nodded. "My cousins and I had gone to the village. Teddy came and warned us through Isabelle that Wyvern had come to the house. And Fionnula."

"Fionnula?" she cried, even more shocked.

"And Uncle Waldrick."

Dani's jaw dropped. "You're joking."

Jake shook his head. "Wyvern broke them out of prison. Surprise, surprise. There is definitely strange business afoot, Dani O'Dell."

"Crikey..."

"I have a lot more to tell you—and I really want to hear about what you've been doing, too. But I can see you need to get yourself, er, de-mudded. So do what you've got to do, but sit by me at supper tonight so we can catch up. Aye?"

She turned bright red at his extraordinary invitation and could only nod, tongue-tied.

In truth, they sat together at meals as often as not, but usually, it was because Dani was a tagalong. Where Jake went, she followed.

Only, this time, it was he, the golden boy of the Order, asking her to sit with him.

Most unusual.

A bit rattled by this unexpected turnabout, Dani lowered her head shyly without another word and finished taking off her boots. Then she rose, muddy boots in one hand.

Jake nodded farewell, taking a step back to get out of her way.

Having collected her wits, more or less, Dani carried her boots with her to her room. She felt like she should say something, though, so she paused at the doorway of her chamber. "Say, Jake?"

"Aye?"

"I'm glad you're back."

That was putting it mildly.

He smiled warmly at her, his blue eyes shining. "It's good to *be* back."

Then he took a deep breath and uttered words Dani never thought that she would hear: "I missed you somethin' awful, carrot-cake."

A gigantic smile spread across her face at his confession—along with a blush. She mumbled something stupid, then fled into her chamber, heart pounding. She shut the door behind her and leaned against it.

But she still couldn't wipe the dreamy smile off her face.

PART IV

CHAPTER 45
A Good Meal

It was grand to be back at the palace, among friends, and safe behind the Veil once more in this place protected by the Order.

True, there was a spy here somewhere in their midst reporting his activities to the Dark Druids—and not everyone was glad to see Jake return. But at least Magick-kind's shock and dismay over the prophecy about him had had a few weeks to die down.

Jake decided to ignore it, and, that evening, enjoyed a lavish supper in the vast, noisy dining hall, catching up with his favorite redhead.

Seated at a round table beneath the blazing chandeliers with the rest of the gang, the two of them were engrossed in their own private conversation.

They talked so much that Jake barely had time to eat the food he'd mounded on his plate: crab- and mushroom-stuffed trout, along with a slice of straccato that nearly fell apart, it was so tender. (Up in the buffet line, Miz Jillian had told him that straccato was a fashionable Italian recipe for pot roast, slow-cooked for hours with tomatoes, herbs, and a hint of cinnamon; she sometimes made it for Sir Peter.)

The man clearly had good taste in women and food, Jake thought, then made a mental note that he should also marry a lady someday who could cook. Clever chap, that wizard. Maybe that was why he was always so happy.

Moving on down the buffet, Jake had been careful to avoid any mishaps this time with his telekinesis. He made it out the other end unscathed. Back for seconds, he loaded up on a generous helping of toad in the hole, a fond favorite of most kids, with sausages peeking up everywhere through a flaky golden crust. Dutifully, he also helped himself to a well-salted pile of roasted vegetables.

He had obviously got back his appetite.

Returning to the table, he sat down, and Dani told him all about her Lightrider classes in between nibbling at her fried fish cakes. It sounded fascinating.

Jake washed down his meal with gulps of warm apple cider and, in turn, related the wild story of finding the secret family vault, and how he could've been crushed to jelly if he hadn't figured out the code.

"Oh, I have to know codes, too!" she said eagerly. "Mine are coordinates, though. Horrid! I've already started memorizing some. It's really hard."

He nodded as he shoveled food into his mouth. "Sounds it."

"So, what was in the vault?" Dani asked.

Jake enjoyed regaling her about some of the family treasures stored there, and how, before leaving Griffon Castle that afternoon, they had moved all the vault's wonders over to Archie's giant underground safe full of prototypes and inventions.

Something between a bunker and an industrial warehouse, the boy genius's underground safe was connected by a tunnel to his lab in an outbuilding at Bradford Park, and protected by dastardly locks he'd invented himself.

Nobody was getting in there.

Dani shook her head, wide-eyed. "I didn't even know he had that."

"Nor did I. But I guess that's the whole point of having a safe, though." He smiled at her, and Dani smiled back.

Only the intriguing dragon-headed vial containing Uncle Waldrick's firepower had come with them to Merlin Hall.

Upon their arrival, Derek had made sure the shimmering little bottle of pyrokinesis was safely stowed away in the potion room of the palace. Jake hadn't even known that Merlin Hall *had* a potion room, but, with all the witches and wizards about, it made sense. Apparently, the high-security chamber lay somewhere on the basement level, along with the guest lab the Elders were letting his cousin use.

For a moment, Dani studied the boy genius from across the table. Archie was gulping down root beer like his mouth was on fire and even sweating mildly from the spicy fried Malabar chicken that he'd chosen.

Dani leaned her head closer to Jake's, and he tingled at her nearness. "How's he been lately, anyway?" she murmured. "Finally getting back to his old self?"

Jake thought it over. "Not really. He actually yelled at Derek and Helena today. All but cursed at them."

"No!" she whispered, scandalized. "Not Mr. Manners?"

Jake shrugged. "He was fearless in front of Wyvern, but afterward, he told Derek to his face that if the adults can't protect us, then, at the very least, they have a moral obligation to warn us of what the blazes is really going on so we can take measures to protect *ourselves.* Otherwise, we're just sitting ducks."

"Crikey," she breathed. "Well...he's right, though. As usual. They should be more honest with you."

Jake seconded that, raising his glass of apple cider.

"How 'bout Isabelle? How's she been? She was a mess when you left." Dani swirled her fork in circles in her mashed potatoes, stirring the gravy around.

Jake gave Dani a penetrating gaze as he recalled his conversation with the empath on the terrace. "Maddox was right," he finally said, keeping his voice low. "She's in love with Janos."

Dani froze, her fork halfway to her mouth. *"What?"* She put the fork down and leaned close again. "She told you that?"

"Not in words. But it's kind of obvious. And...I'd wager it's mutual."

Dani stared at him, wide-eyed. "Well, that's not good."

"I know." He shrugged. "Nevertheless."

She sat there looking dazed for a moment.

Jake frowned, suddenly worried. "You're not going to tell on her, are you?"

"But—I'm her official companion, Jake! Her family hired me to look after her—"

"That doesn't mean you have to act as their spy!" he whispered back. "Lord, I wouldn't have told you if I— Come on, Dani! Everyone hated snitches back in the rookery, remember?"

Oh, she remembered—he saw. Her posture stiffened.

"I'm no snitch. I'm only saying. Nothing can come of it. That's a worse match for her than Maddox."

"She knows that. So does Janos, I wager." Jake frowned, feeling uneasy. He rather wished now he hadn't said anything. He hoped it wasn't a mistake to confide in the carrot-head, but keeping secrets from her was pointless. She always got it out of him in the end. "How's he doing, anyway? Have you seen him?"

She dropped a blob of tartar sauce on her fish cake and shook her head. "He's been keeping to himself. Still holed up in that crypt out on the memorial grounds."

Jake winced. "Poor devil. We should go and see him. Do you know if anyone has talked to him?"

"Sir Peter has tried. Ravyn Vambrace, too. And Aleeyah, I think. But he doesn't want visitors. He barely comes out, even at night." Dani paused. "But, you know, that might be for the best. For his own safety."

"What do you mean?"

She fiddled with her fork. "A lot of people don't like him being here. Some more than others. I heard that Lord Badgerton put up a terrible stink about it—no pun intended," she added wryly, considering the man *was* the uncle of the skunkies. "A lot of people here seem to think Janos is a threat."

"He's not a threat, he's a hero!"

She shrugged. "All I know is that Master Balinor himself gave Janos permission to remain on the premises—after consulting with his owl, of course."

"Well, good. Because he's probably got nowhere else to go." Jake scowled with an angry pang for his vampire friend. "Maybe if they'd reinstate him as a Guardian..."

"I wouldn't hold my breath." Dani took a swallow from her glass of milk while Jake fumed.

"It's so unfair! I wish there was something I could do."

It wasn't as though he could just buy a second mechanical toy monkey to cheer Janos up—although the absurd gift had certainly made Aunt Ramona crack a smile, and that was no easy feat.

The Elder witch had stared at the thing without comprehension for a long moment after Jake wound it up and presented it to her.

The stern old lady had watched the silly toy go marching back and forth across the table in their suite, clapping its cymbals for her and stomping its little monkey feet.

All the kids had fought back laughter watching her stare at it, looking almost offended. And then, abruptly, almost in spite of herself, Aunt Ramona had burst out laughing, unaware of them all waiting to see her reaction.

Relieved she got the joke, Jake and his cousins then passed out the bags of candy they had brought back for the others from the Confectioner's Emporium.

Nixie had been delighted with her candy skulls, Dani scarfed down all her chocolate truffles, and even Maddox broke his no-sweets rule to try the sour lollipop that Isabelle had brought him.

Just when they had finished their candy, the dinner bell chimes had rung throughout the palace, summoning all guests down to the dining hall.

And so here they were, at about eight o'clock in the evening.

By now, the meal was almost over and Jake had managed to eat everything on his plate. Leaning back in his chair, Jake had to admit he was feeling pretty good (other than his guilt over Janos).

He was back with his friends, and, as always, the feast the brownie chefs had prepared had been outrageously delicious. He had eaten like a half-starved hog and was beginning to feel a trifle sleepy as a result. After all, it had been a very hard day.

Reflecting on the afternoon's events was a little unnerving, truth be told. Indeed, despite their in-depth conversation, there were certain things he did not care to discuss even with Dani.

Like his humiliating fight with Lord Wyvern.

It had shaken Jake up more than he cared to admit. Because, deep down, he knew full well that the Nephilim warlock had trounced him with ease.

Aye, Wyvern could have killed them all today if he had wanted to. Instead, he had given Jake that bloodcurdling speech about him becoming the Black Prince.

His son.

Jake shuddered, avoiding his friends' gazes as his grim thoughts churned.

He wanted no part of that so-called destiny, but a part of him wondered if he really had a choice. What if Isabelle had not sent the unicorns when she did, or if they had arrived two minutes later?

Much as he hated to admit it, he was scared. He had not let himself feel it at the time, but it was catching up to him now. Real, cold fear of someone was not an emotion he was used to, and he *really* didn't like the way it felt.

But it was unsettling to think how close he had come to being abducted today—right off the grounds of his own home. If not for the unicorns, he probably would've been carried off to the Black Fortress, possibly forever. And that surely would have started the long-dreaded war.

As Dani chattered on cheerfully beside him, however, he forced himself to remember that all's well that ends well. That was all that mattered. Wyvern and Fionnula had left Griffon Castle empty-handed.

Catastrophe had been averted. And even though his own home wasn't safe for him anymore, at least, here, the Dark Druids couldn't get him.

Aye, Jake mused, slowly scanning the dining hall full of Magickfolk, it was *very* good to be back.

Of course, not everyone looked overjoyed to see him again. Glancing around the huge room, Jake could not help but notice more than a few cold stares.

Most of the kids who spotted him smiled, but many of the adults—djinnis, centaurs, and mages alike—shot disapproving glances in his direction; others, especially the Greenfolk, looked downright fearful at his return.

Jake rolled his eyes at their reaction. *I'm not going to turn into a bloody Dark Druid!* he wanted to yell.

But he dropped his gaze and minded his own business. For, as irked as he was by their suspicion, he realized this was probably nothing compared to what Janos had to deal with around here.

No wonder he stayed holed up in that tomb. Jake couldn't blame him. Blimey, maybe *he* could find another unoccupied crypt out there in the Merlin Hall burial grounds, and the two of them could be neighbors—a couple of outcasts—the doomed living among the dead.

Since his own musings were beginning to depress him, Jake ignored the unfriendly glances and turned his full attention back to the cheerful redhead. The wise thing was to focus on the people who liked him.

"So what else have I missed?" he asked the carrot, forcing a taut smile.

"Let's see..." Chipper as ever, Dani told him about *The Lightrider's Handbook*, her class manual. She gushed on about her endless gratitude to one Mr. Penwick Calavast, who turned out to be the brownie librarian. Jake didn't know he had a name.

Then Dani mentioned her newfound friendship with some kid called Brian.

And Jake's full attention zeroed in.

Hmm. As he listened to her stories from class, she seemed so familiar with this American stranger that Jake wasn't sure how to feel. But jealousy was for idiots.

And yet, the whole time they'd been sitting there, he had not failed to notice how many kids said hello to Dani as they passed by their table on the way to or from the buffet.

She waved to people he didn't even know, and that made him feel odd...and vaguely excluded.

But why was he surprised? She had been chosen for the Lightrider program, and that brought her a whole new status in the eyes of everyone here.

She had clearly become very popular while he was away. Jake was happy for her. And yet...

"So who is this Brian again?" he asked ever so casually.

"Oh—like I said, he's usually my partner when Finnderool makes us team up with the Guardian group."

"Aha," Jake murmured, scrutinizing her.

"Don't worry, you'll like him." She turned around in her chair and began craning her neck, glancing around the vast dining hall. "He's really nice."

Oh, is he?

"Very easy to get along with. He's pretty good at all that Guardian stuff, too. I could introduce you—"

"That's all right! I mean, maybe later," Jake added, not wanting to seem rude. "It's been rather a long day."

That was putting it mildly.

Considering he could still practically feel Wyvern's boot planted on his back, grinding him down into the gravel, Jake was in no mood for meeting new people.

Especially "really nice" boys who had struck up a friendship with his carrot.

Time for a change of subject, Jake thought, before Dani remembered that he, for his part, wasn't always *very nice* at all.

"So." Jake reached for his half-empty glass of cider. "Anything else been happening around here that I should know about? Have they caught the mole?"

"Not that I've heard."

"Hm! Wonder why. You'd think they'd have got him by now. What else?"

"Well...*that* happened, you'll have noticed." She nodded discreetly at Nixie.

Jake looked over at the black-clad witch, hiding his smile. "Yes. I had noticed that." How could he not? Ah, Nixie.

The little non-conformist had given herself another of her ill-advised haircuts. This one involved jaggedy, crooked bangs.

Archie had declared it smashing—but, of course, he too was an eccentric (and her beau).

Jake wasn't sure *what* to call what she'd done to herself.

Nixie either liked her strange new style or was too proud to admit she had made a mistake, for she could've fixed it with a spell.

Dani's green eyes sparkled with mischief. "Personally, I think she pulls it off."

He bit his lip. "If you say so."

"What?" Nixie prompted. She'd been just about to take another bite of her pasta in cream sauce when she'd noticed them talking about her.

"Oh, nothing," Jake said with an innocent smile.

She frowned, but just then, he noticed a flash of a pointy red hat appear for a second in the wedge of empty space between Isabelle's chair and Archie's.

It disappeared, then popped up again an instant later. It remained this time, but wobbled back and forth a bit.

"Um, Izzy?" Jake said in amusement.

"Yes?" Having moved on to the sweets course after finishing her vegetarian risotto, she was savoring spoonfuls of a fluffy vanilla syllabub. Engrossed in her treat, she hadn't noticed the determined red hat.

"I think somebody's trying to get your attention." Jake pointed politely.

Izzy swiveled her head to her right and saw nothing.

"Look down," Jake said.

She did. "Oh! Hello," she said, startled. "I'm sorry, I didn't see you there."

A portion of a blue-sleeved arm and a tiny gnome hand clutching a small envelope were thrust up toward her on an angle.

"Do be careful or you'll fall," she said in alarm.

As she quickly snatched the envelope out of the gnome's grasp, Jake could only surmise that one of the grumpy wee fellows had climbed up on one of his comrades' shoulders in order to reach the table.

"Thank you very much," Izzy added, then opened the note and

read it.

Dani nudged Jake and arched a brow, clearly wondering if the note had come from Janos.

But in the next moment, Izzy glanced around the table. "Everyone! Aunt Ramona says we have to finish eating. We are to join the adults in ten minutes in Parlor 16."

"Why?" Maddox asked, wiping his mouth with his napkin. Jake had noticed the hungry Guardian was on his third helping of hearty lamb stew.

Izzy shrugged. "Aunt Ramona didn't say, but they want us *all* there posthaste."

"I wonder what's going on," Archie said.

Jake slid a dubious glance toward his boy cousin. "Sounds like another family meeting."

"Lord," Dani murmured. "What have they got in store for us now?"

Jake finished his drink and wiped his mouth with a nod, then rose from the table. "Let's go find out."

CHAPTER 46

A New Mission

From the moment Jake and his friends strolled into Parlor 16 down the hallway from the dining room, it was immediately clear that the six adults already present in the gilded drawing room had exchanged harsh words before they arrived.

The elegant sitting room bristled with tension. All the kids sensed it the moment they stepped over the threshold; their jovial mood evaporated as they hurried in and quietly sat down on the gold velvet settees and rose-striped armchairs arranged around the elegant salon.

Only Red's presence calmed the strained atmosphere a bit. The Gryphon had been sitting in the corner, serenely watching what must've been quite a row. When Jake came in, the noble beast left his spot and prowled over to sit next to his chair.

Jake rested his hand atop the Gryphon's head and began scratching his feathers automatically. But he watched the adults with a twist of anxiety in his solar plexus. Adults thought they hid things from kids, but they generally couldn't, and their fighting amongst themselves was never a good sign.

Dani sent Jake a worried look as she got comfortable on the settee next to Isabelle. Jake glanced around at the others. A frown skimmed Maddox's face as he sat down on the other side of the room. Nixie and Archie shared a double seat with a curved back.

Uncle Richard closed the parlor door with a glint of anger in his blue eyes, and the family meeting came to order.

The source of the trouble soon became clear.

Archie and Isabelle's parents were livid over the attack on Griffon Castle.

"This is thoroughly unacceptable!" Aunt Claire exclaimed. "How many more times must I find out only afterward that someone has tried yet again to murder my children?"

Derek mumbled an apology and Miss Helena tried to explain, but the glamorous aristocrat shushed them both.

"No." The viscountess shot the twins and Derek—and even Aunt Ramona—a glare. "You've done your best, I'm sure," she clipped out. "But I see now that Lord Bradford and I have no choice but to keep the children with us if we wish them to survive to adulthood."

"Mother!" Archie said.

"Archimedes, silence," she ordered, turning sharply to her son, her honey-blond side-curls swinging against her cheeks. The rest of her thick hair was gathered and pinned back in elaborate masses of gold curls.

Viscountess Bradford was considered beautiful by many, with her ivory skin, brown eyes fringed with luxurious, dark lashes, and a small, round, rather charming beauty mark above one corner of her mouth.

She waved her fan in agitation as she paced, her peach satin bustle gown trailing out behind her. Lace dripped from the sleeves halfway up her forearms; always supremely fashionable, she also wore a ribbon choker necklace the same shade as her gown.

"We are your parents," she said, "and ultimately, we are the ones responsible for your safety."

"Your mother's right," Uncle Richard chimed in. "The decision's made. We will look after you ourselves. All of you," he added, glancing sternly at Jake.

Jake lowered his gaze. He was not about to argue with his uncle, but he and Dani exchanged a discreet look. Where had these two been this whole time, if they were so concerned?

"Mum, Dad, it's all right, really," Archie said. "You needn't worry. We always manage to come through it right as rain when we work together. There's no need to go flying up into the boughs!"

"Honest!" Isabelle agreed with a wide-eyed nod. "We are quite unscathed, I promise."

"And we mean to *keep* you that way, darling," Uncle Richard said indulgently to his daughter. Looking every inch the aristocrat, the viscount leaned on the table at the front of the room, heels crossed, arms folded across his chest, signet ring gleaming on his pinky finger.

A trim, elegant man in his mid-forties, he was clean-shaven, with firm, classic features. Though he had removed his jacket after dinner, taking his leisure in loose linen shirtsleeves, his light silk waistcoat and pinstriped charcoal trousers were expertly tailored.

With his thatch of wavy sable hair and thoughtful blue eyes, Lord Bradford bore a striking family resemblance to Jake's mother, Elizabeth, as shown in the family portrait in the great hall back at Griffon Castle.

No wonder. They were brother and sister, after all.

"This nonsense has gone on long enough," he declared. "What happened with Waldrick was not your fault, of course. And I suppose there was no harm done with your visit to the giants, in hindsight. But you poor children should never have been subjected to the likes of Garnock the Sorcerer—to say nothing of Davy Jones." The diplomat shuddered. "Now Wyvern's come after you? Who's next? Shemrazul?"

"Father!" Archie muttered.

"No, son. It's too much to place on the shoulders of people your age."

They meant well, Jake supposed. And better late than never. Yet he had a nagging feeling that he and his pals would still end up having to save themselves in the end—and probably his aunt and uncle, too.

Adults. Jake somehow managed not to shake his head.

"Obviously, Richard and I are very disappointed..."

As Aunt Claire resumed her polite rant, Jake and the rest of the kids stared down at the flowery whorls of the carpet or the white marble fireplace, at the gold velvet curtains or the painted glass shades on the tall brass globe lamps flickering on the end tables.

Anywhere but at the four dear adults who usually had charge of them.

A skilled diplomat, Aunt Claire knew exactly how to take them apart without even raising her voice.

Henry was red-faced, with a hangdog look. Miss Helena was ashen, as though she had received a threat of being sacked.

Derek's scowl was guilt-stricken; he also looked a little shocked that he was being yelled at.

Not even Aunt Ramona escaped a tongue-lashing from her angry kinswoman. Jake had long since noticed that the Elder witch always pursed her lips when she was displeased. It made her high cheekbones jut out like knife hilts, and, right now, her thin lips were as puckered as tightly as if she'd been sucking on lemons.

Blimey, thank goodness Red was there.

The stoic presence of the Gryphon, quietly seated next to Jake's armchair, at least brought *some* calming effect to the rigid tension in the room. He continued petting the animal, anxiously playing with Red's feathers. At the end of the day, though, he was just glad that *he* wasn't the one in trouble for once.

Adding to the awkwardness were the occasional outbursts of muffled cheers and laughter coming through the ceiling.

It was parlor game night at Merlin Hall, Jake remembered, and, as usual, the after-dinner fun took place in the salons and music rooms of the second floor, directly above them in the palace.

Normally, Jake somewhat scoffed at it all, being thirteen, but at the moment, he'd have much rather been up there amid the ruckus. It was *kind* of fun, after all. Something to do, watching people make fools of themselves.

The ghosts and clairvoyants loved guessing games like Squeak Piggy Squeak. The shapeshifters (naturally) ruled at charades. The witches and wizards favored chess, while the Guardians played darts or held arm-wrestling matches.

The dwarfs adored a good, rousing sing-along. But the wood elves withdrew to the music room to play flutes and harpsichords and perform their elegant dances; their symmetrical figures shifted and turned like the patterns in a kaleidoscope.

Unfortunately, Parlor 16 seemed to lie right beneath the room where the centaurs were playing their favorite: table tennis. Their hooves stomped back and forth noisily as they wielded their paddles.

After another burst of cheers and a muffled whinny of victory, Aunt Ramona could tolerate no more of Aunt Claire's dressing-down.

"Very well, then." She folded her arms with an air of sour impatience. "Richard, Claire: exactly what do *you* propose?"

Aunt Claire glanced at her husband. "Well, Richard and I have been talking, and since we all know Jake cannot stay at Merlin Hall for reasons we need not discuss—"

Jake knew she meant because of the mole in their midst. Actually, he was surprised they hadn't managed to catch the traitor yet, in the full three weeks he'd been away. The person must be a very devious individual.

"And," she continued, "since we can't send him home anymore, now that Griffon Castle has been compromised, we feel it would be best to take our nephew with us—all the children, actually—on the diplomatic mission the Elders just assigned us."

Dani and Jake looked at each other, wide-eyed.

"We'll keep them on the move," Aunt Claire continued. "That way, the Dark Druids will have a harder time pinpointing Jake's location."

"You'll make yourselves a target," Derek said uneasily.

"A moving target is harder to hit." Uncle Richard cocked the Guardian a glance. "We'll double our security, as well. That should more than suffice. And don't worry about the expense to the Order. As I've already told the Elders, Master Crafanc has graciously agreed to let us fund the mission from the gold vault at the Everton mine."

Red snuffled and nodded in full approval.

"Whatever it takes," Lord Bradford declared, "I will not allow those warlock scoundrels to disrupt these poor youngsters' lives any more than they already have. Children should not have to live out their days under this dark cloud of dread. They deserve to live as normal a life as possible under the circumstances, and that shall be our goal."

He glanced around at the kids reassuringly. "You may continue your studies on the road. I'm sure there'll be time. The trip itself will be an educational experience, one I daresay you will enjoy. Rest assured, children, we will endeavor to help you put this unpleasantness out of your minds and just enjoy...being a youngster."

Right, Jake thought, doing his best to hide his skeptical expression.

How strange it was to grow up for so many years with no father whatsoever, and now, suddenly, he had more of them than he could handle. Not just Derek and Henry, who had become father figures to him in different ways over the past year and a half. Now Uncle Richard wanted to take charge of him, too.

To say nothing of Wyvern's bizarre invitation to become his son and Black Prince.

That had been so unsettling (and oddly embarrassing) that Jake hadn't even told anyone about it yet.

Meanwhile, for the first time, he finally had a shred of actual evidence that his own, true father really *could* still be alive.

As much as he hated to get his hopes up prematurely, Jake could hardly wait to meet him.

Aunt Claire was nodding. "Lord Bradford is right. You needn't worry anymore. Leave everything to us. We will keep you safe. The

Order will see to the spy in the palace while we're away, I'm sure. After all, they've had three weeks." She regarded Aunt Ramona from the corner of her eye, then gave a sniff of restrained indignation. "They can't need much more time in sorting it out, I should hope.

"In the meanwhile," she continued, "we want you with us, where we can see you. I will not have my children living in a state of terror, left open to attack by the foulest of creatures!"

"We're not terrified, Mother!" Isabelle finally burst out, glancing at each parent in exasperation. "We *did* chase them off, you know."

"Yes, dear, and we're very proud of you—"

"But you should not have been put in that position," Uncle Richard finished.

"Your success today does not change the fact that we are your parents, and you are our responsibility. It's our job to protect you, and we shall," Aunt Claire said, brooking no argument. Then she looked at Jake. "Now, I realize, dear nephew, that you, in particular, have good cause not to trust the adults in your life. But if ever there was a time for us to show you that we can and will take care of you, that time has come. The same goes for the rest of you."

As Aunt Claire glanced around with an air of compassion, Nixie sent Jake a skeptical look. She, too, had fended for herself during much of her life.

Well, if the adults wanted their trust, they were going to have to earn it, Jake supposed. But it was nice that at least they wanted to try.

"You see, children," Uncle Richard said somberly, glancing around at the kids, "I am sorry to say that we have to assume not just Jake, but the lot of you have come to the Dark Druids' attention *because* of your friendship with him."

Maddox sent Jake a droll look that seemed to say, *But I don't even like him that much.*

Jake hid his answering smirk, for, in truth, the two boys enjoyed not getting along.

"For that reason," Lord Bradford continued, "you *all* will be traveling with us when we go abroad."

"But sir?" Dani said meekly, lifting a finger. "I have my Lightrider classes."

"This will qualify as hands-on training, Miss O'Dell," he replied. "I've already discussed it with Master Finnderool. He has agreed to count it as an extended field trip. What better opportunity than to see real missions in motion? You'll be quite safe. Besides our additional security, we'll have two Lightriders with us to handle so large a traveling party.

"Agent Ranjit Singh will serve as our primary Lightrider, as usual. But Agent Munroe will also be coming along, now that he is on the mend. I'm sure 'Tex' will be happy to answer your questions as we undertake our journey."

"And the security team?" Derek asked, clearly feeling skeptical about this plan.

"Our usual Guardians are very good," Lord Bradford replied. "But we've been authorized to bring ten battle-tried soldiers with us. That will give us plenty of protection even if we split up. The children may wish to do some sightseeing, but my wife and I have very important diplomatic meetings to attend."

"What sort of meetings, Dad?" Archie asked.

Uncle Richard sighed. "Since it's now sadly clear that war is, indeed, looming on the horizon, we will be traveling to the courts of various key allies to explain they must prepare their defenses and to find out what they might need to be ready."

Jake had sat up straight in his chair; his pulse quickened. He thought it sounded incredibly exciting. But he had a question and lifted his hand.

His uncle nodded to him. "Yes?"

"Sir, aren't many of those rulers already here at Merlin Hall?"

Lord Bradford shook his head. "No, most of the top leaders returned while you were away, Jake. They couldn't neglect their own lands for too many days. And, besides, after the alarming information that Guardian Vambrace, Agent Munroe and Aleeyah brought back from their ordeals and presented to the Fey Parliament, most felt an urgency to return to their own people. We just want to check in on them and see if they have everything they need to secure their lands."

Jake nodded.

"Um, excuse me, sir?" Nixie said. "That is, are we *all* going? Even, um, me?"

Archie's whole demeanor lit up. "Oh yes, Mother, Father—Nixie must come along! She's a crucial member of our team."

His parents seemed amused at his insistence, apparently well aware of their son's partiality to the equally eccentric young witch.

"Of course you will join us, Miss Valentine," Aunt Claire said, then swept a motherly glance over them. “But, mind you, children, this won’t be all fun and games. Consider it part of your education as future members of the Order.”

“Just like your Grand Tour with Aunt Ramona,” Uncle Richard agreed. “Only, this time, you’ll be with us. So...we expect no calamities.”

Aunt Ramona inhaled sharply through her nose, her nostrils flaring. Jake half expected her to go storming out of the room, but the Elder witch stayed.

He frowned to see his beloved old curmudgeon looking upset. Why were his aunt and uncle blaming her for Wyvern’s attack? She’d had nothing to do with it. She wasn’t even there.

Besides, *he* was the one who had nearly been kidnapped, and if he didn’t blame her, then why should they?

On the contrary, Jake was worried about the ol’ girl. Though only three weeks had passed, she looked very tired and worn out. She seemed much older than when he had left.

He had to say something in her defense. “The important thing, sir, is that Wyvern didn’t get what he came for. We found the vault and now Uncle Waldrick will never get his firepower back.”

“Yes. I suppose there is that to be grateful for,” Uncle Richard said. “There’s no question you children did well today. Especially you, nephew.”

“Thank you, sir, but the real credit goes to Isabelle.”

The viscount smiled at his daughter, and Izzy smiled back. “I’m very proud of every one of you. But here, now, right at the outset, let us lay down a few ground rules for our journey to keep everybody safe. My standards are simple. Each and every one of you will obey any orders you are given at all times. Our safety may depend on it. Understood?”

Jake’s eyebrows rose; the kids nodded warily.

“Good. We leave tomorrow morning after breakfast, so you must pack tonight. Our first stop,” he added, “will be the land of the giants.”

“Jugenheim!” Archie yelled.

The meeting turned into chaos as the boys whooped with glee.

Jake turned to Dani. “Oh, you’ve got to see this place!”

The girls hadn’t come along on their previous visit. Maddox hadn’t been with them either; even he smiled at the prospect of seeing the land of the Norse giants.

It was one thing to watch their oversized friends feasting on the lawn at Merlin Hall for a few days, but it was something else entirely to visit *their* land, where everything was huge and you were tiny.

"This is going to be fun!" Jake declared, looking around at his friends with a jovial smile.

Archie waggled his eyebrows and nodded.

"Now, now, there will be no adventures, you two! Do you understand me?" Aunt Claire said, pointing at Jake and Archie. "This is a very serious situation, and I expect you all to do as you're told."

Right, Jake thought, stealing another roguish peek at his cousin.

"Yes, ma'am," Archie said, barely concealing his grin of anticipation.

"Humph." Aunt Ramona sent Richard and Claire a sardonic smile, seemingly wishing the pair of diplomats good luck keeping the lot of them in line.

"Now then," Uncle Richard said, planting his hands on his hips. "While we finish assembling our team for the journey"—he nodded at the other adults, and then glanced back at the kids—"I want you to go up to your rooms and start packing for a week's travel. Tomorrow's a big day, so get a good night's sleep. I recommend you go to bed early. And, Isabelle, do not over-pack, please."

"Who, me, Papa?"

"You needn't bring everything you own," he said with affection. "We'll be traveling light so we can easily stay on the move. That is all. You youngsters may go."

The kids rose and headed for the door while the adults congregated at the front of the room to discuss logistics.

Jake and Archie exchanged another grin.

"Do you think we'll get to see Odin and Thor while we're there?" Archie asked as they headed for the exit, but before Jake could answer, the door of the parlor flew open ahead of them and Janos burst in.

"I just heard the news," he said, looking rather wild and unkempt. "I'm coming with you."

Derek furrowed his brow. "I'm not sure that will be nec—"

"You need me," Janos said. "I'm not asking, Stone. I'm telling you." He glanced at the adults. "Either take me willingly or I will follow of my own accord and kill anything that comes near you."

"Janos," Aunt Ramona chided with a frown.

"What else have I got to do?" he shot back, then nodded at Jake.

"I just heard Wyvern attacked Griffon Castle. Unacceptable! You need me. I'm coming, and that's that."

"Now, look here, monsieur—" Aunt Claire started.

"Madam, with all due respect, Wyvern murdered my children. I'm not going to let him kill yours." Janos sent Derek a piercing stare. "Come on, Stone. Whatever my faults, I'm still the best you have. I'll take the night watch." He swallowed hard, hesitating. "Please."

Jake gave Derek a hopeful look. He could well imagine that Janos desperately needed some sort of task to take his mind off his loss.

"He *is* practically immortal," Archie pointed out.

"Aye, and he saved my life in Italy," Jake reminded them.

Isabelle said not a word. Veiling her gaze behind her lashes, she stared down at the floor.

Janos looked at Uncle Richard. "Well, Bradford?"

Apparently, he was in charge of this mission. And like everyone else at Merlin Hall, he had heard of the vampire's exploits, both good and bad.

"Caw!" Red said, as though reminding Lord Bradford it was Janos who had freed him.

"Hmm." The diplomat flicked a dubious glance over the vampire. "Guardian Stone is still Jake's head of security. If he approves you, then, I suppose, so do I."

Janos turned back to his old team leader. Derek gave him a long, searching stare. "Come on, man. Give me another chance."

"He did save Guardian Vambrace," Isabelle spoke up, much to Jake's surprise.

Dani nodded. "And Dr. Celestus."

Janos gave the carrot-head a grateful glance.

"Fine," Derek grumbled. "Night watch it is."

"Good." Janos gave him a terse nod and marched right back out again, presumably to make his preparations for the journey.

Relieved, Jake nodded his thanks to Derek. But in truth, the Order would be foolish not to accept the help of such a vicious fighter. Even Jake felt safer knowing Janos would be there.

Isabelle still kept her gaze downward as they filed out the door, but Aunt Ramona held up a finger. "Miss O'Dell, I'd like a word with you, please."

"Oh!" Dani turned around. "Yes, ma'am?"

While Dani stayed back to see what Aunt Ramona wanted, Jake

slipped out of the room and ran after the vampire to ask how he was doing. He spotted the ex-Guardian striding down the stone corridor ahead.

"Janos! Wait up!"

The vampire stopped and pivoted slowly as Jake jogged up to him. "Yes?"

"Hey. Thanks for volunteering," Jake said. "I'm bloody glad you'll be coming with us."

Janos just looked at him, remote and withdrawn. There was no trace of his usual cocky humor, not even a smile.

"You all right?" Janos asked tersely. "After Wyvern's attack, I mean."

Jake shrugged. "We survived."

Janos stared intensely at him. "How'd you do it? How'd you beat him?"

"I didn't. Isabelle did."

"What?"

Jake nodded. Now he had the fighter's full attention.

Janos snorted and rested a hand on his hip. "And how exactly did she do that?"

"She summoned the unicorns. The stampede scared Wyvern away."

"Is that right?" Janos first looked startled, then begrudgingly impressed. "Well, good for her."

Jake hesitated. "You kind of hurt her feelings, you know. I heard you were really mean."

"I'm a vampire. I'm supposed to be mean!"

"Not to her," Jake said.

Janos scowled but slowly lowered his head and let out a weary sigh, scratching his cheek.

"Why are you blaming her for what Wyvern did to your family? You know that doesn't make any sense."

"I don't *blame* her!" Janos said hotly. "Did she say that?"

"Yes, she did. She was distraught the whole time we were gone. Because of you."

He spluttered. "Because of—? Don't be ridiculous! Me? Whatever for?"

"She cares about you, man! She did exactly what you asked and then you yelled at her."

"I was a little upset!"

"Yes, I know." Jake lifted his hands. "You had cause. All I'm saying is that you hurt her feelings, mate. And I'm sure you should know that, considering you can read the girl's mind."

Janos looked away and ran his hand restlessly through his hair. "Isabelle and her bloody feelings."

"Look," Jake said. "I, for one, know you didn't mean it. Believe me, I know how it is when you accidentally lash out at one person, when you're really mad at someone else entirely. I do the same blasted thing myself every other day. I try not to, but... Anyway, my cousin, she's very tender-hearted."

Janos frowned. "Is this lecture almost over?"

"I'm not trying to meddle. I just wanted you to know that she's upset. She's very fond of you." Jake stopped himself from saying anything beyond that. "She's a peacemaker. She just wants everyone to get along. You know Izzy. Gentle soul."

Janos harrumphed and studied the floor.

"So, er, not to get in the middle of anything here, I just think...perhaps you owe her an apology."

"Fine." Janos licked his lips as though striving for patience, then cocked a sideways glance down the hallway behind them. "Alas, as you can see, the young lady is busy at the moment. Talking to Stick," he said dryly.

Jake followed his gaze and saw that it was true: Izzy and Maddox were having a conversation halfway down the corridor.

He tried not to smile at the vampire's rude-but-perfect nickname for the overly serious Guardian lad. "Then I guess you're off the hook for the moment."

Janos frowned again before striding off. "Bring that darkling blade I gave you," he said over his shoulder. "You never know."

"Will do!" Jake said. Then he saw his pretty cousin glance wistfully after the vampire as Janos marched out the side door and disappeared into the darkness outside.

He hoped those two made up soon. He didn't like seeing Isabelle in pain, nor Janos still hurting over his loss.

But, more importantly, given the external threats they faced, this disunity within the group was dangerous.

* * *

Maddox stood across from Isabelle, feeling slightly awkward, his thumbs hooked in his pockets as he struggled for words.

Across from him, her arms folded, she had been waiting for him to speak his piece, staring matter-of-factly at him—until the moment Janos walked away.

Then her golden head swiveled so fast that her long curls bounced over her shoulders.

For his part, Maddox had been thinking how glorious she looked with the light from the chandelier sparkling along her delicate profile and shining on her hair. Like an angel standing there, glowing just a little.

"So, maybe, um, tomorrow while we're traveling, we could spend some time together. Catch up," he had been saying. Rather bravely, he thought.

But he lost her attention entirely the moment that insufferable vampire quit the conversation with Jake.

Isabelle looked over with a nosy glance at Janos, like she needed to know what the bloodsucker was doing at every moment.

It infuriated Maddox. His jaw clenched.

What bothered him the most was that she used to look at *him* like that. But not lately.

Not anymore.

His idiotic words trailed off when Izzy glanced back at him, looking bored.

"What?" she prompted, seeing his expression.

Like he'd just been punched in the gut.

Maddox didn't bother answering, just stared impassively at her.

"Oh, you've got to be joking!" she said, reading his face. "Unbelievable. You're jealous?"

Maddox was taken aback by her rude retort. So now she was making fun of him?

"So what if I am, a little?" he said, bristling.

"Well, that would be absurd," she replied.

"Oh really? And why is that absurd?" His pulse had started pounding; he could feel the blood creeping into his cheeks.

This girl really thought she was better than him, didn't she? Just because of her high birth.

Apparently, she didn't know that Maddox was actually the illegitimate son of a bachelor prince whom Ravyn had once been sent to guard.

But, of course, Isabelle's ignorance of his true origins was Maddox's own fault. He was too proud to tell her he was actually a royal bastard.

Nevertheless, his genuine royal blood was part of the reason that he so despised Janos, who'd been very much a commoner up until the night he abandoned the Order and received a bloody kingdom in exchange.

His title, his castle, his lands had been simply handed to him by his filthy vampire brides and their ruler, the foul Red Queen. Janos was one of them. A creature of darkness. He had chosen his path.

And now Isabelle couldn't stop ogling the blackguard. Maddox wondered what that might actually say about *her*.

"Why shouldn't I be jealous with the way you're always pining after him?" Maddox growled.

"Oh, let's see!" she shot back, her tone saucy, her blue eyes ablaze. Drumming her fingers on her arm, she lifted her gaze to the ceiling. "I've been gone for three weeks and I did not receive so much as a single word from you, Maddox. *Jake* even wrote to Dani, but you couldn't spare a single line for me? That told me all I need to know. You don't really care about me. Out of sight, out of mind."

"You wanted me to *write* to you?" he asked.

Her jaw dropped. "Oh—why do I even try? You're right. It was a foolish expectation, considering you've been ignoring me for the past four months."

"No, I haven't."

"Yes, you have."

"My mother was missing!"

"Yes, I know that," she said. "And that is the only reason I didn't give up on you sooner. But I've had it, Maddox! I'm glad your mother's safe—thanks to Janos—but, in the meantime, you completely forgot I existed. You withdrew into your shell and shut me out."

"I didn't want to burden you with my problems!"

"That's exactly what I'm saying—you could've confided in me! That's what people *do* when they care about each other. Instead, you shut me out, withdrew into yourself, and practically abandoned me. Now your mother's back and you think we can simply pick up right where we left off?"

"But—"

“Maddox, a girl is not a toy you can take down off the shelf and play with when it pleases you and then toss aside again whenever it suits your fancy. I’m a person, with feelings, and I will not be treated with such disrespect.

“Besides, what’s the point, anyway? The same Guardian rules that held you back before are still in place. Nothing’s changed.” She waved a hand dismissively. “I just— I see no reason to go through that again. We’ve already *done* that dance, so why waste our time? I’m sorry, Maddox,” she said with crushing finality, “but I’ve moved on.”

Maddox stood there and didn’t know what to say.

A couple of centaurs clip-clopped past the end of the hallway, turning the corner. He hoped they hadn’t heard her scolding him this way.

Rejecting him.

He gritted his teeth.

Didn’t she know lots of other girls liked him quite well, thank you very much? Even Princess Sapphira made it clear she fancied him. But here was haughty Miss Bradford brushing him off like he was some sort of bumbling pest.

A weakling. A nobody.

“All I ask,” she said, “is that if we both have to go on this trip, let’s keep it courteous to spare the others from unnecessary drama.”

“Of course,” he said, seething.

“Good. If you’ll excuse me, I have to pack.”

She started to walk away, but Maddox reached out and grabbed her wrist. “Isabelle, wait.”

She looked down at his possessive hold. “Unhand me at once. What do you want?”

He released her wrist but glared at her. “Why don’t you be honest?”

“I beg your pardon?”

“The only reason you’re saying this is because of that stupid vampire!”

She huffed, but her cheeks turned strawberry red. “No, I’m not!”

“Yes, you are. It’s obvious! Don’t be a fool, Isabelle. You know what he is.”

“How dare you?” she uttered, and for a moment, Maddox thought he was going to get slapped. Clearly appalled, she looked him over from head to foot in utter disgust. “Need I remind you, that ‘stupid vampire’ was the one who risked his life to bring your mother back safe. And it cost him his entire family! You, of all people, have no right to say a single word about him. How monstrously ungrateful."

She shook her head with a withering stare. "You, more than anyone, owe Janos your loyalty, Maddox. I suggest you remember that before he loses patience with you. Because Lord knows I already have."

With that, she pivoted on her heel, her blue skirts swirling around her. Head high, curls bouncing down her back, the Keeper of the Unicorns marched back angrily toward the parlor they had left.

Watching her, Maddox realized two important things.

First: his hot-tempered insults of Janos had, admittedly, been wrong. She was right: his words had been dishonorable. He might despise that creature, but the vampire *had* saved Ravyn's life.

Second, it sank in with great finality that the beautiful Isabelle Bradford was well and truly done with him. He had officially lost his chance, if he'd ever really had one. And there was not a thing he could do about it now.

She was gone.

Her rejection pumped through his veins like a poison spreading through him.

How was this fair?

He had done the right thing, same as always. Had chosen to put the Order's rules ahead of his own wishes. Why, it was the very opposite choice that her precious Janos had once made years ago.

Good God, how did that blasted vampire always get away with everything, when Maddox *never* did? He clamped his jaw shut and clenched his fists at his sides, his temper roiling within him.

Well, he wasn't stupid. He could see exactly what was going on here. The smooth-talking scoundrel had gotten into her head somehow with his unholy charm. Janos had even fooled Derek into giving him another chance.

Why am I the only one who can see he can't be trusted? Now the bloodsucker had cast some sort of glamour over Izzy.

But Maddox made a decision in that moment. After all, he was a Guardian, sworn to protect the innocent and the good. *Fine. Cast me aside. But I'm not going to let him hurt you, Isabelle.*

Even if I have to stake the blackguard myself.

CHAPTER 47
The Snitch

"You wanted to see me, Lady Bradford?" Dani asked nervously back in Parlor 16.

Everyone else had gone, the other kids to pack, the other adults to make their preparations for the trip.

Only the Elder witch remained.

Seated at the elegant writing table at the front of the room, she gave a weary nod. "Don't be alarmed, Miss O'Dell. You are not in any trouble."

Dani was relieved to hear it. She'd been scared to death when the intimidating woman had asked her to stay. She could not recall Her Ladyship ever wanting to speak to her privately before.

Interlocking her bony fingers, the wise old dowager baroness regarded Dani. "How are you finding the Lightrider program so far, Miss O'Dell?"

"Oh, I love it, ma'am," Dani said heartily. "There's so much to learn. It's fun, and Master Finnderool says I'm one of the best in my class."

Her Ladyship's wrinkled face softened with a smile. "I am not at all surprised to hear it. I had a feeling you would be." She glanced down at the Bud of Life on Dani's wrist. "I see you have received your training gauntlet."

She nodded, touching the buckles. "Yes, ma'am. I'm being very careful not to get it wet."

"Good girl," Lady Bradford said, then she came to the point. "Miss O'Dell, I wish to ask a favor of you."

"Me?" Startled, Dani waited attentively. "Of course, my lady. Anything." She owed the old woman so much.

Lady Bradford seemed relieved at her answer and nodded. "I won't be joining the diplomatic mission, as I am needed here. However, I should like for you to keep an eye on my nephew for me during this journey."

"Jake?" Dani smiled. "Oh, I always look out for him, ma'am, and he looks out for me."

"Yes, I know, but, um...that's not exactly what I mean, dear." She paused, pursing her lips slightly. "Jake trusts you more than anyone, Daniela. We all know that. And, so, for his sake, I am charging you with a very serious responsibility."

Dani tilted her head. "Yes, ma'am?"

"I want you to keep me apprised of what he does. Anything unusual you might hear him say. What he's thinking. How he's doing, in general. Particularly if you notice any changes in his behavior. For example...mood swings of, er, a negative sort."

Dani stared at her with a chill of realization tingling down her back. *Oh no.* Her shoulders hunched a little. "Y-you want me to *spy* on Jake for you?"

Her heart began to pound as she recalled their conversation at supper.

Why, barely an hour ago, Jake had warned her not to tattletale on Isabelle's secret bond with Janos. In the rookery, he'd reminded her, snitches were punished ruthlessly.

Rat out a friend? That was the one thing a good rookery lass would never do.

Yet the person asking her to do it was the one soul on earth Dani owed practically everything.

Forget the Lightrider program—Lady Bradford could've sent her back to the rookery at any time. Instead, she had shown Dani the great kindness of letting her stay on as Isabelle's companion. Where she had enough food, a safe place to sleep every night, her friends nearby. Even nice clothes. And books! Education...

Mother Mary, what a horrible dilemma.

Lady Bradford waited for an answer, but Dani felt slightly queasy. Spy on her best friend? She couldn't say yes. But how could she possibly say no?

The Elder witch watched her face as though she could read her mind. For all Dani knew, maybe she could. But, of course, Dani had never been very good at hiding her emotions. She'd always been an open book.

"My dear young lady," the woman said sternly, "you know the stakes. As much as we both adore him, the boy has been prophesied to become a future leader of the Dark Druids. That is why I'm turning to you. If anyone is going to notice wicked tendencies starting to emerge in Jake, it would be you. If you truly care about him, you must tell me if you see anything worrisome taking shape with him so the problem can be dealt with at the earliest stages."

"Dealt with?" Dani echoed, as wary as if ol' Constable Flanagan back in London had asked her to rat out one of her big brothers' misadventures.

"I only mean so we can help him. If signs of evil start arising in my nephew, it is vital that we nip it in the bud, as they say. We daren't risk letting it go untreated. Believe me, I don't like asking this of you, but I really have no choice."

"But don't you think Isabelle would be better at this than me? She is an empath, after all," Dani said meekly.

"Not even Isabelle knows Jake like you do. You're the one he can't survive without."

Dani stared at her, awed that Her Ladyship should think so. "I would never let Jake turn evil. He never would."

"So you agree?"

Dani floundered.

The old woman arched a brow. "My dear, you have been given the extraordinary honor of training to become a Lightrider. I should think your first loyalties now belong to the Order, do they not?" *And I'm the one who got you into the program,* her sharp gaze clearly reminded her.

Despite that fact, Dani dreaded what she was being asked to do. It went against everything she believed in.

It went against *Jake*. Her own best quality in her view was loyalty, and she was being pressured into compromising that. Besides, what if he found out?

She could lose her best friend.

"My dear, I am not asking you to do anything except what is in Jake's best interest and the world's. I can't let my own nephew become another Zolond."

Dani gulped.

"If Jake starts to go bad, I need to know at once."

"But, ma'am, he's always a little bit naughty. I mean, it's a part of what makes him so courageous. How am I supposed to tell if it's just him being his regular rascal self as opposed to...something worse? And if it *does* get worse, well, what will you do to him?"

"Let's not get ahead of ourselves, dear. I am only asking you to monitor him for me during the trip." Lady Bradford tilted her head. "Think of it as if Jake had been exposed to some terrible disease and we weren't sure yet whether or not he had actually *caught* it. You'd be like a nurse, watching for signs of the illness, so the doctors can help him at the first appearance of any symptoms."

"But how exactly do you cure someone from turning evil?" Dani asked, still dubious. Quarantine? Would they lock him away somewhere to prevent his destiny from coming true?

Might they even kill him?

Lady Bradford frowned. "Surely you trust me, Miss O'Dell?"

The pointed question pierced through the cloud of suspicion Dani was feeling, and actually showed her she was probably being silly. Paranoid. A typical rookery fool like her brothers, who refused to trust the police.

But she *wasn't* a rookery lass anymore.

She was a Lightrider-in-training. She was part of something bigger, something good.

And the Elder witch had made it all possible. Jake's Aunt Ramona, of all people, would never ask her to do something bad.

Besides, Dani could not deny that, as much as everyone hated snitches, *they* were the ones who got the fiercest brutes in the rookery locked away where they couldn't prey on poor people anymore.

"Very well." Dani nodded slowly with a gulp. "I'll do it."

"Of course you will," the Elder witch said with a hint of disapproval in her tone that a mere slip of a girl should even question the order. She studied Dani with a frown. "I realize this makes you uncomfortable, Miss O'Dell, but it is vitally important. It is in Jake's best interest, in any case."

"Yes, ma'am." Dani dropped her gaze, but her throat felt strained. "Still, Jake wouldn't like me spyin' on him. If he should ever find out, I'm not sure he will forgive me."

"Then you'll have to be discreet, won't you? Don't tell Archie, of course."

"Oh, certainly not." Everybody knew the boy genius couldn't keep a secret. Dani furrowed her brow. "What about Isabelle, ma'am? What if she senses I'm hiding something? What should I tell her?"

Lady Bradford shrugged. "Tell her you can't discuss it. She'll attribute it to secrets having to do with the Lightrider program. Let her think so; it's easiest that way."

Dani nodded with a sense of unreality. Deep down, she was shocked to hear an adult instructing her to lie—especially to her friends. "And, um, Nixie?"

"Nixie understands the need for secrecy in many things," the Elder witch said cryptically. "Did Master Finnderool show you how to use the communication device embedded in the gauntlet?"

"Yes, ma'am." Dani glanced down at the round black piece right at the bend of her wrist. You could press a button and talk into it.

It had been built into the Bud of Life as a safety mechanism in case any of the young Lightriders accidentally transported themselves to the middle of nowhere. Through the communication device, the stranded student could call back to Merlin Hall so the Order could then send someone to come and fetch them.

"Use it to let me know if you see changes in my nephew, or if you see signs that he's about to do anything...hmm, potentially catastrophic? The Davy Jones debacle comes to mind. Or the Garnock incident. Take your pick."

Wincing at the reminder of the many merry scrapes that Jake had led them on, Dani realized she had no choice but to cooperate, even though it still made her queasy. "Yes, ma'am."

Lady Bradford smiled, pleased that she had secured her spy within the diplomatic party. "That is all, Miss O'Dell. You may go."

Dani sketched a curtsy and turned to go, but, at that moment, the parlor door burst open again.

This time, Isabelle stormed in. "Aunt Ramona!"

Dani saw at once that the older girl was in a rare state of fury.

Izzy acknowledged her with a glance, but her eyes blazed as she marched past Dani to plant her hands on the edge of Lady Bradford's writing table.

"I can't deal with him!" she said.

"Good heavens, who? What on earth is the matter?"

"I don't want Maddox coming with us on this journey," Izzy said flatly. "Can you please make him stay here?"

Lady Bradford raised her pewter eyebrows. "What happened?"

"Nothing *happened*, he's just—rude! He has a chip on his shoulder and a terrible attitude, even now that his mother's back. I just know he's going to be ugly to Janos the whole time we are away. And he isn't nice to me!"

Lady Bradford chuckled at this extraordinary rant from the gentlest of girls. "Not everyone is going to be nice to you all the time, darling."

Isabelle scowled. "Why do we even need him? We have *real* Guardians coming along for our security. We don't need some grouchy boy with no manners getting in the way."

"Dear me," Lady Bradford murmured. "This is most unlike you, Isabelle."

"Maybe I'm just too nice to everyone," Izzy shot back, standing up tall and resting her hands on her hips. "Maybe it's time I stopped."

Even Dani was taken aback to hear this from the ever-virtuous unicorn Keeper. For her part, she lingered uncertainly near the door, unsure if she was supposed to leave the pair to discuss this in private or stay and attend the older girl. Perhaps Isabelle would want some moral support in standing up to her intimidating aunt like this.

"Well?" Izzy demanded.

"Darling, the decision has been made." Lady Bradford shook her head. "Maddox has to go with the group. His safety has been jeopardized too. Just like the rest of you."

"He's going to ruin everything! He's just a dark cloud!"

"Be that as it may," Lady Bradford said, sounding almost amused, "I, for one, am glad the young Guardian will be there."

"Why?" Izzy huffed. "We don't need him."

"Because he will help *you* make sure that the charming Prince Janos keeps his distance."

Dani's eyes widened. It sounded like crafty old Ramona knew exactly what was going on.

Izzy scoffed, sounding shocked and offended, but she wasn't very convincing. She looked away to try to hide her blush. "You needn't worry about Janos, Aunt Ramona. Hadn't you heard? He's not even speaking to me anymore.

"Come on, Dani," Isabelle grumbled, pivoting and stalking back toward the door. "Let's go pack for this wonderful adventure. I'm sure it's going to be *great* fun."

* * *

Some news shook even the Elder witch. And hearing that Wyvern had raided Griffon Castle while the children were there shocked her to the core. This was her fault and she knew it.

She should have seen it coming. But she had been deceived.

With the girls gone, Ramona rose wearily from the chair behind the writing desk in the parlor and walked down the corridor to the lobby, where she headed upstairs to her chamber.

Her body felt heavy and she grew more tired by the day. But the cause was not physical.

The spiritual warfare she had been engaged in for months now was taking a toll on her. All her struggles to pull Geoffrey back toward the light seemed to be having some effect on the Dark Master, but they came at a cost.

Even so, it wasn't as though she could claim perfect moral purity herself.

Just now, for example, she truly regretted pressuring poor Dani into assisting her, but she had no choice.

To be sure, she was also officially out of favor with Richard and Claire at the moment (especially Claire). So be it.

At least Ramona was satisfied that the strategy they had devised—staying on the move with this diplomatic mission—would help keep Jake and the other children a step ahead of the Dark Druids.

Lifting the hem of her skirts as she marched up the grand marble staircase, Ramona still wasn't sure how Fionnula Coralbroom had managed to penetrate the dome of protective magic she had created around the two family estates.

It was slightly unnerving to wonder if she was losing her touch.

Most unsettling of all was the news that Wyvern had tried to lure Jake away to the dark side this very day.

Thankfully, her nephew's reaction, as explained by Derek, had been reassuring to hear. He had resisted with his usual hardheadedness; he had fought back in spades.

Still, the way before him was fraught with peril. They couldn't be too careful. That was why Ramona had tasked Dani O'Dell with keeping an eye on him.

Whatever happened, they could not afford to let this prophecy come true.

It was bad enough that Ramona and her colleagues had still not managed to unmask the spy in their midst. So far, the mole continued to elude them.

In any case, now that the practicalities of their next move had been sorted, she returned to her room to confront Zolond about this latest disturbing development.

Closing the door to her chamber behind her, Ramona brushed off irksome worries that perhaps she shouldn't be doing this.

Maybe *she* was the problem.

Was there some way her old beau might be probing her mind when she went to speak with him?

She did not doubt he had tricks up his sleeve that she had never learned. Geoffrey had always been much more devoted to the craft than she'd had any desire to be.

Sitting down at her table, she knew, as always, to be careful around him.

Yet a suspicion was forming in her mind that it might not be Zolond behind all this trouble after all.

Indeed, Ramona was beginning to think it altogether possible that Wyvern might be doing this without Zolond's knowledge or permission.

That might be mere wishful thinking on her part, but she intended to bring this latest outrage to the Dark Master's attention.

Perhaps he truly didn't know what his henchman was getting up to in his absence.

It was time to find out.

Resting her fingers on the crystal ball, Ramona closed her eyes. After a few deep breaths, it was a simple matter to project herself into the astral realm.

In the next blink, she was once more walking down the white, curled pathway toward the drifting charcoal gazebo.

"Geoffrey," she said firmly, summoning him.

There was no answer for a few minutes. The chimes sang softly on the air. The stars twinkled, all shapes and sizes, purples, silvers, blues.

"Geoffrey!" she repeated, placing her hands on her hips and tapping her toe. "I know you can hear me."

"Well," the cheeky answer finally sounded, echoing into the astral space, "if it isn't my old friend."

The man himself did not appear.

She rolled her eyes impatiently. "A word with you, please."

"My, how polite! That's a change. You must be in a mood. One moment..."

Ramona folded her arms across her chest and paced back and forth impatiently across the runny watercolors of the gazebo. She strove to compose her thoughts, but could not help wondering how much Richard and Claire and, well, the entire Order would disapprove of her if they knew what she was doing right now.

Enough to take her for a traitor and burn her at the stake?

After all, the as-yet-undiscovered mole in the palace wasn't the only one secretly talking to the enemy.

Oh, pish, I know what I'm doing, she thought, annoyed at her own doubts.

"Of course you do," Zolond said almost cheerfully, appearing in a whoosh of gray smoke.

It struck her that the smoke didn't look quite as black as before. *Hmm.*

Then she noticed with amusement that the old man was looking unusually rumpled. His striped waistcoat was unbuttoned, his shirt sleeves rolled up. "What on earth have you been doing?"

"Oh, I was just playing fetch with my reptilians."

She lifted both eyebrows. "Fetch?"

"Yes, they really enjoy it. It's terribly amusing. They are incredibly fast. Did you know they run on all fours at top speed?"

"I did not," she replied, bemused.

"They are descended from Komodo dragons."

"Ah."

"Care to sit?" He conjured two armchairs and gestured to one.

"No."

"Well, I hope you don't mind if I do. Pardon my incivility, plopping myself down in the presence of a lady, but my back hurts. These old bones, you know."

"Oh, believe me, I do." She gestured to the chair as he lowered himself into it with a wince.

"Baal's beard, we're ancient these days, aren't we? What are we now, three hundred and forty?"

"You are," she retorted. "I'm only three-hundred thirty-three."

"Ha. Spring chicken."

They looked at each other and laughed, shaking their heads in mutual despair, or at least resignation, at the absurdity of their unnaturally long lives.

"Honestly, I could strangle you sometimes," she said.

"Yes, I'm sure." He sighed but did not need to state aloud his dread at what awaited him when death finally came. "It's been an interesting journey, at least."

She harrumphed. "It would've been nice to have a choice."

He waved a hand dismissively. "Well, I'm here. Was there something you wanted, dear lady?"

The moment of humor died away as Ramona stared at him.

"Geoffrey, you must rein in your filthy Nephilim henchman. You will not believe what Wyvern's done now."

"If this is about the mole, I told you, I don't involve myself in the day-to-day running of small matters—"

"It's not that. This is something much more serious."

He stopped and stared at her. "Very well. Go on."

"I thought you might want to know that, earlier today, Wyvern raided Griffon Castle and tried to kidnap Jake."

"What?" Zolond murmured, leaning forward in his seat. His idle manner vanished.

Ramona believed that his surprise at this news was genuine. He tried to play it cool, but his bushy gray eyebrows knitted together, and he sat up just a bit straighter.

"Did he, indeed?" he asked uneasily.

"He did. Zolond, this is quite beyond the pale! I know your side likes to claim that it was Jake who broke the truce by thwarting Garnock's return, but the boy was only twelve years old! He did not understand the consequences of his actions. Wyvern, however, is a grown man and knows full well that what he did today completely obliterates the truce."

Her old beau stared grimly at her. "I did not order this."

She nodded with relief. "I thought as much. Apparently, Wyvern did not know my nephew was at home. He went there to try to raid the Everton family vault, but when he saw the boy, he seized the opportunity to try to lure him away. Yes, he nearly resorted to kidnapping! But, thankfully, he failed."

Zolond was silent for a moment. "Was the child hurt?"

"No. They managed to fend him off." Ramona had no desire to give him further details as to how. "Zolond, something must be done about Wyvern or there will be repercussions. If he goes behind your back again and succeeds in abducting my great-great nephew, it'll put *your* great-great grandson in jeopardy as well. I know you don't want that."

He narrowed his eyes, which had begun to smolder. "I will look into the matter." He stood and sighed. "While the cat's away, the mouse will play."

"Bring him to heel," Ramona warned, "or our efforts to avert a war will be for naught."

His expression guarded, Zolond gave her a terse nod. "Thank you for this information. I will see to it. Farewell."

Ramona nodded back. She could feel his anger building, though he'd said little. *Good,* she thought. Wyvern was a powerful foe.

But if anyone could rein in Shemrazul's son, it was the Dark Master.

CHAPTER 48
Scolded

After exiting the astral plane, Zolond sat in grim silence for a moment at the table where his black crystal ball gleamed.

It was time to face up to certain facts. Facts he had long been trying to ignore and still didn't feel like dealing with. Taking a holiday was all very well, but escaping one's troubles was not so easy as merely seeking out some pleasurable new location.

Problems had a way of following a man. Especially regrets, and his multiplied by the day.

Ramona's news about Wyvern was disturbing, of course, but that was not what caused a knot of cold fear to form in the pit of Zolond's stomach as he sat there at the table, staring dully at his obsidian ball.

After all these years, accruing untold power, there was only one thing in the world the Dark Master truly feared, and it wasn't Wyvern. No, it was the freak's father, and to cross the one was to cross the other.

So be it.

As it was, Zolond knew he had cause to worry. Shemrazul had not contacted him in ages. The infernal god he had served for so long had gone silent. And that terrified him. At least, it did when he let himself ponder it.

Most of the time, he ignored that too. But it did not bode well. Perhaps he should do a sacrifice, try to curry favor...

But the thought of slitting the throat of a living thing—some frightened, squirming bird or bleating goat or even a human being—made him grimace with distaste.

Which only went to show the alarming extent of Ramona's growing influence on him.

And yet, even though his dalliance with the Elder witch would likely mean his destruction ere long, Zolond, or Geoffrey—or whoever he was these days—did not regret spending time with her ever since they had met in battle again a few months ago.

No. It was the rest of his three hundred years that he regretted.

In all likelihood, Shemrazul already knew about his unfaithfulness to the dark side. Recent evidence would suggest that was the case. Whenever Zolond donned the ceremonial robes of the Dark Master, for example, and offered up the required prayers and unholy offices to the Horned One, he no longer got a response.

Instead, he was left with eerie silence and the hollow feeling that no one was listening.

What else did he expect? He no longer truly believed. He was merely going through the motions, keeping up the charade, but the sinister heart of the Dark Master had changed.

His rituals were empty. He'd finally lived long enough to realize he had gone the wrong way.

But it was too late, and, sadly, he already knew he was a dead man. With a sigh, the old warlock slumped slightly in his chair. What a wretched situation. Shunned from the light, soon to be banished by the dark.

Where will that leave me, I wonder?

Roaming the realm of the dead, trapped in Limbo as some miserable ghost?

He doubted it would be that easy.

Most likely, he was in for an eternity of fiendish suffering, but it was too late to start backtracking now.

The dark side was not known for mercy. It laughed at such pleas. It reveled in making enemies suffer, and in his heart, Zolond feared he had already become an enemy to Shemrazul.

Ah, how he wished he could simply walk away from it all, take off the mantle of the Dark Master, and become an ordinary old man on a park bench somewhere, feeding the pigeons.

But he was not naïve enough to hope that Shemrazul would ever allow that. No, the dark side ate its own once they ceased to be useful.

He'd been a fool to try to ignore it this long, he supposed, for he knew full well that evil was always at its most dangerous when it went unseen, silently creeping through the shadows, like a spider, a snake.

That was usually when it was preparing to strike. Evil was far too clever to advertise its plans.

Thus, the longer the Horned One gave his longtime servant the cold shoulder, the more fearfully Zolond wondered what torment was being prepared for him.

But he had done this to himself, of course. He was no victim. Hardened souls like him did not pity others, and Zolond had no intention of pitying himself.

Resolved to keep up the charade as long as he could—he scarcely knew why—he beckoned to one of the reptilians stationed by the door. "Bring me the black candle and some matches."

Druk bowed and crossed to fetch them from his old wooden worktable on the opposite wall.

With that, Zolond set his sickening fears aside and focused his mind on the question at hand. Why had Wyvern gone after Jake?

He must've really taken Duradel's prophecy to heart.

No matter.

Zolond might be falling out of favor with the Lord of the Ninth Pit, but, for now, he was still the Dark Master, and when he gave an order, he expected to be obeyed.

"Shall I light it for you, sire?" Druk asked as he set the black pillar candle down on the table before him.

"Please." Zolond pushed aside his obsidian ball and gathered his thoughts about what to say to his wayward second-in-command.

In such situations, it was important to make a strong impression.

The obliging reptilian struck a match, then lit the candle. As the flame grew on the wick, Druk bowed and withdrew to his post beside the door to Zolond's cave.

Zolond closed his eyes for a moment, mentally brushed off a flickering image of Ramona tapping her foot with impatience and glaring at him. She still amused him to no end, that girl.

She was just as feisty as she'd been at nineteen.

Then he focused his thoughts on the situation at hand, his expression growing stern. He murmured his usual incantations, then projected his mind forward, zooming out over the ethers.

He homed in on the Black Fortress, concentrating his will there, until, suddenly, the large black calling candle that was kept at all times waiting on the bridge flamed into life.

The giant calling candle was about two feet high and a foot across. As the smoke from the wick rose, the sorcerer-king cast a large projection of his face into the smoke.

Staring at the bridge crew through the calling candle's smoke, he could see the officers on duty attending to their usual tasks.

No one had noticed him yet.

"May I have your attention?" he boomed in a godlike voice with no warning, and half of them nearly jumped out of their skins.

It was most amusing.

The bridge officers whirled around in surprise to find the head of the Dark Master peering at them from the smoke.

"Sire!" the lieutenant said, his eyes widening.

"Your Majesty!" The others quickly bowed.

Zolond exerted himself to make his appearance as imposing as possible, forcing the smoky image of his head to swell to some three feet across.

That ought to get their attention. Remind them all of who was really in charge around here. The whole crew hurried to bow to him; the pair of Noxu warriors posted by the door grunted and lowered their heads, too.

Satisfied, Zolond stared coldly at them, as though everything was normal. "I wish to speak to Wyvern."

"Y-yes, master, right away. I-I will fetch him for you at once," said the lieutenant.

"No. Bring me to him, wherever he is." *Let me take him unawares.* "I would speak with him privately."

The lieutenant nodded anxiously. "As you wish, sire. H-he is in his chambers, I believe." Then he gestured to the navigator, who had the steadiest hands.

The navigator approached, bowed to Zolond's image in the smoke, and then carefully picked up the sterling silver platter on which the big candle sat.

He carried it with great care out of the bridge and through the halls of the Black Fortress; an entourage of other crew members and Noxu guards went with him out of respect, and in case he needed assistance.

As the solemn procession moved down the wide central corridor, Zolond stared forward: a giant head perched atop the candle, formed from shifting smoke.

He took the opportunity to glance around, right and left, as the navigator carried him with great dignity toward Wyvern's private apartments.

Hmm. Everything appeared to be in order.

But, as Zolond knew all too well, appearances could be deceiving.

* * *

Wyvern, meanwhile, was in the middle of a secret candle call of his own inside his chambers. "Why did you not tell me the boy was at Griffon Castle?" he demanded, still furious over how that debacle had ended this afternoon.

"But I-I didn't know!" Boris Badgerton stammered. "They've all been keeping mum on any information concerning that boy."

Wyvern glared out at him from the ball of smoke atop a normal-sized black candle. "You're an Elder. That's why we chose you."

"Well, he's back now," the shapeshifter snapped. "However...I believe they'll be moving him again."

"Where to this time?"

Badgerton shook his bushy head, his side whiskers twitching. "I believe his relatives are taking him along on a diplomatic mission, but I don't yet know their route."

Wyvern absorbed this with a growl. *They can't hide you forever from me, son.* "Very well," he grumbled. "How is the tunnel coming?"

"Almost done. It'll be ready whenever you are. But, um, I have a bit of a concern, my lord."

"What's that?" Wyvern asked with a frown.

Badgerton glanced around nervously. He was alone in his chamber in Merlin Hall, but he seemed nervous, nonetheless. "I think they know that someone's passing information to your side. Some of the Elders have been acting...strangely. I confess, I'm a bit worried."

"Hmm. When did this begin?"

"I first noticed it about a fortnight ago. It's that Bradford witch. Sir Peter, as well. He hasn't been as unbearably cheerful as usual."

"I see. Well then, you'd better be careful."

"Oh, I will, but I was thinking... If trouble should arise, it would certainly help if you let me take the Proteus power *now.* That way, I could—"

"Out of the question," Wyvern said, turning his eyes to snakelike slits as a warning. "First finish the tunnel. Then you'll receive your reward."

Badgerton scowled but backed down with a huff. "It was just an idea."

"You have to *earn* your place on the Council, Boris. You have yet to prove yourself."

When a knock sounded on Wyvern's door, he glanced over, then turned back to Badgerton. "I have to go. If anything else arises, contact me at once. And remember, be discreet."

The beady-eyed shapeshifter gave an eager nod, then Wyvern cut short their communication, blowing out the flame. Another knock hammered at his door.

"Lord Wyvern?" came a muffled voice. "It's urgent!" It sounded like one of the bridge crew.

"Coming!" With a hurried motion, Wyvern waved away the small smoke cloud lingering over the black candle.

Annoyed but ever dutiful, he marched across his quarters, whose magical mirrors he had conjured today to resemble the ancient catacombs full of skulls and old bones that he enjoyed visiting beneath the streets of Paris.

The macabre setting suited his current mood after his humiliating defeat today at the hands of a few children.

And unicorns. Why was it always unicorns? Horrifying creatures.

But as Wyvern learned in the next moment, his already bad day was about to get worse.

When he opened the door, he nearly jumped to find half the bridge crew standing there, and Zolond's giant head staring coolly at him from atop the large calling candle from the control room.

"Wyvern," the Dark Master said sternly.

"Your Excellency!" Wyvern opened the door all the way. "W-would you care to come in?"

The sorcerer-king didn't answer, but that was clearly his intent. The navigator entered Wyvern's illusory crypt and carried the big black candle over solemnly to the table in the center of the room.

Wyvern hoped no one noticed the small puff of smoke still dissipating around the smaller black candle over on his writing desk.

Then he stood at attention before the giant head, doing his best to clear any trace of treachery off his countenance. "You wished to speak to me, sire?"

"Yes. Alone." The head rotated to nod the dismissal of the bridge crew. They respectfully withdrew.

When the door had closed, Zolond's big, smoky head swiveled around again to stare down at Wyvern. "Now then, commander. How have things been going aboard the ship?"

"Oh, everything's running smoothly." Wyvern forced a smile. "Nothing to report."

He should've known better.

"Funny you should say that, for the strangest reports have reached my ears about your recent activities."

"Oh?" Wyvern rocked on his toes and tried to look innocent.

"Word has it you raided Griffon Castle." Zolond leaned down toward Wyvern a bit. "Now, why would you do such a thing?"

"Well..." Wyvern said slowly, choosing every word with care. "In light of the prophecy about the Griffon lad, I thought it would be...*prudent* to collect a few helpful individuals who might know more about the boy than we do. He has had dealings in the past with the sea-witch, F-Fionnula Coralbroom. The boy's uncle, Waldrick Everton, also knows him very well."

"I see." Zolond scoured Wyvern's face with a knowing stare. "And?"

"Well, they were both imprisoned, so I...I decided to free them. Especially Lady Fionnula. She has been of great use to us in the past. And I know you are no great admirer of the merfolk."

"Hmm. Go on."

"Well, sire, it just seemed to me that any information Waldrick Everton could provide will be of use to us in dealing with the boy. I figured you'd approve, given that the lad is at the heart of Duradel's prophecy."

Wyvern prayed to Shemrazul that the old man was buying his falsehoods.

"I-I took Waldrick to Griffon Castle, you see, because of course he had his price. He demanded certain valuables from the family vault there in exchange for his cooperation. I had no idea the boy himself was at home," Wyvern said truthfully. "I had assumed he was still under guard at Merlin Hall. It is important, however, that we keep tabs on him, don't you agree, sire?"

Zolond let out a snort. "Keeping up to date on Jake's whereabouts is one thing, Wyvern, but I will not have you trying to abduct the lad, especially in front of witnesses. While attempting to lure him to us with the Gryphon is a solid plan, outright kidnapping will start more trouble than we are prepared to deal with right now." The Dark Master paused.

"We must keep to our agreed-upon timetable. Our army needs several more weeks of gestation."

To Wyvern's relief, it seemed Zolond had not caught wind of the whole debacle with that insufferable vampire and the escape of the Gryphon.

Best not to break the news about either of those now. It might be bad for his health.

Wyvern swallowed his frustration with the old man's caution, then sought to placate him.

"I assure you, sire, I have no further intentions of kidnapping Jake."

Zolond's scowl said he didn't believe him.

"Well," Wyvern amended, "at least not until Duradel gives us word that the time has come to act."

The sorcerer-king scrutinized him. "Should the time come when Duradel presents us with a new oracle to guide us on the timing, *then* we can act. Not a moment sooner. Do you understand?" Zolond made his eyes turn to flame as he stared down at Wyvern.

Wyvern lowered his head, resentment stewing. "Of course, Your Majesty. Your word is my command."

"Good."

"And, um..." Wyvern looked up again. "Are you enjoying your holiday?"

"I am thinking perhaps I should return—"

"No, no, take all the time you need. We are perfectly fine here. Nothing else to report." Wyvern bared his teeth in another awkward smile.

"I will not be trifled with, Nathan," Zolond warned quietly, and for a moment, Wyvern trembled in his shoes.

Shemrazul might be incalculably more powerful than the Dark Master, but right now, Wyvern was facing him alone. Clearly, the sorcerer-king was not happy with him.

Wyvern hid his gulp. "I understand."

"Good," Zolond said in his low, chilling rasp. "For if you disobey me, the consequences for you would be...most unpleasant."

Wyvern nodded stiffly and lifted his head, his six-fingered hands clasped behind his back. "Will there be anything else, sire?"

"Dismissed," Zolond replied. Then his face vanished from the smoke cloud and the flame winked out.

Slowly, Wyvern exhaled.

It took a moment, but then fury rose in him like the ocean tide coming in. How the devil had the old snake found out?

Well, talk must be spreading through the magical world.

Wyvern supposed he should probably just count himself lucky that Zolond had not yet heard that Janos had betrayed him and freed the blasted Gryphon, not to mention one of the Lightrider captives. By Beelzebub's hoof, that little matter would be a good deal more difficult to explain.

In any case, if Wyvern thought he was in the clear for the rest of the evening, he was sadly mistaken.

For as he went to pick up the big candle to return it to the bridge, another voice summoned him. The one inside his head. The one that, even more than Zolond's, could not be ignored.

Nathan, Shemrazul spoke into his mind. *Get down here. Now.*

Wyvern blanched. Egads, the Horned One sounded grumpy, even for a demon.

Yes, Father, Wyvern answered. *Right away.*

At once, he left his chamber. In the hallway, he called for one of the Noxu to come and take the big calling candle back to the bridge. He waited until the half-troll had carried it out of his room, then he pulled the door shut and locked it with a tap of his wand.

Pivoting, Wyvern proceeded down the corridor toward the nearest staircase.

As he stalked toward the intersection of two hallways ahead, he saw Fionnula and Waldrick peering curiously around the corner.

"Nathan, darling!" the sea-witch greeted him in a breathy voice. She sidled out from behind the corner, arrayed in a luxurious scarlet gown. "What is going on? We saw—"

"None of your business. Go back to your rooms, both of you."

"But Nathan!" Fionnula said with a pout.

"You heard me. I am in no mood."

She humphed as he strode right past her on his way, but behind him, Wyvern heard Waldrick Everton snicker at her offended reaction.

He ignored them both. Instead, he strove to prepare himself mentally for what he feared was going to be another scolding.

Two in a row!

Ugh, first unicorns, now this. He scoffed and shook his head, but, in truth, the double-barreled dose of disapproval from both of his superiors, the human and the immortal, made him a little queasy.

It was no small thing, disregarding orders from the Dark Master, but, in point of fact, Wyvern knew he had not exactly followed Shemrazul's directions either.

With good reason, his legs felt a little shaky with fear as he jogged down the black staircase. He knew he'd better brace himself for whatever his infernal father had to say.

When he reached the throne room, he nodded, as usual, at the two Noxu warriors stationed there. "He wants to see me."

Better you than me, said the looks on their tusked faces as they uncrossed their spears and opened the door.

The last thing Wyvern wanted to do was go in there at the moment. But he had no choice. Taking a deep breath, he squared his shoulders and marched in, same as always.

Shemrazul was already waiting for him there in a column of flame. The demon had his arms folded across his huge chest and was swaying back and forth as though pacing.

There was only so far he could move, however, with the adamantine chains around his ankles; he was hemmed in, as well, by the ring of arcane symbols engraved in the floor.

Wyvern hurried down the black granite platform to join him, passing in between two of the tall, empty thrones. He bowed at the border of the outer protective ring of floor carvings, his heart thumping.

"You wished to see me, Father?"

Shemrazul fixed him with a deadly stare. The smoke of the pit swirled around his horns as he scowled. "Tell me. Have I been speaking English to you, Wyvern?"

His deep voice rumbled through the room like distant thunder.

"Er, yes, sir." Sweat beaded on his brow from his nearness to the blazing heat as he stood at attention before the fearsome Lord of the Ninth Pit.

"And did I not make myself quite clear as to your instructions? I have been incredibly patient with you for three weeks now," Shemrazul interrupted before Wyvern could answer, "and yet you continue to defy my specific instructions! Such insolence from Zolond is one thing, but from my own son—"

"Father, forgive me!" Wyvern dropped to his knees and prostrated himself on the floor before Shemrazul. It was better than getting flayed alive.

"What have you been doing?" the demon boomed. "I told you, your *first priority* was to gather allies and consolidate support from among the members of the Council, did I not?" He did not wait for an answer. "I was patient. I waited to see how long you would turn a blind eye to my orders. Three weeks?!"

Shemrazul threw up his hands. "Do you think I'm telling you this because I like to hear myself talk? Is it just for my own health? No! These are your orders! This is what you *must* do. Not just if you feel like it! Don't you understand that?"

"Y-yes, Father—"

"Then how dare you disobey me?" Shemrazul thundered in a voice that shook the throne room and could've made the carved devil pillars tremble.

"I-I-I b-beg your forgiveness, Father." Heart pounding, Wyvern kept his gaze down.

"Get up." Shemrazul snorted a sulfurous cloud of disdain. "Quit sniveling and explain yourself. Tell me why you ignored my specific instructions and instead went after the boy and the sea-witch first."

For a fleeting instant, climbing to his feet, Wyvern considered claiming he had merely forgotten the sequence in which Shemrazul wanted the tasks done when he'd commanded him to undertake his coup.

"Don't even think about lying to me," the demon said.

"Sorry, your greatness. I...I can only say that my enthusiasm for becoming a father, l-like you, must've m-marred my judgment. But I"—he gulped—"I won't let it happen again."

"See that you do not." Shemrazul paused, apparently mollified by Wyvern's groveling. "Time grows short, Nathan. Zolond strays ever farther by the hour. Your coronation must occur on the great feast of Samhain, and that is fast approaching."

Wyvern was awed to hear the date was set. *All Hallows' Eve...*

"So, enough of this idiotic dawdling. You must get to work *now* gathering allies. Oh, but I suppose if you are cleverer than I am, then you don't need *my* help—"

"No, I do, mighty Horned One! I am nothing without you. Don't abandon me as you've abandoned Zolond!"

"It was Zolond who abandoned me," he shot back. "Be that as it may. If you do not intend to heed my instructions, then perhaps I should start trying to find someone else to wear the Black Crown—"

"No, sire, please, I beg you!" Wyvern clasped his hands before him. "I was born for this. I will serve you unto my last drop of blood, my final breath. I'll make you proud, Father!"

"Humph." Shemrazul folded his mighty arms and sulked.

"I mean it, sire. Only tell me your will and I'll go at once. Wherever you command."

"That's more like it." Narrowing his fiery eyes, the demon lowered his massive arms to his sides. The tips of his horns bobbed as he nodded. "Very well. But this time, let me spell it out for you clearly so you may understand."

Wyvern nodded, waiting at attention.

"Now, listen carefully," Shemrazul instructed. "Go first to the oracle—he is on your side and may have wisdom to offer. Then pay a visit to the general. You'll need his military expertise for the war..."

CHAPTER 49
Betrayer Betrayed

After Wyvern snarled at Waldrick and Fionnula as he went gusting by, the diva had let out an offended little huff and flounced off to her chamber to sulk. Left alone in the black, polished hallway, Waldrick realized he suddenly had at his disposal a rare opportunity to snoop.

For the moment, he knew where her precious Nathan was: distracted elsewhere. So long as Waldrick stayed clear of the Nephilim's general direction, this was his chance to have a discreet look around and try to figure out what the blazes was going on within the mysterious walls of the Black Fortress.

After all, the revelation earlier today that his brother and sister-in-law were not in their coffins had made it crystal-clear that Wyvern and Fionnula were keeping things from him.

Well, Waldrick Everton would not be played for a nincompoop. If his cohorts would not tell him what was going on, then he would jolly well piece it together for himself.

One way or the other, he thought, *I will get to the bottom of this.*

Then he set out to do just that, sneaking and sauntering along by turns up and down the hallways, acting casual, nose in the air, whenever one of the bridge officers hurried by.

Waldrick strolled past, all but whistling like he had nothing to hide and every right to be there, and, to his relief, none of them bothered him.

Having cleared these hurdles, he pressed on, tiptoeing across intersections, ducking the notice of distant guards. He knew by now to give the Noxu a wide berth—although, the other day, he'd been amused to overhear a knot of the half-trolls grumbling that all humans looked alike to them, except for the few who were easy to distinguish by some obvious feature, like Zolond by his age, or Wyvern by his height, or Fionnula by her flashy-colored gowns.

But the rest of the crew, why, the tusked mercenaries joked among themselves, the only way they could tell the bridge crew members from "the white-coated ones downstairs" was by their uniforms.

Hmm. Waldrick had made a mental note of both pieces of information. He would certainly use their difficulty in telling humans apart if he ran into any trouble with the armored barbarians.

But he was even more intrigued by the comment about white-coated humans somewhere downstairs. Given Zolond's famous proclivities for unholy experiments, blending species, it made sense that there might well be a team of scientists on duty somewhere in the Black Fortress.

So far, Waldrick hadn't noticed anyone of that description. It piqued his curiosity, since it might have something to do with *why* his brother and sister-in-law hadn't been in their coffins.

Determined to look into it and see what he might see, he continued exploring, dodging and darting along between the shadows, making not a sound.

Oh, he was crafty. He rather delighted himself with his sneaking abilities, slipping past closed doorways, peering into open ones, and scanning various uninteresting chambers. Always black! What a dismal place. Would it kill them to use a little color? They had no sense of fashion, these people. Most uncivilized.

Then he spotted the opening to another onyx stairwell ahead. A sign hung over it: *No Unauthorized Personnel.*

Aha, that looked promising. Since it wasn't the same staircase that Wyvern had entered, Waldrick decided to chance it, stealing his way along the corridor to the big, rectangular opening of the stairwell.

When he slipped through it, he found that the stairs went both up and down, zigzagging back and forth. It was impossible to see where either end led to because each flight of steps turned at a landing, then doubled back upon itself.

Waldrick could only see as far as the landings. Intrigued, he opted for the downward stairs, in light of what he'd heard the Noxu mention.

A clammy draft brushed against his face as he crept silently down the steps, sliding his back along the jet-black wall.

As he neared the landing, he heard a strange, low sound coming from somewhere below: a slow, dull, rhythmic *thud-thudding* that seemed to resonate out of the very walls.

What on earth is that? Fear made his heart skip a beat, but Waldrick ventured on. After a dozen steps, he gained the landing and peeked carefully around the corner.

The stairwell ended at the bottom of the next flight, and there appeared to be some sort of room down there, but he was too far away to tell yet what it might hold. Determined to get a closer look, Waldrick sidled down the final flight of stairs, the blood pumping in his veins.

He did not hear anyone speaking or moving around, but he sensed the presence of someone down there. Maybe multiple someones.

The low-pitched rhythm he'd been hearing grew louder and louder as he neared the bottom of the staircase: a deep, continuous *lub-dub* like a giant heartbeat. It made the hairs on his nape stand on end.

Whatever was going on around here, he must be getting close. Drifting to a silent halt near the bottom step, Waldrick held his breath, gathered his courage, and then stole a peek around the side of the wall enclosing the stairwell.

Though he stayed hidden, his quick scan revealed a spacious, kidney-shaped lobby with a black (of course) flagstone floor. On the opposite wall, a bit to his left, were a large and formidable pair of doors.

Guarded by an equally large and formidable pair of Noxu warriors.

Waldrick winced, then continued scanning. He saw that a wide hallway joined the lobby from the left; on the right sat a smaller side room with an open doorway over which hung a sign that said *Cloakroom*.

Pondering all this with a frown, Waldrick withdrew again behind the cover of the stairwell. Suddenly, he heard a distant commotion. The clamor echoed toward the lobby like it was coming from somewhere down that adjoining corridor.

Intrigued, he peeked out again and saw the noises had made the Noxu guards perk up, as though they had been dozing on their feet with boredom.

The barbarians stared in the direction of the hallway as the sounds grew louder. Now distant shouting could be heard—pleading, a few rough cries, and a bevy of hurried footfalls pattering over the flagstone floor. An ear-piercing creak attended the clamor, like a squeaky wheel.

"Guess they caught another one," the larger Noxu grunted to his comrade.

"Better get the door," the shorter, thicker one with a broken tusk replied.

Waldrick stared discreetly around the corner of the stairwell, unnoticed, as the two half-trolls pulled the massive doors open.

As they did so, the heartbeat sound pulsed out louder into the lobby, and, through the open doorway, Waldrick beheld a baffling sight.

A cavernous room yawned, dimly lit, with a tall, massive machine like a giant glass pillar in the middle of the space. A tangle of wires and countless tubes flowed out of the device in all directions, while, inside it, a hydraulic pump of some sort churned, sloshing a soupy green liquid.

He saw that the liquid traveled out through the tubes, but before he could even begin to wonder what the strange device was, the flurry of footfalls and the rhythmic squeak approaching up the hallway suddenly burst into the lobby in the form of four white-coated men rolling a patient on a gurney at top speed, headed toward the big room.

An infuriated man struggled on the gurney, but he was strapped down, awake and kicking as best he could. "Let me go! You won't get away with this! The Order will—"

Brisk and businesslike, the white-coated men ignored his protests, whisking him on toward the Noxu.

"Come through!" The broken-tusked guard waved the team of doctors or scientists or whatever they were into the big room while he and his comrade held the doors open.

"Where'd you get this one?" the larger guard asked.

"A pair of Drow bounty hunters just brought him in," one of the scientists hastily explained as they rolled their struggling captive toward the waiting doorway.

The guard bobbed his head. "Lord Wyvern will be pleased."

"You can't do this!" the bound man hollered. "The Order's waiting for me to check in! When they don't hear from me, they'll send—"

"Oh, shut up," one of the scientists muttered. Then he covered the man's mouth with a cloth apparently doused in chloroform.

The patient stopped struggling as the scientists sped him on through the open doors and into the huge, twilit room beyond.

One of the doctors turned back. "Listen," he said to the Noxu. "Those two Drow mercenaries are still seeing to their horses in the loading bay, but they'll be along shortly. One of you needs to take them up to see Lord Wyvern so they can collect their bounty."

The Noxu grunted in agreement, and when the doctor disappeared, hurrying after his colleagues, they pushed the doors shut and resumed their posts.

Ducking back again behind the stairwell wall, Waldrick's heart pounded as he assessed his situation. *Well, this is inconvenient.*

At any moment now, one barbaric Noxu and two of those keen-eyed, infamously ruthless dark elf mercenaries were going to be coming up this staircase where he stood.

Waldrick knew he needed to get out of there at once, but he could not bear to pry himself away. He had to know what was going on. Who was that poor blackguard they had captured and what did he have to do with the Order?

Never mind him! You have to get out of here before you get caught, his better sense warned.

Ah, but Waldrick had so rarely listened to his better sense in life. Why start now?

Instead, when one of the scientists returned a moment later, he saw his opportunity.

The scrawny, white-coated fellow poked his head out from between the big doors, a frantic look on his face. "Security, come quick! We need some muscle in here! The new Lightrider's stronger than he looks. The sedative's barely working. He's broken his restraints!"

At once, the Noxu rushed into the chamber after the scientist; the doors began drifting closed.

Almost without thinking, Waldrick dashed across the foyer into the cloakroom. He had no idea what he thought he was doing, but as he swept the room with a glance, he found it lined with wooden pegs from which hung more white lab coats.

They reminded him absently of his eccentric little kinsman, Archie. He quickly pulled one on. Hanging from the same peg underneath the lab coat, he discovered a pair of protective goggles. He put these on too, the better to hide his face. His heart thumping like it would jump out of his chest, he spotted a clipboard nearby with a pencil tied to a string. He snatched it up as added props for his disguise, then fled out of the cloakroom.

Stealing across the lobby, he slipped into the big chamber before the Noxu guards could return to their posts.

Nobody even noticed him as he darted to the left, hugging the curved stone wall of the cavelike chamber.

All of the action was happening over on the right-hand side of the room, where the man on the gurney was sitting up, thrashing about, and trying to fight his way free of his captors. It was pointless, of course, but Waldrick used the distraction to blend into the shadows.

While the Noxu wrestled the captive into submission, the scientists crowded around, shouting at one another and arguing about what to do.

Heart pounding, Waldrick sneaked along the opposite wall, heading for the far end of the strange space.

He had no idea how he was going to get out of here, but he needed to get to the bottom of this. Because, clearly, whatever all this was, it had to do with the secrets Wyvern and Fionnula had been keeping about their plans—and his Lightrider brother's fate.

Had the Dark Druids captured Jacob and Elizabeth the same way?

Stealthily following the curve of the stone wall, Waldrick scanned the soaring space as he hurried to put a safer distance between himself and the knot of scientists around the unfortunate Lightrider.

There was nobody else in the room. Well, he wasn't sure it could even be properly called a room, but at least it wasn't black.

The circular walls were the smooth brownish gray of natural rock. Indeed, the whole chamber resembled a giant cave; a domed ceiling of limestone arced some thirty feet overhead.

It was then Waldrick noticed that the walls were honeycombed with countless carved niches.

They reminded him of the dark, spooky catacombs he had once visited underneath the city of Rome. But tucked into each of these hollowed-out recesses was a long glass box...

Like a coffin.

Waldrick froze, narrowed his eyes, and looked harder. His throat closed as he realized there was a person—or, at least, a body—inside each glass case.

Gooseflesh instantly broke out down his arms.

All the while, the heartbeat machine in the center of the chamber pumped on. *Lub-dub!* Time seemed to slow to a drip as Waldrick's gaze followed the course of the tubes flowing out from the device.

A shudder of horror ran through him as he realized that the tubes fed into each one of these countless glass containers.

Still completely confused, he gathered his nerve and began taking closer looks into the coffins nearest him.

Some of the alcoves were at knee, waist, or shoulder level, but there were many rows above, carved into the rock dome. These could only be reached by climbing up the wheeled library ladders that were placed here and there around the huge chamber, apparently for that purpose.

He bent down and peered into several of the alcoves. Upon closer inspection, he saw, to his relief, that the people in the glass boxes were not quite dead. Their chests rose and fell, so, clearly, they were breathing.

They appeared to be asleep, or in some deep, magically induced coma.

Moreover, each one had a tube from the heartbeat machine inserted into his or her wrist.

No—not the wrist, exactly. Waldrick stared, the blood draining out of his face. The tubes were connected to the Flower of Life implant that each prisoner had embedded in his or her forearm.

Icy realization prickled down his spine. They were all Lightriders. Every captive here...

He cast about in a sudden panic, then confirmed his theory by glancing at a few more of the unconscious people in the glass boxes.

They all had a Flower of Life embedded in their arms. He knew what the device looked like because his own brother had been a Lightrider. So had Elizabeth.

Waldrick felt his stomach plummet to his feet as a horrible suspicion blossomed in his mind. *What if he's here? What if they both are?*

What if they've been here all this time? Alive...

Terrified, he turned away from the random Lightrider he had been staring at. His gaze swept the entire cavern.

Impossible. It's been twelve years!

Not even the Dark Master Zolond could keep someone alive for so long in this state, surely.

Waldrick began running from alcove to alcove, searching for the brother he thought he had murdered. Nearly tripping over the endless wires and tubes crisscrossing the chamber, he could barely stop himself from shouting Jacob's name as he hunted.

At least he now realized why they kept the place so dim: they didn't want to wake up their prisoners.

Frantically, Waldrick dragged over a library ladder and began climbing up the rungs, peering into all the alcoves he could see. *Where are you? Are you here?*

There must have been sixty or seventy sleeping men and women in all. Seventy captured Lightriders! He hadn't heard anything about this.

Of course, he had been in prison for the past year... But Waldrick thrust away his myriad questions about how this could've happened. The important thing was his brother might still be alive.

Maybe there's still hope. If anyone could survive this, it would be Jacob. He had always been the strong one.

Waldrick did not stop to wonder what his brother might do to him for his betrayal, if he was still among the living after all this time. The possibility seemed so remote that it was hardly worth worrying about.

Meanwhile, every minute or so, he checked over his shoulder as he worked, making sure that no one had spotted him.

The knot of scientists around the newly captured Lightrider had calmed down. Waldrick supposed they were processing him now, the poor blackguard. He wasn't fighting anymore.

Probably unconscious.

Why? Waldrick wondered. *Why have they kidnapped them? What do they mean to do with them all?*

Then he mounted another rung of the ladder, and that was when he found him.

Waldrick went motionless where he stood, almost forgetting to hold on to the ladder in his shock.

Jacob...?

The glass was dusty, and the tubing looked old. His hand trembling, Waldrick used the sleeve of the lab coat to wipe away the thick layer of dust so he could see the man inside the glass box better.

He drew in his breath as he beheld the handsome face of his comatose elder brother through the glass.

It's you. Waldrick would've recognized that chiseled face anywhere, that shock of golden hair.

But the true Earl of Griffon looked gaunt, frail, aged from having been kept in this state.

And yet the fluid pumping into his body through the Flower of Life implant in the Lightrider's arm was somehow keeping him alive.

As Waldrick stood there in disbelief, feeling like this must be a dream, Jacob's eyes flashed open for a second—searing blue, and glazed a bit, but still full of his usual intensity.

Waldrick jolted backward with an oath and nearly fell off the ladder.

His brother was there but not quite there as he stared back at Waldrick for a second through the glass, as if to say, *I know what you did.*

Then his eyes drifted closed again, and the real Lord Griffon made no further motion, gave no further sign of life.

Trembling violently, his teeth chattering, Waldrick gulped and forced himself to look into the nearby coffins. *No, no, no. Please. Not the woman. Tell me they didn't do* this *to Elizabeth, too...*

But even as he shakily climbed the next rung of the ladder, he could see that the glass box above contained a dark-haired female.

Tears filled his eyes, and he could go no farther. He knew in his heart that it was she, and he could not bear to face her.

Because he knew what he had done. He had shot her in the back while she was fleeing him with her baby. *How could I ever do such a thing? What wicked influence took hold of me that I could ever have justified this?*

Yes, his brother and he had scuffled since boyhood. They'd had their ups and downs, and frankly, Waldrick had often been jealous of Jacob.

But Elizabeth had never once wronged him.

On the contrary, the charming beauty had always done her best to invite him to be a part of the family. Christmases. Easters. The christening of their son. And what thanks had he given her in return?

A bullet in the back.

Apparently, a magical one of some sort, because, clearly, it hadn't killed her. It had only, he surmised, put her into this strange magical coma.

For once in your life, don't be a coward, he thought. *They deserve more from you than that.*

Waldrick clenched his jaw and then forced himself up the next rung.

Again, he had to wipe a circle away in the thick layer of dust on her container before he could see her well.

And then there she was.

Lovely as ever, with her milky skin, pert nose, and her dark, winged eyebrows. The waves of her sable hair flowed past her shoulders down to her waist, overgrown in her long slumber.

I am so, so very sorry.

A tear rolled down Waldrick's face and dripped off his jaw onto his hand as he clutched the ladder rung, staring at his sister-in-law.

You didn't deserve this. And I swear, I will do aught in my power to make it right.

The present moment and his precarious situation came back to Waldrick suddenly, snapping him out of his tearful daze.

He realized he'd better watch his back. The stakes here were obviously higher than he'd had any idea.

Climbing down from the ladder, he gathered his composure for a moment when he reached the floor. Then, hugging the clipboard in his arm, he headed out of the cavernous chamber, moving like he knew exactly what he was doing and had every right to be there, same as always. He was very good at dissembling, after all. An expert at it, really.

His simple ruse worked. The scientists barely looked at him, still fussing over their latest kidnap victim. Together, they were lifting the now-unconscious Lightrider off the gurney and into one of the glass boxes.

Waldrick walked smoothly out the door, sparing an arrogant nod for the larger Noxu, who glanced indifferently at him. He crossed with measured paces to the cloakroom, his heart pounding, but, once inside, he got rid of his disguise.

Taking a deep breath, Waldrick steeled his spine and proceeded back out into the lobby again, crossing to the stairwell.

The Noxu didn't bother him: all humans looked alike. He was just one of the scientists.

Once he was out of view, Waldrick climbed the stairs two at a time in terrified silence, arriving in the black hallway once more.

By some miracle, he made it back to his room without further incident. He didn't even get lost. Finally, he shut the door to his chamber behind him and leaned against it, his legs still trembling beneath him.

He did not know yet what to do, how to fix this. But what had just happened changed everything.

I'm not a murderer after all!

Mawkish tears jumped into his eyes, but he was past caring. What did it matter?

What did anything else matter?

My family is alive.

CHAPTER 50
Gathering Allies

When the diplomatic party walked into King Snorri's great hall at Jugenheim the next day, Jake savored the stunned look on Dani's face.

Nixie and Isabelle were also dumbfounded.

The towering timber hall of the Norse giants was built in the Viking style, with a mighty oak tree growing right up through the center of the floor and passing out overhead through the same opening in the roof that allowed the hearth smoke to escape. The trees had been sacred to them since pagan times.

And speaking of pagans, Archie and Jake had also been tickled by the girls' amazement to meet Odin. The chief Norse god, though retired now, had come in person to let their party into Jugenheim, for he had fixed the seal between the worlds after Snorri had accidentally broken it some time ago.

He'd nodded at Jake when he saw him, a gleam in his remaining eye. The other was covered by an eye patch, for he had sacrificed it at the Well of Wisdom in exchange for the depth of understanding that had made him the chief of the gods.

Jake found him fascinating, an old warrior-king roaming the world in all his disguises, collecting heroes for Valhalla with his retinue of gorgeous, winged Valkyries.

When Jake had first met him, he'd been disguised as a janitor. He was most unpretentious.

"Still have that dagger I gave you, young hero?" he'd asked Jake in amusement, his voice gravelly with a thick Scandinavian accent.

"Oh, yes, sir." Jake pulled out Risker and let Odin examine it again. "I found out the blue stone in the hilt glows in the dark. It's helped me more than once, I can tell you."

Odin nodded. "Take good care of it," he said while the rest of their party walked ahead, marveling at giant land. "Who knows what else it can do? Forged in Asgard, it was made outside of what you mortals call space and time. As for its qualities, hmm, Wayland the Smith does not like to explain his creations. But I would not be surprised if it can do things similar to brightwields and darkling blades."

Jake was awed to hear it. "Thank you, sir."

Odin had given the magical knife back to Jake, then continued on his way, leaving Maddox and even Uncle Richard staring, wide-eyed, after the long-legged, short-skirted Valkyries.

Then it was onward into Jugenheim for their whole party, an entourage of twenty-four people in all. There were two Lightriders, Ranjit and Tex; ten Guardians, plus Derek and Janos; two shapeshifters—Henry and Helena; their official VIPs, Lord and Lady Bradford; and the six kids.

Though the girls had seen giants wandering through the grounds of Merlin Hall now and then, this was not the same as being in their world, where the humans only stood knee-high to the locals and everything was built to *their* scale.

The visiting party had to climb ladders to sit on vast chairs. The giants' dinner plates were so enormous that Jake could've lain down and made snow angels on one.

But it was good to see how well Snorri had taken to the role of king, and, of course, Princess Kaia-of-the-Yellow-Braids had turned into a splendid shield-queen. She was the real power behind the throne. She had been trained for it, while Snorri had been but a lowly shepherd before he'd saved his people from Loki.

The diplomatic party spent two days in Jugenheim, making sure the giants would be ready for any threat from the Dark Druids.

Though the kids were given permission to go exploring during their visit, Jake decided to stay behind while the others ventured out with an escort of giants and Guardians.

They were going to see Smokey the Dragon, but *he* was more interested in observing these diplomatic talks, which Uncle Richard and Aunt Claire had given him permission to do. King Snorri and Queen Kaia knew and trusted him, after all. Given his familiarity with their world, he might even be able to help.

For his part, Jake was very keen to find out exactly how the sophisticated Lord and Lady Bradford went about conducting their various missions as diplomats, what sort of tasks were involved.

He knew for a fact that their magical talents were nothing special. Mediocre at best, Archie had once confided. Uncle Richard's gifts were in the clairvoyant category, just like his sister Elizabeth's had been.

But while Jake's mother had had the full ghost-sight, which she'd passed on to him, her brother's clairvoyance manifested in a more modest way. For Richard, it expressed as a strong discernment when it came to reading other people. It seemed related to the empathic power in his daughter.

Richard's talent no doubt came in handy in his work as a diplomat. He also had a warm affinity with animals (though not as deep as Isabelle's). Every now and then, he would also have dreams about future events, but that was not something he could control, and the visions were very hard to interpret.

As for Aunt Claire, she had received the lesser mage's talent that ran in her lineage, but she was no Nixie. Her magic was limited to charms, hexes, and minor glamours. She was very good at persuading people of things—also a fine skill for a diplomat—but whether that was her magic at work or just her personality was anyone's guess.

But in spite of their limited magical gifts, Jake soon saw for himself that by working together in foreign courts, the smart pair made quite a team.

Sitting in on the meetings with Red by his side, he listened intently as they warned the king and queen of the giants and their panel of advisers about the Dark Druid threat.

"You need to be ready," Aunt Claire said somberly.

"Yes, but for what exactly?" Kaia asked with a worried look. "Considering we're dealing with a bunch of mad warlocks, how can we even predict the nature of their attack? Spells and curses, or armies of monsters or what?"

Aunt Claire shook her head. "I'm afraid we don't yet know, Your Majesty. But we will keep you apprised as we discover more."

"Don't worry," Snorri told them. "The giants will be ready to fight alongside the Order if it comes to that. You are our friends."

Jake smiled, impressed by his confident attitude. "Any more trouble from Loki around here?"

Snorri laughed at the reminder of the battle they'd fought against the Norse god of mischief. "No, he knows when he's beaten."

"It's too bad Thor and Odin can't lend us a hand," Uncle Richard said wistfully. "We could certainly use their fighting skills."

"Unfortunately, they have to stay out of mortal affairs," said Aunt Claire.

Indeed, it was part of the terms of their surrender nearly a thousand years ago, after most of their pagan worshippers had converted to Christianity. They were ordered to stay out of trouble and enjoy their retirement.

It was a shame, thought Jake, for Thor could've probably smashed a hole in the side of the Black Fortress with one throw of his hammer. Ah well...

"Hey, maybe the Valkyries would be allowed to help," Jake blurted out.

Uncle Richard and Aunt Claire exchanged a glance.

"I'll look into it," the viscount said. "Good thinking, Jake."

Jake nodded, pleased to contribute. The work of a diplomat might not be as flashy as that of a Lightrider or as exciting as that of a Guardian, but it was definitely interesting. Jake liked helping to solve practical problems.

In any case, the giants held a feast in their honor both nights they were there. Both times, it turned into a stomping-good sing-along, just like when Archie and Jake had visited Jugenheim alone.

Apparently, some of the giants were still under the impression that Jake and everyone with him were dwarves, and all that the giants knew or cared to know about dwarves was that they were excellent singers.

This was a fact the diplomatic party would soon verify on the next stop in their journey, for the very next morning, they headed off to the Black Mountains in Wales.

It was time to go and see the dwarves.

* * *

Wyvern also set out that morning to seek allies and consolidate support for his overthrow of Zolond, as Shemrazul commanded. He dared not delay any longer.

The bridge crew and the thick-witted Noxu fighters knew nothing of his true purpose, of course. Had no idea of what he was up to, what with all the jumps he led them on over the next few days.

But it wasn't their place to question him.

He let them assume it had something to do with Zolond's recent candle call. That he had received new orders.

In a way, that was true. Why, there was nothing out of the ordinary in his visiting his fellow members of the Dark Druid Council.

Since Shemrazul had ordered him to seek out the Drow prophet, Duradel, first, Wyvern did just that, consulting the dark elf seer in his underground temple.

He was an eerie fellow, with his long, pale hair, fine features, and white, sightless eyes. Dressed in lightweight black armor and flowing midnight robes, Duradel advised Wyvern to destroy any Council members who refused to side with him, lest they betray him to Zolond once they learned of his plans.

Wyvern didn't need to be told twice. After all, empty seats on the future Council could always be filled later by people who owed him.

Already he had promised places to Fionnula, his future queen, and to Badgerton, along with his Proteus power.

But since a proper war could not be conducted without the help of certain key players, he went next to visit General Archeron Raige, per Shemrazul's orders.

The general was a soldier's soldier, an assassin whose favorite pastime was genocide.

When Wyvern went to visit him in the jungles Raige called home, he found the musclebound warrior with a gun in his hands, roaming the wilds of his tropical estate. His square, scarred face painted with camouflage, the stub of a cigar dangling from his lips, Raige never took his fiery eyes off the lush, tangled landscape before him.

"Careful where you step, warlock. I keep the grounds booby-trapped. For trespassers."

Wyvern looked down just in time and saw an open bear trap right in front of his feet. "Thanks for the warning," he muttered.

"Well? Why are you here? Grab a rifle if you'd like a bit of sport, but whatever you do, get to the point, man. The game's afoot. Ah, I love a good hunt in the morning."

Wyvern took him up on his offer and accepted a loaded rifle, though he had too much on his mind to focus on tracking big game. "What exactly are we hunting, general?"

"Pacifists," spat Raige. "They can run, but they can't hide. Follow me." He nodded over his shoulder at Wyvern, then headed down a narrow path crowded with palm trees, hanging vines, and tropical shrubs.

Exotic birds called from the canopy, a monkey mocked from somewhere in the mist, and a large snake slithered on a branch overhead, but neither man paid it any mind.

Raige kept searching the underbrush. "I'm a plainspoken man, Wyvern. None of your sorcerer's double talk. Come straight to the point."

"As you wish." Wyvern didn't mind doing so, since he felt rather sure he could count on the madman to help him.

Raige was always chafing for a war. Still, just in case he refused, Wyvern had brought along not just his wand, but the Altantean cuff with which to kill Raige, if it came to that. The likes of Archeron Raige didn't die easy. Especially given his arsenal of *unusual* weapons.

"So what's on your mind?" He puffed on his cigar and waved off a mosquito.

"General, I've been thinking." Wyvern lifted his rifle into position and followed him into the jungle, scanning the greenery as they stalked their prey. "Zolond's hesitation is beneath us."

The soldier harrumphed like he'd been thinking the same thing.

"I don't know why the Dark Master waits to move against the Order. But I, for one, am running out of patience. It's time to act. With Shemrazul's blessing, I have begun formulating a plan, and I'd be grateful for your support moving forward."

Raige stopped, turned around, and stared at Wyvern, sizing him up.

Wyvern met his gaze evenly.

Raige slowly took the cigar out of his mouth, exhaling smoke. "This a trick? Some kind of test?"

"No." Wyvern shook his head, deadly serious.

"Huh." Raige paused, narrowing his eyes. They were light blue and piercing, contrasting with his camouflaged face. "You double-cross me, I'll kill ya."

Wyvern lifted his hands. "I'm putting myself on the line here too."

"All right, then." Raige flicked ashes off his cigar. "What'd you have in mind?"

"An attack on Merlin Hall," Wyvern replied.

"Oho! Aren't you the cocky one. Nothing like starting small." Raige paused, glancing at movement in the underbrush, but he let it go, looking askance at Wyvern. "Does Zolond know about this?"

Wyvern shook his head. "He's tired," he said in an acid tone. "He's on *holiday.*"

Raige stared at him. "Holiday?"

"You heard me. Shemrazul himself has decided we need new blood at the top—meaning me. If you'll join me, I'll make sure you get what you want."

The general lifted his square chin. "And what exactly do you suppose I want, Nephilim?"

"What you always want. Another war to play with."

The general's eyes glowed with flames for a moment. "The earth's been too quiet these days." He took a puff of his cigar. "Still, your plan is bold. I like bold."

"Indeed. We strike the first blow with a surprise attack when they're least expecting it, and that will provide us with an important psychological victory. Demoralize them."

"The easiest way to win is to demoralize the enemy from the outset," Raige said automatically. "Crush them right from the start in a show of domination."

"You see my vision exactly. So?" Wyvern murmured. "Are you in?"

The smile the general gave him was slightly deranged. "Now you're speaking my language." Raige clapped Wyvern on the shoulder and nearly knocked him into the quicksand beside the path. "Wouldn't miss it for the world."

Sensing motion from the corner of his eye, Raige lifted his rifle quickly and took aim, firing into the thicket. A human yelp issued from somewhere behind the leafy screen of trees.

"Ha!" said Raige as the puff of smoke from his gun filled the air.

"Good shot," Wyvern mumbled.

The general gave him a sardonic salute, then Wyvern continued on his way.

Next, he set a course for Budapest, where he went to pay homage to the Red Queen, Viola Sangray.

In the eyes of human society, Lady Sangray was a ravishing Hungarian countess, but to the underworld, the vicious beauty ruled as the vampire queen.

Again, Wyvern took care to arm himself well when he went to her castle on the Danube that night, for only the most deranged and bloodthirsty vampires climbed the darkling hierarchy to become the ladies and courtiers of the Red Court.

He brought his wand *and* the Atlantean cuff once again, but the latter he hid under his sleeve, for he had murdered Janos's family with it and the vampires were known to be clannish. He hoped she had not heard about that, or, if she had, that Shemrazul was watching over him tonight.

As for the black widow herself, Viola was somewhere between five and six hundred years old, but regular feedings on the blood of the young kept her looking like a woman in her prime.

She had jet-black hair and skin as pale as moonlight, a cruel sense of humor, and no conscience at all.

When Wyvern walked into her crimson throne room that night, with its elaborate but empty gilded mirrors, its chandeliers overhead shaped like spiders or great glass ticks, he was startled by the sight of dazed, half-drained humans lying around on couches and divans, ashen-faced and lethargic.

But he smelled a hint of spiced smoke on the air, and remembered it was an old vampire trick to keep the prey drugged so they wouldn't struggle.

These wretched creatures, however, were here by choice, offering their own veins to feed the thirsty vampires. They had been deluded into thinking that the vampires they served would actually let them join their coven one day from gratitude and live forever young and beautiful.

Little did they know that vampires scoffed at their naiveté. The great fanged family only cared about their own kind—and that, just barely.

He'd say one thing for them, though. Vampires had fine manners, at least these ones. They were almost as elegant as the dark elves. All of them were beautiful, both male and female, and so were their prey.

When Wyvern entered, they bowed and curtsied gracefully to him as the son of Shemrazul. And yet, as he marched up the long red carpet from the doorway to the Red Queen's throne, he could feel their hostility.

If the Horned One weren't his father, he'd probably be dead by now, merely walking in here.

Viola was lounging on her throne and sipping from a skull-shaped goblet. The moment he saw the pout on her ruby lips, Wyvern knew he had trouble.

She must have heard about the hatchlings.

That was the only reason Wyvern swallowed his pride enough to bow to her. "Greetings, dark lady."

"Wyvern," she said, staring coldly at him. "I trust you've come to explain yourself for your barbarous atrocity."

He furrowed his brow. "Um..."

She bared her fangs at him, appearing in a whoosh to stand right in front of him, glaring into his eyes. "You killed six of my beautiful daughters and all of my grand-hatchlings, my darling Janos's brood."

"I can explain—"

"I should hope so."

Lucky for Wyvern, vampires did not hold much value for life. If she were really angry about what he'd done, she'd have come looking for him with several of her deadly followers by her side.

"And where is my son-in-law, anyway? Did you kill him, too?"

"No."

"Then why has he not come to us? We are here for him, ready to comfort our grieving brother." She gestured to her court.

The vampire ladies and gentlemen began approaching from all direction, gathering 'round and staring at him.

Wyvern gulped. "That's just it, Your Majesty," he said. "Janos has betrayed us all. He's gone back to his old friends with the Order."

Viola scowled at him. "Impossible."

"It's true. This is why he had to be punished. I certainly never intended for his family to die."

The other vampires in the room hissed at this obvious lie, but what did they expect?

Just then, Wyvern felt a tug on his sleeve. He looked down and saw a frail waif of a girl who'd come shuffling over to him. She lifted her arm, offering him her wrist to bite.

Wyvern shook his head with distaste. "No, thanks."

"Well, if you see my son-in-law," said Viola, "tell him to come home. I want to talk to him and see for myself if your story is true."

"You'd believe him over me? Don't you realize who I—"

"Tell him it is no trouble for me to make him a new bride, several if he likes. He can have his choice. As for you, Nephilim..." The vampire queen returned to her throne, her ruthless stare fixed on Wyvern. "I had better not hear about you killing Janos or I will be cross."

"Fine," Wyvern said in a dull tone. He'd paid Janos back enough for now. "But be warned: don't trust him if he should appear. Janos is a traitor. In truth, I doubt you would be pleased with how he was raising his children. He was corrupting their minds with compassion, filling their head with all sorts of dangerous notions. He wouldn't even let them feed properly. I saw it for myself."

"What's this?" Viola hissed at the news. "I suppose you have proof of this infamy?"

"Well, not proof, exactly—"

"Then save your excuses," she said. "Blood is thicker than water among my kind. Surely you know that if you were not the son of Shemrazul, you would never leave this chamber alive after what you've done."

Wyvern hid his impatience. "My humblest apologies, Your Majesty."

"If what you say about Janos is true, we will deal with him ourselves. Otherwise, you should have come to me to let me know there was a problem with my favorite son-in-law before you took such action."

"It won't happen again," he said wryly.

She snorted, then took another sip from her goblet. "Well, dragon lord? Why are you really here?"

Wyvern glanced around at their angry audience. "In private, if you please."

Viola flicked a suspicious glance over him, then barked her courtiers' dismissal.

They all left, the vampires gliding out gracefully, their human cattle shuffling out behind them.

Only one large blond male in an impeccably tailored suit remained behind, refusing to leave his queen's side—the royal companion, Wyvern gathered.

He didn't mind. If Viola trusted the imposing fellow, then Wyvern could tolerate him hearing this as well.

Once the three of them were alone, Wyvern explained the situation with Zolond, and how the old man had fallen out of favor with Shemrazul.

Pondering his news, Viola paced across the room. When she reached the edge of the floor, she continued strolling up the side of the wall, her black skirts trailing after her.

It was an impressive display, especially since the black lace train of her gown remained in harmony with her motions, and the contents of her goblet remained in her cup, as though she commanded even gravity.

When she reached the ceiling, she turned a nimble somersault and vaulted down to stand before him. "You really mean to do it? Overthrow Zolond?"

"I mean to try," he answered.

The blond vampire held his tongue, but the look he exchanged with the queen seemed approving of Wyvern's proposal.

"Admittedly, we have been a little disappointed with the Dark Master of late," Viola said, lifting her chin. "He is so absorbed in his experiments that he loses sight of the grand vision. The future. The Master must devote himself to furthering the interests of the dark world. For the sake of our children."

"Exactly," said Wyvern, thinking of Jake.

His son.

Soon.

"But on the other hand"—Viola paced back the other way, sauntering up the opposite wall, and strolling across one of the big mirrors—"old Zolond always was fair to my kind. He's had none of the prejudice others hold against us, you know." She eyed him skeptically from beneath her black lashes. "After what *you* just did to my kin, I am not convinced you hold the proper respect for the darkling race."

"On the contrary, your majesty, what I did proves my respect for your people, your traditions! Janos was betraying everything it means to be a vampire. I made an example of him that will dissuade any more of your children from breaking with the old ways that you hold so dear."

"Humph." She weighed his words, floating back down onto the floor. "Is it really Shemrazul's will that Zolond be cast down?"

"It is," Wyvern said solemnly. "I wouldn't lie to you about something like that."

The male vampire pinned Wyvern with a wary stare in the candlelight, while Viola walked back up the few steps to her throne. Atop the low dais, she took a swirling half step, fluffing her black skirts around her.

"Here is my answer, Nephilim: show me some evidence that this is really Shemrazul's will, then my people will join you in the fight. Obviously, I cannot take you at your word after what you've done to my kin. For all I know, you could be lying. This could be a trap."

"It's not, I promise you. Shall I swear it on my blood?" Wyvern took out his dagger and offered a blood oath, prepared to cut himself to gain this alliance.

Viola's glance flicked to his wrist. A greedy gleam came into her eyes and she licked her lips. "I've never tasted Nephilim blood."

"No, my love. It could be poisonous," her mate murmured, stopping her as she stepped forward. She frowned at him, but the vampire shook his head. "Shall I taste it for you first?"

She paused, then cupped his cheek. "No. I could not bear to lose you. You're right." The male vampire kissed her hand before she lowered it to her side again. "Tempting as your offer is, my companion is right. You don't last six hundred years by being reckless. I'll decline."

"Very well." Wyvern put his dagger away.

She took her seat again while her bodyguard stood at attention right behind her throne. "When I see some sort of proof that your plan has a hope of succeeding, then we will join you, Wyvern, but not a moment sooner. I'm sure you understand. My people believe only in what we can see, hear, smell, touch, and taste. We are open to supporting your coup, but not on blind faith. Never blind faith. Not the vampires."

Wyvern had no choice but to nod. "I can respect that."

Aside from their reputation for clannishness, Wyvern knew that vampires were usually slow to commit, but once they did make up their minds about something, they were wholehearted.

That trait had certainly proved true with Janos. In hindsight, Wyvern realized it had been his killing Urso, the bear shapeshifter, that must've pushed Janos over the edge from friend to foe.

As for Viola, he couldn't blame her for being skeptical of him after the incident with the hatchlings. In truth, this had gone better than he had any right to expect.

"I will see that your people are given special distinctions when I become the Dark Master," he promised her.

"*If* you become the Dark Master," she replied. "We'll see." She raised her glass to him. "To the future, Wyvern, whatever it may hold."

Wyvern murmured agreement, then sketched a bow and took leave of her.

As he left her castle and returned to the Black Fortress, he stewed a bit on their exchange. Her answer hadn't been quite what he'd hoped for, but he could work with this.

It was worth showing a little patience, anyway, because having an army of undead killers by his side would bring him a huge advantage over anything the Order could produce.

Then he gave the bridge crew a new set of coordinates. Next, he would drop in for an unannounced visit to his next potential ally—two for one this time.

The Cataclysm Twins.

* * *

The next day, Jake was delighted to return to Waterfall Village behind the thundering cascade in the Welsh mountains.

Though it was dim in the dwarves' underground realm, the cozy little city they had hewn for themselves right into the rock had a welcoming feel, with its cubbyhole shops, quaint town square, and winding walkways, all lit by hanging lanterns both day and night.

The dwarves received them in a formal ceremony headed up by Emrys, the hearty, dark-eyed chief of Jake's gold mine. Charming old Ufudd was there too. He had woven a red ribbon braided into his long white beard for the occasion.

All the dwarves rejoiced to see Red again, though they preferred to call him by his true Welsh name, Crafanc-y-Gwrool. The dwarves had a great esteem for the Gryphon. After all, it had been Red's mother who had shown Jake's ancestors the vein of gold in the mountain that became the mine and eventually spawned the entire village here—all because of her gratitude to Jake's medieval ancestor, Sir Reginald Everton, for saving the Gryphon egg and returning it to the nest instead of delivering it to his king.

Red pranced in delight at the dwarves' adulation. They spoiled him here, really. The noble beast made such a ham of himself that even Maddox laughed.

Then their jolly hosts welcomed the diplomatic party with a concert, just like they had when Jake had first come here and met them all.

As before, the dwarves cast powdered handfuls of the mysterious mineral known as Illuminium up into the air. It began to sparkle and glisten in the resonant frequencies of their song.

Jake watched Dani staring up at the glittering dust in wonder. She had always been fascinated by Illuminium.

As he recalled, she had sprinkled some of it on Teddy once for laughs and made him glow. But as pretty as the twinkling cloud of dust was at the concert, the redhead's delight at it was prettier still.

The following day, after the concert and the welcome feast, Jake was allowed to sit in on the official meetings again, since he knew the dwarves well—and, indeed, owned the land on which they lived.

He watched and listened, impressed with his aunt and uncle's diplomatic skills. The dwarven folk could be a little grumpy, as he had learned last time he was here. They especially did not like to hear about anything that might interfere with their work schedules.

"Ah, no one even thinks about us out here! We keep to ourselves," one of the town leaders insisted. "Why should a bunch of warlocks bother us?"

They pooh-poohed the threat from the Dark Druids at first, but Jake knew they were really just annoyed at the prospect of having to pause production in order to shore up their defenses.

Hard workers, they hated missing their quotas. Growing testy at Uncle Richard when he tried to stress the danger, they quit listening to him—and Aunt Claire they all but ignored, for, in their view, what did an aristocratic human lady know about mining, let alone the affairs of dwarves?

They could be a little touchy when they felt anyone was questioning their expertise. They grumped and harrumphed about having to change their busy mining schedule, until Jake finally spoke up to reason with them. What they cared about most was the gold they worked so hard to unearth, so...

"My friends," he said, "what if the enemy were to mobilize that tribe of gold goblins out in the woods against you?"

"Those parasites? Bah, they don't scare us," said the deputy mayor. "We know how to manage them. You know how stupid they are."

"W-well, yes, I...I know they're usually pretty docile," Jake admitted. "But we're dealing with highly skilled warlocks. The Dark Druids could put a spell on the goblins to make them more aggressive, or even make them clever temporarily. What if creatures like *that* started sneaking in here to steal from you?"

"That could never happen," someone muttered.

Jake hadn't seen which one had said it, but the dwarves' resistance made him all the more determined to convince them of the seriousness of this situation.

Inspiration struck without warning, and suddenly, he realized how to motivate them.

Jake leaned forward. "Armies need funding, you know. Even evil ones. There's a lot of gold in these mines that our enemies would love to get their hands on to support their dark operations. A well-run mining enterprise like this could easily become a prime target."

"Hmm," said the dwarves, stroking their beards.

Jake saw his uncle send him a discreet nod of approval. Why, the diplomat looked quite impressed.

Encouraged, Jake looked around sincerely at the dwarves. "I'm not the expert that you are, sirs, but, to me, it seems most economical to take precautions now instead of waiting for a crisis."

"The lad speaks sense," Ufudd declared, nodding at Jake.

"Very well, Lord Griffon," the mayor said begrudgingly. "How would *you* suggest that we proceed?"

"Um..." Jake floundered for a moment. He knew that as Red's owner, the dwarves gave him extra respect.

His large, feathered pet looked at him expectantly.

Better think of something quick.

Aunt Claire arched a brow in amusement, waiting to hear his response.

"Well," he ventured, "perhaps you all could work in shifts. Half of your usual crew continuing with your mining output, as planned, while the other half sees to the defenses. I would have them check armaments, make sure you're well supplied, survey the walls for any weakened sections that might be vulnerable to attack. I'm sure you'd want to set a watchman over the water entrances, as well—the underground rivers and such."

The dwarf leaders looked at each other, then began murmuring among themselves.

"If we could keep production going, then maybe we wouldn't fall too badly behind..."

"Doesn't sound too *terribly* impractical..."

"Warlocks aside, I have noticed a few spots were the walls could use some shoring up. Maintenance..."

Uncle Richard sent Jake a proud wink as the dwarves convinced themselves of the wisdom of his plan and came out acting like the whole thing had been their own idea from the beginning.

Jake hid his grin, happy to be of help. He might never be chosen for a Lightrider, but maybe, just maybe, if he followed in his aunt and uncle's footsteps, he could be a half-decent diplomat someday.

Later that evening, when he shared that possibility with Dani, she gave him a playful shove. "That's fantastic! I can be your Lightrider and you can be my Princess Pansy!"

He scowled at her. "Princess Pansy, eh?"

"Hurry, they're coming!" she teased.

In reply, Jake levitated her off the ground, hardly for the first time.

"Put me down!" She screeched and kicked her feet, to no avail, giggling indignantly—until he floated her out over the little subterranean river where Emrys and Ufudd had once taken them on a boat ride.

"No, Jake, no!" Her pleas turned genuinely panicked. "The Bud of Life! I can't get it wet! Put me back!"

"Oops, sorry. Forgot." He quickly returned her to dry ground, whereupon she whacked him in the arm.

"Ow." He rubbed his biceps. "Guess I deserved that."

"Yes, you did!" she declared.

Later that night, she sat beside him again as the dwarves treated them to another concert, but the kids had already been given the order that the diplomatic party would be moving on in the morning. Now that the dwarves had made their defense plan, the leaders of Waterfall Village were eager for their guests to leave, for there was much work to be done.

You wouldn't know it by their fine hospitality, though. The second night's kingly feast was even more delicious than the first, and a different group sang to entertain them—a large, all-ages choir.

Their music was simply beautiful, powerful, swirling harmonies deep with emotion. An orchestra accompanied them, and as their poignant melodies resonated through the soaring stone cavern, the Illuminium sparkled overhead.

They finished a wistful song, and the whole audience held its breath for a moment, still enraptured—and it was then, during that brief pause, that Jake heard a small sob to his right.

As thunderous applause erupted, he looked over and saw Izzy rise and hurry out, brushing away a tear.

Good Lord! The poor girl was bawling from the music. The heartfelt songs of the dwarves must have stirred her sensitive emotions, forcing her to leave in embarrassment so she could regain her composure in private.

Poor thing, Jake thought. He knew she had been tightly wound of late. All the darkness gathering in the world was really starting to get to her.

When she quietly slipped out of the concert hall by herself, Janos glanced after her, then sent Jake an annoyed frown.

"I'll keep an eye on her," the vampire whispered, then rose and left without a sound.

Maddox scowled as Janos followed Isabelle.

"Oh, relax," Jake chided under his breath. "He's on security detail."

Maddox gave Jake a dubious look, but resisted the urge to go after them and remained in his chair.

Jake would've stopped his friend from following them, anyway, because Janos and Izzy still hadn't made up. They were both clearly suffering, and it was obvious they really needed to talk.

Maybe once those two cleared the air, then the dark cloud the whole group seemed to be traveling under would finally abate. Their hosts' hospitality was flawless, but feasting and song could only fix so much.

He hoped the pair managed to make peace. He hated seeing people he cared about in pain, and those two usually made each other so happy.

CHAPTER 51
Discovery by Moonlight

Isabelle wiped away the tears flowing hotly down her cheeks as the dwarves' gorgeous song faded behind her. She didn't really know why she was crying, could not put it into words. The music had stirred some deep well of feeling in her heart and she couldn't seem to help it.

God, it was embarrassing to be so oversensitive.

She knew she ought to toughen up somehow. But who else could she be than who she was?

And who she was right now could not *stand* being underground one moment longer. She needed to see the sky, smell the breeze...

Having walked out blindly through an iron-reinforced side door of the mine, she welcomed the cool night air on her face. It soothed her.

Silver moonlight danced on the meadow before her, beyond which lay the unicorn forest.

Finally quieting her sobs, Izzy dabbed at her nose and decided to go and check on the herd that lived on this additional family property.

Jake owned a few thousand acres here as part of his charming woodland estate called Plass-y-Fforest. While the dwarves inhabited the underground spaces, the woods had been set aside as another safe unicorn preserve, like Bradford Park.

The herd here had been doing well last time they'd visited, she recalled. It seemed a lifetime ago.

Taking a deep breath to try to shake off her emotional outburst, she began walking out across the wildflower field, through the tall grass, savoring the night breeze.

When she reached the middle of the meadow, she paused and tilted her head, gazing up at the starry skies.

She just stood that way for a long moment, counting

constellations, marveling at the moon, and then, gradually, although she'd heard nothing, she sensed Janos from some distance behind her.

Stealthy vampire, she had not even heard him come out.

She turned around and saw him standing back by the iron door. Watching over her from a distance with those keen eyes of his.

Izzy stared at him, wondering why he even bothered, since it was clear that he despised her now for whatever reason. With that thought, she suddenly wondered if she was quite safe. If he really hated her, perhaps he might hurt her.

He must've read that fleeting worry in her mind, for he snorted aloud.

"You shouldn't be out here by yourself," he said. "Come back inside."

She bristled. "Don't tell me what to do."

He let out a weary sigh at her retort. But Isabelle did not know what to say to him, so she just turned away and started walking through the tall grass toward the woods.

In a heartbeat, he whooshed across the field in a puff of smoke to rematerialize beside her, and the next thing she knew, he was strolling along by her side as though nothing had changed between them.

She huffed at his intrusion, looking askance at him. "What are you doing?"

"What does it look like? I'm guarding you. I'm a Guardian, remember?"

"Is that what you are?" she said under her breath.

"Isabelle." His tone was cajoling.

"What?" she retorted, turning to him with a mutinous stare and folding her arms across her chest.

Janos stopped as well, gazing at her with a mix of sadness and frustration. "Isabelle...I didn't mean to hurt your feelings. Surely you know that. I was hurt. Badly."

"Of course you were, and of *course* I know that. But why then did you—"

"Fine. Do you really want to know?" he interrupted, looking vexed to have to answer for his actions.

"Yes! Why were you so mean to me?" She gazed up at him imploringly. The moonlight glimmered on his chiseled face, dancing across his high cheekbones and smooth, pale forehead. He looked away.

"I dunno... I guess I wanted someone else to feel the pain too." He looked back at her, a flicker of shame in his eyes. "It was more than I could carry on my own at just that moment, but— Oh, never mind! Excuses won't do. I was wrong. I was rude. And I am sorry."

She stared at him, still confused.

He tilted his head. "What?"

"I don't understand you," she whispered. "You reached into my mind; you placed your own thoughts there, and did I not respond as you desired? I immediately helped you. You knew I would. And then you turned around and cut me to the quick. It makes no sense. What did I do that was so wrong?"

"Nothing!" He gripped her shoulders and searched her eyes. "Izzy, I promise, you did nothing wrong. Nothing at all. It was all me." He released his hold on her too quickly and dropped his gaze. "As I've told you, I'm a bad person. Everybody knows that."

She did not know what to say to that. Many believed so. He clearly did. It did not feel true to her.

"Would you stop reading me?" he said in exasperation.

"Stop reading *me*!" she cried, blushing that he'd caught her.

Janos shook his head, staring deep into her eyes. "You see too much, little one."

"So do you," she replied. Then—she hardly knew why—she inwardly opened her heart and mind and gazed at him, devoid of defenses.

She had nothing to hide. And since he could read her mind, he probably knew by now how much her feelings toward him had changed.

His green eyes flickered, but he shook his head slowly. "You are too young, sweet."

"But I will catch up to you someday," she whispered. "You don't age; I do. It won't be long now."

He turned away and swallowed hard. "You mustn't say such things," he said in a hollow voice. "It's foolishness."

"Then why can't I forget you?" She trembled a little as the words tumbled out. "This is terrible. It hurts all the time."

"Isabelle, it's delusion. You know that. It's probably just some stupid glamour that comes with the fangs, one I can't even control—"

"I don't believe that! All your flirting with me..."

"I wish I'd never done it. I was joking!" He turned back to her.

“No, you weren’t,” she said. “I’m an empath, Janos. I *know*. You need me.” Her heart pounded as she trapped him in his lies. “You love me,” she added slowly, shocked at her own boldness. “You don’t want to; I realize that. All the same, I am glad.”

Janos shut his eyes.

As her gaze traveled down his strong shoulders and chest, Izzy almost dared to reach out and touch him, but thought better of it.

“Fine,” he said in a low, rather tormented voice. “You want to know why I blamed you? Because I did it for you. The things that got my family killed.”

He stared at her with fierce intensity. “I’m no hero, Isabelle. Left to my own devices, I’d have been quite content to go on living in the gray zone between good and evil, only looking out for myself. But then he had to go and threaten you. Wyvern.”

The way he said the warlock’s name sent a shiver down her spine.

“I couldn’t let him hurt you. So I went with him to the Black Fortress. He made me choose, and I chose you. Just once, I wanted to do what was right. But I never expected the cost to be quite so high. He killed my children.”

Her heart clenched. “I’m so sorry,” she whispered.

Tilting his head with a sad smile, Janos lifted his hand and cupped her cheek in his palm. His touch was cool and smooth.

“You have nothing to apologize for. When I came back that night, it wasn’t you I was angry at, but at him. And, most of all, myself.”

It was just like Jake had theorized, she thought. But she wanted to hear it from Janos. “Why were you angry at yourself? For not being able to protect them?”

“No. Not in the main.” Dropping his hand back down to his side, he let out a great sigh. He was silent for a long moment. “It was because when they died, a part of me was glad.” He shook his head. “I really am a monster.”

“No, you’re not.”

He gazed at the trees, clearly wrestling with himself. “They were mine and I loved them in my way, but they never should have existed… The fruit of all my sins.” He looked at her grimly again, very much a Guardian once more, stoic and blunt. “The hard truth is, the world is better off without them. Just as it would be better off without me.”

“No! Janos, don’t say that.” She clutched his forearm.

“Why not? It’s true.”

"*I* wouldn't be better off! Janos—sometimes I feel as though you're the only one who really understands me."

His lips quirked with a careworn smile. *Likewise,* he admitted telepathically, as if he dared not say it out loud.

She stepped closer. "Janos, I really think—"

"Isabelle, no." He shook his head, set her back gently at arm's length, and gave her a pained look. "You are as dear to me as the memory of dawn. But that is all it can *ever* be."

He sounded very sure.

She drew back, wounded. "But why?"

"You know perfectly well why, Isabelle," he said, forcing his usual sardonic cheer.

"Because you're a vampire."

"Obviously."

"But I cannot leave you alone forever in the darkness!" she cried.

He arched a brow, then chuckled at her dramatic announcement. "Eh, I'll be fine," he said with a wave, making light of his own damnation.

"But Janos—"

"No, Isabelle," he said firmly, though his gaze was tender. "I'll never drag you down with me."

"But I already know I will love you forever!"

"Oh, God," he muttered, rolling his eyes. "Listen to me." With an indulgent smile, he gathered both of her hands in his and held them as lightly as if they were baby birds with the most delicate bones. "Here's what you must do."

"Yes?" she asked eagerly, ready to promise him anything.

"Go have a Season or two or three. Dance with a hundred suitors. Break a few hearts. Grow up for a while, yes? If you still remember me at that point, then maybe we'll talk."

"Janos!"

"It's too soon, love. You're too young. And, besides, to be perfectly frank, I have no real plans of surviving this war."

"What?"

He ignored her horrified question and rambled on blithely, as if he had said nothing earth-shattering. "After you've had your fun as a Society belle for a few years and, if you can't find some other fool to marry you, don't worry, if all else fails, I won't leave you a wallflower. Poor, homely thing." He chucked her under the chin. "On that, you can rely."

She yanked her other hand out of his light, chilly hold. "Stop treating me like a child and tell me what you meant by that. Not surviving the war?"

Janos just looked at her.

She was reminded of the young gentlemen who had crowded around her at the harvest ball. All of their boasts about winning the war amounted to nothing compared to this one's lethal silence.

They could brag; he could actually do it.

"Why would you say such a thing?" she demanded.

He rested his hands on his hips and shrugged. "Well, you know, dear, people do die in wars. So I've heard."

"You're immortal."

"Not entirely."

"Do you *want* to die, Janos?"

"Oh, I dunno." He lifted his head and gazed up at the stars. "It's more a matter of duty. Besides, I really have nothing to live for."

Her eyes widened. "Nothing at all? Not even me?"

"You're what I *fight* for, Isabelle. What I'd die for," he said quietly. "It's different."

Izzy was so upset by his words that she turned and walked away, reeling. *But I don't want that.*

I'm sorry, he answered, uninvited. *It changes nothing. It's just who I am.*

She whirled around, infuriated. "Stay out of my head! You obviously don't care about me at all if you actually *hope* to die in some battle, you vainglorious fool! Don't you have any idea what that would do to me?"

"Hmm." He lowered his head and finally stopped looking so maddeningly self-assured. "Hadn't thought of that."

"Of course you didn't. Males never do." Isabelle pivoted and continued marching on across the field. *Stupid suicidal vampire.*

He laughed at her silent rant. "Isabelle, where are you going?"

"To see the unicorns! I am their Keeper, after all."

At once, Izzy sensed him getting nervous to hear this.

"Uh, I don't think that's such a good idea!"

"Why not?" she drawled, turning back, her hand on her hip. "Worried they'll impale you, prince? Maybe you deserve it."

"Really? A stake-through-the-heart joke? Not funny!" he called after her as she marched on, but the humor in his tone was hard to resist.

He made her want to scream, and yet somehow his charm lured her back inevitably to their former mutual teasing in spite of herself.

Ignore him, she advised herself.

You can't ignore me.

I hate you.

I hear that a lot from females. Right before they throw themselves at me.

Fuming, Isabelle shook her head and thrust him out of her mind.

He followed at a respectful distance, still on Guardian duty. After all, if the unicorns charged, he could always turn himself into a cloud of smoke.

Determined to put some distance between them so she could at least think straight, Izzy strode on across the moonlit meadow. But when she came to the medieval ruins of the abbey that had once stood on Jake's property, she was drawn toward its lonely beauty.

She wandered into the ruins, glancing at old, broken pillars and hollowed-out archways of stone in what had been the chapel's nave.

Before long, she found herself looking up at the moonlight shining in through the last remaining stained-glass window in the place.

Tall and narrow, it had been oddly preserved through the ages, probably by some sort of magic. There were unicorns in range, after all.

The stained glass actually showed a life-sized portrait of an angel. One they knew well.

At that moment, Janos drifted into the ruins several paces behind her, glancing around at the toppled chunks of timeworn stone.

> *"But my Soul wanders,"* he quoted as he approached.
> *"I demand it back*
> *To meditate amongst decay, and stand*
> *A ruin amidst ruins; there to track*
> *Fall'n states and buried greatness..."*

Isabelle turned with a rueful smile in spite of herself. "Lord Byron."

He looked impressed. "You know the work?"

"*Childe Harold's Pilgrimage.*" She returned her guarded gaze to the window. "Interesting poem. Dreadful man."

"Ah, that's a bit harsh," he said lightly. "A great poet. A rebel."

"Mad, bad, and dangerous to know?" She slanted Janos a pointed glance.

"What are you looking at me for?" he asked innocently.

"Oh, no reason."

"Humph. To be sure, you're safer with me right now than you'd have been out here with Byron. Hold on—" Janos suddenly noticed the window, and his eyebrows shot up. "Is that...?"

She nodded. "Dr. Celestus."

"Really?" Janos stepped past her, studying the window. "It *does* look like him. Though he was in considerably worse shape last time I saw him."

"It's him." Izzy nodded. "Apparently, he's had a connection to Jake's family line for centuries."

"What, like a guardian angel?"

She shrugged. "Something like that, I believe."

"Huh." Janos stood gazing up at the window.

As portrayed in colorful glass, the angel was blond and tall, fine-featured. He had white-feathered wings, wore a simple white robe with a gold cord around his waist, and carried a sword in his hand.

"Ooh, look at that." Janos stepped closer, then pointed at the weapon. "That's a brightwield! Oh, I should've loved to have one of those in hand when I..."

His words trailed off, but not before Izzy saw the images that flashed through his mind because of their bond.

Dreadful spatters of blood. Dying demons falling before the darkling blade in Janos's hand. Terrible howls; fearsome Noxu baring their teeth at him; fire, chaos, and rage all around.

And there, slumped in a cell, the poor, maimed Light Being in chains, his glow dimmed, bloody stumps on his back in place of wings.

"Oh my God," Izzy whispered at the sickening sight.

As she reached out to steady herself on a hunk of stone, Janos turned to her sharply.

"Isabelle!" He rushed to her side. "You saw that?"

"You really did that?" she countered, dizzied by the scenes from his memory. "You slew those demons and saved him? I heard that you had..."

"You should sit down. I'm so sorry." He took her elbow and steered her over to the nearest fallen pillar, where he made her sit down. "I didn't mean for you to witness any of th—"

"It's all right," she said. She was still a bit shaky, but the nauseating wave of lightheadedness at all those flashing violent images was already passing.

"Should I go get some smelling salts?"

"I'm fine," she said, amused at his solicitude. "Stop making a fuss."

Standing in front of her, Janos leaned forward, bracing his hands on his thighs. He searched her face with a frown. "But you're pale."

"Look who's talking."

His eyebrow arched, then he smirked.

Shaking her head to clear it, Izzy was already feeling better when she looked at him with a sudden inspiration. "Janos!"

"What?"

She pointed at the glass portrait. "You saved Celestus! Don't you see what this means?" Hope flooded her heart.

He shook his head.

She took hold of his shoulders as an eager smile broke out across her face. "Maybe Dr. Celestus can help you! Once he gets well, of course."

"Help me what?" he asked, wrinkling his nose.

She actually wasn't sure. "I don't know! But something. Maybe there's a way to un-vampire you."

"Un-vampire?"

She nodded eagerly. "Maybe! I mean, if anyone could, he's an angel! He has *connections*, if you take my meaning. To someone who can always take evil and use it for good."

For some reason, her hopeful suggestion seemed to sadden him. "You would say that," he murmured with a wistful smile. Then he straightened up. "Don't you ever lose faith, Izzy?"

"No," she said. "I don't let myself." She rose from her cold stone seat.

Janos stepped back to give her room, but still studied her. "Are you sure you're all right?"

"Are you?" she countered. "After that battle in the Black Fortress, I mean. You killed the worst creatures there. It looked beyond horrible. So, how are you?"

He looked surprised at her question. "Nobody's ever asked me that before."

"Well? Do you need to see a healer?"

"I'm looking at one," he whispered.

She smiled uncertainly. It was true that the Order usually lumped the empaths in with the healers' category.

"Of course," he added with a roguish smile. "I'm a big boy."

Isabelle tilted her head and studied him, amazed.

"What?" he asked. He really had no idea how much of a hero he was.

"Read my mind," she said softly, staring at him. "I dare you."

He looked at her for a long moment, already sensing her thoughts. "No," he said, "I don't think I will."

"Then I'll tell you aloud." She reached up and caressed his cheek. "I love you, Janos."

He stared at her, stock-still. She could see he was astonished, but for once, he didn't make a joke.

She moved closer, her stare locked on his. "Thank you for saving Celestus. Thank you for rescuing Red and bringing Ravyn and Tex home safe. Thank you for doing all of that…for me."

His eyes dipped to her lips, but he remained perfectly motionless, almost as though he was holding his breath.

"You're welcome," he said.

When she tilted her head back, coyly offering her lips, he looked away.

"Don't do this to me, Isabelle. Please," he said quietly. "Leave me just one thing I can know for sure I did right."

Izzy stopped cold as understanding flooded in, shredding her romantic haze. Good Lord! What was she doing? Tempting him to throw away his last shred of honor? Who was being selfish now? Her usually strict conscience must have nodded off, but it came roaring back and was appalled at her.

Janos was unmoving, clearly wanting to kiss her as much as she wanted to be kissed.

But, with clarity returning not a moment too soon, Izzy realized what would happen if either of them acted on the impulse.

They'd send him away.

Derek. Her parents. Aunt Ramona. Dani would tattle. Someone would find out, because she was no good at lying.

And she'd never see him again. Janos would be banished from their party and maybe Merlin Hall, shunned forever.

He would no longer be allowed to serve as any sort of Guardian, even an unofficial one—and, if that happened, he'd be utterly alone.

And the darkness would swallow him.

"I'm sorry," she forced out as she stepped away sharply and turned aside, her pulse pounding. "You're right, of course—I apologize. How dreadfully forward of me."

Janos closed his eyes with a flinch, both pained and relieved she had moved out of range.

Disaster avoided—but only just.

Izzy still tingled from his nearness. "Please forgive me," she added, still trembling with her back to him. "I-I didn't understand."

"Now you do," he said quietly.

"Yes." She nodded, too ashamed of her own recklessness to look at him.

"Good." Janos paused. "We should be getting back."

Then he stepped out of the ruins and went out into the moonlight to wait for her, leaving her alone for a moment to collect herself.

Izzy was deeply shaken by her own lapse in judgment. Celestus seemed to frown down at her from the stained-glass window.

She closed her eyes and shook off her attraction to the most unsuitable of all suitors as best she could.

Through one of the glassless windows on the other side of the crumbling ancient church, she could see him standing out there.

How alone he was. Tenderness filled her as she realized how badly he needed to stay with their group. The lot of them were the closest thing he had left to a family. And, to be sure, if he lost Derek's trust all over again because of her, Janos would lose what little self-respect he still possessed.

He'd never say it aloud, but she got the feeling that Derek was more or less his idol. Gazing at the beautiful vampire silvered by moonlight, Izzy's heart throbbed with the desire to protect him.

Though he was nigh indestructible, he had known so little kindness.

She finally understood that what Janos really needed was something innocent in his life. Something good. Not just another smitten female drooling over him. He had chosen to pin his last few chivalrous ideals on her; now it was up to Isabelle to prove worthy of them.

She took a deep, steadying breath and blew it out, smoothing her hair. *Fine, then. Just friends.* Since he had been adamant that she was too young, and, since she knew, deep down, that he was probably right, Izzy made her peace with it.

A sensible girl really ought not to love a vampire, after all, if she could help it. It was hardly what Mother would call a suitable match.

She would just have to content herself with going back to how it had been between them before.

Let the future take care of itself. Instead of kissing him senseless, she could help him, the poor benighted warrior, see the beauty in life again, help him find new reasons for joy.

That she could do without ruining either of them.

Squaring her shoulders, Isabelle finally managed to recapture her runaway heart and pin it back safely onto her sleeve, where it usually lived.

Only then, once she had composed herself, did she rejoin Janos outside.

"Shall we?" He avoided her eyes when she returned and gestured toward the distant iron doorway to the mine.

She nodded, resolute. "Let's."

They began walking back across the field.

Neither spoke.

She wondered if he was angry at her again because of this. In truth, she felt a little stupid. "Um, sorry about that."

"About what?" he asked, sending her a private little smile that said all was forgiven.

Izzy smiled back in relief; the glimmer in his green eyes made her heart dance. But yes, it was best to pretend that spellbinding moment of temptation had never happened.

They strode on in silence, their steps perfectly matched.

"You know," he said with a wary glance at the woods, "I can feel those bloody unicorns stalking us."

She laughed, grateful for his quip breaking the tension after all the awkwardness. "They're not stalking us!" She smacked him in the arm. "They're hoping I'll come and see them."

He gave a mock shudder. "You're on your own there, sister."

"No one invited you anyway."

"Hold on..." He drifted to a halt, glancing to the right. "What's that?"

"What's what?"

He walked about ten feet to the right, the tall grasses whispering as he passed.

Izzy looked up curiously as Janos bent down, reaching for something concealed amid the wildflowers. He picked it up with a low exclamation of wonder.

It looked like a white wand, glistening in the moonlight.

Izzy lit up at the sight of it and hurried over to join him.

"What is this?" he asked.

"I'll give you one guess."

He frowned at her. "A unicorn's horn?"

She nodded. "Let me see it."

"Here." His hand brushed hers as he gave it to her. They both ignored the jolt of awareness.

"One of the colts must have shed it this past spring," she said, examining it.

"They do that?"

"Only once, as they approach full maturity. Then the adult horn grows in." She marveled at the pearl-white spire. "Oh, it's beautiful. It's nearly perfect! Bravo to those sharp vampire eyes of yours. Do you know how valuable this is? Unicorn horn has extraordinary healing properties."

"I'd heard that. May I?" Janos took it back from her and inspected it, testing its durability and lightly touching the tip. "Sharp! You know, personally, I'd have this made into a dagger if I were you."

"A dagger?" She shook her head, resting her hands on her hips. "Guardians."

"What? Bits of unicorn horn have been embedded in bladed weapons for centuries."

"Yes, for added power, I know. But what would I do with a dagger?"

"Er, we're about to go to war?" He sent her a sardonic look.

"Oh, right." She sighed. "I'd almost forgotten for a moment."

"I daresay this would make a fine weapon." He held it like a spike, gauging its weight in his grasp. "It would put my mind at ease if you had something more practical to defend yourself with than just that Keeper's staff of yours, anyway."

"Maybe you're right." She took it back from him and studied the unicorn horn in the moon-glow. "Maybe it would make a good knife."

"You should have Maddox fashion it into a weapon for you," he said with a nod.

She gave him a coquettish smile. "Or you could do it."

Janos snorted. "If I cut myself on that thing, it'd probably poison me. Besides, the blacksmith's son is better at making weapons than I am. I'm sure he'd be honored to do it for you. Speak of the devil," he added, nodding toward the iron door several yards away.

"Miss Bradford!" Maddox barked, marching out with his shoulders bristling. "Come back inside! The concert's over. Your governess is looking for you." He paused but couldn't seem to help himself. "I don't think she'd be very happy with you if she found you out here alone with *him*."

"He's right, of course," Janos said cheerfully to her. "I'm a terrible influence."

She tossed her head. "I don't care. I'm still mad at him."

"Aw," Janos chided with a teasing glance. Then he snatched the unicorn horn out of her hand and started striding toward Maddox. "Ho, Stick!"

Izzy followed reluctantly. She would rather stay out here with Janos than go back underground.

"Bet you can't make Isabelle a dagger out of this." He tossed it to the lad, which nearly gave Izzy an apoplectic fit, but they were Guardians, both of them, and Maddox's well-honed instincts allowed him to shoot his hand out in time to catch the horn before it stabbed him or even hit the ground.

He examined it. "What is this?"

"Give you two guesses," Janos drawled.

"A unicorn horn?"

"Clever lad! Miss Bradford was just saying how she'd love to have it made into a dagger. Think you could manage that?"

Maddox studied the horn with fascination, then sent her a wary look as she joined them. "I don't think Isabelle would really want that."

"She does," Isabelle replied.

"For self-defense," Janos said. "And who can blame her, what, with all the nasty folk who'd like to see her dead?"

"Thanks for the reminder," she said lightly.

"My pleasure." Janos looked at Maddox again. "Of course, if you don't think you can do it, I could try to muddle my way through, but I'm not as good at this as—"

"No, no, of course I can do it," Maddox said. "I've never worked with this material before..." He sent Izzy a hopeful look. "But I'd be happy to try."

Janos smiled broadly. "There you are, Miss Bradford! You see? I knew this fine young fellow would agree. I have no doubt you shall soon find yourself in possession of a capital blade, and, as for you, Stick, impress her with your work, and you might still have a chance with the lady."

Izzy pursed her lips as Janos clapped Maddox on the shoulder, ignoring his scowl, then headed back inside.

Rogue. She knew what he was up to. He was trying to shove Maddox at her as a preferable replacement for himself. But it wasn't going to work.

Sure, Maddox might be closer to her own age, but Izzy didn't care. Her heart was already lost to the scoundrel.

"Come along, children! It's not much of a party without us, so we'd better get back inside. Spit-spot!"

Maddox shook his head at the vampire's carefree air, but Isabelle supposed she didn't mind going back in. Especially if Miss Helena was looking for her.

The Guardian lad gestured to her to go ahead of him. Isabelle nodded prim gratitude to him and went. She was not eager to go back down into the gloom of the mine. But now that things were somewhat fixed between her and Janos, she felt a lot better about everything.

She stole one last glance up at the stars before she went through the iron doorway. They seemed to shine a little brighter, their silver magic piercing through the dark.

CHAPTER 52
Brood of Vipers

For Wyvern, the excitement was building. He had not heard anything further from Zolond since his obnoxious candle call. Shemrazul continued to encourage him, so he pressed on in his quest to gather allies for when the time came to act.

It wouldn't be long now.

He was pleased to have gained the full cooperation of the Cataclysm Twins, an eccentric brother-sister pair in their early thirties who tended to wreak havoc everywhere they went, either separately or together.

Simeon, the elder twin, was a reckless, dark-haired chap with a talent for generating natural disasters. He could stomp earthquakes into being, wake up sleeping volcanoes, and manipulate water in all its phases, so blizzards, hurricanes, and tsunamis were all hobbies of his.

Amaranth, the younger twin, was a clever, educated miss with spectacles and a dusting of freckles across her nose. Never mind her harmless appearance—the lady scientist specialized in plagues, poison, and disease.

She tended to follow in her brother's wake, adding a wave of human misery to further complicate the trouble he had started. Outbreaks of malaria after floods. Influenza after ice storms.

They worked well together. Powerful as they were, the pair saw the overthrow of Zolond as an adventure.

That left only a few more members of the Council for Wyvern to visit.

The following night, he parked the Black Fortress near the White Cliffs of Dover and walked out to the windy ledge to meet with Captain Inigo Dread. Having set up the meeting in advance, he looked up eagerly, with Thanatos seated by his side.

The manticore hissed nervously as Dread's vessel, *The Dream Wraith,* came sputtering down from the clouds toward the cliff's edge, while the cold Atlantic waves crashed below.

Wyvern's long coat blew around his body in the breeze. The descending airship was a sight to behold, chugging and whirring down from the dark skies.

Floating out behind the vessel was an even more curious sight. *The Dream Wraith* pulled great fishing nets through the skies, but instead of fish, its nets captured the prayers and dreams, hopes and wishes of the innocent, especially children, intercepting them on the way up.

Captain Inigo Dread and his grim crew harvested despair, as all of those hopes and prayers were never answered—not because no one was listening, but because they had been stolen by the dream fishers halfway up the skies. These precious raw materials were then turned into food for many breeds of monsters.

The airship's haul of captured hopes and dreams floated out behind it as the *Wraith* drifted down to hover across from the cliffs. The one-eyed captain clomped out onto the narrow wooden deck on his peg leg.

"Wyvern!" he yelled down over the noise of the propellers, waving from the railing.

"Good to see you!" Wyvern called back.

Dread threw down a rope ladder and beckoned Wyvern aboard. After all, the English Channel was infamously windy. Not even a crew as experienced as Dread's sky pirates could force the great dirigible to hover precisely in place.

Leaving Thanatos behind, Wyvern climbed up the rope ladder with only one nervous glance down at the dark, crashing waves below. It was cold in the biting breeze. Behind the ship, the captured dreams and wishes glowed in the nets with an aura of sadness.

Ignoring it, he clambered aboard the airship, then met with the captain in his private quarters. The captain's wood-paneled stateroom with its curved sides was surprisingly cozy.

Dread offered Wyvern a drink, then they got down to business. His wand by his side in case the captain didn't like his plan, Wyvern explained the situation. But, to his relief, a canny grin slowly spread across the sky pirate's face.

"Aye, I won't stand in the way. I mean, it's a shame about Zolond, in'nt it? But I reckon he done it to himself. We all gotta die sometime."

"Indeed."

"You really think you can take 'im?"

Wyvern smiled with cool confidence, but kept his tone modest. "We'll see."

"Humph." Dread scrutinized him with a searching, one-eyed stare. The other eye was covered by a patch.

Wyvern had heard the grizzled old salt lost the use of his other eye when he was struck by lightning while tending his ship.

As for the missing lower portion of his left leg, that had become dinner for a shark once when *The Dream Wraith* had made a crash landing in some Australian bay.

"Very well," the sky pirate said after a brief silence. "You let me harvest the rich pickings to be had above Merlin Hall the night of your attack, and you've got yourself a deal. The dreams and hopes of Magick-folk aren't easy to come by."

"You'll provide cover from above? I know you've got the guns for it."

"Aye." *The Dream Wraith* was fitted with several cannons, including two small but effective swivel-guns fore and aft.

Wyvern nodded. "Then it seems we have an understanding."

"Done." Dread spat in his palm, then offered Wyvern a handshake.

Though Wyvern found this crude little ritual rather disgusting, he followed suit, clasping the sky pirate's hand in his six-fingered grasp.

From there, it was on to Vienna, Austria, where he tracked down the most unassuming member of the Dark Druid Council, Professor Richard Labyrinth.

A little academic in a tweed coat with elbow patches, the doctor taught at the university and also saw patients at the lunatic asylum.

A humorless middle-aged man, pale and balding, he wore small, round spectacles and a pointed beard. But, as dry and mild-mannered as he seemed, in some ways, Dr. Labyrinth was even more dangerous than Raige.

The general could overcome the enemy by force, but Dr. Labyrinth knew how to get into their psyches and twist their minds until they questioned their own sanity. He didn't *cure* mental patients; on the contrary, he drove perfectly sane clients mad.

Lately Wyvern had heard that Labyrinth had been going after

newspaper writers and politicians, the better to spread his insanity on a wider scale.

When he welcomed Wyvern into his office at the university, Dr. Labyrinth sat down on an armchair by his desk, leaving Wyvern nowhere to sit but on a padded leather couch across from him.

"Please, make yourself comfortable. You may lie down if you like. Now, tell me. Why are you here?" His voice was a lulling monotone with a slight Germanic accent. "Why are you *really* here?"

Wyvern glowered. "Spare me your mind games, doctor. I am here on business."

Wyvern then explained the purpose of his visit.

Labyrinth heard him out, listening in detached silence, slowly turning his pencil end over end on his cluttered desk.

"Well?" Wyvern finally said.

The professor adjusted his spectacles. "You say your father has given you this mission."

"Yes, that is correct."

"But what do you want, Wyvern? What does *Nathan* really want, deep down?"

Wyvern gave him a blank stare. "I beg your pardon?"

"Well," Labyrinth said in his faint accent, shifting in his chair, "it sounds inordinately important to you to please your father. Why is that?"

"Have you *seen* him?" Wyvern retorted.

"Hmm. You are afraid of Shemrazul?"

Wyvern sat straight on the couch. "All nine circles of Hell are afraid of him, you idiot!"

"Now, now, zhere is no need for violent outbursts. It is very plain you suffer from ze megalomania, and a strong case of ze paranoia, as well. But why zis urge to please your father, hmm? Perhaps you think you are still just a little child, ja? One who may not measure up in his eyes?"

"Enough of your nonsense." Wyvern shot to his feet. "Are you with me or not, Labyrinth?"

The professor sighed. "It would not be rational behavior to risk turning everything to chaos when all is working smoothly. I would need...an incentive."

And there it was. Wyvern snorted.

No matter how many fancy words or convoluted justifications the brilliant doctor wished to supply, it always boiled down to that one same question with every human being: *What's in it for me?*

Wyvern didn't need to be some sort of scientific genius to know that much.

"What would make *you* happy, doctor?" he asked, glad to turn the tables on him.

"Why, Nathan, you know me. All I ever wanted was to help ze human race improve itself. By *any means necessary.*" Labyrinth's tone was kind, but his eyes were merciless.

Utopians were terrifying.

"If I were given greater latitude to pursue my studies, and perhaps a steady supply of new test subjects to work with—"

"Consider it done," Wyvern said. The less he knew about the doctor's unnerving experiments on the human mind, the better.

"Hmm, zhen of course I will assist. Always I am pleased to further Progress. Care for a sherry? Shall we toast?"

Wyvern nodded, then accepted a small glass of the strong amber cordial from the bottle that the professor kept tucked inside his desk.

"To ze future," Dr. Labyrinth said.

"And the Black Crown," Wyvern answered heartily. Then he clinked his dainty cut-crystal glass to the professor's and downed his drink.

Relieved to get out of Vienna with his wits intact, Wyvern hastened on the next day in his quest, this time transporting the Black Fortress all the way to America.

It slammed down on a sleepy rural stretch of Long Island, New York. That was as close as he dared land to the great city.

After a tedious two-hour carriage ride, he finally arrived on bustling Wall Street.

No one could win the war without money, and flashy Mabus Marshwood was the Dark Druids' alchemist-in-chief.

Rumor had it the financier was one-quarter goblin, but it did not show in his very human appearance. He looked the part of the wealthy American gent, with slicked-back hair and a trim figure bedecked in fine clothes copied from French and English tailors.

He lived in a Gilded Age mansion down the street from the Vanderbilts and rubbed elbows in New York society with all the great robber barons of the age.

Aside from his secret recipe for turning lead into gold, he was wonderfully ambitious.

And blunt.

"Oh, I can really make this work for me!" he responded to Wyvern's explanation of the plan afoot. Marshwood clapped his hands together with typical American enthusiasm. "I like it! How exciting. You know money doesn't like to stand still, Wyvern. It must flow like water—always moving—but in Zolond's time, it's grown a little stagnant, dull.

"Believe me, I love to capitalize on something I know is happening in advance. But I abhor wasting resources or, worse, backing a scheme that won't pay off. So let me run some numbers..."

Wyvern strolled around admiring the paintings that adorned Marshwood's drawing room while the man himself scribbled columns of figures on a notepad and tapped away on an adding machine, mumbling to himself about dividends and compound interest.

Eyeing him, Wyvern actually *could* see a hint of gold goblin in the alchemist's face.

Of course, he'd never say so. He needed the money mage's cooperation.

When Marshwood had finished calculating odds and probabilities, he straightened up, chewing his lip. "Here's the thing, ol' man," he said. "You have my backing, but I need a bit of reassurance that it'll work. I'm afraid I'm with Viola on this. But, unlike her, you see, I don't have an army of vampires at my defense. I can't afford to face the likes of Zolond by myself if you should fail. I'll place my bets on you, Wyvern. But for now, I'll have to stick to the role of silent partner. I hope you understand. It's nothing personal; just business."

"Of course." Wyvern nodded. "For a mage of your standing, my dear Marshwood, that will have to do."

"Good luck," Marshwood whispered. Then he brightened and cheerfully flipped a coin. "Stay for dinner? The wife's hosting ambassadors or something."

"I must be on my way, but thank you."

Wyvern still had one more Council member left to visit, and he wanted to get it over with, because in many ways, he had saved the hardest for last.

Not yet finished in America, he jumped the Black Fortress more than a thousand miles to the south, splashing down at the edge of the vast and mysterious Louisiana bayou.

Steeling his spine that overcast afternoon, with thoughts of the

Black Crown and his newly assigned wife and son, he walked out across the precarious wooden footbridges to the swamp witch's cottage deep in the cypress marsh.

Mother Octavia Fouldon served as head witch of the Americas, with final authority over all practitioners of the craft, from the Salem witches of New England to the voodoo priestesses of New Orleans and the devotees of Santeria throughout the South.

One never would've thought the plump old Cajun crone was nearly so important, living humbly out here on the swamp with her mangy cat, Miasma.

But, in fact, Mother Fouldon was the most senior member of the Council, second only to Zolond himself.

She was a nasty old soul, worse than her horrid distant cousin with the sweet tooth—Grismelda of the Black Forest, who was always luring careless children to their doom in her gingerbread house.

Witches at this level, Wyvern knew, were almost always cannibals, if only for ritualistic purposes.

Himself, he found the practice unhealthy and distasteful, but he dared not move forward with his coup until he knew where Mother Fouldon stood on the matter of overthrowing Zolond. He did not need a witch of her power as an enemy.

Best to kill her now before she suspected anything if she showed signs of opposing his plan.

Frankly, he wasn't optimistic. Mother Fouldon and the Dark Master had known each other for at least a century. The swamp witch respected Zolond as one of the few mages on the planet superior to her.

As Wyvern cautiously approached her rambling wooden shack, he wondered why she did not conjure some palatial mansion for herself. Instead, her poky wooden cottage stood on stilts above the stagnant water, hemmed in by cypress trees veiled with Spanish moss.

Just then, a ripple in the water underneath the footbridge caught his eye. Blanching, Wyvern only now noticed huge alligators drifting slowly through the black water.

Despite his being a dragon lord with some inborn authority over such beasts, he took out his wand anyway, just in case any of Mother Fouldon's monstrous pets decided to attack.

Fortunately, he made it onto the wooden porch of her cottage, where he noticed a horned goat tied up, munching on some hay, and a big red tabby cat lying on the railing, gnawing on a catfish head.

It stank.

Then Mother Fouldon herself came clomping out through the screen door, her face wreathed in wrinkles, a kerchief tied around her head, and a yarn shawl draped around her shoulders.

A wand as well as a chatelaine's purse dangled from the belt around her thick waist; she looked at him with a belligerent glint in her hazel eyes.

"Well, if it ain't young Wyvern," she drawled. "What brings you out to my neck o' the woods, boy?"

The Nephilim warlock lifted his eyebrows, not exactly accustomed to being addressed as "boy."

The pugnacious old witch was chewing tobacco and spat brown juice that dinged into a can, still half glaring at him, sizing him up like he was some sort of an unsatisfactory grandson.

Though she barely came up to his solar plexus, the intensity of her stare was a little unnerving.

The goat bleated at that moment, breaking the tension.

"Nice goat," Wyvern said, welcoming the distraction, for she was difficult to read and it made him uneasy. "A pet?"

She glanced at the animal, then nodded at Wyvern, baring her brown teeth in a smile. "Every night I feed a goat to the gators." Then she gave him the evil eye. "Not always a goat."

Wyvern hid his gulp; he was fairly sure that had been a veiled threat. "I see."

As if on cue, an alligator angled itself perpendicular to the porch, where it floated in the brackish water with an air of nonchalance, as though it wished to listen in on their conversation.

Considering he had an Orange-Ruffed Darter pulling his personal chariot, Wyvern wasn't sure why he found the monstrous creatures so intimidating. Probably because his expensive carriage dragon was trained and these were wild.

The massive alligators were also under the command of a woman who might well be his mortal enemy.

When Wyvern cleared his throat, gathered his thoughts, and started to explain the reason for his visit, Mother Fouldon interrupted.

"I already know why ye're here, devil's whelp."

"You do?"

She scowled up at him and poked him in the chest. "Old Z's been a good leader for three hundred years. Why you throwin' him over?"

"Because he has been too lenient on the Order of the Yew Tree, Mother Fouldon," he said in a serious tone. "Why does he let our enemies continue to grow powerful when we could snuff them out and expand our influence? What is he waiting for?"

"Have you talked to him about it? Give him a chance to explain hisself?"

"I've tried. He doesn't listen." He hesitated. "I fear the Dark Master has come under an unsavory influence in recent weeks."

She gave him a searching look. "Ramona Bradford."

Wyvern nodded. "That's what I've been told."

"Humph. She ain't nothin'."

Wyvern kept his mouth shut, but he had heard rumors that the Elder witch had once blasted Mother Fouldon into a stupor during a wand battle about a century ago.

"Him and his hoity-toity English wench..." Clearly in a bad mood now, the swamp hag clomped away from Wyvern to the goat's end of the porch. She reached up and pulled the rope on a cowbell hanging from the corner of the porch roof.

The water came alive, rippling in all directions. Wyvern gripped his wand and backed away from the railing, moving toward the cottage wall as Mother Fouldon untied the goat.

"Chick, chick, chickies!" She clucked her tongue toward the water as she opened a little gate built into the railing. "Suppertime, y'all!"

She unceremoniously kicked the bleating goat into the water, where a great thrashing ensued.

Wyvern barely breathed as the alligators feasted. But the swamp witch seemed mollified when she shut the gate and came marching back to him.

"This is a dumb idear," she informed him. "Yer wet behind the ears yet. But seeing as how the others have agreed, I ain't sticking my neck out for Zolond. I reckon he wouldn't stick his neck out none for me. And a plague on that Ramona Bradford!" She spat tobacco again, and once more, it dinged angrily into the tin can. "You get it done," she ordered him. "Don't muck it up. But me, I'm stayin' out of it. Mind you, I won't tolerate no foolishness once *you're* the Dark Master, ya ken?"

"Yes, ma'am."

"Humph! Ya better say that." She scrutinized him as twilight began to settle over the swamp. "Truth is, I had me a little visit from Shemrazul the other night."

"You did?" He waved off a mosquito.

Mother Fouldon pointed into the murky distance amid the cypress trees and hanging moss. "See them swamp lights yonder?"

Wyvern followed the direction that her crooked finger pointed. A weird, bluish glow of gases flickered over the bog.

"The Horned One appeared to me in the shape of one of them there will-o'-wisps. Told me what you're up to. Said I ought to help. He's the boss, so..." She shrugged. "Don't mean I gotta like it none."

The alligators finished their supper and the black waters grew still.

"I understand," Wyvern said. "Thank you, Mother Fouldon. I won't let you down."

"Just make it quick on the ol' coot when ya put him down. Quick and painless. It's the least he deserves."

Wyvern nodded, relieved by her cooperation.

Yet the swamp hag's request that he kill Zolond in a fast and painless way made the reality of Wyvern's goal truly sink in—maybe for the first time.

Not until that moment had he pondered the actuality of it: killing Zolond.

He had killed plenty of people before. And it was not the Druid way to become emotionally attached to anyone, of course.

Still, as he returned to the Black Fortress, it made Wyvern feel slightly queasy just for a moment to contemplate killing the old man he had grown to know so well.

Zolond wasn't so bad.

If Wyvern had had a conscience, it would've started plaguing him from that moment forward.

But the queasy feeling dissipated within a few moments. In its place, a sense of accomplishment filled him. Indeed, a smile spread across Wyvern's face as he headed down the ink-black stairs to the throne room to tell his father the good news.

He had completed the task Shemrazul had set for him: Wyvern had secured his allies.

There were only two Council members he didn't bother with. Deathhand the Abomination and Lady Nebula Vail were Zolond loyalists and would only blow his cover prematurely. He would deal with them later.

All of which meant he was now ready to initialize the next phase of his coup.

Some of his co-conspirators wanted proof that he was Dark Master material?

Oh, he'd give them all the proof that they required. A grand demonstration of his power.

Very soon, he would launch a show of force that all of Magick-kind would talk about for centuries.

And the Order would never forget.

CHAPTER 53
Blue Waters

It was good to be adventuring again, Jake thought several days later as he strolled toward the bow of *The Wind Dancer*, the large wooden sailing yacht that Uncle Richard had borrowed from the Elders for their party's transport out to Poseidonia.

The Order owned the small, elegant ship and employed its capable captain and worthy crew, so there was no need to try to hide magical matters from them.

The fine teak deck rocked gently under Jake's feet until he reached the prow of the vessel and leaned on the rails. Gazing seaward, he let the balmy Mediterranean breeze ripple through his hair.

Dolphins swam along casually beside the sleek hundred-foot vessel as the wind puffed the three tiers of sails on both masts, fore and aft.

Though autumn had taken over the northern regions of the world, summer lingered around Southern Italy, Sicily, and the Greek islands, near their next stop.

The golden sunshine was a welcome reprieve from gray skies, and the turquoise water was still quite warm, so it would be a comfortable swim down to Poseidonia, ruled by Sapphira's father, King Nereus.

Jake was looking forward to seeing the merfolk's kingdom again—especially now that they wouldn't be having any more trouble from ol' Captain Davy Jones. Aye, it would take the infamous Lord of the Locker a good hundred years to put himself back together after Jake and Archie had blown him to smithereens on their last trip here.

At least they had stopped him from stealing the Atlantean orb that Sapphira had found near the Calypso Deep.

Musing on wild memories from that trip, Jake was glad to have something else to do other than worry about the prophecy and Wyvern's chilling wish to claim him for a son—something else to think about other than the swirling undercurrents of tension occurring in their group.

Janos and Isabelle were back to being friends, thankfully, but the news from Merlin Hall wasn't terribly encouraging.

The kids were able to talk to Aunt Ramona now and then through the communication device embedded in Dani's training gauntlet. The little Lightrider-to-be would click it on, then hold out her arm as they all stood around her.

This way, they were able to hear Aunt Ramona and speak to her if they wished. The Elder witch had asked how they were enjoying their first official diplomatic trip, and they told her they were having fun.

But when Jake wanted to know if they'd caught the mole, she had wearily admitted they'd had no success. Neither she nor Sir Peter nor Dame Oriel's team of ghosts had managed to uncover the Dark Druids' spy yet.

The ghosts had too much ground to cover between them, and, as for the spells and potions, nothing they had tried so far had worked.

Nixie asked for details about which spells they'd selected.

Aunt Ramona indulged her star pupil—for educational reasons, no doubt. "We've done a variety of truth-telling potions, silencing spells, aura revealers, finders' incantations... In truth, we're running out of options."

"But ma'am," Nixie said, "surely the mole is hidden behind multilayered masking or cloaking spells. Wouldn't these need to be peeled away first, before anything like that could be applied?"

Aunt Ramona had gone silent for a moment at that. No sound came from Dani's gauntlet but the crackling of the ethers.

"You may be onto something, Miss Valentine. An excellent suggestion. We'll try that."

It was too bad Aunt Ramona couldn't see Nixie's grin at that moment. Such smiles were rare from the young cynic.

"Happy to help," Nixie had said, while Archie slapped her shoulder and mouthed, *Atta girl!*

After the conversation ended, Nixie had told them that, unfortunately, unmasking spells took a few days to work—the more layers, the more time.

"But after that, then they should be able to have their spells sink in. I wonder what they'll try," she mused aloud. "A truth-teller or a silencing spell...? Personally, I'd choose the latter."

"What does that do?" Dani asked.

"Exactly what it sounds like," Nixie said with a shrug. "It'll mute the spy's voice so they can't tell the enemy what they know."

"Does it hurt?" Jake asked.

"I've never experimented with it myself, but I've heard it tickles."

Jake and Dani exchanged a startled look.

Then Isabelle glanced mischievously at her little brother. "Did someone say ticklish?"

She reached over and squeezed Archie's side. The boy genius folded sideways with a yelp.

Nixie joined in tickling Archie until he ran away in tears of laughter, shrieking, "Leave me alone!"

But such moments of levity were rare.

An undercurrent of anxiety gnawed at the group, especially after Aunt Ramona's frustrating news.

Uncle Richard and Aunt Claire were obviously concerned about larger matters, focused on their mission. And half the time, Jake could swear that Archie was hiding something.

The boy genius just seemed a little...off.

Jake asked him if something was bothering him, but Archie had mumbled indecipherably and pooh-poohed the question.

Whatever it was, he clearly wished to hide it, and Jake wasn't one to pry. Nixie seemed glum about it, too. Jake could only gather that Archie wasn't confiding in her, either. Maddox was still disgruntled about Isabelle rejecting him for once and for all—if that was the case. Jake wasn't sure.

Though their head Lightrider, the affable Sikh agent, Ranjit, was always calm and collected, serene, Tex was restless, still angry over what the Dark Druids had done to him and the other Lightriders.

Sometimes he peered into the distance with his ominous Texas squint, chewing a toothpick, as though, deep down, he was plotting revenge.

Only Dani remained generally cheerful, though she was anxious about missing her Lightrider classes and falling behind. Tex gave her some pointers, while Jake tried to pretend he wasn't eavesdropping on them, but of course he was.

Red, for his part, was not happy about being near the ocean again.

Since lions couldn't swim, he was afraid of boat travel even on a luxurious yacht, but he was making progress. Instead of flatly refusing to leave the beach, he was cowering in the boys' cabin, hiding his head under Jake's blanket.

The big baby, Jake thought affectionately.

Janos remained in his bat form during daylight hours and slept in his little black box until the sun went down. Isabelle had taken it upon herself to make sure the box stayed safely locked while their deadly friend was at his most vulnerable.

Derek and the twins conferred frequently in low tones about everything that was happening, trying hard "not to worry the children," but their furtiveness put the kids even more on edge.

Indeed, the only one who seemed perfectly at ease in all this was little Teddy.

He had become quite the traveler, that dog. Nails tapping, he scampered around the boat's deck in his little doggy life vest, enjoying their tour of magical places immensely.

Jake could only guess that the wee terrier was disappointed that the dreadful Piscean potion they'd all have to take didn't work on canines.

Alas, Teddy had to remain on the boat that day with Red and Miss Helena, whose inner feline wanted no part of visiting any sort of underwater destination. Janos also wasn't coming, since he couldn't go out in the daytime.

Isabelle also stayed behind. She claimed she didn't want to get her hair wet, but Jake knew she was merely being polite, offering that excuse. The empath clearly needed a break from the group and the burden of all their churning emotions.

In any case, there hadn't been much love lost between his beautiful blond cousin and the equally gorgeous, raven-haired Princess Sapphira.

For the rest of the diplomatic party, it was time to take the disgusting but effective Piscean potion.

Dani had gotten special permission from Finnderool to remove the Bud of Life so she could go along.

All of them dressed in their bathing costumes and jumped into the turquoise waves. Then Isabelle handed out vials of the potion from her perch on the ship's ladder and watched them swallow it with a wince.

Even though Jake knew for a fact that the Piscean potion worked, it was painful and scary going through that horrid process again, sprouting amphibious webbing between his fingers and toes, feeling gills open like gashes along the sides of his neck, and those few terrifying moments of being sure that he was drowning. His eyes grew strange, semi-transparent lids, then bulged a bit like a frog's to help him see better underwater.

Thankfully, the change only took about a minute, and when they had all recovered from transforming into mer-humans, off they swam.

Then everything was fine. The dolphins remained nearby to escort them down; Sapphira must've sent them.

What a funny-looking entourage they made, Jake thought, as they glided down and down through the water, passing by the dark, mysterious Seaweed Forest, where they had given Jones's shark-men the slip the last time they were here.

The kids hid their knowing smiles from Uncle Richard and Aunt Claire as they passed the overgrown colony of kelp. Archie and Isabelle's parents were already scandalized enough about the few brushes with doom that they *knew* about. Others, it seemed best not to reveal, especially not now.

Leave the diplomats their sanity, they all had agreed. But for their part, the rest of them remembered their dangerous adventure here all too well.

As they pressed on through ever deeper water, the beautiful seashell city of the merfolk and the king's coral palace soon came into sight.

Crown Princess Sapphira herself swam out with a retinue of brawny merman guards and more smiley dolphins to greet them. Her younger sister, Princess Liliana, hurried by her side on her seahorse Wallace, her braids floating out behind her.

Barely nine years old, Princess Lil had not come to Merlin Hall with the others who'd taken the Landwalker spell, but had stayed home to attend to her studies under Professor Pomodori. It was nice seeing the younger mermaid now. She hugged Dani; those two had become fast friends on their last visit here.

Greetings were exchanged, then they all swam down together to the palace, where King Nereus received them with full royal pomp.

The merman king still treated Jake like a returning hero after he and the others had saved their watery kingdom this past summer. Jake had even won the respect of Tyndaris, the stern captain of the palace guard.

The gray-haired and bespectacled Professor Pomodori, meanwhile, presented Archie with a Latin translation of an ancient book on Atlantis that he had found in the royal library.

The old scholar said it represented the bulk of his people's knowledge about the lost empire, so it was not to be shared with landers at large. But, as a token of his thanks to the boy genius for *his* role in saving the underwater kingdom, Pomodori had faithfully copied all the sketches as well as the text of the book onto the insides of clamshells.

"Mind you, you won't be able to see the letters once you go above the surface," Pomodori reminded his fellow scholar. "You'll have to put it in salt water in order for them to appear."

"I understand. Professor, truly, I am honored." Archie shook the old tutor's hand. "I will take good care of it, I promise."

"I know you will, my lad. So tell me about your latest experiments..."

Meanwhile, Maddox and Sapphira took a strolling sort of swim together in the undersea gardens to catch up on what each had been doing. Since both were stubborn, hard-nosed fighters, they got along well.

It was no secret that the royal mermaid had taken a bit of a fancy to the older lad. And no doubt the attentions of Bellissima helped to soothe the sting of Isabelle's rejection.

At the edge of the gardens, Dani was learning how to ride a seahorse from Princess Lil. The smaller princess had brought over her usual mount, Wallace, along with a second, larger seahorse with frilly purple fins for the redhead to try riding.

Neither the carrot nor the seahorse looked too sure about this. Jake watched in amusement, then decided to join them.

Unlike on the other stops on their journey, this time, he left the strategizing to the adults. He'd already saved the world once in this place. This time, why not just relax and have fun?

Everything they had gone through here this past summer reminded him that he might as well enjoy just being a kid.

While it lasted.

* * *

Meanwhile, far away in England, Lord Badgerton was laughing over supper with the skunkies. They'd had their soup and salad in the first course, and now dug into the main course, a marvelous roasted pheasant with tasty stuffing. Scarfing it down with speedy bites, Badgerton tried not to laugh with his mouth full over the antics of his clever niece and lively pair of nephews.

It was then, with his fork halfway to his mouth, that Badgerton suddenly felt an odd tickle in his throat. He paused and took a drink of hard cider. The tickle remained. In fact, it got stronger.

Oh dear. Tugging at his cravat, the shapeshifter lord glanced down nervously at his plate. *I hope there aren't walnuts in this stuffing.*

Prue continued rambling on about how she was the best student in shapeshifter class, to which both Charlie and Welton noisily objected.

"Uncle Boris, tell her to stop bragging!" Welton said.

"I'm better than both of you," Charlie declared through a mouthful of potatoes.

"Well, now—" Badgerton tried to speak, determined to keep the peace among the little rascals, but the itch in his throat intensified.

Since the cider had failed, he reached for his glass of water and quickly took a gulp.

The water went down easily enough. That was a relief. It meant his throat wasn't swelling up. He had an allergy to nuts.

Prue was smirking. "It's true, Uncle Boris. The teacher likes me best."

"Brown-noser!" Welton retorted.

"Now, children, I'm sure you are all equally—" Badgerton started, but he stopped with his mouth open, confused. Because no sound came out.

The kids were looking at him, as though waiting for him to speak.

He cleared his throat and tried again, but all that came out was a faint squeak like the air going out of the balloon.

"Uncle Boris, what's wrong with you?" Welton asked, scrunching up his big, pointy nose.

Alarmed, Badgerton took another drink of water and forced out a cough. He wanted to answer them, but again, nothing came out.

He could only mouth, *I seem to have lost my voice.*

All three children looked puzzled and astonished, and then they burst out laughing, not realizing the seriousness of the situation.

"Uncle Boris, stop teasing us!" Welton said.

"I dunno." Charlie scrutinized Badgerton. "He looks a little...funny."

"You're thick," Prue retorted. "Uncle Boris just doesn't want to admit he *knows* I'm the best because he doesn't want to hurt your feelings."

But, in truth, Uncle Boris was starting to panic.

He gulped down the rest of his water, cleared his throat a few more times to no avail, and then, heart pounding, throat itching madly, he excused himself from the table by crude sign language.

The triplets whined at his abrupt departure, but he had to get back to his own rooms. This was no allergic reaction. He was only a shapeshifter, but he knew magic when it was inflicted on him.

Who could do such a thing to an Elder? Who would dare?

Could Wyvern be behind this?

The thought filled Badgerton with dread.

True, the tunnel he'd promised the Nephilim lord was not yet finished, but why would that madman resort to this sort of low, dirty trick? Just to get his attention?

Unfortunately, when Badgerton fled back to his private suite, he got an answer that he desperately despised.

Upon opening the door to his apartments, the first thing he saw was a sealed letter lying on the floor, just beyond the threshold. Someone must have pushed it under the door.

Stepping in, he quickly shut the door behind him, then bent and picked up the note.

Perhaps this would contain some sort of explanation for his intolerable predicament.

His throat itching away, he quickly tore the letter open, and there, lo and behold, was an official communique from none other than Sir Peter Quince.

MEMORANDUM
FROM THE DESK OF THE CHANCELLOR

To: All Elders and Department Heads

Dear Ladies and Gentlemen:

In the coming days, all Elders and department heads are hereby requested to make themselves available for an interview with our panel of empaths. A security concern has arisen, and we wish to remove all possibility of suspicion from your names. We regret to inform you that while, rest assured, these interviews are only a formality, they are mandatory. All staff members will submit to questioning.

We thank you in advance for your cooperation. Should you wish to bring legal representation, you may do so at your own expense.

Please notify Jillian with your availability so we can add you to the schedule. The interviews will require less than an hour of your time.

Full transparency is advised.

Cordially yours,
Sir Peter Quince

Badgerton clutched his chest and felt himself turn white as soon as he finished reading. He skimmed the letter again all the way through twice, then flung it away from him with a silent shriek.

His mind raced. *They know! They clearly know now there's an informant. They've done a silencing spell and now they want to question us.*

As soon as they see I've lost my voice, they'll know it's me!

A cold sweat sprang out on his brow as he realized he was as good as caught already.

Locking the door behind him, he walked on shaky legs over to the cabinet where he had hidden the black calling candle Wyvern had given him. Lord, Badgerton wished he'd never laid eyes on that dreadful Nephilim, but it was too late to find his conscience now.

Badgerton tried three times to light the candle, but his hands were shaking too badly. Then he realized he did not even have a voice with which to tell Wyvern the situation.

He gave up on the candle for the moment and yanked out a piece of paper and a pencil, then wrote out a simple message in big block letters:

> HELP! SILENCING SPELL!
> I'M ABOUT TO GET CAUGHT!

He pressed so hard in his fright that he snapped the pencil tip, but the message was clear enough. *Short, to the point. I like it.*

Now the candle.

Again, he burned through several matches, striking one after another in his effort to light the blasted thing, his throat itching madly all the while. If he were in possession of his voice, he'd be cursing up a storm at that moment.

Finally, he managed to get the stupid thing lit after a few more tries.

To his relief, the wick caught; the flame gleamed in the dim of a chilly October evening. As the smoke curled in a gray cloud above the calling candle the warlock had given him, Badgerton waited anxiously for his co-conspirator to appear. He rubbed his hands together, frigid with fear as he sat down across from his desk where the sinister candle sent out its message through the ethers.

It seemed to take forever, but finally, Wyvern's face appeared in the smoke.

"Who's there?" he demanded, squinting out of the smoke. "Oh. It's you."

Badgerton threw up his hands in frustration.

"Well? What do you want?" Wyvern demanded.

Badgerton held up the message he'd written for Wyvern to see.

The warlock didn't look. "Why aren't you talking? Don't be annoying, Badgerton. I'm busy. Tell me what's the matter."

Badgerton gestured frantically at his mouth and pointed to his throat, made a few choking sounds to demonstrate, then held up the note insistently again.

"What's this?" Wyvern's smoky head leaned closer as he peered at the note, looking irritated.

Badgerton moved the paper closer so he could see, nearly catching it on fire.

"Oh bloody— A silencing spell? When did this happen?"

Badgerton tried to gesture that it had just occurred, but Wyvern quickly grew frustrated by this vexing game of charades.

"Hold on. Let me get my wand. I'll fix you." Wyvern shook his smoky head at him, then withdrew.

Badgerton sat very still and waited, wide-eyed with anxiety. A moment later, Wyvern reappeared with his wand. He closed his eyes for a long moment, inhaled through his Roman nose, then spoke an incantation in low, garbled syllables, as though he were speaking backward.

It was dreadful to listen to, that warlock language. But the itching in Badgerton's throat eased, and all of a sudden, he could talk again.

"Ack!" he said. He coughed a few times and cleared his throat. "Oh, thank goodness!"

Wyvern stared dully at him. "Explain. Now."

"Ahem! They must've realized there's a spy in the palace, my lord," Badgerton whispered as loudly as he dared. "I was at dinner with the children when my voice disappeared for no reason!"

Wyvern gave a sage nod. "A silencing spell. Probably what I would do to a spy. For starters."

"Then I came back to my rooms and there was a letter under the door. They're assembling a panel of empaths to interrogate all of the staff members. They want everyone to schedule with them. Including me!"

"Calm down. At least now you can talk," Wyvern said. He thought for a moment. "I daresay we ought to turn their suspicions onto someone else, don't you think?"

Badgerton's eyes widened. "Oh yes, good idea, my lord!"

"Who do you think cast this spell on you? The Bradford witch?"

He frowned. "Hmm, no, I doubt it. She's reluctant to use magic except in emergencies. It had to be Sir Peter. He's the one who sent out this letter."

"Quince," Wyvern said with a sneer. A snaky gleam came into his eyes. "Wants you to schedule with his wife, you say?"

Badgerton nodded anxiously.

"Dear Sir Peter's quite smitten with the little lady. Isn't he?" Wyvern hissed, his pupils flickering longwise.

"Y-yes, my lord. Revoltingly so—even though she's nothing but a common mortal."

"Perfect," Wyvern murmured. "Leave this to me. As for you, *Boris,* you need you get out there and finish the blasted tunnel. Tonight."

"Tonight? You can't be serious—"

"You said it's almost done."

"Yes, b-but— Don't you understand? They know there's a mole! You've got to get me out of here before I'm caught!"

"Boris. Calm down and listen carefully." Wyvern's smoky head grew larger and stared imposingly at Badgerton. "That memorandum from Peter Quince proves the time has come to act. They already know they have a mole. I don't intend to give the Elders any more time to prepare for my attack.

"We are coming. Tonight. And, by Shemrazul's horns, if that tunnel is not finished when I get there, well, you remember my owl."

Badgerton gulped. Oh, he remembered.

"You would never dream of reneging on our agreement, I'm sure?" Wyvern said.

"N-n-no, o-of course not, my lord. I-I just thought it might be prudent to postpone until things calm down around here—"

"No. My hour is at hand. You go finish the tunnel while I cast suspicion elsewhere to distract and confuse them. How long do you need until you can break through to the other side?"

Badgerton thought about it. "Four hours."

"Perfect," Wyvern growled. He glanced downward, probably at his fob watch. "It's seven now. We'll be there by midnight. And my lord shapeshifter?"

"Yes, sir?" Badgerton asked, cringing.

"Do not forget the deal we made. The Proteus power awaits you, along with a seat on my Council. But if you fail me: my owl eats your precious skunkies alive."

With this dire warning, Wyvern's head vanished from the candle smoke.

Badgerton slumped in his chair, his heart still pounding. For a long moment, he pondered the enormity of what he had got himself tangled up in. What he stood to lose…

And what he still could gain.

A member of the Dark Druid Council! Why, in that position, imbued with the Proteus power, he would rule over all dark-leaning shapeshifters in the world!

He could even lose this homely, pudgy shape forever and transform himself into a chap as good-looking as, say, that insufferable vampire.

The possibilities were endless...

Steeling his resolve, Badgerton took the memo from Sir Peter, held it over the calling candle, and took cold pleasure in watching it burn.

Those nosy empaths could go to Hades before they would ever interrogate him.

To blazes with them all. He was sick of everybody here, so many who thought they were better than him and his kind. They'd soon learn who was really their superior.

Ha. He could hardly wait to see the looks on the other Elders' faces when Wyvern showed up at Merlin Hall with his army of Noxu.

Then Badgerton rose from the chair, blew out the candle, and changed himself into his animal form.

Scampering out of the palace for the last time, he bade a scoffing farewell to Merlin Hall. Then he scurried off into the night to uphold his end of the deal he had made with the devil's son.

* * *

Turning from the black candle, Wyvern continued to balance the glowing ball of magic he had extracted from Badgerton on the tip of his wand.

He wasn't finished with it yet. Time to redirect it.

The contained and isolated silencing spell shone in the gloom of his chamber, a pale blue sphere. Wyvern grimaced, for he could taste the magical signature, as it were, of the wizard who had cast it.

Bloody Peter Quince.

Ugh. Wyvern couldn't stand him. He saw no reason why any man should be so annoyingly happy. Suffice to say, they had tangled before. All too well he remembered the impressive Thunderfist that Quince had created to pound on the doors of the Black Fortress in that battle back in June.

Ah well. The trick that Wyvern was about to pay Quince back with was subtler but much more amusing.

It was an easy solution, too, considering that Wyvern's own spells could not penetrate the countless layers of enchantment that, for centuries, had formed a protective magical dome over Merlin Hall.

The blasted dome was the reason he had needed Badgerton's help in the first place.

If the Dark Druids could not shatter the dome from the air or pound their way through it from ground level (they'd tried numerous times over the centuries), then Wyvern would simply tunnel under it and come up inside, thanks to the badger man's particular skills as a burrowing expert.

Wyvern was fortunate that Badgerton was such a malcontent; it hadn't been very difficult persuading him.

Then Wyvern took a deep breath and let it out, clearing his mind for the task at hand.

Still containing and controlling Quince's silencing spell on the tip of his wand, he closed his eyes and concentrated.

Long-distance spells took a great deal of power, but at least Sir Peter's spell would have no trouble sailing right back in through the dome.

With a few pointed incantations and a sudden burst of power, Wyvern recast the silencing spell onto its *new* target.

The silvery-blue orb of magic sped away from his wand at lightning speed.

It zoomed out of his chamber, right through the wall, exiting the Black Fortress to speed out into the night.

Wyvern kept his mind fixed carefully on his intended target as he waited for the orb to travel from here to there.

In his mind's eye, he saw it fly over the North Sea like a shooting star. Then the green isle of his homeland zoomed into sight: England.

He would be there soon. In the blink of an eye, the spell careened across several counties heading for Wiltshire.

Wyvern saw the white outline of Aelfric the Long Man in the dark, the towering guardian of Merlin Hall, his silhouette scored into the chalk hill behind which the palace was hidden.

They'd have to be prepared to deal with Aelfric tonight, too...

Wyvern smiled as he sensed the orb pierce the dome without the slightest friction, given that it was Sir Peter's working; then it plunged down through the roof of Merlin Hall and began rushing through the palace, seeking its target.

It careened down hallways, past opulent chambers, whizzing by countless Order idiots who barely noticed it.

The bright little ball of magic whooshed out the far end of the palace and zoomed up a path, heading toward the stately manor that stood apart from the palace. The Chancellor's House.

Sir Peter's home, where he lived in such sickening domestic bliss.

The shiny orb penetrated the front door and raced through the cushy chambers, seeking the person Wyvern had chosen.

His lips curled and his eyes flicked open with pleasure as he felt the spell hit its intended mark.

He could see her bustling about the kitchen, a slim lady in a frilly apron with her blond hair pinned up. Quite pretty.

He watched her pull the oven door open and peek in at some biscuits, then pick up a wooden spoon and stir a hearty stew simmering atop the stove. Why, he could almost smell the hint of nutmeg and bay leaf in the stew, almost feel the warmth of the wife's cozy domain.

Jillian Quince had not yet realized she'd been stricken.

Since she was alone, she hadn't tried speaking yet; there was no one to talk to. But soon she'd realize her voice had gone missing.

And so would her mate.

Though it would have been delightful to watch the coming drama in the Quince household unfold, Wyvern had work to do.

He rose, slid his wand back into its holster, then strode out of his chamber to go ready the troops for battle. He would check in with Shemrazul to confirm his plan, of course, but he knew in his bones that the hour of his destiny had come.

At last, he would show the rest of the Council what a *real* Dark Master could do.

Tonight he was taking Merlin Hall.

CHAPTER 54

The Night Watch

There was far too much sun in this place, but Isabelle's light knock on his little wooden bat-coffin each evening of their journey woke Janos with the signal that it was safe to come out now: night had fallen.

As per their habit, she unlocked the box with the key he had entrusted to her; she'd been wearing it on a fine silver chain around her neck for safekeeping. She would then retreat from his room to leave him his privacy as he readied himself for his overnight shift on sentry duty.

On that particular evening, it was about seven o'clock when she gave him the signal.

"Morning!" she called cheerfully, and if a bat could smile, Janos smiled.

Then he listened to her leaving, heard every soft footfall with his intense hearing as she climbed up the hatch and returned abovedeck.

Only then did he emerge from the box, for young ladies didn't like icky creatures like bats. Everybody knew that.

Returning to his human form, Janos stretched a bit, yawned and washed up, then dressed for the night, taking care to arm himself well. Vampire or not, he was on Guardian duty here, after all. It rather shocked him to realize how good it felt to have a sense of purpose again.

He buckled his weapons belt around his waist, checked his darkling blade, then tossed back a glass of his usual stag's blood breakfast. It was not fresh, but it was sufficient to keep him alive.

At last, he climbed up the hatch onto the moonlit deck of the fine yacht, where a beautiful sight greeted him.

On all sides, the silvered waves rippled out gently while the tide whispered in the moonlight. Even a ruined Guardian could appreciate the smell of the sea salt in the silky night air, the sparkling stars clustered overhead against a black sky.

The pearly sails hugged the yardarms, still furled while *The Wind Dancer* drifted at anchor.

It was such a beautiful night that he was tempted to change himself back into a bat for a few minutes just so he could fly around and see it all from above. But he had an important duty here. He was the night watch, and if anyone came near this vessel, he'd tear them limb from limb.

Especially with *her* here.

He walked across the gently swaying decks to where Isabelle stood at the rails, staring down at the water while the breeze played with her long hair. "Hullo, you."

She looked over her shoulder with a warm smile as he approached. "There you are."

Janos smiled back. He had a feeling that she was the reason he had had such a good day's sleep again on this trip. He liked being around her. It was soothing and soft and made him feel strangely safe—which was odd, indeed, considering he was the one who was supposed to be the protector here.

Ah well. Nothing about his reaction to the unicorn girl made any sense to him. All he knew was that her presence comforted him somehow. The burden of his tragedy weighed less heavily on him these days.

"Surprised they're not back yet," Janos remarked as he leaned on the ship's railing beside her.

She chuckled. "King Nereus is probably making them watch a turtle ballet."

"Oh? That sounds interesting."

"It is. For about ten minutes," she said. "Unfortunately, it normally drags on for two hours."

"Aha. So, you don't regret missing out, eh?"

"Not at all. But if you still want to go down and see Coral City, there's more of that potion left." She gestured toward the potion box. "The merfolk kingdom is an amazing sight."

He gave her a mock frown. "Then who would look after you and your governess, Miss Bradford?"

Izzy smiled. "I don't think anyone's going to attack us out here on the boat, Janos."

He groaned and dropped his head back. "Oh, you had to say that."

She laughed.

He smiled. "Where is Miss Helena, anyway?"

"I'm afraid our poor leopard lady had been seasick all day," Izzy said. "She's lying down in her cabin. She was looking quite green the last I saw her."

"Oh, that is unfortunate." Janos glanced around at the lamp-lit decks. Everything seemed to be in order. "Anything else going on today that I should know about?"

"No." She shook her head. "It's been wonderfully quiet. The group will probably be back soon, but I, for one, am glad to have had a break." With that, she sat down, folded her arms on the lower railing, and gazed at the waves in contentment, dangling her feet over the side.

Janos noticed with amusement that she had taken off her shoes. "What are we doing, then?"

"Enjoying the sea spray."

"Aha. Why? Is it fun?"

"It will be when I summon some dolphins." She sent him a twinkling smile. "Do you like dolphins, Janos?"

"I dunno, never tried one. They're warm-blooded, aren't they? Could be tasty."

She smacked him on the arm as he swung down to sit beside her. "You are terrible!"

"Yes, yes, that's been well established," he said, laughing.

"Now be quiet and let me fetch them."

He snorted. "Yes, ma'am."

Then Izzy closed her eyes, held her hand out over the waves, and sent forth a telepathic message to any dolphins nearby to come and play with her.

Apparently, Janos wasn't the only one who couldn't seem to resist her, for a trio of dolphins promptly arrived. She didn't even have to bribe them with sardines. They swam right over to the side of the boat, shy at first, but encouraged by her soft words.

From the moment the creatures surfaced, Janos was utterly amazed.

They were huge animals, ten feet long and several hundred pounds each, but as friendly and playful as oversized, watery dogs.

Soon they were clicking and squeaking and waving their flippers at the two of them, much to his delight. The dolphins bobbed upright in the water beside the boat, tossing their heads, whistling and chattering at Isabelle like eager children all talking to her at once.

After a little while, she somehow got them doing tricks. The silly creatures seemed eager to amuse her and Janos with their antics.

The dolphins leaped and danced, splashed about and wobbled upright across the water. Janos laughed, then let out a wordless exclamation as one of them corkscrewed through the air. Not to be outdone, another rocketed up from the waves and somersaulted six feet above the surface, landing with a great splash.

"Bravo!" Isabelle cheered and applauded while Janos wiped salt water out of his eyes.

"Now I'm awake," he muttered.

"I'm so tempted to jump in with them!"

"No, no, no, don't do that."

"But they're so adorable!" She continued chuckling and reaching down to pet them, praising the creatures.

It was good to see her smile again, he thought. In truth, he'd been a little worried about her the past few days. All of the tensions roiling their party seemed to be wearing her down.

She never complained, so he'd taken it upon himself to keep an eye on her.

All Janos knew was that *he* would not have wanted her gift. His own telepathic power was different—colder, more detached.

It was one thing to be able to read people's thoughts when he put forth the effort, but it must be a burden always sensing others' feelings—as if one's own weren't difficult enough. He was glad, in any case, that she'd had some time to recover today. This dolphin show had been just the thing to lift both their spirits.

Though their splashy new friends settled down a bit at that point, they did not leave. Instead, the dolphins lingered around the boat, swimming back and forth below the spot where Izzy and Janos sat side by side.

They lapsed into companionable silence.

Janos savored the rare moment of peace. Then she giggled and pointed at one of the dolphins, who rudely bumped his pals aside as he swam.

"Rudesby! Did you see that?" She glanced at Janos, her eyes shining, so full of innocent joy.

He gazed at her, wonderstruck. God, when was the last time he had even witnessed real joy, let alone felt it? But somehow she had given that gift to him tonight.

"We should name him Jake. What?" she asked, a curious smile tugging at her lips as she noticed his starstruck gaze.

"Nothing." Janos smiled at her, captivated. But if he did not get away from her this instant, he was going to do something rash. "I, ah, I think I'd better go take a turn around the decks. Make sure everything's in order."

"Wait. I have something for you." She captured his hand to stop him from leaving.

"What is it?" he asked, lingering, against his better judgment.

"Hold on. I'll be right back." She climbed to her feet.

Janos turned from the railing, watching her pad over to where the potion box sat. She moved it aside, lifting a second, larger wooden case that had been stacked underneath it. She brought it back to him and sat down again.

"What's this?"

She flipped the latch and opened it. "A set of magical toys that Aunt Ramona gave me when I was little."

"You're still little."

She scowled at him for that, then picked up one of the colorful items inside and handed it to him: a little paper lantern in the shape of a flower.

A pink lotus, to be exact.

Janos furrowed his brow as she also took one—a daisy. "What do you do with these?"

She turned the daisy upside down to show him. "One twist of the stem makes them light up, then you pinch the base, and that makes them float like helium balloons. They're called Floating Flowers. Look."

She demonstrated, twisting the daisy's stem so that a softly glowing light popped on inside of it, illuminating its white petals and yellow center. Then she squeezed the green base and opened her hand to release it.

Sure enough, the illuminated daisy slowly righted itself, floating between them in midair.

She captured it as it started rising, before it floated away.

"Uh-huh," Janos said, charmed at the toy but puzzled, as always, with this girl. "And you packed these why?"

Izzy hesitated. "I don't mean to overstep my bounds, but I...I thought we could use them in a little ceremony together, just you and me, to commemorate your hatchlings. D-do you think that would be suitable?"

Janos stared at her, taken aback.

"As you said," she added earnestly, "they were only innocent children."

Janos felt a lump rise in his throat, but managed to nod. "Yes. They would have liked that."

For the next short while, Isabelle lit up the floating flowers in solemn silence and handed them to him.

Janos pinched the base and reached out over the waves with one cupped lightly in his grasp. Then he loosened his fingers and whispered the name of each child in succession, remembering them as the flower floated up and up toward the moon.

Tiny glowing roses. Dahlias. Marigolds and pansies. Peonies, buttercups, lilacs, and begonias. Carnations, daffodils...whichever bloom seemed to fit each child.

His heart was no less broken, but honoring them helped.

Isabelle and he repeated this ritual over and over again with no sound but the lapping of the waves against the boat, until the case was empty and dozens of floating flowers hung in the dark sky, glowing in soft, ethereal colors to rival the moon. Already, they were drifting away on the wind, traveling off the port stern, out beyond the anchor.

Janos stared after them with a mist of tears in his eyes, but what could he do but let them go? Having given the urchins at least some semblance of a memorial, he felt some of the burden of his grief float away with the flower lanterns on the soft night breeze.

At last, he turned to Isabelle. Her gaze poured out compassion on him.

Janos captured her hand and kissed it reverently, closing his eyes. "Thank you."

When he opened them again and looked at her, she nodded once, tears in her eyes. She clasped his hand as he held on to hers. "You loved them, I know."

He took a deep breath, nodded, and lowered his gaze.

"What of their mothers?" she murmured after a moment. "Do you miss them, too?"

He looked askance at her, finding his way back somehow to his usual wry humor at last. "Immortal bloodsucking witches?" He shuddered half in jest and shook his head. “Clearly, I have dreadful taste in women.”

“It’s improving,” she teased with a sparkle in her eyes that said, *You’re mine. Eventually.*

He begged to differ, at least on the outside, so he pinched her cheek as one would an adorable toddler. “Behave yourself, pipsqueak. I have to go to work.”

“What, over there?” she asked, glancing toward the rest of the yacht’s long, moonlit deck.

“Yes. *Aaaall* the way over there.” *A safe distance from you.* Janos gave her a smile.

“If you must.” Her smile said she didn’t want him to go—and that was exactly why he should. “And I am not a pipsqueak, I’ll have you know.”

“Yes, you are. Don’t fall in,” he advised, climbing to his feet.

She gave him a salute. “Aye-aye, cap’n.”

He snorted and walked away, squaring his shoulders after that poignant ordeal and returning his attention firmly to his duties.

What she’d said earlier was right, of course: it was quiet out here on the water, far from danger. Nevertheless, he began walking the perimeter of the deck, scanning in all directions.

He could still see the Floating Flowers in the sky, but in the farther distance, across a gulf of watery blackness, clusters of tiny lights marked the town of Taormina. Right alongside the hull, the yacht’s own lanterns spilled blotches of illumination onto the waves like liquid gold.

Somewhere behind them, Janos supposed, was the beautiful Villa da Palma, a beachside mansion owned by the Order.

The villa’s elegant terrace was built around a waypoint; their traveling party had arrived there before sailing off on *The Wind Dancer.*

Janos wasn’t sure what their next stop would be after this. He mused on it as he continued scanning the horizon, both to starboard and port. Dotting the listless sea here and there, he saw the green or red sidelights of other vessels moored for the night.

They did not concern him. They were far off, and none showed any signs of coming nearer.

He walked on. The deck rocked gently beneath his feet, but Janos compensated for its motion with ease. Overhead, a few isolated clouds wandered across the sky, giving the moon a wide berth. He listened to the lulling rhythm of the waves patting the hull and the steady creaking of weathered wood and ropes.

At his back now, he could hear the dolphins splashing again, jumping and clowning around to amuse Isabelle. The music of her laughter lilted over the deck and made Janos smile in spite of himself.

When he reached the back of the boat, he let his gaze follow the taut, heavy chain that angled down from the stern and disappeared beneath the waves. On the other end, somewhere below, was the anchor, holding the ship steady.

For some reason, the thought of the anchor reminded him of Derek, an immovable object in a constantly shifting sea.

Janos checked his fob watch, then rounded the stern, heading back up the starboard side of the deck, where he exchanged polite nods with a seaman on duty.

Strolling back toward the bow, he was about midship when he heard a splash a few yards out from the side of the boat. It was just one of the dolphins surfacing, puffing water out of its blowhole. He paused for a minute, turning toward the sea and resting his elbows on the railing.

The dolphin swam toward him, then passed under the boat and disappeared. Janos gazed into the distance, where the Floating Flowers had begun to wink out of sight.

He savored the balmy night breeze caressing his cheek, not missing the cold weather up north. It would only be worse when they returned.

Winter was coming. In more ways than one.

For a moment, he thought of his ruined castle and the fact that there was no one to go home to anymore.

But he let the wind take his sorrow with it and surrendered to the first truly peaceful moment he had known in ages. Certainly since the night of the fire.

Unfortunately, it was short-lived. For it all began to unravel when a shiver of premonition ran through his body.

Still leaning at the rails, he went very still and listened inwardly.

What made a person a Guardian was the ability to sense danger in advance, so he could get there before it arrived.

The sensation of danger approaching grew stronger. Janos straightened up from the railing, turned around, and scanned the ship with sharpening alertness.

Still, nothing. But something was wrong. He could feel it.

Without warning, his Guardian instincts suddenly ignited. An overwhelming certainty of danger pulsated through him.

But where, and to whom?

His first thought was of Isabelle.

In a flash, blending vampire prowess with Guardian abilities, he launched himself forward in a vertical leap up onto the lowest yardarm of the foremast, balanced there just long enough to draw his blade, his gaze homing in on her.

She had risen to her feet and backed away from the rails.

Was something coming toward the boat?

Janos vaulted down a few feet away from her on the deck. She wore a look of dread on her face, and as he landed, she let out a small cry of pain and bent forward slightly, clutching her temples.

That was not what he'd expected.

"Isabelle! What's wrong?" In the blink of an eye, he whooshed to her side, closing the distance between them. He clasped her elbow to steady her. "What happened? Answer me!"

She reached for him, holding on to his arm and the lapel of his jacket. "The most dreadful feeling. Something's wrong. Something terrible."

Her answer amazed him. "You felt it too?"

She looked likewise startled. "What *was* that?"

"I don't know," he said. "I thought you were under attack. Did you see something in the water?"

"No." She shook her head, still looking dazed.

"Then what did you sense?" he asked.

"I'm not sure. But it felt horrible. Like something evil drawing near."

Janos clenched his jaw, putting his arm around her protectively as he glanced in all directions, his darkling blade in his other hand. If only he had some idea of what the source of the threat might be!

"Unfortunately, my instincts aren't what they used to be," he said in a taut voice.

"Perhaps if we both try at the same time, we can figure out where it's coming from," she said, still looking pale and a little queasy.

"Very well." He closed his eyes and leaned his forehead against hers.

Silent, motionless, they both concentrated on homing in on the source of the danger. With her beside him, clarity pierced through the fog that had long muffled his Guardian instincts. Their combined efforts seem to multiply his abilities.

Perhaps it did the same to hers, for they opened their eyes at the same time, looked at each other, and spoke simultaneously: "Merlin Hall."

"Something's wrong at the palace," Janos clipped out.

Izzy nodded. "I could swear one of my relatives is in danger."

"Who? Ramona's at Merlin Hall."

She furrowed her brow, her gaze faraway as her mind turned over the problem. "It didn't feel like it was coming from Aunt Ramona."

Janos tensed. "Jake."

He released her, striding over to the rails and peering down into the black water. "We have to get the group back up here, now. Where's that underwater potion? I'll take it immediately and swim down to fetch them—"

"No need! I can send the dolphins. They'll give Sapphira the message, then Derek can bring everyone back to the boat. Don't worry, King Nereus has loads of security," she added, hurrying back to the rails. "The head of his palace guard, Captain Tyndaris, is trustworthy. Once the dolphins communicate the threat, I'm sure he'll send a contingent to escort our party back."

Janos frowned, but Isabelle was already hanging over the edge of the boat, summoning the dolphins near to give them their instructions.

Having seen the creatures' silly antics, he was not at all sure about entrusting so vital a message to a bunch of fish.

"Trust me. They can do it," she said, sensing his doubt. "They are extremely intelligent."

"Izzy, they're animals!"

"They are pure, loving spirits! Such creatures will always help the cause of good."

Well, that was a subject where Janos was out of his depth, so he kept his mouth shut.

Since the dolphins were still loitering around the boat, Izzy stretched her hand out over the water once more, sending her thoughts telepathically into the animals' minds.

The dolphins clicked and squeaked and bobbed their heads as if they understood. A moment later, they dove through the waves with a splash of their tails and darted off into the deep.

Janos stared after them, frowning with uncertainty as Isabelle rose and turned around. “You’re sure about this?”

She nodded. “Trust me.”

He looked deep into her eyes and decided to give it a chance. “Very well. You should go below, just in case the threat is closer than it seems. Check in on Miss Helena—and tell the Gryphon to quit being a baby and get up here. I could use his eagle eyes to help keep watch.”

“What are you going to do?” she asked, already heading for the hatch while he strode off down the deck.

“I’m going to let the captain know to rouse the crew and get ready to make sail. As soon as the rest of our party arrives, we head for the Villa di Palma. We need to get to the waypoint and return to Merlin Hall posthaste.”

CHAPTER 55
Treachery

Unbeknownst to Isabelle, she was right: the intense dread and horror she had sensed indeed came from one of her own kin. But it wasn't Jake whose feelings she was sensing. If that were the case, she would only have felt utter boredom at the turtle ballet.

No, the terror she had tasted came not from her cousin, but her felonious uncle.

Waldrick was aghast, gripping the metal railing before him as he stared down at the army of Noxu warriors assembled in the vast onyx hall below, just behind the closed drawbridge.

Standing alone on an upper gallery with a view down into the huge space, he could not believe what he saw unfolding within the walls of the Black Fortress.

The half-troll barbarians were beating their shields and sending up a clamor of chants and battle-hungry yowls, some two hundred strong—the full regiment of the palace guards.

Whipping the tusked horde into a frenzy was none other than General Archeron Raige. The Dark Druids' legendary military expert had arrived earlier today. Presently, Raige swaggered back and forth in front of his troops, the stump of a cigar hanging out of his lips as he rallied them for an apparent attack on Merlin Hall.

"No mercy, boys. Destroy everything in your path..."

Waldrick's terror tripled upon hearing that. Dry-mouthed, he could feel his heart slamming like it might crack his ribs.

But if the legendary Archeron Raige wasn't bad enough, alas, he wasn't the only freak show to arrive here over the past few days. There were more.

Wyvern had been jumping the Fortress all over the globe in recent days, Waldrick had noticed. But he hadn't thought much about it at the time, still shaken after finding his brother and the rest of the comatose Lightriders in that bizarre cavern in the base of the Black Fortress.

It was only this evening that Waldrick realized that something huge was about to happen.

He couldn't decide which one of the new arrivals was most terrifying. He looked around slowly at them all, his heart in his throat.

Raige was pure brute force.

Duradel, by contrast, the blind oracle, was quiet and unnerving. When wood elves went bad, they joined their evil counterparts, an eerie folk known as the Drow.

Wyvern was speaking to the pale-haired prophet with his manticore by his side in a shadowy corner of the huge hall below, near the mechanisms for raising and lowering the drawbridge.

The mysterious dark elf seer wore a hooded black cloak that offered a glimpse of his moon-pale hair. Duradel gripped a staff covered in carvings and listened to Wyvern's confidences with white, staring eyes.

Meanwhile, standing closer by, almost underneath Waldrick's balcony, Fionnula twirled her wand idly in her fingers as she swapped beauty secrets with the ageless Red Queen. He could hear a little of the ladies' conversation despite the Noxu clamor, thanks to the hall's acoustics.

"I'm really looking forward to raiding that library of theirs," the sea-witch was saying. "Their collection of grimoires is second to none."

Viola Sangray nodded, but looked bored.

The vampire queen had glided in just tonight, as soon as it got dark, with an entourage of half a dozen elegant courtiers, male and female.

The other well-dressed vampires sauntered around restlessly here and there, sharpening their blades...and licking their fangs for the taste of blood.

Order blood.

Waldrick could not believe the Nephilim really meant to do this. Invade Merlin Hall? It was impossible. Madness.

It would never work. The Dark Druids would never win. They were all going to die—and Waldrick feared he would die alongside them, even though he'd barely had a choice in this.

But then, even worse was the thought of their plot succeeding.

Waldrick did his best to hide his horror at the prospect of evil finally and truly overcoming good, since he, too, was supposed to be a villain.

But he was petrified.

"Let's just hope that stupid beaver gets his tunnel done on time," the vampire queen said to the sea-witch. "What did Wyvern promise him, anyway?"

"The Proteus power *and* a seat on the Council ruling over all shapeshifters."

"Really?" Viola let out a cynical laugh. "That's all it took to corrupt an Elder of the Order?"

"It would seem so!" Fionnula laughed along with her fellow villainess.

But Waldrick's eyes widened and his hammering pulse jolted with newfound horror. *A traitor among the Elders?*

It was unthinkable.

Well, that changed everything.

That meant these crazies might actually succeed! It was true, then. Evil might be on the verge of beating good this very night for once and for all.

But they can't. They mustn't, he thought, his stomach churning.

And yet there was no sign of Zolond being involved in all this. How could Wyvern undertake such a huge move without the Dark Master's oversight?

Waldrick finally realized that Wyvern was doing all this as part of that mad goal he'd hinted at the first night the two of them met inside the Order prison.

The Nephilim actually meant to overthrow Zolond. And tonight, Wyvern was making his move.

Awed, Waldrick looked around with fresh eyes at what was going on. The handful of other Dark Druids who had recently arrived at the Black Fortress were apparently in on the coup.

One was madder than the next. Waldrick had at least enough sense to stay out of their way. One wrong move, and any one of them might kill him just for giggles. After all, he was of little use to this sinister lot without his pyrokinesis.

Moreover, now that Fionnula had attached herself to her precious Nathan, it wasn't as though Waldrick could count on the sea-witch to defend him against her new friends.

No, after what he had seen in the basement, Waldrick now understood all too clearly that the opera diva had always been out for herself.

As for him, he knew what he had to do.

There was no way these loon-bats could take over Merlin Hall. He had to believe that the Elders would beat them back.

Surely.

Even his own ancient kinswoman, Aunt Ramona, had the ability to inflict massive damage when she roused herself in her fury. She didn't like using magic, but when she resorted to it, he'd heard she was second only to Zolond himself.

But, for his part, Waldrick made a plan. A somewhat cowardly plan, he admitted, but sensible for once.

He decided with all his will that, sometime during the heat of battle, he would wait for his chance and run away.

He would defect to the other side.

Thanks to his sojourn in prison, Waldrick had had plenty of time to contemplate all his wrong choices and past misdeeds.

But now he knew for a fact that he was not actually a murderer. His brother was still alive, though only just barely.

That meant there was still time—and still hope—to fix what he had done.

Yes. When the battle came, he was going to find his moment and flee toward the enemy. Hands up, he'd surrender; they'd have to spare his life and take him prisoner.

He'd been a turncoat once; he could change sides again, could he not? He didn't expect any sort of hero's welcome from the Order, but they would spare his life. And he would not be tortured.

He would not be hunted for sport the way Raige would probably do to him if he hung around here. No one would suck his blood or use a spell to turn him into something unpleasant.

His mind was made up. He would defect and tell the Order everything he knew.

If he survived.

* * *

Meanwhile, beneath the moonlit pastures a mile away from Merlin

Hall, almost outside the dome of protective spells, Badgerton dug with all his might. He threw the dirt carelessly aside as his sharp claws whipped through the soil. He stopped and yanked out stones, then kept on, his blistered paws whirring away with maniacal speed.

He knew he was doomed if he should be found out now. Also doomed if he should fail.

Just a few more feet...

Wyvern had said he wanted the tunnel tall enough for a man. This was not easy to accomplish, but few creatures were more determined than a badger once they had set their minds to something.

Focused on his task, Badgerton did not let himself think about what Wyvern meant to *do* with the tunnel.

What he might be bringing through.

That was no longer Badgerton's concern. He had made his choice months ago. No, he was just the engineer. His rewards would be great—the Proteus power, a seat on the Council. Anything to save the skunkies from Wyvern's horrid owl.

Thrusting these thoughts from his mind, sweat and grime coating his face, Badgerton just kept plowing grimly forward.

It was much too late to turn back now.

* * *

"Jilly-bean, I'm home! And I've brought the birthday girl with me."

"Oh, Peter!" Ramona tut-tutted him while Dame Oriel laughed behind her.

The three of them headed into the Chancellor's House, having just finished their duties at the palace.

"I told you not to make a fuss," Ramona chided, though she couldn't help smiling. "This is hardly the time for celebration, with all that's going on."

"Nonsense, young lady! It's exactly what we need right now." The cheery wizard held the door for both older women. "And shame on you for trying to hide it, anyway. A birthday must be celebrated—even if belatedly."

"Especially a three hundred and thirty-third birthday," Oriel chimed in, following Ramona into his handsome, wood-paneled foyer of the manor house. "I agree with you, Peter."

"Of course you do, dear lady." Peter tapped his temple. "Great minds. Just wait until you taste Jillian's cooking. And people think she has no magical powers! Ha."

Ramona chuckled at the smitten husband while Oriel took a deep inhalation.

"Oh, it smells wonderful in here!"

It did. Aromas danced on the air. The sweetness of a cake baking, the tempting tang of beef roasting, and the cozy scent of soup simmering on the stove mingled with the smell of wood logs crackling in the fireplace.

Magical meals were easy to conjure, but there was just something special about real home cooking.

The warmth of the Quince family home enveloped them as Sir Peter set the books under his arm aside on the deep windowsill, then took the ladies' wraps and hung them on the coat tree by the door.

Ramona gave him an arch smile. "You know I only came because we have serious matters to discuss."

Like their plan of attack on the upcoming clairvoyant interviews.

"Besides," she added, "the dreaded occasion was nearly a fortnight ago."

"Then we must delay the celebration no longer!" Sir Peter slipped off his usual black wizard's robe and hung it on the coat tree as well.

It was rare to see him without it, but underneath was the casual but gentlemanly garb of a typical professor. He wore brown tweed trousers and a paisley vest of autumn colors over a tidy linen shirt with an ascot around his neck in a subdued shade of the mage's hallmark color: orange.

"Welcome once more to our humble abode," he said with a smile. He gestured to them to go ahead of him toward the stairs. "Can I invite you ladies up to the drawing room for an aperitif before dinner?"

"That sounds lovely," Oriel said, her plum-colored hair burnished in the glow of the small chandelier overhead.

But Ramona eyed the ceiling skeptically. "There had better not be a surprise party up there."

"Never!" Peter laughed and threw his arm around her bony shoulders. "As I promised you, nothing but a quiet celebratory dinner with friends. However, there will be cake," he warned. "And possibly the singing of a *certain* tune."

"Singing will not be necessary," Ramona said sternly.

"But I have an excellent voice," Peter said with a frown.

"I'm sure you do."

"He does." Oriel nodded.

"Nevertheless," Ramona said. "Let's keep the birthday silliness to a minimum, shall we?"

"Oh, very well." Their host gave her a mock pout and lowered his arm from Ramona's shoulders.

"Killjoy," Oriel teased.

Ramona snorted. "Old age has made me cranky."

"Shall we, ladies?" Sir Peter gestured toward the staircase that led up to the drawing room. "I'll pour us our drinks, then check on my good lady wife and see if she needs any assistance in the kitchen."

"You actually cook?" Oriel asked.

"When she lets me." He took off his spectacles and polished them on his sleeve before putting them back on. "I'm always on cleanup duty afterwards. She doesn't mind me using magic for that."

"I daresay." Ramona laughed.

"Must be nice." Oriel sighed. "Lucky mages."

Still chatting, they headed across the cozy foyer, when, suddenly, Jillian herself came rushing down the first-floor hallway in her apron.

"Hullo, darl—" Peter started, then he saw the look of panic on her face. "Jill?"

The prim blonde flew past Ramona and Oriel with barely a glance. Rushing over to her husband, she gripped his forearms with an air of desperation.

"Jilly, what's wrong?" Peter asked, searching her face. "Did you burn the roast? Drop the cake? What is it? It's all right. Tell me what's the matter."

With a stricken look, she opened her mouth to answer, but no words came out. She began gesticulating frantically to her mouth and throat, and before Ramona's eyes, the blood drained from Peter's face.

He jolted back from his wife with a look of stunned accusation. *"No."*

Oriel gasped and covered her mouth, realizing what it signified.

Ramona froze with shock.

Jillian Quince was the mole?

All three Elders just stood there staring at the young woman in horror.

"Oh, Jillian...! There must be some mistake." Peter sounded like someone had just punched him in the stomach. He stared at his wife for a long, incredulous moment.

Oriel's jaw hung open.

Watching the dean's wife with hawklike intensity, Ramona reached for her wand, just in case.

Jillian stood motionless, looking around at them slowly with confusion.

Peter suddenly turned away. "Oh, Jillian, how could you?"

He sent Ramona a devastated look. Then rage filled his eyes. He spun back to his wife and roared, *"How could you betray me?"*

A terrified shriek would've torn from Jillian's lips, but no sound came out on account of the silencing spell that Peter had personally created to expose the spy.

Jillian quickly pulled free of his hold on her arm, looking overwhelmed. *Help me!* she mouthed, giving him a wounded look.

The wizard shook his head bitterly. "You, of all people!" he cried. "Why?"

Ramona laid her hand firmly on his shoulder. "There's no point in frightening her, Peter," she said. "The spell has served its purpose."

What spell? Jillian mouthed.

Ramona barely had the heart to answer. Even she would never have suspected that their mole might turn out to be the dean's wife.

But perhaps it made sense.

As a non-magical person married to a wizard of great power, constantly surrounded by people with supernatural gifts, perhaps jealousy had gnawed away at Jillian until it had poisoned her heart and corrupted her judgment.

Oriel glanced from Jillian to Ramona and back again with a wide-eyed look.

Sir Peter suddenly pivoted and strode toward the stairs. "Forgive me, ladies. I...I require a moment to collect my thoughts. Then I'll remove the spell, and this *traitor* can confess to her perfidy."

Jillian's eyes welled up with tears of disbelief. As Peter jogged up the creaking wooden steps, she stood there clutching her apron, looking bewildered and quite at a loss.

What is going on? she mouthed at the ladies.

Ramona stared coldly at her, insulted that the woman saw fit to keep up the act. Whom did she think she was fooling?

"When Ravyn Vambrace returned from the Black Fortress," Ramona said, "she brought back information that the Dark Druids have a mole at Merlin Hall. Your husband performed a silencing spell that would stop the traitor from reporting to the enemy, exposing him or *her* by the loss of their voice."

Jillian's jaw dropped. She clutched her chest. *Me?*

"It would seem so," Ramona said.

Jillian shook her head, earnest horror stamped on her face. She glanced toward the stairs, then ran after her husband.

Oriel gave Ramona a stunned look.

"Stay away from me, cursed woman!" they heard Peter bark at Jillian a moment later. "You two-faced—! I don't even know you!"

"What do we do now?" Oriel murmured.

"I hardly know," Ramona replied. "I could've never foreseen this."

"Perhaps one of us should go and fetch the Guardians to come and take her away," Oriel said grimly.

"Perhaps we should send Peter to fetch them," Ramona said in a low voice. "Get him out of here for a bit, so he can cool off."

"I've never seen him like this before," Oriel whispered.

Ramona wondered if the lovelorn wizard had remembered yet that the punishment for traitors was burning at the stake. With a shudder, she headed for the stairs. "I'll tell him to go get the Guardians."

"Hold on. We've got company, Ramona." Oriel lifted her hand, turning toward the wall. "Yes, Constanzio? What is it?"

Ramona saw nothing, but understood they now had a spectral visitor.

"What?" Oriel drew in her breath.

Ramona looked at her in alarm. "What's he saying?"

"Can you show yourself?" Oriel asked the ghost. "You've got to tell her this in person." She looked darkly at Ramona. "Best if you hear it from him."

It took a ghost vast quantities of energy to become visible even briefly to non-clairvoyants, but Constanzio began doing just that.

The warmth of the room drained away, leaving a chill as the opera ghost pulled the energy out of the atmosphere and channeled it into materializing.

Ramona nodded to the wispy gray ghost in greeting as his portly form floated halfway through the wood-paneled wall.

"It's Badgerton!" His famous voice, though muffled, seemed to echo backward from a great distance. "Badgerton's the traitor!"

"What?" Ramona asked.

"He has a black candle in his room!" said Constanzio, floating by the fireplace. "I saw him use it to contact the enemy just tonight."

Ramona froze. "Zolond?"

"No, Wyvern. At first, he couldn't speak at all."

"The silencing spell!" Oriel said.

"Oh no," Ramona breathed as she realized their mistake. *Jillian...*

"But Wyvern removed it," the ghost said. "Then Badgerton could talk."

"Peter, get down here!" Ramona shouted, then looked at her friend. "Wyvern must've redirected Peter's silencing spell onto Jillian."

Constanzio started fading as Peter rushed back to them, pounding back down the staircase.

"What is it?" the wizard demanded, then saw the ghost. "Constanzio!"

"Tell Sir Peter the name of the real traitor," Ramona ordered the fading specter.

The ghost turned to the wizard. "It's Badgerton."

"What?" Peter answered, visibly jolting.

"There's more." Constanzio had almost disappeared, but he used the last of his strength to continue. "After Badgerton ended the candle call with Wyvern, he turned himself into a badger and fled the palace. So I followed."

"Where?" Ramona asked swiftly as Constanzio continued to fade.

"I'm not sure. I lost him outside somewhere around the zoo. I think he went underground." The ghost shook his head. "The black candle's still in his room—proof of what I say!"

Then Constanzio vanished.

"Badgerton...?" Peter echoed, at a loss.

Ramona squeezed his arm. "It wasn't Jillian."

Peter turned and saw his teary-eyed wife standing on the stairs. Jillian must've followed him down from the parlor without any of them hearing her.

She looked at her husband as if he was the one who'd committed the betrayal—and, indeed, he had.

"Jill?" Peter took a hapless step toward her, still dazed. "Jill, I'm sorry—"

Turning away from his apology, she fled back up the stairs with a muted sob. Peter closed his eyes and hung his head, more deeply wounded than if Wyvern had plunged a dagger in his back.

"I'll go fetch that candle Constanzio mentioned. Make sure it's there," Oriel said. "We don't need anyone else getting hold of it."

Ramona slipped her wand back into its holster. "I'll send the Guardians to hunt down Lord Badgerton."

Peter dragged his eyes open, his face ashen. He looked downright queasy over the false accusations he had hurled at the woman he loved. "I'll go remove the silencing spell from my wife. I doubt she'll have much to say to me, but maybe then we can get to the bottom of this."

Ramona nodded, but frankly, she doubted Jillian would be forgiving him anytime soon. With that, the three of them split up to see to their separate tasks.

* * *

Three of Badgerton's front claws were torn and bleeding by the time his paw punched through the endless wall of soil to empty space on the other side.

Panting and covered in dirt, he paused with relief, but only long enough to wipe the sweat off his brow. He peered with one eye through the small hole he had made. He saw more meadows, some sheep.

Through the fist-sized hole, the cool night air began pouring into the tunnel. It helped to revive him, for he was more than exhausted.

He was not sure how much time had passed, but he had worked at a feverish pace, not taking breaks.

Encouraged to have finally arrived at the end of his tunnel, he worked on widening the hole, ignoring the pain in his front paws and screaming shoulder muscles. Somehow, he summoned up a final burst of strength, and soon, the opening was as big as his whole body.

Though by now he trembled with pain, he told himself that the Proteus power would be worth it, as would his future seat on the Dark Druid Council.

Wyvern had specified that the tunnel must be tall enough for a large man to walk through. Well, that large man would simply have to duck his head a bit, Badgerton thought, for after widening the opening to about five and a half feet in diameter, he'd done all he could do. He'd worked until he couldn't lift his arms anymore.

At last, he changed himself back into a human. Wincing and grimacing, he looked down at his filthy, blistered hands, then gingerly pulled on the clothes he'd stashed in the tunnel along with some other supplies he figured he might need.

Once he was decent, though covered in dirt and grime, he shuffled out of the tunnel, bone-tired, his shoulders slumping.

No wonder it had taken him four bloody months to finish, he thought as he stepped out into a grassy meadow beyond the magical boundaries of Merlin Hall.

He'd dug his way through a whole blasted mile of earth, pushing forward an average of forty-five feet per night. Rather proud of himself, Badgerton turned to look back toward his starting point near the magical zoo, but, of course, Merlin Hall—the palace and all its outbuildings—had become invisible now that he was outside the Veil.

The important thing was that he was in the clear. It seemed he had gotten away with it.

Worn out from his task, Badgerton glanced around at the rolling countryside with its moonlit patchwork of sweeping sheep pastures and stubbled cornfields hemmed in by stone fences.

The late October chill kept him moving after all his sweaty toil. His hands still on fire with pain, he returned to his supplies and lit a pair of lanterns, setting one near the mouth of the tunnel to help his co-conspirators find their way in the dark. The other he carried with him as he left the tunnel.

He then staggered up to the top of the hillock under which he had just burrowed, determined to get a better view into the distance.

Wyvern ought to be arriving soon. Perhaps he was out there somewhere already.

Trudging to the top of the smooth green mound, Badgerton was panting by the time he reached the hillcrest. But when he looked across the dale, he could not believe what he saw.

He jerked with an oath of astonishment, then he stared in shock.

Wyvern had landed the Black Fortress right on top of poor Aelfric!

The three-hundred-foot-tall chalk man in the hillside, chief protector of Merlin Hall, struggled uselessly, trying to get up, his white-outlined feet kicking, hands flailing.

Pinned beneath the castle's spiky towers, poor Aelfric could do nothing. The huge building had landed square on his chest, holding him down.

Meanwhile, the drawbridge of the Black Fortress stood open, and an army of Noxu barbarians were marching out bearing torches and spears.

Badgerton felt a tingle of dread run down his spine. His heart jumped up into his throat. *What have I done?*

But a deal was a deal. It was too late for regret now.

The invasion was here.

CHAPTER 56

A Hasty Exit

Dani enjoyed the turtle ballet. For the first half-hour.

It was a lovely spectacle, at least for a while, especially when the turtles trailed long, colorful ribbons from their mouths as they swam through their swirling shapes and figures. The small amphitheater inside the Coral Palace had a sandy floor and a half-circle of white stone columns that formed the backdrop for the sea turtles' performance.

But, ribbons or no, there were only so many spins and pirouettes a person could take before utter boredom set in.

It had arrived much sooner for Jake than for Dani. Sitting beside her, his elbow resting on his chair arm, he leaned his cheek on his fist with a glazed stare.

At the end of the row, Sapphira had practically fallen asleep.

Dani felt sorry for the mermaid princess for having to sit through this all the time because of her father.

Up on his coral throne, King Nereus was still enjoying every moment of the show. Same with Lord and Lady Bradford—though, of course, they were diplomats, so perhaps they were just being nice.

Smooth as they were, it was hard to tell how they really felt about most things, unless it was one of those rare occasions when they chose to be frank.

In any case, since the underwater orchestra continued sawing away on their strange musical instruments, Dani decided now was the perfect time to tell Jake something private that had been on her mind for days.

Something she had not had the chance to say yet, with all that had been happening. But it was important that he knew.

Perhaps, also, she had been keeping her distance from him a little lately, guilty over the knowledge that she was keeping tabs on him for his Aunt Ramona.

But so far, Jake had been perfectly well behaved, so there had been nothing controversial for her to report.

Dani had noticed he seemed fascinated by his uncle and aunt's role as diplomats, and had duly reported that to Her Ladyship.

Nothing to feel guilty about there. With her conscience relatively clean, she leaned a bit closer and gave him a nudge with her arm.

He jolted upright, blinking. "Huh?"

"I don't believe it, you know," she whispered. "Not for an instant."

He looked at her with confusion.

"The prophecy," she whispered while the turtles spun. "It's rubbish. You could never turn evil. I just wanted you to know that I know. We all do. No matter what other people think."

He gave her a smile. "Thanks, carrot." Then he sighed, a stream of small bubbles rising from his lips. "I wouldn't mind if the flipside of that prophecy came true, though. If I could find some way to destroy them."

She nodded, quite willing to agree that if anyone could do it, it was probably Jake. But what an ominous destiny to have to carry around from the age of thirteen.

"Well," she assured him, "you're still just a kid. I'm sure you don't even need to worry about it till you're old. Like, thirty or something."

"I hope so," he murmured, though he didn't look convinced. "It would be nice to get it out of the way, though. Rather than have it hanging over my head my whole life."

She nodded at that.

The turtles wove in layered figure eights around the columns.

"Jake?" Dani whispered after a moment, ignoring an offended courtier who gave her a dirty look for talking during the performance.

Jake leaned near. "Aye, carrot?"

She pursed her lips for a moment, straightening her spine. "I just want you to know that, when the time comes, however old we are, you can count on me."

He looked surprised.

"If there's any way I can help you do it, you know I will."

Jake's blue eyes crinkled at the corners as he smiled at her as only he could.

He captured her hand, and Dani started to link her fingers through his, but they had both forgotten they had webbed hands and feet at the moment on account of the Piscean potion, so it didn't work.

Stifling laughter, they gave up on holding hands and exchanged a grin as another courtier shushed them. They tried to sit quietly for a moment.

"Ugh, how much longer is this thing?" Jake whispered.

Dani shrugged. "I don't know. They're turtles. They're slow at everything."

At that moment, some movement caught her eye over by the round porthole window in one of the pinkish coral walls. She elbowed Jake again and nodded toward it. "What's happening over there?"

He looked over.

One, two, three large dolphins zoomed in through the porthole.

Ignoring the turtles' performance, they swam overtop of the audience, arcing down to crowd around Princess Sapphira in the front row.

The first dolphin woke the sleeping mermaid princess with a nudge of his snout, then all three began clicking at her and squeaking up a storm.

Jake and Dani both looked on with interest.

The other two dolphins hovered nearby, not even caring that they were blocking the king's view and interrupting the whole court's entertainment.

"Daughter, get those noisy pets of yours out of here this instant!" the brawny, white-bearded mer-king commanded while the sea turtles got out of formation and started bumping into each other.

"I beg your pardon, Father, please hold on..." Sapphira rose from her seat, turning to the dolphins. "What's this you're saying?"

The dolphins whistled and squealed with great excitement.

"Are you sure?" the princess asked.

The middle dolphin bobbed his head.

"Oh no," Sapphira murmured. "Did she say anything else?"

The dolphin wagged his head back and forth.

Jake and Dani exchanged a surprised glance.

Then the first dolphin chirped and whistled to his friends, and all three swam off again as quickly as they'd come.

The turtles looked a little offended at the interruption, Dani thought. Some kept swimming through their practiced choreography, but others stopped and floated in place, flippers waving; they seemed unsure of what to do.

Then she noticed that Sapphira looked worried all of a sudden. With a swish of her tail, the mermaid princess sped over to her father's side and whispered in his ear.

King Nereus turned to his daughter, then lifted his hand. "I am sorry, everyone. We will have to cut tonight's performance short."

"Oh thank God," Jake said quietly.

"What is it, sire?" Lord Bradford asked. "Is something wrong?"

Even Maddox was awake now.

"It appears so, my lord. We just received a message from your ship." King Nereus rose with a frown. "Your daughter, Isabelle, implores you all to return to the surface immediately. It was she who sent the dolphins. She says it's some sort of emergency. That you all must hurry back to Merlin Hall at once."

Dani turned to Jake with wide-eyed alarm, but he just shrugged.

* * *

Grateful as Jake was to escape the turtle ballet, trouble back at Merlin Hall was not the sort of interruption he'd had in mind. Uncle Richard and Aunt Claire and the rest of their entourage said hasty farewells to their hosts, anxious to return to their vessel and find out what was the matter.

It had to be something quite serious, or Isabelle would never have dared interrupt a royal visit.

Soon, they set out through the night-dark waters. Escorting the diplomatic party back to their ship was the brawny Captain Tyndaris and a contingent of his armed mermen guards. The seas were dangerous at night.

To help light their way, each guest had been given one of the glowing, phosphorescent sea anemones that served as underwater lanterns. Sea candles, Sapphira had called them.

The mer-soldiers had small ones affixed to the front of their Roman-like helmets. This kept their hands free for wielding their stingray spears in case the group crossed paths with any night-hunting sharks.

Surrounding their guests in a protective ring, the mermen conducted them back up to the yacht, Tyndaris himself leading the way.

Swimming through the eerie darkness of the night sea, Jake wondered with gnawing anxiety just what this "emergency" was back at Merlin Hall.

His friends and he exchanged worried glances as they glided upward through the waves. Nobody knew what to expect.

When they reached the surface, arriving beside the towering vessel, Jake lifted his head, blinked salt water out of his eyes, and saw that all the ship's lanterns were lit up. The crew was running around the decks getting ready to sail.

To his surprise, Isabelle was down on the water in one of the ship's dinghies, Janos holding the oars steady; she had a second box of Nixie's vials open on her lap, this time, to reverse the effects of the Piscean potion.

At Aunt Claire's request, Nixie had brewed up doses of the reversal potion for each of them, just in case something came up.

Smart lady, Jake thought. But, of course, his aunt was an experienced diplomat. She obviously knew from many such missions to expect the unexpected and had become accustomed to managing crises on the road.

Her daughter, meanwhile, had the vials ready and waiting to turn each of them back into their regular selves.

"Queue up, everyone!" Izzy said.

From the edge of the rowboat, she handed out the vials, explaining the situation to her parents, Ranjit, Derek, and Tex as she worked.

Treading water nearby, Jake overheard what she was saying.

"We aren't sure what's the matter, but Janos and I both had the strongest premonition about half an hour ago that we need to get to Merlin Hall as quickly as possible. He could feel it with his Guardian instincts, and I sensed it empathically, as well. Something's wrong back there, but neither of us has any idea what it might be."

"I guess we'd better go find out." Uncle Richard passed the next vial of potion to Archie. "Back up onto the boat, son."

"Yes, sir," Archie said, and, not for the first time, Jake felt a twinge of envy at the easy relationship between his cousins and their parents.

Would he ever get to know what that was like? It was hard to believe so.

Jake shoved off the unhappy thought and accepted the next vial of potion.

The reversal spell did not taste nearly as disgusting as the first one. It took only seconds to work, and, better still, it didn't hurt as the gills in the sides of his neck closed and the webbing between his fingers disappeared.

Good riddance, he thought. Then he joined the queue of once-more human passengers treading water at the foot of the ship's ladder.

One by one, they climbed up, shivering in their bathing costumes.

Up on deck, a crew member waited to assist them, steadying each returning passenger as they climbed over the bulwark; Miss Helena handed out towels.

The girls went up first, including Nixie, which was fortunate. For, as soon as Aunt Ramona's protégée was aboard once more, she rushed to the girls' shared cabin and fetched her wand.

Once again, Nixie put her magic to good use, tapping each returning passenger with a drying spell—no need to catch cold with wet hair.

As for Dani, the moment she was dry, she thanked Nixie, then raced off to get the Bud of Life and dutifully put it back on. When Jake arrived, climbing back onto the boat, he saw and heard her breathlessly telling Aunt Claire that as soon as she had refastened it onto her wrist, she had tried to contact Merlin Hall with the communication device to find out what was going on.

"But there was nobody there!" Dani said. "No one answered."

"It's all right, dear." Aunt Claire laid a hand on Dani's shoulder. "Just keep trying. Aunt Ramona must be away from her room right now, that's all. If you do manage to connect, come and get me or Lord Bradford at once."

"Yes, my lady," Dani said with an anxious nod.

Nixie dried Jake with a flick of her wand. He nodded his thanks, then strode over to Red, who was waiting for him nearby.

"Any thoughts on all this?" Jake murmured to his wise pet.

"Becaw." The Gryphon shook his feathered head, but at least he'd found his courage and stopped cowering under the blankets.

As soon as everyone was safely aboard, the captain of *The Wind Dancer* ordered the anchor drawn up.

Lord Bradford went to the rails and waved down to the mermen, who had waited to make sure they had everything they needed. "Thank you! We're all set!"

"Safe journeys, sir!" Tyndaris called back, saluting him. Then the mer-soldiers sank back down beneath the waves and retreated in formation to swim back to Coral City.

"Make sail!" the ship's captain shouted to the crew.

Jake drew in his breath as the broad white sails on both masts came tumbling down; it was a beautiful sight to behold.

The sailors locked the ropes into position, and the sleek little ship began drifting forward.

"Unfortunately," the captain said to everyone standing around, "the wind's only at eight knots tonight. I'm afraid this could take a while."

Uncle Richard frowned at that, but Nixie arched a brow.

"Perhaps not," she murmured.

Archie grinned at her. "Think you can do something about it, Nix?"

"Child's play," she said with a savvy smile.

Nearly their entire party followed Nixie to the stern.

Jake and Archie exchanged a knowing glance. They had seen many times what the little witch could do, but it was fun to watch the adults' reactions.

The boy genius folded his arms over his chest, unable to wipe the proud grin off his face. He looked almost smug, eyeing his parents. "Mum, Dad, wait till you see this."

Nixie lifted her wand and had, oh, a little private talk with the night sky.

Nothing happened at first, so she spoke to it more sternly, very Aunt Ramona-like. Commanding.

In mere minutes, the wind picked up and the sails puffed out with what the captain announced was a moderate breeze of sixteen knots. "She's doubled our speed!"

"Becaw!" the Gryphon congratulated her.

"Thank you, Red." Nixie turned to the captain. "Need any more?"

"No, miss! Any faster than this, we'd risk running aground when we near the shore."

She nodded. "Let me know if you need anything else."

As she sauntered off, Jake started a round of applause for their own weather mage.

Nixie waved it off, embarrassed. "It was nothing!"

Lord Bradford nudged Archie; he grinned at his father. "Isn't she great?"

Even Aunt Claire looked impressed.

The hour-long sail back to the cove from which they'd set out was uneventful but nerve-racking, but at least it gave them time to change out of their bathing costumes into normal clothes.

The whole time, questions about what sort of trouble was afoot kept everyone on edge. Dani kept trying to contact Merlin Hall, to no avail. Still, nobody answered.

It wasn't a good sign.

The Guardians readied themselves for danger and tried their best to home in on what was happening through their heightened senses. But Maddox told Jake and the other kids that that wasn't really how it worked.

Those with his gift rarely got details on what they might face. Their usual way of doing things was to focus on whomever they were assigned to protect; they were trained to discern when and where that person might ever be in trouble, and their duty was to show up at the right place and time, ready for anything.

"It's probably different for Janos because he's also a vampire," Maddox said. "The bloodsuckers have telepathic abilities; Guardians don't. How those two aspects of him must mix, I have no idea. Weird, though, that Izzy sensed it too."

Jake sat next to Dani while she kept trying to hail Merlin Hall.

Finally, *The Wind Dancer* dropped anchor a few hundred yards out from the private beach below the Villa di Palma. The captain ordered the ship's three rowboats to be lowered, then the sailors rowed the passengers ashore.

Their baggage would soon follow, but no one dared wait for it. They simply grabbed any essentials and went.

Red flew off to the beach first and arrived ahead of everyone else. Jake could've ridden on his Gryphon, but instead, he carried Teddy on the rowboat for Dani. She was busy being paranoid about not getting her training gauntlet wet.

At last, the whole group hurried across the pearly sand, and then up the stone stairs to the graceful seaside villa where Jake and the others had stayed before.

The tension was building. While Lightrider Ranjit went out to the terrace and stood at the waypoint, prepared to conduct their party through the portal, Isabelle rushed inside to see if there was any Inkbug messages from Merlin Hall.

There were none.

Lord only knew what was waiting for them on the other end of that portal.

After just a couple of minutes to organize themselves, the whole party gathered on the terrace overlooking the beach. Ranjit waved them back to a safe distance from the waypoint, just like Sir Peter always did on the other end, at Merlin Hall.

The stately Sikh Lightrider walked over to the brass waypoint marker alone. He rolled up his left sleeve and began punching the coordinates for Merlin Hall into the Flower of Life embedded in his left arm.

Waiting for the portal to open, everyone seemed to hold their breath. The tension was extreme.

Archie rubbed his sweaty palms on his waistcoat and gave Jake a hapless smile.

Even Uncle Richard looked a little nervous, and Aunt Claire clearly expected the worst. After changing out of their bathing costumes, the viscountess had reappeared, not in one of her usual satin gowns, but in boyish garb closer to what Ravyn Vambrace might don for a mission.

Miss Helena was obviously glad to return to dry land, and though she gave the kids reassuring smiles, the way she and Henry prowled around them, Jake could see that both governess and tutor stood ready to shapeshift into their fierce animal forms at the first sign of trouble.

Jake and Dani exchanged a grim look.

It sort of bothered him, how the adults were acting so protective. They meant well, of course, but it was a little insulting to his pride. Didn't they realize the sorts of dangers that he and the others had already dealt with on their own, thank you very much?

Thirty-foot-tall rock golems, for heaven's sake.

Wyvern's rock golems, Jake reminded himself, and his mood turned darker still. For he suddenly had a feeling that, whatever was happening, that Nephilim freak might well be the source of the problem once again.

At that thought, Jake reached out and laid his hand on Red's neck, recalling how close he had come to losing his Gryphon to that lunatic.

"Red?" he murmured to his pet.

"Becaw?" Red's golden eyes gleamed with warlike readiness as he tilted his head to glance at Jake. His windblown feathers were bristling a bit in anticipation of trouble ahead.

"Whatever happens, I want you to stay by my side this time," Jake said. Teddy peeked over Dani's shoulder from his brown satchel, as though eavesdropping. "I can't risk losing you again."

Red nodded, much to Jake's relief.

"Good boy." In the final seconds before the portal opened, Jake glanced around at his loved ones. He had a feeling that once that portal opened, things would never be the same.

Dani was carefully observing Ranjit's procedures; Archie was straightening his lucky bowtie; Nixie twirled her wand restlessly in her hand.

Isabelle stayed near her father, who turned to her and whispered, "I'm so proud of you, darling. You did the right thing, sending for us. Whatever awaits us, look out for your little brother."

"Yes, Papa."

Derek cracked his knuckles; Maddox clenched his fists; Tex tipped back his hat, then rested his hands on his six-guns like a gunfighter at high noon, waiting for the signal to draw.

Aunt Claire lifted her chin expectantly, but Janos scanned the party with a focused gaze.

When it met Jake's, Janos sent him a sardonic smile. "Are we having fun yet?" he murmured.

Jake flashed a smile at the gallows humor.

Then the portal flashed open, and its mirror-brightness dazzled everyone, since their eyes had grown accustomed to the dark.

"I'll go first," Derek said gruffly, nodding to the other Guardians.

"No, let me." Janos reached out to stop him. "You've got to look after Jake."

"I can take care of myself!" Jake insisted, stepping forward.

Both fighters sent him pointed looks, needing no words to remind him about the stupid prophecy and the Dark Druids' desire to recruit him.

Jake rolled his eyes. "Fine," he grumbled. "Forget it."

Janos seemed amused at his lack of fear, then strode toward the portal, Isabelle anxiously gazing after him.

The other Guardians followed the vampire, weapons drawn. Janos glanced at Ranjit, making sure it was safe to proceed. The white-clad Sikh gestured politely to the shining, upright entrance into the Grid.

Janos squared his shoulders, his lean silhouette black against the portal's brightness. Then he calmly stepped through.

One by one, the other Guardians went, but Derek stayed back with Jake, determined to watch over him and the other kids. Uncle Richard and Henry went next, then Miss Helena and Aunt Claire.

Derek beckoned to the girls to proceed. "Ladies first."

Isabelle. Nixie. Dani clutching her dog. The redhead sent Jake a fearful glance, but he gave her a bolstering nod, and off she went.

"I'll look after 'em." Tex followed the girls, his long brown duster coat blowing ominously.

Red and Maddox flanked Jake. Archie stood by.

Derek glanced at the lads. "You boys ready?"

"Yes, sir," Maddox said firmly. He nodded and strode over to the portal, marching right in.

"Righty-ho," Archie said nervously.

Jake clapped his cousin on the back as Archie walked over, jumping into the portal.

Except for Ranjit, who was still holding the portal open, Derek brought up the rear, prepared to defend Jake from whatever they might face.

Jake wished they wouldn't make such a fuss over him, but he understood.

Because of this ridiculous prophecy, they believed his safety had larger ramifications for the Order and the world beyond just his own personal preference of remaining, well, *alive.*

He gave his trusty mentor a grateful glance, because, after all, Derek was only doing his duty. Red flew into the shining circle ahead of him.

Then Jake charged into the portal.

The next thing he knew, he was a cloud of tingling molecules hurtling northward up the shimmering tunnel of the ley line.

As Jake whizzed toward England, even this blink-of-an-eye speed of travel did not feel fast enough. His worry multiplied exponentially with every hundred miles he covered as Gaia sent him and the others rocketing homeward. Jake could feel the Earth energies throbbing through his atoms.

And then, in little more than the twinkling of an eye, the ley line spat each traveler out in succession at the far end of the tunnel, dumping them onto the vast, dark lawn of Merlin Hall.

Jake stumbled out of the portal—thankfully, in one piece. He nearly landed on Archie, who was straightening his glasses.

Someone yanked both boys out of the way so Derek wouldn't smash them when he came hurling out next.

Immediately, Jake knew something was wrong. Chaos filled the air all around him. Booms and screams. Roars and shouts.

Good Lord, was that cannon fire?

He ducked instinctively, the jolting reverberations vibrating in his chest. Shrieks went up from some of the girls. Still dizzy, queasy, Jake strove to see and to steady himself. His head was still reeling from the portal travel, and his eyes had not yet adjusted to the dark after the tunnel's dazzling light.

But dread gripped him as tightly as Dani now did, screeching beside him as she clung to his arm, the terrible sounds of battle raging all around them.

"It's all right. Get down! Stay together, kids." It was Janos, cool and firm, speaking loudly over the clamor. "Nixie, dear, can you do a shielding spell of some sort?"

Jake did not hear her answer in the crashes and the din. Teddy was barking by his ear. The earth seemed to shake under his feet; he smelled smoke. Finally, with a few more blinks, he forced his vision to adjust to the night.

And what he saw horrified him.

Tusked monsters in leather armor were battling Order folk all around them. Beyond their clashes, the palace was on fire.

The maze was burning.

"Dear God," Jake whispered, holding on to Dani with one hand, Red with the other.

Merlin Hall was under attack.

CHAPTER 57
War

Sheer pandemonium surrounded them in the blazing night. Everything was happening at once.

Jake was not normally one to duck, cower, or cringe, but even he let out a curse to find that he had stepped out of the portal into the middle of a raging battle.

His breath came in short, rapid puffs from pure shock at what they had stumbled into. His pulse slammed. They had known there was trouble at Merlin Hall, but no one could've predicted this.

The headquarters of the Order was supposed to be invulnerable to attack—safe behind the Veil!

Well, it seemed the Veil had been torn, or at least had a serious hole in it, as of tonight, Jake thought.

No wonder there had been no answer to Dani's attempts to hail the palace with her training gauntlet. People here were fighting for their lives.

Jake pulled the carrot-head closer automatically, his gaze darting about as he tried to take it all in at once.

He had been in many bad situations before, but never anything like this.

This was war.

The air was thick with shouts and explosions, screams and choking smoke clouds. Roaring fires were even now consuming portions of the great maze housing the Old Father Yew.

Jagged lightning flashes from dueling wands lit up the night. Naiads hurled spears and threats from the nearby stream at the tusked, gray-skinned monsters storming across the grounds. Their barbaric war drums throbbed through the darkness.

Red roared, his feathered mane bristling. The Gryphon scored the ground angrily with his claws beside Jake, clearly wanting to fight.

But there was no way Jake would allow that, after his beloved pet had already been captured once. "No, Red! You stay by my side."

The Guardians had already moved into position.

Weapons drawn, their party's ten well-trained soldiers plus Derek and Janos formed a ring around the rest of them. Archie and Isabelle huddled next to their parents.

Again, the earth shook.

"What was that?" Dani cried.

Jake looked over his shoulder into the distance. "Aelfric," he whispered.

Dani followed his gaze. They both gaped at four spiky black castle towers peeking over the hill where the mighty Long Man stood guard over Merlin Hall.

They could see Aelfric's chalk-outlined arms and legs flailing as he tried to shove the building off him, to no avail.

The Black Fortress.

Jake stared at the enemy stronghold with a chill of foreboding down his spine. The Dark Druids must have landed it right on top of him. Electrical currents flickered like lightning now and then between its sharp corner towers.

But when another explosion slammed into the small grove of trees on the lawn where he and Maddox had once bickered over a stick, Jake ducked.

Glancing upward with a flinch, he saw a strange, bulbous, propeller-driven vehicle chugging noisily through the sky overhead, trailing long, billowing fishing nets out behind it.

"Look at that!" Archie exclaimed, pointing up at it, but the airship or dirigible, or whatever it was, continued pounding the palace roof, the maze, and the sculpted grounds with cannon fire from above.

Nixie was ashen-faced. She had her wand in her hand but looked too scared to remember any of her spells that might have been helpful at the moment.

Meanwhile, at the front of their party, the Guardians fended off a knot of tusked barbarian invaders, who charged.

It seemed the diplomatic party's arrival via the bright, shiny portal had drawn the enemy's attention.

They repelled the attack, but Jake heard Derek curse as he kicked one of the creatures backward. "Filthy Noxu!"

"Oh," Archie said with a gulp. "So, *that's* a Noxu."

The brutish half-trolls smelled terrible. Their musky odor mingled with the smell of the smoke from all the fires. The bulky creatures wore leather armor and had beady eyes, and snouts like wild boars.

Jake was glad to let the adult warriors handle them. The Guardians were focused on their fight, but seemed to have matters under control.

Relatively safe in the middle of the ring with the rest of the civilians in their party, Jake continued scanning. He was pained by the sight of dead gnomes strewn across the grass here and there.

Over by the maze, he saw that Dr. Plantagenet had mobilized a bucket line. The Green Folk were terrified of fire, but that did not stop dozens of their kind from passing pails of water along, working to douse some of the tall flames that threatened to consume the whole maze. Big, clumsy Ogden Trumbull was helping.

Next, his gaze zoomed toward the palace, where the gnomes of Merlin Hall were working catapults stationed on the roof to assist the embattled Guardians trying to beat back the horde of Noxu surging around the entrance.

Taking in the whole violent panorama, Jake turned around slowly and watched with a sense of unreality as a centaur on the bridge jumped forward like a donkey, kicked out with both hind legs, and sent one of the invaders flying into the river.

There, the naiads fell upon the creature and held it underwater until it stopped thrashing.

Blimey.

The younger members of the diplomatic party huddled together, unsure what to do while the rattled adults strove to get their bearings.

The iron ring of Guardians around them continued beating back the tusked barbarians. The soldiers almost seemed to be enjoying themselves—except for Derek, who was outraged.

Red reared up, unsheathing his front claws as his golden eyes gleamed. Clearly chafing to join the battle, the Gryphon let out a war cry. Even little Teddy started barking more viciously, like he was keen to bite somebody's ankles.

Dani quickly quieted her dog, but Henry and Helena exchanged a nod, then turned themselves into their animal forms. It seemed the twins, too, burned to join the battle to defend Merlin Hall—or, at least, to protect their charges.

In the next instant, the kids had a black leopard defending them on one side, a snarling wolf on the other, as well as an angry Gryphon.

It was then that Jake spotted the over-tall Nephilim madman, his would-be father. Wyvern was battling Sir Peter near the fountain in the middle of the courtyard, out in front of the palace.

Jake looked on anxiously, worried that the easygoing headmaster was no match for the son of Shemrazul.

But without his usual black academic robes, the cheery dean looked like a different person. He fought with a vengeance. By the lurid glow from the burning maze, Jake could see the snarl of fury on Sir Peter's face.

Feet braced, he gripped his wand with both hands. Jagged arrows of bright magic flew out of it at Wyvern, who answered in kind.

Jake did not want to look away, but seeing their duel made him all the more desperate to find Aunt Ramona out there, wherever she was, and make sure she was safe.

Another sweep of the grounds did not reveal her, but Jake caught snatches of treacherous singing in the distance.

Oh, he knew that voice.

Fionnula.

Still, Jake did not see either witch yet. Instead, as he scanned past the duel of warlock and wizard up to the front stairs of Merlin Hall, he saw the towering master Guardian, Ebrahim, planted in front of the palace doors.

The powerful black man was mowing down Noxu on all sides and bellowing orders to the many other Guardians fighting with him there to fend off the horde.

The Noxu clearly meant to storm the palace. Jake thought he glimpsed Ravyn among the knot of Guardians there, but he lost her again when Archie jostled him from behind.

"Look out!" Archie pulled Jake out of the way as a pair of fighters tumbled into their midst, right past the ring of Guardians surrounding them.

A half-troll and a very angry, brawny dwarf warrior were beating the daylights out of each other. Absorbed in their battle, the pair rolled right through the children's midst and out the other side of the Guardians' circle, then jumped to their feet and continued banging on each other with all their might.

Jake wondered if the stout-hearted dwarf was one of Laird Broadbuckle's men from the Deep Delves. Probably so.

"Thanks, Arch," Jake mumbled.

The boys exchanged an ominous glance.

Mad things were happening everywhere they looked.

A herd of centaurs armed with swords launched a cavalry charge against a group of the invaders, rushing at them with thundering hooves. But the Noxu quickly formed an infantry square, pointing a phalanx of spears at the onslaught. The centaurs had no choice but to gallop around them, flowing by on both sides.

Across the lawns, Guardians flipped and spun with dazzling attacks against the brutish enemy troops.

The airship blasted Merlin Hall's roof, blowing up one of the catapults and sending gnomes flying.

All around the palace, curtains or, in some places, flames billowed out from the broken windows. Jake could see ghosts pulling energy from the fires to make themselves visible. In poltergeist form, they did their best to scare away some of the Noxu.

Overhead, witches careened on brooms, throwing bolts of magic from their wands at the dirigible, only to flee from a giant owl that swooped after them, chasing them through the dark skies.

Jake realized the witches were trying to bring the odd vehicle down and, thereby, stop the attack from the air. Studying the airship, Jake felt an idea begin stirring in his head...

One that would likely get him killed—or, at the very least, infuriate his mentor.

Still glancing around worriedly trying to spot Aunt Ramona, he noticed old Master Balinor engaged in some high strangeness.

The aged head wizard walked out from around the corner of the palace. His kingly owl followed him—a normal-sized one. Its majestic head swiveled all around, as though the bird were watching out for sneak attacks on his master from behind.

Raising his arms, Balinor conjured a gushing waterfall that appeared out of thin air above the palace.

Aiming the torrent at a section of the roof that was on fire, the wizard blasted the flames with water; at the same time, Jake saw that Balinor was controlling someone he had apparently trapped inside of what looked like a man-sized snow globe swirling with wisps of black smoke.

Inside this translucent orb, a large, furious man pounded on the glass, his shouts and curses at the wizard muffled.

Jake had no idea who the fellow was, but he looked rather terrifying.

A soldier of some sort, the herculean fellow was covered in more weapons than even Derek would've carried into battle. His face was smeared with greenish-brown war paint.

Calmly ignoring the warrior's muffled curses and threats, Balinor put out the blaze and walked on, repeating the waterfall exercise on the next section of the burning palace, several yards away. The old wizard simply floated the angry man in the ball along with him.

Unfortunately, mere moments after Balinor moved on, the section of the fire he thought he'd just extinguished flickered back to life.

Jake looked on with concern, unsure if Balinor even noticed.

Janos certainly had. He stood nearby, having kept close to the kids in the battle.

Pausing, the vampire guardian stared grimly toward the roof. "That is no ordinary fire. I have seen that before..." Turning, Janos glared at the Nephilim, who was still battling Sir Peter. "Someone's got to get that cursed Atlantean cuff off Wyvern!"

Suddenly, Aleeyah appeared in their midst with a tinkling of silvery bells. "You're right," she said to Janos, her fellow spy. "Those are not normal flames. I just took a closer look up on the roof."

"And?" Janos prompted.

"I believe it's Greek fire," the djinni said with an ominous look. "I've seen it used in many wars throughout the Near East, but not for an age."

"Greek fire?" Jake echoed, mystified.

"The secret weapon of the Byzantine Empire!" Archie shoved his way over to the djinni. "Did you say Greek fire?"

Aleeyah nodded.

"Then water's of no use. That'll never put it out!" The boy genius straightened his glasses. "Tell Balinor he needs to use potassium. Potassium salts! And if that doesn't work, tell him to try carbon dioxide."

Jake and Janos exchanged a startled glance.

Aleeyah furrowed her brow. "Come again?"

"Arch, not even Balinor can conjure something unless he can first picture it in his mind." Nixie grasped his elbow. "What does this stuff look like? Describe what you mean so Aleeyah can tell Balinor."

Archie shrugged. "Baking soda! That's basically all it is, give or take a molecule. A whole blizzard of it dumped upon the fire should do the trick. It'll smother the flames."

Janos looked wryly at the djinni. "You heard the boy genius."

Aleeyah seemed amused. "Excellent. I will tell him now. Thank you once again, Dr. Bradford," she said, then vanished.

"I daresay." Archie tugged on his waistcoat. "Hasn't anyone around here studied chemistry besides me?"

After the djinni had gone, Jake suddenly hoped she didn't get stuck in her smoke form again—it was brave of her to risk it. But desperate times and all.

Then Aunt Claire turned to their primary Lightrider. "Ranjit, take the children out of here! You've got to take them someplace safe."

"I will send them where you wish, my lady, but I cannot leave," said the white-uniformed Sikh.

"But—"

"You see what is happening!" He gestured at the field. "I am sorry, my lady. All are needed here."

"Stone! Lord Bradford! What are you doing here?" an angry male voice shouted from somewhere out amid the chaos.

Jake looked over and saw Finnderool nimbly ducking blows as he ran toward the group, shooting Noxu warriors with his bow along the way.

"How did this happen?" Uncle Richard exclaimed as the wood elf slipped past Janos, who dropped a Noxu after snapping its neck.

"Badgerton's betrayed us," Finnderool replied. "He dug a tunnel out beneath the dome and let the blackguards in."

Aunt Claire gasped. Even the wolf and the leopard looked shocked, since Badgerton was a shapeshifter too.

Jake and Dani exchanged a wide-eyed look.

"You shouldn't be here," Finnderool said to Uncle Richard. "But, frankly, I'm glad you are." He eyed Derek and Janos. "We are badly outnumbered. The Noxu are about to storm the palace, and have already reached the center of the maze."

"Oh no. The Old Father Yew," Isabelle murmured. She closed her eyes, lifting her hand to her temple. "He's dying..."

"Traps in the maze have taken out dozens of these brutes," the wood elf continued, "but I swear Wyvern brought every stinking half-troll mercenary he could hire. What's worse, he's got several other Dark Druids with him."

Aunt Claire recoiled. "Not Zolond!"

"No, my lady. I have not seen the Dark Master," Finnderool said. "But Archeron Raige is directing Wyvern's forces. At least, he was, until Balinor contained him." The wood elf nodded at the furious man in the magical snow globe. "And"—he added with a grim glance at Janos—"Viola Sangray has come."

"Oh, perfect," Janos mumbled.

Jake had never heard of either one.

"Fionnula Coralbroom is here. You might've heard her. Remember, don't listen to her songs. Inigo Dread arrived in *The Dream Wraith*, as you've no doubt noticed." Finnderool nodded at the dirigible floating overhead.

"How did he penetrate the dome?" Derek exclaimed, gesturing at the sky.

"Fionnula used her singing to weaken the dome from the inside as soon as she arrived with Wyvern," Finnderool said, then he glanced around. "As for Duradel, I haven't seen the prophet, but I can feel him somewhere close by."

"Never mind them! Where is Aunt Ramona?" Archie demanded, the flames reflected in his glasses.

"Dealing with Fionnula, Master Archie." Then Finnderool looked at his fellow Lightriders. "Ranjit, Tex: I need you both to come with me. We've lost track of some of the children."

"What?" Aunt Claire clutched her heart.

Miss Helena roared with concern.

"It all happened so suddenly!" the wood elf said. "Right now, we've got about a hundred schoolchildren sheltering in the library basement with Jillian Quince and the librarians. But dozens more of our students are hiding wherever they can all over the grounds. Many are still hunkered down in the palace—which, as you've noticed, is on fire. Aleeyah's been helping, but I could use a hand finding the rest of the children and getting them down into that shelter as quickly as possible."

Ranjit nodded. "I am with you."

"What can I do?" Uncle Richard asked.

The elf pointed at the woods surrounding the lawns. "Some of the kids are hiding in the forest, I believe. The Noxu haven't made it that far yet. Gather them up as best you can; I'll be there with a retinue of Guardians as soon as possible."

"Done," said Uncle Richard. The viscount exchanged a glance with his wife, who gave him a firm nod.

"Miss O'Dell?" Finnderool turned to Dani. "Take your friends someplace safe."

"Who, me?" the carrot said with a blink. She had been huddled beside Jake in a terrified daze.

But the cool-nerved wood elf sent her a pointed look. "Yes, *you.*" Then he nodded to his colleagues. "Shall we?"

"Go on, Ranj," Tex said. "I'll give the lil gal a hand. Be right behind ya."

As the cowboy took Dani aside to help her open the portal, Ranjit centered himself amid the chaos, then clapped his hands together and conjured a rifle. He nodded to Finnderool, who nocked an arrow in his bow, then both Lightriders ran off toward the palace to find the stray schoolkids.

"Guardians, two of you go with them!" Derek ordered, pointing. "Remember, the enemy's collecting Lightriders! Kill anything that tries to lay a hand on them."

"Yes, sir!" Two of the bodyguards from the trip jogged after the pair.

The remaining Guardians redistributed themselves evenly around the diplomatic party, along with the two snarling shapeshifters.

Tex turned to Dani, laying a steadying hand on her shoulder. "Now, don't fret, tumbleweed. Let's send you on your way."

"Tex, I-I can't."

"Yes, ya can."

"Sure you can, carrot," Jake chimed in.

"Munroe, you send those kids somewhere the enemy won't think to look for them," Janos said, his tone dire. "We know they want Jake and Isabelle—they'd probably like to get their hands on Archie, too."

"Well, don't I feel special," the boy genius quipped.

"Easy, fangs," Tex drawled at the vampire. "You do your job; I'll do mine." Then he gazed down kindly at Dani. "You got some coordinates memorized, honey? Someplace no one will find ya."

"Y-yes, sir," Dani said, wide-eyed. "I'm going to take them to—"

"No!" Aunt Claire interrupted.

The viscountess strode over to Dani, sword in hand, while

explosions crashed overhead. "Keep the location to yourself, please, Miss O'Dell. It's better if we don't know where you're taking them—just in case."

"In case *what*, Mother?" Archie turned to her in alarm. "Surely you don't mean in case you're captured?"

Isabelle gasped and grabbed her arm. "Mother, no! You can't risk it. You need to come with us!"

"Children, I will brook no argument—"

"Izzy's right, Mum. You have no business being at a battle. You can't fight!"

"I can help your father find the children, though. You heard what Finnderool said."

Archie looked half panicked that his mother, let alone his sire, should remain so close to danger. Perhaps he had seen enough of what Jake had gone through as an orphan...

"Father! Talk sense to her!"

"You heard your mother," the viscount replied, reloading his pistol. "Don't worry, son." He smiled at his wife. "The lady is full of surprises."

Aunt Claire gave her two children a quick hug and cupped Jake's cheek. "Be brave, children. I know I hardly need say that to you, of all people—"

She hesitated again, clearly pained to leave them, then glanced at their little Lightrider-in-training. "Look after them, Miss O'Dell. All of you, take care of one another, as you've done so many times before. Someone will be in contact with you at the first opportunity."

"Yes, ma'am," Dani said gravely.

Though her emerald eyes were round with fear, her face pale beneath her freckles, a businesslike attitude came over her as she set about opening the portal.

Jake watched her for a second with open admiration. The little redhead had always been one to keep her wits about her in a fight, but having been given her assignment and reminded of her training, she seemed to turn quite fearless.

Standing boldly by the waypoint, Dani began carefully turning the series of dials embedded on her leather training gauntlet.

"You're sure that thing really works?" Jake asked while the battle crashed around them.

"Shh! I'm concentrating." She shot him a quick scowl. "Stand back so you don't get fried."

"Claire, let's go. There's a break in the action." Uncle Richard tugged on Aunt Claire's arm, gesturing toward the woods. "Stay safe, children."

"All my love!" Though her face was anguished, the viscountess blew them all a kiss, then she and Uncle Richard both headed for the tree line, ready to shoot or stab anything that stepped into their path.

"Two of you, go with them!" Again, Derek gestured at the ring of Guardians surrounding them.

"Yes, sir!" Two more of their security team ran off to assist the diplomats.

Derek apparently felt that they could spare them, since they still had half a dozen men, plus Janos, the shapeshifters, Red, and himself.

Suddenly, Isabelle groaned and hung her head. "Oh—poor Father Yew." The empath wove on her feet like she might faint; both Jake and Maddox reached out to steady her. "He's burning…suffering… They're killing him as the symbol of all we hold dear. They're so evil. So full of hate."

"Get Isabelle out of here!" Janos barked. "She can't be exposed to this much longer!"

Jake did his best to comfort his cousin, though her pretty face was anguished.

Janos was right. She couldn't take much more. Jake could only imagine what the sensitive soul of an empath must be experiencing in the midst of all this chaos and fury.

"Hurry up, Dani!" Maddox said.

"I'm trying!"

"Give her a second!" Tex shot back, standing by the little redhead. "She's almost got it. You try recalling bunches of numbers under pressure. Don't listen to him, honey. Just stay calm."

Jake exchanged a dark glance with Nixie. The news that the Old Father Yew was being burned alive infuriated him. The angry look on the young witch's face suggested she was thinking the same thing.

Now that their initial terror had passed, they were torn between following their orders to leave through the portal and the growing urge to join the fight. Of course, Jake knew he was forbidden to do so. Wyvern was here, and the Dark Druids wanted to abduct him.

At that moment, Red let out a full-throated roar that took all of them off guard, even Jake.

Dani jumped, so badly startled that her hand flailed across the

Bud of Life. "Blast it, Red, look what you made me do!"

Judging by the string of rookery expletives to come flying out of her mouth, Jake gathered she had hit something she shouldn't have.

"It's all right, darlin', cool yer heels," Tex said. "It wasn't your fault. Just be patient."

"Bigmouth Gryphon!" Dani muttered, sending Red a dirty look.

"Just concentrate on your vectors, and we'll try again in a minute when the device resets."

"What's he yawping about, anyway?" Dani demanded, flustered, as she waited for the Bud to reset.

Jake shook his head. "I'm not sure..."

As Red continued growling, Jake followed the Gryphon's golden-eyed glare across the battlefield and found himself looking at a horrifying animal. A large, tawny lion with a kingly mane...

And a scorpion's tail.

The dark, segmented tail with a venomous stinger on the end angled forward above the lion's back, long enough to strike over its head. The lion prowled in a wide circle around Lord Wyvern, as though protecting him.

Although it stayed clear of its master's duel with Sir Peter, the creature seemed determined to stop anyone else from interfering.

Jake grimaced with revulsion. "What *is* that thing?"

Janos grabbed a Noxu by one tusk, punched it in the face, kneed it in the stomach, and sent it reeling backward. Chest heaving, he looked in the direction Jake indicated and growled. "Thanatos."

"What?"

"Wyvern's manticore," Janos said grimly. "That foul beast was guarding Red's cage inside the Black Fortress when I got there. Blast it, I thought Ravyn and I killed it!" Then he glanced around. "Where is Ravyn, anyway? Has anyone spotted her yet?"

"Aye, I think I saw her over there, by the palace doors, with Master Ebrahim." Jake pointed.

Maddox took a step forward, peering in that direction. He had been strangely quiet ever since they arrived—even for him. Jake now realized it was because the lad was worried about his Guardian mother.

Maddox's dark eyes homed in on the tumult around the palace entrance. "I see her!"

The fight shifted, and Jake saw the warrior woman too. Ravyn was brawling with fists and blades against the half-troll barbarians.

But then one towering brute with exceptionally long tusks came at her. The barbarian must've been three times the slim fighter's weight in pure muscle.

Maddox tensed as the big Noxu grabbed Ravyn by the throat and lifted her high off her feet. She struggled to no avail, legs kicking.

Without warning, the older lad sprinted away from the group, heading straight for his birth mum.

Izzy screamed his name.

"Maddox, what are you doing?" Jake yelled.

"Get back here, St. Trinian!" Derek thundered, turning from his own battle, chest heaving.

But Maddox kept running—flagrantly disobeying the master Guardian's orders.

"Is he always this much of a problem?" Janos yelled angrily over his shoulder.

"No worse than you!" Derek retorted.

"You want me to go after him?"

"Don't leave us!" Izzy cried.

Jake, meanwhile, anxiously searched the seething knot of fighters around the palace doors.

He picked Maddox out of the chaos just in time to see his friend pull off an astonishing feat. The Guardian apprentice literally ran up the huge Noxu's back, punched the brute in the side of the head, then leaped off its shoulder as it staggered from the blow.

The Noxu dropped Ravyn; Maddox spun around, drew his blade, and stabbed it in the stomach, then gave his mother a hand up.

Jumping to her feet, Ravyn looked pleased with her son.

Admittedly, even Jake was impressed.

Derek wasn't. The master Guardian glowered in the young fighter's direction. "If he gets himself killed, I'm going to throttle him."

"Don't even say that," Izzy whispered.

While they were all looking toward the palace doors, Jake noticed that, in the courtyard outside the entrance, Wyvern's battle with Sir Peter continued to intensify.

Wyvern conjured a massive fist out of swirling green smoke and punched the headmaster with it. Sir Peter went crashing back against the stone rim of the fountain, his wand temporarily flung from his hand, his glasses knocked off his face.

He shook his head as though dazed while the Nephilim laughed, but Sir Peter quickly summoned his wand back into his grasp. Then he picked his glasses up off the gravel and put them back on.

"I owed you that!" Wyvern shouted.

Sir Peter struck back, lunging with his wand to release a volley of arrows. Wyvern turned himself into smoke for a moment—just like when he had vanished from the grounds of Griffon Castle, fleeing the unicorn stampede.

The arrows swept right through him and slammed harmlessly into a tall shrubbery behind him. The warlock reappeared with a smirk.

Sir Peter looked enraged and shouted, "If you *ever* target my wife again—!" He raised his wand upright over his head, bellowed a command, and then swept the tip downward.

An explosion cracked the ground in a seam before him that ran toward Wyvern like an earthquake; the courtyard suddenly split beneath the Nephilim.

The manticore roared as Wyvern plunged straight down into the long, jagged crack in the earth.

Red tensed beside Jake as the manticore charged Sir Peter; the wizard saw it coming and froze the beast mid-motion, much like Fionnula had done to Henry in wolf form.

Wasting no time while the monster was immobilized, Sir Peter began chanting to force the split ground back together to crush Wyvern inside the artificial crevasse.

But as the earth began to rumble slowly back together, Wyvern came levitating back up out of the ground, his eyes burning nearly orange with rage.

With a flick of his wrist and some magical command, Wyvern turned his wand into a long leather bullwhip that flew out and wrapped around Sir Peter's neck.

Wyvern yanked the smaller man off his feet and began dragging the wizard toward himself, raking Sir Peter across the gravel and slowly choking the air out of him.

"Oh no," Nixie said, standing, frozen, between Archie and Jake.

Meanwhile, Master Balinor was still putting out fires along the front face of the palace, calling powdery white avalanches of banking soda down upon the roof.

But when his owl screeched, apparently warning him that his right-hand man was in trouble, the aged head wizard turned around, saw the situation, and frowned.

Still controlling the angry general in the smoky snow globe, Balinor let out a visible sigh, as though he was growing weary of all this.

Then he aimed his wand at the manticore and uttered a low incantation that made a small puff of wind blow across the entire battlefield. It blew Jake's forelock back from his face...

And unfroze the manticore.

The creature landed on the gravel, finishing its jump.

"Oh, Lord! Is he senile?" Archie exclaimed. "Why would Balinor do that?"

"Just wait," Nixie said with a gulp, though she sounded unsure.

The manticore shook itself as though it had forgotten what it was doing.

Still staring at the manticore, Master Balinor repeated his incantation, and the creature turned slowly toward its master.

All of a sudden, it lifted its horrible tail and hissed at Lord Wyvern.

The warlock stopped dragging Sir Peter and looked at his pet.

The manticore prowled closer, its tail poised to strike.

"Oh," Archie murmured. "That's why..."

"Thanatos! Sit!" Wyvern's order rumbled across the field.

The beast ignored it.

Wyvern changed his bullwhip back into a wand just in time to defend himself as the manticore leaped on him and threw him to the ground.

Sir Peter rolled away from them and scrambled to his feet, coughing and rubbing his throat. "Thank you!"

"Anytime, dear boy." Balinor waved. Meanwhile, the manticore kept trying to bite Wyvern and stab him with its tail.

Sir Peter jogged toward the palace, looking exhausted. The Guardians kept the Noxu away and parted ranks to let him slip inside, whether to catch his breath or move on to another task, Jake did not know.

Some of the Guardians jeered to see the haughty Lord Wyvern calling on all his Nephilim strength to hold his own pet at bay. Even a few of the ugly Noxu looked amused.

Balinor simply went back to conjuring cascades of baking soda to squelch the roof fires.

What he didn't notice, intent on his task, was that, in the next moment, Wyvern broke the spell the manticore was under.

Shoving his confused pet off him, the furious warlock sat up, shot forth a crackling bolt of magic from his wand, and shattered the magical snow globe, releasing Archeron Raige.

The warrior stepped out in a swirl of black smoke. The moment he was free, he hurled a large dagger with glowing green symbols on the blade.

The wizard's owl screamed as the knife plunged into Balinor's back.

Everybody with the diplomatic party gasped in horror as the old man fell.

The Guardians defending the palace reacted too late. Although a few ran to surround the head wizard, the scene around the front of Merlin Hall turned to chaos.

The Noxu began cheering. Action halted across the battlefield as everyone started to realize what had happened. Balinor's owl, meanwhile, went berserk, flapping all around and letting out ear-piercing screeches.

When one of the Noxu moved toward the bird's fallen master, the owl flew at the brute and tried to gouge its eyes out. The half-troll screamed and fled with bloody scratches on its face.

Meanwhile, the brawny warrior from inside the snow globe lit a cigar, warded off blows from numerous Guardians at once, then started barking orders at the Noxu.

The tusked horde began hurling themselves against the palace doors with newfound zeal.

Dani gave Jake a terrified look, forgetting all about the portal. Her face was white beneath her freckles. They needed no words to confirm that neither could believe what had just happened.

The head of the Order had just been cut down before their very eyes.

Everyone was staring at the cluster of Guardians that had gathered around the fallen chief wizard.

"Do you think he's dead?" Nixie asked.

"Maybe the healers can get to him in time," Derek said, but his tone was murderous.

Jake glanced around. You didn't need to be an empath to feel the sudden plunge in morale across the field. Defeat at the hands of the Dark Druids suddenly seemed very possible. Maybe even imminent.

But Jake felt his anger at the enemy rising like a flood. His hands tingled with the readiness to use his telekinesis somehow to help in this fight.

I have to do something.

Janos seemed to share his sentiments. His eyes had turned black; the tips of his fangs were showing.

Even Derek lost patience. "Hang it, Tex, is she going to get that portal open anytime soon?"

"I'm sorry, Guardian Stone! I'm doing my best!" Dani cried.

"It's all right, honey." Tex turned and sent the Guardian a frown. "She had a little trouble, is all. Almost there. The Bud just needs a few more seconds to reset."

"Fine. Then, when it does, do it *for* her!" Derek said.

"And how's that supposed to teach 'er anything?" Tex replied.

"This is no time for a lesson, Munroe!"

"Yeah, well, reckon she might need to do it again real soon on the other end without us. Ya never know. So hold yer horses, muchacho. Give the kid another minute."

Derek glared at the Lightrider but did not argue further.

Jake realized the cowboy was probably right. Wherever Dani was taking them, they might arrive only to find they weren't safe there, either. If she needed to transport them again quickly somewhere else, she'd have to be able to do it herself, without adult supervision.

Meanwhile, over by the front of the palace, the manticore had fully recovered from Balinor's spell. It now began attacking the crowd. Fangs bared, tail whipping about, it didn't seem to care whether it struck friend or foe.

It bit one Guardian and stabbed another with its tail. Teeth gnashing, the monstrous beast did not withdraw until none other than Maddox St. Trinian snatched up one of the fallen Noxu's spears and sent it hurtling through the air, nailing the creature in the side.

The manticore roared and ran off into an untouched opening of the maze, the spear still dragging from its side.

Wyvern swore, glancing after his pet. He'd been busy casting curses and spells that had turned several Guardians to ashes—until some keen-eyed wood elf in an upper window of the palace peppered the warlock with six arrows in quick succession.

The Nephilim bellowed, but the arrows did not kill him. They only slowed him down. He retreated from the fight, limping off into the maze after his wounded pet.

"Look!" Isabelle suddenly pointed. "There's Aunt Ramona!"

Finnderool had told them that the Elder witch was battling Fionnula somewhere in the fray, but seeing their clash firsthand was something else altogether. The two great witches chased, knocked, and blasted each other into view at last, emerging from the quadrangle.

Fionnula was in full diva form, from her frilly, low-cut gown to her red high-heeled shoes. But, clearly, the sea-witch meant business.

Wand in hand, she flung her arm forward, hurling crackling blue orbs of magic at Aunt Ramona. The Elder witch cast each volley of Fionnula's attack into the ground; the spheres landed like grenades, blowing up chunks of turf.

When Aunt Ramona struck back, bright purple lightning tinged with silver and gold blasted from her wand. The rocketing force of it threw the sea-witch to the ground and sent her rolling several feet across the grass.

Fionnula recovered with a vicious snarl, jumping to her feet, her pale cheek bloodied, her long sable tresses smoking. Visibly furious, she hammered back at the Elder witch, to no avail.

Her gray hair blowing, her skirts whipping in the witches' wind, Aunt Ramona stood planted like an iron rod in a storm.

Jake stared at her in awe—yet uneasiness filled him. If Balinor could be felled, so could she.

Suddenly, from the corner of his eye, he noticed a Noxu spear hurtling straight toward their group. He reacted instantly, knocking it away with his telekinesis like he was swatting a fly.

The spear plunged into the ground nearby, where it stuck upright.

Dani blanched at the near-miss, but, for Jake, that was the last straw.

The Order's forces were wavering after seeing Balinor cut down. He had a notion for how to turn the tide.

Derek wasn't going to like it, but Jake had been a *very* good boy for quite long enough.

"C'mon, Red. Fly." Jake jumped on the Gryphon's back and seized hold of his collar. "Take me up to that airship."

CHAPTER 58
A Leap of Faith

Jake leaned forward over the Gryphon's feathery mane as Red galloped free of the Guardians' ring around them and launched into the air. Jake refused to look back, but winced to hear his party's reaction behind him.

Determined to stay focused on his task, he fixed his stare on the dirigible above and did his best to ignore Dani shrieking his name.

"I'll be right back," he mumbled with a frown. "Doesn't she know that?"

"Becaw," Red said.

"Yes, I noticed."

The whole group was, er, a little displeased.

Derek was thundering threats to ground Jake till the end of time. Wolf-Henry was barking, practically howling at him, as if to say, *Come back down here this instant, young man!*

Even Archie was shouting: "Have you gone insane?"

Uncle Richard and Aunt Claire left the edge of the woods to peer up at him, aghast.

As for Aunt Ramona, well, he didn't even want to think about what her reaction might be. Forget grounding him; the Elder witch would turn him into a toad.

But stealing a glance behind him, Jake saw that at least Janos was laughing. And when Tex lifted his fist and punched the air, Jake caught a distant *"Yee-haw!"*

Ha. At least some of them knew not to treat him like a baby. He could do this. They'd see.

In fact, he was already fifty feet in the air when it occurred to him that if he succeeded, the Order folk across the grounds below would see for themselves that he was no villain—that he was on their side, no matter what the Dark Druids' foolish prophecy said. Anyone with lingering doubts would realize he was loyal to the Order, just like his famous parents.

Determined to clear his name of their unfounded suspicions and protect his family's reputation, Jake continued ascending on his Gryphon, his stare fixed on the airship.

The Dream Wraith was still pounding Merlin Hall with fiery artillery strikes.

But not for long, if he had anything to say about it. Jake clenched his jaw and rode on.

Red seemed to sense his intentions; his scarlet wings beat powerfully as he climbed toward the moon.

Well aware they'd be an easy target up here in the open, Jake kept an eye out for anyone taking aim at them from the ground.

Ahead, black columns of smoke rose before him, clouding the night sky over the maze. Red wove among them, angling back and forth. Higher, partly hidden in the haze, Jake could see the dirigible lit by a series of dully glowing lanterns spaced out along the hull.

He coughed as he held on tight to the Gryphon's collar, his eyes watering, his lungs burning from the smoke. The smell of it singed his nostrils. Blinking rapidly to clear his vision, he glanced down at the sprawling maze below.

What he saw appalled him.

Noxu were running through its green corridors with torches, spreading ordinary blazes in addition to the Greek fire that Janos said Wyvern had started with the Atlantean cuff.

And Isabelle was right. The Old Father Yew was burning. Thousands of years old and some seventy feet tall, the very symbol of the Order, its branches stretched out amid the writhing flames like a burning man's arms.

Scores of evil creatures danced before the flames consuming the Old Father Yew, throwing twisted goblin shadows across the trampled green.

Fury filled Jake. It was bad enough the enemy had likely slain Master Balinor. But this?

This was not just a crime; it was a violation, a sacrilege.

Furious and hurt by the senseless destruction, Jake forced himself to focus on the task at hand. But the instant he lifted his gaze off the Hades-like inferno below and looked forward again, his eyes suddenly widened.

The giant owl appeared right in front of him and Red, swooping out of the smoke bellows with an ear-splitting screech.

The Gryphon roared, nearly colliding with the giant bird of prey. The owl swept down on them, angling its talons as if it meant to seize Jake right off Red's back.

Jake reacted without forethought. He was not a cruel person, and would never intentionally harm an animal, but pure training kicked in; his response was automatic. He hurled a bolt of energy at the monstrous bird, breaking its left wing.

The owl screamed and plummeted, spiraling helplessly toward the ground.

Jake stared, startled at what he'd just done, but the witches cheered as the giant owl landed in a furious puff of feathers.

Uneasy with the pain he'd inflicted, Jake looked down anxiously and saw the owl still screeching and flapping its one good wing. It looked dazed.

One of the wood elves moved in to shoot it with his bow, but when Dr. Plantagenet ran over and stopped him before he could release the arrow, Jake had to admit he was relieved. After all, maybe it wasn't the owl's fault.

Maybe it was just an ordinary barn owl that Wyvern or the Dark Master had enchanted and could be saved. The important thing was that the fearsome bird was no longer guarding the dirigible.

With that, Jake swallowed hard and set his mind once more on his purpose: robbing Wyvern of his air support.

The witches swerved out of Jake's way on their brooms as he approached, but, thankfully, did not try to stop him. They merely looked on with curious stares as he and Red flew by.

"Be careful of those nets!" one called after him. "Don't get tangled up in them, or you'll never escape."

Jake waved his thanks for the helpful tip and urged Red on toward *The Dream Wraith.* As they approached, they duly took care to steer clear of the long fishing nets trailing out behind the dirigible.

The nets were secured by ropes all around the ship but floated out behind it on the night breeze. They seemed as gauzy and fine as butterfly nets, but he did not intend to test the witches' puzzling claim that there was no escape from them.

What the nets were for, Jake had no idea, but that scarcely mattered at the moment, for the sky pirates now saw him coming.

The grubby crewmen quickly loaded another lead ball the size of a grapefruit into the small, swivel-mounted cannon affixed to the back corner of the ship's deck.

What a clamor the odd vessel made as Red and he approached! Its noisy, chugging engines belched steam. Its whirring propellers generated a wind that ruffled Jake's hair and Red's feathers, and its huge wooden rudder creaked left and right, guiding it through the dark sky.

"What do you think you're doing, lad?" one of the pirates shouted down at him with a mocking grin, his gold tooth flashing. He wore a black bandana knotted around his head; its long ends blew in the breeze. "Hope you're ready to die!"

Jake didn't reply. Instead, he leaned lower over the Gryphon's neck. "Prepare for evasive maneuvers, Red."

"Caw!"

Jake gulped but held on tight as the sky pirates aimed the muzzle right at them. *You better make it a good shot, you mumpers, because it's the last one you're gonna get.*

He narrowed his eyes, flying on fearlessly, headlong into danger—for Balinor. For the Old Father Yew. For Dani and everyone here.

The gold tooth pirate lit the fuse...

BOOM!

The cannonball exploded out of the muzzle and came screaming straight at him and Red, trailing sparks and plumes of smoke. Jake stared at a cannonball nearly the size of his head speeding toward him.

Then Red dove, banking to the right.

The ball flew by just inches above them. The witches scattered as it careened through the air to slam down in an empty field on the far side of the Naiads' stream.

Still holding on to Red's collar for dear life, Jake had leaned all the way forward, jockey-like, fully committed to the Gryphon's steep, nose-down angle.

But as Red evened out, Jake glanced back and saw the gun crew peering over the rails, trying to figure out where he and the Gryphon were headed next.

"That was close," Jake said with a shudder. "Now it's our turn, boy. What do you say to a counterstrike?"

Red let out a particularly bellicose *"Caw!"*

Jake smiled grimly, the wind whipping through his hair. "Ready when you are."

Red pumped his wings, then glided underneath the vessel on a diagonal. They passed between the huge wooden rudder near the back and the landing gear in the middle.

Maneuvering deftly in between the ropes securing the fishing nets, the Gryphon spun in a corkscrew motion, briefly flying upside down. Jake's stomach heaved, but he was clutching Red's collar with a death grip and holding on tight with his legs. The moment they cleared the tangle of fishing lines, the Gryphon swooped back upward on a graceful arc, banking to the right again, zooming Jake toward the stern.

Heart pounding, Jake let go of the collar with his right hand, his fingers already tingling as he summoned up the full force of his telekinesis.

Those sky pirates obviously didn't know who they were dealing with.

Several rude, swarthy, and tattooed fellows jeered at him from the rails as he sped past. By the dull glow of the ship's lanterns, Jake could see the gun crew swiveling the cannon around, waiting for him to fly back into range.

They took aim at him and his Gryphon, but Jake did not give them time to fire.

Zeroing in on his target, he hurled a handful of concentrated telekinetic force from his right palm across the stern deck at the cannon, knocking the swivel gun clean off its metal base. Wood cracked and splintered as the cannon tore free of the deck and toppled overboard, taking out a section of the wooden railing as it fell.

The sudden loss of several hundred pounds of iron on one side unbalanced the vessel and made the deck lurch, pitching all three members of the gun crew overboard.

Jake gasped; the other pirates standing around shouted; the witches cheered and zoomed in to press the fight.

While the Gryphon carried him clear of the fray with a victorious eagle's cry, Jake stared down, stricken, as the men fell, following the cannon, which had just now landed on the grass below. One slipped sternward and instantly got tangled up in the fishing nets, struggling like a fly trapped in a spiderweb.

The second somersaulted end over end toward the lawn,

screaming all the way down. Lucky for him, a quick-thinking Order mage stopped the pirate's fall before he splatted on the battlefield. Suspended a few feet off the ground, he was quickly captured and taken into custody.

But the third...the third, Jake knew, would haunt his dreams.

The very man who had fired the cannonball. Jake recognized him by his black bandana.

For a hair-raising moment, the pirate dangled over the edge of the broken deck, feet kicking. He held on for a heartbeat, then dropped. His mates screamed, but, tough as he was, the pirate somehow managed to catch hold of one of the trailing ropes.

He swung wildly back and forth.

Jake considered going to his aid with his telekinesis, but, at once, the man's crewmates grabbed hold of the rope and started pulling him up.

Since it seemed like they had the situation under control, Jake shook it off and went on about his business of disabling the ship.

The Dream Wraith had continued drifting on a northwesterly course over the grounds of Merlin Hall. It was now directly over the maze. The smoke grew thicker, and the cold October sky actually felt a few degrees warmer above the inferno.

All of a sudden, Jake heard a bloodcurdling scream. From the corner of his eye, he saw it happen.

The pirate lost his grip on the rope and fell, dropping like a stone into the fiery heart of the maze before Jake could even react.

In the blink of an eye, the man was simply gone, and in one spot, the inferno blazed up, incinerating him.

The crew wailed.

"Blast it, where did that brat on the Gryphon go?" one bellowed. "I'll kill him!"

"Red! Quick, get under the ship!" Jake said. "They're going to start shooting any minute now. We need to get out of range."

"Becaw!"

Thanks to the witches, who were now zooming all around the airship on their brooms, hectoring the crewmen, Jake was able to get close to the vessel again, urging Red lower.

He noticed that his Gryphon did not seem at all bothered by the gunner's fate, but for his part, Jake felt ill.

As Red swooped, gliding under the ship for cover, thoughts of the prophecy returned with a vengeance.

He could barely wrap his wits around the fact that he was responsible for a man's death. Killing anyone had not been his intention! He had only wanted to make them stop firing on the people below.

Pulse pounding, Jake swallowed hard and strove to refocus his mind as Red hovered under the dirigible. Because the fact was, he wasn't done yet.

For the moment, the pirates were still in chaos, dealing with the unbalanced weight on the stern and taking care not to fall through the broken section of the slanted deck themselves. But it wouldn't be long before they regrouped.

Jake knew he'd have to act quickly. Steeling his resolve, he turned his attention to the giant rudder on the back part of the dirigible's underbelly.

He dared not try to crush one of the propellers with his telekinesis. The last thing he wanted to do was bring the airship crashing down in a fiery heap on the lawn with all those people down there.

But during their Italian beach holiday, Jake had spent enough time tooling around with Maddox on the little sailboat that came with the villa to understand that cracking the rudder would strip *The Dream Wraith* of its ability to steer.

While the propellers powered the ship forward, the rudder controlled its direction. If he could damage *that*, the ship would have no choice but to keep on drifting forward in a straight line until the captain figured out where and how to land.

Suddenly, a burst of dazzling brightness on the lawn below drew Jake's eye.

She did it!

"Well done, carrot," he whispered.

The portal was open at last, shiny and waiting. The sight of it helped to clear his head.

Better hurry.

Time was ticking.

Thanks to the witches, who were now zooming all around the airship on their brooms, Jake was able to get close to the massive rudder, urging Red toward the back end of the airship.

There, he dealt the giant wooden rudder several massive wallops with his telekinesis, hammering the base until it cracked off the tiller and hung as useless as a broken arm.

As soon as this was accomplished, he headed Red back down to the ground. The portal was waiting; he left sky duty to the witches and hurried toward the light.

As Red glided down from the dark sky, Jake was startled to notice people across the fire-lit grounds cheering for him and his Gryphon.

He hadn't heard their jubilation while he was up there. It seemed his success in thwarting *The Dream Wraith* had not only saved lives, but had stoked the Order's flagging morale.

Across the palace grounds, they fought with renewed vigor, pounding the Noxu.

Jake was glad to see it. Still, when he swung off Red's back and jogged over to the group, his legs felt wobbly beneath him.

"Son, you're somethin' else!" Tex thumped him on the back as Jake returned to the fold, slipping past the ring of sweaty, bloodied Guardians.

Janos sent him a wink, but Derek scowled, Henry barked, and Archie cried, "You're a madman!"

Dani just shook her head.

The little Lightrider stood proudly by the portal she had opened, fists planted on her hips. "Finally! Come on, everybody. Let's get out of here. Who wants to go first?"

She didn't notice that no one volunteered because she was glancing around, doing a quick head count. "Hold on—where's Maddox?"

"Never mind him, just *go*!" Janos exclaimed.

"But we need a Guardian for our party! It's protocol! Could *you* come?"

"No!" the vampire retorted, though he sent her an apologetic look. "I'm needed here. Please, hurry. Isabelle can't take much more of this."

While Dani searched the grounds, trying to spot Maddox, Jake looked at his cousin and gasped to see that her nose was bleeding.

"Izzy!" He went over to her at once.

Good Lord, that sort of thing only happened to him when he'd pressed his talents to maximum exertion. Archie had given her his handkerchief to manage the nosebleed, but Janos was right: their empath was in trouble with all the fury and hatred in the air.

Jake turned to Dani. "Forget about a Guardian. I'll protect you," he said, but she paid him no mind.

"Oh, look!" She suddenly brightened. "There's my friend Brian!"

"Brian?" Jake echoed, following her gaze.

"Brian!" She waved madly to a dark-haired boy in a short brown jacket who was running to and fro about the lawn, looking lost. "Brian, over here! Come with us!"

"Brian!" Derek also beckoned to the bewildered-looking lad.

The wide-eyed boy ran toward them. He looked a little younger than Jake—maybe eleven or twelve, closer to Dani's age.

He also looked half scared out of his wits. "Dani! Guardian Stone!"

"Brian, what are you doing out here?" Derek exclaimed as the tousle-headed boy slipped past the ring of Guardians surrounding them.

"I-I don't know—I got separated from my class!" Though pale with fear, he recovered quickly once Derek laid a steadying hand on his shoulder. He gulped and glanced anxiously at the portal. "S-so, what are we doing, then?"

"Leaving," Dani said firmly. "Want to come?"

"Gladly!" He gave her a wide-eyed nod.

"Good." Dani looked relieved. "We've got a Guardian. *Now* we can go."

Jake cocked a brow.

That kid's supposed to protect us? He sent a dubious glance up at the dirigible that was now drifting off course, unable to steer. *Didn't she just see me...?*

Oh, never mind.

Izzy was weaving on her feet. "We can't just leave Maddox behind," she said weakly, but it was obvious the older boy had no intention of returning.

"We have no choice." Dani looked around at them. "Well, then? It's time. Who wants to go first?"

Archie and Nixie took a step backward; everyone looked at Jake.

"Who, me?" he said, startled. "Naw, that's all right." He gestured politely to their great new protector to go ahead of him. "Be my guest."

Blimey, if anyone's molecules were going to get scrambled from entering a portal opened by a baby Lightrider who may or may *not* know what she was doing, let it be the stranger, Jake thought. That seemed reasonable to him.

But Brian shook his head and moved aside. "No, sir! I mean, unless you're scared, then I could try—"

"I'm not *scared*!" Jake said.

Derek scowled over his shoulder. "Somebody go, or I'm going to start *throwing* you all through the blasted thing!" Then he blocked a resounding blow from a Noxu who took a chop at him with an axe.

Indeed, their protectors were being peeled away one by one, drawn into the battle. Derek began battling two Noxu warriors at once.

"Dame Oriel's in trouble." Janos glanced toward them. "Stay alive," he said, mostly to Isabelle. Then he raced off, donning his full, terrifying vampire appearance as he ran to save the purple-haired Elder.

Thankfully, his back was to them, so the empath couldn't see his face.

No doubt that was for the best.

Jake had seen him once like that; he shuddered at the memory.

Janos leaped over the battle with a soaring, preternatural bound and landed somewhere on the far end of the field.

Red roared a warning as more enemies headed for their group, drawn by the light of the portal.

"Come *on*, Jake!" Dani said to him through gritted teeth. "You have to go first, or no one else will follow." Desperation shone in her big green eyes. "Don't you trust me?"

Jake tore his stare away from the fight and looked at her in surprise. He suddenly realized how much she needed him to believe in her right now.

"Of course I do, carrot," he said abruptly. In that moment, with the others waiting for his signal, he felt the full responsibility of being the leader. It cleared his mind with sudden and absolute force.

All conflicting arguments about what *he* would've preferred to do—stay and help the Order win—simply melted away.

He realized if he didn't go with his friends, they'd have no one to protect them but Nixie with her wand and this Brian kid.

Besides, if he stayed and the Dark Druids managed to capture him—and if there *was* any truth to this prophecy—then everyone was doomed.

With that, his mind was made up.

"C'mon, you lot," he said, striding forward. "Let's get out of here." When he reached Dani's side, standing close to her, he looked into her eyes. "You're sure you know where this thing goes?"

"Trust me," she said, but Jake knew her too well.

He could see the fear and uncertainty that glimmered in her eyes. She wasn't a hundred percent sure about this herself.

Oh, perfect.

Jake knew for a fact that she had only done this once before in her entire life.

He had no idea where the tunnel would take him, or if the carrot actually knew what she was doing, but he decided to take a leap of faith.

He owed her that much. Lord knew she had believed in *him* enough times, had trusted his harebrained schemes.

Besides, if he balked, the others wouldn't want to risk it either, and it was simply too dangerous for them to stay a moment longer. Isabelle looked weaker by the minute, wilting like a flower. Archie was supporting his sister, but now droplets of blood had begun leaking from her ear. She seemed about to faint.

Stepping up to the bright, watery disk, half sure he was going to end up in Timbuktu (wherever that was), Jake gathered his nerve, only praying that his molecules came back together properly on the other end of this thing.

But before he leaped, he gave their little Lightrider's hand a reassuring squeeze, then glanced over his shoulder. "C'mon, Red!"

"Becaw!" said the Gryphon.

Jake took a deep breath, then ran at the portal with a whoop, just like Tex had taught them. *"Yee-haw!"*

Then he leaped.

Dissolving into light, he went whooshing down the tunnel at a thousand miles an hour, headed heaven only knew where.

EPILOGUE
The Devil's Due

Did you see him, Nathan? Did you see your son? As Wyvern surveyed the battlefield with glowing pride, the devil in his head sounded positively giddy with delight.

"I certainly did, Father." Wyvern glanced up as the ponderous dirigible floated away, useless. Yes, he had lost his air support, but he had gained so much more here tonight.

Only thirteen, and he crippled The Dream Wraith*!* Shemrazul enthused. *Now, there's a lad after my own heart.*

"Maybe thirteen's the boy's lucky number," Wyvern murmured, though, in truth, he did not see why Shemrazul had to make such a fuss over Jake at the moment.

He was the victor here tonight.

Merlin Hall had not been penetrated in centuries, let alone sacked and pillaged. But he, Wyvern—he alone—had dared to do what the Dark Master himself had never attempted, and it had paid off in spades.

Balinor had fallen. The Old Yew was dead. The Order had lost its smug superiority. Wyvern smiled at how he had humiliated them.

Best of all, he had impressed his fiery father. He had given the devil his due, and he knew he would soon be rewarded.

With the Black Crown.

I'm coming for you next, Zolond, he thought. But having accomplished his purpose, there was no need to linger. He trusted he had made his point.

After tonight, there would be no more question about who was really in charge of the Dark Druids.

It hadn't come easy. But he looked around slowly, assessing the scene. It was tempting simply to take over Merlin Hall, but he wasn't a fool. Attacking old wizards and schoolchildren was one thing. If he attempted to occupy the Order's headquarters, allied armies would be here by morning.

No, best to strike quickly and retreat to safety, like the serpents his side so admired. Besides, in truth, he was weary. He was covered in sweat from exertion. Dried blood where that wood elf had shot him made his clothes stick to his skin.

No matter. Out of sight in the maze, Wyvern had simply pulled the arrows out of his agonized body and healed his half-dozen savage wounds. Then he had healed Thanatos again. This done, his gaze was drawn skyward.

From his hiding place in an unburned aisle of the labyrinth, he'd had a fine view of his future son wreaking havoc on the sky pirates. It had filled Wyvern's dark heart with pride when the boy had sent that one useless fellow to his doom.

Oh yes, young Jake would make an excellent addition to the family.

"A good night's work, Thanatos."

The manticore hissed in agreement.

Ah, they were not so easily broken, either of them. His loyal pet stood by his side, guarding him with occasional growls.

Nostrils flaring, Wyvern inhaled the gratifying scene of gunpowder and smoke, smiling to see that the Noxu forces had now battled their way past the weary Guardians on the front stairs and had stormed the palace, trampling countless Merlin Hall gnomes underfoot.

Many Noxu had died tonight, but now the survivors collected their well-earned plunder from the rich chambers and salons of the lavish place.

When a burst of elegant laughter drew his attention, Wyvern looked over and saw the Red Queen and four of her beautiful courtiers toying with a terrified Dame Oriel. Wyvern recognized the clairvoyant Elder by her ridiculous purple hair.

"Where are your ghosts? Why will they not help you?" the vampires taunted, shoving the older woman back and forth among them, mocking her and baring their fangs.

She shrieked when a beautiful courtier snapped his jaws at her.

In all fairness, a few palace ghosts did show up to try to aid their medium friend. Summoning all of their poltergeist strength, they formed a ring around her, especially one fat fellow who shouted at the vampires in Italian with the most magnificent spectral voice.

But the spirits could not maintain their force field around her for very long, and the moment they faded away, the vampires moved in again.

This time, in earnest.

At that moment, one of their own bounded into their midst from somewhere on high.

Janos landed among them with his darkling blade in hand and, whirling like a top, lopped off two of the vampires' heads in one spinning blow.

Wyvern's eyes widened. Viola cried out in horror, but the other two vampires retreated slightly, into the shadows.

Janos threw his arm around Dame Oriel's waist and leaped away with her, removing the clairvoyant to safety on the roof.

Well—relative safety, considering that *The Dream Wraith* had blown holes in it. To Wyvern's annoyance, it was no longer burning. Balinor had managed to put out many of the lovely fires he had started up there with the Atlantean cuff.

After the old wizard died, that irksome Sir Peter had continued his work, conjuring torrents of some white powder that had somehow snuffed out the flames. He hadn't seen the younger wizard since.

In any case, the moment Janos released the purple-haired lady, she rushed into the palace through a rooftop door.

The traitorous double agent turned around, prepared to fend off Viola's two remaining courtiers as they joined him with massive leaps. The Red Queen herself was crying over her slain followers—and, no doubt, over her favorite son-in-law's treachery.

I told her, Wyvern thought. *She should've believed me.*

Just then, Archeron Raige came stomping out of the palace with a fearsome long gun under one arm. Sweat had caused his camouflage face paint to smear almost all the way off. His olive-green shirt was in tatters over his massive upper body, but his eyes shone with pleasure at all the fun he'd had tonight.

"Any luck?" Wyvern asked.

He had instructed the general to make a sweep of the palace to collect any remaining Lightriders he could find for their project in the basement of the Black Fortress.

Raige shook his head and threw the nub of his stinky cigar down on the ground. "Nah. They've either fled through the portal or holed up in that blasted library. Can't get to 'em. Too much magic on that place." He spat. "We got enough of 'em now anyway, don't we?"

"We do," Wyvern admitted with a grimace of distaste. Yes, the general had inhaled a lot of smoke tonight, but that was no excuse for such dreadful manners.

As for the Lightriders, ah well. Though a few more to add to the collection wouldn't hurt, what Raige said was true. They already had enough to accomplish their aims.

And it wouldn't be long now before it was time to bring their great, secret project to fruition...

Once more, Wyvern surveyed the fast-moving field.

Viola Sangray had exchanged her tears for fury, rocketed onto the roof, and was now engaged in a deadly dance with Janos along the edge of it, doing her best to destroy him.

Out on the dark lawn, off to Wyvern's left as he faced the palace, Fionnula was still locked in combat with old Ramona Bradford.

Wyvern wondered if he ought to give his good lady wife a little help or if she'd be insulted by his interference. She could be so touchy, and the last thing he wanted to deal with when they returned to the Black Fortress was one of Fionnula's sulks.

It was then that Wyvern suddenly spotted a most unlikely participant on the battlefield.

None other than Waldrick Everton was barreling across the grass, his lanky legs pumping at top speed.

Wyvern wrinkled his brow as Jake's uncle sprinted toward a knot of Guardians still clashing with some of the Noxu.

What on earth is he doing?

Frankly, Wyvern couldn't believe the lily-livered coward had even ventured out of the Black Fortress. The last Wyvern had seen him, Waldrick had been waving goodbye from the safety of the castle, along with the newly arrived Boris Badgerton.

Yet now here he was, running pell-mell toward some of the Order's warriors. Wyvern watched, half amused.

Suicide mission? Eh, not him. Wyvern scoffed. *He'd never kill his favorite person.*

Did the weasel wish to prove his valor now that the battle was almost done and it was safe to come out?

Except...he wasn't carrying a weapon.

Then, across the distance, Wyvern heard Waldrick shouting. The ex-earl lifted his hands in the air as he raced toward a brawny figure. Squinting, Wyvern recognized him as the Guardian he'd had so much fun torturing a few months back.

Then Waldrick's words carried to him in a lull of the gunfire.

"Derek, it's me! It's Waldrick! Don't shoot! I surrender, I defect! Please—Jacob's alive!" Waldrick skidded onto his knees in front of the master Guardian, nearly face-planting on the grass.

Order soldiers instantly surrounded him. Wyvern's heart welled up with stunned fury.

"Fionnula!" he bellowed.

His future wife turned in surprise at his thunderous tone.

"Forget her!" He pointed. "Kill Waldrick! *Now!*"

She surely understood. *He knows too much!*

Unfortunately, all Wyvern's shout accomplished was to distract his future wife, allowing the Elder witch to slam Fionnula with a mighty magical blow.

She went tumbling across the lawn.

Wyvern fumed. *Incompetent.*

"Raige!" he bellowed. But the general had just received a skull-cracking head butt from a huge, bald, dark-skinned Guardian who was actually as tall as Raige. That was rare.

Fine. I'll do it myself, Wyvern thought, stewing with fury.

But just as he started toward the group of Guardians surrounding the traitor, Peter Quince stepped out of the maze behind him and threw a net over Wyvern.

Too late he realized it was a dreaded Entangler's Net. The blasted thing yanked his feet out from under him and toppled him onto his face in the gravel with an *"Oof!"*

As its golden latticework sucked in against his body from his head to his knees, the more he struggled, the tighter it got. His arms were bound by his sides; only his six-fingered hands flailed beneath his wrists.

"I'll kill you for this!"

"Yes, yes. You are certainly welcome to try." Casual leather shoes strolled into view right beside his head.

Wyvern cocked his eyes up to the side and saw the bespectacled wizard smiling down at him, hands in pockets.

The smile did not reach Sir Peter's eyes. "You've been a real problem this evening, do you know that?"

Wyvern cursed at him, writhing and wriggling like a snake in his determination to break free. He knew this was impossible, of course.

Entangler's Nets were exceedingly rare and almost impossible to escape without help. If only he realized the Order had one! But, blast it, he couldn't think of everything all by himself.

Fortunately, the general was only just now climbing to his feet after the head butt. He glanced over at Wyvern.

"Fall back!" Raige roared toward the palace, and the Noxu quickly started to obey.

Good, Wyvern thought as the tusked mercenaries began pouring out of the palace, carrying their loot. As much as the brutes enjoyed raiding, to defy one of the general's orders meant a very nasty death.

Raige pointed them toward Wyvern.

Fionnula was on her way, thankfully, though she looked a little dazed. She wasn't quite running straight in her high-heeled shoes. Ramona Bradford strode after her, disheveled and out for blood.

For his part, helpless for the moment, his hands secured at his sides, Wyvern could just make out Derek Stone and a couple of other Guardians hustling Waldrick out of view across the distant lawn.

He wanted to scream with frustration, but he refused to give Peter Quince the satisfaction. The irritating fellow smiled again.

"Night, night, Wyvern." This time, the chancellor blasted him with a white-hot orb that flashed from his wand, knocking Wyvern nearly senseless.

The night buckled; the world turned double before his eyes. He smelled burning human hair and feared that it was his. The boom of Quince's spell reverberated in his ears, dizzying him.

Then, much to his chagrin, Wyvern lost consciousness...

When he eventually came to, Quince was gone, and a bloodied Fionnula was on her knees beside him, anxiously tapping his cheek. "Nathan, wake up! We've got to get out of here!"

Double images of her false, lovely face rotated before Wyvern's eyes.

Raige was also bent over him, peering down skeptically into his face. No wonder Wyvern smelled cigar smoke.

Viola kicked Wyvern in the leg. "Get up! We're done here," the vampire queen said in disgust. "I trust we've made our point. Let's quit while we're ahead."

Wyvern nodded, still dazed.

Fionnula pulled him to his feet. "Come along, dear," she said through gritted teeth.

Raige straightened up and turned to his troops. "Back to the Fortress! Double-time it!"

A steady stream of grunting Noxu continued flowing out of the ransacked palace, jogging back toward Badgerton's tunnel, their hands laden with all they could steal. Some carried jewels, others sacks of gold. Still more had stolen the magical paintings off the walls, but one Noxu with a ring in his snout had carried off a schoolchild.

The tot kicked the half-troll in the spleen and ran for its life as soon as the warrior dropped it. The Greenfolk trying to save the maze quickly took the child under their protection.

Still a little dazed, Wyvern looked around, wondering what had happened while he was out.

His gaze homed in on Ramona Bradford standing on the top step of the palace entrance, wand in hand.

Something in her stare made him realize the Elder witch must've had something to do with his allies' eagerness to leave. What the devil had she done to them while he was out?

It didn't matter, he quickly decided, in no mood to test her wrath, now that his allies had got him out of the Entangler's Net. He'd accomplished his purpose here. The palace had been looted, the sculpted grounds savaged.

He'd taught the Order its place.

Of course, that witless Waldrick Everton's defection to the other side boded ill, but even Shemrazul knew there were few unmixed victories in life.

The important thing was that the show of strength Wyvern had carried out here would solidify his position and seal his followers' loyalty.

All that was left now would be to take care of Zolond and claim the Black Crown.

"Let's get out of here," he muttered to his allies. He grabbed Viola's arm, while Fionnula caught hold of Raige, then they both performed transport spells, whisking themselves back to the safety of the Black Fortress.

In two shakes of a rattler's tail.

* * *

"Well done, Nathan! Ha ha!" Shemrazul wore a devil's grin from ear to ear, horn to horn. His laughter reverberated through the Ninth Pit. "My boys! Did you see them?"

Ignoring the groans of the damned all around him, he turned to his court of imps and lesser devils at the bottom of the canyon, where the lava river flowed.

"I'll be free in no time." Once Wyvern took power, Shemrazul knew that his loyal son would gladly give him full possession of his body.

His consciousness in a willing servant's body—like in the old days, how it used to be with Garnock.

He could hardly wait.

And then, for the rest of Wyvern's natural existence, Shemrazul would be grooming Jake as the next body for him to inhabit.

Ah, it was going to be great fun breaking out of here in the not-too-distant future and becoming the Dark Master himself, more or less. After all, if you want something done right...

It was then Shemrazul noticed that his buoyant mood seemed to have alarmed his slavish followers.

They awaited orders; he was always happy to give them.

"Find my grandson," he commanded the strange collection of creatures gathered around his cloven hooves. "I want to know where Jake and his little friends went."

"Shall we kill them, master?" a hunchbacked imp with blue, pointy ears asked eagerly.

Shemrazul hissed and swatted the idiot into the river of lava with his dragon tail. "Anyone else care to ask a stupid question?"

"N-no, master! No questions!"

"You are *tracking* him! That is all," Shemrazul said, rolling his eyes. "Do not lay one claw on that boy. He is mine."

"*Buuuut* sire? Didn't the lad just spend the whole battle fighting against us?" asked a monstrous blob.

Shemrazul narrowed his eyes and exploded the blob with a wave of his clawed finger just for annoying him. "How many eons have we been here, and still, you understand nothing? Dunces! The boy now has blood on his hands. Remember?"

With that, Shemrazul smiled down at the cowering, doomed soul of a gold-toothed pirate in a black bandana.

Dead scarcely twenty minutes after falling off *The Dream Wraith* into the fire, the pirate's ghost looked bewildered. He didn't seem to realize yet quite where he was, what was going on.

Oh, he'd learn. Shemrazul smiled at his latest victim. The pirate had been a criminal and a murderer in life. Where else did he expect to land?

"Er, but sire?" One of the hook-nosed red devils in attendance scratched his head with his pitchfork, looking confused.

"What?" Shemrazul growled. What a cruel punishment it was, being confined for all time with such frustrating henchmen.

The red devil lowered his pitchfork. "It's just—the boy didn't *mean* to kill this man, Your Awfulness."

"So?" Shemrazul retorted. "When has that ever stopped me?"

Indeed, undeserved guilt was his specialty. They didn't call him the Accuser for nothing.

"Aye, he's right, sire!" said a thing with two skinny legs attached to a globular body with one eye. Even after several thousand years, Shemrazul still wasn't sure what it was. It gestured at the pirate. "Jake's killing this chap was just an accident."

"Besides," the blue-eared imp chimed in, climbing out of the river of lava, his flesh already growing back, "this fellow *did* try to take the lad's head off with a cannonball."

"Oh really?" Shemrazul rumbled. Leaning forward on his skull-covered throne, he peered down at the dead pirate. "Is this true?" he demanded with a scowl, pretending like he didn't already know. Terrifying new arrivals was one of the few joys left to him. "You tried to shoot the future leader of the Dark Druids with a cannon? My *grandson*?"

The pirate yelped, stammered, and backed away.

Shemrazul's endless adamantine chains clanked and uncoiled as he lifted a cloven hoof high and smushed the pirate with a deafening bang. "That'll teach you."

His henchmen laughed and cheered.

"Now, go!" he ordered them. "Find Jake! Search the globe, but tell me where he's gone. Keep your eyes on him, once you've tracked him down. And when the time is right, we'll bring the dear boy home..."

The End

Coming Soon!

Wickedness has seized the upper hand.

Will goodness fall? Join Jake and his friends in the next pulse-pounding Gryphon Chronicles adventure as the gang is thrust into an unimaginable confrontation with the forces of evil, and where the young Lord Griffon will ultimately come face to face with his most menacing enemy yet...

THE DRAGON LORD

The Gryphon Chronicles: Book 7

* * *

The Complete Gryphon Chronicles Series:

Book 1 – THE LOST HEIR
Book 2 – JAKE & THE GIANT
Book 3 – THE DARK PORTAL
Book 3.5 – THE GINGERBREAD WARS
Book 4 – RISE OF ALLIES
Book 5 – SECRETS OF THE DEEP
Book 6 – THE BLACK FORTRESS
Book 7 – THE DRAGON LORD

In case you missed it…

It's Jake's first Christmas with a family, but nothing's ever quite what you'd expect. Celebrate a Victorian Christmas with a Gryphon Chronicles holiday novella.

JAKE & THE GINGERBREAD WARS

Peace on Earth, Goodwill to Men...And Gingerbread Men?!

Santa's Horrid Little Helper

Wanted! Humbug, the disgruntled Christmas elf.
Reward: One Christmas wish granted, courtesy of Santa.

Humbug hates being a Christmas elf. Instead of making toys, he'd rather make mischief. Angling for a new job in Halloween Town, he sets out to prove he's frightful enough for the task by ruining Christmas for as many people as possible—until Jake and his friends capture him. The kids set out on a rip-roaring adventure to the North Pole to hand the troublemaker over to Santa and collect the reward. But the way is fraught with danger, leaving them to wonder if they'll make it back in time for Christmas…or if they'll even make it back alive!

ABOUT THE AUTHORS

E.G. FOLEY is the pen name for a husband-and-wife writing team who live in Pennsylvania. They've been finishing each other's sentences since they were teens, so it was only a matter of time till they were writing together, too.

Like his kid readers, "E" (Eric) can't sit still for too long! A bit of a renaissance man, he's picked up hobbies from kenpo to carpentry to classical guitar over the years, and holds multiple degrees in math, science, and education. He treated patients as a chiropractor for nearly a decade, then switched careers to venture into the wild-and-woolly world of teaching middle school, where he was often voted favorite teacher. His students helped inspire him to start dreaming up great stories for kids, until he recently switched gears again and left teaching to become a full-time writer and author entrepreneur.

By contrast, "G" (Gael, aka Gaelen Foley) has had *one* dream all her life and has pursued it with maniacal intensity since the age of seventeen: writing fiction! After earning her Lit degree at SUNY Fredonia, she waited tables at night for nearly six years as a "starving artist" to keep her days free for honing her craft, until she finally got The Call in 1997. Today, with millions of her twenty-plus romances from Ballantine and HarperCollins sold in many languages worldwide, she's been hitting bestseller lists regularly since 2001. Although she loves all her readers, young and old, she admits there's just something magical about writing for children.

You can find the Foleys on Facebook/EGFoleyAuthor or visit their website at www.EGFoley.com. They are hard at work on their next book.

Thanks for Reading!

CPSIA information can be obtained
at www.ICGtesting.com
Printed in the USA
LVHW021624301220
675428LV00004B/39